The Complete Escapades of The Scarlet Pimpernel

Volume 3

The Complete Escapades of The Scarlet Pimpernel
Volume 3

Lord Tony's Wife

and

The Triumph of the Scarlet Pimpernel

Baroness Orczy

LEONAUR

The Complete Escapades of The Scarlet Pimpernel
Volume 3
Lord Tony's Wife
and
The Triumph of the Scarlet Pimpernel
by Baroness Orczy

FIRST EDITION

First published under the titles
Lord Tony's Wife
and
The Triumph of the Scarlet Pimpernel

Leonaur is an imprint of Oakpast Ltd

Copyright in this form © 2018 Oakpast Ltd

ISBN: 978-1-78282-734-4 (hardcover)
ISBN: 978-1-78282-735-1 (softcover)

http://www.leonaur.com

Publisher's Notes

Contents

Lord Tony's Wife   7

The Triumph of the Scarlet Pimpernel   219

Lord Tony's Wife

To

Dora Countess of Chesterfield

A Token of Friendship

And Love.

Emmuska Orczy

Contents

Prologue: Nantes, 1789   11

The Moor   30

The Bottom Inn   35

The Assembly Rooms   54

The Father   68

The Nest   74

The Scarlet Pimpernel   82

Marguerite   87

The Road to Portishead   90

The Coast of France   98

The Tiger's Lair   106

Le Bouffay   127

The Fowlers   138

The Net   153

The Message of Hope   168

The Rat Mort   175

The Fracas in the Tavern   182

The English Adventurers   195

The Proconsul   205

Lord Tony   214

Prologue: Nantes, 1789

"Tyrant! tyrant! tyrant!"

It was Pierre who spoke, his voice was hardly raised above a murmur, but there was such an intensity of passion expressed in his face, in the fingers of his hand which closed slowly and convulsively as if they were clutching the throat of a struggling viper, there was so much hate in those muttered words, so much power, such compelling and awesome determination that an ominous silence fell upon the village lads and the men who sat with him in the low narrow room of the *auberge des Trois Vertus.*

Even the man in the tattered coat and threadbare breeches, who—perched upon the centre table—had been haranguing the company on the subject of the Rights of Man, paused in his peroration and looked down on Pierre half afraid of that fierce flame of passionate hate which his own words had helped to kindle.

The silence, however, had only lasted a few moments, the next Pierre was on his feet, and a cry like that of a bull in a slaughter-house escaped his throat.

"In the name of God!" he shouted, "let us cease all that senseless talking. Haven't we planned enough and talked enough to satisfy our puling consciences? The time has come to strike, *mes amis,* to strike I say, to strike at those cursed aristocrats, who have made us what we are—ignorant, wretched, downtrodden—senseless clods to work our fingers to the bone, our bodies till they break so that they may wallow in their pleasures and their luxuries! Strike, I say!" he reiterated while his eyes glowed and his breath came and went through his throat with a hissing sound. "Strike! as the men and women struck in Paris on that great day in July. To them the Bastille stood for tyranny, and they struck at it as they would at the head of a tyrant—and the tyrant cowered, cringed, made terms—he was frightened at the wrath of the people! That is what happened in Paris! That is what must happen in Nantes. The *château* of the Duc de Kernogan is our Bastille! Let us strike at it tonight, and if the arrogant aristocrat resists, we'll raze his

11

house to the ground. The hour, the day, the darkness are all propitious. The arrangements hold good. The neighbours are ready. Strike, I say!"

He brought his hard fist crashing down upon the table, so that mugs and bottles rattled: his enthusiasm had fired all his hearers: his hatred and his lust of revenge had done more in five minutes than all the tirades of the agitators sent down from Paris to instil revolutionary ideas into the slow-moving brains of village lads.

"Who will give the signal?" queried one of the older men quietly.

"I will!" came a lusty response from Pierre.

He strode to the door, and all the men jumped to their feet, ready to follow him, dragged into this hot-headed venture by the mere force of one man's towering passion. They followed Pierre like sheep— sheep that have momentarily become intoxicated—sheep that have become fierce—a strange sight truly—and yet one that the man in the tattered coat who had done so much speechifying lately, watched with eager interest and presently related with great wealth of detail to M. de Mirabeau the champion of the people.

"It all came about through the death of a pair of pigeons," he said.

The death of the pigeons, however, was only the spark which set all these turbulent passions ablaze. They had been smouldering for half a century and had been ready to burst into flames for the past decade.

Antoine Melun, the wheelwright, who was to have married Louise, Pierre's sister, had trapped a pair of pigeons in the woods of M. le Duc de Kernogan. He had done it to assert his rights as a man—he did not want the pigeons. Though he was a poor man, he was no poorer than hundreds of peasants for miles around: but he paid imposts and taxes until every particle of profit which he gleaned from his miserable little plot of land went into the hands of the collectors, whilst M. le Duc de Kernogan paid not one *sou* towards the costs of the State, and he had to live on what was left of his own rye and wheat after *M. le Duc's* pigeons had had their fill of them.

Antoine Melun did not want to eat the pigeons which he had trapped, but he desired to let M. le Duc de Kernogan know that God and Nature had never intended all the beasts and birds of the woods to be the exclusive property of one man, rather than another. So, he trapped and killed two pigeons and *M. le Duc's* head-bailiff caught him in the act of carrying those pigeons home.

Whereupon Antoine was arrested for poaching and thieving: he was tried at Nantes under the presidency of M. le Duc de Kernogan, and ten minutes ago, while the man in the tattered coat was declaiming to a number of peasant lads in the coffee-room of the *Auberge des Trois Vertus* on the subject of their rights as men and citizens, someone brought the news that Antoine Melun had just been condemned to death and would be hanged on the morrow.

That was the spark which had fanned Pierre Adet's hatred of the aristocrats to a veritable conflagration: the news of Antoine Melun's fate was the bleat which rallied all those human sheep around their leader. For Pierre had naturally become their leader because his hatred of *M. le Duc* was more tangible, more powerful than theirs. Pierre had had more education than they. His father, Jean Adet the miller, had sent him to a school in Nantes, and when Pierre came home *M. le Curé* of Vertou took an interest in him and taught him all he knew himself—which was not much—in the way of philosophy and the classics. But later on, Pierre took to reading the writings of M. Jean-Jacques Rousseau and soon knew the *Contrat Social* almost by heart. He had also read the articles in M. Marat's newspaper *L'ami du Peuple!* and, like Antoine Melun, the wheelwright, he had got it into his head that it was not God, nor yet Nature who had intended one man to starve while another gorged himself on all the good things of this world.

He did not, however, speak of these matters, either to his father or to his sister or to *M. le Curé*, but he brooded over them, and when the price of bread rose to four *sous* he muttered curses against M. le Duc de Kernogan, and when famine prices ruled throughout the district those curses became overt threats; and by the time that the pinch of hunger was felt in Vertou Pierre's passion of fury against the Duc de Kernogan had turned to a frenzy of hate against the entire *noblesse* of France.

Still he said nothing to his father, nothing to his mother and sister. But his father knew. Old Jean would watch the storm-clouds which gathered on Pierre's lowering brow; he heard the muttered curses which escaped from Pierre's lips whilst he worked for the liege-lord whom he hated. But Jean was a wise man and knew how useless it is to put out a feeble hand in order to stem the onrush of a torrent. He knew how useless, are the words of wisdom from an old man, to quell the rebellious spirit of the young.

Jean was on the watch. And evening after evening when the work on the farm was done, Pierre would sit in the small low room of the *auberge* with other lads from the village talking, talking of their wrongs, of the arrogance of the aristocrats, the sins of *M. le Duc* and his family, the evil conduct of the king and the immorality of the queen: and men in ragged coats and tattered breeches came in from Nantes, and even from Paris, in order to harangue these village lads and told them yet further tales of innumerable wrongs suffered by the people at the hands of the *aristos*, and stuffed their heads full of schemes for getting even once and for all with those men and women who fattened on the sweat of the poor and drew their luxury from the hunger and the toil of the peasantry.

Pierre sucked in these harangues through every pore: they were meat and drink to him. His hate and passions fed upon these effusions till his whole being was consumed by a maddening desire for reprisals, for vengeance—for the lust of triumph over those whom he had been taught to fear.

And in the low, narrow room of the *auberge* the fevered heads of village lads were bent together in conclave, and the ravings and shoutings of a while ago were changed to whisperings and low murmurings behind barred doors and shuttered windows. Men exchanged cryptic greetings when they met in the village street, enigmatical signs passed between them while they worked: strangers came and went at dead of night to and from the neighbouring villages. *M. le Duc's* overseers saw nothing, heard nothing, guessed nothing. *M. le Curé* saw much and old Jean Adet guessed a great deal, but they said nothing, for nothing then would have availed.

Then came the catastrophe.

Pierre pushed open the outer door of the *Auberge des Trois Vertus* and stepped out under the porch. A gust of wind caught him in the face. The night, so the chronicles of the time tell us, was as dark as pitch: on ahead lay the lights of the city flickering in the gale: to the left the wide tawny ribbon of the river wound its turbulent course toward the ocean, the booming of the waters swollen by the recent melting of the snow sounded like the weird echoes of invisible cannons far away.

Without hesitation Pierre advanced. His little troop followed him in silence. They were a little sobered now that they came out into the open and that the fumes of cider and of hot, perspiring humanity no longer obscured their vision or inflamed their brain.

They knew whither Pierre was going. It had all been pre-arranged—throughout this past summer, in the musty parlour of the *auberge*, behind barred doors and shuttered windows—all they had to do was to follow Pierre, whom they had tacitly chosen as their leader.

They walked on behind him, their hands buried in the pockets of their thin, tattered breeches, their heads bent forward against the fury of the gale.

Pierre made straight for the mill—his home—where his father lived and where Louise was even now crying her eyes out because Antoine Melun, her sweetheart, had been condemned to be hanged for killing two pigeons.

At the back of the mill was the dwelling house and beyond it a small farmery, for Jean Adet owned a little bit of land and would have been fairly well off if the taxes had not swallowed up all the money that he made out of the sale of his rye and his hay. Just here the ground rose sharply to a little hillock which dominated the flat valley of the Loire and commanded a fine view over the more distant villages.

Pierre skirted the mill and without looking round to see if the others followed him he struck squarely to the right up a narrow lane bordered by tall poplars, and which led upwards to the summit of the little hillock around which clustered the tumble-down barns of his father's farmery.

The gale lashed the straight, tall stems of the poplars until they bent nearly double, and each tiny bare twig sighed and whispered as if in pain. Pierre strode on and the others followed in silence. They were chilled to the bone under their scanty clothes, but they followed on with grim determination, set teeth, and anger and hate seething in their hearts.

The top of the rising ground was reached. It was pitch dark, and the men when they halted fell up against one another trying to get a foothold on the sodden ground. But Pierre seemed to have eyes like a cat. He only paused one moment to get his bearings, then—still without a word—he set to work. A large barn and a group of small circular straw ricks loomed like solid masses out of the darkness—black, silhouetted against the black of the stormy sky. Pierre turned toward the barn: those of his comrades who were in the forefront of the small crowd saw him disappearing inside one of those solid shadowy masses that looked so ghostlike in the night.

Anon those who watched and who happened to be facing the interior of the barn saw sparks from a tinder flying in every direction: the next moment they could see Pierre himself quite clearly. He was standing in the middle of the barn and intent on lighting a roughly-fashioned torch with his tinder: soon the resin caught a spark and Pierre held the torch inclined toward the ground so that the flames could lick their way up the shaft. The flickering light cast a weird glow and deep grotesque shadows upon the face and figure of the young man. His hair, lanky and dishevelled, fell over his eyes; his mouth and jaw, illumined from below by the torch, looked unnaturally large, and showed his teeth gleaming white, like the fangs of a beast of prey. His shirt was torn open at the neck, and the sleeves of his coat were rolled up to the elbow. He seemed not to feel either the cold from without or the scorching heat of the flaming torch in his hand. But he worked deliberately and calmly, without haste or febrile movements: grim determination held his excitement in check.

At last his work was done. The men who had pressed forward, in order to watch him, fell back as he advanced, torch in hand. They knew exactly what he was going to do, they had thought it all out, planned it, spoken of it till even their unimaginative minds had visualised this coming scene with absolutely realistic perception. And yet, now that the supreme hour had come, now that they saw Pierre—torch in hand—prepared to give the signal which would set ablaze the seething revolt of the countryside, their heart seemed to stop its beating within their body; they held their breath, their toil-worn hands went up to their throats as if to repress that awful choking sensation which was so like fear.

But Pierre had no such hesitations; if his breath seemed to choke him as it reached his throat, if it escaped through his set teeth with a strange whistling sound, it was because his excitement was that of a hungry beast who had sighted his prey and is ready to spring and devour. His hand did not shake, his step was firm: the gusts of wind caught the flame of his torch till the sparks flew in every direction and scorched his hair and his hands, and while the others recoiled he strode on, to the straw-rick that was nearest.

For one moment he held the torch aloft. There was triumph now in his eyes, in his whole attitude. He looked out into the darkness far away which seemed all the more impenetrable beyond the restricted circle of flickering torchlight. It seemed as if he would wrest from that inky blackness all the secrets which it hid—all the enthusiasm, the excitement, the passions, the hatred which he would have liked to set ablaze as he would the straw-ricks *anon*.

"Are you ready, *mes amis?*" he called.

"Aye! aye!" they replied—not gaily, not lustily, but calmly and under their breath.

One touch of the torch and the dry straw began to crackle; a gust of wind caught the flame and whipped it into energy; it crept up the side of the little rick like a glowing python that wraps its prey in its embrace. Another gust of wind, and the flame leapt joyously up to the pinnacle of the rick and sent forth other tongues to lick and to lick, to enfold the straw, to devour, to consume.

But Pierre did not wait to see the consummation of his work of destruction. Already with a few rapid strides he had reached his father's second straw-rick, and this too he set alight, and then another and another, until six blazing furnaces sent their lurid tongues of flames, twisting and twirling, writhing and hissing through the stormy night.

Within the space of two minutes the whole summit of the hillock seemed to be ablaze, and Pierre, like a god of fire, torch in hand, seemed to preside over and command a multitude of ever-spreading flames to his will. Excitement had overmastered him now, the lust to destroy was upon him, and excitement had seized all the others too.

There was shouting and cursing, and laughter that sounded mirthless and forced, and calls to Pierre, and oaths of revenge. Memory, like an evil-intentioned witch, was riding invisibly in the darkness, and she touched each seething brain with her fever-giving wand. Every man had an outrage to remember, an injustice to recall, and strong, brown fists were shaken aloft in the direction of the *château* de Kernogan, whose lights glimmered feebly in the distance beyond the Loire.

"Death to the tyrant! À *la lanterne les aristos!* The people's hour has come at last! No more starvation! No more injustice! Equality! Liberty! À *mort les aristos!*"

The shouts, the curses, the crackling flames, the howling of the wind, the soughing of the trees, made up a confusion of sounds which seemed hardly of this earth; the blazing ricks, the flickering, red light of the flames had finally transformed the little hillock behind the mill into another Brocken on whose summit witches and devils do of a truth hold their revels.

"À *moi!*" shouted Pierre again, and he threw his torch down upon the ground and once more made for the barn. The others followed him. In the barn were such weapons as these wretched, penniless peasants had managed to collect—scythes, poles, axes, saws, anything that would prove useful for the destruction of the *château* de Kernogan and the proposed brow-beating of *M. le Duc* and his family. All the men trooped in in the wake of Pierre. The entire hillock was now a blaze of light—lurid and red and flickering—alternately teased and fanned and subdued by the gale, so that at times every object stood out clearly cut, every blade of grass, every stone in bold relief, and in the ruts and fissures, every tiny pool of muddy water shimmered like strings of fire-opals: whilst at others, a pall of inky darkness, smoke-laden and impenetrable would lie over the ground and erase the outline of farm-buildings and distant mill and of the pushing and struggling mass of humanity inside the barn.

But Pierre, heedless of light and darkness, of heat or of cold, proceeded quietly and methodically to distribute the primitive implements of warfare to this crowd of ignorant men, who were by now over ready for mischief: and with every weapon which he placed in willing hands, he found the right words for willing ears—words which would kindle passion and lust of vengeance most readily where they lay dormant, or would fan them into greater vigour where they smouldered.

"For thee this scythe, Hector Lebrun," he would say to a tall, lanky youth whose emaciated arms and bony hands were stretched with longing toward the bright piece of steel; "remember last year's harvest, the heavy tax thou wert forced to pay, so that not one *sou* of profit went into thy pocket, and thy mother starved whilst *M. le Duc* and his brood feasted and danced, and shiploads of corn were sunk in the Loire lest abundance made bread too cheap for the poor!

"For thee this pick-axe, Henri Meunier! Remember the new roof on thy hut, which thou didst build to keep the wet off thy wife's bed, who was crippled with ague—and the heavy impost levied on thee by the tax-collector for this improvement to thy miserable hovel.

"This pole for thee, Charles Blanc! Remember the beating administered to thee by the *duc's* bailiff for daring to keep a tame rabbit to amuse thy children!

"Remember! Remember, *mes amis!*" he added exultantly, remember every wrong you have endured, every injustice, every blow! remember your poverty and his wealth, your crusts of dry bread and his succulent meals, your rags and his silks and velvets, remember your starving children and ailing mother, your care-laden wife and toil-worn daughters! Forget nothing, *mes amis*, tonight, and at the gates of the *château* de Kernogan demand of its arrogant owner wrong for wrong and outrage for outrage."

A deafening cry of triumph greeted this peroration, scythes and sickles and axes and poles were brandished in the air and several scores of hands were stretched out to Pierre and clasped in this newly-formed bond of vengeful fraternity.

Then it was that with vigorous play of the elbows, Jean Adet, the miller, forced his way through the crowd till he stood face to face with his son.

"Unfortunate!" he cried, "what is all this? What dost thou propose to do? Whither are ye all going?"

"To Kernogan!" they all shouted in response.

"*En avant*, Pierre! we follow!" cried some of them impatiently.

But Jean Adet—who was a powerful man despite his years—had seized Pierre by the arm and dragged him to a distant corner of the barn:

"Pierre!" he said in tones of command, "I forbid thee in the name of thy duty and the obedience which thou dost owe to me and to thy mother, to move another step in this hot-headed adventure. I was on the high-road, walking homewards, when that conflagration and the senseless cries of these poor lads warned me that some awful mischief was afoot. Pierre! my son! I command thee to lay that weapon down."

But Pierre—who in his normal state was a dutiful son and sincerely fond of his father—shook himself free from Jean Adet's grasp.

"Father!" he said loudly and firmly, "this is no time for interference. We are all of us men here and know our own minds. What we mean to do tonight we have thought on and planned for weeks and months. I pray you, father, let me be! I am not a child and I have work to do."

"Not a child?" exclaimed the old man as he turned appealingly to the lads who had stood by, silent and sullen during this little scene. "Not a child? But you are all only children, my lads. You don't know what you are doing. You don't know what terrible consequences this mad escapade will bring upon us all, upon the whole village, aye! and the countryside. Do you suppose for one moment that the *château* of Kernogan will fall at the mercy of a few ignorant unarmed lads like yourselves? Why! four hundred of you would not succeed in forcing your way even as far as the courtyard of the palace. *M. le Duc* has had wind for some time of your turbulent meetings at the *auberge*: he has kept an armed guard inside his castle yard for weeks past, a company of artillery with two guns hoisted upon his walls. My poor lads! you are running straight to ruin! Go home, I beg of you! Forget this night's escapade! Nothing but misery to you and yours can result from it."

They listened quietly, if surlily, to Jean Adet's impassioned words. Far be it from their thoughts to flout or to mock him. Paternal authority commanded respect even among the most rough; but they all felt that they had gone too far now to draw back: the savour of anticipated revenge had been too sweet to be forgone quite so readily, and Pierre with his vigorous personality, his glowing eloquence, his compelling power had more influence over them than the sober counsels of prudence and the wise admonitions of old Jean Adet. Not one word was spoken, but with an instinctive gesture every man grasped his weapon more firmly and then turned to Pierre, thus electing him their spokesman.

Pierre too had listened in silence to all that his father said, striving to hide the burning anxiety which was gnawing at his heart, lest his comrades allowed themselves to be persuaded by the old man's counsels and their ardour be cooled by the wise dictates of prudence. But when Jean Adet had finished speaking, and Pierre saw each man thus grasping his weapon all the more firmly and in silence, a cry of triumph escaped his lips.

"It is all in vain, father," he cried, "our minds are made up. A host of angels from heaven would not bar our way now to victory and to vengeance."

"Pierre!" admonished the old man.

"It is too late, my father," said Pierre firmly, "*en avant*, lads!"

"Yes! *en avant! en avant!*" assented some, "we have wasted too much time as it is."

"But, unfortunate lads," admonished the old man, "what are you going to do?—a handful of you—where are you going?"

"We go straight to the cross-roads now, father," said Pierre, firmly. "The firing of your ricks—for which I humbly crave your pardon—is the preconcerted signal which will bring the lads from all the neighbouring villages—from Goulaine and les Sorinières and Doulon and Tourne-Bride to our meeting place. Never you fear! There will be more than four hundred of us and a company of paid soldiers is not like to frighten us. Eh, lads?"

"No! no! *en avant!*" they shouted and murmured impatiently, "there has been too much talking already and we have wasted precious time."

"Pierre!" entreated the miller.

But no one listened to the old man now. A general movement down the hillock had already begun and Pierre, turning his back on his father, had pushed his way to the front of the crowd and was now leading the way down the slope. Up on the summit the fire was already burning low; only from time to time an imprisoned tongue of flame would dart out of the dying embers and leap fitfully up into the night. A dull red glow illumined the small farmery and the mill and the slowly moving mass of men along the narrow road, whilst clouds of black, dense smoke were tossed about by the gale. Pierre walked with head erect. He ceased to think of his father and he never looked back to see if the others followed him. He knew that they did: like the straw-ricks a while ago, they had become the prey of a consuming fire: the fire of their own passion which had caught them and held them and would not leave them now until their ardour was consumed in victory or defeat.

M. le Duc de Kernogan had just finished dinner when Jacques Labrunière, his head-bailiff, came to him with the news that a rabble crowd, composed of the peasantry of Goulaine and Vertou and the neighbouring villages, had assembled at the cross-roads, there held revolutionary speeches, and was even now marching toward the castle still shouting and singing and brandishing a miscellaneous collection of weapons chiefly consisting of scythes and axes.

"The guard is under arms, I imagine," was *M. le Duc's* comment on this not altogether unforeseen piece of news.

"Everything is in perfect order," replied the head-bailiff coolly, "for the defence of *M. le Duc* and his property—and of *Mademoiselle.*"

M. le Duc, who had been lounging in one of the big armchairs in the stately hall of Kernogan, jumped to his feet at these words: his cheeks suddenly pallid, and a look of deadly fear in his eyes.

"*Mademoiselle,*" he said hurriedly, "by G—d, Labrunière, I had forgotten—momentarily——"

"*M. le Duc?*" stammered the bailiff in anxious inquiry.

"Mademoiselle de Kernogan is on her way home—even now—she spent the day with Mme. le Marquise d'Herbignac—she was to return at about eight o'clock—If those devils meet her carriage on the road—"

"There is no cause for anxiety, *M. le Duc,*" broke in Labrunière hurriedly. "I will see that half a dozen men get to horse at once and go and meet *Mademoiselle* and escort her home—"

"Yes—yes—Labrunière," murmured the *duc,* who seemed very much overcome with terror now that his daughter's safety was in jeopardy, "see to it at once. Quick! quick! I shall wax crazy with anxiety."

While Labrunière ran to make the necessary arrangements for an efficient escort for Mademoiselle de Kernogan and gave the sergeant in charge of the posse the necessary directions, *M. le Duc* remained motionless, huddled up in the capacious armchair, his head buried in his hand, shivering in front of the huge fire which burned in the monumental hearth, himself the prey of nameless, overwhelming terror.

He knew—none better—the appalling hatred wherewith he and all his family and belongings were regarded by the local peasantry. Astride upon his manifold rights—feudal, territorial, seignorial rights—he had all his life ridden roughshod over the prejudices, the miseries, the undoubted rights of the poor people, who were little better than serfs in the possession of the high and mighty Duc de Kernogan. He also knew—none better—that gradually, very gradually it is true, but with unerring certainty, those same downtrodden, ignorant, miserable and half-starved peasants were turning against their oppressors, that riots and outrages had occurred in many rural districts in the North and that the insidious poison of social revolution was gradually creeping toward the South and West, and had already infected the villages and small townships which were situated quite unpleasantly close to Nantes and to Kernogan.

For this reason, he had kept a company of artillery at his own expense inside the precincts of his *château*, and with the aristocrat's open contempt for this peasantry which it had not yet learned to fear, he had disdained to take further measures for the repression of local gatherings, and would not pay the village rabble the compliment of being afraid of them in any way.

But with his daughter Yvonne in the open roadway on the very night when an assembly of that same rabble was obviously bent on mischief, matters became very serious. Insult, outrage or worse might befall the proud aristocrat's only child, and knowing that from these people, whom she had been taught to look upon as little better than beasts, she could expect neither mercy nor chivalry, the Duc de Kernogan within his unassailable castle felt for his daughter's safety the most abject, the most deadly fear which hath ever unnerved any man.

Labrunière a few minutes later did his best to reassure his master.

"I have ordered the men to take the best horses out of the stables, *M. le Duc*," he said, "and to cut across the fields toward la Gramoire so as to intercept *Mademoiselle's* coach ere it reach the cross-roads. I feel confident that there is no cause for alarm," he added emphatically.

"Pray God you are right, Labrunière," murmured the *duc* feebly. "Do you know how strong the rabble crowd is?"

"No, *Monseigneur*, not exactly. Camille the under-bailiff, who brought me the news, was riding homewards across the meadows about an hour ago when he saw a huge conflagration which seemed to come from the back of Adet's mill: the whole sky has been lit up by a lurid light for the past hour, and I fancied myself that Adet's straw must be on fire. But Camille pushed his horse up the rising ground which culminates at Adet's farmery. It seems that he heard a great deal of shouting which did not seem to be accompanied by any attempt at putting out the fire. So, he dismounted and led his horse round the hillock skirting Adet's farm buildings so that he should not be seen. Under cover of darkness he heard and saw the old miller with his son Pierre engaged in distributing scythes, poles and axes to a crowd of youngsters and haranguing them wildly all the time. He also heard Pierre Adet speak of the conflagration as a preconcerted signal and say that he and his mates would meet the lads of the neighbouring villages at the cross-roads—and that four hundred of them would then march on Kernogan and pillage the castle."

"Bah!" quoth *M. le Duc* in a voice hoarse with execration and contempt, "a lot of oafs who will give the hangman plenty of trouble tomorrow. As for that Adet and his son, they shall suffer for this—I can promise them that—If only *Mademoiselle* were home!" he added with a heartrending sigh.

Indeed, had M. le Duc de Kernogan been gifted with second sight, the agony of mind which he was enduring would have been aggravated an hundredfold. At the very moment when the head-bailiff was doing his best to reassure his liege-lord as to the safety of Mlle. de Kernogan, her coach was speeding along from the *château* of Herbignac toward those same cross-roads where a couple of hundred hot-headed peasant lads were planning as much mischief as their unimaginative minds could conceive.

The fury of the gale had in no way abated, and now a heavy rain was falling—a drenching, sopping rain which in the space of half an hour had added five centimetres to the depth of the mud on the roads and had in that same space of time considerably damped the enthusiasm of some of the poor lads. Three score or so had assembled from Goulaine, two score from les Sorinières, some three dozen from Doulon: they had rallied to the signal in hot haste, gathered their scythes and spades, very eager and excited, and had reached the cross-roads which were much nearer to their respective villages than to Jean Adet's farm and the mill, even while the old man was admonishing his son and the lads of Vertou on the summit of the blazing hillock. Here they had spent half an hour in cooling their heels and their tempers under the drenching rain—wet to the skin—fuming and fretting at the delay.

But even so—damped in ardour and chilled to the marrow—they were still a dangerous crowd and prudence ought to have dictated to Mademoiselle de Kernogan the wiser course of ordering her coachman Jean-Marie to head his horses back toward Herbignac the moment that the outrider reported that a mob, armed with scythes, spades and axes, held the cross-roads, and that it would be dangerous for the coach to advance any further.

Already for the past few minutes the sound of loud shouting had been heard even above the tramp of the horses and the clatter of the coach. Jean-Marie had pulled up and sent one of the outriders on ahead to see what was amiss: the man returned with very unpleasant tidings—in his opinion it certainly would be dangerous to go any further. The mob appeared bent on mischief: he had heard threats and curses all levelled against M. le Duc de Kernogan—the conflagration up at Vertou was evidently a signal which would bring along a crowd of malcontents from all the neighbouring villages. He was for turning back forthwith. But *Mademoiselle* put her head out of the window just then and asked what was amiss. On hearing that Jean-Marie and the postilion and outriders were inclined to be afraid of a mob of peasant lads who had assembled at the cross-roads, and were apparently threatening to do mischief, she chided them for their cowardice.

"Jean-Marie," she called scornfully to the old coachman, who had been in her father's service for close on half a century, "do you really mean to tell me that you are afraid of that rabble!"

"Why no! *Mademoiselle*, so please you," replied the old man, nettled in his pride by the taunt, "but the temper of the peasantry round here has been ugly of late, and 'tis your safety I have got to guard."

"'Tis my commands you have got to obey," retorted *Mademoiselle* with a gay little laugh which mitigated the peremptoriness of her tone. "If my father should hear that there's trouble on the road he will die of anxiety if I do not return: so, whip up the horses, Jean-Marie. No one will dare to attack the coach."

"But *Mademoiselle*——" remonstrated the old man.

"*Ah çà!*" she broke in more impatiently, "am I to be openly disobeyed? Best join that rabble, Jean-Marie, if you have no respect for my commands."

Thus, twitted by *Mademoiselle's* sharp tongue, Jean-Marie could not help but obey. He tried to peer into the distance through the veil of blinding rain which beat against his face and stung the horses to restlessness. But the light from the coach lanthorns prevented his seeing clearly into the darkness beyond. Still it seemed to him that on ahead a dense and solid mass was moving toward the coach, also that the sound of shouting and of excited humanity was considerably nearer than it had been before. No doubt the mob had perceived the lights of the coach, and was even now making towards it, with what intent Jean-Marie divined all too accurately.

But he had his orders, and, though he was an old and trusted servant, disobedience these days was not even to be thought of. So, he did as he was bid. He whipped up his horses, which were high-spirited and answered to the lash with a bound and a plunge forward. Mlle. de Kernogan leaned back on the cushions of the coach. She was satisfied that Jean-Marie had done as he was told, and she was not in the least afraid.

But less than five minutes later she had a rude awakening. The coach gave a terrific lurch. The horses reared and plunged, there was a deafening clamour all around: men were shouting and cursing: there was the clash of wood and iron and the cracking of whips: the tramp of horses' hoofs in the soft ground, and the dull thud of human bodies falling in the mud, followed by loud cries of pain. There was the sudden crash of broken glass, the coach lanthorns had been seized and broken: it seemed to Yvonne de Kernogan that out of the darkness faces distorted with fury were peering at her through the window-panes. But through all the confusion, the coach kept moving on. Jean-Marie stuck to his post, as did also the postilion and the four outriders, and with whip and tongue they urged their horses to break through the crowd regardless of human lives, knocking and trampling down men and lads heedless of curses and blasphemies which were hurled on them and on the occupants of the coach, whoever they might be.

The next moment, however, the coach came to a sudden halt, and a wild cry of triumph drowned the groans of the injured and the dying.

"Kernogan! Kernogan!" was shouted from every side.

"Adet! Adet!"

"You limbs of Satan," cried Jean-Marie, "you'll rue this night's work and weep tears of blood for the rest of your lives. Let me tell you that! *Mademoiselle* is in the coach. When *M. le Duc* hears of this, there will be work for the hangman—"

"*Mademoiselle* in the coach," broke in a hoarse voice with a rough tone of command. "Let's look at her—"

"Aye! Aye! let's have a look at *Mademoiselle*," came with a volley of

25

objurgations and curses from the crowd.

"You devils—you would dare?" protested Jean-Marie.

Within the coach Yvonne de Kernogan hardly dared to breathe. She sat bolt upright, her cape held tightly round her shoulders: her eyes dilated now with excitement, if not with fear, were fixed upon the darkness beyond the window-panes. She could see nothing, but she *felt* the presence of that hostile crowd who had succeeded in over-powering Jean-Marie and were intent on doing her harm.

But she belonged to a caste which never reckoned cowardice amongst its many faults. During these few moments when she knew that her life hung on the merest thread of chance, she neither screamed nor fainted but sat rigidly still, her heart beating in unison with the agonising seconds which went so fatefully by. And even now, when the carriage door was torn violently open and even through the darkness she discerned vaguely the forms of these avowed enemies close beside her, and anon felt a rough hand seize her wrist, she did not move, but said quite calmly, with hardly a tremor in her voice:

"Who are you? and what do you want?"

An outburst of harsh and ironical laughter came in response.

"Who are we, my fine lady?" said the foremost man in the crowd, he who had seized her wrist and was half in and half out of the coach at this moment, "we are the men who throughout our lives have toiled and starved whilst you and such as you travel in fine coaches and eat your fill. What we want? Why, just the spectacle of such a fine lady as you are being knocked down into the mud just as our wives and daughters are if they happen to be in the way when your coach is passing. Isn't that it, *mes amis?*"

"Aye! aye!" they replied, shouting lustily. "Into the mud with the fine lady. Out with her, Adet. Let's have a look at *Mademoiselle* how she will look with her face in the mud. Out with her, quick!"

But the man who was still half in and half out of the coach, and who had hold of *Mademoiselle's* wrist did not obey his mates imme-diately. He drew her nearer to him and suddenly threw his rough, begrimed arms round her, and with one hand pulled back her hood, then placing two fingers under her chin, he jerked it up till her face was level with his own.

Yvonne de Kernogan was certainly no coward, but at the loath-some contact of this infuriated and vengeful creature, she was over-come with such a hideous sense of fear that for the moment con-sciousness almost left her: not completely alas! for though she could not distinguish his face she could feel his hot breath upon her cheeks, she could smell the nauseating odour of his damp clothes, and she could hear his hoarse mutterings as for the space of a few seconds he held her thus close to him in an embrace which to her was far more awesome than that of death.

"And just to punish you, my fine lady," he said in a whisper which sent a shudder of horror right through her, "to punish you for what you are, the brood of tyrants, proud, disdainful, a budding tyrant yourself, to punish you for every misery my mother and sister have had to endure, for every luxury which you have enjoyed, I will kiss you on the lips and the cheeks and just between your white throat and chin and never as long as you live if you die this night or live to be an hundred will you be able to wash off those kisses showered upon you by one who hates and loathes you—a miserable peasant whom you despise and who in your sight is lower far than your dogs."

Yvonne, with eyes closed, hardly breathed, but through the veil of semi-consciousness which mercifully wrapped her senses, she could still hear those awful words, and feel the pollution of those loath-some kisses with which—true to his threat—this creature—half man, wholly devil, whom she could not see, but whom she hated and feared as she would Satan himself—now covered her face and throat.

After that she remembered nothing more. Consciousness mer-cifully forsook her altogether. When she recovered her senses, she was within the precincts of the castle: a confused murmur of voices reached her ears, and her father's arms were round her. Gradually she distinguished what was being said: she gathered the threads of the story which Jean-Marie and the postilion and outriders were hastily unravelling in response to *M. le Duc's* commands.

These men of course knew nothing of the poignant little drama which had been enacted inside the coach. All they knew was that they had been surrounded by a rough crowd—a hundred or so strong—who brandished scythes and spades, that they had made valiant efforts to break through the crowd by whipping up their horses, but that suddenly some of those devils more plucky than the others seized the horses by their bits and rendered poor Jean-Marie quite helpless. He thought then that all would be up with the lot of them and was think-ing of scrambling down from his box in order to protect *Mademoiselle* with his body, and the pistols which he had in the boot, when happily for everyone concerned, he heard in the distance—above the clat-ter which that abominable rabble was making, the hurried tramp of horses. At once he jumped to the conclusion that these could be none other than a company of soldiers sent by *M. le Duc.* This spurred him to a fresh effort and gave him a new idea. To Carmail the postilion who had a pistol in his holster he gave the peremptory order to fire a shot into the air or into the crowd, Jean-Marie cared not which. This Carmail did, and at once the horses, already maddened by the crowd, plunged and reared wildly, shaking themselves free. Jean-Marie, however, had them well in hand, and from far away there came the cries of encouragement from the advancing horsemen who were bearing down on them full tilt. The next moment there was a general *mêlée.* Jean-Marie saw nothing save his horses' heads, but the outriders declared that men were trampled down like flies all around, while others vanished into the night.

What happened after that none of the men knew or cared. Jean-Marie galloped his horses all the way to the castle and never drew rein until the precincts were reached.

Had M. de Kernogan had his way and a free hand to mete out retributive justice in the proportion that he desired, there is no doubt that the hangman of Nantes would have been kept exceedingly busy. As it was a number of arrests were effected the following day—half the manhood of the countryside was implicated in the aborted *Jacquerie* and the city prison was not large enough to hold it all.

A court of justice presided over by *M. le Duc* and composed of half a dozen men who were directly or indirectly in his employ, pronounced summary sentences on the rioters which were to have been carried out as soon as the necessary arrangements for such wholesale executions could be made. Nantes was turned into a city of wailing; peasant-women—mothers, sisters, daughters, wives of the condemned, trooped from their villages into the city, loudly calling on *M. le Duc* for mercy, besieging the improvised court-house, the prison gates, the town residence of *M. le Duc*, the palace of the bishop: they pushed their way into the courtyards and the very corridors of those buildings—flunkeys could not cope with them—they fought with fists and elbows for the right to make a direct appeal to the liege-lord who had power of life and death over their men.

The municipality of Nantes held aloof from this distressful state of things, and the town councillors, the city functionaries and their families shut themselves up in their houses in order to avoid being a witness to the heartrending scenes which took place uninterruptedly round the court-house and the prison. The mayor himself was powerless to interfere, but it is averred that he sent a secret courier to Paris to M. de Mirabeau, who was known to be a personal friend of his, with a detailed account of the *Jacquerie* and of the terrible measures of reprisal contemplated by M. le Duc de Kernogan, together with an earnest request that pressure from the highest possible quarters be brought to bear upon His Grace so that he should abate something of his vengeful rigours.

Poor King Louis, who in these days was being terrorised by the National Assembly and swept off his feet by the eloquence of M. de Mirabeau, was only too ready to make concessions to the democratic spirit of the day. He also desired his *noblesse* to be equally ready with such concessions. He sent a personal letter to *M. le Duc*, not only asking him, but commanding him, to show grace and mercy to a lot of misguided peasant lads whose loyalty and adherence—he urged— might be won by a gracious and unexpected act of clemency.

The king's commands could not in the nature of things be disobeyed: the same stroke of the pen which was about to send half a hundred young countrymen to the gallows granted them *M. le Duc's* gracious pardon and their liberty: the only exception to this general amnesty being Pierre Adet, the son of the miller. *M. le Duc's* servants had deposed to seeing him pull open the door of the coach and stand for some time half in and half out of the carriage, obviously trying to terrorise *Mademoiselle*. *Mademoiselle* refused either to corroborate or to deny this statement, but she had arrived fainting at the gate of the *château*, and she had been very ill ever since. She had sustained a serious shock to her nerves, so the doctor hastily summoned from Paris had averred, and it was supposed that she had lost all recollection of the terrible incidents of that night.

But *M. le Duc* was satisfied that it was Pierre Adet's presence inside the coach which had brought about his daughter's mysterious illness and that heartrending look of nameless horror which had dwelt in her eyes ever since. Therefore, with regard to that man *M. le Duc* remained implacable and as a concession to a father's outraged feelings both the mayor of Nantes and the city functionaries accepted Adet's condemnation without a murmur of dissent.

The sentence of death finally passed upon Pierre, the son of Jean Adet, miller of Vertou, could not, however, be executed, for the simple reason that Pierre had disappeared and that the most rigorous search instituted in the neighbourhood and for miles around failed to bring him to justice. One of the outriders who had been in attendance on

Mademoiselle on that fateful night declared that when Jean-Marie finally whipped up his horses at the approach of the party of soldiers, Adet fell backwards from the step of the carriage and was run over by the hind wheels and instantly killed. But his body was never found among the score or so which were left lying there in the mud of the road until the women and old men came to seek their loved ones among the dead.

Pierre Adet had disappeared. But *M. le Duc's* vengeance had need of a prey. The outrage which he was quite convinced had been perpetrated against his daughter must be punished by death—if not by the death of the chief offender, then by that of the one who stood nearest to him. Thus was Jean Adet the miller dragged from his home and cast into prison. Was he not implicated himself in the riots? Camille the bailiff had seen and heard him among the insurgents on the hillock that night. At first it was stated that he would be held as hostage for the reappearance of his son. But Pierre Adet had evidently fled the countryside: he was obviously ignorant of the terrible fate which his own folly had brought upon his father. Many thought that he had gone to seek his fortune in Paris where his talents and erudition would ensure him a good place in the present mad rush for equality amongst all men. Certain it is that he did not return and that with merciless hate and vengeful relentlessness M. le Duc de Kernogan had Jean Adet hanged for a supposed crime said to be committed by his son.

Jean Adet died protesting his innocence. But the outburst of indignation and revolt aroused by this crying injustice was swamped by the torrent of the revolution which, gathering force by these very acts of tyranny and of injustice, soon swept innocent and guilty alike into a vast whirlpool of blood and shame and tears.

BOOK ONE: BATH, 1793

CHAPTER 1

The Moor

Silence. Loneliness. Desolation.

And the darkness of late afternoon in November, when the fog from the Bristol Channel has laid its pall upon moor and valley and hill: the last grey glimmer of a wintry sunset has faded in the west: earth and sky are wrapped in the gloomy veils of oncoming night. Some little way ahead, a tiny light, flickers feebly.

"Surely we cannot be far now."

"A little more patience, *Mounzeer*. Twenty minutes and we be there."

"Twenty minutes, *mordieu*. And I have ridden since the morning. And you tell me it was not far."

"Not far, *Mounzeer*. But we be not 'orzemen either of us. We doan't travel very fast."

"How can I ride fast on this heavy beast? And in this *satané* mud. My horse is up to his knees in it. And I am wet—ah! wet to my skin in this *sacré* fog of yours."

The other made no reply. Indeed he seemed little inclined for conversation: his whole attention appeared to be riveted on the business of keeping in his saddle, and holding his horse's head turned in the direction in which he wished it to go: he was riding a yard or two ahead of his companion, and it did not need any assurance on his part that he was no horseman: he sat very loosely in his saddle, his broad shoulders bent, his head thrust forward, his knees turned out, his hands clinging alternately to the reins and to the pommel with that ludicrous inconsequent gesture peculiar to those who are wholly unaccustomed to horse exercise.

His attitude, in fact, as well as the promiscuous set of clothes which he wore—a labourer's smock, a battered high hat, threadbare corduroys and fisherman's boots—at once suggested the loafer, the do-nothing who hangs round the yards of half-way houses and posting inns on the chance of earning a few coppers by an easy job which does not entail too much exertion on his part and which will not take him too far from his favourite haunts. When he spoke—which was not often—the soft burr in the pronunciation of the sibilants betrayed the Westcountryman.

His companion, on the other hand, was obviously a stranger: high of stature, and broadly built, his wide shoulders and large hands and feet, his square head set upon a short thick neck, all bespoke the physique of a labouring man, whilst his town-made clothes—his heavy caped coat, admirably tailored, his buckskin breeches and boots of fine leather—suggested, if not absolutely the gentleman, at any rate one belonging to the well-to-do classes. Though obviously not quite so inexperienced in the saddle as the other man appeared to be, he did not look very much at home in the saddle either: he held himself very rigid and upright and squared his shoulders with a visible effort at seeming at ease, like a townsman out for a constitutional on the fashionable promenade of his own city, or a cavalry subaltern but lately

31

emerged from a riding school. He spoke English quite fluently, even colloquially at times, but with a marked Gallic accent.

The road along which the two cavaliers were riding was unspeakably lonely and desolate—an offshoot from the main Bath to Weston road. It had been quite a good secondary road once. The accounts of the county administration under date 1725 go to prove that it was completed in that year at considerable expense and with stone brought over for the purpose all the way from Draycott quarries, and for twenty years after that a coach used to ply along it between Chelwood and Redhill as well as two or three carriers, and of course there was all the traffic in connexion with the Stanton markets and the Norton Fairs. But that was nigh on fifty years ago now, and somehow—once the mail-coach was discontinued—it had never seemed worthwhile to keep the road in decent repair. It had gone from bad to worse since then and travelling on it these days either ahorse or afoot had become very unpleasant. It was full of ruts and crevasses and knee-deep in mud, as the stranger had very appositely remarked, and the stone parapet which bordered it on either side, and which had once given it such an air of solidity and of value, was broken down in very many places and threatened soon to disappear altogether.

The country round was as lonely and desolate as the road. And that sense of desolation seemed to pervade the very atmosphere right through the darkness which had descended on upland and valley and hill. Though nothing now could be seen through the gloom and the mist, the senses were conscious that even in broad daylight there would be nothing to see. Loneliness dwelt in the air as well as upon the moor. There were no homesteads for miles around, no cattle grazing, no pastures, no hedges, nothing—just arid wasteland with here and there a group of stunted trees or an isolated yew, and tracts of rough, coarse grass not nearly good enough for cattle to eat.

There are vast stretches of upland equally desolate in many parts of Europe—notably in Northern Spain—but in England, where they are rare, they seem to gain an additional air of loneliness through the very life which pulsates in their vicinity. This bit of Somersetshire was one of them in this year of grace 1793. Despite the proximity of Bath and its fashionable life, its gaieties and vitality, distant only a little over twenty miles, and of Bristol distant less than thirty, it had remained wild and forlorn, almost savage in its grim isolation, primitive in the grandeur of its solitude.

The road at the point now reached by the travellers begins to slope in a gentle gradient down to the level of the Chew, a couple of miles further on: it was midway down this slope that the only sign of living humanity could be perceived in that tiny light which glimmered persistently. The air itself under its mantle of fog had become very still, only the water of some tiny moorland stream murmured feebly in its stony bed ere it lost its entity in the bosom of the river far away.

"Five more minutes and we be at th' Bottom Inn," quoth the man who was ahead in response to another impatient ejaculation from his companion.

"If we don't break our necks meanwhile in this confounded darkness," retorted the other, for his horse had just stumbled and the inexperienced rider had been very nearly pitched over into the mud.

"I be as anxious to arrive as you are, *Mounzeer*," observed the countryman laconically.

"I thought you knew the way," muttered the stranger.

"'Ave I not brought you safely through the darkness?" retorted the other; "you was pretty well ztranded at Chelwood, *Mounzeer*, or I be much mistaken. Who else would 'ave brought you out 'ere at this time o' night, I'd like to know—and in this weather too? You wanted to get to th' Bottom Inn and didn't know 'ow to zet about it: none o' the gaffers up to Chelwood 'peared eager to 'elp you when I come along. Well, I've brought you to th' Bottom Inn and—Whoa! Whoa! my beauty! Whoa, confound you! Whoa!"

And for the next moment or two the whole of his attention had perforce to be concentrated on the business of sticking to his saddle whilst he brought his fagged-out, ill-conditioned nag to a standstill.

The little glimmer of light had suddenly revealed itself in the shape of a lanthorn hung inside the wooden porch of a small house which had loomed out of the darkness and the fog. It stood at an angle of the road where a narrow lane had its beginnings ere it plunged into the moor beyond and was swallowed up by the all-enveloping gloom. The house was small and ugly; square like a box and built of grey stone, its front flush with the road, its rear flanked by several small outbuildings. Above the porch hung a plain sign-board bearing the legend: "The Bottom Inn" in white letters upon a black ground: to right and left of the porch there was a window with closed shutters, and on the floor above two more windows—also shuttered—completed the architectural features of the Bottom Inn.

It was uncompromisingly ugly and uninviting, for beyond the faint glimmer of the lanthorn only one or two narrow streaks of light filtrated through the chinks of the shutters.

The travellers, after some difference of opinion with their respective horses, contrived to pull up and to dismount without any untoward accident. The stranger looked about him, peering into the darkness. The place indeed appeared dismal and inhospitable enough: its solitary aspect suggested footpads and the abode of cut-throats. The silence of the moor, the pall of mist and gloom that hung over upland and valley sent a shiver through his spine.

"You are sure this is the place?" he queried.

"Can't ye zee the zign?" retorted the other gruffly.

"Can you hold the horses while I go in?"

"I doan't know as 'ow I can, *Mounzeer*. I've never 'eld two 'orzes all at once. Suppose they was to start kickin' or thought o' runnin' away?"

"Running away, you fool!" muttered the stranger, whose temper had evidently suffered grievously during the weary, cold journey from Chelwood. "I'll break your *satané* head if anything happens to the beasts. How can I get back to Bath save the way I came? Do you think I want to spend the night in this God-forsaken hole?"

Without waiting to hear any further protests from the lout, he turned into the porch and with his riding whip gave three consecutive raps against the door of the inn, followed by two more. The next moment there was the sound of a rattling of bolts and chains, the door was cautiously opened and a timid voice queried:

"Is it *Mounzeer?*"

"*Pardieu!* Who else?" growled the stranger. "Open the door, woman. I am perished with cold."

With an unceremonious kick he pushed the door further open and strode in. A woman was standing in the dimly lighted passage. As the stranger walked in she bobbed him a respectful curtsey.

"It is all right, *Mounzeer*," she said; "the Captain's in the coffee-room. He came over from Bristol early this afternoon."

"No one else here, I hope," he queried curtly.

"No one, zir. It ain't their hour not yet. You'll 'ave the 'ouse to yourself till after midnight. After that there'll be a bustle, I reckon. Two shiploads come into Watchet last night—brandy and cloth, *Mounzeer*, so the Captain says, and worth a mint o' money. The pack 'orzes will be through yere in the small hours."

"That's all right, then. Send me in a bite and a mug of hot ale."

"I'll see to it, *Mounzeer*."

"And stay—have you some sort of stabling where the man can put the two horses up for an hour's rest?"

"Aye, aye, zir."

"Very well then, see to that too: and see that the horses get a feed and a drink and give the man something to eat."

"Very good, *Mounzeer*. This way, zir. I'll see the man presently. Straight down the passage, zir. The coffee-room is on the right. The Captain's there, waiting for ye."

She closed the front door carefully, then followed the stranger to the door of the coffee-room. Outside an anxious voice was heard muttering a string of inconsequent and wholly superfluous "Whoa's!" Of a truth the two wearied nags were only too anxious for a little rest.

Chapter 2

The Bottom Inn

A man was sitting, huddled up in the ingle-nook of the small coffee-room, sipping hot ale from a tankard which he had in his hand.

Anything less suggestive of a rough sea-faring life than his appearance it would be difficult to conceive; and how he came by the appellation "the Captain" must for ever remain a mystery. He was small and spare, with thin delicate face and slender hands: though dressed in very rough garments, he was obviously ill at ease in them; his narrow shoulders scarcely appeared able to bear the weight of the coarsely made coat, and his thin legs did not begin to fill the big fisherman's boots which reached midway up his lean thighs. His hair was lank and plentifully sprinkled with grey: he wore it tied at the nape of the neck with a silk bow which certainly did not harmonise with the rest of his clothing. A wide-brimmed felt hat something the shape of a sailor's, but with higher crown—of the shape worn by the peasantry in Brittany—lay on the bench beside him.

When the stranger entered he had greeted him curtly, speaking in French.

The room was inexpressibly stuffy, and reeked of the fumes of stale tobacco, stale victuals and stale beer; but it was warm, and the stranger, stiff to the marrow and wet to the skin, uttered an exclamation of well-being as he turned to the hearth, wherein a bright fire burned cheerily. He had put his hat down when first he entered and had divested himself of his big coat: now he held one foot and then the other to the blaze and tried to infuse new life into his numbed hands.

"The Captain" took scant notice of his comings and goings. He did not attempt to help him off with his coat, nor did he make an effort to add another log to the fire. He sat silent and practically motion-less, save when from time to time he took a sip out of his mug of ale. But whenever the new-comer came within his immediate circle of vision he shot a glance at the latter's elegant attire—the well-cut coat, the striped waistcoat, the boots of fine leather—the glance was quick and comprehensive and full of scorn, a flash that lasted only an instant and was at once veiled again by the droop of the flaccid lids which hid the pale, keen eyes.

"When the woman has brought me something to eat and drink," the stranger said after a while, "we can talk. I have a good hour to spare, as those miserable nags must have some rest."

He too spoke in French and with an air of authority, not to say arrogance, which caused "the Captain's" glance of scorn to light up with an added gleam of hate and almost of cruelty. But he made no remark and continued to sip his ale in silence, and for the next half-hour the two men took no more notice of one another, just as if they had never travelled all those miles and come to this desolate spot for the sole purpose of speaking with one another. During the course of that half-hour the woman brought in a dish of mutton stew, a chunk of bread, a piece of cheese and a jug of spiced ale and placed them on the table: all of these good things the stranger consumed with an obviously keen appetite. When he had eaten and drunk his fill, he rose from the table, drew a bench into the ingle-nook and sat down so that his profile only was visible to his friend "the Captain."

"Now, Citizen Chauvelin," he said with at attempt at ease and familiarity not unmixed with condescension, "I am ready for your news."

Chauvelin had winced perceptibly both at the condescension and the familiarity. It was such a very little while ago that men had trem-bled at a look, a word from him: his silence had been wont to strike terror in quaking hearts. It was such a very little while ago that he had been president of the Committee of Public Safety, all powerful, the right hand of citizen Robespierre, the master sleuth-hound who could track an unfortunate "suspect" down to his most hidden lair, before whose keen, pale eyes the innermost secrets of a soul stood revealed, who guessed at treason ere it was wholly born, who scented treachery ere it was formulated. A year ago, he had with a word sent scores of men, women and children to the guillotine—he had with a sign brought the whole machinery of the ruthless Committee to work against innocent or guilty alike on mere suspicion, or to gratify his own hatred against all those whom he considered to be the enemies of that bloody revolution which he had helped to make. Now his presence, his silence, had not even the power to ruffle the self-assurance of an upstart.

But in the hard school both of success and of failure through which he had passed during the last decade, there was one lesson which Armand once Marquis de Chauvelin had learned to the last letter, and that was the lesson of self-control. He had winced at the other's familiarity, but neither by word nor gesture did he betray what he felt.

"I can tell you," he merely said quite curtly, "all I have to say in far less time than it has taken you to eat and drink, citizen Adet—"

But suddenly, at sound of that name, the other had put a warning hand on Chauvelin's arm, even as he cast a rapid, anxious look all round the narrow room.

"Hush, man!" he murmured hurriedly, "you know quite well that that name must never be pronounced here in England. I am Martin-Roget now," he added, as he shook off his momentary fright with equal suddenness, and once more resumed his tone of easy condescension, "and try not to forget it."

Chauvelin without any haste quietly freed his arm from the other's grasp. His pale face was quite expressionless, only the thin lips were drawn tightly over the teeth now, and a curious hissing sound escaped faintly from them as he said:

"I'll try and remember, citizen, that here in England you are an *aristo*, the same as all these confounded English whom may the devil sweep into a bottomless sea."

Martin-Roget gave a short, complacent laugh.

"Ah," he said lightly, "no wonder you hate them, Citizen Chauvelin. You too were an *aristo* here in England once—not so very long ago, I am thinking—special envoy to His Majesty King George, what?—until failure to bring one of these *satané* Britishers to book made you—er—well, made you what you are now."

He drew up his tall, broad figure as he spoke and squared his massive shoulders as he looked down with a fatuous smile and no small measure of scorn on the hunched-up little figure beside him. It had seemed to him that something in the nature of a threat had crept into Chauvelin's attitude, and he, still flushed with his own importance, his immeasurable belief in himself, at once chose to measure his strength against this man who was the personification of failure and disgrace—this man whom so many people had feared for so long and whom it

37

might not be wise to defy even now.

"No offence meant, Citizen Chauvelin," he added with an air of patronage which once more made the other wince. "I had no wish to wound your susceptibilities. I only desired to give you timely warning that what I do here is no one's concern, and that I will brook interference and criticism from no man."

And Chauvelin, who in the past had oft with a nod sent a man to the guillotine, made no reply to this arrogant taunt. His small figure seemed to shrink still further within itself: and anon he passed his thin, claw-like hand over his face as if to obliterate from its surface any expression which might war with the utter humility wherewith he now spoke.

"Nor was there any offence meant on my part, citizen Martin-Roget," he said suavely. "Do we not both labour for the same end? The glory of the Republic and the destruction of her foes?"

Martin-Roget gave a sigh of satisfaction. The battle had been won: he felt himself strong again—stronger than before through that very act of deference paid to him by the once all-powerful Chauvelin. Now he was quite prepared to be condescending and jovial once again:

"Of course, of course," he said pleasantly, as he once more bent his tall figure to the fire. "We are both servants of the Republic, and I may yet help you to retrieve your past failures, citizen, by giving you an active part in the work I have in hand. And now," he added in a calm, business-like manner, the manner of a master addressing a servant who has been found at fault and is taken into favour again, "let me hear your news."

"I have made all the arrangements about the ship," said Chauvelin quietly.

"Ah! that is good news indeed. What is she?"

"She is a Dutch ship. Her master and crew are all Dutch—"

"That's a pity. A Danish master and crew would have been safer."

"I could not come across any Danish ship willing to take the risks," said Chauvelin dryly.

"Well! And what about this Dutch ship then?"

"She is called the *Hollandia* and is habitually engaged in the sugar trade: but her master does a lot of contraband—more that than fair trading, I imagine: anyway, he is willing for the sum you originally named to take every risk and incidentally to hold his tongue about the whole business."

"For two thousand *francs?*"

"Yes."

"And he will run the *Hollandia* into Le Croisic?"

"When you command."

"And there is suitable accommodation on board her for a lady and her woman?"

"I don't know what you call suitable," said Chauvelin with a sarcastic tone, which the other failed or was unwilling to note, "and I don't know what you call a lady. The accommodation available on board the *Hollandia* will be sufficient for two men and two women."

"And her master's name?" queried Martin-Roget.

"Some outlandish Dutch name," replied Chauvelin. "It is spelt K U Y P E R. The devil only knows how it is pronounced."

"Well! And does Captain K U Y P E R understand exactly what I want?"

"He says he does. The *Hollandia* will put into Portishead on the last day of this month. You and your guests can get aboard her any day after that you choose. She will be there at your disposal and can start within an hour of your getting aboard. Her master will have all his papers ready. He will have a cargo of West Indian sugar on board—destination Amsterdam, consignee Mynheer van Smeer—everything perfectly straight and square. French *aristos*, *émigrés* on board on their way to join the army of the princes. There will be no difficulty in England."

"And none in Le Croisic. The man is running no risks."

"He thinks he is. France does not make Dutch ships and Dutch crews exactly welcome just now, does she?"

"Certainly not. But in Le Croisic and with Citizen Adet on board—"

"I thought that name was not to be mentioned here," retorted Chauvelin dryly.

"You are right, citizen," whispered the other, "it escaped me and—"

Already he had jumped to his feet, his face suddenly pale, his whole manner changed from easy, arrogant self-assurance to uncertainty and obvious dread. He moved to the window, trying to subdue the sound of his footsteps upon the uneven floor.

"Are you afraid of eavesdroppers, Citizen Roget?" queried Chauvelin with a shrug of his narrow shoulders.

"No. There is no one there. Only a lout from Chelwood who brought me here. The people of the house are safe enough. They have plenty of secrets of their own to keep."

He was obviously saying all this in order to reassure himself, for there was no doubt that his fears were on the alert. With a febrile gesture he unfastened the shutters, and pushed them open, peering out into the night.

"Hallo!" he called.

But he received no answer.

"It has started to rain," he said more calmly. "I imagine that lout has found shelter in an outhouse with the horses."

"Very likely," commented Chauvelin laconically.

"Then if you have nothing more to tell me," quoth Martin-Roget, "I may as well think about getting back. Rain or no rain, I want to be in Bath before midnight."

"Ball or supper-party at one of your duchesses?" queried the other with a sneer. "I know them."

To this Martin-Roget vouchsafed no reply.

"How are things at Nantes?" he asked.

"Splendid! Carrier is like a wild beast let loose. The prisons are over-full: the surplus of accused, condemned and suspect fills the cellars and warehouses along the wharf. Priests and suchlike trash are kept on disused galliots up stream. The guillotine is never idle, and friend Carrier fearing that she might give out—get tired, what?—or break down—has invented a wonderful way of getting rid of shoals of undesirable people at one magnificent swoop. You have heard tell of it no doubt."

"Yes. I have heard of it," remarked the other curtly.

"He began with a load of priests. Requisitioned an old barge. Ordered Baudet the shipbuilder to construct half a dozen portholes in her bottom. Baudet demurred: he could not understand what the order could possibly mean. But Foucaud and Lamberty—Carrier's agents—you know them—explained that the barge would be towed down the Loire and then up one of the smaller navigable streams which it was feared the royalists were preparing to use as a way for making a descent upon Nantes, and that the idea was to sink the barge in midstream in order to obstruct the passage of their army. Baudet, satisfied, put five of his men to the task. Everything was ready on the 16th of last month. I know the woman Pichot, who keeps a small tavern opposite La Sécherie.

"She saw the barge glide up the river toward the *galliot* where twenty-five priests of the diocese of Nantes had been living for the past two months in the company of rats and other vermin as noxious as themselves. Most lovely moonlight there was that night. The Loire looked like a living ribbon of silver. Foucaud and Lamberty directed operations, and Carrier had given them full instructions. They tied the *calotins* up two and two and transferred them from the galliot to the barge. It seems they were quite pleased to go. Had enough of the rats, I presume. The only thing they didn't like was being searched. Some had managed to secrete silver ornaments about their person when they were arrested. Crucifixes and such like. They didn't like to part with these, it seems. But Foucaud and Lamberty relieved them of everything but the necessary clothing, and they didn't want much of that, seeing whither they were going. Foucaud made a good pile, so they say. Self-seeking, avaricious brute! He'll learn the way to one of Carrier's barges too one day, I'll bet."

He rose and with quick footsteps moved to the table. There was some ale left in the jug which the woman had brought for Martin-Roget a while ago. Chauvelin poured the contents of it down his throat. He had talked uninterruptedly, in short, jerky sentences, without the slightest expression of horror at the atrocities which he recounted. His whole appearance had become transfigured while he spoke. Gone was the urbane manner which he had learnt at courts long ago, gone was the last instinct of the gentleman sunk to proletarianism through stress of circumstances, or financial straits or even political convictions. The erstwhile Marquis de Chauvelin—envoy of the Republic at the Court of St. James'—had become Citizen Chauvelin in deed and in fact, a part of that rabble which he had elected to serve, one of that vile crowd of bloodthirsty revolutionaries who had sullied the pure robes of Liberty and of Fraternity by spattering them with blood. Now he smacked his lips, wiped his mouth with his sleeve, and burying his hands in the pockets of his breeches he stood with legs wide apart and a look of savage satisfaction settled upon his pale face. Martin-Roget had made no comment upon the narrative. He had resumed his seat by the fire and was listening attentively. Now while the other drank and paused, he showed no sign of impatience, but there was something in the look of the bent shoulders, in the rigidity of the attitude, in the large, square hands tightly clasped together which suggested the deepest interest and an intentness that was almost painful.

"I was at the woman Pichot's tavern that night," resumed Chauvelin after a while. "I saw the barge—a moving coffin, what?—gliding downstream towed by the galliot and escorted by a small boat. The floating battery at La Samaritaine challenged her as she passed, for

Carrier had prohibited all navigation up or down the Loire until further notice. Foucaud, Lamberty, Fouquet and O'Sullivan the armourer were in the boat: they rowed up to the pontoon and Vailly the chief gunner of the battery challenged them once more.

"However, they had some sort of written authorisation from Carrier, for they were allowed to pass. Vailly remained on guard. He saw the barge glide further downstream. It seems that the moon on that time was hidden by a cloud. But the night was not dark and Vailly watched the barge till she was out of sight. She was towed past Trentemoult and Chantenay into the wide reach of the river just below Cheviré where, as you know, the Loire is nearly two thousand feet wide."

Once more he paused, looking down with grim amusement on the bent shoulders of the other man.

"Well?"

Chauvelin laughed. The query sounded choked and hoarse, whether through horror, excitement or mere impatient curiosity it were impossible to say.

"Well!" he retorted with a careless shrug of the shoulders. "I was too far up stream to see anything and Vailly saw nothing either. But he heard. So, did others who happened to be on the shore close by."

"What did they hear?"

"The hammering," replied Chauvelin curtly, "when the portholes were knocked open to let in the flood of water. And the screams and yells of five and twenty drowning priests."

"Not one of them escaped, I suppose?"

"Not one."

Once more Chauvelin laughed. He had a way of laughing—just like that—in a peculiar mirthless, derisive manner, as if with joy at another man's discomfiture, at another's material or moral downfall. There is only one language in the world which has a word to express that type of mirth; the word is *Schadenfreude*.

It was Chauvelin's turn to triumph now. He had distinctly perceived the signs of an inward shudder which had gone right through Martin-Roget's spine: he had also perceived through the man's bent shoulders, his silence, his rigidity that his soul was filled with horror at the story of that abominable crime which he—Chauvelin—had so blandly retailed and that he was afraid to show the horror which he felt. And the man who is afraid can never climb the ladder of success above the man who is fearless.

There was silence in the low raftered room for a while: silence only broken by the crackling and sizzling of damp logs in the hearth, and the tap-tapping of a loosely fastened shutter which sounded weird and ghoulish like the knocking of ghosts against the window-frame. Martin-Roget bending still closer to the fire knew that Chauvelin was watching him and that Chauvelin had triumphed, for—despite failure, despite humiliation and disgrace—that man's heart and will had never softened: he had remained as merciless, as fanatical, as before and still looked upon every sign of pity and humanity for a victim of that bloody revolution—which was his child, the thing of his creation, yet worshipped by him, its creator—as a crime against patriotism and against the Republic.

And Martin-Roget fought within himself lest something he might say or do, a look, a gesture should give the other man an indication that the horrible account of a hideous crime perpetrated against twenty-five defenceless men had roused a feeling of unspeakable horror in his heart. That was the punishment of these callous makers of a ruthless revolution—that was their hell upon earth, that they were doomed to hate and to fear one another; every man feeling that the other's hand was up against him as it had been against law and order, against the guilty and the innocent, the rebel and the defenceless; every man knowing that the other was always there on the alert, ready to pounce like a beast of prey upon any victim—friend, comrade, brother—who came within reach of his hand.

Like many men stronger than himself, Pierre Adet—or Martin-Roget as he now called himself—had been drawn into the vortex of bloodshed and of tyranny out of which now he no longer had the power to extricate himself. Nor had he any wish to extricate himself. He had too many past wrongs to avenge, too much injustice on the part of Fate and Circumstance to make good, to wish to draw back now that a newly-found power had been placed in the hands of men such as he through the revolt of an entire people. The sickening sense of horror which a moment ago had caused him to shudder and to turn away in loathing from Chauvelin was only like the feeble flicker of a light before it wholly dies down—the light of something purer, early lessons of childhood, former ideals, earlier aspirations, now smothered beneath the passions of revenge and of hate.

And he would not give Chauvelin the satisfaction of seeing him wince. He was himself ashamed of his own weakness. He had deliberately thrown in his lot with these men and he was determined not to

43

fall a victim to their denunciations and to their jealousies. So now he made a great effort to pull himself together, to bring back before his mind those memory-pictures of past tyranny and oppression which had effectually killed all sense of pity in his heart, and it was in a tone of perfect indifference which gave no loophole to Chauvelin's sneers that he asked after a while:

"And was Citizen Carrier altogether pleased with the result of his patriotic efforts?"

"Oh, quite!" replied the other. "He has no one's orders to take. He is proconsul—virtual dictator in Nantes: and he has vowed that he will purge the city from all save its most deserving citizens. The cargo of priests was followed by one of malefactors, night-birds, cut-throats and such like. That is where Carrier's patriotism shines out in all its glory. It is not only priests and *aristos*, you see—other miscreants are treated with equal fairness."

"Yes! I see he is quite impartial," remarked Martin-Roget coolly.

"Quite," retorted Chauvelin, as he once more sat down in the ingle-nook. And, leaning his elbows upon his knees he looked straight and deliberately into the other man's face, and added slowly: "You will have no cause to complain of Carrier's want of patriotism when you hand over your bag of birds to him."

This time Martin-Roget had obviously winced, and Chauvelin had the satisfaction of seeing that his thrust had gone home: though Martin-Roget's face was in shadow, there was something now in his whole attitude, in the clasping and unclasping of his large, square hands which indicated that the man was labouring under the stress of a violent emotion. In spite of this he managed to say quite coolly: "What do you mean exactly by that, Citizen Chauvelin?"

"Oh!" replied the other, "you know well enough what I mean—I am no fool, what?—or the Revolution would have no use for me. If after my many failures she still commands my services and employs me to keep my eyes and ears open, it is because she knows that she can count on me. I do keep my eyes and ears open, Citizen Adet or Martin-Roget, whatever you like to call yourself, and also my mind—and I have a way of putting two and two together to make four. There are few people in Nantes who do not know that old Jean Adet, the miller, was hanged four years ago, because his son Pierre had taken part in some kind of open revolt against the tyranny of the *ci-devant* Duc de Kernogan and was not there to take his punishment himself. I knew old Jean Adet—I was on the Place du Bouffay at Nantes when he was hanged—"

But already Martin-Roget had jumped to his feet with a muttered blasphemy.

"Have done, man," he said roughly, "have done!" And he started pacing up and down the narrow room like a caged panther, snarling and showing his teeth, whilst his rough, toil-worn hands quivered with the desire to clutch an unseen enemy by the throat and to squeeze the life out of him. "Think you," he added hoarsely, "that I need reminding of that?"

"No. I do not think that, citizen," replied Chauvelin calmly, "I only desired to warn you."

"Warn me? Of what?"

Nervous, agitated, restless, Martin-Roget had once more gone back to his seat: his hands were trembling as he held them up mechanically to the blaze and his face was the colour of lead. In contrast with his restlessness Chauvelin appeared the more calm and bland.

"Why should you wish to warn me?" asked the other querulously, but with an attempt at his former over-bearing manner. "What are my affairs to you—what do you know about them?"

"Oh, nothing, nothing, citizen Martin-Roget," replied Chauvelin pleasantly, "I was only indulging the fancy I spoke to you about just now of putting two and two together in order to make four. The chartering of a smuggler's craft—*aristos* on board her—her ostensible destination Holland—her real objective Le Croisic—Le Croisic is now the port for Nantes and we don't bring *aristos* into Nantes these days for the object of providing them with a feather-bed and a competence, what?"

"And," retorted Martin-Roget quietly, "if your surmises are correct, Citizen Chauvelin, what then?"

"Oh, nothing!" replied the other indifferently. "Only—take care, citizen—that is all."

"Take care of what?"

"Of the man who brought me, Chauvelin, to ruin and disgrace."

"Oh! I have heard of that legend before now," said Martin-Roget with a contemptuous shrug of the shoulders. "The man they call the Scarlet Pimpernel you mean?"

"Why, yes!"

"What have I to do with him?"

"I don't know. But remember that I myself have twice been after that man here in England; that twice he slipped through my fingers when I thought I held him so tightly that he could not possibly escape and that twice in consequence I was brought to humiliation and to shame. I am a marked man now—the guillotine will soon claim me for her future use. Your affairs, citizen, are no concern of mine, but I have marked that Scarlet Pimpernel for mine own. I won't have any blunderings on your part give him yet another triumph over us all."

Once more Martin-Roget swore one of his favourite oaths.

"By Satan and all his brood, man," he cried in a passion of fury, "have done with this interference. Have done, I say. I have nothing to do, I tell you, with your *satané* Scarlet Pimpernel. My concern is with—"

"With the Duc de Kernogan," broke in Chauvelin calmly, "and with his daughter; I know that well enough. You want to be even with them over the murder of your father. I know that too. All that is your affair. But beware, I tell you. To begin with, the secrecy of your identity is absolutely essential to the success of your plan. What?"

"Of course, it is. But—"

"But nevertheless, your identity is known to the most astute, the keenest enemy of the Republic."

"Impossible," asserted Martin-Roget hotly.

"The Duc de Kernogan—"

"Bah! He had never the slightest suspicion of me. Think you his High and Mightiness in those far-off days ever looked twice at a village lad so that he would know him again four years later? I came into this country as an *émigré* stowed away in a smuggler's ship like a bundle of contraband goods. I have papers to prove that my name is Martin-Roget and that I am a banker from Brest. The worthy bishop of Brest—denounced to the Committee of Public Safety for treason against the Republic—was given his life and a safe conduct into Spain on the condition that he gave me—Martin-Roget—letters of personal introduction to various high-born *émigrés* in Holland, in Germany and in England. Armed with these I am invulnerable. I have been presented to His Royal Highness the Regent, and to the *élite* of English society in Bath. I am the friend of M. le Duc de Kernogan now and the accredited suitor for his daughter's hand."

"His daughter!" broke in Chauvelin with a sneer, and his pale, keen eyes had in them a spark of malicious mockery.

Martin-Roget made no immediate retort to the sneer. A curious hot flush had spread over his forehead and his ears, leaving his cheeks wan and livid.

"What about the daughter?" reiterated Chauvelin.

"Yvonne de Kernogan has never seen Pierre Adet the miller's son," replied the other curtly. "She is now the affianced wife of Martin-Roget the millionaire banker of Brest. Tonight, I shall persuade *M. le Duc* to allow my marriage with his daughter to take place within the week. I shall plead pressing business in Holland and my desire that my wife shall accompany me thither. The duke will consent and Yvonne de Kernogan will not be consulted. The day after my wedding I shall be on board the *Hollandia* with my wife and father-in-law, and together we will be on our way to Nantes where Carrier will deal with them both."

"You are quite satisfied that this plan of yours is known to no one, that no one at the present moment is aware of the fact that Pierre Adet, the miller's son, and Martin-Roget, banker of Brest, are one and the same?"

"Quite satisfied," replied Martin-Roget emphatically.

"Very well, then, let me tell you this, citizen," rejoined Chauvelin slowly and deliberately, "that in spite of what you say I am as convinced as that I am here, alive, that your real identity will be known—if it is not known already—to a gentleman who is at this present moment in Bath, and who is known to you, to me, to the whole of France as the Scarlet Pimpernel."

Martin-Roget laughed and shrugged his shoulders.

"Impossible!" he retorted. "Pierre Adet no longer exists—he never existed—much—Anyhow, he ceased to be on that stormy day in September, 1789. Unless your pet enemy is a wizard he cannot know."

"There is nothing that my pet enemy—as you call him—cannot ferret out if he has a mind to. Beware of him, citizen Martin-Roget. Beware, I tell you."

"How can I," laughed the other contemptuously, "if I don't know who he is?"

"If you did," retorted Chauvelin, "it wouldn't help you—much. But beware of every man you don't know; beware of every stranger you meet; trust no one; above all, follow no one. He is there where you least expect him under a disguise you would scarcely dream of."

"Tell me who he is then—since you know him—so that I may duly beware of him."

"No," rejoined Chauvelin with the same slow deliberation, "I will not tell you who he is. Knowledge in this case would be a very dangerous thing."

"Dangerous? To whom?"

"To yourself probably. To me and to the Republic most undoubtedly. No! I will not tell you who the Scarlet Pimpernel is. But take my advice, citizen Martin-Roget," he added emphatically, "go back to Paris or to Nantes and strive there to serve your country rather than run your head into a noose by meddling with things here in England and running after your own schemes of revenge."

"My own schemes of revenge!" exclaimed Martin-Roget with a hoarse cry that was like a snarl—It seemed as if he wanted to say something more, but that the words choked him even before they reached his lips. The hot flush died down from his forehead and his face was once more the colour of lead. He took up a log from the corner of the hearth and threw it with a savage, defiant gesture into the fire.

Somewhere in the house a clock struck nine.

Martin-Roget waited until the last echo of the gong had died away, then he said very slowly and very quietly:

"Forgo my own schemes of revenge? Can you even remotely guess, Citizen Chauvelin, what it would mean to a man of my temperament and of my calibre to give up that for which I have toiled and striven for the past four years? Think of what I was on that day when a conglomeration of adverse circumstances turned our proposed expedition against the *château* de Kernogan into a disaster for our village lads, and a triumph for the *duc*. I was knocked down and crushed all but to death by the wheels of Mlle. de Kernogan's coach. I managed to crawl in the mud and the cold and the rain, on my hands and knees, hurt, bleeding, half dead, as far as the presbytery of Vertou where the *cure* kept me hidden at risk of his own life for two days until I was able to crawl farther away out of sight.

"The *cure* did not know, I did not know then of the devilish revenge which the Duc de Kernogan meant to wreak against my father. The news reached me when it was all over and I had worked my way to Paris with the few *sous* in my pocket which that good *cure* had given me, earning bed and bread as I went along. I was an ignorant lout when I arrived in Paris. I had been one of the *ci-devant* Kernogan's labourers—his chattel, what?—little better or somewhat worse off than a slave. There I heard that my father had been foully murdered—hung for a crime which I was supposed to have committed, for which I had not even been tried. Then the change in me began. For four years I starved in a garret, toiling like a galley-slave with my hands and muscles by day and at my books by night.

"And what am I now? I have worked at books, at philosophy, at science: I am a man of education. I can talk and discuss with the best of those d——d *aristos* who flaunt their caprices and their mincing manners in the face of the outraged democracy of two continents. I speak English—almost like a native—and Danish and German too. I can quote English poets and criticise M. de Voltaire. I am an *aristo*, what? For this I have worked, Citizen Chauvelin—day and night— oh! those nights! how I have slaved to make myself what I now am! And all for the one object—the sole object without which exist- ence would have been absolutely unendurable. That object guided me, helped me to bear and to toil, it cheered and comforted me! To be even one day with the Duc de Kernogan and with his daughter! to be their master! to hold them at my mercy!—to destroy or pardon as I choose!—to be the arbiter of their fate!—I have worked for four years: now my goal is in sight, and you talk glibly of forgoing my own schemes of revenge! Believe me, Citizen Chauvelin," he concluded, "it would be easier for me to hold my right hand into those flames until it hath burned to a cinder than to forgo the hope of that vengeance which has eaten into my soul. It would hurt much less."

He had spoken thus at great length, but with extraordinary re- straint. Never once did he raise his voice or indulge in gesture. He spoke in even, monotonous tones, like one who is reciting a lesson; and he sat straight in front of the fire, his elbow on his knee, his chin resting in his hand and his eyes fixed upon the flames.

Chauvelin had listened in perfect silence. The scorn, the resentful anger, the ill-concealed envy of the fallen man for the successful up- start had died out of his glance. Martin-Roget's story, the intensity of feeling betrayed in that absolute, outward calm had caused a chord of sympathy to vibrate in the other's atrophied heart. How well he un- derstood that vibrant passion of hate, that longing to exact an eye for an eye, an outrage for an outrage! Was not his own life given over now to just such a longing?—a mad aching desire to be even once with that hated enemy, that maddening, mocking, elusive Scarlet Pimpernel who had fooled and baffled him so often?

Some few moments had gone by since Martin-Roget's harsh, mo- notonous voice had ceased to echo through the low raftered room: silence had fallen between the two men—there was indeed nothing more to say; the one had unburthened his over-full heart and the other had understood. They were of a truth made to understand one another, and the silence between them betokened sympathy.

Around them all was still, the stillness of a mist-laden night; in the house no one stirred: the shutter even had ceased to creak; only the crackling of the wood fire broke that silence which soon became oppressive.

Martin-Roget was the first to rouse himself from this trance-like state wherein memory was holding such ruthless sway: he brought his hands sharply down on his knees, turned to look for a moment on his companion, gave a short laugh and finally rose, saying briskly the while:

"And now, citizen, I shall have to bid you *adieu* and make my way back to Bath. The nags have had the rest they needed and I cannot spend the night here."

He went to the door and opening it called a loud "Hallo, there!"

The same woman who had waited on him on his arrival came slowly down the stairs in response.

"The man with the horses," commanded Martin-Roget peremptorily. "Tell him I'll be ready in two minutes."

He returned to the room and proceeded to struggle into his heavy coat, Chauvelin as before making no attempt to help him. He sat once more huddled up in the ingle-nook hugging his elbows with his thin white hands. There was a smile half scornful, but not wholly dissatisfied around his bloodless lips. When Martin-Roget was ready to go he called out quietly after him:

"The *Hollandia* remember! At Portishead on the last day of the month. Captain K U Y P E R."

"Quite right," replied Martin-Roget laconically. "I'm not like to forget."

He then picked up his hat and riding whip and went out.

Outside in the porch he found the woman bending over the recumbent figure of his guide.

"He be azleep, *Mounzeer,*" she said placidly, "fast azleep, I do believe."

"Asleep?" cried Martin-Roget roughly, "we'll soon see about waking him up."

He gave the man a violent kick with the toe of his boot. The man groaned, stretched himself, turned over and rubbed his eyes. The light of the swinging lanthorn showed him the wrathful face of his employer. He struggled to his feet very quickly after that.

"Stir yourself, man," cried Martin-Roget savagely, as he gripped the fellow by the shoulder and gave him a vigorous shaking. "Bring the horses along now, and don't keep me waiting, or there'll be trouble."

"All right, *Mounzeer*, all right," muttered the man placidly, as he shook himself free from the uncomfortable clutch on his shoulder and leisurely made his way out of the porch.

"Haven't you got a boy or a man who can give that lout a hand with those *sacré* horses?" queried Martin-Roget impatiently. "He hardly knows a horse's head from its tail."

"No, zir, I've no one tonight," replied the woman gently. "My man and my son they be gone down to Watchet to 'elp with the cargo and the pack-'orzes. They won't be 'ere neither till after midnight. But," she added more cheerfully, "I can straighten a saddle if you want it."

"That's all right then—but—"

He paused suddenly, for a loud cry of "Hallo! Well! I'm—" rang through the night from the direction of the rear of the house. The cry expressed both surprise and dismay.

"What the —— is it?" called Martin-Roget loudly in response.

"The 'orzes!"

"What about them?"

To this there was no reply, and with a savage oath and calling to the woman to show him the way Martin-Roget ran out in the direction whence had come the cry of dismay. He fell straight into the arms of his guide, who promptly set up another cry, more dismal, more expressive of bewilderment than the first.

"They be gone," he shouted excitedly.

"Who have gone?" queried the Frenchman.

"The 'orzes!"

"The horses? What in —— do you mean?"

"The 'orzes have gone, *Mounzeer*. There was no door to the ztables and they be gone."

"You're a fool," growled Martin-Roget, who of a truth had not taken in as yet the full significance of the man's jerky sentences. "Horses don't walk out of the stables like that. They can't have done if you tied them up properly."

"I didn't tie them up," protested the man. "I didn't know 'ow to tie the beastly nags up, and there was no one to 'elp me. I didn't think they'd walk out like that."

"Well! if they're gone you'll have to go and get them back somehow, that's all," said Martin-Roget, whose temper by now was beyond his control, and who was quite ready to give the lout a furious thrashing.

"Get them back, *Mounzeer*," wailed the man, "'ow can I? In the dark, too. Besides, if I did come nose to nose wi' 'em I shouldn't know 'ow to get 'em. Would you, *Mounzeer?*" he added with bland impertinence.

"I shall know how to lay you out, you *satané* idiot," growled Martin-Roget, "if I have to spend the night in this hole."

He strode on in the darkness in the direction where a little glimmer of light showed the entrance to a wide barn which obviously was used as a rough stabling. He stumbled through a yard and over a miscellaneous lot of rubbish. It was hardly possible to see one's hands before one's eyes in the darkness and the fog. The woman followed him, offering consolation in the shape of a seat in the coffee-room whereon to pass the night, for indeed she had no bed to spare, and the man from Chelwood brought up the rear—still ejaculating cries of astonishment rather than distress.

"You are that careless, man!" the woman admonished him placidly, "and I give you a lanthorn and all for to look after your 'orzes properly."

"But you didn't give me a 'and for to tie 'em up in their stalls and give 'em their feed. Drat 'em! I 'ate 'orzes and all to do with 'em."

"Didn't you give 'em the feed I give you for 'em then?"

"No, I didn't. Think you I'd go into one o' them narrow stalls and get kicked for my pains."

"Then they was 'ungry, pore things," she concluded, "and went out after the 'ay what's just outside. I don't know 'ow you'll ever get 'em back in this fog."

There was indeed no doubt that the nags had made their way out of the stables, in that irresponsible fashion peculiar to animals, and that they had gone astray in the dark. There certainly was no sound in the night to denote their presence anywhere near.

"We'll get 'em all right in the morning," remarked the woman with her exasperating placidity.

"Tomorrow morning!" exclaimed Martin-Roget in a passion of fury. "And what the d——l am I going to do in the meanwhile?"

The woman reiterated her offers of a seat by the fire in the coffee-room.

"The men won't mind ye, zir," she said, "heaps of 'em are Frenchies like yourself, and I'll tell 'em you ain't a spying on 'em."

"It's no more than five mile to Chelwood," said the man blandly, "and maybe you get a better shakedown there."

"A five-mile tramp," growled Martin-Roget, whose wrath seemed to have spent itself before the hopelessness of his situation, "in this fog and gloom, and knee-deep in mud—There'll be a sovereign for you, woman," he added curtly, "if you can give me a clean bed for the night."

The woman hesitated for a second or two.

"Well! a zovereign is tempting, zir," she said at last. "You shall 'ave my son's bed. I know 'e'd rather 'ave the zovereign if 'e was ever zo tired. This way, zir," she added, as she once more turned toward the house, "mind them 'urdles there."

"And where am I goin' to zleep?" called the man from Chelwood after the two retreating figures.

"I'll look after the man for you, zir," said the woman; "for a matter of a shillin' 'e can sleep in the coffee-room, and I'll give 'im 'is breakfast too."

"Not one farthing will I pay for the idiot," retorted Martin-Roget savagely. "Let him look after himself."

He had once more reached the porch. Without another word, and not heeding the protests and curses of the unfortunate man whom he had left standing shelterless in the middle of the yard, he pushed open the front door of the house and once more found himself in the passage outside the coffee-room.

But the woman had turned back a little before she followed her guest into the house, and she called out to the man in the darkness:

"You may zleep in any of them outhouses and welcome, and zure there'll be a bit o' porridge for ye in the mornin'!"

"Think ye I'll stop," came in a furious growl out of the gloom, "and conduct that d———d frog-eater back to Chelwood? No fear. Five miles ain't nothin' to me, and 'e can keep the miserable shillin' 'e'd 'ave give me for my pains. Let 'im get 'is 'orzes back 'izelf and get to Chelwood as best 'e can. I'm off, and you can tell 'im zo from me. It'll make 'im sleep all the better, I reckon."

The woman was obviously not of a disposition that would ever argue a matter of this sort out. She had done her best, she reckoned, both for master and man, and if they chose to quarrel between themselves that was their business and not hers.

So, she quietly went into the house again; barred and bolted the door, and finding the stranger still waiting for her in the passage she conducted him to a tiny room on the floor above.

"My son's room, *Mounzeer*," she said; "I 'ope as 'ow ye'll be comfortable."

"It will do all right," assented Martin-Roget. "Is 'the Captain' sleeping in the house tonight?" he added as with an afterthought.

"Only in the coffee-room, *Mounzeer*. I couldn't give 'im a bed. 'The Captain' will be leaving with the pack 'orzes a couple of hours before dawn. Shall I tell 'im you be 'ere."

"No, no," he replied promptly. "Don't tell him anything. I don't want to see him again: and he'll be gone before I'm awake, I reckon."

"That 'e will, zir, most like. Goodnight, zir."

"Goodnight. And—mind—that lout gets the two horses back again for my use in the morning. I shall have to make my way to Chelwood as early as may be."

"Aye, aye, zir," assented the woman placidly. It were no use, she thought, to upset the *Mounzeer's* temper once more by telling him that his guide had decamped. Time enough in the morning, when she would be less busy.

"And my John can see 'im as far as Chelwood," she thought to herself as she finally closed the door on the stranger and made her way slowly down the creaking stairs.

CHAPTER 3

The Assembly Rooms

The sigh of satisfaction was quite unmistakable.

It could be heard from end to end, from corner to corner of the building. It sounded above the din of the orchestra who had just attacked with vigour the opening bars of a *schottische*, above the *brouhaha* of moving dancers and the *frou-frou* of skirts: it travelled from the small octagon hall, through the central *salon* to the tearoom, the ballroom and the cardroom: it reverberated from the gallery in the ballroom to the maids' gallery: it distracted the ladies from their gossip and the gentlemen from their cards.

It was a universal, heartfelt "Ah!" of intense and pleasurable satisfaction.

Sir Percy Blakeney and his lady had just arrived. It was close on midnight, and the ball had positively languished. What was a ball without the presence of Sir Percy? His Royal Highness too had been expected earlier than this. But it was not thought that he would come at all, despite his promise, if the spoilt pet of Bath society remained

54

unaccountably absent; and the Assembly Rooms had worn an air of woe even in the face of the gaily dressed throng which filled every vast room in its remotest angle.

But now Sir Percy Blakeney had arrived, just before the clocks had struck midnight, and exactly one minute before His Royal Highness drove up himself from the Royal Apartments. Lady Blakeney was looking more radiant and beautiful than ever before, so everyone remarked, when a few moments later she appeared in the crowded ballroom on the arm of His Royal Highness and closely followed by my lord Anthony Dewhurst and by Sir Percy himself, who had the young Duchess of Flintshire on his arm.

"What do you mean, you incorrigible rogue," Her Grace was saying with playful severity to her cavalier, "by coming so late to the ball? Another two minutes and you would have arrived after His Royal Highness himself: and how would you have justified such solecism, I would like to know."

"By swearing that thoughts of your grace had completely addled my poor brain," he retorted gaily, "and that in the mental contemplation of such charms I forgot time, place, social duties, everything."

"Even the homage due to truth," she laughed. "Cannot you for once in your life be serious, Sir Percy?"

"Impossible, dear lady, whilst your dainty hand rests upon mine arm."

It was not often that His Royal Highness graced Bath with his presence, and the occasion was made the excuse for quite exceptional gaiety and brilliancy. The new fashions of this memorable year of 1793 had defied the declaration of war and filtrated through from Paris: London milliners had not been backward in taking the hint, and though most of the more starchy dowagers obstinately adhered to the pre-war fashions—the huge hooped skirts, stiff stomachers, pointed waists, voluminous panniers and monumental head erections—the young and smart matrons were everywhere to be seen in the new gracefully flowing skirts innocent of steel constructions, the high waist line, the pouter pigeon-like draperies over their pretty bosoms.

Her Grace of Flintshire looked ravishing with her curly fair hair entirely free from powder, and Lady Betty Draitune's waist seemed to be nestling under her arm-pits. Of course, Lady Blakeney wore the very latest thing in striped silks and gossamer-like muslin and lace, and it was hard to enumerate all the pretty *débutantes* and young brides who fluttered about the Assembly Rooms this night.

And gliding through that motley throng, bright-plumaged like a swarm of butterflies, there were a few figures dressed in sober blacks and greys—the *émigrés* over from France—men, women, young girls and gilded youth from out that seething cauldron of revolutionary France—who had shaken the dust of that rampant demagogism from off their buckled shoes, taking away with them little else but their lives. Mostly chary of speech, grave in their demeanour, bearing upon their wan faces traces of that horror which had seized them when they saw all the traditions of their past tottering around them, the proletariat whom they had despised turning against them with all the fury of caged beasts let loose, their kindred and friends massacred, their king and queen murdered. The shelter and security which hospitable England had extended to them, had not altogether removed from their hearts the awful sense of terror and of gloom.

Many of them had come to Bath because the more genial climate of the West of England consoled them for the inclemencies of London's fogs. Received with open arms and with that lavish hospitality which the refugees and the oppressed had already learned to look for in England, they had gradually allowed themselves to be drawn into the fashionable life of the gay little city. The Comtesse de Tournai was here and her daughter, Lady Ffoulkes, Sir Andrew's charming and happy bride, and M. Paul Déroulède and his wife—beautiful Juliette Déroulède with the strange, haunted look in her large eyes, as of one who has looked closely on death; and M. le Duc de Kernogan with his exquisite daughter, whose pretty air of seriousness and of repose sat so quaintly upon her young face.

But everyone remarked as soon as *M. le Duc* entered the rooms that M. Martin-Roget was not in attendance upon *Mademoiselle*, which was quite against the order of things; also, that *M. le Duc* appeared to keep a more sharp eye than usual upon his daughter in consequence, and that he asked somewhat anxiously if milor Anthony Dewhurst was in the room, and looked obviously relieved when the reply was in the negative.

At which trifling incident everyone who was in the know smiled and whispered, for *M. le Duc* made it no secret that he favoured his own compatriot's suit for Mademoiselle Yvonne's hand rather than that of my Lord Tony—which—as old Euclid has it—is absurd.

But with the arrival of the royal party M. de Kernogan's troubles began. To begin with, though M. Martin-Roget had not arrived, my Lord Tony undoubtedly had. He had come in, in the wake of Lady

Blakeney, but very soon he began wandering round the room obviously in search of someone. Immediately there appeared to be quite a conspiracy among the young folk in the ballroom to keep both Lord Tony's and Mlle. Yvonne's movements hidden from the prying eyes of *M. le Duc*: and anon His Royal Highness, after a comprehensive survey of the ball-room and a few gracious words to his more intimate circle, wandered away to the card-room, and as luck would have it he claimed M. le Duc de Kernogan for a partner at *faro*.

Now *M. le Duc* was a courtier of the old *régime*: to have disobeyed the royal summons would in his eyes have been nothing short of a crime. He followed the royal party to the card-room, and on his way thither had one gleam of comfort in that he saw Lady Blakeney sitting on a sofa in the octagon hall engaged in conversation with his daughter, whilst Lord Anthony Dewhurst was nowhere in sight.

However, the gleam of comfort was very brief, for less than a quarter of an hour after he had sat down at His Highness' table, Lady Blakeney came into the card-room and stood thereafter for some little while close beside the prince's chair. The next hour after that was one of special martyrdom for the anxious father, for he knew that his daughter was in all probability sitting out in a specially secluded corner in the company of my Lord Tony.

If only Martin-Roget were here!

Martin-Roget with the eagle eyes and the airs of an accredited suitor would surely have intervened when my lord Tony in the face of the whole brilliant assembly in the ballroom, drew Mlle. de Kernogan into the seclusion of the recess underneath the gallery.

My Lord Tony was never very glib of tongue. That peculiar dignified shyness which is one of the chief characteristics of well-bred Englishmen caused him to be tongue-tied when he had most to say. It was just with gesture and an appealing pressure of his hand upon her arm that he persuaded Yvonne de Kernogan to sit down beside him on the sofa in the remotest and darkest corner of the recess, and there she remained beside him silent and grave for a moment or two and stole timid glances from time to time through the veil of her lashes at the finely-chiselled, expressive face of her young English lover.

He was pining to put a question to her, and so great was his excitement that his tongue refused him service, and she, knowing what was hovering on his lips, would not help him out, but a humorous twinkle in her dark eyes, and a faint smile round her lips lit up the habitual seriousness of her young face.

"*Mademoiselle*—" he managed to stammer at last. "Mademoiselle Yvonne—you have seen Lady Blakeney?"

"Yes," she replied demurely, "I have seen Lady Blakeney."

"And—and—she told you?"

"Yes. Lady Blakeney told me many things."

"She told you that—that—In God's name, Mademoiselle Yvonne," he added desperately, "do help me out—it is cruel to tease me! Can't you see that I'm nearly crazy with anxiety?"

Then she looked up at him, her dark eyes glowing and brilliant, her face shining with the light of a great tenderness.

"Nay, milor," she said earnestly, "I had no wish to tease you. But you will own 'tis a grave and serious step which Lady Blakeney suggested that I should take. I have had no time to think—as yet."

"But there is no time for thinking, Mademoiselle Yvonne," he said *naïvely*. "If you will consent—Oh! you will consent, will you not?" he pleaded.

She made no immediate reply, but gradually her hand which rested upon the sofa stole nearer and then nearer to his; and with a quiver of exquisite happiness his hand closed upon hers. The tips of his fingers touched the smooth warm palm and poor Lord Tony had to close his eyes for a moment as his sense of superlative ecstasy threatened to make him faint. Slowly he lifted that soft white hand to his lips.

"Upon my word, Yvonne," he said with quiet fervour, "you will never have cause to regret that you have trusted me."

"I know that well, milor," she replied demurely.

She settled down a shade or two closer to him still.

They were now like two birds in a cosy nest—secluded from the rest of the assembly, who appeared to them like dream-figures flitting in some other world that had nothing to do with their happiness. The strains of the orchestra who had struck the measure of the first figure of a *contredanse* sounded like fairy-music, distant, unreal in their ears. Only their love was real, their joy in one another's company, their hands clasped closely together!

"Tell me," she said after a while, "how it all came about. It is all so terribly sudden—so exquisitely sudden. I was prepared of course—but not so soon—and certainly not tonight. Tell me just how it happened."

She spoke English quite fluently, with just a charming slight accent, which he thought the most adorable thing he had ever heard.

"You see, dear heart," he replied, and there was a quiver of intense feeling in his voice as he spoke, "there is a man who not only is the friend whom I love best in all the world, but is also the one whom I trust absolutely, more than myself. Two hours ago, he sent for me and told me that grave danger threatened you—threatened our love and our happiness, and he begged me to urge you to consent to a secret marriage—at once—tonight."

"And you think this—this friend knew?"

"I know," he replied earnestly, "that he knew, or he would not have spoken to me as he did. He knows that my whole life is in your exquisite hands—he knows that our happiness is somehow threatened by that man Martin-Roget. How he obtained that information I could not guess—he had not the time or the inclination to tell me. I flew to make all arrangements for our marriage tonight and prayed to God—as I have never prayed in my life before—that you, dear heart, would deign to consent."

"How could I refuse when Lady Blakeney advised? She is the kindest and dearest friend I possess. She and your friend ought to know one another. Will you not tell me who he is?"

"I will present him to you, dear heart, as soon as we are married," he replied with awkward evasiveness. Then suddenly he exclaimed with boyish enthusiasm: "I can't believe it! I can't believe it! It is the most extraordinary thing in the world—"

"What is that, milor?" she asked.

"That you should have cared for me at all. For of course you must care, or you wouldn't be sitting here with me now—you would not have consented—would you?"

"You know that I do care, milor," she said in her grave quiet way. "How could it be otherwise?"

"But I am so stupid and so slow," he said *naïvely.* "Why! look at me now. My heart is simply bursting with all that I want to say to you, but I just can't find the words, and I do nothing but talk rubbish and feel how you must despise me."

Once more that humorous little smile played for a moment round Yvonne de Kernogan's serious mouth. She didn't say anything just then, but her delicate fingers gave his hand an expressive squeeze.

"You are not frightened?" he asked abruptly.

"Frightened? Of what?" she rejoined.

"At the step you are going to take?"

"Would I take it," she retorted gently, "if I had any misgivings?"

"Oh! if you had—Do you know that even now—" he continued clumsily and haltingly, "now that I have realised just what it will mean to have you—and just what it would mean to me, God help me—if I were to lose you—well!—that even now I would rather go through that hell than that you should feel the least bit doubtful or unhappy about it all."

Again, she smiled, gently, tenderly up into his eager, boyish face.

"The only unhappiness," she said gravely, "that could ever overtake me in the future would be parting from you, milor."

"Oh! God bless you for that, my dear! God bless you for that! But for pity's sake turn your dear eyes away from me or I vow I shall go crazy with joy. Men do go crazy with joy sometimes, you know, and I feel that in another moment I shall stand up and shout at the top of my voice to all the people in the room that within the next few hours the loveliest girl in all the world is going to be my wife."

"She certainly won't be that, if you do shout it at the top of your voice, milor, for father would hear you and there would be an end to our beautiful adventure."

"It will be a beautiful adventure, won't it?" he sighed with unconcealed ecstasy.

"So beautiful, my dear lord," she replied with gentle earnestness, "so perfect, in fact, that I am almost afraid something must happen presently to upset it all."

"Nothing can happen," he assured her. "M. Martin-Roget is not here, and His Royal Highness is even now monopolising M. le Duc de Kernogan so that he cannot get away."

"Your friend must be very clever to manipulate so many strings on our behalf!"

"It is long past midnight now, sweetheart," he said with sudden irrelevance.

"Yes, I know. I have been watching the time: and I have already thought everything out for the best. I very often go home from balls and routs in the company of Lady Ffoulkes and sleep in her house those nights. Father is always quite satisfied, when I do that, and to-night he will be doubly satisfied feeling that I shall be taken away from your society. Lady Ffoulkes is in the secret, of course, so Lady Blakeney told me, and she will be ready for me in a few minutes now: she'll take me home with her and there I will change my dress and rest for a while, waiting for the happy hour. She will come to the church with me and then—oh then! Oh! my dear milor!" she added suddenly with a deep sigh whilst her whole face became irradiated with a light of intense happiness, "as you say it is the most wonderful thing in all the world—this—our beautiful adventure together."

"The parson will be ready at half-past six, dear heart, it was the earliest hour that I could secure—after that we go at once to your church and the priest will tie up any loose threads which our English parson failed to make tight. After those two ceremonies we shall be very much married, shan't we?—and nothing can come between us, dear heart, can it?" he queried with a look of intense anxiety on his young face.

"Nothing," she replied. Then she added with a short sigh: "Poor father!"

"Dear heart, he will only fret for a little while. I don't believe he can really want you to marry that man Martin-Roget. It is just obstinacy on his part. He can't have anything against me really—save of course that I am not clever and that I shall never do anything very big in the world—except to love you, Yvonne, with my whole heart and soul and with every fibre and muscle in me—Oh! I'll do that," he added with boyish enthusiasm, "better than anyone else in all the world could do! And your father will, I'll be bound, forgive me for stealing you, when he sees that you are happy, and contented, and have everything you want and—and—"

As usual Lord Tony's eloquence was not equal to all that it should have expressed. He blushed furiously and with a quaint, shy gesture, passed his large, well-shaped hand over his smooth, brown hair. "I am not much, I know," he continued with a winning air of self-deprecation, "and you are far above me as the stars—you are so wonderful, so clever, so accomplished and I am nothing at all—but—but I have plenty of high-born connexions, and I have plenty of money and influential friends—and—and Sir Percy Blakeney, who is the most accomplished and finest gentleman in England, calls me his friend."

She smiled at his eagerness. She loved him for his clumsy little ways, his halting speech, that big loving heart of his which was too full of fine and noble feelings to find vent in mere words.

"Have you ever met a finer man in all the world?" he added enthusiastically.

Yvonne de Kernogan smiled once more. Her recollections of Sir Percy Blakeney showed her an elegant man of the world, whose mind seemed chiefly occupied on the devising and the wearing of exquisite clothes, in the uttering of lively witticisms for the entertainment of his royal friend and the ladies of his entourage: it showed her a man of great wealth and vast possessions who seemed willing to spend both in the mere pursuit of pleasures. She liked Sir Percy Blakeney well enough, but she could not understand clever and charming Marguerite Blakeney's adoration for her inane and foppish husband, nor the whole-hearted admiration openly lavished upon him by men like Sir Andrew Ffoulkes, my lord Hastings, and others. She would gladly have seen her own dear milor choose a more sober and intellectual friend. But then she loved him for his marvellous power of whole-hearted friendship, for his loyalty to those he cared for, for everything in fact that made up the sum total of his winning personality, and she pinned her faith on that other mysterious friend whose individuality vastly intrigued her.

"I am more interested in your anonymous friend," she said quaintly, "than in Sir Percy Blakeney. But he too is kindness itself and Lady Blakeney is an angel. I like to think that the happiest days of my life— our honeymoon, my dear lord—will be spent in their house."

"Blakeney has lent me Combwich Hall for as long as we like to stay there. We'll drive thither directly after the service, dear heart, and then we'll send a courier to your father and ask for his blessing and his forgiveness."

"Poor father!" sighed Yvonne again. But evidently compassion for the father whom she had elected to deceive did not weigh over heavily in the balance of her happiness. Her little hand once more stole like a timid and confiding bird into the shelter of his firm grasp.

In the card-room at His Highness' table Sir Percy Blakeney was holding the bank and seemingly luck was dead against him. Around the various tables the ladies stood about, chattering and hindering the players. Nothing appeared serious tonight, not even the capricious chances of hazard.

His Royal Highness was in rare good humour, for he was winning prodigiously.

Her Grace of Flintshire placed her perfumed and beringed hand upon Sir Percy Blakeney's shoulder; she stood behind his chair, chattering incessantly in a high flutey treble just like a canary. Blakeney vowed that she was so ravishing that she had put Dame Fortune to flight.

"You have not yet told us, Sir Percy," she said roguishly, "how you came to arrive so late at the ball."

"Alas, madam," he sighed dolefully, "'twas the fault of my cravat."

"Your cravat?"

"Aye indeed! You see I spent the whole of today in perfecting my new method for tying a butterfly bow, so as to give the neck an appearance of utmost elegance with a minimum of discomfort. Lady Blakeney will bear me out when I say that I set my whole mind to my task. Was I not busy all day m'dear?" he added, making a formal appeal to Marguerite, who stood immediately behind His Highness' chair, and with her luminous eyes, full of merriment and shining with happiness fixed upon her husband.

"You certainly spent a considerable time in front of the looking-glass," she said gaily, "with two valets in attendance and my lord Tony an interested spectator in the proceedings."

"There now!" rejoined Sir Percy triumphantly, "her ladyship's testimony thoroughly bears me out. And now you shall see what Tony says on the matter. Tony! Where's Tony!" he added as his lazy grey eyes sought the brilliant crowd in the cardroom. "Tony, where the devil are you?"

There was no reply, and *anon* Sir Percy's merry gaze encountered that of M. le Duc de Kernogan who, dressed in sober black, looked strangely conspicuous in the midst of this throng of bright-coloured butterflies, and whose grave eyes, as they rested on the gorgeous figure of the English exquisite, held a world of contempt in their glance.

"Ah! *M. le Duc*," continued Blakeney, returning that scornful look with his habitual good-humoured one, "I had not noticed that Mademoiselle Yvonne was not with you, else I had not thought of inquiring so loudly for my friend Tony."

"My Lord Antoine is dancing with my daughter, Sir Percy," said the other man gravely, in excellent if somewhat laboured English, "he had my permission to ask her."

"And is a thrice happy man in consequence," retorted Blakeney lightly, "though I fear me M. Martin-Roget's wrath will descend upon my poor Tony's head with unexampled vigour in consequence."

"M. Martin-Roget is not here this evening," broke in the duchess, "and methought," she added in a discreet whisper, "that my lord Tony was all the happier for his absence. The two young people have spent a considerable time together under the shadow of the gallery in the ballroom, and, if I mistake not, Lord Tony is making the most of his time."

She talked very volubly and with a slight North-country brogue which no doubt made it a little difficult for the stranger to catch her every word. But evidently *M. le Duc* had understood the drift of what she said, for now he rejoined with some acerbity:

"Mlle. de Kernogan is too well educated, I hope, to allow the attentions of any gentleman, against her father's will."

"Come, come, M. de Kernogan," here interposed His Royal Highness with easy familiarity, "Lord Anthony Dewhurst is the son of my old friend the Marquis of Atiltone: one of our most distinguished families in this country, who have helped to make English history. He has moreover inherited a large fortune from his mother, who was a Cruche of Crewkerne and one of the richest heiresses in the land. He is a splendid fellow—a fine sportsman, a loyal gentleman. His attentions to any young lady, however high-born, can be but flattering—and I should say welcome to those who have her future welfare at heart."

But in response to this gracious tirade, M. le Duc de Kernogan bowed gravely, and his stern features did not relax as he said coldly:

"Your Royal Highness is pleased to take an interest in the affairs of my daughter. I am deeply grateful."

There was a second's awkward pause, for everyone felt that despite his obvious respect and deference M. le Duc de Kernogan had endeavoured to inflict a snub upon the royal personage, and one or two hot-headed young fops in the immediate entourage even muttered the word: "Impertinence!" inaudibly through their teeth. Only His Royal Highness appeared not to notice anything unusual or disrespectful in *M. le Duc's* attitude. It seemed as if he was determined to remain good-humoured and pleasant. At any rate he chose to ignore the remark which had offended the ears of his entourage. Only those who stood opposite to His Highness, on the other side of the card table, declared afterwards that the prince had frowned and that a haughty rejoinder undoubtedly hovered on his lips.

Be that as it may, he certainly did not show the slightest sign of ill-humour: quite gaily and unconcernedly he scooped up his winnings which Sir Percy Blakeney, who held the Bank, was at this moment pushing towards him.

"Don't go yet, M. de Kernogan," he said as the Frenchman made a movement to work his way out of the crowd, feeling no doubt that the atmosphere round him had become somewhat frigid if not exactly inimical, "don't go yet, I beg of you. *Pardi!* Can't you see that you have been bringing me luck? As a rule, Blakeney, who can so well afford to lose, has the devil's own good fortune, but tonight I have succeeded in getting some of my own back from him. Do not, I entreat you, break the run of my luck by going."

"Oh, *Monseigneur*," rejoined the old courtier suavely, "how can my poor presence influence the gods, who of a surety always preside over Your Highness' fortunes?"

"Don't attempt to explain it, my dear sir," quoth the prince gaily. "I only know that if you go now, my luck may go with you and I shall blame you for my losses."

"Oh! in that case, *Monseigneur*—"

"And with all that, Blakeney," continued His Highness, once more taking up the cards and turning to his friend, "remember that we still await your explanation as to your coming so late to the ball."

"An omission, your Royal Highness," rejoined Blakeney, "an absence of mind brought about by your severity, and that of Her Grace. The trouble was that all my calculations with regard to the exact adjustment of the butterfly bow were upset when I realised that the set of the present-day waistcoat would not harmonise with it. Less than two hours before I was due to appear at this ball my mind had to make a complete *volte-face* in the matter of cravats. I became bewildered, lost, utterly confused. I have only just recovered, and one word of criticism on my final efforts would plunge me now into the depths of despair."

"Blakeney, you are absolutely incorrigible," retorted His Highness with a laugh. "*M. le Duc*," he added, once more turning to the grave Frenchman with his wonted graciousness, "I pray you do not form your judgment on the gilded youth of England by the example of my friend Blakeney. Some of us can be serious when occasion demands, you know."

"Your Highness is pleased to jest," said M. de Kernogan stiffly. "What greater occasion for seriousness can there be than the present one. True, England has never suffered as France is suffering now, but she has engaged in a conflict against the most powerful democracy the world has ever known, she has thrown down the gauntlet to a set of human beasts of prey who are as determined as they are ferocious. England will not emerge victorious from this conflict, *Monseigneur*, if her sons do not realise that war is not mere sport and that victory can only be attained by the sacrifice of levity and of pleasure."

He had dropped into French in response to His Highness' remark, in order to express his thoughts more accurately. The prince—a little bored no doubt—seemed disinclined to pursue the subject. Nevertheless, it seemed as if once again he made a decided effort not to show ill-humour. He even gave a knowing wink—a wink!—in the direction of his friend Blakeney and of Her Grace as if to beg them to set the ball of conversation rolling once more along a smoother—a less boring—path. He was obviously quite determined not to release M. de Kernogan from attendance near his royal person.

As usual Sir Percy threw himself in the breach, filling the sudden pause with his infectious laugh:

"*La!*" he said gaily, "how beautifully *M. le Duc* does talk. Ffoulkes," he added, addressing Sir Andrew, who was standing close by, "I'll wager you ten pounds to a pinch of snuff that you couldn't deliver yourself of such splendid sentiments, even in your own native lingo."

"I won't take you, Blakeney," retorted Sir Andrew with a laugh. "I'm no good at peroration."

"You should hear our distinguished guest M. Martin-Roget on the same subject," continued Sir Percy with mock gravity. "By Gad! can't he talk? I feel a d——d worm when he talks about our national levity, our insane worship of sport, our—our—*M. le Duc*," he added with becoming seriousness and in atrocious French, "I appeal to you. Does not M. Martin-Roget talk beautifully?"

"M. Martin-Roget," replied the duc gravely, "is a man of marvellous eloquence, fired by overwhelming patriotism. He is a man who must command respect wherever he goes."

"You have known him long, *M. le Duc?*" queried His Royal Highness graciously.

"Indeed, not very long, *Monseigneur*. He came over as an *émigré* from Brest some three months ago, hidden in a smuggler's ship. He had been denounced as an aristocrat who was furthering the cause of the royalists in Brittany by helping them plentifully with money, but he succeeded in escaping, not only with his life, but also with the bulk of his fortune."

"Ah! M. Martin-Roget is rich?"

"He is sole owner of a rich banking business in Brest, *Monseigneur*, which has an important branch in America and correspondents all over Europe. *Monseigneur* the Bishop of Brest recommended him specially to my notice in a very warm letter of introduction, wherein he speaks of M. Martin-Roget as a gentleman of the highest patriotism and integrity. Were I not quite satisfied as to M. Martin-Roget's antecedents and present connexions I would not have ventured to present him to Your Highness."

"Nor would you have accepted him as a suitor for your daughter, *M. le Duc, c'est entendu!*" concluded His Highness urbanely. "M. Martin-Roget's wealth will no doubt cover his lack of birth."

"There are plenty of high-born gentlemen devoted to the royalist cause, *Monseigneur*," rejoined the *duc* in his grave, formal manner. "But the most just and purest of causes must at times be helped with money. The Vendéens in Brittany, the Princes at Coblentz are all sorely in need of funds—"

"And M. Martin-Roget son-in-law of M. le Duc de Kernogan is more likely to feed those funds than M. Martin-Roget the plain business man who has no aristocratic connexions," concluded His Royal Highness dryly. "But even so, *M. le Duc*," he added more gravely, "surely you cannot be so absolutely certain as you would wish that M. Martin-Roget's antecedents are just as he has told you. *Monseigneur* the Bishop of Brest may have acted in perfect good faith—"

"*Monseigneur* the Bishop of Brest, your Highness, is a man who has our cause, the cause of our King and of our Faith, as much at heart as I have myself. He would know that on his recommendation I would trust any man absolutely. He was not like to make careless use of such knowledge."

"And you are quite satisfied that the worthy bishop did not act under some dire pressure—?"

"Quite satisfied, *Monseigneur*," replied the *duc* firmly. "What pressure could there be that would influence a prelate of such high integrity as *Monseigneur* the Bishop of Brest?"

There was silence for a moment or two, during which the heavy bracket clock over the door struck the first hour after midnight. His Royal Highness looked round at Lady Blakeney, and she gave him a smile and an almost imperceptible nod. Sir Andrew Ffoulkes had in the meanwhile quietly slipped away.

"I understand," said His Royal Highness quite gravely, turning back to *M. le Duc*, "and I must crave your pardon, sir, for what must have seemed to you an indiscretion. You have given me a very clear *exposé* of the situation. I confess that until tonight it had seemed to me—and to all your friends, *Monsieur*, a trifle obscure. In fact, it had been my intention to intercede with you in favour of my young friend Lord Anthony Dewhurst, who of a truth is deeply enamoured of your daughter."

"Though Your Highness' wishes are tantamount to a command, yet would I humbly assert that my wishes with regard to my daughter are based upon my loyalty and my duty to my Sovereign King Louis XVII, whom may God guard and protect, and that therefore it is beyond my power now to modify them."

"May God trounce you for an obstinate fool," murmured His Highness in English, and turning his head away so that the other should not hear him. But aloud and with studied graciousness he said:

"*M. le Duc*, will you not take a hand at hazard? My luck is turning, and I have faith in yours. We must fleece Blakeney tonight. He has had Satan's own luck these past few weeks. Such good fortune becomes positively revolting."

There was no more talk of Mlle. de Kernogan after that. Indeed, her father felt that her future had already been discussed far too freely by all these well-wishers who of a truth were not a little indiscreet. He thought that the manners and customs of good society were very peculiar here in this fog-ridden England. What business was it of all these high-born ladies and gentlemen—of His Royal Highness himself for that matter—what plans he had made for Yvonne's future? Martin-Roget was *bourgeois* by birth, but he was vastly rich and had promised to pour a couple of millions into the coffers of the Royalist Army if Mlle. de Kernogan became his wife. A couple of millions with more to follow, no doubt, and a loyal adherence to the royalist cause was worth these days all the blue blood that flowed in my lord Anthony Dewhurst's veins.

So, at any rate thought *M. le Duc* this night, while His Royal Highness kept him at cards until the late hours of the morning

CHAPTER 4

The Father

It was close on ten o'clock now in the morning on the following day, and M. le Duc de Kernogan was at breakfast in his lodgings in Laura Place, when a courier was announced who was the bearer of a letter for *M. le Duc*.

He thought the man must have been sent by Martin-Roget, who mayhap was sick, seeing that he had not been present at the Assembly Rooms last night, and the *duc* took the letter and opened it without misgivings. He read the address on the top of the letter: "Combwich Hall"—a place unknown to him, and the first words of the letter: "Dear father!" And even then, he had no misgivings.

In fact, he had to read the letter through three times before the full meaning of its contents had penetrated into his brain. Whilst he read, he sat quite still, and even the hand which held the paper had not the slightest tremor. When he had finished he spoke quite quietly to his valet:

"Give the courier a glass of ale, Frédérick," he said, "and tell him he can go; there is no answer. And—stay," he added, "I want you to go round at once to M. Martin-Roget's lodgings and ask him to come and speak with me as early as possible."

The valet left the room, and *M. le Duc* deliberately read through the letter from end to end for the fourth time. There was no doubt, no possible misapprehension. His daughter Yvonne de Kernogan had eloped clandestinely with my Lord Anthony Dewhurst and had been secretly married to him in the small hours of the morning in the Protestant church of St. James, and subsequently before a priest of her own religion in the Priory Church of St. John the Evangelist.

She apprised her father of this fact in a few sentences which purported to be dictated by profound affection and filial respect, but in which M. de Kernogan failed to detect the slightest trace of contrition. Yvonne! his Yvonne! the sole representative now of the old race—eloped like a kitchen-wench! Yvonne! his daughter! his asset for the future! his thing! his fortune! that which he meant with perfect egoism to sacrifice on the altar of his own beliefs and his own loyalty to the kingship of France! Yvonne had taken her future in her own hands! She knew that her hand, her person, were the purchase price of so many millions to be poured into the coffers of the royalist cause, and she had disposed of both, in direct defiance of her father's will and of her duty to her king and to his cause!

Yvonne de Kernogan was false to her traditions, false to her father! false to her king and country! In the years to come when the chroniclers of the time came to write the histories of the great families that had rallied round their king in the hour of his deadly peril, the name of Kernogan would be erased from those glorious pages. The Kernogans will have failed in their duty, failed in their loyalty! Oh! the shame of it all! The shame!!

The *duc* was far too proud a gentleman to allow his valet to see him under the stress of violent emotion, but now that he was alone his thin, hard face—with that air of gravity which he had transmitted to his daughter—became distorted with the passion of unbridled fury; he tore the letter up into a thousand little pieces and threw the fragments into the fire. On the bureau beside him there stood a miniature of Yvonne de Kernogan painted by Hall three years ago and framed in a circlet of brilliants. *M. le Duc's* eyes casually fell upon it; he picked it up and with a violent gesture of rage threw it on the floor and stamped upon it with his heel, destroying in this paroxysm of silent fury a work of art worth many hundred pounds.

His daughter had deceived him. She had also upset all his plans whereby the army of M. le Prince de Condé would have been enriched by a couple of million *francs*. In addition to the shame upon her father, she had also brought disgrace upon herself and her good name, for she was a minor and this clandestine marriage, contracted without her father's consent, was illegal in France, illegal everywhere: save perhaps in England—of this M. de Kernogan was not quite sure, but he certainly didn't care. And in this solemn moment he registered a vow that never as long as he lived would he be reconciled to that English nincompoop who had dared to filch his daughter from him, and never—as long as he lived—would he by his consent render the marriage legal, and the children born of that wedlock legitimate in the eyes of his country's laws.

A calm akin to apathy had followed his first outbreak of fury. He sat down in front of the fire and buried his chin in his hand. Something of course must be done to get his daughter back. If only Martin-Roget were here, he would know better how to act. Would Martin-Roget stick to his bargain and accept the girl for wife, now that her fame and honour had been irretrievably tarnished? There was the question which the next half-hour would decide. M. de Kernogan cast a feverish, anxious look on the clock. Half an hour had gone by since Frédérick went to seek Martin-Roget, and the latter had not yet appeared.

Until he had seen Martin-Roget and spoken with Martin-Roget M. de Kernogan could decide nothing. For one brief, mad moment, the project had formed itself in his disordered brain to rush down to Combwich Hall and provoke that impudent Englishman who had stolen his daughter: to kill him or be killed by him; in either case Yvonne would then be parted from him for ever. But even then, the thought of Martin-Roget brought more sober reflection. Martin-Roget would see to it. Martin-Roget would know what to do. After all, the outrage had hit the accredited lover just as hard as the father.

But why in the name of —— did Martin-Roget not come?

It was past midday when at last Martin-Roget knocked at the door of *M. le Duc's* lodgings in Laura Place. The older man had in the meanwhile gone through every phase of overwhelming emotions. The outbreak of unreasoning fury—when like a maddened beast that bites and tears he had broken his daughter's miniature and trampled it under foot—had been followed by a kind of dull apathy, when for close upon an hour he had sat staring into the flames, trying to grapple with an awful reality which seemed to elude him all the time.

He could not believe that this thing had really happened: that Yvonne, his well-bred dutiful daughter, who had shown such marvellous courage and presence of mind when the necessity of flight and of exile had first presented itself in the wake of the awful massacres and wholesale executions of her own friends and kindred, that she should have eloped—like some flirtatious wench—and outraged her father in this monstrous fashion, by a clandestine marriage with a man of alien race and of a heretical religion! M. de Kernogan could not realise it. It passed the bounds of possibility. The very flames in the hearth seemed to dance and to mock the bare suggestion of such an atrocious transgression.

To this gloomy numbing of the senses had succeeded the inevitable morbid restlessness: the pacing up and down the narrow room, the furtive glances at the clock, the frequent orders to Frédérick to go out and see if M. Martin-Roget was not yet home. For Frédérick had come back after his first errand with the astounding news that M. Martin-Roget had left his lodgings the previous day at about four o'clock and had not been seen or heard of since. In fact, his landlady was very anxious about him and was sorely tempted to see the town-crier on the subject.

Four times did Frédérick have to go from Laura Place to the Bear Inn in Union Street, where M. Martin-Roget lodged, and three times he returned with the news that nothing had been heard of *Mounzeer* yet. The fourth time—it was then close on midday—he came back running—thankful to bring back the good tidings, since he was tired of that walk from Laura Place to the Bear Inn. M. Martin-Roget had come home. He appeared very tired and in rare ill-humour: but Frédérick had delivered the message from *M. le Duc*, whereupon M. Martin-Roget had become most affable and promised that he would come round immediately. In fact, he was even then treading hard on Frédérick's heels.

"My daughter has gone! She left the ball clandestinely last night, and was married to Lord Anthony Dewhurst in the small hours of the morning. She is now at a place called Combwich Hall—with him!"

M. le Duc de Kernogan literally threw these words in Martin-Roget's face, the moment the latter had entered the room, and Frédérick had discreetly closed the door.

"What? What?" stammered the other vaguely. "I don't understand. What do you mean?" he added, bewildered at the *duc's* violence, tired after his night's adventure and the long ride in the early morning, irritable with want of sleep and decent food. He stared, uncomprehending, at the *duc*, who had once more started pacing up and down the room, like a caged beast, with hands tightly clenched behind his back, his eyes glowering both at the newcomer and at the imaginary presence of his most bitter enemy—the man who had dared to come between him and his projects for his daughter.

Martin-Roget passed his hand across his brow like a man who is not yet fully awake.

"What do you mean?" he reiterated hazily.

"Just what I say," retorted the other roughly. "Yvonne has eloped with that nincompoop Lord Anthony Dewhurst. They have gone through some sort of marriage ceremony together. And she writes me a letter this morning to tell me that she is quite happy and contented and spending her honeymoon at a place called Combwich Hall. Honeymoon!" he repeated savagely, as if to lash his fury up anew, "Tsha!"

Martin-Roget on the other hand was not the man to allow himself to fall into a state of frenzy, which would necessarily interfere with calm consideration.

He had taken the fact in now. Yvonne's elopement with his English rival, the clandestine marriage, everything. But he was not going to allow his inward rage to obscure his vision of the future. He did not spend the next precious seconds—as men of his race are wont to do—in smashing things around him, in raving and fuming and gesticulating. No. That was not the temper M. Martin-Roget was in at this moment when Fate and a girl's folly were ranging themselves against his plans. His friend, Citizen Chauvelin, would have envied him his calm in the face of this disaster.

Whilst *M. le Duc* still stormed and raved, Martin-Roget sat down quietly in front of the fire, rested his chin in his hand and waited for a lull in the other man's paroxysm ere he spoke.

"From your attitude, *M. le Duc*," he then said quietly, hiding obvious sarcasm behind a veil of studied deference, "from your attitude I gather that your wishes with regard to Mlle. de Kernogan have undergone no modification. You would still honour me by desiring that she should become my wife?"

"I am not in the habit of changing my mind," said *M. le Duc* gruffly. He desired the marriage, he coveted Martin-Roget's millions for the royalist cause, but he had no love for the man. All the pride of the Kernogans, their long line of ancestry, rebelled against the thought of a fair descendant of this glorious race being allied to a *roturier*—a *bourgeois*—a tradesman, what? and the cause of king and country counted few greater martyrdoms than that of the Duc de Kernogan whenever he met the banker Martin-Roget on an equal social footing.

"Then there is not much harm done," rejoined the latter coolly; "the marriage is not a legal one. It need not even be dissolved—Mademoiselle de Kernogan is still Mademoiselle de Kernogan and I her humble and faithful adorer."

M. le Duc paused in his restless walk.

"You would—" he stammered, then checked himself, turning abruptly away. He had some difficulty in hiding the scorn wherewith he regarded the other's coolness. *Bourgeois* blood was not to be gainsaid. The tradesman—or banker, whatever he was—who hankered after an alliance with Mademoiselle de Kernogan and was ready to lay down a couple of millions for the privilege—was not to be deterred from his purpose by any considerations of pride or of honour. *M. le Duc* was satisfied and re-assured, but he despised the man for his leniency for all that.

"The marriage is no marriage at all according to the laws of France," reiterated Martin-Roget calmly.

"No, it is not," assented the *duc* roughly.

For a while there was silence: Martin-Roget seemed immersed in his own thoughts and not to notice the febrile comings and goings of the other man.

"What we have to do, *M. le Duc*," he said after a while, "is to induce Mlle. de Kernogan to return here immediately."

"How are you going to accomplish that?" sneered the *duc*.

"Oh! I was not suggesting that I should appear in the matter at all," rejoined Martin-Roget with a shrug of the shoulders.

"Then how can I—?"

"Surely—" argued the younger man tentatively.

"You mean—?"

Martin-Roget nodded. Despite these ambiguous half-spoken sentences, the two men had understood one another.

"We must get her back, of course," assented the *duc*, who had suddenly become as calm as the other man.

"There is no harm done," reiterated Martin-Roget with slow and earnest emphasis.

Whereupon the *duc*, completely pacified, drew a chair close to the hearth and sat down, leaning his elbows on his knees and holding his fine, aristocratic hands to the blaze.

Frédérick came in half an hour later to ask if *M. le Duc* would have his luncheon. He found the two gentlemen sitting quite close together over the dying embers of a fire that had not been fed for close upon an hour: and that prince of valets was glad to note that *M. le Duc's* temper had quite cooled down and that he was talking calmly and very affably to M. Martin-Roget.

CHAPTER 5

The Nest

There are lovely days in England sometimes in November or December, days when the departing year strives to make us forget that winter is nigh, and autumn smiles, gentle and benignant, caressing with a still tender kiss the last leaves of the scarlet oak which linger on the boughs and touching up with a vivid brush the evergreen verdure of bay trees, of ilex and of yew. The sky is of that pale, translucent blue which dwellers in the South never see, with the soft transparency of an aquamarine as it fades into the misty horizon at midday. And at dusk the thrushes sing: "Kiss me quick! kiss me quick! kiss me quick" in the naked branches of old acacias and chestnuts, and the robins don their crimson waistcoats and dart in and out among the coppice and through the feathery arms of larch and pine. And the sun which tips the prickly points of holly leaves with gold, joins in this merry make-believe that winter is still a very, very long way off, and that mayhap he has lost his way altogether, and is never coming to this balmy beautiful land again.

Just such a day was the penultimate one of November, 1793, when Lady Anthony Dewhurst sat at a desk in the wide bay window of the drawing-room in Combwich Hall, trying to put into a letter to Lady Blakeney all that her heart would have wished to express of love and gratitude and happiness.

Three whole days had gone by since that exciting night, when before break of day in the dimly-lighted old church, in the presence of two or three faithful friends, she had plighted her troth to Lord Anthony: even whilst other kind friends—including His Royal Highness—formed part of the little conspiracy which kept her father occupied and, if necessary, would have kept M. Martin-Roget out of the way. Since then her life had been one continuous dream of perfect bliss. From the moment when after the second religious ceremony in the Roman Catholic church she found herself alone in the carriage with milor, and felt his arms—so strong and yet so tender—closing round her and his lips pressed to hers in the first masterful kiss of complete possession, until this hour when she saw his tall, elegant figure hurrying across the garden toward the gate and suddenly turning toward the window whence he knew that she was watching him, every hour and every minute had been nothing but unalloyed happiness.

Even there where she had looked for sorrow and difficulty her path had been made smooth for her. Her father, who she had feared would prove hard and irreconcilable, had been tender and forgiving to such an extent that tears almost of shame would gather in her eyes whenever she thought of him.

As soon as she arrived at Combwich Hall she had written a long and deeply affectionate letter to her father, imploring his forgiveness for the deception and unfilial conduct which on her part must so deeply have grieved him. She pleaded for her right to happiness in words of impassioned eloquence, she pleaded for her right to love and to be loved, for her right to a home, which a husband's devotion would make a paradise for her.

This letter she had sent by special courier to her father and the very next day she had his reply. She had opened the letter with trembling fingers, fearful lest her father's harshness should mar the perfect serenity of her life. She was afraid of what he would say, for she knew her father well: knew his faults as well as his qualities, his pride, his obstinacy, his unswerving determination and his loyalty to the king's cause—all of which must have been deeply outraged by his daughter's high-handed action. But as she began to read, astonishment, amazement at once filled her soul: she could hardly trust her comprehension, hardly believe that what she read could indeed be reality, and not just the continuance of the happy dream wherein she was dwelling these days.

Her father—gently reproachful—had not one single harsh word to utter. He would not, he said, at the close of his life, after so many bitter disappointments, stand in the way of his daughter's happiness: "You should have trusted me, my child," he wrote: and indeed, Yvonne could not believe her eyes. "I had no idea that your happiness was at stake in this marriage, or I should never have pressed the claims of my own wishes in the matter. I have only you in the world left, now that misery and exile are to be my portion! Is it likely that I would allow any personal desires to weigh against my love for you?"

Happy as she was Yvonne cried—cried bitterly with remorse and shame when she read that letter. How could she have been so blind, so senseless as to misjudge her father so? Her young husband found her in tears and had much ado to console her: he too read the letter and was deeply touched by the kind reference to himself contained therein: "My Lord Anthony is a gallant gentleman," wrote M. le Duc de Kernogan, "he will make you happy, my child, and your old father will be more than satisfied. All that grieves me is that you did not trust me sooner. A clandestine marriage is not worthy of a daughter of the Kernogans."

"I did speak most earnestly to *M. le Duc*," said Lord Tony reflectively, "when I begged him to allow me to pay my addresses to you. But then," he added cheerfully, "I am such a clumsy lout when I have to talk at any length—and especially clumsy when I have to plead my own cause. I suppose I put my case so badly before your father, m'dear, that he thought me three parts an idiot and would not listen to me."

"I too begged and entreated him, dear," she said with a smile, "but he was very determined then and vowed that I should marry M. Martin-Roget despite my tears and protestations. Dear father! I suppose he didn't realise that I was in earnest."

"He has certainly accepted the inevitable very gracefully," was my Lord Tony's final comment.

Then they read the letter through once more, sitting close together, he with one arm round her shoulder, she nestling against his chest, her hair brushing against his lips and with the letter in her hands which she could scarcely read for the tears of joy which filled her eyes.

"I don't feel very well today," the letter concluded; "the dampness and the cold have got into my bones: moreover, you two young love birds will not desire company just yet, but tomorrow if the weather is more genial I will drive over to Combwich in the afternoon, and perhaps you will give me supper and a bed for the night. Send me word by the courier who will forthwith return to Bath if this will be agreeable to you both."

Could anything be more adorable, more delightful? It was just the last drop that filled Yvonne's cup of happiness right up to the brim.

The next afternoon she sat at her desk in order to tell Lady Blakeney all about it. She made out a copy of her father's letter and put that in with her own and begged dear Lady Blakeney to see Lady Ffoulkes forthwith and tell her all that had happened. She herself was expecting her father every minute and milor Tony had gone as far as the gate to see if the *barouche* was in sight.

Half an hour later M. de Kernogan had arrived and his daughter lay in his arms, happy, beyond the dreams of men. He looked rather tired and wan and still complained that the cold had got into his bones: evidently, he was not very well and Yvonne after the excitement of the meeting felt not a little anxious about him. As the evening wore on he became more and more silent; he hardly would eat anything and soon after eight o'clock he announced his desire to retire to bed.

"I am not ill," he said as he kissed his daughter and bade her a fond "Goodnight," "only a little wearied—with emotion no doubt. I shall be better after a night's rest."

He had been quite cordial with my Lord Tony, though not effusive, which was only natural—he was at all times a very reserved man, and—unlike those of his race—never demonstrative in his manner: but with his daughter he had been singularly tender, with a wistful affection which almost suggested remorse, even though it was she who, on his arrival, had knelt down before him and had begged for his blessing and his forgiveness.

But the following morning he appeared to be really ill: his cheeks looked sunken, almost livid, his eyes dim and hollow. Nevertheless, he would not hear of staying on another day or so.

"No, no," he declared emphatically, "I shall be better in Bath. It is more sheltered there, here the north winds would drive me to my bed very quickly. I shall take a course of baths at once. They did me a great deal of good before, you remember, Yvonne—in September, when I caught a chill—they soon put me right. That is all that ails me now—I've caught a chill."

He did his best to reassure his daughter, but she was far from satisfied: more especially as he hardly would touch the cup of chocolate which she had prepared for him with her own hands.

"I shall be quite myself again in Bath," he declared, "and in a day or two when you can spare the time—or when milor can spare you—perhaps you will drive over to see how the old father is getting on, eh?"

"Indeed," she said firmly, "I shall not allow you to go to Bath alone. If you will go, I shall accompany you."

"Nay!" he protested, "that is foolishness, my child. The *barouche* will take me back quite comfortably. It is less than two hours' drive and I shall be quite safe and comfortable."

"You will be quite safe and comfortable in my company," she retorted with a tender, anxious glance at his pale face and the nervous tremor of his hands. "I have consulted with my dear husband and he has given his consent that I should accompany you."

"But you can't leave milor like that, my child," he protested once more. "He will be lonely and miserable without you."

"Yes. I think he will," she said wistfully. "But he will be all the happier when you are well again, and I can return to Combwich satisfied."

Whereupon *M. le Duc* yielded. He kissed and thanked his daughter and seemed even relieved at the prospect of her company. The *barouche* was ordered for eleven o'clock, and a quarter of an hour before that time Lord Tony had his young wife in his arms, bidding her a sad farewell.

"I hate your going from me, sweetheart," he said as he kissed her eyes, her hair, her lips. "I cannot bear you out of my sight even for an hour—let alone a couple of days."

"Yet I must go, dear heart," she retorted, looking up with that sweet, grave smile of hers into his eager young face. "I could not let him travel alone—could I?"

"No, no," he assented somewhat dubiously, "but remember, dear heart, that you are infinitely precious and that I shall scarce live for sheer anxiety until I have you here, safe, once more in my arms."

"I'll send you a courier this evening," she rejoined, as she extricated herself gently from his embrace, "and if I can come back tomorrow—"

"I'll ride over to Bath in any case in the morning so that I may escort you back if you really can come."

"I will come if I am reassured about father. Oh, my dear lord," she added with a wistful little sigh, "I knew yesterday morning that I was too happy, and that something would happen to mar the perfect felicity of these last few days."

"You are not seriously anxious about *M. le Duc's* health, dear heart?"

"No, not seriously anxious. Farewell, milor. It is *au revoir*—a few hours and we'll resume our dream."

There was nothing in all that to arouse my Lord Tony's suspicions. All day he was miserable and forlorn because Yvonne was not there—but he was not suspicious.

Fate had a blow in store for him, from which he was destined never wholly to recover, but she gave him no warning, no premonition. He spent the day in making up arrears of correspondence, for he had a large private fortune to administer—trust funds on behalf of brothers and sisters who were minors—and he always did it conscientiously and to the best of his ability. The last few days he had lived in a dream and there was an accumulation of business to go through. In the evening he expected the promised courier, who did not arrive: but his was not the sort of disposition that would fret and fume because of a contretemps which might be attributable to the weather—it had rained heavily since afternoon—or to sundry trifling causes which he at Combwich, ten or a dozen miles from Bath, could not estimate. He had no suspicions even then. How could he have? How could he guess? Nevertheless, when he ultimately went to bed, it was with the firm resolve that he would in any case go over to Bath in the morning and remain there until Yvonne was able to come back with him.

Combwich without her was anyhow unendurable.

He started for Bath at nine o'clock in the morning. It was still raining hard. It had rained all night and the roads were very muddy. He started out without a groom. A little after half-past ten, he drew rein outside his house in Chandos Buildings, and having changed his clothes he started to walk to Laura Place. The rain had momentarily left off, and a pale wintry sun peeped out through rolling banks of grey clouds. He went round by way of Saw Close and the Upper Borough Walls, as he wanted to avoid the fashionable throng that crowded the neighbourhood of the Pump Room and the Baths. His intention was to seek out the Blakeneys at their residence in the Circus after he had seen Yvonne and obtained news of *M. le Duc*.

He had no suspicions. Why should he have?

The Abbey clock struck a quarter-past eleven when finally, he knocked at the house in Laura Place. Long afterwards he remembered how just at that moment a dense grey mist descended into the valley. He had not noticed it before, now he saw that it had enveloped this part of the city so that he could not even see clearly across the Place.

A woman came to open the door. Lord Tony then thought this strange considering how particular *M. le Duc* always was about everything pertaining to the management of his household: "The house of a poor exile," he was wont to say, "but nevertheless that of a gentleman."

"Can I go straight up?" he asked the woman, who he thought was standing ostentatiously in the hall as if to bar his way. "I desire to see *M. le Duc.*"

"Ye can walk upstairs, zir," said the woman, speaking with a broad Somersetshire accent, "but I doubt me if ye'll see 'is Grace the Duke. 'Es been gone these two days."

Tony had paid no heed to her at first; he had walked across the narrow hall to the oak staircase, and was half-way up the first flight when her last words struck upon his ear—quite without meaning for the moment—but nevertheless he paused, one foot on one tread, and the other two treads below—and he turned round to look at the woman, a swift frown across his smooth forehead.

"Gone these two days," he repeated mechanically; "what do you mean?"

"Well! 'Is Grace left the day afore yesterday—Thursday it was—'Is man went yesterday afternoon with luggage and sich—'e went by coach 'e did—Leave off," she cried suddenly; "what are ye doin'? Ye're 'urtin' me."

For Lord Tony had rushed down the stairs again and was across the hall, gripping the unoffending woman by the wrist and glaring into her expressionless face until she screamed with fright.

"I beg your pardon," he said humbly as he released her wrist: all the instincts of the courteous gentleman arrayed against his loss of control. "I—I forgot myself for the moment," he stammered; "would you mind telling me again—what—what you said just now?"

The woman was prepared to put on the airs of outraged dignity, she even glanced up at the malapert with scorn expressed in her small beady eyes. But at sight of his face her anger and her fears both fell away from her. Lord Tony was white to the lips, his cheeks were the colour of dead ashes, his mouth trembled, his eyes alone glowed with ill-repressed anxiety.

"'Is Grace," she said with slow emphasis, for of a truth she thought that the young gentleman was either sick or daft, "'Is Grace left this 'ouse the day afore yesterday in a hired *barouche*. 'Is man—Frederick—went yesterday afternoon with the luggage. 'E caught the Bristol coach at two o'clock. I was 'Is Grace's 'ousekeeper and I am to look after the 'ouse and the zervants until I 'ear from 'Is Grace again. Them's my orders. I know no more than I'm tellin' ye."

"But His Grace returned here yesterday forenoon," argued Lord Tony calmly, mechanically, as one who would wish to convince an obstinate child. "And my lady—Mademoiselle Yvonne, you know—was with him."

"Noa! Noa!" said the woman placidly. "'Is Grace 'asn't been near this 'ouse come Thursday afternoon, and 'is man left yesterday wi' th' luggage. Why!" she added confidentially, "'e ain't gone far. It was all zettled that zuddint I didn't know nothing about it myzelf till I zeed

80

Mr. Frederick start off wi' th' luggage. Not much luggage neither it wasn't. Sure but 'Is Grace'll be 'ome zoon. 'E can't 'ave gone far. Not wi' that bit o' luggage. Zure."

"But my lady—Mademoiselle Yvonne—"

"Lor, zir, didn't ye know? Why 'twas all over th' town o' Tuesday as 'ow *Mademozell* 'ad eloped with my Lord Anthony Dew'urst, and—"

"Yes! yes! But you have seen my lady since?"

"Not clapped eyes on 'er, zir, since she went to the ball come Monday evenin'. An' a picture she looked in 'er white gown—"

"And—did His Grace leave no message—for—for anyone?—no letter?"

"Ah, yes, now you come to mention it, zir. Mr. Frederick 'e give me a letter yesterday. ''Is Grace,' sez 'e, 'left this yere letter on 'is desk. I just found it,' sez 'e. 'If my Lord Anthony Dew'urst calls,' sez 'e, 'give it to 'im.' I've got the letter zomewhere, zir. What may your name be?"

"I am Lord Anthony Dewhurst," replied the young man mechanically.

"Your pardon, my lord, I'll go fetch th' letter."

Lord Tony never moved while the woman shuffled across the passage and down the back stairs. He was like a man who has received a knock-out blow and has not yet had time to recover his scattered senses. At first when the woman spoke, his mind had jumped to fears of some awful accident—runaway horses—a broken *barouche*—or a sudden aggravation of the *duc's* ill-health. But soon he was forced to reject what now would have seemed a consoling thought: had there been an accident, he would have heard—a rumour would have reached him—Yvonne would have sent a courier. He did not know yet what to think, his mind was like a slate over which a clumsy hand had passed a wet sponge—impressions, recollections, above all a hideous, nameless fear, were all blurred and confused within his brain.

The woman came back carrying a letter which was crumpled and greasy from a prolonged sojourn in the pocket of her apron. Lord Tony took the letter and broke its heavy seal. The woman watched him, curiously, pityingly now, for he was good to look on, and she scented the significance of the tragedy which she had been the means of revealing to him. But he had become quite unconscious of her presence, of everything in fact save those few sentences, written in French, in a cramped hand, and which seemed to dance a wild saraband before his eyes:

"Milor,—

"You tried to steal my daughter from me, but I have taken her from you now. By the time this reaches you we shall be on the high seas on our way to Holland, thence to Coblentz, where Mademoiselle de Kernogan will in accordance with my wishes be united in lawful marriage to M. Martin-Roget whom I have chosen to be her husband. She is not and never was your wife. As far as one may look into the future, I can assure you that you will never in life see her again."

And to this monstrous document of appalling callousness and cold-blooded cruelty there was appended the signature of André Dieudonné Duc de Kernogan.

But unlike the writer thereof Lord Anthony Dewhurst neither stormed nor raged: he did not even tear the execrable letter into an hundred fragments. His firm hand closed over it with one convulsive clutch, and that was all. Then he slipped the crumpled paper into his pocket. Quite deliberately he took out some money and gave a piece of silver to the woman.

"I thank you very much," he said somewhat haltingly. "I quite understand everything now."

The woman curtseyed and thanked him; tears were in her eyes, for it seemed to her that never had she seen such grief depicted upon any human face. She preceded him to the hall door and held it open for him, while he passed out. After the brief gleam of sunshine, it had started to rain again, but he didn't seem to care. The woman suggested fetching a hackney coach, but he refused quite politely, quite gently: he even lifted his hat as he went out. Obviously, he did not know what he was doing. Then he went out into the rain and strode slowly across the Place.

CHAPTER 6

The Scarlet Pimpernel

Instinct kept him away from the more frequented streets—and instinct after a while drew him in the direction of his friend's house at the corner of The Circus. Sir Percy Blakeney had not gone out fortunately: the lacquey who opened the door to my Lord Tony stared astonished and almost paralysed for the moment at the extraordinary appearance of his lordship. Rain dropped down from the brim of his hat on to his shoulders: his boots were muddy to the knees, his clothes wringing wet. His eyes were wild and hazy and there was a curious tremor round his mouth.

The lacquey declared with a knowing wink afterwards that his

82

lordship must 'ave been drinkin'!

But at the moment his sense of duty urged him to show my lord—who was his master's friend—into the library, whatever condition he was in. He took his dripping coat and hat from him and marshalled him across the large, square hall.

Sir Percy Blakeney was sitting at his desk, writing, when Lord Tony was shown in. He looked up and at once rose and went to his friend.

"Sit down, Tony," he said quietly, "while I get you some brandy."

He forced the young man down gently into a chair in front of the fire and threw another log into the blaze. Then from a cupboard he fetched a flask of brandy and a glass, poured some out and held it to Tony's lips. The latter drank—unresisting—like a child. Then as some warmth penetrated into his bones, he leaned forward, resting his elbows on his knees and buried his face in his hands. Blakeney waited quietly, sitting down opposite to him, until his friend should be able to speak.

"And after all that you told me on Monday night!" were the first words which came from Tony's quivering lips, "and the letter you sent me over on Tuesday! Oh! I was prepared to mistrust Martin-Roget. Why! I never allowed her out of my sight!—But her father!—How could I guess?"

"Can you tell me exactly what happened?"

Lord Tony drew himself up and staring vacantly into the fire told his friend the events of the past four days. On Wednesday the courier with M. de Kernogan's letter, breathing kindness and forgiveness. On Thursday his arrival and seeming ill-health, on Friday his departure with Yvonne. Tony spoke quite calmly. He had never been anything but calm since first, in the house in Laura Place, he had received that awful blow.

"I ought to have known," he concluded dully, "I ought to have guessed. Especially since you warned me."

"I warned you that Martin-Roget was not the man he pretended to be," said Blakeney gently, "I warned you against him. But I too failed to suspect the Duc de Kernogan. We are Britishers, you and I, my dear Tony," he added with a quaint little laugh, "our minds will never be quite equal to the tortuous ways of these Latin races. But we are not going to waste time now talking about the past. We have got to find your wife before those brutes have time to wreak their devilries against her."

"On the high seas—on the way to Holland—thence to Coblentz—" murmured Tony, "I have not yet shown you the *duc's* letter to me."

He drew from his pocket the crumpled, damp piece of paper on which the ink had run into patches and blotches, and which had become almost undecipherable now. Sir Percy took it from him and read it through:

"The Duc de Kernogan and Lady Anthony Dewhurst are not on their way to Holland and to Coblentz," he said quietly as he handed the letter back to Lord Tony.

"Not on their way to Holland?" queried the young man with a puzzled frown. "What do you mean?"

Blakeney drew his chair closer to his friend: a marvellous and subtle change had suddenly taken place in his individuality. Only a few moments ago he was the polished, elegant man of the world, then the kindly and understanding friend—self-contained, reserved, with a perfect manner redolent of sympathy and dignity. Suddenly all that was changed. His manner was still perfect and outwardly calm, his gestures scarce, his speech deliberate, but the compelling power of the leader—which is the birth-right of such men—glowed and sparkled now in his deep-set eyes: the spirit of adventure and reckless daring was awake—insistent and rampant—and subtle effluvia of enthusiasm and audacity emanated from his entire personality.

Sir Percy Blakeney had sunk his individuality in that of the Scarlet Pimpernel.

"I mean," he said, returning his friend's anxious look with one that was inspiring in its unshakable confidence, "I mean that on Monday last, the night before your wedding—when I urged you to obtain Yvonne de Kernogan's consent to an immediate marriage—I had followed Martin-Roget to a place called "The Bottom Inn" on Goblin Combe—a place well known to every smuggler in the county."

"You, Percy!" exclaimed Tony in amazement.

"Yes, I," laughed the other lightly. "Why not? I had had my suspicions of him for some time. As luck would have it he started off on the Monday afternoon by hired coach to Chelwood. I followed. From Chelwood he wanted to go on to Redhill: but the roads were axle deep in mud, and evening was gathering in very fast. Nobody would take him. He wanted a horse and a guide. I was on the spot—as disreputable a bar-loafer as you ever saw in your life. I offered to take him. He had no choice. He had to take me. No one else had offered. I took him to the Bottom Inn. There he met our esteemed friend M.

Chauvelin—"

"Chauvelin!" cried Tony, suddenly roused from the dull apathy of his immeasurable grief, at sound of that name which recalled so many exciting adventures, such mad, wild, hair-breadth escapes. "Chauvelin! What in the world is he doing here in England?"

"Brewing mischief, of course," replied Blakeney dryly. "In disgrace, discredited, a marked man—what you will—my friend M. Chauvelin has still an infinite capacity for mischief. Through the interstices of a badly fastened shutter I heard two blackguards devising infinite dev- ilry. That is why, Tony," he added, "I urged an immediate marriage as the only real protection for Yvonne de Kernogan against those black- guards."

"Would to God you had been more explicit!" exclaimed Tony with a bitter sigh.

"Would to God I had," rejoined the other, "but there was so little time, with licences and what not all to arrange for, and less than an hour to do it in. And would you have suspected the *duc* himself of such execrable duplicity even if you had known, as I did then, that the so- called Martin-Roget hath name Adet, and that he matures thoughts of deadly revenge against the Duc de Kernogan and his daughter?"

"Martin-Roget? the banker—the exiled royalist who—"

"He may be a banker now—but he certainly is no royalist—he is the son of a peasant who was unjustly put to death four years ago by the Duc de Kernogan."

"Ye gods!"

"He came over to England plentifully supplied with money—I could not gather if the money is his or if it has been entrusted to him by the revolutionary government for purposes of spying and corrup- tion—but he came to England in order to ingratiate himself with the Duc de Kernogan and his daughter, and then to lure them back to France, for what purpose you may well imagine."

"Good God, man—you can't mean—?"

"He has chartered a smuggler's craft—or rather Chauvelin has done it for him. Her name is the *Hollandia*, her master hath name Kuyper. She was to be in Portishead harbour on the last day of No- vember: all her papers in order. Cargo of West India sugar, destination Amsterdam, consignee some Mynheer over there. But Martin-Roget, or whatever his name may be, and no doubt our friend Chauvelin too, were to be aboard her, and also M. le Duc de Kernogan and his daughter. And the *Hollandia* is to put into Le Croisic for Nantes, whose revolutionary proconsul, that infamous Carrier, is of course Chauvelin's bosom friend."

Sir Percy Blakeney finished speaking. Lord Tony had listened to him quietly and in silence: now he rose and turned resolutely to his friend. There was no longer any trace in him of that stunned apathy which had been the primary result of the terrible blow. His young face was still almost unrecognisable from the lines of grief and horror which marred its habitual fresh, boyish look. He looked twenty years older than he had done a few hours ago, but there was also in his whole attitude now the virility of more mature manhood, its determination and unswerving purpose.

"And what can I do now?" he asked simply, knowing that he could trust his friend and leader with what he held dearest in all the world. "Without you, Blakeney, I am of course impotent and lost. I haven't the head to think. I haven't sufficient brains to pit against those cunning devils. But if you will help me—"

Then he checked himself abruptly, and the look of hopeless despair once more crept into his eyes.

"I am mad, Percy," he said with a self-deprecating shrug of the shoulders, "gone crazy with grief, I suppose, or I shouldn't talk of asking your help, of risking your life in my cause."

"Tony, if you talk that rubbish, I shall be forced to punch your head," retorted Blakeney with his light laugh. "Why man," he added gaily, "can't you see that I am aching to have at my old friend Chauvelin again?"

And indeed, the zest of adventure, the zest to fight, never dormant, was glowing with compelling vigour now in those lazy eyes of his which were resting with such kindliness upon his stricken friend. "Go home, Tony!" he added, "go, you rascal, and collect what things you want, while I send for Hastings and Ffoulkes, and see that four good horses are ready for us within the hour. Tonight, we sleep at Portishead, Tony. The *Daydream* is lying off there, ready to sail at any hour of the day or night. The *Hollandia* has twenty-four hour's start of us, alas! and we cannot overtake her now: but we'll be in Nantes ere those devils can do much mischief: and once in Nantes!—Why, Tony man! think of the glorious escapes we've had together, you and I! Think of the gay, mad rides across the north of France, with half-fainting women and swooning children across our saddle-bows! Think of the day when we smuggled the de Tournais out of Calais harbour, the day we snatched Juliette Déroulède and her Paul out of the tumbril and tore across Paris with that howling mob at our heels! Think! think, Tony! of all the happiest, merriest moments of your life and they will seem dull and lifeless beside what is in store for you, when with your dear wife's arms clinging round your neck, we'll fly along the quays of Nantes on the road to liberty! Ah, Tony lad! were it not for the anxiety which I know is gnawing at your heart, I would count this one of the happiest hours of my happy life!"

He was so full of enthusiasm, so full of vitality, that life itself seemed to emanate from him and to communicate itself to the very atmosphere around. Hope lit up my lord Tony's wan face: he believed in his friend as medieval ascetics believed in the saints whom they adored. Enthusiasm had crept into his veins dull despair fell away from him like a mantle.

"God bless you, Percy," he exclaimed as his firm and loyal hand grasped that of the leader whom he revered.

"Nay!" retorted Blakeney with sudden gravity. "He hath done that already. Pray for His help today, lad, as you have never prayed before."

Chapter 7

Marguerite

Lord Tony had gone, and for the space of five minutes Sir Percy Blakeney stood in front of the hearth staring into the fire. Something lay before him, something had to be done now, which represented the heavy price that had to be paid for those mad and happy adventures, for that reckless daring, aye for that selfless supreme sacrifice which was as the very breath of life to the Scarlet Pimpernel.

And in the dancing flames he could see Marguerite's blue eyes, her ardent hair, her tender smile all pleading with him not to go. She had so much to give him—so much happiness, such an infinity of love, and he was all that she had in the world! It seemed to him as if he could feel her arms around him even now, as if he could hear her voice whispering appealingly: "Do not go! Am I nothing to you that thoughts of others should triumph over my pleading? that the need of others should outweigh mine own most pressing need? I want you, Percy! aye! even I! You have done so much for others—it is my turn now."

But even as in a kind of trance those words seemed to reach his strained senses, he knew that he must go, that he must tear himself away once more from the clinging embrace of her dear arms and shut his eyes to the tears which *anon* would fill her own. Destiny demanded that he should go. He had chosen his path in life himself, at first only in a spirit of wild recklessness, a mad tossing of his life into the scales of Fate. But now that same destiny which he had chosen had become his master: he no longer could draw back. What he had done once, twenty times, an hundred times, that he must do again, all the while that the weak and the defenceless called mutely to him from across the seas, all the while that innocent women suffered and orphaned children cried.

And today it was his friend, his comrade, who had come to him in his distress: the young wife whom he idolised was in the most dire peril that could possibly threaten any woman: she was at the mercy of a man who, driven by the passion of revenge, meant to show her no mercy, and the devil alone knew these days to what lengths of infamy a man so driven would go.

The minutes sped on. Blakeney's eyes grew hot and wearied from staring into the fire. He closed them for a moment and then quietly turned to go.

All those who knew Marguerite Blakeney these days marvelled if she was ever unhappy. Lady Ffoulkes, who was her most trusted friend, vowed that she was not. She had moments—days—sometimes weeks of intense anxiety, which amounted to acute agony. Whenever she saw her husband start on one of those expeditions to France wherein every minute, every hour, he risked his life and more in order to snatch yet another threatened victim from the awful clutches of those merciless Terrorists, she endured soul-torture such as few women could have withstood who had not her splendid courage and her boundless faith. But against such crushing sorrow she had to set off the happiness of those reunions with the man whom she loved so passionately—happiness which was so great, that it overrode and conquered the very memory of past anxieties.

Marguerite Blakeney suffered terribly at times—at others she was overwhelmingly happy—the measure of her life was made up of the bitter dregs of sorrow and the sparkling wine of joy! No! she was not altogether unhappy: and gradually that enthusiasm which irradiated from the whole personality of the valiant Scarlet Pimpernel, which dominated his every action, entered into Marguerite Blakeney's blood too. His vitality was so compelling, those impulses which carried him headlong into unknown dangers were so generous and were actuated by such pure selflessness, that the noble-hearted woman whose very soul was wrapped up in the idolised husband, allowed herself to ride by his side on the buoyant waves of his enthusiasm and of his desires: she smothered every expression of anxiety, she swallowed her tears, she learned to say the word "Goodbye" and forgot the word "Stay!"

It was half an hour after midday when Percy knocked at the door of her *boudoir*. She had just come in from a walk in the meadows round the town and along the bank of the river: the rain had overtaken her and she had come in very wet, but none the less exhilarated by the movement and the keen, damp, salt-laden air which came straight over the hills from the Channel. She had taken off her hat and her mantle and was laughing gaily with her maid who was shaking the wet out of a feather. She looked round at her husband when he entered, and with a quick gesture ordered the maid out of the room.

She had learned to read every line on Percy's face, every expression of his lazy, heavy-lidded eyes. She saw that he was dressed with more than his usual fastidiousness, but in dark clothes and travelling mantle. She knew, moreover, by that subtle instinct which had become a second nature and which warned her whenever he meant to go.

Nor did he announce his departure to her in so many words. As soon as the maid had gone, he took his beloved in his arms.

"They have stolen Tony's wife from him," he said with that light, quaint laugh of his. "I told you that the man Martin-Roget had planned some devilish mischief—well! he has succeeded so far, thanks to that unspeakable fool the Duc de Kernogan."

He told her briefly the history of the past few days.

"Tony did not take my warning seriously enough," he concluded with a sigh; "he ought never to have allowed his wife out of his sight."

Marguerite had not interrupted him while he spoke. At first, she just lay in his arms, quiescent and listening, nerving herself by a supreme effort not to utter one sigh of misery or one word of appeal. Then, as her knees shook under her, she sank back into a chair by the hearth and he knelt beside her with his arms clasped tightly round her shoulders, his cheek pressed against hers. He had no need to tell her that duty and friendship called, that the call of honour was once again—as it so often has been in the world—louder than that of love.

She understood and she knew, and he, with that supersensitive instinct of his, understood the heroic effort which she made.

"Your love, dear heart," he whispered, "will draw me back safely home as it hath so often done before. You believe that, do you not?"

And she had the supreme courage to murmur: "Yes!"

CHAPTER 8

The Road to Portishead

It was not until Bath had very obviously been left behind that Yvonne de Kernogan—Lady Anthony Dewhurst—realised that she had been trapped.

During the first half-hour of the journey her father had lain back against the cushions of the carriage with eyes closed, his face pale and wan as if with great suffering. Yvonne, her mind a prey to the gravest anxiety, sat beside him, holding his limp cold hand in hers. Once or twice she ventured on a timid question as to his health and he invariably murmured a feeble assurance that he felt well, only very tired and disinclined to talk. *Anon* she suggested—diffidently, for she did not mean to disturb him—that the driver did not appear to know his way into Bath, he had turned into a side road which she felt sure was not the right one. *M. le Duc* then roused himself for a moment from his lethargy. He leaned forward and gazed out of the window.

"The man is quite right, Yvonne," he said quietly, "he knows his way. He brought me along this road yesterday. He gets into Bath by a slight *détour* but it is pleasanter driving."

This reply satisfied her. She was a stranger in the land and knew little or nothing of the environs of Bath. True, last Monday morning after the ceremony of her marriage she had driven out to Combwich, but dawn was only just breaking then, and she had lain for the most part—wearied and happy—in her young husband's arms. She had taken scant note of roads and signposts.

A few minutes later the coach came to a halt and Yvonne, looking through the window, saw a man who was muffled up to the chin and enveloped in a huge travelling cape, mount swiftly up beside the driver.

"Who is that man?" she queried sharply.

"Some friend of the coachman's, no doubt," murmured her father in reply, "to whom he is giving a lift as far as Bath."

The *barouche* had moved on again.

Yvonne could not have told you why, but at her father's last words she had felt a sudden cold grip at her heart—the first since she started. It was neither fear nor yet suspicion, but a chill seemed to go right through her. She gazed anxiously through the window, and then looked at her father with eyes that challenged and that doubted. But *M. le Duc* would not meet her gaze. He had once more closed his eyes and sat quite still, pale and haggard, like a man who is suffering acutely.

"Father we are going back to Bath, are we not?"

The query came out trenchant and hard from her throat which now felt hoarse and choked. Her whole being was suddenly pervaded by a vast and nameless fear. Time had gone on, and there was no sign in the distance of the great city. M. de Kernogan made no reply, but he opened his eyes and a curious glance shot from them at the terror-stricken face of his daughter.

Then she knew—knew that she had been tricked and trapped—that her father had played a hideous and complicated *rôle* of hypocrisy and duplicity in order to take her away from the husband whom she idolised.

Fear and her love for the man of her choice gave her initiative and strength. Before M. de Kernogan could realise what she was doing, before he could make a movement to stop her, she had seized the handle of the carriage door, wrenched the door open and jumped out into the road. She fell on her face in the mud, but the next moment she picked herself up again and started to run—down the road which the carriage had just traversed, on and on as fast as she could go. She ran on blindly, unreasoningly, impelled by a purely physical instinct to escape, not thinking how childish, how futile such an attempt was bound to be.

Already after the first few minutes of this swift career over the muddy road, she heard quick, heavy footsteps behind her. Her father could not run like that—the coachman could not have thus left his horses—but still she could hear those footsteps at a run—a quicker run than hers—and they were gaining on her—every minute, every second. The next, she felt two powerful arms suddenly seizing her by the shoulders. She stumbled and would once more have fallen, but for those same strong arms which held her close.

"Let me go! Let me go!" she cried, panting.

But she was held and could no longer move. She looked up into the face of Martin-Roget, who without any hesitation or compunction lifted her up as if she had been a bale of light goods and carried her back toward the coach. She had forgotten the man who had been picked up on the road a while ago and had been sitting beside the coachman since.

He deposited her in the *barouche* beside her father, then quietly closed the door and once more mounted to his seat on the box. The carriage moved on again. M. de Kernogan was no longer lethargic, he looked down on his daughter's inert form beside him, and not one look of tenderness or compassion softened the hard callousness of his face.

"Any resistance, my child," he said coldly, "will as you see be useless as well as undignified. I deplore this necessary violence, but I should be forced once more to requisition M. Martin-Roget's help if you attempted such foolish tricks again. When you are a little more calm, we will talk openly together."

For the moment she was lying back against the cushions of the carriage; her nerves having momentarily given way before this appalling catastrophe which had overtaken her and the hideous outrage to which she was being subjected by her own father. She was sobbing convulsively. But in the face of his abominable callousness, she made a great effort to regain her self-control. Her pride, her dignity came to the rescue. She had had time in those few seconds to realise that she was indeed more helpless than any bird in a fowler's net, and that only absolute calm and presence of mind could possibly save her now.

If indeed there was the slightest hope of salvation.

She drew herself up and resolutely dried her eyes and readjusted her hair and her hood and mantle.

"We can talk openly at once, sir," she said coldly. "I am ready to hear what explanation you can offer for this monstrous outrage."

"I owe you no explanation, my child," he retorted calmly. "Presently when you are restored to your own sense of dignity and of self-respect you will remember that a lady of the house of Kernogan does not elope in the night with a stranger and a heretic like some kitchen-wench. Having so far forgotten herself my daughter must, alas! take the consequences, which I deplore, of her own sins and lack of honour."

"And no doubt, father," she retorted, stung to the quick by his insults, "that you too will *anon* be restored to your own sense of self-respect and remember that hitherto no gentleman of the house of Kernogan has acted the part of a liar and of a hypocrite!"

"Silence!" he commanded sternly.

"Yes!" she reiterated wildly, "it was the *rôle* of a liar and of a hypocrite that you played from the moment when you sat down to pen that letter full of protestations of affection and forgiveness, until like a veritable Judas you betrayed your own daughter with a kiss. Shame on you, father!" she cried. "Shame!"

"Enough!" he said, as he seized her wrist so roughly that the cry of pain which involuntarily escaped her effectually checked the words in her mouth. "You are mad, beside yourself, a thoughtless, senseless creature whom I shall have to coerce more effectually if you do not cease your ravings. Do not force me to have recourse once again to M. Martin-Roget's assistance to keep your undignified outburst in check."

The name of the man whom she had learned to hate and fear more than any other human being in the world was sufficient to restore to her that measure of self-control which had again threatened to leave her.

"Enough indeed," she said more calmly; "the brain that could devise and carry out such infamy in cold blood is not like to be influenced by a defenceless woman's tears. Will you at least tell me whither you are taking me?"

"We go to a place on the coast now," he replied coldly, "the outlandish name of which has escaped me. There we embark for Holland, from whence we shall join their Royal Highnesses at Coblentz. It is at Coblentz that your marriage with M. Martin-Roget will take place, and—"

"Stay, father," she broke in, speaking quite as calmly as he did, "ere you go any further. Understand me clearly, for I mean every word that I say. In the sight of God—if not in that of the laws of France—I am the wife of Lord Anthony Dewhurst. By everything that I hold most sacred and most dear I swear to you that I will never become Martin-Roget's wife. I would die first," she added with burning but resolutely suppressed passion.

He shrugged his shoulders.

"Pshaw, my child," he said quietly, "many a time since the world began have women registered such solemn and sacred vows, only to break them when force of circumstance and their own good sense made them ashamed of their own folly."

"How little you know me, father," was all that she said in reply.

Indeed, Yvonne de Kernogan—Yvonne Dewhurst as she was now in sight of God and men—had far too much innate dignity and self-respect to continue this discussion, seeing that in any case she was physically the weaker, and that she was absolutely helpless and defenceless in the hands of two men, one of whom—her own father—who should have been her protector, was leagued with her bitterest enemy against her.

That Martin-Roget was her enemy—aye and her father's too—she had absolutely no doubt. Some obscure yet keen instinct was working in her heart, urging her to mistrust him even more wholly than she had done before. Just now, when he laid ruthless hands on her and carried her, inert and half-swooning, back into the coach, and she lay with closed eyes, her very soul in revolt against this contact with him, against the feel of his arms around her, a vague memory surcharged with horror and with dread stirred within her brain: and over the vista of the past few years she looked back upon an evening in the autumn—a rough night with the wind from the Atlantic blowing across the lowlands of Poitou and soughing in the willow trees that bordered the Loire—she seemed to hear the tumultuous cries of enraged human creatures dominating the sound of the gale, she felt the crowd of evil-intentioned men around the closed carriage wherein she sat, calm and unafraid. Darkness then was all around her. She could not see. She could only hear and feel. And she heard the carriage door being wrenched open, and she felt the cold breath of the wind upon her cheek, and also the hot breath of a man in a passion of fury and of hate.

She had seen nothing then, and mercifully semi-unconsciousness had dulled her aching senses, but even now her soul shrunk with horror at the vague remembrance of that ghostlike form—the spirit of hate and of revenge—of its rough arms encircling her shoulders, its fingers under her chin—and then that awful, loathsome, contaminating kiss which she thought then would have smirched her for ever. It had taken all the pure, sweet kisses of a brave and loyal man whom she loved and revered, to make her forget that hideous, indelible stain: and in the arms of her dear milor she had forgotten that one terrible moment, when she had felt that the embrace of death must be more endurable than that of this unknown and hated man.

It was the memory of that awful night which had come back to her as in a flash while she lay passive and broken in Martin-Roget's arms. Of course, for the moment she had no thought of connecting the rich banker from Brest, the enthusiastic royalist and *émigré*, with one of those turbulent, uneducated peasant lads who had attacked her carriage that night: all that she was conscious of was that she was outraged by his presence, just as she had been outraged then, and that the contact of his hands, of his arms, was absolutely unendurable.

To fight against the physical power which held her a helpless prisoner in the hands of the enemy was sheer impossibility. She knew that and was too proud to make feeble and futile efforts which could only end in defeat and further humiliation. She felt hideously wretched and lonely—thoughts of her husband, who at this hour was still serenely unconscious of the terrible catastrophe which had befallen him, brought tears of acute misery to her eyes. What would he do when—tomorrow, perhaps—he realised that his bride had been stolen from him, that he had been fooled and duped as she had been too. What could he do when he knew?

She tried to solace her own soul-agony by thinking of his influential friends who, of course, would help him as soon as they knew. There was that mysterious and potent friend of whom he spoke so little, who already had warned him of coming danger and urged on the secret marriage which should have proved a protection. There was Sir Percy Blakeney, of whom he spoke much, who was enormously rich, independent, the most intimate friend of the Regent himself. There was—

But what was the use of clinging even for one instant to those feeble cords of Hope's broken lyre? By the time her dear lord knew that she was gone, she would be on the high seas, far out of his reach.

And she had not even the solace of tears—heartbroken sobs rose in her throat, but she resolutely kept them back. Her father's cold, impassive face, the callous glitter in his eyes told her that every tear would be in vain, her most earnest appeal an object for his sneers.

As to how long the journey in the coach lasted after that Yvonne Dewhurst could not have said. It may have been a few hours, it may have been a cycle of years. She had been young—a happy bride, a dutiful daughter—when she left Combwich Hall. She was an old woman now, a supremely unhappy one, parted from the man she loved without hope of ever seeing him again in life, and feeling nothing but hatred and contempt for the father who had planned such infamy against her.

She offered no resistance whatever to any of her father's commands. After the first outburst of revolt and indignation she had not even spoken to him.

There was a halt somewhere on the way, when in the low-raftered room of a posting-inn, she had to sit table with the two men who had compassed her misery. She was thirsty, feverish and weak: she drank some milk in silence. She felt ill physically as well as mentally, and the constant effort not to break down had helped to shatter her nerves. As she had stepped out of the *barouche* without a word, so she stepped into it again when it stood outside, ready with a fresh relay of horses to take her further, still further, away from the cosy little nest where even now her young husband was waiting longingly for her return. The people of the inn—a kindly-looking woman, a portly middle-aged man, one or two young ostlers and serving-maids were standing about in the yard when her father led her to the coach. For a moment the wild idea rushed to her mind to run to these people and demand their protection, to proclaim at the top of her voice the infamous act which was dragging her away from her husband and her home and lead her a helpless prisoner to a fate that was infinitely worse than death. She even ran to the woman who looked so benevolent and so kind, she placed her small quivering hand on the other's rough toil-worn one and in hurried, appealing words begged for her help and the shelter of a home till she could communicate with her husband.

The woman listened with a look of kindly pity upon her homely face, she patted the small, trembling hand and stroked it gently, tears of compassion gathered in her eyes:

"Yes, yes, my dear," she said soothingly, speaking as she would to a sick woman or to a child, "I quite understand. I wouldna' fret if I was you. I would jess go quietly with your pore father: 'e knows what's best for you, that 'e do. You come 'long wi' me," she added as she drew Yvonne's hands through her arm, "I'll see ye're comfortable in the coach."

Yvonne, bewildered, could not at first understand either the woman's sympathy or her obvious indifference to the pitiable tale, until— Oh! the shame of it!—she saw the two young serving-maids looking on her with equal pity expressed in their round eyes, and heard one of them whispering to the other:

"Pore lady! so zad ain't it? I'm that zorry for the pore father!"

And the girl with a significant gesture indicated her own forehead and glanced knowingly at her companion. Yvonne felt a hot flush rise to the very roots of her hair. So, her father and Martin-Roget had thought of everything, and had taken every precaution to cut the ground from under her feet. Wherever a halt was necessary, wherever the party might come in contact with the curious or the indifferent, it would be given out that the poor young lady was crazed, that she talked wildly, and had to be kept under restraint.

Yvonne as she turned away from that last faint glimmer of hope, encountered Martin-Roget's glance of triumph and saw the sneer which curled his full lips. Her father came up to her just then and took her over from the kindly hostess, with the ostentatious manner of one who has charge of a sick person and must take every precaution for her welfare.

"Another loss of dignity, my child," he said to her in French, so that none but Martin-Roget could catch what he said. "I guessed that you would commit some indiscretion, you see, so M. Martin-Roget and myself warned all the people at the inn the moment we arrived. We told them that I was travelling with a sick daughter who had become crazed through the death of her lover and believed herself—like most crazed persons do—to be persecuted and oppressed. You have seen the result. They pitied you. Even the serving-maids smiled. It would have been wiser to remain silent."

Whereupon he handed her into the *barouche* with loving care, a crowd of sympathetic onlookers gazing with obvious compassion on the poor crazed lady and her sorely tried father.

After this episode Yvonne gave up the struggle.

No one but God could help her, if He chose to perform a miracle.

The rest of the journey was accomplished in silence. Yvonne gazed, unseeing, through the carriage window as the *barouche* rattled on the cobble-stones of the streets of Bristol. She marvelled at the number of people who went gaily by along the streets, unheeding, unknowing that the greatest depths of misery to which any human being could sink had been probed by the unfortunate young girl who wide-eyed, mute and broken-hearted gazed out upon the busy world without.

Portishead was reached just when the grey light of day turned to a gloomy twilight. Yvonne unresisting, insentient, went whither she was bidden to go. Better that, than to feel Martin-Roget's coercive grip on her arm, or to hear her father's curt words of command.

She walked along the pier and *anon* stepped into a boat, hardly knowing what she was doing: the twilight was welcome to her, for it hid much from her view and her eyes—hot with unshed tears—ached for the restful gloom. She realised that the boat was being rowed along for some little way down the stream, that Frédérick, who had come she knew not how or whence, was in the boat too with some luggage which she recognised as being familiar: that another woman was there whom she did not know, but who appeared to look after her comforts, wrapped a shawl closer round her knees and drew the hood of her mantle closer round her neck. But it was all like an ugly dream: the voices of her father and of Martin-Roget, who were talking in monosyllables, the sound of the oars as they struck the water, or creaked in their rowlocks, came to her as from an ever-receding distance.

A couple of hours later she came back to complete conciousness. She was in a narrow place, which at first appeared to her like a cupboard: the atmosphere was both cold and stuffy and reeked of tar and of oil. She was lying on a hard bed with her mantle and a shawl wrapped round her. It was very dark save where the feeble glimmer of a lamp threw a circle of light around. Above her head there was a constant and heavy tramping of feet, and the sound of incessant and varied creakings and groanings of wood, cordage and metal filled the night air with their weird and dismal sounds. A slow feeling of movement coupled with a gentle oscillation confirmed the unfortunate girl's first waking impression that she was on board a ship. How she had got there she did not know. She must ultimately have fainted in the small boat and been carried aboard. She raised herself slightly on her elbow and peered round her into the dark corners of the cabin: opposite to her upon a bench, also wrapped up in shawl and mantle, lay the woman who had been in attendance on her in the boat.

The woman's heavy breathing indicated that she was fast asleep.

Loneliness! Misery! Desolation encompassed the happy bride of yesterday. With a moan of exquisite soul-agony she fell back against the hard cushions, and for the first time this day a convulsive flow of tears eased the super-acuteness of her misery.

CHAPTER 9

The Coast of France

The whole of that wretched mournful day Yvonne Dewhurst spent upon the deck of the ship which was bearing her away every hour, every minute, further and still further from home and happiness. She seldom spoke: she ate and drank when food was brought to her: she was conscious neither of cold nor of wet, of well-being or ill. She sat upon a pile of cordages in the stern of the ship leaning against the taffrail and in imagination seeing the coast of England fade into illimitable space.

Part of the time it rained, and then she sat huddled up in the shawls and tarpaulins which the woman placed about her: then, when the sun came out, she still sat huddled up, closing her eyes against the glare.

When daylight faded into dusk, and then twilight into night she gazed into nothingness as she had gazed on water and sky before, thinking, thinking, thinking! This could not be the end—it could not. So much happiness, such pure love, such perfect companionship as she had had with the young husband whom she idolised could not all be wrenched from her like that, without previous foreboding and without some warning from Fate. This miserable, sordid, wretched journey to an unknown land could not be the epilogue to the exquisite romance which had suddenly changed the dreary monotony of her life into one long, glowing dream of joy and of happiness! This could not be the end!

And gazing into the immensity of the far horizon she thought and thought and racked her memory for every word, every look which she had had from her dear milor. And upon the grey background of sea and sky she seemed to perceive the vague and dim outline of that mysterious friend—the man who knew everything—who foresaw everything, even and above all the dangers that threatened those whom he loved. He had foreseen this awful danger too! Oh! if only milor and she herself had realised its full extent! But now surely! surely! he would help, he would know what to do. Milor was wont to speak of him as being omniscient and having marvellous powers.

Once or twice during the day M. le Duc de Kernogan came to sit beside his daughter and tried to speak a few words of comfort and of sympathy. Of a truth—here on the open sea—far both from home and kindred and from the new friends he had found in hospitable England—his heart smote him for all the wrong he had done to his only child. He dared not think of the gentle and patient wife who lay at rest in the churchyard of Kernogan, for he feared that with his thoughts he would conjure up her pale, avenging ghost who would demand an account of what he had done with her child.

Cold and exposure—the discomfort of the long sea-journey in this rough trading ship had somewhat damped M. de Kernogan's pride and obstinacy: his loyalty to the cause of his king had paled before the demands of a father's duty toward his helpless daughter.

It was close on six o'clock and the night, after the turbulent and capricious alternations of rain and sunshine, promised to be beautifully clear, though very cold. The pale crescent of the moon had just emerged from behind the thick veil of cloud and mist which still hung threateningly upon the horizon: a fitful sheen of silver danced upon the waves.

M. le Duc stood beside his daughter. He had inquired after her health and well-being and received her monosyllabic reply with an impatient sigh. M. Martin-Roget was pacing up and down the deck with restless and vigorous strides: he had just gone by and made a loud and cheery comment on the weather and the beauty of the night.

Could Yvonne Dewhurst have seen her father's face now, or had she cared to study it, she would have perceived that he was gazing out to sea in the direction to which the schooner was heading with an intent look of puzzlement, and that there was a deep furrow between his brows.

Half an hour went by and he still stood there, silent and absorbed: then suddenly a curious exclamation escaped his lips: he stooped and seized his daughter by the wrist.

"Yvonne!" he said excitedly, "tell me! am I dreaming, or am I crazed?"

"What is it?" she asked coldly.

"Out there! Look! Just tell me what you see?"

He appeared so excited and his pressure on her wrist was so insistent that she dragged herself to her feet and looked out to sea in the direction to which he was pointing.

"Tell me what you see," he reiterated with ever-growing excitement, and she felt that the hand which held her wrist trembled violently.

"The light from a lighthouse, I think," she said.

"And besides that?"

"Another light—a much smaller one—considerably higher up. It must be perched up on some cliffs."

"Anything else?"

"Yes. There are lights dotted about here and there. Some village on the coast."

"On the coast?" he murmured hoarsely, "and we are heading towards it."

"So, it appears," she said indifferently. What cared she to what shore she was being taken: every land save England was exile to her now.

Just at this moment M. Martin-Roget in his restless wanderings once more passed by.

"M. Martin-Roget!" called the *duc*.

And vaguely Yvonne wondered why his voice trembled so.

"At your service, *M. le Duc*," replied the other as he came to a halt, and then stood with legs wide apart firmly planted upon the deck, his hands buried in the pockets of his heavy mantle, his head thrown back, as if defiantly, his whole attitude that of a master condescending to talk with slaves.

"What are those lights over there, ahead of us?" asked *M. le Duc* quietly.

"The lighthouse of Le Croisic, *M. le Duc*," replied Martin-Roget dryly, "and of the guard-house above and the harbour below. All at your service," he added, with a sneer.

"*Monsieur*—" exclaimed the *duc*.

"Eh? what?" queried the other blandly.

"What does this mean?"

In the vague, dim light of the moon Yvonne could just distinguish the two men as they stood confronting one another. Martin-Roget, tall, massive, with arms now folded across his breast, shrugging his broad shoulders at the *duc's* impassioned query—and her father who suddenly appeared to have shrunk within himself, who raised one trembling hand to his forehead and with the other sought with pathetic entreaty the support of his daughter's arm.

"What does this mean?" he murmured again.

"Only," replied Martin-Roget with a laugh, "that we are close to the coast of France and that with this unpleasant but useful north-westerly wind we shall be in Nantes two hours before midnight."

"In Nantes?" queried the *duc* vaguely, not understanding, speaking tonelessly like a somnambulist or a man in a trance. He was leaning heavily now on his daughter's arm, and she with that motherly instinct which is ever present in a good woman's heart even in the presence of her most cruel enemy, drew him tenderly towards her, gave him the support he needed, not quite understanding herself yet what it was that had befallen them both.

"Yes, in Nantes, *M. le Duc*," reiterated Martin-Roget with a sneer.

"But 'twas to Holland we were going."

"To Nantes, *M. le Duc*," retorted the other with a ringing note of triumph in his voice, "to Nantes, from which you fled like a coward when you realised that the vengeance of an outraged people had at last overtaken you and your kind."

"I do not understand," stammered the *duc*, and mechanically now—instinctively—father and daughter clung to one another as if each was striving to protect the other from the raving fury of this madman. Never for a moment did they believe that he was sane. Excitement, they thought, had turned his brain: he was acting and speaking like one possessed.

"I dare say it would take far longer than the next four hours while we glide gently along the Loire, to make such as you understand that your arrogance and your pride are destined to be humbled at last and that you are now in the power of those men who a while ago you did not deem worthy to lick your boots. I dare say," he continued calmly, "you think that I am crazed. Well! perhaps I am, but sane enough anyhow, *M. le Duc*, to enjoy the full flavour of revenge."

"Revenge?—what have we done?—what has my daughter done?—" stammered the *duc* incoherently. "You swore you loved her—desired to make her your wife—I consented—she—"

Martin-Roget's harsh laugh broke in on his vague murmurings.

"And like an arrogant fool you fell into the trap," he said with calm irony, "and you were too blind to see in Martin-Roget, suitor for your daughter's hand, Pierre Adet, the son of the victim of your execrable tyranny, the innocent man murdered at your bidding."

"Pierre Adet—I don't understand."

"'Tis but little meseems that you do understand, *M. le Duc*," sneered the other. "But turn your memory back, I pray you, to the night four years ago when a few hot-headed peasant lads planned to give you a fright in your castle of Kernogan—the plan failed and Pierre Adet, the leader of that unfortunate band, managed to fly the country, whilst you, like a crazed and blind tyrant, administered punishment right and left for the fright which you had had. Just think of it! those boors! those louts! that swinish herd of human cattle had dared to raise a cry of revolt against you! To death with them all! to death! Where is Pierre Adet, the leader of those hogs? to him an exemplary punishment must be meted! a deterrent against any other attempt at revolt.

"Well, *M. le Duc*, do you remember what happened then? Pierre Adet, severely injured in the *mêlée*, had managed to crawl away into safety. While he lay betwixt life and death, first in the presbytery of Vertou, then in various ditches on his way to Paris, he knew nothing of what happened at Nantes. When he returned to consciousness and to active life he heard that his father, Jean Adet the miller, who was innocent of any share in the revolt, had been hanged by order of M. le Duc de Kernogan."

He paused awhile and a curious laugh—half-convulsive and not unmixed with sobs—shook his broad shoulders. Neither the *duc* nor Yvonne made any comment on what they heard: the *duc* felt like a fly caught in a death-dealing web. He was dazed with the horror of his position, dazed above all with the rush of bitter remorse which had surged up in his heart and mind, when he realised that it was his own folly, his obstinacy—aye! and his heartlessness which had brought this awful fate upon his daughter. And Yvonne felt that whatever she might endure of misery and hopelessness was nothing in comparison with what her father must feel with the addition of bitter self-reproach.

"Are you beginning to understand the position better now, *M. le Duc?*" queried Martin-Roget after a while.

The *duc* sank back nerveless upon the pile of cordages close by. Yvonne was leaning with her back against the taffrail, her two arms outstretched, the north-west wind blowing her soft brown hair about her face whilst her eyes sought through the gloom to read the lines of cruelty and hatred which must be distorting Martin-Roget's face now.

"And," she said quietly after a while, "you have waited all these years, *Monsieur,* nursing thoughts of revenge and of hate against us. Ah! believe me," she added earnestly, "though God knows my heart is full of misery at this moment, and though I know that at your bidding death will so soon claim me and my father as his own, yet would I not change my wretchedness for yours."

"And I, citizeness," he said roughly, addressing her for the first time in the manner prescribed by the revolutionary government, "would not change places with any king or other tyrant on earth. Yes," he added as he came a step or two closer to her, "I have waited all these years. For four years I have thought and striven and planned, planned to be even with your father and with you one day. You had fled the country—like cowards, bah!—ready to lend your arms to the foreigner against your own country in order to re-establish a tyrant upon the throne whom the whole of the people of France loathed and detested. You had fled, but soon I learned whither you had gone.

"Then I set to work to gain access to you—I learned English—I too went to England—under an assumed name—with the necessary introductions so as to gain a footing in the circles in which you moved. I won your father's condescension—almost his friendship!—The rich banker from Brest should be fleeced in order to provide funds for the armies that were to devastate France—and the rich banker of Brest refused to be fleeced unless he was lured by the promise of Mlle. de Kernogan's hand in marriage."

"You need not, *Monsieur,*" rejoined Yvonne coldly, while Martin-Roget paused in order to draw breath, "you need not, believe me, take the trouble to recount all the machinations which you carried through in order to gain your ends. Enough that my father was so foolish as to trust you, and that we are now completely in your power, but—"

"There is no 'but,'" he broke in gruffly, "you are in my power and will be made to learn the law of the *talion* which demands an eye for an eye, a life for a life: that is the law which the people are applying to that herd of *aristos* who were arrogant tyrants once and are shrinking, cowering slaves now. Oh! you were very proud that night, Mademoiselle Yvonne de Kernogan, when a few peasant lads told you some home truths while you sat disdainful and callous in your carriage, but there is one fact that you can never efface from your memory, strive how you may, and that is that for a few minutes I held you in my arms and that I kissed you, my fine lady, aye! kissed you like I would any pert kitchen wench, even I, Pierre Adet, the miller's son."

He drew nearer and nearer to her as he spoke; she, leaning against the taffrail, could not retreat any further from him. He laughed.

"If you fall over into the water, I shall not complain," he said, "it will save our proconsul the trouble, and the guillotine some work. But you need not fear. I am not trying to kiss you again. You are nothing to me, you and your father, less than nothing. Your death in misery and wretchedness is all I want, whether you find a dishonoured grave in the Loire or by suicide I care less than nothing. But let me tell you this," he added, and his voice came now like a hissing sound through his set teeth, "that there is no intention on my part to make glorious martyrs of you both. I dare say you have heard some pretty stories over in England of *aristos* climbing the steps of the guillotine with an ecstatic look of martyrdom upon their face: and tales of the tumbrils of Paris laden with men and women going to their death and shouting "God save the King" all the way. That is not the sort of paltry revenge which would satisfy me.

"My father was hanged by yours as a malefactor—hanged, I say, like a common thief! he, a man who had never wronged a single soul in the whole course of his life, who had been an example of fine living, of hard work, of noble courage through many adversities. My mother was left a widow—not the honoured widow of an honourable man—but a pariah, the relict of a malefactor who had died of the hangman's rope—my sister was left an orphan—dishonoured—without hope of gaining the love of a respectable man. All that I and my family owe to *ci-devant* M. le Duc de Kernogan, and therefore I tell you, that both he and his daughter shall not die like martyrs but like malefactors too—shamed—dishonoured—loathed and execrated even by their own kindred!

"Take note of that, M. le Duc de Kernogan! You have sown shame, shame shall you reap! and the name of which you are so proud will be dragged in the mire until it has become a by-word in the land for all

104

that is despicable and base."

Perhaps at no time of his life had Martin-Roget, erstwhile Pierre Adet, spoken with such an intensity of passion, even though he was at all times turbulent and a ready prey to his own emotions. But all that he had kept hidden in the inmost recesses of his heart, ever since as a young stripling he had chafed at the social conditions of his country, now welled forth in that wild harangue. For the first time in his life he felt that he was really master of those who had once despised and oppressed him. He held them and was the arbiter of their fate. The sense of possession and of power had gone to his head like wine: he was intoxicated with his own feeling of triumphant revenge, and this impassioned rhetoric flowed from his mouth like the insentient babble of a drunken man.

The Duc de Kernogan, sitting on the coil of cordages with his elbows on his knees and his head buried in his hands, had no thought of breaking in on the other man's ravings. The bitterness of remorse paralysed his thinking faculties. Martin-Roget's savage words struck upon his senses like blows from a sledge-hammer. He knew that nothing but his own folly was the cause of Yvonne's and his own misfortune.

Yvonne had been safe from all evil fortune under the protection of her fine young English husband; he—the father who should have been her chief protector—had dragged her by brute force away from that husband's care and had landed her—where?—A shudder like acute ague went through the unfortunate man's whole body as he thought of the future. Nor did Yvonne Dewhurst attempt to make reply to her enemy's delirious talk. She would not give him even the paltry satisfaction of feeling that he had stung her into a retort. She did not fear him—she hated him too much for that—but like her father she had no illusions as to his power over them both. While he stormed and raved she kept her eyes steadily fixed upon him. She could only just barely distinguish him in the gloom, and he no doubt failed to see the expression of lofty indifference wherewith she contrived to regard him: but he *felt* her contempt, and but for the presence of the sailors on the deck he probably would have struck her.

As it was when, from sheer lack of breath, he had to pause, he gave one last look of hate on the huddled figure of the *duc*, and the proud, upstanding one of Yvonne, then with a laugh which sounded like that of a fiend—so cruel, so callous was it, he turned on his heel, and as he strode away towards the bow his tall figure was soon absorbed in the surrounding gloom.

The Duc de Kernogan and his daughter saw little or nothing of Martin-Roget after that. For a while longer they caught sight of him from time to time as he walked up and down the deck with ceaseless restlessness and in the company of another man, who was much shorter and slimmer than himself and whom they had not noticed hitherto. Martin-Roget talked most of the time in a loud and excited voice, the other appearing to listen to him with a certain air of deference.

Whether the conversation between these two was actually intended for the ears of the two unfortunates, or whether it was merely chance which brought certain phrases to their ears when the two men passed closely by, it were impossible to say. Certain it is that from such chance phrases they gathered that the *barque* would not put into Nantes, as the navigation of the Loire was suspended for the nonce by order of Proconsul Carrier. He had need of the river for his awesome and nefarious deeds. Yvonne's ears were regaled with tales—told with loud ostentation—of the terrible *noyades*, the wholesale drowning of men, women and children, malefactors and traitors, so as to ease the burden of the guillotine.

After three bells it got so bitterly cold that Yvonne, fearing that her father would become seriously ill, suggested their going down to their stuffy cabins together. After all, even the foul and shut-up atmosphere of these close, airless cupboards was preferable to the propinquity of those two human fiends up on deck and the tales of horror and brutality which they loved to tell.

And for two hours after that, father and daughter sat in the narrow cell-like place, locked in each other's arms. She had everything to forgive, and he everything to atone for: but Yvonne suffered so acutely, her misery was so great that she found it in her heart to pity the father whose misery must have been even greater than hers. The supreme solace of bestowing love and forgiveness and of easing the racking paroxysms of remorse which brought the unfortunate man to the verge of dementia, warmed her heart towards him and brought surcease to her own sorrow.

BOOK TWO: NANTES, DECEMBER, 1793

CHAPTER 1

The Tiger's Lair

Nantes is in the grip of the tiger.

Representative Carrier—with powers as of a proconsul—has been sent down to stamp out the lingering remnants of the counter-revolution. La Vendée is temporarily subdued; the army of the royalists driven back across the Loire; but traitors still abound—this the National Convention in Paris hath decreed—there are traitors everywhere. They were not *all* massacred at Cholet and Savenay. Disbanded, yes! but not exterminated, and wolves must not be allowed to run loose, lest they band again, and try to devour the flocks.

Therefore, extermination is the order of the day. Every traitor or would-be traitor—every son and daughter and father and mother of traitors must be destroyed ere they do more mischief. And Carrier—Carrier the coward who turned tail and bolted at Cholet—is sent to Nantes to carry on the work of destruction. Wolves and wolflings all! Let none survive. Give them fair trial, of course. As traitors they have deserved death—have they not taken up arms against the Republic and against the Will and the Reign of the People? But let a court of justice sit in Nantes town; let the whole nation know how traitors are dealt with: let the nation see that her rulers are both wise and just. Let wolves and wolflings be brought up for trial and set up the guillotine on Place du Bouffay with four executioners appointed to do her work. There would be too much work for two, or even three. Let there be four—and let the work of extermination be complete.

And Carrier—with powers as of a proconsul—arrives in Nantes town and sets to work to organise his household. Civil and military—with pomp and circumstance—for the son of a small farmer, destined originally for the Church and for obscurity is now virtual autocrat in one of the great cities of France. He has power of life and death over thousands of citizens—under the direction of justice, of course! So now he has citizens of the bedchamber, and citizens of the household, he has a guard of honour and a company of citizens of the guard. And above all he has a crowd of spies around him—servants of the Committee of Public Safety so they are called—they style themselves *"La Compagnie Marat"* in honour of the great patriot who was foully murdered by a female wolfling.

So, *la Compagnie Marat* is formed—they wear red bonnets on their heads—no stockings on their feet—short breeches to display their bare shins: their captain, Fleury, has access at all times to the person of the proconsul, to make report on the raids which his company effect at all hours of the day or night. Their powers are supreme too. In and out of houses—however private—up and down the streets—through shops, taverns and warehouses, along the quays and the yards—everywhere they go. Everywhere they have the right to go! to ferret and to spy, to listen, to search, to interrogate—the red-capped Company is paid for what it can find. Piece-work, what? Work for the guillotine!

And they it is who keep the guillotine busy. Too busy in fact. And the court of justice sitting in the Hôtel du Département is overworked too. Carrier gets impatient. Why waste the time of patriots by so much paraphernalia of justice? Wolves and wolflings can be exterminated so much more quickly, more easily than that. It only needs a stroke of genius, one stroke, and Carrier has it.

He invents the *Noyades*!

The Drownages we may call them!

They are so simple! An old flat-bottomed barge. The work of two or three ship's carpenters! Portholes below the water-line and made to open at a given moment. All so very, very simple. Then a journey downstream as far as Belle Isle or la Maréchale, and "sentence of deportation" executed without any trouble on a whole crowd of traitors—"vertical deportation" Carrier calls it facetiously and is mightily proud of his invention and of his witticism too.

The first attempt was highly successful. Ninety priests, and not one escaped. Think of the work it would have entailed on the guillotine—and on the friends of Carrier who sit in justice in the Hôtel du Département! Ninety heads! Bah! That old flat-bottomed barge is the most wonderful labour-saving machine.

After that the "Drownages" become the order of the day. The red-capped Company recruits victims for the hecatomb, and over Nantes Town there hangs a pall of unspeakable horror. The prisons are not vast enough to hold all the victims, so the huge *entrepôt*, the bonded warehouse on the quay, is converted: instead of chests of coffee it is now encumbered with human freight: into it pell-mell are thrown all those who are destined to assuage Carrier's passion for killing: ten thousand of them: men, women, and young children, counter-revolutionists, innocent tradesmen, thieves, aristocrats, criminals and women of evil fame—they are herded together like cattle, without straw whereon to lie, without water, without fire, with barely food enough to keep up the last attenuated thread of a miserable existence.

And when the warehouse gets over full, to the Loire with them!—a hundred or two at a time! Pestilence, dysentery decimates their numbers. Under pretence of hygienic requirements two hundred are flung into the river on the 14th day of December. Two hundred—many of them women—crowds of children and a batch of parish priests.

Some there are among Carrier's colleagues—those up in Paris—who protest! Such wholesale butchery will not redound to the credit of any revolutionary government—it even savours of treachery—it is unpatriotic! There are the emissaries of the National Convention, deputed from Paris to supervise and control—they protest as much as they dare—but such men are swept off their feet by the torrent of Carrier's gluttony for blood. Carrier's mission is to "purge the political body of every evil that infests it." Vague and yet precise! He reckons that he has full powers and thinks he can flaunt those powers in the face of those sent to control him. He does it too for three whole months ere he in his turn meets his doom. But for the moment he is omnipotent. He has to make report every week to the Committee of Public Safety, and he sends brief, garbled versions of his doings. "He is pacifying La Vendée! he is stamping out the remnants of the rebellion! he is purging the political body of every evil that infests it." *Anon* he succeeds in getting the emissaries of the National Convention re-called. He is impatient of control. "They are weak, pusillanimous, un-patriotic! He must have freedom to act for the best."

After that he remains virtual dictator, with none but obsequious, terrified myrmidons around him: these are too weak to oppose him in any way. And the municipality dare not protest either—nor the district council—nor the departmental. They are merely sheep who watch others of their flock being sent to the slaughter.

After that from within his lair the man tiger decides that it is a pity to waste good barges on the cattle: "Fling them out!" he cries. "Fling them out! Tie two and two together. Man and woman! criminal and *aristo!* the thief with the *ci-devant* duke's daughter! the *ci-devant* marquis with the slut from the streets! Fling them all out together into the Loire and pour a hail of grape shot above them until the last strug-gler has disappeared!" "Equality!" he cries, "Equality for all! Fraternity! Unity in death!"

His friends call this new invention of his: "*Marriage Républicain!*" and he is pleased with the *mot.*

And Republican marriages become the order of the day.

Nantes itself now is akin to a desert—a desert wherein the air is filled with weird sounds of cries and of moans, of furtive footsteps scurrying away into dark and secluded byways, of musketry and con-fused noises, of sorrow and of lamentations.

Nantes is a city of the dead—a city of sleepers. Only Carrier is awake—thinking and devising and planning shorter ways and swifter, for the extermination of traitors.

In the Hôtel de la Villestreux the tiger has built his lair: at the apex of the island of Feydeau, with the windows of the hotel facing straight down the Loire. From here there is a magnificent view downstream upon the quays which are now deserted and upon the once prosperous port of Nantes.

The staircase of the hotel which leads up to the apartments of the proconsul is crowded every day and all day with suppliants and with petitioners, with the citizens of the household and the members of the Compagnie Marat.

But no one has access to the person of the dictator. He stands aloof, apart, hidden from the eyes of the world, a mysterious personality whose word sends hundreds to their death, whose arbitrary will has reduced a once flourishing city to abject poverty and squalor. No tyrant has ever surrounded himself with a greater paraphernalia of pomp and circumstance—no *aristo* has ever dwelt in greater luxury: the spoils of churches and *châteaux* fill the Hôtel de la Villestreux from attic to cellar, gold and silver plate adorn his table, priceless works of art hang upon his walls, he lolls on couches and chairs which have been the resting-place of kings. The wholesale spoliation of the entire country-side has filled the demagogue's abode with all that is most sumptuous in the land.

And he himself is far more inaccessible than was *le Roi Soleil* in the days of his most towering arrogance, than were the Popes in the glorious days of medieval Rome. Jean Baptiste Carrier, the son of a small farmer, the obscure deputy for Cantal in the National Convention, dwells in the Hôtel de la Villestreux as in a stronghold. No one is allowed near him save a few—a very few—intimates: his valet, two or three women, Fleury the commander of the Marats, and that strange and abominable youngster, Jacques Lalouët, about whom the chroniclers of that tragic epoch can tell us so little—a cynical young braggart, said to be a cousin of Robespierre and the son of a midwife of Nantes, beardless, handsome and vicious: the only human being—so we are told—who had any influence over the sinister proconsul: mere hanger-on of Carrier or spy of the National Convention, no one can say—a malignant personality which has remained an enigma and a mystery to this hour.

None but these few are ever allowed now inside the inner sanctuary wherein dwells and schemes the dictator. Even Lamberty, Fouquet and the others of the staff are kept at arm's length. Martin-Roget,

Chauvelin and other strangers are only allowed as far as the ante-room. The door of the inner chamber is left open and they hear the proconsul's voice and see his silhouette pass and repass in front of them, but that is all.

Fear of assassination—the inevitable destiny of the tyrant—haunts the man-tiger even within the fastnesses of his lair. Day and night a carriage with four horses stands in readiness on La Petite Hollande, the great, open, tree-bordered Place at the extreme end of the Isle Feydeau and on which give the windows of the Hôtel de la Ville-streux. Day and night the carriage is ready—with coachman on the box and postillion in the saddle, who are relieved every two hours lest they get sleepy or slack—with luggage in the boot and provisions always kept fresh inside the coach; everything always ready lest something—a warning from a friend or a threat from an enemy, or merely a sudden access of unreasoning terror, the haunting memory of a bloody act—should decide the tyrant at a moment's notice to fly from the scenes of his brutalities.

Carrier in the small room which he has fitted up for himself as a sumptuous *boudoir*, paces up and down just like a wild beast in its cage: and he rubs his large bony hands together with the excitement engendered by his own cruelties, by the success of this wholesale butchery which he has invented and carried through.

There never was an uglier man than Carrier, with that long hatchet-face of his, those abnormally high cheekbones, that stiff, lanky hair, that drooping, flaccid mouth and protruding underlip. Nature seemed to have set herself the task of making the face a true mirror of the soul—the dark and hideous soul on which of a surety Satan had already set his stamp. But he is dressed with scrupulous care—not to say elegance—and with a display of jewellery the provenance of which is as unjustifiable as that of the works of art which fill his private sanctum in every nook and cranny.

In front of the tall window, heavy curtains of crimson damask are drawn closely together, in order to shut out the light of day: the room is in all but total darkness: for that is the proconsul's latest caprice: that no one shall see him save in semi-obscurity.

Captain Fleury has stumbled into the room, swearing lustily as he barks his shins against the angle of a priceless Louis XV bureau. He has to make report on the work done by the Compagnie Marat. Fifty-three priests from the department of Anjou who have refused to take the new oath of obedience to the government of the Republic. The red-capped Company who tracked them down and arrested them, vow that all these *calotins* have precious objects—money, jewellery, gold plate—concealed about their persons. What is to be done about these things? Are the *calotins* to be allowed to keep them or to dispose of them for their own profit?

Carrier is highly delighted. What a haul!

"Confiscate everything," he cries, "then ship the whole crowd of that pestilential rabble, and don't let me hear another word about them."

Fleury goes. And that same night fifty-three priests are "shipped" in accordance with the orders of the proconsul, and Carrier, still rubbing his large bony hands contentedly together, exclaims with glee:

"What a torrent, eh! What a torrent! What a revolution!"

And he sends a letter to Robespierre. And to the Committee of Public Safety he makes report:

"Public spirit in Nantes," he writes, "is magnificent: it has risen to the most sublime heights of revolutionary ideals."

After the departure of Fleury, Carrier suddenly turned to a slender youth, who was standing close by the window, gazing out through the folds of the curtain on the fine vista of the Loire and the quays which stretched out before him.

"Introduce Citizen Martin-Roget into the ante-room now, Lalouët," he said loftily. "I will hear what he has to say, and Citizen Chauvelin may present himself at the same time."

Young Lalouët lolled across the room, smothering a yawn.

"Why should you trouble about all that rabble?" he said roughly, "it is nearly dinner-time and you know that the chef hates the soup to be kept waiting."

"I shall not trouble about them very long," replied Carrier, who had just started picking his teeth with a tiny gold tool. "Open the door, boy, and let the two men come."

Lalouët did as he was told. The door through which he passed he left wide open, he then crossed the ante-room to a further door, threw it open and called in a loud voice:

"Citizen Chauvelin! Citizen Martin-Roget!"

For all the world like the ceremonious audiences at Versailles in the days of the great Louis.

There was sound of eager whisperings, of shuffling of feet, of chairs dragged across the polished floor. Young Lalouët had already and quite unconcernedly turned his back on the two men who, at his call, had entered the room.

Two chairs were placed in front of the door which led to the private sanctuary—still wrapped in religious obscurity—where Carrier sat enthroned. The youth curtly pointed to the two chairs, then went back to the inner room. The two men advanced. The full light of midday fell upon them from the tall window on their right—the pale, grey, colourless light of December. They bowed slightly in the direction of the audience chamber where the vague silhouette of the proconsul was alone visible.

The whole thing was a farce. Martin-Roget held his lips tightly closed together lest a curse or a sneer escaped them. Chauvelin's face was impenetrable—but it is worthy of note that just one year later when the half-demented tyrant was in his turn brought before the bar of the Convention and sentenced to the guillotine, it was Citizen Chauvelin's testimony which weighed most heavily against him.

There was silence for a time: Martin-Roget and Chauvelin were waiting for the dictator's word. He sat at his desk with the scanty light, which filtrated between the curtains, immediately behind him, his ungainly form with the high shoulders and mop-like, shaggy hair half swallowed up by the surrounding gloom. He was deliberately keeping the other two men waiting and busied himself with turning over desultorily the papers and writing tools upon his desk, in the intervals of picking at his teeth and muttering to himself all the time as was his wont. Young Lalouët had resumed his post beside the curtained window and he was giving sundry signs of his growing impatience.

At last Carrier spoke:

"And now, Citizen Martin-Roget," he said in tones of that lofty condescension which he loved to affect, "I am prepared to hear what you have to tell me with regard to the cattle which you brought into our city the other day. Where are the *aristos* now? and why have they not been handed over to Commandant Fleury?"

"The girl," replied Martin-Roget, who had much ado to keep his vehement temper in check, and who chose for the moment to ignore the second of Carrier's peremptory queries, "the girl is in lodgings in the *Carrefour de la Poissonnerie*. The house is kept by my sister, whose lover was hanged four years ago by the *ci-devant* Duc de Kernogan for trapping two pigeons. A dozen or so lads from our old village—men who worked with my father and others who were my friends—lodge in my sister's house. They keep a watchful eye over the wench for the sake of the past, for my sake and for the sake of my sister Louise. The *ci-devant* Kernogan woman is well-guarded. I am satisfied as to that."

"And where is the *ci-devant duc?*"

"In the house next door—a tavern at the sign of the Rat Mort—a place which is none too reputable, but the landlord—Lemoine—is a good patriot and he is keeping a close eye on the *aristo* for me."

"And now will you tell me, citizen," rejoined Carrier with that unctuous suavity which always veiled a threat, "will you tell me how it comes that you are keeping a couple of traitors alive all this while at the country's expense?"

"At mine," broke in Martin-Roget curtly.

"At the country's expense," reiterated the proconsul inflexibly. "Bread is scarce in Nantes. What traitors eat is stolen from good patriots. If you can afford to fill two mouths at your expense, I can supply you with some that have never done aught but proclaim their adherence to the Republic. You have had those two *aristos* inside the city nearly a week and——"

"Only three days," interposed Martin-Roget, "and you must have patience with me, Citizen Carrier. Remember I have done well by you, by bringing such high game to your bag——"

"Your high game will be no use to me," retorted the other with a harsh laugh, "if I am not to have the cooking of it. You have talked of disgrace for the rabble and of your own desire for vengeance over them, but——"

"Wait, citizen," broke in Martin-Roget firmly, "let us understand one another. Before I embarked on this business you gave me your promise that no one—not even you—would interfere between me and my booty."

"And no one has done so hitherto to my knowledge, citizen," rejoined Carrier blandly. "The Kernogan rabble has been yours to do with what you like—er—so far," he added significantly. "I said that I would not interfere and I have not done so up to now, even though the pestilential crowd stinks in the nostrils of every good patriot in Nantes. But I don't deny that it was a bargain that you should have a free hand with them—for a time, and Jean Baptiste Carrier has never yet gone back on a given word."

Martin-Roget made no comment on this peroration. He shrugged his broad shoulders and suddenly fell to contemplating the distant landscape. He had turned his head away in order to hide the sneer which curled his lips at the recollection of that "bargain" struck with the imperious proconsul. It was a matter of five thousand *francs* which had passed from one pocket to the other and had bound Carrier down to a definite promise.

After a brief while Carrier resumed: "At the same time," he said, "my promise was conditional, remember. I want that cattle out of Nantes—I want the bread they eat—I want the room they occupy. I can't allow you to play fast and loose with them indefinitely—a week is quite long enough———"

"Three days," corrected Martin-Roget once more.

"Well! three days or eight," rejoined the other roughly. "Too long in any case. I must be rid of them out of this city or I shall have all the spies of the Convention about mine ears. I am beset with spies, Citizen Martin-Roget, yes, even I—Jean Baptiste Carrier—the most selfless the most devoted patriot the Republic has ever known! Mine enemies up in Paris send spies to dog my footsteps, to watch mine every action. They are ready to pounce upon me at the slightest slip, to denounce me, to drag me to their bar—they have already whetted the knife of the guillotine which is to lay low the head of the finest patriot in France———"

"Hold on! hold on, Jean Baptiste my friend," here broke in young Lalouët with a sneer, "we don't want protestations of your patriotism just now. It is nearly dinner time."

Carrier had been carried away by his own eloquence. At Lalouët's mocking words he pulled himself together: murmured: "You young viper!" in tones of tigerish affection, and then turned back to Martin-Roget and resumed more calmly:

"They'll be saying that I harbour *aristos* in Nantes if I keep that Kernogan rabble here any longer. So, I must be rid of them, Citizen Martin-Roget—say within the next four-and-twenty hours—" He paused for a moment or two, then added drily: "That is my last word, and you must see to it. What is it you do want to do with them *enfin?*"

"I want their death," replied Martin-Roget with a curse, and he brought his heavy fist crashing down upon the arm of his chair, "but not a martyr's death, understand? I don't want the pathetic figure of Yvonne Kernogan and her father to remain as a picture of patient resignation in the hearts and minds of every other *aristo* in the land. I don't want it to excite pity or admiration. Death is nothing for such as they! they glory in it! they are proud to die. The guillotine is their final triumph! What I want for them is shame—degradation—a sensational trial that will cover them with dishonour—I want their name dragged in the mire—themselves an object of derision or of loathing. I want

115

articles in the *Moniteur* giving account of the trial of the *ci-devant* Duc de Kernogan and his daughter for something that is ignominious and base. I want shame and mud slung at them—noise and beating of drums to proclaim their dishonour. Noise! noise! that will reach every corner of the land, aye that will reach Coblentz and Germany and England. It is that which they would resent—the shame of it—the disgrace to their name!"

"Tshaw!" exclaimed Carrier. "Why don't you marry the wench, citizen Martin-Roget? That would be disgrace enough for her, I'll warrant," he added with a loud laugh, enchanted at his witticism.

"I would tomorrow," replied the other, who chose to ignore the coarse insult, "if she would consent. That is why I have kept her at my sister's house these three days."

"Bah! you have no need of a traitor's consent. My consent is sufficient—I'll give it if you like. The laws of the Republic permit, nay desire every good patriot to ally himself with an *aristo*, if he have a mind. And the Kernogan wench face to face with the guillotine—or worse—would surely prefer your embraces, citizen, what?"

A deep frown settled between Martin-Roget's glowering eyes and gave his face a sinister expression.

"I wonder—" he muttered between his teeth.

"Then cease wondering, citizen," retorted Carrier cynically, "and try our Republican marriage on your Kernogans—thief linked to *aristo*, cut-throat to a proud wench—and then the Loire! Shame? Dishonour? *Fal lal* I say! Death, swift and sure and unerring. Nothing better has yet been invented for traitors."

Martin-Roget shrugged his shoulders.

"You have never known," he said quietly, "what it is to hate."

Carrier uttered an exclamation of impatience.

"Bah!" he said, "that is all talk and nonsense. Theories, what? Citizen Chauvelin is a living example of the futility of all that rubbish. He too has an enemy it seems whom he hates more thoroughly than any good patriot has ever hated the enemies of the Republic. And hath this deadly hatred availed him, forsooth? He too wanted the disgrace and dishonour of that confounded Englishman whom I would simply have tossed into the Loire long ago, without further process. What is the result? The Englishman is over in England, safe and sound, making long noses at Citizen Chauvelin, who has much ado to keep his own head out of the guillotine."

Martin-Roget once more was silent: a look of sullen obstinacy had settled upon his face.

"You may be right, Citizen Carrier," he muttered after a while.

"I am always right," broke in Carrier curtly.

"Exactly—but I have your promise."

"And I'll keep it, as I have said, for another four and twenty hours. Curse you for a mulish fool," added the proconsul with a snarl, "what in the d——l's name do you want to do? You have talked a vast deal of rubbish but you have told me nothing of your plans. Have you any—that are worthy of my attention?"

Martin-Roget rose from his seat and began pacing up and down the narrow room. His nerves were obviously on edge. It was difficult for any man—let alone one of his temperament and half-tutored disposition—to remain calm and deferential in face of the over-bearance of this brutal Jack-in-office, Martin-Roget—himself an upstart—loathed the offensive self-assertion of that uneducated and bestial parvenu, who had become all-powerful through the sole might of his savagery, and it cost him a mighty effort to keep a violent retort from escaping his lips—a retort which probably would have cost him his head.

Chauvelin, on the other hand, appeared perfectly unconcerned. He possessed the art of outward placidity to a masterly degree. Throughout all this while he had taken no part in the discussion. He sat silent and all but motionless, facing the darkened room in front of him, as if he had done nothing else in all his life but interview great dictators who chose to keep their sacred persons in the dark. Only from time to time did his slender fingers drum a tattoo on the arm of his chair.

Carrier had resumed his interesting occupation of picking his teeth: his long, thin legs were stretched out before him; from beneath his flaccid lids he shot swift glances upwards, whenever Martin-Roget in his restless pacing crossed and recrossed in front of the open door. But *anon*, when the latter came to a halt under the lintel and with his foot almost across the threshold, young Lalouët was upon him in an instant, barring the way to the inner sanctum.

"Keep your distance, citizen," he said drily, "no one is allowed to enter here."

Instinctively Martin-Roget had drawn back—suddenly awed despite himself by the air of mystery which hung over that darkened room, and by the dim silhouette of the sinister tyrant who at his approach had with equal suddenness cowered in his lair, drawing his limbs together and thrusting his head forward, low down over the desk, like a leopard crouching for a spring. But this spell of awe only

117

lasted a few seconds, during which Martin-Roget's unsteady gaze encountered the half-mocking, wholly supercilious glance of young Lalouët.

The next, he had recovered his presence of mind. But this crowning act of audacious insolence broke the barrier of his self-restraint. An angry oath escaped him.

"Are we," he exclaimed roughly, "back in the days of Capet, the tyrant, and of Versailles, that patriots and citizens are treated like menials and obtrusive slaves? *Pardieu*, citizen Carrier, let me tell you this—"

"*Pardieu*, Citizen Martin-Roget," retorted Carrier with a growl like that of a savage dog, "let *me* tell *you* that for less than two pins I'll throw you into the next barge that will float with open portholes down the Loire. Get out of my presence, you swine, ere I call Fleury to throw you out."

Martin-Roget at the insult and the threat had become as pale as the linen at his throat: a cold sweat broke out upon his forehead and he passed his hand two or three times across his brow like a man dazed with a sudden and violent blow. His nerves, already overstrained and very much on edge, gave way completely. He staggered and would have measured his length across the floor, but that his hand encountered the back of his chair and he just contrived to sink into it, sick and faint, horror-struck and pallid.

A low cackle—something like a laugh—broke from Chauvelin's thin lips. As usual he had witnessed the scene quite unmoved.

"My friend Martin-Roget forgot himself for the moment, Citizen Carrier," he said suavely, "already he is ready to make amends."

Jacques Lalouët looked down for a moment with infinite scorn expressed in his fine eyes, on the presumptuous creature who had dared to defy the omnipotent representative of the People. Then he turned on his heel, but he did not go far this time: he remained standing close beside the door—the terrier guarding his master.

Carrier laughed loud and long. It was a hideous, strident laugh which had not a tone of merriment in it.

"Wake up, friend Martin-Roget," he said harshly, "I bear no malice: I am a good dog when I am treated the right way. But if anyone pulls my tail or treads on my paws, why! I snarl and growl of course. If the offence is repeated—I bite—remember that; and now let us resume our discourse, though I confess I am getting tired of your Kernogan rabble."

While the great man spoke, Martin-Roget had succeeded in pulling himself together. His throat felt parched, his hands hot and moist: he was like a man who had been stumbling along a road in the dark and been suddenly pulled up on the edge of a yawning abyss into which he had all but fallen. With a few harsh words, with a monstrous insult Carrier had made him feel the gigantic power which could hurl any man from the heights of self-assurance and of ambition to the lowest depths of degradation: he had shown him the glint of steel upon the guillotine.

He had been hit as with a sledge-hammer—the blow hurt terribly, for it had knocked all his self-esteem into nothingness and pulverised his self-conceit. It had in one moment turned him into a humble and cringing sycophant.

"I had no mind," he began tentatively, "to give offence. My thoughts were bent on the Kernogans. They are a fine haul for us both, Citizen Carrier, and I worked hard and long to obtain their confidence over in England and to induce them to come with me to Nantes."

"No one denies that you have done well," retorted Carrier gruffly and not yet wholly pacified. "If the haul had not been worth having you would have received no help from me."

"I have shown my gratitude for your help, citizen Carrier. I would show it again—more substantially if you desire—"

He spoke slowly and quite deferentially but the suggestion was obvious. Carrier looked up into his face: the light of measureless cupidity—the cupidity of the coarse-grained, enriched peasant—glittered in his pale eyes. It was by a great effort of will that he succeeded in concealing his eagerness beneath his habitual air of lofty condescension:

"Eh? What?" he queried airily.

"If another five thousand *francs* is of any use to you—"

"You seem passing rich, Citizen Martin-Roget," sneered Carrier.

"I have slaved and saved for four years. What I have amassed I will sacrifice for the completion of my revenge."

"Well!" rejoined Carrier with an expressive wave of the hand, "it certainly is not good for a pure-minded republican to own too much wealth. Have we not fought," he continued with a grandiloquent gesture, "for equality of fortune as well as of privileges—"

A sardonic laugh from young Lalouët broke in on the proconsul's eloquent effusion.

Carrier swore as was his wont, but after a second or two he began again more quietly:

"I will accept a further six thousand *francs* from you, Citizen Martin-Roget, in the name of the Republic and all her needs. The Republic of France is up in arms against the entire world. She hath need of men, of arms, of—"

"Oh! cut that," interposed young Lalouët roughly.

But the over-vain, high and mighty despot who was ready to lash out with unbridled fury against the slightest show of disrespect on the part of any other man, only laughed at the boy's impudence.

"Curse you, you young viper," he said with that rude familiarity which he seemed to reserve for the boy, "you presume too much on my forbearance. These children you know, citizen.... Name of a dog!" he added roughly, "we are wasting time! What was I saying—?"

"That you would take six thousand *francs*," replied Martin-Roget curtly, "in return for further help in the matter of the Kernogans."

"Why, yes!" rejoined Carrier blandly, "I was forgetting. But I'll show you what a good dog I am. I'll help you with those Kernogans—but you mistook my words, citizen: 'tis ten thousand *francs* you must pour into the coffers of the Republic, for her servants will have to be placed at the disposal of your private schemes of vengeance."

"Ten thousand *francs* is a large sum," said Martin-Roget. "Let me hear what you will do for me for that."

He had regained something of his former complacency. The man who buys—be it goods, consciences or services—is always for the moment master of the man who sells. Carrier, despite his dictatorial ways, felt this disadvantage, no doubt, for his tone was more bland, his manner less curt. Only young Jacques Lalouët stood by—like a snarling terrier—still arrogant and still disdainful—the master of the situation—seeing that neither schemes of vengeance nor those of corruption had ruffled his self-assurance. He remained beside the door, ready to pounce on either of the two intruders if they showed the slightest sign of forgetting the majesty of the great proconsul.

"I told you just now, Citizen Martin-Roget," resumed Carrier after a brief pause, "and I suppose you knew it already, that I am surrounded with spies."

"Spies, citizen?" murmured Martin-Roget, somewhat taken aback by this sudden irrelevance. "I didn't know—I imagine—Anyone in your position—"

"That's just it," broke in Carrier roughly. "My position is envied by those who are less competent, less patriotic than I am. Nantes is swarming with spies. Mine enemies in Paris are working against me.

They want to undermine the confidence which the National Convention reposes in her accredited representative."

"Preposterous," ejaculated young Lalouët solemnly.

"Well!" rejoined Carrier with a savage oath, "you would have thought that the Convention would be only too thankful to get a strong man at the head of affairs in this hotbed of treason and of rebellion. You would have thought that it was no one's affair to interfere with the manner in which I administer the powers that have been given me. I command in Nantes, what? Yet some busybodies up in Paris, some fools, seem to think that we are going too fast in Nantes. They have become weaklings over there since Marat has gone. It seems that they have heard rumours of our flat-bottomed barges and of our fine Republican marriages: apparently, they disapprove of both. They don't realise that we have to purge an entire city of every kind of rabble—traitors as well as criminals. They don't understand my aspirations, my ideals," he added loftily and with a wide, sweeping gesture of his arm, "which is to make Nantes a model city, to free her from the taint of crime and of treachery, and—"

An impatient exclamation from young Lalouët once again broke in on Carrier's rhetoric, and Martin-Roget was able to slip in the query which had been hovering on his lips:

"And is this relevant, Citizen Carrier," he asked, "to the subject which we have been discussing?"

"It is," replied Carrier drily, "as you will see in a moment. Learn then, that it has been my purpose for some time to silence mine enemies by sending to the National Convention a tangible reply to all the accusations which have been levelled against me. It is my purpose to explain to the Assembly my reasons for mine actions in Nantes, my Drownages, my Republican marriages, all the coercive measures which I have been forced to take in order to purge the city from all that is undesirable."

"And think you, Citizen Carrier," queried Martin-Roget without the slightest trace of a sneer, "that up in Paris they will understand your explanations?"

"Yes! they will—they must when they realise that everything that I have done has been necessitated by the exigencies of public safety."

"They will be slow to realise that," mused the other. "The National Convention today is not what the Constitutional Assembly was in '92. It has become soft and sentimental. Many there are who will disapprove of your doings—Robespierre talks loftily of the dignity of the

Republic—her impartial justice—The Girondins—"

Carrier interposed with a coarse imprecation. He suddenly leaned forward, sprawling right across the desk. A shaft of light from between the damask curtains caught the end of his nose and the tip of his protruding chin, distorting his face and making it seem grotesque as well as hideous in the dim light. He appeared excited and inflated with vanity. He always gloried in the atrocities which he committed, and though he professed to look with contempt on every one of his colleagues, he was always glad of an opportunity to display his inventive powers before them, and to obtain their fulsome eulogy.

"I know well enough what they talk about in Paris," he said, "but I have an answer—a substantial, definite answer for all their rubbish. Dignity of the Republic? Bah! Impartial justice? 'Tis force, strength, Spartan vigour that we want—and I'll show them—Listen to my plan, Citizen Martin-Roget, and see how it will work in with yours. My idea is to collect together all the most disreputable and notorious evildoers of this city—there are plenty in the *entrepôt* at the present moment, and there are plenty more still at large in the streets of Nantes—thieves, malefactors, forgers of State bonds, assassins and women of evil fame—and to send them in a batch to Paris to appear before the Committee of Public Safety, whilst I will send to my colleagues there a letter couched in terms of gentle reproach: 'See!' I shall say, 'what I have to contend with in Nantes. See! the moral pestilence that infests the city. These evil-doers are but a few among the hundreds and thousands of whom I am vainly trying to purge this city which you have entrusted to my care!' They won't know how to deal with the rabble," he continued with his harsh strident laugh. "They may send them to the guillotine wholesale or deport them to Cayenne, and they will have to give them some semblance of a trial in any case. But they will have to admit that my severe measures are justified, and in future, I imagine, they will leave me more severely alone."

"If as you say," urged Martin-Roget, "the National Convention give your crowd a trial, you will have to produce some witnesses."

"So, I will," retorted Carrier cynically. "So, I will. Have I not said that I will round up all the most noted evil-doers in the town? There are plenty of them I assure you. Lately, my Company Marat have not greatly troubled about them. After Savenay there was such a crowd of rebels to deal with, there was no room in our prisons for malefactors as well. But we can easily lay our hands on a couple of hundred or so, and members of the municipality or of the district council, or tradespeople of substance in the city will only be too glad to be rid of them and will testify against those that were actually caught red-handed. Not one but has suffered from the pestilential rabble that has infested the streets at night, and lately I have been pestered with complaints of all these night-birds—men and women and—"

Suddenly he paused. He had caught Martin-Roget's feverish gaze fixed excitedly upon him. Whereupon he leaned back in his chair, threw his head back and broke into loud and immoderate laughter.

"By the devil and all his myrmidons, citizen!" he said, as soon as he had recovered his breath, "meseems you have tumbled to my meaning as a pig into a heap of garbage. Is not ten thousand *francs* far too small a sum to pay for such a perfect realisation of all your dreams? We'll send the Kernogan girl and her father to Paris with the herd, what?... I promise you that such filth and mud will be thrown on them and on their precious name that no one will care to bear it for centuries to come."

Martin-Roget of a truth had much ado to control his own excitement. As the proconsul unfolded his infamous plan, he had at once seen as in a vision the realisation of all his hopes. What more awful humiliation, what more dire disgrace could be devised for proud Kernogan and his daughter than being herded together with the vilest scum that could be gathered together among the flotsam and jetsam of the population of a seaport town? What more perfect retaliation could there be for the ignominious death of Jean Adet the miller?

Martin-Roget leaned forward in his chair. The hideous figure of Carrier was no longer hideous to him. He saw in that misshapen, gawky form the very embodiment of the god of vengeance, the wielder of the flail of retributive justice which was about to strike the guilty at last.

"You are right, Citizen Carrier," he said, and his voice was thick and hoarse with excitement. He rested his elbow on his knee and his chin in his hand. He hammered his nails against his teeth. "That was exactly in my mind while you spoke."

"I am always right," retorted Carrier loftily. "No one knows better than I do how to deal with traitors."

"And how is the whole thing to be accomplished? The wench is in my sister's house at present—the father is in the Rat Mort—"

"And the Rat Mort is an excellent place—I know of none better. It is one of the worst-famed houses in the whole of Nantes—the meeting-place of all the vagabonds, the thieves and the cut-throats of

123

the city."

"Yes! I know that to my cost. My sister's house is next door to it. At night the street is not safe for decent females to be abroad: and though there is a platoon of Marats on guard at Le Bouffay close by, they do nothing to free the neighbourhood of that pest."

"Bah!" retorted Carrier with cynical indifference, "they have more important quarry to net. Rebels and traitors swarm in Nantes, what? Commandant Fleury has had no time hitherto to waste on mere cut-throats, although I had thoughts before now of razing the place to the ground. Citizen Lamberty has his lodgings on the other side and he does nothing but complain of the brawls that go on there o' nights. Sure, it is that while a stone of the Rat Mort remains standing all the night-hawks of Nantes will congregate around it and brew mischief there which is no good to me and no good to the Republic."

"Yes! I know all about the Rat Mort. I found a night's shelter there four years ago when—"

"When the *ci-devant* Duc de Kernogan was busy hanging your father—the miller—for a crime which he never committed. Well then, citizen Martin-Roget," continued Carrier with one of his hideous leers, "since you know the Rat Mort so well what say you to your fair and stately Yvonne de Kernogan and her father being captured there in the company of the lowest scum of the population of Nantes?"

"You mean—?" murmured Martin-Roget, who had become livid with excitement.

"I mean that my Marats have orders to raid some of the haunts of our Nantese cut-throats, and that they may as well begin tonight and with the Rat Mort. They will make a descent on the house and a thorough perquisition, and every person—man, woman and child—found on the premises will be arrested and sent with a batch of malefactors to Paris, there to be tried as felons and criminals and deported to Cayenne where they will, I trust, rot as convicts in that pestilential climate. Think you," concluded the odious creature with a sneer, "that when put face to face with the alternative, your Kernogan wench will still refuse to become the wife of a fine patriot like yourself?"

"I don't know," murmured Martin-Roget. "I—I—"

"But I do know," broke in Carrier roughly, "that ten thousand *francs* is far too little to pay for so brilliant a realisation of all one's hopes. Ten thousand *francs*? 'Tis an hundred thousand you should give to show your gratitude."

Martin-Roget rose and stretched his large, heavy figure to its full height. He was at great pains to conceal the utter contempt which he felt for the abominable wretch before whom he was forced to cringe.

"You shall have ten thousand *francs*, Citizen Carrier," he said slowly; "it is all that I possess in the world now—the last remaining fragment of a sum of twenty-five thousand *francs* which I earned and scraped together for the past four years. You have had five thousand *francs* already. And you shall have the other ten. I do not grudge it. If twenty years of my life were any use to you, I would give you that, in exchange for the help you are giving me in what means far more than life to me."

The proconsul laughed and shrugged his shoulders—of a truth he thought Citizen Martin-Roget an awful fool.

"Very well then," he said, "we will call the matter settled. I confess that it amuses me, although remember that I have warned you. With all these *aristos*, I believe in the potency of my barges rather than in your elaborate schemes. Still! it shall never be said that Jean Baptiste Carrier has left a friend in the lurch."

"I am grateful for your help, Citizen Carrier," said Martin-Roget coldly. Then he added slowly, as if reviewing the situation in his own mind: "Tonight, you say?"

"Yes. Tonight. My Marats under the command of citizen Fleury will make a descent upon the Rat Mort. Those shall be my orders. The place will be swept clean of every man, woman and child who is inside. If your two Kernogans are there—well!" he said with a cynical laugh and a shrug of his shoulders, "they can be sent up to Paris with the rest of the herd."

"The dinner bell has gone long ago," here interposed young Lalouët drily, "the soup will be stone-cold and the chef red-hot with anger."

"You are right, Citizen Lalouët," said Carrier as he leaned back in his chair once more and stretched out his long legs at his ease. "We have wasted far too much time already over the affairs of a couple of *aristos*, who ought to have been at the bottom of the Loire a week ago. The audience is ended," he added airily, and he made a gesture of overweening condescension, for all the world like the one wherewith the *Grand Monarque* was wont to dismiss his courtiers.

Chauvelin rose too and quietly turned to the door. He had not spoken a word for the past half-hour, ever since in fact he had put in a conciliatory word on behalf of his impetuous colleague. Whether he had taken an active interest in the conversation or not it were impossible to say. But now, just as he was ready to go, and young Lalouët prepared to close the doors of the audience chamber, something seemed suddenly to occur to him and he called somewhat peremptorily to the young man.

"One moment, citizen," he said.

"What is it now?" queried the youth insolently, and from his fine eyes there shot a glance of contempt on the meagre figure of the once powerful Terrorist.

"About the Kernogan wench," continued Chauvelin. "She will have to be conveyed some time before night to the tavern next door. There may be agencies at work on her behalf—"

"Agencies?" broke in the boy gruffly. "What agencies?"

"Oh!" said Chauvelin vaguely, "we all know that *aristos* have powerful friends these days. It will not be over safe to take the girl across after dark from one house to another—the alley is badly lighted: the wench will not go willingly. She might scream and create a disturbance and draw—er—those same unknown agencies to her rescue. I think a body of Marats should be told off to convey her to the Rat Mort—"

Young Lalouët shrugged his shoulders.

"That's your affair," he said curtly. "Eh, Carrier?" And he glanced over his shoulder at the proconsul, who at once assented.

Martin-Roget—struck by his colleague's argument—would have interposed, but Carrier broke in with one of his uncontrolled outbursts of fury.

"*Ah ça*," he exclaimed, "enough of this now. Citizen Lalouët is right and I have done enough for you already. If you want the Kernogan wench to be at the Rat Mort, you must see to getting her there yourself. She is next door, what? I won't have anything to do with it and I won't have my Marats implicated in the affair either. Name of a dog! have I not told you that I am beset with spies? It would of a truth be a climax if I was denounced as having dragged *aristos* to a house of ill-fame and then had them arrested there as malefactors! Now out with you! I have had enough of this! If your rabble is at the Rat Mort tonight, they shall be arrested with all the other cutthroats. That is my last word. The rest is your affair. Lalouët! the door!"

And without another word, and without listening to further protests from Martin-Roget or Chauvelin, Jacques Lalouët closed the doors of the audience chamber in their face.

Outside on the landing, Martin-Roget swore a violent, all comprehensive oath.

"To think that we are under the heel of that skunk!" he said.

"And that in the pursuit of our own ends we have need of his help!" added Chauvelin with a sigh.

"If it were not for that—And even now," continued Martin-Roget moodily, "I doubt what I can do. Yvonne de Kernogan will not follow me willingly either to the Rat Mort or elsewhere, and if I am not to have her conveyed by the guard—"

He paused and swore again. His companion's silence appeared to irritate him.

"What do you advise me to do, Citizen Chauvelin?" he asked.

"For the moment," replied Chauvelin imperturbably, "I should advise you to join me in a walk along the quay as far as Le Bouffay. I have work to see to inside the building and the north-westerly wind is sure to be of good counsel."

An angry retort hovered on Martin-Roget's lips, but after a second or two he succeeded in holding his irascible temper in check. He gave a quick sigh of impatience.

"Very well," he said curtly. "Let us to Le Bouffay by all means. I have much to think on, and as you say the north-westerly wind may blow away the cobwebs which for the nonce do o'ercloud my brain."

And the two men wrapped their mantles closely round their shoulders, for the air was keen. Then they descended the staircase of the hotel and went out into the street.

CHAPTER 2

Le Bouffay

In the centre of the Place the guillotine stood idle—the paint had worn off her sides—she looked weather-beaten and forlorn—stern and forbidding still, but in a kind of sullen loneliness, with the ugly stains of crimson on her, turned to rust and grime.

The Place itself was deserted, in strange contrast to the bustle and the movement which characterised it in the days when the death of men, women and children was a daily spectacle here for the crowd. Then a constant stream of traffic, of carts and of tumbrils, of soldiers and gaffers encumbered it in every corner, now a few tumble-down booths set up against the frontage of the grim edifice—once the stronghold of the Dukes of Brittany, now little else but a huge prison—a few vendors and still fewer purchasers of the scanty wares displayed under their ragged awnings, one or two idlers loafing against the mud-stained walls, one or two urchins playing in the gutters were the only signs of life.

Martin-Roget with his colleague Chauvelin turned into the Place from the quay—they walked rapidly and kept their mantles closely wrapped under their chin, for the afternoon had turned bitterly cold. It was then close upon five o'clock—a dark, moonless, starless night had set in with only a suspicion of frost in the damp air; but a blustering north-westerly wind blowing down the river and tearing round the narrow streets and the open Place, caused passers-by to muffle themselves, shivering, yet tighter in their cloaks.

Martin-Roget was talking volubly and excitedly, his tall, broad figure towering above the slender form of his companion. From time to time he tossed his mantle aside with an impatient, febrile gesture and then paused in the middle of the Place, with one hand on the other man's shoulder, marking a point in his discourse or emphasising his argument with short *staccato* sentences and brief, emphatic words. Chauvelin—placid and impenetrable as usual—listened much and talked little. He was ready to stand still or to walk along just as his colleague's mood demanded; in the darkness, and with the collar of a large mantle pulled tightly up to his ears, it was impossible to guess by any sign in his face what was going on in his mind.

They were a strange contrast these two men—temperamentally as well as physically—even though they had so much in common and were both the direct products of that same social upheaval which was shaking the archaic dominion of France to its very foundations. Martin-Roget, tall, broad-shouldered, bull-necked, the typical self-educated peasant, with square jaw and flat head, with wide bony hands and spatulated fingers: and Chauvelin—the aristocrat turned demagogue, thin and frail-looking, bland of manner and suave of speech, with delicate hands and pale, almost ascetic face.

The one represented all that was most brutish and sensual in this fight of one caste against the other, the thirst for the other's blood, the human beast that has been brought to bay through wrongs perpetrated against it by others and has turned upon its oppressors, lashing out right and left with blind and lustful fury at the crowd of tyrants that had kept him in subjection for so long. Whilst Chauvelin was the personification of the spiritual side of this bloody Revolution—the spirit of cool and calculating reprisals that would demand an eye for an eye and see that it got two. The idealist who dreams of the righteousness of his own cause and the destruction of its enemies, but who leaves to others the accomplishment of all the carnage and the bloodshed which his idealism has demanded, and which his reason has appraised as necessary for the triumph of which he dreams.

Chauvelin was the man of thought and Martin-Roget the man of action. With the one, revenge and reprisals were selfish desires, the avenging of wrongs done to himself or to his caste, hatred for those who had injured him or his kindred. The other had no personal feelings of hatred: he had no personal wrongs to avenge: his enemies were the enemies of his party, the erstwhile tyrants who in the past had oppressed an entire people. Every man, woman or child who was not satisfied with the present Reign of Terror, who plotted or planned for its overthrow, who was not ready to see husband, father, wife or child sacrificed for the ultimate triumph of the Revolution was in Chauvelin's sight a noxious creature, fit only to be trodden under heel and ground into subjection or annihilation as a danger to the State.

Martin-Roget was the personification of *sans-culottism*, of rough manners and foul speech—he chafed against the conventions which forced him to wear decent clothes and boots on his feet—he would gladly have seen everyone go about the streets half-naked, unwashed, a living sign of that downward levelling of castes which he and his friends stood for, and for which they had fought and striven and committed every crime which human passions let loose could invent. Chauvelin, on the other hand, was one of those who wore fine linen and buckled shoes and whose hands were delicately washed and perfumed whilst they signed decrees which sent hundreds of women and children to a violent and cruel death.

The one trod in the paths of Danton: the other followed in the footsteps of Robespierre.

Together the two men mounted the outside staircase which leads up past the lodge of the concierge and through the clerk's office to the interior of the stronghold. Outside the monumental doors they had to wait a moment or two while the clerk examined their permits to enter.

"Will you come into my office with me?" asked Chauvelin of his companion; "I have a word or two to add to my report for the Paris courier tonight. I won't be long."

"You are still in touch with the Committee of Public Safety then?" asked Martin-Roget.

"Always," replied the other curtly.

Martin-Roget threw a quick, suspicious glance on his companion. Darkness and the broad brim of his sugar-loaf hat effectually concealed even the outlines of Chauvelin's face, and Martin-Roget fell to musing over one or two things which Carrier had blurted out a while ago. The whole of France was overrun with spies these days—ever one was under suspicion, everyone had to be on his guard. Every word was overheard, every glance seen, every sign noted.

What was this man Chauvelin doing here in Nantes? What reports did he send up to Paris by special courier? He, the miserable failure who had ceased to count was nevertheless in constant touch with that awful Committee of Public Safety which was wont to strike at all times and unexpectedly in the dark. Martin-Roget shivered beneath his mantle. For the first time since his schemes of vengeance had wholly absorbed his mind he regretted the freedom and safety which he had enjoyed in England, and he marvelled if the miserable game which he was playing would be worth the winning in the end. Nevertheless, he had followed Chauvelin without comment. The man appeared to exercise a fascination over him—a kind of subtle power, which emanated from his small shrunken figure, from his pale keen eyes and his well-modulated, suave mode of speech.

The clerk had handed the two men their permits back. They were allowed to pass through the gates.

In the hall some half-dozen men were nominally on guard—nominally, because discipline was not over strict these days, and the men sat or lolled about the place; two of them were intent on a game of dominoes, another was watching them, whilst the other three were settling some sort of quarrel among themselves which necessitated vigorous and emphatic gestures and the copious use of expletives. One man, who appeared to be in command, divided his time impartially between the domino-players and those who were quarrelling.

The vast place was insufficiently lighted by a chandelier which hung from the ceiling and a couple of small oil-lamps placed in the circular niches in the wall opposite the front door.

No one took any notice of Martin-Roget or of Chauvelin as they crossed the hall, and presently the latter pushed open a door on the left of the main gates and held it open for his colleague to pass through.

"You are sure that I shall not be disturbing you?" queried Martin-Roget.

"Quite sure," replied the other curtly. "And there is something which I must say to you—where I know that I shall not be overheard."

Then he followed Martin-Roget into the room and closed the door behind him. The room was scantily furnished with a square deal table in the centre, two or three chairs, a broken-down bureau leaning against one wall and an iron stove wherein a meagre fire sent a stream of malodorous smoke through sundry cracks in its chimney-pipe. From the ceiling there hung an oil-lamp the light of which was thrown down upon the table, by a large green shade made of cardboard.

Chauvelin drew a chair to the bureau and sat down; he pointed to another and Martin-Roget took a seat beside the table. He felt restless and excited—his nerves all on the jar: his colleague's calm, sardonic glance acted as a further irritant to his temper.

"What is it that you wished to say to me, Citizen Chauvelin?" he asked at last.

"Just a word, citizen," replied the other in his quiet urbane manner. "I have accompanied you faithfully on your journey to England: I have placed my feeble powers at your disposal: a while ago I stood between you and the proconsul's wrath. This, I think, has earned me the right of asking what you intend to do."

"I don't know about the right," retorted Martin-Roget gruffly, "but I don't mind telling you. As you remarked a while ago the North-West wind is wont to be of good counsel. I have thought the matter over whilst I walked with you along the quay and I have decided to act on Carrier's suggestion. Our eminent proconsul said just now that it was the duty of every true patriot to marry an *aristo*, an he be free and Chance puts a comely wench in his way. I mean," he added with a cynical laugh, "to act on that advice and marry Yvonne de Kernogan—if I can."

"She has refused you up to now?"

"Yes—up to now."

"You have threatened her—and her father?"

"Yes—both. Not only with death but with shame."

"And still she refuses?"

"Apparently," said Martin-Roget with ever-growing irritation.

"It is often difficult," rejoined Chauvelin meditatively, "to compel these *aristos*. They are obstinate—"

"Oh! don't forget that I am in a position now to bring additional pressure on the wench. That lout Carrier has splendid ideas—a brute, what? but clever and full of resource. That suggestion of his about the Rat Mort is splendid—"

"You mean to try and act on it?"

"Of course, I do," said Martin-Roget roughly. "I am going over

131

presently to my sister's house to see the Kernogan wench again, and to have another talk with her. Then if she still refuses, if she still chooses to scorn the honourable position which I offer her, I shall act on Carrier's suggestion. It will be at the Rat Mort tonight that she and I will have our final interview, and there when I dangle the prospect of Cayenne and the convict's brand before her, she may not prove so obdurate as she has been up to now."

"H'm! That is as may be," was Chauvelin's dry comment. "Personally, I am inclined to agree with Carrier. Death, swift and sure—the Loire or the guillotine—is the best that has yet been invented for traitors and aristos. But we won't discuss that again. I know your feelings in the matter and in a measure, I respect them. But if you will allow me I would like to be present at your interview with the *soi-disant* Lady Anthony Dewhurst. I won't disturb you and I won't say a word—but there is something I would like to make sure of—"

"What is that?"

"Whether the wench has any hopes—" said Chauvelin slowly, "whether she has received a message or has any premonition—whether in short she thinks that outside agencies are at work on her behalf."

"Tshaw!" exclaimed Martin-Roget impatiently, "you are still harping on that Scarlet Pimpernel idea."

"I am," retorted the other drily.

"As you please. But understand, Citizen Chauvelin, that I will not allow you to interfere with my plans, whilst you go off on one of those wild-goose chases which have already twice brought you into disrepute."

"I will not interfere with your plans, citizen," rejoined Chauvelin with unwonted gentleness, "but let me in my turn impress one thing upon you, and that is that unless you are as wary as the serpent, as cunning as the fox, all your precious plans will be upset by that interfering Englishman whom you choose to disregard."

"What do you mean?"

"I mean that I know him—to my cost—and you do not. But you will, an I am not gravely mistaken, make acquaintance with him ere your great adventure with these Kernogan people is successfully at an end. Believe me, citizen Martin-Roget," he added impressively, "you would have been far wiser to accept Carrier's suggestion and let him fling that rabble into the Loire for you."

"Pshaw! you are not childish enough to imagine, Citizen Chauvelin, that your Englishman can spirit away that wench from under my sister's eyes? Do you know what my sister suffered at the hands of the Kernogans? Do you think that she is like to forget my father's igno-minious death any more than I am? And she mourns a lover as well as a father—she mourns her youth, her happiness, the mother whom she worshipped. Think you a better gaoler could be found anywhere? And there are friends of mine—lads of our own village, men who hate the Kernogans as bitterly as I do myself—who are only too ready to lend Louise a hand in case of violence. And after that—suppose your magnificent Scarlet Pimpernel succeeded in hoodwinking my sister and in evading the vigilance of a score of determined village lads, who would sooner die one by one than see the Kernogan escape—sup-pose all that, I say, there would still be the guard at every city gate to challenge. No! no! it couldn't be done, Citizen Chauvelin," he added with a complacent laugh. "Your Englishman would need the help of a legion of angels, what? to get the wench out of Nantes this time."

Chauvelin made no comment on his colleague's impassioned ha-rangue. Memory had taken him back to that one day in September in Boulogne when he too had set one prisoner to guard a precious hostage: it brought back to his mind a vision of a strangely pictur-esque figure as it appeared to him in the window-embrasure of the old castle-hall, (see *The Elusive Pimpernel* in volume 1): it brought back to his ears the echo of that quaint, irresponsible laughter, of that lazy, drawling speech, of all that had acted as an irritant on his nerves ere he found himself baffled, foiled, eating out his heart with vain reproach at his own folly.

"I see you are unconvinced, citizen Martin-Roget," he said quietly, "and I know that it is the fashion nowadays among young politicians to sneer at Chauvelin—the living embodiment of failure. But let me just add this. When you and I talked matters over together at the Bot-tom Inn, in the wilds of Somersetshire, I warned you that not only was your identity known to the man who calls himself the Scarlet Pimpernel, but also that he knew every one of your plans with regard to the Kernogan wench and her father. You laughed at me then—do you remember?—you shrugged your shoulders and jeered at what you call my far-fetched ideas—just as you do now. Well! will you let me remind you of what happened within four-and-twenty hours of that warning which you chose to disregard?—Yvonne de Kernogan was married to Lord Anthony Dewhurst and—"

"I know all that, man," broke in Martin-Roget impatiently. "It was all a mere coincidence—the marriage must have been planned long before that—your Scarlet Pimpernel could not possibly have had anything to do with it."

"Perhaps not," rejoined Chauvelin drily. "But mark what has happened since. Just now when we crossed the Place I saw in the distance a figure flitting past—the gorgeous figure of an exquisite who of a surety is a stranger in Nantes: and carried upon the wings of the north-westerly wind there came to me the sound of a voice which, of late, I have only heard in my dreams. On my soul, citizen Martin-Roget," he added with earnest emphasis, "I assure you that the Scarlet Pimpernel is in Nantes at the present moment, that he is scheming, plotting, planning to rescue the Kernogan wench out of your clutches. He will not leave her in your power, on this I would stake my life; she is the wife of one of his dearest friends: he will not abandon her, not while he keeps that resourceful head of his on his shoulders. Unless you are desperately careful he will outwit you; of that I am as convinced as that I am alive."

"Bah! you have been dreaming, Citizen Chauvelin," rejoined Martin-Roget with a laugh and shrugging his broad shoulders; "your mysterious Englishman in Nantes? Why man! the navigation of the Loire has been totally prohibited these last fourteen days—no carriage, van or vehicle of any kind is allowed to enter the city—no man, woman or child to pass the barriers without special permit signed either by the proconsul himself or by Fleury the captain of the Marats. Why! even I, when I brought the Kernogans in overland from Le Croisic, I was detained two hours outside Nantes while my papers were sent in to Carrier for inspection. You know that, you were with me."

"I know it," replied Chauvelin drily, "and yet—"

He paused, with one claw-like finger held erect to demand attention. The door of the small room in which they sat gave on the big hall where the half-dozen Marats were stationed, the single window at right angles to the door looked out upon the Place below. It was from there that suddenly there came the sound of a loud peal of laughter—quaint and merry—somewhat inane and affected, and at the sound Chauvelin's pale face took on the hue of ashes and even Martin-Roget felt a strange sensation of cold creeping down his spine.

For a few seconds the two men remained quite still, as if a spell had been cast over them through that light-hearted peal of rippling laughter. Then equally suddenly the younger man shook himself free of the spell; with a few long strides he was already at the door and out in the vast hall; Chauvelin following closely on his heels.

The clock in the tower of the edifice was even then striking five. The Marats in the hall looked up with lazy indifference at the two men who had come rushing out in such an abrupt and excited manner.

"Any stranger been through here?" queried Chauvelin peremptorily of the sergeant in command.

"No," replied the latter curtly. "How could they, without a permit?"

He shrugged his shoulders and the men resumed their game and their argument. Martin-Roget would have parleyed with them but Chauvelin had already crossed the hall and was striding past the clerk's office and the lodge of the concierge out toward the open. Martin-Roget, after a moment's hesitation, followed him.

The Place was wrapped in gloom. From the platform of the guillotine an oil-lamp hoisted on a post threw a small circle of light around. Small pieces of tallow candle, set in pewter sconces, glimmered feebly under the awnings of the booths, and there was a street-lamp affixed to the wall of the old *château* immediately below the parapet of the staircase, and others at the angles of the Rue de la Monnaye and the narrow Ruelle des Jacobins.

Chauvelin's keen eyes tried to pierce the surrounding darkness. He leaned over the parapet and peered into the remote angles of the building and round the booths below him.

There were a few people on the Place, some walking rapidly across from one end to the other, intent on business, others pausing in order to make purchases at the booths. Up and down the steps of the guillotine a group of street urchins were playing hide-and-seek. Round the angles of the narrow streets the vague figures of passers-by flitted to and fro, now easily discernible in the light of the street lanthorns, anon swallowed up again in the darkness beyond. Whilst immediately below the parapet two or three men of the Company Marat were lounging against the walls. Their red bonnets showed up clearly in the flickering light of the street lamps, as did their bare shins and the polished points of their sabots. But of an elegant, picturesque figure such as Chauvelin had described a while ago there was not a sign.

Martin-Roget leaned over the parapet and called peremptorily:

"Hey there! citizens of the Company Marat!"

One of the red-capped men looked up leisurely.

"Your desire, citizen?" he queried with insolent deliberation, for they were mighty men, this bodyguard of the great proconsul, his spies and tools in the awesome work of frightfulness which he carried on so ruthlessly.

"Is that you Paul Friche?" queried Martin-Roget in response.

"At your service, citizen," came the glib reply, delivered not without mock deference.

"Then come up here. I wish to speak with you."

"I can't leave my post, nor can my mates," retorted the man who had answered to the name of Paul Friche. "Come down, citizen, an you desire to speak with us."

Martin-Roget swore lustily.

"The insolence of that rabble—" he murmured.

"Hush! I'll go," interposed Chauvelin quickly. "Do you know that man Friche? Is he trustworthy?"

"Yes, I know him. As for being trustworthy—" added Martin-Roget with a shrug of the shoulders. "He is a corporal in the Marats and high in favour with Commandant Fleury."

Every second was of value, and Chauvelin was not the man to waste time in useless parleyings. He ran down the stairs at the foot of which one of the red-capped gentry deigned to speak with him.

"Have you seen any strangers across the Place just now?" he queried in a whisper.

"Yes," replied the man Friche. "Two!"

Then he spat upon the ground and added spitefully: "*Aristos*, what? In fine clothes—like yourself, citizen—"

"Which way did they go?"

"Down the Ruelle des Jacobins."

"When?"

"Two minutes ago."

"Why did you not follow them?—*Aristos* and—"

"I would have followed," retorted Paul Friche with studied insolence; "'twas you called me away from my duty."

"After them then!" urged Chauvelin peremptorily. "They cannot have gone far. They are English spies, and remember, citizen, that there's a reward for their apprehension."

The man grunted an eager assent. The word "reward" had fired his zeal. In a trice he had called to his mates and the three Marats soon sped across the Place and down the Ruelle des Jacobins where the surrounding gloom quickly swallowed them up.

Chauvelin watched them till they were out of sight, then he rejoined his colleague on the landing at the top of the stairs. For a second or two longer the click of the men's *sabots* upon the stones resounded on the adjoining streets and across the Place, and suddenly that same quaint, merry, somewhat inane laugh woke the echoes of the grim buildings around and caused many a head to turn inquiringly, marvelling who it could be that had the heart to laugh these days in the streets of Nantes.

Five minutes or so later the three Marats could vaguely be seen recrossing the Place and making their way back to Le Bouffay, where Martin-Roget and Chauvelin still stood on the top of the stairs excited and expectant. At sight of the men Chauvelin ran down the steps to meet them.

"Well?" he queried in an eager whisper.

"We never saw them," replied Paul Friche gruffly, "though we could hear them clearly enough, talking, laughing and walking very rapidly toward the quay. Then suddenly the earth or the river swallowed them up. We saw and heard nothing more."

Chauvelin swore and a curious hissing sound escaped his thin lips.

"Don't be too disappointed, citizen," added the man with a coarse laugh, "my mate picked this up at the corner of the Ruelle, when, I fancy, we were pressing the *aristos* pretty closely."

He held out a small bundle of papers tied together with a piece of red ribbon: the bundle had evidently rolled in the mud, for the papers were covered with grime. Chauvelin's thin, claw-like fingers had at once closed over them.

"You must give me back those papers, citizen," said the man, "they are my booty. I can only give them up to Citizen-Captain Fleury."

"I'll give them to the citizen-captain myself," retorted Chauvelin. "For the moment you had best not leave your post of duty," he added more peremptorily, seeing that the man made as he would follow him.

"I take orders from no one except—" protested the man gruffly.

"You will take them from me now," broke in Chauvelin with a sudden assumption of command and authority which sat with weird strangeness upon his thin shrunken figure. "Go back to your post at once, ere I lodge a complaint against you for neglect of duty, with the citizen proconsul."

He turned on his heel and, without paying further heed to the man and his mutterings, he remounted the stone stairs.

"No success, I suppose?" queried Martin-Roget.

"None," replied Chauvelin curtly.

He had the packet of papers tightly clasped in his hand. He was debating in his mind whether he would speak of them to his colleague or not.

"What did Friche say?" asked the latter impatiently.

"Oh! very little. He and his mates caught sight of the strangers and followed them as far as the quays. But they were walking very fast and suddenly the Marats lost their trace in the darkness. It seemed, according to Paul Friche, as if the earth or the night had swallowed them up."

"And was that all?"

"Yes. That was all."

"I wonder," added Martin-Roget with a light laugh and a careless shrug of his wide shoulders, "I wonder if you and I, Citizen Chauvelin—and Paul Friche too for that matter—have been the victims of our nerves."

"I wonder," assented Chauvelin drily. And—quite quietly—he slipped the packet of papers in the pocket of his coat.

"Then we may as well adjourn. There is nothing else you wish to say to me about that enigmatic Scarlet Pimpernel of yours?"

"No—nothing."

"And you still would like to hear what the Kernogan wench will say and see how she will look when I put my final proposal before her?"

"If you will allow me."

"Then come," said Martin-Roget. "My sister's house is close by."

CHAPTER 3

The Fowlers

In order to reach the *Carrefour de la Poissonnerie* the two men had to skirt the whole edifice of Le Bouffay, walk a little along the quay and turn up the narrow alley opposite the bridge. They walked on in silence, each absorbed in his own thoughts.

The house occupied by the citizeness Adet lay back a little from the others in the street. It was one of an irregular row of mean, squalid, tumble-down houses, some of them little more than lean-to sheds built into the walls of Le Bouffay. Most of them had overhanging roofs which stretched out like awnings more than half way across the road, and even at midday shut out any little ray of sunshine which, might have a tendency, to peep into the street below.

In this year II of the Republic the *Carrefour de la Poissonnerie* was unpaved, dark and evil-smelling. For two thirds of the year it was ankle-deep in mud: the rest of the time the mud was baked into cakes

and emitted clouds of sticky dust under the shuffling feet of the passers-by. At night it was dimly lighted by one or two broken-down
lanthorns which were hung on transverse chains overhead from house
to house. These lanthorns only made a very small circle of light immediately below them: the rest of the street was left in darkness, save
for the faint glimmer which filtrated through an occasional ill-fitting
doorway or through the chinks of some insecurely fastened shutter.

The *Carrefour de la Poissonnerie* was practically deserted in the day-
time; only a few children—miserable little atoms of humanity showing
their meagre, emaciated bodies through the scanty rags which failed
to cover their nakedness—played weird, mirthless games in the mud
and filth of the street. But at night it became strangely peopled with
vague and furtive forms that were wont to glide swiftly by, beneath
the hanging lanthorns, in order to lose themselves again in the welcome obscurity beyond: men and women—ill-clothed and unshod,
with hands buried in pockets or beneath scanty shawls—their feet,
oft-times bare, making no sound as they went squishing through the
mud. A perpetual silence used to reign in this kingdom of squalor and
of darkness, where night-hawks alone fluttered their wings; only from
time to time a joyless greeting of boon-companions, or the hoarse
cough of some wretched consumptive would wake the dormant echoes that lingered in the gloom.

Martin-Roget knew his way about the murky street well enough.
He went up to the house which lay a little back from the others. It appeared even more squalid than the rest, not a sound came from within—hardly a light—only a narrow glimmer found its way through
the chink of a shutter on the floor above. To right and left of it the
houses were tall, with walls that reeked of damp and of filth: from one
of these—the one on the left—an iron sign dangled and creaked dis-
mally as it swung in the wind. Just above the sign there was a window
with partially closed shutters: through it came the sound of two husky
voices raised in heated argument.

In the open space in front of Louise Adet's house vague forms
standing about or lounging against the walls of the neighbouring
houses were vaguely discernible in the gloom. Martin-Roget and
Chauvelin as they approached were challenged by a raucous voice
which came to them out of the inky blackness around.

"Halt! who goes there?"

"Friends!" replied Martin-Roget promptly. "Is Citizeness Adet
within?"

"Yes! she is!" retorted the man bluntly; "excuse me, friend Adet—I did not know you in this confounded darkness."

"No harm done," said Martin-Roget. "And it is I who am grateful to you all for your vigilance."

"Oh!" said the other with a laugh, "there's not much fear of your bird getting out of its cage. Have no fear, friend Adet! That Kernogan rabble is well looked after."

The small group dispersed in the darkness and Martin-Roget rapped against the door of his sister's house with his knuckles.

"That is the Rat Mort," he said, indicating the building on his left with a nod of the head. "A very unpleasant neighbourhood for my sister, and she has oft complained of it—but name of a dog! won't it prove useful this night?"

Chauvelin had as usual followed his colleague in silence, but his keen eyes had not failed to note the presence of the village lads of whom Martin-Roget had spoken. There are no eyes so watchful as those of hate, nor is there aught so incorruptible. Every one of these men here had an old wrong to avenge, an old score to settle with those *ci-devant* Kernogans who had once been their masters and who were so completely in their power now. Louise Adet had gathered round her a far more efficient bodyguard than even the proconsul could hope to have.

A moment or two later the door was opened, softly and cautiously, and Martin-Roget asked: "Is that you, Louise?" for of a truth the darkness was almost deeper within than without, and he could not see who it was that was standing by the door.

"Yes! it is," replied a weary and querulous voice. "Enter quickly. The wind is cruel, and I can't keep myself warm. Who is with you, Pierre?"

"A friend," said Martin-Roget drily. "We want to see the *aristo*."

The woman without further comment closed the door behind the newcomers. The place now was as dark as pitch, but she seemed to know her way about like a cat, for her shuffling footsteps were heard moving about unerringly. A moment or two later she opened another door opposite the front entrance, revealing an inner room—a sort of kitchen—which was lighted by a small lamp.

"You can go straight up," she called curtly to the two men.

The narrow, winding staircase was divided from this kitchen by a wooden partition. Martin-Roget, closely followed by Chauvelin, went up the stairs. On the top of these there was a tiny landing with a door on either side of it. Martin-Roget without any ceremony pushed open the door on his right with his foot.

A tallow candle fixed in a bottle and placed in the centre of a table in the middle of the room flickered in the draught as the door flew open. It was bare of everything save a table and a chair, and a bundle of straw in one corner. The tiny window at right angles to the door was innocent of glass, and the north-westerly wind came in an icy stream through the aperture. On the table, in addition to the candle, there was a broken pitcher half-filled with water, and a small chunk of brown bread blotched with stains of mould.

On the chair beside the table and immediately facing the door sat Yvonne Lady Dewhurst. On the wall above her head a hand unused to calligraphy had traced in clumsy characters the words: "*Liberté! Fraternité! Egalité!*" and below that "*ou la Mort.*"

The men entered the narrow room and Chauvelin carefully closed the door behind him. He at once withdrew into a remote corner of the room and stood there quite still, wrapped in his mantle, a small, silent, mysterious figure on which Yvonne fixed dark, inquiring eyes.

Martin-Roget, restless and excited, paced up and down the small space like a wild animal in a cage. From time to time exclamations of impatience escaped him and he struck one fist repeatedly against his open palm. Yvonne followed his movements with a quiet, uninterested glance, but Chauvelin paid no heed whatever to him.

He was watching Yvonne ceaselessly, and closely.

Three days' incarceration in this wind-swept attic, the lack of decent food and of warmth, the want of sleep and the horror of her present position all following upon the soul-agony which she had endured when she was forcibly torn away from her dear milor, had left their mark on Yvonne Dewhurst's fresh young face. The look of gravity which had always sat so quaintly on her piquant features had now changed to one of deep and abiding sorrow; her large dark eyes were circled and sunk; they had in them the unnatural glow of fever, as well as the settled look of horror and of pathetic resignation. Her soft brown hair had lost its lustre; her cheeks were drawn and absolutely colourless.

Martin-Roget paused in his restless walk. For a moment he stood silent and absorbed, contemplating by the flickering light of the candle all the havoc which his brutality had wrought upon Yvonne's dainty face.

But Yvonne after a while ceased to look at him—she appeared to be unconscious of the gaze of these two men, each of whom was at this moment only thinking of the evil which he meant to inflict upon her—each of whom only thought of her as a helpless bird whom he had at last ensnared and whom he could crush to death as soon as he felt so inclined.

She kept her lips tightly closed and her head averted. She was gazing across at the unglazed window into the obscurity beyond, marvelling in what direction lay the sea and the shores of England.

Martin-Roget crossed his arms over his broad chest and clutched his elbows with his hands with an obvious effort to keep control over his movements and his temper in check. The quiet, almost indifferent attitude of the girl was exasperating to his over-strung nerves.

"Look here, my girl," he said at last, roughly and peremptorily, "I had an interview with the proconsul this afternoon. He chides me for my leniency toward you. Three days he thinks is far too long to keep traitors eating the bread of honest citizens and taking up valuable space in our city. Yesterday I made a proposal to you. Have you thought on it?"

Yvonne made no reply. She was still gazing out into nothingness and just at that moment she was very far away from the narrow, squalid room and the company of these two inhuman brutes. She was thinking of her dear milor and of that lovely home at Combwich wherein she had spent three such unforgettable days. She was remembering how beautiful, had been the colour of the bare twigs, in the chestnut coppice when the wintry sun danced through and in between them and drew fantastic patterns of living gold upon the carpet of dead leaves; and she remembered too how exquisite were the tints of russet and blue on the distant hills, and how quaintly the thrushes had called: "Kiss me quick!" She saw again those trembling leaves of a delicious faintly crimson hue which still hung upon the branches of the scarlet oak, and the early flowering heath which clothed the moors with a gorgeous mantle of rosy amethyst.

Martin-Roget's harsh voice brought her abruptly back to the hideous reality of the moment.

"Your obstinacy will avail you nothing," he said, speaking quietly, even though a note of intense irritation was distinctly perceptible in his voice. "The proconsul has given me a further delay wherein to deal leniently with you and with your father if I am so minded. You know what I have proposed to you: Life with me as my wife—in which case your father will be free to return to England or to go to the devil as

142

he pleases—or the death of a malefactor for you both in the company of all the thieves and evil-doers who are mouldering in the prisons of Nantes at this moment. Another delay wherein to choose between an honourable life and a shameful death. The proconsul waits. But tonight, he must have his answer."

Then Yvonne turned her head slowly and looked calmly on her enemy.

"The tyrant who murders innocent men, women and children," she said, "can have his answer now. I choose death which is inevitable in preference to a life of shame."

"You seem," he retorted, "to have lost sight of the fact that the law gives me the right to take by force that which you so obstinately refuse."

"Have I not said," she replied, "that death is my choice? Life with you would be a life of shame."

"I can get a priest to marry us without your consent: and your religion forbids you to take your own life," he said with a sneer.

To this she made no reply, but he knew that he had his answer. Smothering a curse, he resumed after a while:

"So, you prefer to drag your father to death with you? Yet he has begged you to consider your decision and to listen to reason. He has given his consent to our marriage."

"Let me see my father," she retorted firmly, "and hear him say that with his own lips.

"Ah!" she added quickly, for at her words Martin-Roget had turned his head away and shrugged his shoulders with well-assumed indifference, "you cannot and dare not let me see him. For three days now, you have kept us apart and no doubt fed us both up with your lies. My father is Duc de Kernogan, Marquis de Trentemoult," she added proudly, "he would far rather die side by side with his daughter than see her wedded to a criminal."

"And you, my girl," rejoined Martin-Roget coldly, "would you see your father branded as a malefactor, linked to a thief and sent to perish in the Loire?"

"My father," she retorted, "will die as he has lived, a brave and honourable gentleman. The brand of a malefactor cannot cling to his name. Sorrow we are ready to endure—death is less than nothing to us—we will but follow in the footsteps of our king and of our queen and of many whom we care for and whom you and your proconsul and your colleagues have brutally murdered. Shame cannot touch us, and our honour and our pride are so far beyond your reach that your impious and blood-stained hands can never sully them."

She had spoken very slowly and very quietly. There were no heroics about her attitude. Even Martin-Roget—callous brute though he was—felt that she had only spoken just as she felt, and that nothing that he might say, no plea that he might urge, would ever shake her determination.

"Then it seems to me," he said, "that I am only wasting my time by trying to make you see reason and common-sense. You look upon me as a brute. Well! perhaps I am. At any rate I am that which your father and you have made me. Four years ago, when you had power over me and over mine, you brutalised us. Today we—the people—are your masters and we make you suffer, not for all—that were impossible—but for part of what you made us suffer. That, after all, is only bare justice. By making you my wife I would have saved you from death—not from humiliation, for that you must endure, and at my hands in a full measure—but I would have made you my wife because I still have pleasant recollections of that kiss which I snatched from you on that never-to-be-forgotten night and in the darkness—a kiss for which you would gladly have seen me hang then, if you could have laid hands on me."

He paused, trying to read what was going on behind those fine eyes of hers, with their vacant, far-seeing gaze which seemed like another barrier between her and him. At this rough allusion to that moment of horror and of shame, she had not moved a muscle, nor did her gaze lose its fixity.

He laughed.

"It is an unpleasant recollection, eh, my proud lady? The first kiss of passion was not implanted on your exquisite lips by that fine gentleman whom you deemed worthy of your hand and your love, but by Pierre Adet, the miller's son, what? a creature not quite so human as your horse or your pet dog. Neither you nor I are like to forget that methinks—"

Yvonne vouchsafed no reply to the taunt, and for a moment there was silence in the room, until Chauvelin's thin, suave voice broke in quite gently:

"Do not lose your patience with the wench, citizen Martin-Roget. Your time is too precious to be wasted in useless recriminations."

"I have finished with her," retorted the other sullenly. "She shall be dealt with now as I think best. I agree with Citizen Carrier. He is right after all. To the Loire with the lot of that foul brood!"

"Nay!" here rejoined Chauvelin with placid urbanity, "are you not a little harsh, citizen, with our fair Yvonne? Remember! Women have moods and megrims. What they indignantly refuse to yield to us one day, they will grant with a smile the next. Our beautiful Yvonne is no exception to this rule, I'll warrant."

Even while he spoke he threw a glance of warning on his colleague. There was something enigmatic in his manner at this moment, in the strange suavity wherewith he spoke these words of conciliation and of gentleness. Martin-Roget was as usual ready with an impatient retort. He was in a mood to bully and to brutalise, to heap threat upon threat, to win by frightfulness that which he could not gain by persuasion. Perhaps that at this moment he desired Yvonne de Kernogan for wife, more even than he desired her death. At any rate his headstrong temper was ready to chafe against any warning or advice. But once again Chauvelin's stronger mentality dominated over his less resolute colleague. Martin-Roget—the fowler—was in his turn caught in the net of a keener snarer than himself, and whilst—with the obstinacy of the weak—he was making mental resolutions to rebuke Chauvelin for his interference later on, he had already fallen in with the latter's attitude.

"The wench has had three whole days wherein to alter her present mood," he said more quietly, "and you know yourself, citizen, that the proconsul will not wait after today."

"The day is young yet," rejoined Chauvelin. "It still hath six hours to its credit—Six hours—Three hundred and sixty minutes!" he continued with a pleasant little laugh; "time enough for a woman to change her mind three hundred and sixty times. Let me advise you, citizen, to leave the wench to her own meditations for the present, and I trust that she will accept the advice of a man who has a sincere regard for her beauty and her charms and who is old enough to be her father, and seriously think the situation over in a conciliatory spirit. M. le Duc de Kernogan will be grateful to her, for of a truth he is not over happy either at the moment—and will be still less happy in the *dépôt* tomorrow: it is overcrowded, and typhus, I fear me, is rampant among the prisoners. He has, I am convinced—in spite of what the citizeness says to the contrary—a rooted objection to being hurled into the Loire, or to be arraigned before the bar of the Convention, not as an aristocrat and a traitor but as an unit of an undesirable herd of criminals sent up to Paris for trial, by an anxious and harried proconsul. There! there!" he added benignly, "we will not worry our fair Yvonne any longer, will we, citizen? I think she has grasped the alternative and will soon realise that marriage with an honourable patriot is not such an untoward fate after all."

"And now, citizen Martin-Roget," he concluded, "I pray you allow me to take my leave of the fair lady and to give you the wise recommendation to do likewise. She will be far better alone for a while. Night brings good counsel, so they say."

He watched the girl keenly while he spoke. Her impassivity had not deserted her for a single moment: but whether her calmness was of hope or of despair he was unable to decide. On the whole he thought it must be the latter: hope would have kindled a spark in those dark, purple-rimmed eyes, it would have brought moisture to the lips, a tremor to the hand.

The Scarlet Pimpernel was in Nantes—that fact was established beyond a doubt—but Chauvelin had come to the conclusion that so far as Yvonne Dewhurst herself was concerned, she knew nothing of the mysterious agencies that were working on her behalf.

Chauvelin's hand closed with a nervous contraction over the packet of papers in his pocket. Something of the secret of that enigmatic English adventurer lay revealed within its folds. Chauvelin had not yet had the opportunity of examining them: the interview with Yvonne had been the most important business for the moment.

From somewhere in the distance a city clock struck six. The afternoon was wearing on. The keenest brain in Europe was on the watch to drag one woman and one man from the deadly trap which had been so successfully set for them. A few hours more and Chauvelin in his turn would be pitting his wits against the resources of that intricate brain, and he felt like a war-horse scenting blood and battle. He was aching to get to work—aching to form his plans—to lay his snares— to dispose his trap so that the noble English quarry should not fail to be caught within its meshes.

He gave a last look to Yvonne, who was still sitting quite impassive, gazing through the squalid walls into some beautiful distance, the reflection of which gave to her pale, wan face an added beauty.

"Let us go, Citizen Martin-Roget," he said peremptorily. "There is nothing else that we can do here."

And Martin-Roget, the weaker morally of the two, yielded to the stronger personality of his colleague. He would have liked to stay on for a while, to gloat for a few moments longer over the helplessness of the woman who to him represented the root of every evil which had ever befallen him and his family. But Chauvelin commanded and he felt impelled to obey. He gave one long, last look on Yvonne—a look that was as full of triumph as of mockery—he looked round the four dank walls, the unglazed window, the broken pitcher, the mouldy bread. Revenge was of a truth the sweetest emotion of the human heart. Pierre Adet—son of the miller who had been hanged by orders of the Duc de Kernogan for a crime which he had never committed—would not at this moment have changed places with Fortune's Benjamin.

Downstairs in Louise Adet's kitchen, Martin-Roget seized his colleague by the arm.

"Sit down a moment, citizen," he said persuasively, "and tell me what you think of it all."

Chauvelin sat down at the other's invitation. All his movements were slow, deliberate, perfectly calm.

"I think," he said drily, "as far as your marriage with the wench is concerned, that you are beaten, my friend."

"Tshaw!" The exclamation, raucous and surcharged with hate came from Louise Adet. She, too, like Pierre—more so than Pierre mayhap—had cause to hate the Kernogans. She, too, like Pierre had lived the last three days in the full enjoyment of the thought that Fate and Chance were about to level things at last between herself and those detested *aristos*. Silent and sullen she was shuffling about in the room, among her pots and pans, but she kept an eye upon her brother's movements and an ear on what he said. Men were apt to lose grit where a pretty wench was concerned. It takes a woman's rancour and a woman's determination to carry a scheme of vengeance against another to a successful end.

Martin-Roget rejoined more calmly:

"I knew that she would still be obstinate," he said. "If I forced her into a marriage, which I have the right to do, she might take her own life and make me look a fool. So, I don't want to do that. I believe in the persuasiveness of the Rat Mort tonight," he added with a cynical laugh, "and if that fails—Well! I was never really in love with the fair Yvonne, and now she has even ceased to be desirable—If the Rat Mort fails to act on her sensibilities as I would wish, I can easily console myself by following Carrier's herd to Paris. Louise shall come with me—eh, little sister?—and we'll give ourselves the satisfaction of seeing M. le Duc de Kernogan and his exquisite daughter stand in the felon's dock—tried for malpractices and for evil living. We'll see them branded as convicts and packed off like so much cattle to Cayenne. That will be a sight," he concluded with a deep sigh of satisfaction, "which will bring rest to my soul."

He paused: his face looked sullen and evil under the domination of that passion which tortured him.

Louise Adet had shuffled up close to her brother. In one hand she held the wooden spoon wherewith she had been stirring the soup: with the other she brushed away the dark, lank hair which hung in strands over her high, pale forehead. In appearance she was a woman immeasurably older than her years. Her face had the colour of yellow parchment, her skin was stretched tightly over her high cheekbones—her lips were colourless and her eyes large, wide-open, were pale in hue and circled with red. Just now a deep frown of puzzlement between her brows added a sinister expression to her cadaverous face:

"The Rat Mort?" she queried in that tired voice of hers, "*Cayenne?* What is all that about?"

"A splendid scheme of Carrier's, my Louise," replied Martin-Roget airily. "We convey the Kernogan woman to the Rat Mort. Tonight, a descent will be made on that tavern of ill-fame by a company of Marats and every man, woman and child within it will be arrested and sent to Paris as undesirable inhabitants of this most moral city: in Paris they will be tried as malefactors or evil-doers—cut throats, thieves, what? and deported as convicts to Cayenne, or else sent to the guillotine. The Kernogans among that herd! What sayest thou to that, little sister? Thy father, thy lover, hung as thieves! *M. le Duc* and *Mademoiselle* branded as convicts! 'Tis pleasant to think on, eh?"

Louise made no reply. She stood looking at her brother, her pale, red-rimmed eyes seemed to drink in every word that he uttered, while her bony hand wandered mechanically across and across her forehead as if in a pathetic endeavour to clear the brain from everything save of the satisfying thoughts which this prospect of revenge had engendered.

Chauvelin's gentle voice broke in on her meditations.

"In the meanwhile," he said placidly, "remember my warning, Citizen Martin-Roget. There are passing clever and mighty agencies at work, even at this hour, to wrest your prey from you. How will you convey the wench to the Rat Mort? Carrier has warned you of spies—but I have warned you against a crowd of English adventurers far more dangerous than an army of spies. Three pairs of eyes—probably more, and one pair the keenest in Europe—will be on the watch to seize upon the woman and to carry her off under your very nose."

Martin-Roget uttered a savage oath.

"That brute Carrier has left me in the lurch," he said roughly. "I don't believe in your nightmares and your English adventurers, still it would have been better if I could have had the woman conveyed to the tavern under armed escort."

"Armed escort has been denied you, and anyway it would not be much use. You and I, Citizen Martin-Roget, must act independently of Carrier. Your friends down there," he added, indicating the street with a jerk of the head, "must redouble their watchfulness. The village lads of Vertou are of a truth no match intellectually with our English adventurers, but they have vigorous fists in case there is an attack on the wench while she walks across to the Rat Mort."

"It would be simpler," here interposed Louise roughly, "if we were to knock the wench on the head and then let the lads carry her across."

"It would not be simpler," retorted Chauvelin drily, "for Carrier might at any moment turn against us. Commandant Fleury with half a company of Marats will be posted round the Rat Mort, remember. They may interfere with the lads and arrest them and snatch the wench from us, when all our plans may fall to the ground—one never knows what double game Carrier may be playing. No! no! the girl must not be dragged or carried to the Rat Mort. She must walk into the trap of her own free will."

"But name of a dog! how is it to be done?" ejaculated Martin-Roget, and he brought his clenched fist crashing down upon the table. "The woman will not follow me—or Louise either—anywhere willingly."

"She must follow a stranger then—or one whom she thinks a stranger—someone who will have gained her confidence—"

"Impossible."

"Oh! nothing is impossible, citizen," rejoined Chauvelin blandly.

"Do you know a way then?" queried the other with a sneer.

"I think I do. If you will trust me that is——"

"I don't know that I do. Your mind is so intent on those English adventurers, you are like as not to let the *aristos* slip through your fingers."

"Well, citizen," retorted Chauvelin imperturbably, "will you take the risk of conveying the fair Yvonne to the Rat Mort by twelve o'clock tonight? I have very many things to see to, I confess that I should be glad if you will ease me from that responsibility."

"I have already told you that I see no way," retorted Martin-Roget with a snarl.

"Then why not let me act?"

"What are you going to do?"

"For the moment I am going for a walk on the quay and once more will commune with the North-West wind."

"Tshaw!" ejaculated Martin-Roget savagely.

"Nay, citizen," resumed Chauvelin blandly, "the winds of heaven are excellent counsellors. I told you so just now and you agreed with me. They blow away the cobwebs of the mind and clear the brain for serious thinking. You want the Kernogan girl to be arrested inside the Rat Mort and you see no way of conveying her thither save by the use of violence, which for obvious reasons is to be deprecated: Carrier, for equally obvious reasons, will not have her taken to the place by force. On the other hand, you admit that the wench would not follow you willingly——Well, citizen, we must find a way out of that impasse, for it is too unimportant an one to stand in the way of our plans: for this I must hold a consultation with the North-West wind."

"I won't allow you to do anything without consulting me."

"Am I likely to do that? To begin with I shall have need of your co-operation and that of the citizeness."

"In that case——" muttered Martin-Roget grudgingly. "But remember," he added with a return to his usual self-assured manner, "remember that Yvonne and her father belong to me and not to you. I brought them into Nantes for mine own purposes—not for yours. I will not have my revenge jeopardised so that your schemes may be furthered."

"Who spoke of my schemes, citizen Martin-Roget?" broke in Chauvelin with perfect urbanity. "Surely not I? What am I but an humble tool in the service of the Republic?—a tool that has proved useless—a failure, what? My only desire is to help you to the best of my abilities. Your enemies are the enemies of the Republic: my ambition is to help you in destroying them."

For a moment longer, Martin-Roget hesitated: he abominated this suggestion of becoming a mere instrument in the hands of this man whom he still would have affected to despise—had he dared. But here came the difficulty: he no longer dared to despise Chauvelin. He felt the strength of the man—the clearness of his intellect, and though he—Martin-Roget—still chose to disregard every warning in connexion with the English spies, he could not wholly divest his mind from the possibility of their presence in Nantes. Carrier's scheme was so magnificent, so satisfying, that the ex-miller's son was ready to humble his pride and set his arrogance aside in order to see it carried through successfully.

So after a moment or two, despite the fact that he positively ached to shut Chauvelin out of the whole business, Martin-Roget gave a grudging assent to his proposal.

"Very well!" he said, "you see to it. So long as it does not interfere with my plans—"

"It can but help them," rejoined Chauvelin suavely. "If you will act as I shall direct I pledge you my word that the wench will walk to the Rat Mort of her free will and at the hour when you want her. What else is there to say?"

"When and where shall we meet again?"

"Within the hour I will return here and explain to you and to the citizeness what I want you to do. We will get the *aristos* inside the Rat Mort, never fear; and after that I think that we may safely leave Carrier to do the rest, what?"

He picked up his hat and wrapped his mantle round him. He took no further heed of Martin-Roget or of Louise, for suddenly he had felt the crackling of crisp paper inside the breast-pocket of his coat and in a moment the spirit of the man had gone a-roaming out of the narrow confines of this squalid abode. It had crossed the English Channel and wandered once more into a brilliantly-lighted ball-room where an exquisitely dressed dandy declaimed inanities and doggrel rhymes for the delectation of a flippant assembly: it heard once more the lazy, drawling speech, the inane, affected laugh, it caught the glance of a pair of lazy, grey eyes fixed mockingly upon him.

Chauvelin's thin claw-like hand went back to his pocket: it felt that packet of papers, it closed over it like a vulture's talon does upon a prey. He no longer heard Martin-Roget's obstinate murmurings, he no longer felt himself to be the disgraced, humiliated servant of the State: rather did he feel once more the master, the leader, the success-ful weaver of an hundred clever intrigues. The enemy who had baf-fled him so often had chosen once more to throw down the glove of mocking defiance. So be it! The battle would be fought this night—a decisive one—and long live the Republic and the power of the peo-ple!

With a curt nod of the head Chauvelin turned on his heel and without waiting for Martin-Roget to follow him, or for Louise to light him on his way, he strode from the room, and out of the house, and had soon disappeared in the darkness in the direction of the quay.

Once more, free from the encumbering companionship of Martin-Roget, Chauvelin felt free to breathe and to think. He, the obscure and impassive servant of the Republic, the cold-blooded Terrorist who had gone through every phrase of an exciting career without moving a muscle of his grave countenance, felt as if every one of his arteries was on fire. He strode along the quay in the teeth of the north-westerly wind, grateful for the cold blast which lashed his face and cooled his throbbing temples.

The packet of papers inside his coat seemed to sear his breast.

Before turning to go along the quay he paused, hesitating for a moment what he would do. His very humble lodgings were at the far end of the town, and every minute of time was precious. Inside Le Bouffay, where he had a small room allotted to him as a minor representative in Nantes of the Committee of Public Safety, there was the ever-present danger of prying eyes.

On the whole—since time was so precious—he decided on returning to Le Bouffay. The *concierge* and the clerk fortunately let him through without those official delays which he—Chauvelin—was wont to find so galling ever since his disgrace had put a bar against the opening of every door at the bare mention of his name or the display of his tricolour scarf.

He strode rapidly across the hall: the men on guard eyed him with lazy indifference as he passed. Once inside his own sanctum he looked carefully around him; he drew the curtain closer across the window and dragged the table and a chair well away from the range which might be covered by an eye at the keyhole. It was only when he had thoroughly assured himself that no searching eye or inquisitive ear could possibly be watching over him that he at last drew the precious packet of papers from his pocket. He undid the red ribbon which held it together and spread the papers out on the table before him. Then he examined them carefully one by one.

As he did so an exclamation of wrath or of impatience escaped him from time to time, once he laughed—involuntarily—aloud.

The examination of the papers took him some time. When he had finished he gathered them all together again, retied the bit of ribbon round them and slipped the packet back into the pocket of his coat. There was a look of grim determination on his face, even though a bitter sigh escaped his set lips.

"Oh! for the power," he muttered to himself, "which I had a year ago! for the power to deal with mine enemy myself. So, you have come to Nantes, my valiant Sir Percy Blakeney?" he added while a short, sardonic laugh escaped his thin, set lips: "and you are determined that I shall know how and why you came! Do you reckon, I wonder, that I have no longer the power to deal with you? Well!—"

He sighed again but with more satisfaction this time.

"Well!—" he reiterated with obvious complacency. "Unless that oaf Carrier is a bigger fool than I imagine him to be I think I have you this time, my elusive Scarlet Pimpernel."

CHAPTER 4

The Net

It was not an easy thing to obtain an audience of the great proconsul at this hour of the night, nor was Chauvelin, the disgraced servant of the Committee of Public Safety, a man to be considered. Carrier, with his love of ostentation and of tyranny, found great delight in keeping his colleagues waiting upon his pleasure, and he knew that he could trust young Jacques Lalouët to be as insolent as any tyrant's flunkey of yore.

"I must speak with the proconsul at once," had been Chauvelin's urgent request of Fleury, the commandant of the great man's bodyguard.

"The proconsul dines at this hour," had been Fleury's curt reply.

"'Tis a matter which concerns the welfare and the safety of the State!"

"The proconsul's health is the concern of the State too, and he dines at this hour and must not be disturbed."

"Commandant Fleury!" urged Chauvelin, "you risk being implicated in a disaster. Danger and disgrace threaten the proconsul and all his adherents. I must speak with Citizen Carrier at once."

Fortunately for Chauvelin there were two keys which, when all else failed, were apt to open the doors of Carrier's stronghold: the key of fear and that of cupidity. He tried both and succeeded. He bribed and he threatened: he endured Fleury's brutality and Lalouët's impertinence but he got his way. After an hour's weary waiting and ceaseless parleyings he was once more ushered into the antechamber where he had sat earlier in the day. The doors leading to the inner sanctuary were open. Young Jacques Lalouët stood by them on guard. Carrier, fuming and raging at having been disturbed, vented his spleen and ill-temper on Chauvelin.

"If the news that you bring me is not worth my consideration," he cried savagely, "I'll send you to moulder in Le Bouffay or to drink the waters of the Loire."

Chauvelin silent, self-effaced, allowed the flood of the great man's wrath to spend itself in threats. Then he said quietly:

"Citizen proconsul I have come to tell you that the English spy, who is called the Scarlet Pimpernel, is now in Nantes. There is a re-ward of twenty thousand *francs* for his capture and I want your help to lay him by the heels."

Carrier suddenly paused in his ravings. He sank into a chair and a livid hue spread over his face.

"It's not true!" he murmured hoarsely.

"I saw him—not an hour ago—"

"What proof have you?"

"I'll show them to you—but not across this threshold. Let me enter, citizen proconsul, and close your sanctuary doors behind me rather than before. What I have come hither to tell you, can only be said between four walls."

"I'll make you tell me," broke in Carrier in a raucous voice, which excitement and fear caused almost to choke in his throat. "I'll make you—curse you for the traitor that you are.... Curse you!" he cried more vigorously, "I'll make you speak. Will you shield a spy by your silence, you miserable traitor? If you do I'll send you to rot in the mud of the Loire with other traitors less accursed than yourself."

"If you only knew," was Chauvelin's calm rejoinder to the other's ravings, "how little I care for life. I only live to be even one day with an enemy whom I hate. That enemy is now in Nantes, but I am like a bird of prey whose wings have been clipped. If you do not help me mine enemy will again go free—and death in that case matters little or nothing to me."

For a moment longer, Carrier hesitated. Fear had gripped him by the throat. Chauvelin's earnestness seemed to vouch for the truth of his assertion, and if this were so—if those English spies were indeed in Nantes—then his own life was in deadly danger. He—like every one of those bloodthirsty tyrants who had misused the sacred names of Fraternity and of Equality—had learned to dread the machinations of those mysterious Englishmen and of their unconquerable leader. Popular superstition had it that they were spies of the English Government and that they were not only bent on saving traitors from well-merited punishment but that they were hired assassins paid by Mr. Pitt to murder every faithful servant of the Republic. The name of the Scarlet Pimpernel, so significantly uttered by Chauvelin, had turned Carrier's sallow cheeks to a livid hue. Sick with terror now he called Lalouët to him. He clung to the boy with both arms as to the one being in this world whom he trusted.

"What shall we do, Jacques?" he murmured hoarsely, "shall we let him in?"

The boy roughly shook himself free from the embrace of the great proconsul.

"If you want twenty thousand *francs*," he said with a dry laugh, "I should listen quietly to what Citizen Chauvelin has to say."

Terror and rapacity were ranged on one side against inordinate vanity. The thought of twenty thousand francs made Carrier's ugly mouth water. Money was ever scarce these days: also, the fear of assassination was a spectre which haunted him at all hours of the day and night. On the other hand, he positively worshipped the mystery wherewith he surrounded himself. It had been his boast for some time now that no one save the chosen few had crossed the threshold of his private chamber: and he was miserably afraid not only of Chauvelin's possible evil intentions, but also that this despicable ex-*aristo* and equally despicable failure would boast in the future of an ascendancy over him.

He thought the matter over for fully five minutes, during which there was dead silence in the two rooms—silence only broken by the stertorous breathing of that wretched coward, and the measured ticking of the fine Buhl clock behind him. Chauvelin's pale eyes were fixed upon the darkness, through which he could vaguely discern the uncouth figure of the proconsul, sprawling over his desk. Which way would his passions sway him? Chauvelin as he watched and waited felt that his habitual self-control was perhaps more severely taxed at this moment than it had ever been before. Upon the swaying of those passions, the passions of a man infinitely craven and infinitely base, depended all his—Chauvelin's—hopes of getting even at last with a daring and resourceful foe. Terror and rapacity were the counsellors which ranged themselves on the side of his schemes, but mere vanity and caprice fought a hard battle too.

In the end it was rapacity that gained the victory. An impatient exclamation from young Lalouët roused Carrier from his sombre brooding and hastened on a decision which was destined to have such momentous consequences for the future of both these men.

"Introduce Citizen Chauvelin in here, Lalouët," said the proconsul grudgingly. "I will listen to what he has to say."

Chauvelin crossed the threshold of the tyrant's sanctuary, in no way awed by the majesty of that dreaded presence or confused by the air of mystery which hung about the room.

He did not even bestow a glance on the multitudinous objects of art and the priceless furniture which littered the tiger's lair. His pale face remained quite expressionless as he bowed solemnly before Carrier and then took the chair which was indicated to him. Young Lalouët fetched a candelabra from the ante-room and carried it into the audience chamber: then he closed the communicating doors. The candelabra he placed on a console-table immediately behind Carrier's desk and chair, so that the latter's face remained in complete shadow, whilst the light fell full upon Chauvelin.

"Well! what is it?" queried the proconsul roughly. "What is this story of English spies inside Nantes? How did they get here? Who is responsible for keeping such rabble out of our city? Name of a dog, but someone has been careless of duty! and carelessness these days is closely allied to treason."

He talked loudly and volubly—his inordinate terror causing the words to come tumbling, almost incoherently, out of his mouth. Finally, he turned on Chauvelin with a snarl like an angry cat:

"And how comes it, citizen," he added savagely, "that you alone here in Nantes are acquainted with the whereabouts of those dangerous spies?"

"I caught sight of them," rejoined Chauvelin calmly, "this afternoon after I left you. I knew we should have them here, the moment citizen Martin-Roget brought the Kernogans into the city. The woman is the wife of one of them."

"Curse that blundering fool Martin-Roget for bringing that rabble about our ears, and those assassins inside our gates."

"Nay! Why should you complain, citizen proconsul?" rejoined Chauvelin in his blandest manner. "Surely you are not going to let the English spies escape this time? And if you succeed in laying them by the heels—there where everyone else has failed—you will have earned twenty thousand *francs* and the thanks of the entire Committee of Public Safety."

He paused: and young Lalouët interposed with his impudent laugh:

"Go on, Citizen Chauvelin," he said, "if there is twenty thousand *francs* to be made out of this game, I'll warrant that the proconsul will take a hand in it—eh, Carrier?"

And with the insolent familiarity of a terrier teasing a grizzly he tweaked the great man's ear.

Chauvelin in the meanwhile had drawn the packet of papers from his pocket and untied the ribbon that held them together. He now spread the papers out on the desk.

"What are these?" queried Carrier.

"A few papers," replied Chauvelin, "which one of your Marats, Paul Friche by name, picked up in the wake of the Englishmen. I caught sight of them in the far distance and sent the Marats after them. For a while Paul Friche kept on their track, but after that they disappeared in the darkness."

"Who were the senseless louts," growled Carrier, "who allowed a pack of foreign assassins to escape? I'll soon make them disappear—in the Loire."

"You will do what you like about that, citizen Carrier," retorted Chauvelin drily; "in the meanwhile you would do well to examine these papers."

He sorted these out, examined them one by one, then passed them across to Carrier. Lalouët, impudent and inquisitive, sat on the corner of the desk, dangling his legs. With scant ceremony he snatched one paper after another out of Carrier's hands and examined them curiously.

"Can you understand all this gibberish?" he asked airily. "Jean Baptiste, my friend, how much English do you know?"

"Not much," replied the proconsul, "but enough to recognise that abominable doggrel rhyme which has gone the round of the Committees of Public Safety throughout the country."

"I know it by heart," rejoined young Lalouët. "I was in Paris once, when citizen Robespierre received a copy of it. Name of a dog!" added the youngster with a coarse laugh, "how he cursed!"

It is doubtful however if citizen Robespierre did on that occasion curse quite so volubly as Carrier did now.

"If I only knew why that *satané* Englishman throws so much calligraphy about," he said, "I would be easier in my mind. Now this senseless rhyme—I don't see—"

"Its importance?" broke in Chauvelin quietly. "I dare say not. On the face of it, it appears foolish and childish: but it is intended as a taunt and is really a poor attempt at humour. They are a queer people these English. If you knew them as I do, you would not be surprised to see a man scribbling off a cheap joke before embarking on an enterprise which may cost him his head."

"And this inane rubbish is of that sort," concluded young Lalouët. And in his thin high treble he began reciting:

"We seek him here;
We seek him there!
Those Frenchies seek him everywhere.
Is he in heaven?
Is he in h——ll?
That demmed elusive Pimpernel?"

"Pointless and offensive," he said as he tossed the paper back on the table.

"A cursed *aristo* that Englishman of yours," growled Carrier. "Oh! when I get him—"

He made an expressive gesture which made Lalouët laugh.

"What else have we got in the way of documents, Citizen Chauvelin?" he asked.

"There is a letter," replied the latter.

"Read it," commanded Carrier. "Or rather translate it as you read. I don't understand the whole of the gibberish."

And Chauvelin, taking up a sheet of paper which was covered with neat, minute writing, began to read aloud, translating the English into French as he went along:

"'Here we are at last, my dear Tony! Didn't I tell you that we can get in anywhere despite all precautions taken against us!'"

"The impudent devils!" broke in Carrier.

"'Did you really think that they could keep us out of Nantes while Lady Anthony Dewhurst is a prisoner in their hands?'"

"Who is that?"

"The Kernogan woman. As I told you just now, she is married to an Englishman who is named Dewhurst and who is one of the members of that thrice cursed League."

Then he continued to read:

"'And did you really suppose that they would spot half a dozen English gentlemen in the guise of peat-gatherers, returning at dusk and covered with grime from their work? Not like, friend Tony! Not like! If you happen to meet mine engaging friend M. Chambertin before I have that privilege myself, tell him I pray you, with my regards, that I am looking forward to the pleasure of making a long nose at him once more. Calais, Boulogne, Paris—now Nantes—the scenes of his triumphs multiply exceedingly.'"

"What in the devil's name does all this mean?" queried Carrier with an oath.

"You don't understand it?" rejoined Chauvelin quietly.

"No. I do not."

"Yet I translated quite clearly."

"It is not the language that puzzles me. The contents seem to me such drivel. The man wants secrecy, what? He is supposed to be astute, resourceful, above all mysterious and enigmatic. Yet he writes to his friend—matter of no importance between them, recollections of the past, known to them both—and threats for the future, equally futile and senseless. I cannot reconcile it all. It puzzles me."

"And it would puzzle me," rejoined Chauvelin, while the ghost of a smile curled his thin lips, "did I not know the man. Futile? Senseless, you say? Well, he does futile and senseless things one moment and amazing deeds of personal bravery and of astuteness the next. He is three parts a braggart too. He wanted you, me—all of us to know how he and his followers succeeded in eluding our vigilance and entered our closely-guarded city in the guise of grimy peat-gatherers. Now I come to think of it, it was easy enough for them to do that.

"Those peat-gatherers who live inside the city boundaries return from their work as the night falls in. Those cursed English adventurers are passing clever at disguise—they are born mountebanks the lot of them. Money and impudence, they have in plenty. They could easily borrow or purchase some filthy rags from the cottages on the dunes, then mix with the crowd on its return to the city. I dare say it was cleverly done. That Scarlet Pimpernel is just a clever adventurer and nothing more. So far, his marvellous good luck has carried him through. Now we shall see."

Carrier had listened in silence. Something of his colleague's calm had by this time communicated itself to him too. He was no longer raving like an infuriated bull—his terror no longer made a half-cringing, wholly savage brute of him. He was sprawling across the desk—his arms folded, his deep-set eyes studying closely the well-nigh inscrutable face of Chauvelin. Young Lalouët too had lost something of his impudence. That mysterious spell which seemed to emanate from the elusive personality of the bold English adventurer had been cast over these two callous, bestial natures, humbling their arrogance and making them feel that here was no ordinary situation to be dealt with by smashing, senseless hitting and the spilling of innocent blood. Both felt instinctively too that this man Chauvelin, however wholly he may have failed in the past, was nevertheless still the only man who might grapple successfully with the elusive and adventurous foe.

"Are you assuming, Citizen Chauvelin," queried Carrier after a while, "that this packet of papers was dropped purposely by the Englishman, so that it might get into our hands?"

"There is always such a possibility," replied Chauvelin drily. "With that type of man, one must be prepared to meet the unexpected."

"Then go on, Citizen Chauvelin. What else is there among those *satané* papers?"

"Nothing further of importance. There is a map of Nantes, and one of the coast and of Le Croisic. There is a cutting from *Le Moniteur* dated last September, and one from the *London Gazette* dated three years ago. The *Moniteur* makes reference to the production of *Athalie* at the Théâtre Molière, and the *London Gazette* to the sale of fat cattle at an Agricultural Show. There is a receipted account from a London tailor for two hundred pounds worth of clothes supplied, and one from a Lyons mercer for an hundred *francs* worth of silk cravats. Then there is the one letter which alone amidst all this rubbish appears to be of any consequence—"

He took up the last paper; his hand was still quite steady.

"Read the letter," said Carrier.

"It is addressed in the English fashion to Lady Anthony Dewhurst," continued Chauvelin slowly, "the Kernogan woman, you know, citizen. It says:

"'Keep up your courage. Your friends are inside the city and on the watch. Try the door of your prison every evening at one hour before midnight. Once you will find it yield. Slip out and creep noiselessly down the stairs. At the bottom a friendly hand will be stretched out to you. Take it with confidence—it will lead you to safety and to freedom. Courage and secrecy.'"

Lalouët had been looking over his shoulder while he read: now he pointed to the bottom of the letter.

"And there is the device," he said, "we have heard so much about of late—a five-petalled flower drawn in red ink—the Scarlet Pimpernel, I presume."

"Aye! the Scarlet Pimpernel," murmured Chauvelin, "as you say!

Braggadocio on his part or accident, his letters are certainly in our hands now and will prove—must prove, the tool whereby we can be even with him once and for all."

"And you, Citizen Chauvelin," interposed Carrier with a sneer, "are mighty lucky to have me to help you this time. I am not going to be fooled, as Candeille and you were fooled last September, as you were fooled in Calais and Héron in Paris. I shall be seeing this time to the capture of those English adventurers."

"And that capture should not be difficult," added Lalouët with a complacent laugh. "Your famous adventurer's luck hath deserted him this time: an all-powerful proconsul is pitted against him and the loss of his papers hath destroyed the anonymity on which he reckons."

Chauvelin paid no heed to the fatuous remarks.

How little did this flippant young braggart and this coarse-grained bully understand the subtle workings of that same adventurer's brain! He himself—one of the most astute men of the day—found it difficult. Even now—the losing of those letters in the open streets of Nantes—it was part of a plan. Chauvelin could have staked his head on that—a part of a plan for the liberation of Lady Anthony Dewhurst—but what plan?—what plan?

He took up the letter which his colleague had thrown down: he fingered it, handled it, letting the paper crackle through his fingers, as if he expected it to yield up the secret which it contained. The time had come—of that he felt no doubt—when he could at last be even with his enemy. He had endured more bitter humiliation at the hands of this elusive Pimpernel than he would have thought himself capable of bearing a couple of years ago. But the time had come at last—if only he kept his every faculty on the alert, if Fate helped him and his own nerves stood the strain. Above all if this blundering, self-satisfied Carrier could be reckoned on!...

There lay the one great source of trouble! He—Chauvelin—had no power: he was disgraced—a failure—a nonentity to be sneered at. He might protest, entreat, wring his hands, weep tears of blood and not one man would stir a finger to help him: this brute who sprawled here across his desk would not lend him half a dozen men to enable him to lay by the heels the most powerful enemy the Government of the Terror had ever known. Chauvelin inwardly ground his teeth with rage at his own impotence, at his own dependence on this clumsy lout, who was at this moment possessed of powers which he himself would give half his life to obtain.

But on the other hand, he did possess a power which no one could take from him—the power to use others for the furtherance of his own aims—to efface himself while others danced as puppets to his piping. Carrier had the power: he had spies, Marats, prison-guards at his disposal. He was greedy for the reward, and cupidity and fear would make of him a willing instrument. All that Chauvelin need do was to use that instrument for his own ends. One would be the head to direct, the other—a mere insentient tool.

From this moment onwards every minute, every second and every fraction of a second would be full of portent, full of possibilities. Sir Percy Blakeney was in Nantes with at least three or four members of his League: he was at this very moment taxing every fibre of his resourceful brain in order to devise a means whereby he could rescue his friend's wife from the fate which was awaiting her: to gain this end he would dare everything, risk everything—risk and dare a great deal more than he had ever dared and risked before.

Chauvelin was finding a grim pleasure in reviewing the situation, in envisaging the danger of failure which he knew lay in wait for him, unless he too was able to call to his aid all the astuteness, all the daring, all the resource of his own fertile brain. He studied his colleague's face keenly—that sullen, savage expression in it, the arrogance, the blundering vanity. It was terrible to have to humour and fawn to a creature of that stamp when all one's hopes, all one's future, one's ideals and the welfare of one's country were at stake.

But this additional difficulty only served to whet the man's appetite for action. He drew in a long breath of delight, like a captive who first after many days and months of weary anguish scents freedom and ozone. He straightened out his shoulders. A gleam of triumph and of hope shot out of his keen pale eyes. He studied Carrier and he studied Lalouët and he felt that he could master them both—quietly, diplomatically, with subtle skill that would not alarm the proconsul's rampant self-esteem: and whilst this coarse-fibred brute gloated in anticipatory pleasure over the handling of a few thousand *francs*, and whilst Martin-Roget dreamed of a clumsy revenge against one woman and one man who had wronged him four years ago, he—Chauvelin—would pursue his work of striking at the enemy of the Revolution—of bringing to his knees the man who spent life and fortune in combating its ideals and in frustrating its aims. The destruction of such a foe was worthy a patriot's ambition.

On the other hand, some of Carrier's bullying arrogance had gone.

He was terrified to the very depths of his cowardly heart, and for once he was turning away from his favourite Jacques Lalouët and inclined to lean on Chauvelin for advice. Robespierre had been known to tremble at sight of that small scarlet device, how much more had he—Carrier—cause to be afraid. He knew his own limitations and he was terrified of the assassin's dagger. As Marat had perished, so he too might end his days, and the English spies were credited with murderous intentions and superhuman power. In his innermost self, Carrier knew that despite countless failures Chauvelin was mentally his superior, and though he never would own to this and at this moment did not attempt to shed his over-bearing manner, he was watching the other keenly and anxiously, ready to follow the guidance of an intellect stronger than his own.

At last Carrier elected to speak.

"And now, Citizen Chauvelin," he said, "we know how we stand. We know that the English assassins are in Nantes. The question is how are we going to lay them by the heels?"

Chauvelin gave him no direct reply. He was busy collecting his precious papers together and thrusting them back into the pocket of his coat. Then he said quietly:

"It is through the Kernogan woman that we can get hold of him."

"How?"

"Where she is, there will the Englishmen be. They are in Nantes for the sole purpose of getting the woman and her father out of your clutches—"

"Then it will be a fine haul inside the Rat Mort," ejaculated Carrier with a chuckle. "Eh, Jacques, you young scamp? You and I must go and see that, what? You have been complaining that life was getting monotonous. Drownages—Republican marriages! They have all palled in their turn on your jaded appetite—But the capture of the English assassins, eh?—of that League of the Scarlet Pimpernel which has even caused citizen Robespierre much uneasiness—that will stir up your sluggish blood, you lazy young vermin!—Go on, go on, Citizen Chauvelin, I am vastly interested!"

He rubbed his dry, bony hands together and cackled with glee. Chauvelin interposed quietly:

"Inside the Rat Mort, eh, citizen?" he queried.

"Why, yes. Citizen Martin-Roget means to convey the Kernogan woman to the Rat Mort, doesn't he?"

"He does."

"And you say that where the Kernogan woman is there the Englishmen will be—"

"The inference is obvious."

"Which means ten thousand *francs* from that fool Martin-Roget for having the wench and her father arrested inside the Rat Mort! and twenty thousand for the capture of the English spies—Have you forgotten, Citizen Chauvelin," he added with a raucous cry of triumph, "that Commandant Fleury has my orders to make a raid on the Rat Mort this night with half a company of my Marats, and to arrest every one whom they find inside?"

"The Kernogan wench is not at the Rat Mort yet," quoth Chauvelin drily, "and you have refused to lend a hand in having her conveyed thither."

"I can't do it, my little Chauvelin," rejoined Carrier, somewhat sobered by this reminder. "I can't do it—you understand—my Marats taking an *aristo* to a house of ill-fame where presently I have her arrested—it won't do—it won't do—you don't know how I am spied upon just now—It really would not do—I can't be mixed up in that part of the affair. The wench must go to the Rat Mort of her own free will, or the whole plan falls to the ground—That fool Martin-Roget must think of a way—it's his affair, after all. He must see to it—Or you can think of a way," he added, assuming the coaxing ways of a tiger-cat; "you are so clever, my little Chauvelin."

"Yes," replied Chauvelin quietly, "I can think of a way. The Kernogan wench shall leave the house of Citizeness Adet and walk into the tavern of the Rat Mort of her own free will. Your reputation, citizen Carrier," he added without the slightest apparent trace of a sneer, "your reputation shall be safeguarded in this matter. But supposing that in the interval of going from the one house to the other the English adventurer succeeds in kidnapping her—"

"Pah! is that likely?" quoth Carrier with a shrug of the shoulders.

"Exceedingly likely, citizen; and you would not doubt it if you knew this Scarlet Pimpernel as I do. I have seen him at his nefarious work. I know what he can do. There is nothing that he would not venture—there are few ventures in which he does not succeed. He is as strong as an ox, as agile as a cat. He can see in the dark and he can always vanish in a crowd. Here, there and everywhere, you never know where he will appear. He is a past master in the art of disguise and he is a born mountebank. Believe me, citizen, we shall want all the resources of our joint intellects to frustrate the machinations of such a foe."

Carrier mused for a moment in silence.

"H'm!" he said after a while, and with a sardonic laugh. "You may be right, Citizen Chauvelin. You have had experience with the rascal—you ought to know him. We won't leave anything to chance—don't be afraid of that. My Marats will be keen on the capture. We'll promise commandant Fleury a thousand *francs* for himself and another thousand to be distributed among his men if we lay hands on the English assassins tonight. We'll leave nothing to chance," he reiterated with an oath.

"In which case, Citizen Carrier, you must on your side agree to two things," rejoined Chauvelin firmly.

"What are they?"

"You must order Commandant Fleury to place himself and half a company of his Marats at my disposal."

"What else?"

"You must allow them to lend a hand if there is an attempt to kidnap the Kernogan wench while she is being conveyed to the Rat Mort—"

Carrier hesitated for a second or two, but only for form's sake: it was his nature whenever he was forced to yield to do so grudgingly.

"Very well!" he said at last. "I'll order Fleury to be on the watch and to interfere if there is any street-brawling outside or near the Rat Mort. Will that suit you?"

"Perfectly. I shall be on the watch too—somewhere close by—I'll warn commandant Fleury if I suspect that the English are making ready for a coup outside the tavern. Personally, I think it unlikely—because the Duc de Kernogan will be inside the Rat Mort all the time, and he too will be the object of the Englishmen's attacks on his behalf. Citizen Martin-Roget too has about a score or so of his friends posted outside his sister's house: they are lads from his village who hate the Kernogans as much as he does himself. Still! I shall feel easier in my mind now that I am certain of Commandant Fleury's co-operation."

"Then it seems to me that we have arranged everything satisfactorily, what?"

"Everything, except the exact moment when Commandant Fleury shall advance with his men to the door of the tavern and demand admittance in the name of the Republic."

"Yes, he will have to make quite sure that the whole of our quarry is inside the net, eh?—before he draws the strings—or all our pretty plans fall to nought."

"As you say," rejoined Chauvelin, "we must make sure. Supposing therefore that we get the wench safely into the tavern, that we have her there with her father, what we shall want will be someone in observation—someone who can help us to draw our birds into the snare just when we are ready for them. Now there is a man whom I have in my mind: he hath name Paul Friche and is one of your Marats—a surly, ill-conditioned giant—he was on guard outside Le Bouffay this afternoon—I spoke to him—he would suit our purpose admirably."

"What do you want him to do?"

"Only to make himself look as like a Nantese cutthroat as he can—"

"He looks like one already," broke in Jacques Lalouët with a laugh.

"So much the better. He'll excite no suspicion in that case in the minds of the frequenters of the Rat Mort. Then I'll instruct him to start a brawl—a fracas—soon after the arrival of the Kernogan wench. The row will inevitably draw the English adventurers hot-haste to the spot, either in the hope of getting the Kernogans away during the *mêlée* or with a view to protecting them. As soon as they have appeared upon the scene, the half company of the Marats will descend on the house and arrest everyone inside it."

"It all sounds remarkably simple," rejoined Carrier, and with a leer of satisfaction he turned to Jacques Lalouët.

"What think you of it, citizen?" he asked.

"That it sounds so remarkably simple," replied young Lalouët, "that personally I should be half afraid—"

"Of what?" queried Chauvelin blandly.

"If you fail, Citizen Chauvelin—"

"Impossible!"

"If the Englishmen do not appear?"

"Even so the citizen proconsul will have lost nothing. He will merely have failed to gain the twenty thousand *francs*. But the Kernogans will still be in his power and Citizen Martin-Roget's ten thousand *francs* are in any case assured."

"Friend Jean-Baptiste," concluded Lalouët with his habitual insolent familiarity, "you had better do what Citizen Chauvelin wants. Ten thousand *francs* are good—and thirty better still. Our privy purse has been empty far too long, and I for one would like the handling of a few brisk notes."

"It will only be twenty-eight, citizen Lalouët," interposed Chauvelin blandly, "for Commandant Fleury will want one thousand *francs* and his men another thousand to stimulate their zeal. Still! I imagine that these hard times twenty-eight thousand *francs* are worth fighting for."

"You seem to be fighting and planning and scheming for nothing, Citizen Chauvelin," retorted young Lalouët with a sneer. "What are you going to gain, I should like to know, by the capture of that daredevil Englishman?"

"Oh!" replied Chauvelin suavely, "I shall gain the citizen proconsul's regard, I hope—and yours too, Citizen Lalouët. I want nothing more except the success of my plan."

Young Lalouët jumped down to his feet. He shrugged his shoulders and through his fine eyes shot a glance of mockery and scorn on the thin, shrunken figure of the Terrorist.

"How you do hate that Englishman, Citizen Chauvelin," he said with a light laugh.

Carrier having fully realised that he in any case stood to make a vast sum of money out of the capture of the band of English spies, gave his support generously to Chauvelin's scheme. Fleury, summoned into his presence, was ordered to place himself and half a company of Marats at the disposal of Citizen Chauvelin. He demurred and growled like a bear with a sore head at being placed under the orders of a civilian, but it was not easy to run counter to the proconsul's will. A good deal of swearing, one or two overt threats and the citizen *commandant* was reduced to submission. The promise of a thousand *francs*, when the reward for the capture of the English spies was paid out by a grateful government, overcame his last objections.

"I think you should rid yourself of that obstinate oaf," was young Lalouët's cynical comment, when Fleury had finally left the audience chamber; "he is too argumentative for my taste."

Chauvelin smiled quietly to himself. He cared little what became of every one of these Nantese louts once his great object had been attained.

"I need not trouble you further, Citizen Carrier," he said as he finally rose to take his leave. "I shall have my hands full until I myself lay that meddlesome Englishman bound and gagged at your feet."

The phrase delighted Carrier's insensate vanity. He was over-gracious to Chauvelin now.

"You shall do that at the Rat Mort, Citizen Chauvelin," he said with marked affability, "and I myself will commend you for your zeal to the Committee of Public Safety."

"Always supposing," interposed Jacques Lalouët with his cynical laugh, "that Citizen Chauvelin does not let the whole rabble slip through his fingers."

"If I do," concluded Chauvelin drily, "you may drag the Loire for my body tomorrow."

"Oh!" laughed Carrier, "we won't trouble to do that. *Au revoir*, Citizen Chauvelin," he added with one of his grandiloquent gestures of dismissal, "I wish you luck at the Rat Mort tonight."

Jacques Lalouët ushered Chauvelin out. When he was finally left standing alone at the head of the stairs and young Lalouët's footsteps had ceased to resound across the floors of the rooms beyond, he remained quite still for a while, his eyes fixed into vacancy, his face set and expressionless; and through his lips there came a long-drawn-out sigh of intense satisfaction.

"And now, my fine Scarlet Pimpernel," he murmured softly, "once more *à nous deux*."

Then he ran swiftly down the stairs and a moment later was once more speeding toward Le Bouffay.

CHAPTER 5

The Message of Hope

After Martin-Roget and Chauvelin had left her, Yvonne had sat for a long time motionless, almost unconscious. It seemed as if gradually, hour by hour, minute by minute, her every feeling of courage and of hope were deserting her. Three days now she had been separated from her father—three days she had been under the constant supervision of a woman who had not a single thought of compassion or of mercy for the "aristocrat" whom she hated so bitterly.

At night, curled up on a small bundle of dank straw Yvonne had made vain efforts to snatch a little sleep. Ever since the day when she had been ruthlessly torn away from the protection of her dear milor, she had persistently clung to the belief that he would find the means to come to her, to wrest her from the cruel fate which her pitiless enemies had devised for her. She had clung to that hope throughout that dreary journey from dear England to this abominable city. She had clung to it even whilst her father knelt at her feet in an agony of remorse. She had clung to hope while Martin-Roget alternately coaxed and terrorised her, while her father was dragged away from her, while she endured untold misery, starvation, humiliation at the hands of Louise Adet: but now—quite unaccountably—that hope seemed suddenly to have fled from her, leaving her lonely and inexpressibly desolate. That small, shrunken figure which, wrapped in a dark mantle, had stood in the corner of the room watching her like a serpent watches its prey, had seemed like the forerunner of the fate with which Martin-Roget, gloating over her helplessness, had already threatened her.

She knew, of course, that neither from him, nor from the callous brute who governed Nantes, could she expect the slightest justice or mercy. She had been brought here by Martin-Roget not only to die, but to suffer grievously at his hands in return for a crime for which she personally was in no way responsible. To hope for mercy from him at the eleventh hour were worse than futile. Her already overburdened heart ached at thought of her father: he suffered all that she suffered, and in addition he must be tortured with anxiety for her and with remorse. Sometimes she was afraid that under the stress of desperate soul-agony he might perhaps have been led to suicide. She knew nothing of what had happened to him, where he was, nor whether privations and lack of food or sleep, together with Martin-Roget's threats, had by now weakened his morale and turned his pride into humiliating submission.

A distant tower-clock struck the evening hours one after the other. Yvonne for the past three days had only been vaguely conscious of time. Martin-Roget had spoken of a few hours' respite only, of the proconsul's desire to be soon rid of her. Well! this meant no doubt that the morrow would see the end of it all—the end of her life which such a brief while ago seemed so full of delight, of love and of happiness.

The end of her life! She had hardly begun to live and her dear milor had whispered to her such sweet promises of endless vistas of bliss.

Yvonne shivered beneath her thin gown. The north-westerly blast came in cruel gusts through the unglazed window and a vague instinct of self-preservation caused Yvonne to seek shelter in the one corner of the room where the icy draught did not penetrate quite so freely.

Eight, nine and ten struck from the tower-clock far away: she heard these sounds as in a dream. Tired, cold and hungry her vitality at that moment was at its lowest ebb—and, with her back resting against the wall she fell presently into a torpor-like sleep.

Suddenly something roused her, and in an instant, she sat up—wide-awake and wide-eyed, every one of her senses conscious and on the alert. Something had roused her—at first, she could not say what it was—or remember. Then presently individual sounds detached themselves from the buzzing in her ears. Hitherto the house had always been so still; except on the isolated occasions when Martin-Roget had come to visit her and his heavy tread had caused every loose board in the tumble-down house to creak, it was only Louise Adet's shuffling footsteps which had roused the dormant echoes, when she crept upstairs either to her own room, or to throw a piece of stale bread to her prisoner.

But now—it was neither Martin-Roget's heavy footfall nor the shuffling gait of Louise Adet which had roused Yvonne from her trance-like sleep. It was a gentle, soft, creeping step which was slowly, cautiously mounting the stairs. Yvonne crouching against the wall could count every tread—now and then a board creaked—now and then the footsteps halted.

Yvonne, wide-eyed, her heart stirred by a nameless terror was watching the door.

The piece of tallow-candle flickered in the draught. Its feeble light just touched the remote corner of the room. And Yvonne heard those soft, creeping footsteps as they reached the landing and came to a halt outside the door.

Every drop of blood in her seemed to be frozen by terror: her knees shook: her heart almost stopped its beating.

Under the door something small and white had just been introduced—a scrap of paper; and there it remained—white against the darkness of the unwashed boards—a mysterious message left here by an unknown hand, whilst the unknown footsteps softly crept down the stairs again.

For a while longer Yvonne remained as she was—cowering against the wall—like a timid little animal, fearful lest that innocent-looking object hid some unthought-of danger. Then at last she gathered courage. Trembling with excitement she raised herself to her knees and then on hands and knees—for she was very weak and faint—she crawled up to that mysterious piece of paper and picked it up.

Her trembling hand closed over it. With wide staring terror-filled eyes she looked all round the narrow room, ere she dared cast one more glance on that mysterious scrap of paper. Then she struggled to her feet and tottered up to the table. She sat down and with fingers numbed with cold she smoothed out the paper and held it close to the light, trying to read what was written on it.

Her sight was blurred. She had to pull herself resolutely together, for suddenly she felt ashamed of her weakness and her overwhelming terror yielded to feverish excitement.

The scrap of paper contained a message—a message addressed to her in that name of which she was so proud—the name which she thought she would never be allowed to bear again: Lady Anthony Dewhurst. She reiterated the words several times, her lips clinging lovingly to them—and just below them there was a small device, drawn in red ink—a tiny flower with five petals—

Yvonne frowned and murmured, vaguely puzzled—no longer frightened now: "A flower—drawn in red—what can it mean?"

And as a vague memory struggled for expression in her troubled mind she added half aloud: "Oh! if it should be—!"

But now suddenly all her fears fell away from her. Hope was once more knocking at the gates of her heart—vague memories had taken definite shape—the mysterious letter—the message of hope—the red flower—all were gaining significance. She stooped low to read the letter by the feeble light of the flickering candle. She read it through with her eyes first—then with her lips in a soft murmur, while her mind gradually took in all that it meant for her.

"Keep up your courage. Your friends are inside the city and on the watch. Try the door of your prison every evening at one hour before midnight. Once you will find it yield. Slip out and creep noiselessly down the stairs. At the bottom a friendly hand will be stretched out for you. Take it with confidence—it will lead you to safety and to freedom. Courage and secrecy."

When she had finished reading, her eyes were swimming in tears. There was no longer any doubt in her mind about the message now, for her dear milor had so often spoken to her about the brave Scarlet Pimpernel who had risked his precious life many a time ere this, in order to render service to the innocent and the oppressed. And now, of a surety, this message came from him: from her dear milor and from his gallant chief. There was the small device—the little red flower which had so often brought hope to despairing hearts. And it was more than hope that it brought to Yvonne. It brought certitude and happiness, and a sweet, tender remorse that she should ever have doubted. She ought to have known all along that everything would be for the best: she had no right ever to have given way to despair. In her heart she prayed for forgiveness from her dear absent milor.

How could she ever doubt him? Was it likely that he would abandon her?—he and that brave friend of his whose powers were indeed magical. Why! she ought to have done her best to keep up her physical as well as her mental faculties—who knows? But perhaps physical strength might be of inestimable value both to herself and to her gallant rescuers presently.

She took up the stale brown bread and ate it resolutely. She drank some water and then stamped round the room to get some warmth into her limbs.

A distant clock had struck ten a while ago—and if possible, she ought to get an hour's rest before the time came for her to be strong and to act: so, she shook up her meagre straw paillasse and lay down, determined if possible to get a little sleep—for indeed she felt that that was just what her dear milor would have wished her to do.

Thus, time went by—waking or dreaming, Yvonne could never afterwards have said in what state she waited during that one long hour which separated her from the great, blissful moment. The bit of candle burnt low and presently died out. After that Yvonne remained quite still upon the straw, in total darkness: no light came in through the tiny window, only the cold north-westerly wind blew in in gusts. But of a surety the prisoner who was within sight of freedom felt neither cold nor fatigue now.

The tower-clock in the distance struck the quarters with dreary monotony.

The last stroke of eleven ceased to vibrate through the stillness of the winter's night.

Yvonne roused herself from the torpor-like state into which she had fallen. She tried to struggle to her feet, but intensity of excitement had caused a strange numbness to invade her limbs. She could hardly move. A second or two ago it had seemed to her that she heard a gentle scraping noise at the door—a drawing of bolts—the grating of a key in the lock—then again, soft, shuffling footsteps that came and went and that were not those of Louise Adet.

At last Yvonne contrived to stand on her feet; but she had to close her eyes and to remain quite still for a while after that, for her ears were buzzing and her head swimming: she thought that she must fall if she moved and mayhap lose consciousness.

But this state of weakness only lasted a few seconds: the next she had groped her way to the door and her hand had found the iron latch. It yielded. Then she waited, calling up all her strength—for the hour had come wherein she must not only think and act for herself, but think of every possibility which might occur, and act as she imagined her dear lord would require it of her.

She pressed the clumsy iron latch further: it yielded again, and anon she was able to push open the door.

Excited yet confident she tiptoed out of the room. The darkness—like unto pitch—was terribly disconcerting. With the exception of her narrow prison Yvonne had only once seen the interior of the house and that was when, half fainting, she had been dragged across its threshold and up the stairs. She had therefore only a very vague idea as to where the stairs lay and how she was to get about without stumbling.

Slowly and cautiously she crept a few paces forward, then she turned and carefully closed the door behind her. There was not a sound inside the house: everything was silent around her: neither footfall nor whisperings reached her straining ears. She felt about her with her hands, she crouched down on her knees: anon she discovered the head of the stairs.

Then suddenly she drew back, like a frightened hare conscious of danger. All the blood rushed back to her heart, making it beat so violently that she once more felt sick and faint. A sound—gentle as a breath—had broken that absolute and dead silence which up to now had given her confidence. She felt suddenly that she was no longer alone in the darkness—that somewhere close by there was someone—friend or foe—who was lying in watch for her—that somewhere in the darkness something moved and breathed.

The crackling of the paper inside her kerchief served to remind her that her dear milor was on the watch and that the blessed message had spoken of a friendly hand which would be stretched out to her and which she was enjoined to take with confidence. Reassured she crept on again, and *anon* a softly murmured: "Hush—sh!—sh!—" reached her ear. It seemed to come from down below—not very far—and Yvonne, having once more located the head of the stairs with her hands, began slowly to creep downstairs—softly as a mouse—step by step—but every time that a board creaked she paused, terrified, listening for Louise Adet's heavy footstep, for a sound that would mean the near approach of danger.

"Hush—sh—sh" came again as a gentle murmur from below and the something that moved and breathed in the darkness seemed to draw nearer to Yvonne.

A few more seconds of soul-racking suspense, a few more steps

173

down the creaking stairs and she felt a strong hand laid upon her wrist and heard a muffled voice whisper in English:

"All is well! Trust me! Follow me!"

She did not recognise the voice, even though there was something vaguely familiar in its intonation. Yvonne did not pause to conjecture: she had been made happy by the very sound of the language which stood to her for every word of love she had ever heard: it restored her courage and her confidence in their fullest measure.

Obeying the whispered command, Yvonne was content now to follow her mysterious guide who had hold of her hand. The stairs were steep and winding—at a turn she perceived a feeble light at their foot down below. Up against this feeble light the form of her guide was silhouetted in a broad, dark mass. Yvonne could see nothing of him beyond the square outline of his shoulders and that of his sugar-loaf hat. Her mind now was thrilled with excitement and her fingers closed almost convulsively round his hand. He led her across Louise Adet's back kitchen. It was from here that the feeble light came—from a small oil lamp which stood on the centre table. It helped to guide Yvonne and her mysterious friend to the bottom of the stairs, then across the kitchen to the front door, where again complete darkness reigned. But soon Yvonne—who was following blindly whithersoever she was led— heard the click of a latch and the grating of a door upon its hinges: a cold current of air caught her straight in the face. She could see nothing, for it seemed to be as dark out of doors as in: but she had the sensation of that open door, of a threshold to cross, of freedom and happiness beckoning to her straight out of the gloom. Within the next second or two she would be out of this terrible place; its squalid and dank walls would be behind her. On ahead in that thrice welcome obscurity her dear milor and his powerful friend were beckoning to her to come boldly on—their protecting arms were already stretched out for her; it seemed to her excited fancy as if the cold night-wind brought to her ears the echo of their endearing words.

She filled her lungs with the keen winter air: hope, happiness, excitement thrilled her every nerve.

"A short walk, my lady," whispered the guide, still speaking in English; "you are not cold?"

"No, no, I am not cold," she whispered in reply. "I am conscious of nothing save that I am free."

"And you are not afraid?"

"Indeed, indeed I am not afraid," she murmured fervently. "May

God reward you, sir, for what you do."

Again, there had been that certain something—vaguely familiar—in the way the man spoke which for the moment piqued Yvonne's curiosity. She did not, of a truth, know English well enough to detect the very obvious foreign intonation; she only felt that sometime in the dim and happy past she had heard this man speak. But even this vague sense of puzzlement she dismissed very quickly from her mind. Was she not taking everything on trust? Indeed, hope and confidence had a very firm hold on her at last.

CHAPTER 6

The Rat Mort

The guide had stepped out of the house into the street, Yvonne following closely on his heels. The night was very dark and the narrow little *Carrefour de la Poissonnerie* very sparsely lighted. Somewhere overhead on the right, something groaned and creaked persistently in the wind. A little further on a street lanthorn was swinging aloft, throwing a small circle of dim, yellowish light on the unpaved street below. By its fitful glimmer Yvonne could vaguely perceive the tall figure of her guide as he stepped out with noiseless yet firm tread, his shoulder brushing against the side of the nearest house as he kept closely within the shadow of its high wall. The sight of his broad back thrilled her. She had fallen to imagining whether this was not perchance that gallant and all-powerful Scarlet Pimpernel himself: the mysterious friend of whom her dear milor so often spoke with an admiration that was akin to worship. He too was probably tall and broad—for English gentlemen were usually built that way; and Yvonne's over-excited mind went galloping on the wings of fancy, and in her heart, she felt that she was glad that she had suffered so much, and then lived through such a glorious moment as this.

Now from the narrow unpaved yard in front of the house the guide turned sharply to the right. Yvonne could only distinguish outlines. The streets of Nantes were familiar to her, and she knew pretty well where she was. The lanthorn inside the clock tower of Le Bouffay guided her—it was now on her right—the house wherein she had been kept a prisoner, these past three days, was built against the walls of the great prison house. She knew that she was in the *Carrefour de la Poissonnerie.*

She felt neither fatigue nor cold, for she was wildly excited. The keen north-westerly wind searched all the weak places in her worn clothing and her thin shoes were wet through. But her courage up to this point had never once forsaken her. Hope and the feeling of freedom gave her marvellous strength, and when her guide paused a moment ere he turned the angle of the high wall and whispered hurriedly: "You have courage, my lady?" she was able to answer serenely: "In plenty, sir."

She tried to peer into the darkness in order to realise whither she was being led. The guide had come to a halt in front of the house which was next to that of Louise Adet: it projected several feet in front of the latter: the thing that had creaked so weirdly in the wind turned out to be a painted sign, which swung out from an iron bracket fixed into the wall. Yvonne could not read the writing on the sign, but she noticed that just above it there was a small window dimly lighted from within.

What sort of a house it was Yvonne could not, of course, see. The frontage was dark save for narrow streaks of light which peeped through the interstices of the door and through the chinks of ill-fastened shutters on either side. Not a sound came from within, but now that the guide had come to a halt it seemed to Yvonne—whose nerves and senses had become preternaturally acute—that the whole air around her was filled with muffled sounds, and when she stood still and strained her ears to listen she was conscious right through the inky blackness of vague forms—shapeless and silent—that glided past her in the gloom.

"Your friends will meet you here," the guide whispered as he pointed to the door of the house in front of him. "The door is on the latch. Push it open and walk in boldly. Then gather up all your courage, for you will find yourself in the company of poor people, whose manners are somewhat rougher than those to which you have been accustomed. But though the people are uncouth, you will find them kind. Above all you will find that they will pay no heed to you. So, I entreat you do not be afraid. Your friends would have arranged for a more refined place wherein to come and find you, but as you may well imagine they had no choice."

"I quite understand, sir," said Yvonne quietly, "and I am not afraid."

"Ah! that's brave!" he rejoined. "Then do as I tell you. I give you my word that inside that house you will be perfectly safe until such time as your friends are able to get to you. You may have to wait an hour, or even two; you must have patience. Find a quiet place in one of the corners of the room and sit there quietly, taking no notice of what goes on around you. You will be quite safe, and the arrival of your friends is only a question of time."

"My friends, sir?" she said earnestly, and her voice shook slightly as she spoke, "are you not one of the most devoted friends I can ever hope to have? I cannot find the words now wherewith to thank you, but—"

"I pray you do not thank me," he broke in gruffly, "and do not waste time in parleying. The open street is none too safe a place for you just now. The house is."

His hand was on the latch and he was about to push open the door, when Yvonne stopped him with a word.

"My father?" she whispered with passionate entreaty. "Will you help him too?"

"M. le Duc de Kernogan is as safe as you are, my lady," he replied. "He will join you *anon*. I pray you have no fears for him. Your friends are caring for him in the same way as they care for you."

"Then I shall see him—soon?"

"Very soon. And in the meanwhile," he added, "I pray you to sit quite still and to wait events—despite anything you may see or hear. Your father's safety and your own—not to speak of that of your friends—hangs on your quiescence, your silence, your obedience."

"I will remember, sir," rejoined Yvonne quietly. "I in my turn entreat you to have no fears for me."

Even while she said this, the man pushed the door open.

Yvonne had meant to be brave. Above all she had meant to be obedient. But even so, she could not help recoiling at sight of the place where she had just been told she must wait patiently and silently for an hour, or even two.

The room into which her guide now gently urged her forward was large and low, only dimly lighted by an oil-lamp which hung from the ceiling and emitted a thin stream of black smoke and evil smell. Such air as there was, was foul and reeked of the fumes of alcohol and charcoal, of the smoking lamp and of rancid grease. The walls had no doubt been whitewashed once, now they were of a dull greyish tint, with here and there hideous stains of red or the marks of a set of greasy fingers. The plaster was hanging in strips and lumps from the ceiling; it had fallen away in patches from the walls where it displayed the skeleton laths beneath. There were two doors in the wall immediately facing the front entrance, and on each side of the latter there was a small window, both insecurely shuttered. To Yvonne the whole place appeared unspeakably squalid and noisome. Even as she entered her ears caught the sound of hideous muttered blasphemy, followed by quickly suppressed hoarse and mirthless laughter and the piteous cry of an infant at the breast.

There were perhaps sixteen to twenty people in the room— amongst them a goodly number of women, some of whom had tiny, miserable atoms of humanity clinging to their ragged skirts. A group of men in tattered shirts, bare shins and sabots stood in the centre of the room and had apparently been in conclave when the entrance of Yvonne and her guide caused them to turn quickly to the door and to scan the new-comers with a furtive, suspicious look which would have been pathetic had it not been so full of evil intent. The muttered blasphemy had come from this group; one or two of the men spat upon the ground in the direction of the door, where Yvonne instinctively had remained rooted to the spot.

As for the women, they only betrayed their sex by the ragged clothes which they wore: there was not a face here which had on it a single line of softness or of gentleness: they might have been old women or young: their hair was of a uniform, nondescript colour, lank and unkempt, hanging in thin strands over their brows; their eyes were sunken, their cheeks either flaccid or haggard—there was no individuality amongst them—just one uniform sisterhood of wretchedness which had already gone hand in hand with crime.

Across one angle of the room there was a high wooden counter like a bar, on which stood a number of jugs and bottles, some chunks of bread and pieces of cheese, and a collection of pewter mugs. An old man and a fat, coarse-featured, middle-aged woman stood behind it and dispensed various noxious-looking liquors. Above their heads upon the grimy, tumble-down wall the Republican device "*Liberté! Egalité! Fraternité!*" was scrawled in charcoal in huge characters, and below it was scribbled the hideous doggrel which an impious mind had fashioned last autumn on the subject of the martyred queen.

Yvonne had closed her eyes for a moment as she entered; now she turned appealingly toward her guide.

"Must it be in here?" she asked.

"I am afraid it must," he replied with a sigh. "You told me that you would be brave."

She pulled herself together resolutely. "I will be brave," she said quietly.

"Ah! that's better," he rejoined. "I give you my word that you will be absolutely safe in here until such time as your friends can get to you. I entreat you to gather up your courage. I assure you that these wretched people are not unkind: misery—not unlike that which you yourself have endured—has made them what they are. No doubt we should have arranged for a better place for you wherein to await your friends if we had the choice. But you will understand that your safety and our own had to be our paramount consideration, and we had no choice."

"I quite understand, sir," said Yvonne valiantly, "and am already ashamed of my fears."

And without another word of protest she stepped boldly into the room.

For a moment or two the guide remained standing on the threshold, watching Yvonne's progress. She had already perceived an empty bench in the furthest angle of the room, up against the door opposite, where she hoped or believed that she could remain unmolested while she waited patiently and in silence as she had been ordered to do. She skirted the groups of men in the centre of the room as she went, but even so she felt more than she heard that muttered insults accompanied the furtive and glowering looks wherewith she was regarded. More than one wretch spat upon her skirts on the way.

But now she was in no sense frightened, only wildly excited; even her feeling of horror she contrived to conquer. The knowledge that her own attitude, and above all her obedience, would help her gallant rescuers in their work gave her enduring strength. She felt quite confident that within an hour or two she would be in the arms of her dear milor who had risked his life in order to come to her. It was indeed well worthwhile to have suffered as she had done, to endure all that she might yet have to endure, for the sake of the happiness which was in store for her.

She turned to give a last look at her guide—a look which was intended to reassure him completely as to her courage and her obedience: but already he had gone and had closed the door behind him, and quite against her will the sudden sense of loneliness and helplessness clutched at her heart with a grip that made it ache. She wished that she had succeeded in catching sight of the face of so valiant a friend: the fact that she was safely out of Louise Adet's vengeful clutches was due to the man who had just disappeared behind that door. It would be thanks to him presently if she saw her father again. Yvonne felt more convinced than ever that he was the Scarlet Pimpernel—milor's friend—who kept his valiant personality a mystery, even to those who owed their lives to him. She had seen the outline of his broad figure, she had felt the touch of his hand. Would she recognise these again when she met him in England in the happy days that were to come? In any case she thought that she would recognise the voice and the manner of speaking, so unlike that of any English gentleman she had known.

The man who had so mysteriously led Yvonne de Kernogan from the house of Louise Adet to the Rat Mort, turned away from the door of the tavern as soon as it had closed on the young girl, and started to go back the way he came.

At the angle formed by the high wall of the tavern he paused; a moving form had detached itself from the surrounding gloom and hailed him with a cautious whisper.

"Hist! citizen Martin-Roget, is that you?"

"Yes."

"Everything just as we anticipated?"

"Everything."

"And the wench safely inside?"

"Quite safely."

The other gave a low cackle, which might have been intended for a laugh.

"The simplest means," he said, "are always the best."

"She never suspected me. It was all perfectly simple. You are a magician, Citizen Chauvelin," added Martin-Roget grudgingly. "I never would have thought of such a clever ruse."

"You see," rejoined Chauvelin drily, "I graduated in the school of a master of all ruses—a master of daring and a past master in the art of mimicry. And hope was our great ally—the hope that never forsakes a prisoner—that of getting free. Your fair Yvonne had boundless faith in the power of her English friends, therefore she fell into our trap like a bird."

"And like a bird she shall struggle in vain after this," said Martin-Roget slowly. "Oh! that I could hasten the flight of time—the next few minutes will hang on me like hours. And I wish too it were not so bitterly cold," he added with a curse; "this north-westerly wind has got into my bones."

"On to your nerves, I imagine, citizen," retorted Chauvelin with a laugh; "for my part I feel as warm and comfortable as on a lovely day in June."

"Hark! Who goes there?" broke in the other man abruptly, as a solitary moving form detached itself from the surrounding inky blackness and the sound of measured footsteps broke the silence of the night.

"Quite in order, citizen!" was the prompt reply.

The shadowy form came a step or two further forward.

"Is it you, Citizen Fleury?" queried Chauvelin.

"Himself, citizen," replied the other.

The men had spoken in a whisper. Fleury now placed his hand on Chauvelin's arm.

"We had best not stand so close to the tavern," he said, "the night hawks are already about and we don't want to scare them."

He led the others up the yard, then into a very narrow passage which lay between Louise Adet's house and the Rat Mort and was bordered by the high walls of the houses on either side.

"This is a blind alley," he whispered. "We have the wall of Le Bouffay in front of us: the wall of the Rat Mort is on one side and the house of the Citizeness Adet on the other. We can talk here undisturbed."

Overhead there was a tiny window dimly lighted from within. Chauvelin pointed up to it.

"What is that?" he asked.

"An aperture too small for any human being to pass through," replied Fleury drily. "It gives on a small landing at the foot of the stairs. I told Friche to try and manoeuvre so that the wench and her father are pushed in there out of the way while the worst of the fracas is going on. That was your suggestion, Citizen Chauvelin."

"It was. I was afraid the two *aristos* might get spirited away while your men were tackling the crowd in the tap-room. I wanted them put away in a safe place."

"The staircase is safe enough," rejoined Fleury; "it has no egress save that on the tap-room and only leads to the upper story and the attic. The house has no back entrance—it is built against the wall of Le Bouffay."

"And what about your Marats, citizen *commandant?*"

"Oh! I have them all along the street—entirely under cover but closely on the watch—half a company and all keen after the game. The thousand *francs* you promised them has stimulated their zeal most marvellously, and as soon as Paul Friche in there has whipped up the tempers of the frequenters of the Rat Mort, we shall be ready to rush the place and I assure you, Citizen Chauvelin, that only a disembodied ghost—if there be one in the place—will succeed in evading arrest."

"Is Paul Friche already at his post then?"

"And at work—or I'm much mistaken," replied Fleury as he suddenly gripped Chauvelin by the arm.

For just at this moment the silence of the winter's night was broken by loud cries which came from the interior of the Rat Mort—voices were raised to hoarse and raucous cries—men and women all appeared to be shrieking together, and presently there was a loud crash as of overturned furniture and broken glass.

"A few minutes longer, citizen Fleury," said Chauvelin, as the *commandant* of the Marats turned on his heel and started to go back to the *Carrefour de la Poissonnerie.*

"Oh yes!" whispered the latter, "we'll wait awhile longer to give the Englishmen time to arrive on the scene. The coast is clear for them—my Marats are hidden from sight behind the doorways and shop-fronts of the houses opposite. In about three minutes from now I'll send them forward."

"And good luck to your hunting, citizen," whispered Chauvelin in response.

Fleury very quickly disappeared in the darkness and the other two men followed in his wake. They hugged the wall of the Rat Mort as they went along and its shadow enveloped them completely: their shoes made no sound on the unpaved ground. Chauvelin's nostrils quivered as he drew the keen, cold air into his lungs and faced the north-westerly blast which at this moment also lashed the face of his enemy. His keen eyes tried to pierce the gloom, his ears were strained to hear that merry peal of laughter which in the unforgettable past had been wont to proclaim the presence of the reckless adventurer. He knew—he felt—as certainly as he felt the air which he breathed, that the man whom he hated beyond everything on earth was somewhere close by, wrapped in the murkiness of the night—thinking, planning, intriguing, pitting his sharp wits, his indomitable pluck, his impudent dare-devilry against the sure and patient trap which had been set for him.

Half a company of Marats in front—the walls of Le Bouffay in the rear! Chauvelin rubbed his thin hands together!

"You are not a disembodied ghost, my fine Scarlet Pimpernel," he murmured, "and this time I really think——"

CHAPTER 7

The Fracas in the Tavern

Yvonne had settled herself in a corner of the tap-room on a bench and had tried to lose consciousness of her surroundings.

182

It was not easy! Glances charged with rancour were levelled at her dainty appearance—dainty and refined despite the look of starvation and of weariness on her face and the miserable state of her clothing—and not a few muttered insults waited on those glances.

As soon as she was seated Yvonne noticed that the old man and the coarse, fat woman behind the bar started an animated conversation together, of which she was very obviously the object, for the two heads—the lean and the round—were jerked more than once in her direction. Presently the man—it was George Lemoine, the proprietor of the Rat Mort—came up to where she was sitting: his lank figure was bent so that his lean back formed the best part of an arc, and an expression of mock deference further distorted his ugly face.

He came up quite close to Yvonne and she found it passing difficult not to draw away from him, for the leer on his face was appalling: his eyes, which were set very near to his hooked nose, had a horrible squint, his lips were thick and moist, and his breath reeked of alcohol.

"What will the noble lady deign to drink?" he now asked in an oily, suave voice.

And Yvonne, remembering the guide's admonitions, contrived to smile unconcernedly into the hideous face.

"I would very much like some wine," she said cheerfully, "but I am afraid that I have no money wherewith to pay you for it."

The creature with a gesture of abject humility rubbed his greasy hands together.

"And may I respectfully ask," he queried blandly, "what are the intentions of the noble lady in coming to this humble abode, if she hath no desire to partake of refreshments?"

"I am expecting friends," replied Yvonne bravely; "they will be here very soon and will gladly repay you lavishly for all the kindness which you may be inclined to show to me the while."

She was very brave indeed and looked this awful misshapen specimen of a man quite boldly in the face: she even contrived to smile, though she was well aware that a number of men and women—perhaps a dozen altogether—had congregated in front of her in a compact group around the landlord, that they were nudging one another and pointing derisively—malevolently—at her. It was impossible, despite all attempts at valour, to mistake the hostile attitude of these people. Some of the most obscene words, coined during these last horrible days of the Revolution, were freely hurled at her, and one woman suddenly cried out in a shrill treble:

"Throw her out, Citizen Lemoine! We don't want spies in here!"

"Indeed, indeed," said Yvonne as quietly as she could, "I am no spy. I am poor and wretched like yourselves! and desperately lonely, save for the kind friends who will meet me here *anon*."

"*Aristos* like yourself!" growled one of the men. "This is no place for you or for them."

"No! No! This is no place for *aristos*," cried one of the women in a voice which many excesses and many vices had rendered hoarse and rough. "Spy or not, we don't want you in here. Do we?" she added as with arms *akimbo* she turned to face those of her own sex, who behind the men had come up in order to see what was going on.

"Throw her out, Lemoine," reiterated a man who appeared to be an oracle amongst the others.

"Please! please let me stop here!" pleaded Yvonne; "if you turn me out I shall not know what to do: I shall not know where to meet my friends—"

"Pretty story about those friends," broke in Lemoine roughly. "How do I know if you're lying or not?"

From the opposite angle of the room, the woman behind the bar had been watching the little scene with eyes that glistened with cupidity. Now she emerged from behind her stronghold of bottles and mugs and slowly waddled across the room. She pushed her way unceremoniously past her customers, elbowing men, women and children vigorously aside with a deft play of her large, muscular arms. Having reached the forefront of the little group she came to a standstill immediately in front of Yvonne and crossing her mighty arms over her ponderous chest she eyed the "*aristo*" with unconcealed malignity.

"We do know that the slut is lying—that is where you make the mistake, Lemoine. A slut, that's what she is—and the friend whom she's going to meet—? Well!" she added, turning with an ugly leer toward the other women, "we all know what sort of friend that one is likely to be, eh, *mesdames?* Bringing evil fame on this house, that's what the wench is after—so as to bring the police about our ears—I wouldn't trust her, not another minute. Out with you and at once—do you hear?—this instant—Lemoine has parleyed quite long enough with you already!"

Despite all her resolutions Yvonne was terribly frightened. While the hideous old hag talked and screamed and waved her coarse, red arms about, the unfortunate young girl with a great effort of will, kept repeating to herself: "I am not frightened—I must not be frightened.

He assured me that these people would do me no harm—" But now when the woman had ceased speaking there was a general murmur of:

"Throw her out! Spy or *aristo* we don't want her here!" whilst some of the men added significantly: "I am sure that she is one of Carrier's spies and in league with his Marats! We shall have those devils in here in a moment if we don't look out! Throw her out before she can signal to the Marats!"

Ugly faces charged with hatred and virulence were thrust threateningly forward—one or two of the women were obviously looking forward to joining in the scramble, when this "stuck-up wench" would presently be hurled out into the street.

"Now then, my girl, out you get," concluded the woman Lemoine, as with an expressive gesture she proceeded to roll her sleeves higher up her arm. She was about to lay her dirty hands on Yvonne, and the poor girl was nearly sick with horror, when one of the men—a huge, coarse giant, whose muscular torso, covered with grease and grime showed almost naked through a ragged shirt which hung from his shoulders in strips—seized the woman Lemoine by the arm and dragged her back a step or two away from Yvonne.

"Don't be a fool, *petite mère*," he said, accompanying this admonition with a blasphemous oath. "Slut or no, the wench may as well pay you something for the privilege of staying here. Look at that cloak she's wearing—the shoe-leather on her feet. Aren't they worth a bottle of your sour wine?"

"What's that to you, Paul Friche?" retorted the woman roughly, as with a vigorous gesture she freed her arm from the man's grasp. "Is this my house or yours?"

"Yours, of course," replied the man with a coarse laugh and a still coarser jest, "but this won't be the first time that I have saved you from impulsive folly. Yesterday you were for harbouring a couple of rogues who were Marats in disguise: if I hadn't given you warning, you would now have swallowed more water from the Loire than you would care to hold. But for me two days ago you would have received the goods pinched by Ferté out of Balaze's shop and been thrown to the fishes in consequence for the entertainment of the proconsul and his friends. You must admit that I've been a good friend to you before now."

"And if you have, Paul Friche," retorted the hag obstinately, "I paid you well for your friendship, both yesterday and the day before, didn't I?"

"You did," assented Friche imperturbably. "That's why I want to

185

serve you again tonight."

"Don't listen to him, *petite mère*," interposed one of two out of the crowd. "He is a white-livered skunk to talk to you like that."

"Very well! Very well!" quoth Paul Friche, and he spat vigorously on the ground in token that henceforth he divested himself from any responsibility in this matter, "don't listen to me. Lose a benefit of twenty, perhaps forty *francs* for the sake of a bit of fun. Very well! Very well!" he continued as he turned and slouched out of the group to the further end of the room, where he sat down on a barrel. He drew the stump of a clay pipe out of the pocket of his breeches, stuffed it into his mouth, stretched his long legs out before him and sucked away at his pipe with complacent detachment. "I didn't know," he added with biting sarcasm by way of a parting shot, "that you and Lemoine had come into a fortune recently and that forty or fifty *francs* are nothing to you now."

"Forty or fifty? Come! come!" protested Lemoine feebly.

Yvonne's fate was hanging in the balance. The attitude of the small crowd was no less threatening than before, but immediate action was withheld while the Lemoines obviously debated in their minds what was best to be done. The instinct to "have at" an *aristo* with all the ac-cumulated hatred of many generations was warring with the innate rapacity of the Breton peasant.

"Forty or fifty?" reiterated Paul Friche emphatically. "Can't you see that the wench is an *aristo* escaped out of Le Bouffay or the *entrepôt?*" he added contemptuously.

"I know that she is an *aristo*," said the woman, "that's why I want to throw her out."

"And get nothing for your pains," retorted Friche roughly. "If you wait for her friends we may all of us get as much as twenty *francs* each to hold our tongues."

"Twenty *francs* each—" The murmur was repeated with many a sigh of savage gluttony, by everyone in the room—and repeated again and again—especially by the women.

"You are a fool, Paul Friche—" commented Lemoine.

"A fool am I?" retorted the giant. "Then let me tell you, that 'tis you who are a fool and worse. I happen to know," he added, as he once more rose and rejoined the group in the centre of the room, "I happen to know that you and everyone here is heading straight for a trap ar-ranged by the Committee of Public Safety, whose chief emissary came into Nantes a while ago and is named Chauvelin. It is a trap which will land you all in the criminal dock first and on the way to Cayenne or the guillotine afterwards. This place is surrounded with Marats, and orders have been issued to them to make a descent on this place, as soon as papa Lemoine's customers are assembled. There are two members of the accursed company amongst us at the present moment—"

He was standing right in the middle of the room, immediately beneath the hanging lamp. At his words—spoken with such firm confidence, as one who knows and is therefore empowered to speak—a sudden change came over the spirit of the whole assembly. Everything was forgotten in the face of this new danger—two Marats, the sleuthhounds of the proconsul—here present, as spies and as informants! Every face became more haggard—every cheek more livid. There was a quick and furtive scurrying toward the front door.

"Two Marats here?" shouted one man, who was bolder than the rest. "Where are they?"

Paul Friche, who towered above his friends, stood at this moment quite close to a small man, dressed like the others in ragged breeches and shirt, and wearing the broad-brimmed hat usually affected by the Breton peasantry.

"Two Marats? Two spies?" screeched a woman. "Where are they?"

"Here is one," replied Paul Friche with a loud laugh: and with his large grimy hand he lifted the hat from his neighbour's head and threw it on the ground; "and there," he added as with long, bony finger he pointed to the front door, where another man—a square-built youngster with tow-coloured hair somewhat resembling a shaggy dog—was endeavouring to effect a surreptitious exit, "there is the other; and he is on the point of slipping quietly away in order to report to his captain what he has seen and heard at the Rat Mort. One moment, citizen," he added, and with a couple of giant strides he too had reached the door; his large rough hand had come down heavily on the shoulder of the youth with the tow-coloured hair and had forced him to veer round and to face the angry, gesticulating crowd.

"Two Marats! Two spies!" shouted the men. "Now we'll soon settle their little business for them!"

"Marat yourself," cried the small man who had first been denounced by Friche. "I am no Marat, as a good many of you here know. Maman Lemoine," he added pleading, "you know me. Am I a Marat?"

But the Lemoines—man and wife—at the first suggestion of police had turned a deaf ear to all their customers. Their own safety being in jeopardy they cared little what happened to anybody else.

187

They had retired behind their counter and were in close consultation together, no doubt as to the best means of escape if indeed the man Paul Friche spoke the truth.

"I know nothing about him," the woman was saying, but he certainly was right last night about those two men who came ferreting in here—and last week too—"

"Am I a Marat, Maman Lemoine?" shouted the small man as he hammered his fists upon the counter. "For ten years and more I have been a customer in this place and—"

"Am I a Marat?" shouted the youth with the tow-coloured hair addressing the assembly indiscriminately. "Some of you here know me well enough. Jean Paul, you know—Ledouble, you too—"

"Of course! Of course, I know you well enough, Jacques Leroux," came with a loud laugh from one of the crowd. "Who said you were a Marat?"

"Am I a Marat, Maman Lemoine?" reiterated the small man at the counter.

"Oh! leave me alone with your quarrels," shouted the woman Lemoine in reply. "Settle them among yourselves."

"Then if Jacques Leroux is not a Marat," now came in a bibulous voice from a distant corner of the room, "and this compeer here is known to Maman Lemoine, where are the real Marats who according to this fellow Friche, whom we none of us know, are spying upon us?"

"Yes! where are they?" suggested another. "Show 'em to us, Paul Friche, or whatever your accursed name happens to be."

"Tell us where you come from yourself," screamed the woman with the shrill treble, "it seems to me quite possible that you're a Marat yourself."

This suggestion was at once taken up.

"Marat yourself!" shouted the crowd, and the two men who a moment ago had been accused of being spies in disguise shouted louder than the rest: "Marat yourself!"

After that, pandemonium reigned.

The words "police" and "Marats" had aroused the terror of all these night-hawks, who were wont to think themselves immune inside their lair: and terror is at all times an evil counsellor. In the space of a few seconds confusion held undisputed sway. Everyone screamed, waved arms, stamped feet, struck out with heavy bare fists at his nearest neighbour. Everyone's hand was against everyone else.

"Spy! Marat! Informer!" were the three words that detached themselves most clearly from out the babel of vituperations freely hurled from end to end of the room.

The children screamed, the women's shrill or hoarse treble mingled with the cries and imprecations of the men.

Paul Friche had noted that the turn of the tide was against him, long before the first naked fist had been brandished in his face. Agile as a monkey he had pushed his way through to the bar, and placing his two hands upon it, with a swift leap he had taken up a sitting position in the very middle of the table amongst the jugs and bottles, which he promptly seized and used as missiles and weapons, whilst with his dangling feet encased in heavy sabots he kicked out vigorously and unceasingly against the shins of his foremost assailants.

He had the advantage of position and used it cleverly. In his right hand he held a pewter mug by the handle and used it as a swivel against his aggressors with great effect.

"The Loire for you—you blackmailer! liar! traitor!" shouted some of the women who, bolder than the men, thrust shaking fists at Paul Friche as closely as that pewter mug would allow.

"Break his jaw before he can yell for the police," admonished one of the men from the rear, "before he can save his own skin."

But those who shouted loudest had only their fists by way of weapon and Paul Friche had mugs and bottles, and those *sabots* of his kicked out with uncomfortable agility.

"Break my jaw, will you," he shouted every time that a blow from the mug went home, "a spy am I? Very well then, here's for you, Jacques Leroux; go and nurse your cracked skull at home. You want a row," he added hitting at a youth who brandished a heavy fist in his face, "well! you shall have it and as much of it as you like! as much of it as will bring the patrols of police comfortably about your ears."

Bang! went the pewter mug crashing against a man's hard skull! *Bang* went Paul Friche's naked fist against the chest of another. He was a hard hitter and swift.

The Lemoines from behind their bar shouted louder than the rest, doing as much as their lungs would allow them in the way of admonishing, entreating, protesting—cursing every one for a set of fools who were playing straight into the hands of the police.

"Now then! Now then, children, stop that bellowing, will you? There are no spies here. Paul Friche was only having his little joke! We all know one another, what?"

"Camels!" added Lemoine more forcibly. "They'll bring the patrols

189

about our ears for sure."

Paul Friche was not by any means the only man who was being vigorously attacked. After the first two or three minutes of this kingdom of pandemonium, it was difficult to say who was quarrelling with whom. Old grudges were revived, old feuds taken up there, where they had previously been interrupted. Accusations of spying were followed by abuse for some past wrong of black-legging or cheating a *confrère*. The temperature of the room became suffocating. All these violent passions seething within these four walls seemed to become tangible and to mingle with the atmosphere already surcharged with the fumes of alcohol, of tobacco and of perspiring humanity. There was many a black-eye already, many a contusion: more than one knife—surreptitiously drawn—was already stained with red.

There was also a stampede for the door. One man gave the signal. Seeing that his mates were wasting precious time by venting their wrath against Paul Friche and then quarrelling among themselves, he hoped to effect an escape ere the police came to stop the noise. No one believed in the place being surrounded. Why should it be? The Marats were far too busy hunting up rebels and *aristos* to trouble much about the Rat Mort and its customers, but it was quite possible that a brawl would bring a patrol along, and then 'ware the *police correctionnelle* and the possibility of deportation or worse. Retreat was undoubtedly safer while there was time. One man first: then one or two more on his heels, and those among the women who had children in their arms or clinging to their skirts: they turned stealthily to the door—almost ashamed of their cowardice, ashamed lest they were seen abandoning the field of combat.

It was while confusion reigned unchecked that Yvonne—who was cowering, frankly terrified at last, in the corner of the room, became aware that the door close beside her—the door situated immediately opposite the front entrance—was surreptitiously opened. She turned quickly to look—for she was like a terror-stricken little animal now—one that scents and feels and fears danger from every quarter round. The door was being pushed open very slowly by what was still to Yvonne an unseen hand. Somehow that opening door fascinated her: for the moment she forgot the noise and the confusion around her.

Then suddenly with a great effort of will she checked the scream which had forced itself up to her throat.

"Father!" was all that she contrived to say in a hoarse and passionate murmur.

Fortunately, as he peered cautiously round the room, *M. le Duc* caught sight of his daughter. She was staring at him—wide-eyed, her lips bloodless, her cheeks the colour of ashes. He looked but the ghost now of that proud aristocrat who little more than a week ago was the centre of a group of courtiers round the person of the heir to the English throne. Starved, emaciated, livid, he was the shadow of his former self, and there was a haunted look in his purple-rimmed eyes which spoke with pathetic eloquence of sleepless nights and of a soul tortured with remorse.

Just for the moment no one took any notice of him—everyone was shrieking, everyone was quarrelling, and *M. le Duc*, placing a finger to his lips, stole cautiously round to his daughter. The next instant they were clinging to one another, these two, who had endured so much together—he the father who had wrought such an unspeakable wrong, and she the child who was so lonely, so forlorn and almost happy in finding someone who belonged to her, someone to whom she could cling.

"Father, dear! what shall we do?" Yvonne murmured, for she felt the last shred of her fictitious courage oozing out of her, in face of this awful lawlessness which literally paralysed her thinking faculties.

"Sh! dear!" whispered *M. le Duc* in reply. "We must get out of this loathsome place while this hideous row is going on. I heard it all from the filthy garret up above, where those devils have kept me these three days. The door was not locked—I crept downstairs—No one is paying heed to us—We can creep out. Come."

But at the suggestion, Yvonne's spirits, which had been stunned by the events of the past few moments, revived with truly mercurial rapidity.

"No! no! dear," she urged. "We must stay here—You don't know—I have had a message—from my own dear milor—my husband—he sent a friend to take me out of the hideous prison where that awful Pierre Adet was keeping me—a friend who assured me that my dear milor was watching over me—he brought me to this place—and begged me not to be frightened—but to wait patiently—and I must wait, dear—I must wait!"

She spoke rapidly in whispers and in short jerky sentences. *M. le Duc* listened to her wide-eyed, a deep line of puzzlement between his brows. Sorrow, remorse, starvation, misery had in a measure numbed his mind. The thought of help, of hope, of friends could not penetrate into his brain.

"A message," he murmured inanely, "a message. No! no! my girl, you must trust no one—Pierre Adet—Pierre Adet is full of evil tricks—he will trap you—he means to destroy us both—he has brought you here so that you should be murdered by these ferocious devils."

"Impossible, father dear," she said, still striving to speak bravely. "We have both of us been all this while in the power of Pierre Adet; he could have had no object in bringing me here tonight."

But the father who had been an insentient tool in the schemes of that miserable intriguer, who had been the means of bringing his only child to this terrible and deadly pass—the man who had listened to the lying counsels and proposals of his own most bitter enemy, could only groan now in terror and in doubt.

"Who can probe the depths of that abominable villain's plans?" he murmured vaguely.

In the meanwhile, the little group who had thought prudence the better part of valour had reached the door. The foremost man amongst them opened it and peered cautiously out into the darkness. He turned back to those behind him, put a finger to his lip and beckoned to them to follow him in silence.

"Yvonne, let us go!" whispered the *duc*, who had seized his daughter by the hand.

"But father—"

"Let us go!" he reiterated pitiably. "I shall die if we stay here!"

"It won't be for long, father dear," she entreated; "if milor should come with his friend, and find us gone, we should be endangering his life as well as our own."

"I don't believe it," he rejoined with the obstinacy of weakness. "I don't believe in your message—how could milor or anyone come to your rescue, my child?—No one knows that you are here, in this hell in Nantes."

Yvonne clung to him with the strength of despair. She too was as terrified as any human creature could be and live, but terror had not altogether swept away her belief in that mysterious message, in that tall guide who had led her hither, in that scarlet device—the five-petalled flower which stood for everything that was most gallant and most brave.

She desired with all her might to remain here—despite everything, despite the awful brawl that was raging round her and which sickened her, despite the horror of the whole thing—to remain here and to wait. She put her arms round her father: she dragged him back every time that he tried to move. But a sort of unnatural strength seemed to have conquered his former debility. His attempts to get away became more and more determined and more and more febrile.

"Come, Yvonne! we must go!" he continued to murmur intermittently and with ever-growing obstinacy. "No one will notice us—I heard the noise from my garret upstairs—I crept down—I knew no one would notice me—Come—we must go—now is our time."

"Father, dear, whither could we go? Once in the streets of Nantes what would happen to us?"

"We can find our way to the Loire!" he retorted almost brutally. He shook himself free from her restraining arms and gripped her firmly by the hand. He tried to drag her toward the door, whilst she still struggled to keep him back. He had just caught sight of the group of men and women at the front door: their leader was standing upon the threshold and was still peering out into the darkness.

But the next moment they all came to a halt: what their leader had perceived through the darkness did not evidently quite satisfy him: he turned and held a whispered consultation with the others. *M. le Duc* strove with all his might to join in with that group. He felt that in its wake would lie the road to freedom. He would have struck Yvonne for standing in the way of her own safety.

"Father dear," she contrived finally to say to him, "if you go hence, you will go alone. Nothing will move me from here, because I know that milor will come."

"Curse you for your obstinacy," retorted the *duc*, "you jeopardise my life and yours."

Then suddenly from the angle of the room where wrangling and fighting were at their fiercest, there came a loud call:

"Look out, Père Lemoine, your *aristos* are running away. You are losing your last chance of those fifty *francs*."

It was Paul Friche who had shouted. His position on the table was giving him a commanding view over the heads of the threatening, shouting, perspiring crowd, and he had just caught sight of *M. le Duc* dragging his daughter by force toward the door.

"The authors of all this pother," he added with an oath, "and they will get away whilst we have the police about our ears."

"Name of a name of a dog," swore Lemoine from behind his bar, "that shall not be. Come along, *maman*, let us bring those *aristos* along here. Quick now."

It was all done in a second. Lemoine and his wife, with the weight and authority of the masters of the establishment, contrived to elbow their way through the crowd. The next moment Yvonne felt herself forcibly dragged away from her father.

"This way, my girl, and no screaming," a bibulous voice said in her ear, "no screaming, or I'll smash some of those front teeth of yours. You said some rich friends were coming along for you presently. Well then! come and wait for them out of the crowd!"

Indeed, Yvonne had no desire to struggle or to scream. Salvation she thought had come to her and to her father in this rough guise. In another moment mayhap, he would have forced her to follow him, to leave milor in the lurch, to jeopardise for ever every chance of safety.

"It is all for the best, father dear," she managed to cry out over her shoulder, for she had just caught sight of him being seized round the shoulders by Lemoine and heard him protesting loudly:

"I'll not go! I'll not go! Let me go!" he shouted hoarsely. "My daughter! Yvonne! Let me go! You devil!"

But Lemoine had twice the vigour of the Duc de Kernogan, nor did he care one jot about the other's protests. He hated all this row inside his house, but there had been rows in it before and he was beginning to hope that nothing serious would come of it. On the other hand, Paul Friche might be right about these *aristos*; there might be forty or fifty *francs* to be made out of them, and in any case, they had one or two things upon their persons which might be worth a few *francs*—and who knows? they might even have something in their pockets worth taking.

This hope and thought gave Lemoine additional strength, and seeing that the *aristo* struggled so desperately, he thought to silence him by bringing his heavy fist with a crash upon the old man's head.

"Yvonne! À moi!" shouted M. le Duc ere he fell back senseless.

That awful cry, Yvonne heard it as she was being dragged through the noisome crowd. It mingled in her ear with the other awful sounds—the oaths and blasphemies which filled the air with their hideousness. It died away just as a formidable crash against the entrance door suddenly silenced every cry within.

"All hands up!" came with a peremptory word of command from the doorway.

"Mercy on us!" murmured the woman Lemoine, who still had Yvonne by the hand, "we are undone this time."

There was a clatter and grounding of arms—a scurrying of bare feet and sabots upon the floor, the mingled sounds of men trying to fly and being caught in the act and hurled back: screams of terror from the women, one or two pitiable calls, a few shrill cries from frightened children, a few dull thuds as of human bodies falling—It was all so confused, so unspeakably horrible. Yvonne was hardly conscious. Near her someone whispered hurriedly:

"Put the *aristos* away somewhere, Maman Lemoine—the whole thing may only be a scare—the Marats may only be here about the *aristos*—they will probably leave you alone if you give them up—perhaps you'll get a reward—Put them away till some of this row subsides—I'll talk to Commandant Fleury if I can."

Yvonne felt her knees giving way under her. There was nothing more to hope for now—nothing. She felt herself lifted from the ground—she was too sick and faint to realise what was happening: through the din which filled her ears she vainly tried to distinguish her father's voice again.

A moment or two later she found herself squatting somewhere on the ground. How she got here she did not know—where she was she knew still less. She was in total darkness. A fusty, close smell of food and wine gave her a wretched feeling of nausea—her head ached intolerably, her eyes were hot, her throat dry: there was a constant buzzing in her ears.

The terrible sounds of fighting and screaming and cursing, the crash of broken glass and overturned benches came to her as through a partition—close by but muffled.

In the immediate nearness all was silence and darkness.

Chapter 8

The English Adventurers

It was with that muffled din still ringing in her ear and with the conception of all that was going on, on the other side of the partition, standing like an awesome spectre of evil before her mind, that Yvonne woke to the consciousness that her father was dead.

He lay along the last half-dozen steps of a narrow wooden staircase which had its base in the narrow, cupboard-like landing on to which the Lemoines had just thrust them both. Through a small heart-shaped hole cut in the door of the partition-wall, a shaft of feeble light struck straight across to the foot of the stairs: it lit up the recumbent figure of the last of the Ducs de Kernogan, killed in a brawl in a house of evil fame.

Weakened by starvation, by the hardships of the past few days, his constitution undermined by privations and mayhap too by gnawing remorse, he had succumbed to the stunning blow dealt to him by a half drunken brute. His cry: "Yvonne! *À moi!*" was the last despairing call of a soul racked with remorse to the daughter whom he had so cruelly wronged.

When first that feeble shaft of light had revealed to her the presence of that inert form upon the steps, she had struggled to her feet and—dazed—had tottered up to it. Even before she had touched the face, the hands, before she had bent her ear to the half-closed mouth and failed to catch the slightest breath, she knew the full extent of her misery. The look in the wide-open eyes did not terrify her, but they told her the truth, and since then she had cowered beside her dead father on the bottom step of the narrow stairs, her fingers tightly closed over that one hand which never would be raised against her.

An unspeakable sense of horror filled her soul. The thought that he—the proud father, the haughty aristocrat, should lie like this and in such a spot, dragged in and thrown down—no doubt by Lemoine—like a parcel of rubbish and left here to be dragged away again and thrown again like a dog into some unhallowed ground—that thought was so horrible, so monstrous, that at first it dominated even sorrow. Then came the heartrending sense of loneliness. Yvonne Dewhurst had endured so much these past few days that a while ago she would have affirmed that nothing could appal her in the future. But this was indeed the awful and overwhelming climax to what had already been a surfeit of misery.

This! she, Yvonne, cowering beside her dead father, with no one to stand between her and any insult, any outrage which might be put upon her, with nothing now but a few laths between her and that yelling, screeching mob outside.

Oh! the loneliness! the utter, utter loneliness!

She kissed the inert hand, the pale forehead: with gentle, reverent fingers she tried to smooth out those lines of horror and of fear which gave such a pitiful expression to the face. Of all the wrongs which her father had done her she never thought for a moment. It was he who had brought her to this terrible pass: he who had betrayed her into the hands of her deadliest enemy: he who had torn her from the protecting arms of her dear milor and flung her and himself at the mercy of a set of inhuman wretches who knew neither compunction nor pity.

But all this she forgot, as she knelt beside the lifeless form—the last thing on earth that belonged to her—the last protection to which she might have clung.

Out of the confusion of sounds which came—deadened by the intervening partition—to her ear, it was impossible to distinguish anything very clearly. All that Yvonne could do, as soon as she had in a measure collected her scattered senses, was to try and piece together the events of the last few minutes—minutes which indeed seemed like days and even years to her.

Instinctively she gave to the inert hand which she held an additional tender touch. At any rate her father was out of it all. He was at rest and at peace. As for the rest, it was in God's hands. Having only herself to think of now, she ceased to care what became of her. He was out of it all: and those wretches after all could not do more than kill her. A complete numbness of senses and of mind had succeeded the feverish excitement of the past few hours: whether hope still survived at this moment in Yvonne Dewhurst's mind it were impossible to say. Certain it is that it lay dormant—buried beneath the overwhelming misery of her loneliness.

She took the *fichu* from her shoulders and laid it reverently over the dead man's face: she folded the hands across the breast. She could not cry: she could only pray, and that quite mechanically.

The thought of her dear milor, of his clever friend, of the message which she had received in prison, of the guide who had led her to this awful place, was relegated—almost as a memory—in the furthermost cell of her brain.

But after a while outraged nature, still full of vitality and of youth, re-asserted itself. She felt numb and cold and struggled to her feet. From somewhere close to her a continuous current of air indicated the presence of some sort of window. Yvonne, faint with the close and sickly smell, which even that current failed to disperse, felt her way all round the walls of the narrow landing.

The window was in the wall between the partition and the staircase, it was small and quite low down. It was crossed with heavy iron bars. Yvonne leaned up against it, grateful for the breath of pure air.

For a while yet she remained unconscious of everything save the confused din which still went on inside the tavern, and at first the sounds which came through the grated window mingled with those on the other side of the partition. But gradually as she contrived to fill her lungs with the cold breath of heaven, it seemed as if a curtain was being slowly drawn away from her atrophied senses.

Just below the window two men were speaking. She could hear

them quite distinctly now—and soon one of the voices—clearer than the other—struck her ear with unmistakable familiarity.

"I told Paul Friche to come out here and speak to me," Yvonne heard that same voice say.

"Then he should be here," replied the other, "and if I am not mistaken—"

There was a pause, and then the first voice was raised again.

"Halt! Is that Paul Friche?"

"At your service, citizen," came in reply.

"Well! Is everything working smoothly inside?"

"Quite smoothly; but your Englishmen are not there."

"How do you know?"

"Bah! I know most of the faces that are to be found inside the Rat Mort at this hour: there are no strangers among them."

The voice that had sounded so familiar to Yvonne was raised now in loud and coarse laughter.

"Name of a dog! I never for a moment thought that there were any Englishmen about. Citizen Chauvelin was suffering from nightmare."

"It is early yet," came in response from a gentle bland voice, "you must have patience, citizen."

"Patience? Bah!" ejaculated the other roughly. "As I told you before 'tis but little I care about your English spies. 'Tis the Kernogans I am interested in. What have you done with them, citizen?"

"I got that blundering fool Lemoine to lock them up on the landing at the bottom of the stairs."

"Is that safe?"

"Absolutely. It has no egress save into the tap-room and up the stairs, to the rooms above. Your English spies if they came now would have to fly in and out of those top windows ere they could get to the *aristos*."

"Then in Satan's name keep them there awhile," urged the more gentle, insinuating voice, "until we can make sure of the English spies."

"Tshaw! What foolery!" interjected the other, who appeared to be in a towering passion. "Bring them out at once, Citizen Friche—bring them out—right into the middle of the rabble in the tap-room—Commandant Fleury is directing the perquisition—he is taking down the names of all that cattle which he is arresting inside the premises—let the *ci-devant* Duc de Kernogan and his exquisite daughter figure among the vilest cutthroats of Nantes."

"Citizen, let me urge on you once more—" came in earnest persuasive accents from that gentle voice.

"Nothing!" broke in the other savagely. "To h—ll with your English spies. It is the Kernogans that I want."

Yvonne, half-crazed with horror, had heard the whole of this abominable conversation wherein she had not failed to recognise the voice of Martin-Roget or Pierre-Adet, as she now knew him to be. Who the other two men were she could easily conjecture. The soft bland voice she had heard twice during these past few days, which had been so full of misery, of terror and of surprise: once she had heard it on board the ship which had taken her away from England and once again a few hours since, inside the narrow room which had been her prison. The third man who had subsequently arrived on the scene was that coarse and grimy creature who had seemed to be the moving evil spirit of that awful brawl in the tavern.

What the conversation meant to her she could not fail to guess. Pierre Adet had by what he said made the whole of his abominable intrigue against her palpably clear. Her father had been right, after all. It was Pierre Adet who through some clever trickery had lured her to this place of evil. How it was all done she could not guess. The message—the device—her walk across the street—the silence—the mysterious guide—which of these had been the trickery?—which had been concocted by her enemy?—which devised by her dear milor?

Enough that the whole thing was a trap, a trap all the more hideous as she, Yvonne, who would have given her heart's blood for her beloved, was obviously the bait wherewith these friends meant to capture him and his noble chief. They knew evidently of the presence of the gallant Scarlet Pimpernel and his band of heroes here in Nantes—they seemed to expect their appearance at this abominable place tonight. She, Yvonne, was to be the decoy which was to lure to this hideous lair those noble eagles who were still out of reach.

And if that was so—if indeed her beloved and his valiant friends had followed her hither, then some part of the message of hope must have come from them or from their chief—and milor and his friend must even now be somewhere close by, watching their opportunity to come to her rescue—heedless of the awful danger which lay in wait for them—ignorant mayhap of the abominable trap which had been so cunningly set for them by these astute and ferocious brutes.

Yvonne a prisoner in this narrow space, clinging to the bars of what was perhaps the most cruel prison in which she had yet been confined, bruised her hands and arms against those bars in a wild desire to get out. She longed with all her might to utter one long, loud and piercing cry of warning to her dear milor not to come nigh her now, to fly, to run while there was yet time; and all the while she knew that if she did utter such a cry he would hurry hot-haste to her side. One moment she would have had him near—another she wished him an hundred miles away.

In the tap-room a more ordered medley of sounds had followed on the wild pandemonium of a while ago. Brief, peremptory words of command, steady tramping of feet, loud harsh questions and subdued answers, occasionally a moan or a few words of protest quickly suppressed, came through the partition to Yvonne's straining ears.

"Your name?"

"Where do you live?"

"Your occupation?"

"That's enough. Silence. The next."

"Your name?"

"Where do you live?"

Men, women and even children were being questioned, classified, packed off, God knew whither. Sometimes a child would cry, a man utter an oath, a woman shriek: then would come harsh orders delivered in a gruff voice, more swearing, the grounding of arms and more often than not a dull, flat sound like a blow struck against human flesh, followed by a volley of curses, or a cry of pain.

"Your name?"

"George Amédé Lemoine."

"Where do you live?"

"In this house."

"Your occupation?"

"I am the proprietor of the tavern, citizen. I am an honest man and a patriot. The Republic—"

"That's enough."

"But I protest."

"Silence. The next."

All with dreary, ceaseless monotony: and Yvonne like a trapped bird was bruising her wings against the bars of her cage. Outside the window Chauvelin and Martin-Roget were still speaking in whispers: the fowlers were still watching for their prey. The third man had apparently gone away. What went on beyond the range of her prison window—out in the darkness of the night which Yvonne's aching eyes could not pierce—she, the miserable watcher, the bait set here to catch the noble game, could not even conjecture. The window was small and her vision was further obstructed by heavy bars. She could see nothing—hear nothing save those two men talking in whispers. Now and again she caught a few words:

"A little while longer, citizen—you lose nothing by waiting. Your Kernogans are safe enough. Paul Friche has assured you that the landing where they are now has no egress save through the tap-room, and to the floor above. Wait at least until Commandant Fleury has got the crowd together, after which he will send his Marats to search the house. It won't be too late then to lay hands on your *aristos*, if in the meanwhile—"

"'Tis futile to wait," here interrupted Martin-Roget roughly, "and you are a fool, citizen, if you think that those Englishmen exist elsewhere than in your imagination."

"Hark!" broke in the gentle voice abruptly and with forceful command.

And as Yvonne too in instinctive response to that peremptory call was further straining her every sense in order to listen, there came from somewhere, not very far away, right through the stillness of the night, a sound which caused her pulses to still their beating and her throat to choke with the cry which rose from her breast.

It was only the sound of a quaint and drawly voice saying loudly and in English:

"Egad, Tony! ain't you getting demmed sleepy?"

Just for the space of two or three seconds Yvonne had remained quite still while this unexpected sound sent its dulcet echo on the wings of the north-westerly blast. The next—stumbling in the dark— she had run to the stairs even while she heard Martin-Roget calling loudly and excitedly to Paul Friche.

One reverent pause beside her dead father, one mute prayer commending his soul to the mercy of his Maker, one agonised entreaty to God to protect her beloved and his friend, and then she ran swiftly up the winding steps.

At the top of the stairs, immediately in front of her, a door—slightly ajar—showed a feeble light through its aperture. Yvonne pushed the door further open and slipped into the room beyond. She did not pause to look round but went straight to the window and throwing open the rickety sash she peeped out. For the moment she felt that she would gladly have bartered away twenty years of her life to know exactly whence had come that quaint and drawling voice. She leaned far out of the window trying to see. It gave on the side of the Rat Mort over against Louise Adet's house—the space below seemed to her to be swarming with men: there were hurried and whispered calls—orders were given to stand at close attention, whilst Martin-Roget had apparently been questioning Paul Friche, for Yvonne heard the latter declare emphatically:

"I am certain that it came either from inside the house or from the roof. And with your permission, citizen, I would like to make assurance doubly sure."

Then one of the men must suddenly have caught sight of the vague silhouette leaning out of the window, for Martin-Roget and Friche uttered a simultaneous cry, whilst Chauvelin said hurriedly:

"You are right, citizen, something is going on inside the house."

"What can we do?" queried Martin-Roget excitedly.

"Nothing for the moment but wait. The Englishmen are caught sure enough like rats in their holes."

"Wait!" ejaculated Martin-Roget with a savage oath, "wait! always wait! while the quarry slips through one's fingers."

"It shall not slip through mine," retorted Paul Friche. "I was a steeple-jack by trade in my day: it won't be the first time that I have climbed the side of a house by the gutter-pipe. À moi Jean-Pierre," he added, "and may I be drowned in the Loire if between us two we do not lay those cursed English spies low."

"An hundred *francs* for each of you," called Chauvelin lustily, "if you succeed."

Yvonne did not think to close the window again. Vigorous shouting and laughter from below testified that that hideous creature Friche and his mate had put their project in immediate execution; she turned and ran down the stairs—feeling now like an animal at bay; by the time that she had reached the bottom, she heard a prolonged, hoarse cry of triumph from below and guessed that Paul Friche and his mate had reached the window-sill: the next moment there was a crash overhead of broken window-glass and of furniture kicked from one end of the room to the other, immediately followed by the sound of heavy footsteps running helter-skelter down the stairs.

Yvonne, half-crazed with terror, faint and sick, fell unconscious over the body of her father.

Inside the tap-room Commandant Fleury was still at work.

"Your name?"

"Where do you live?"

"Your occupation?"

The low room was filled to suffocation: the walls lined with Marats, the doors and windows which were wide open were closely guarded, whilst in the corner of the room, huddled together like bales of rubbish, was the human cattle that had been driven together, preparatory to being sent for a trial to Paris in vindication of Carrier's brutalities against the city.

Fleury for form's sake made entries in a notebook—the whole thing was a mere farce—these wretched people were not likely to get a fair trial—what did the whole thing matter? Still! the *commandant* of the Marats went solemnly through the farce which Carrier had invented with a view to his own justification.

Lemoine and his wife had protested and been silenced: men had struggled and women had fought—some of them like wild cats—in trying to get away. Now there were only half a dozen or so more to docket. Fleury swore, for he was tired and hot.

"This place is like a pest-house," he said.

Just then came the sound of that lusty cry of triumph from outside, followed by all the clatter and the breaking of window glass.

"What's that?" queried Fleury.

The heavy footsteps running down the stairs caused him to look up from his work and to call briefly to a sergeant of the Marats who stood beside his chair:

"Go and see what that *sacré* row is about," he commanded. "In there," he added as he indicated the door of the landing with a jerk of the head.

But before the man could reach the door, it was thrown open from within with a vigorous kick from the point of a *sabot*, and Paul Friche appeared under the lintel with the *aristo* wench thrown over his shoulder like a sack of potatoes, his thick, muscular arms encircling her knees. His scarlet bonnet was cocked over one eye, his face was smeared with dirt, his breeches were torn at the knees, his shirt hung in strips from his powerful shoulders. Behind him his mate—who had climbed up the gutter-pipe into the house in his wake—was tottering under the load of the *ci-devant* Duc de Kernogan's body which he had slung across his back and was holding on to by the wrists.

Fleury jumped to his feet—the appearance of these two men, each with his burden, caused him to frown with anger and to demand peremptorily: "What is the meaning of this?"

"The *aristos*," said Paul Friche curtly; "they were trying to escape."

He strode into the room, carrying the unconscious form of the girl as if it were a load of feathers. He was a huge, massive-looking giant: the girl's shoulders nearly touched the low ceiling as he swung forward facing the angry *commandant*.

"How did you get into the house? and by whose orders?" demanded Fleury roughly.

"Climbed in by the window, *pardi*," retorted the man, "and by the orders of Citizen Martin-Roget."

"A corporal of the Company Marat takes orders only from me; you should know that, Citizen Friche."

"Nay!" interposed the sergeant quickly, "this man is not a corporal of the Company Marat, citizen *commandant*. As for Corporal Friche, why! he was taken to the infirmary some hours ago with a cracked skull, he—"

"Not Corporal Friche," exclaimed Fleury with an oath, "then who in the devil's name is this man?"

"The Scarlet Pimpernel, at your service, citizen *commandant*," came loudly and with a merry laugh from the pseudo Friche.

And before either Fleury or the sergeant or any of the Marats could even begin to realise what was happening, he had literally bounded across the room, and as he did so he knocked against the hanging lamp which fell with a crash to the floor, scattering oil and broken glass in every direction and by its fall plunging the place into total darkness. At once there arose a confusion and medley of terrified screams, of piercing shrieks from the women and the children, and of loud imprecations from the men. These mingled with the hasty words of command, with quick orders from Fleury and the sergeant, with the grounding of arms and the tramping of many feet, and with the fall of human bodies that happened to be in the way of the reckless adventurer and his flight.

"He is through the door," cried the men who had been there on guard.

"After him then!" shouted Fleury. "Curse you all for cowards and for fools."

The order had no need to be repeated. The confusion, though great, had only been momentary. Within a second or less, Fleury and his sergeant had fought their way through to the door, urging the men to follow.

"After him—quick!—he is heavily loaded—he cannot have got far—" commanded Fleury as soon as he had crossed the threshold.

"Sergeant, keep order within, and on your life see that no one else escapes."

CHAPTER 9

The Proconsul

From round the angle of the house Martin-Roget and Chauvelin were already speeding along at a rapid pace.

"What does it all mean?" queried the latter hastily.

"The Englishman—with the wench on his back? have you seen him?"

"Malediction! what do you mean?"

"Have you seen him?" reiterated Fleury hoarsely.

"No."

"He couldn't have passed you?"

"Impossible."

"Then unless some of us here have eyes like cats that limb of Satan will get away. On to him, my men," he called once more. "Can you see him?"

The darkness outside was intense. The north-westerly wind was whistling down the narrow street, drowning the sound of every distant footfall: it tore mercilessly round the men's heads, snatching the bonnets from off their heads, dragging at their loose shirts and breeches, adding to the confusion which already reigned.

"He went this way—" shouted one.

"No! that!" cried another.

"There he is!" came finally in chorus from several lusty throats. "Just crossing the bridge."

"After him," cried Fleury, "an hundred *francs* to the man who first lays hands on that devil."

Then the chase began. The Englishman on ahead was unmistakable with that burden on his shoulder. He had just reached the foot of the bridge where a street lanthorn fixed on a tall bracket on the corner stone had suddenly thrown him into bold relief. He had less than an hundred metres start of his pursuers and with a wild cry of excitement they started in his wake.

He was now in the middle of the bridge—an unmistakable figure of a giant vaguely silhouetted against the light from the lanthorns on the further end of the bridge—seeming preternaturally tall and misshapen with that hump upon his back.

From right and left, from under the doorways of the houses in the

205

Carrefour de la Poissonnerie the Marats who had been left on guard in the street now joined in the chase. Overhead windows were thrown open—the good *burghers* of Nantes, awakened from their sleep, forgetful for the nonce of all their anxieties, their squalor and their miseries, leaned out to see what this new kind of din might mean. From everywhere—it almost seemed as if some sprang out of the earth—men, either of the town-guard or Marats on patrol duty, or merely idlers and night hawks who happened to be about, yielded to that primeval instinct of brutality which causes men as well as beasts to join in a pursuit against a fellow creature.

Fleury was in the rear of his posse. Martin-Roget and Chauvelin, walking as rapidly as they could by his side, tried to glean some information out of the *commandant's* breathless and scrappy narrative:

"What happened exactly?"

"It was the man Paul Friche—with the *aristo* wench on his back—and another man carrying the *ci-devant aristo*—they were the English spies—in disguise—they knocked over the lamp—and got away—"

"Name of a—"

"No use swearing, citizen Martin-Roget," retorted Fleury as hotly as his agitated movements would allow. "You and Citizen Chauvelin are responsible for the affair. It was you, Citizen Chauvelin, who placed Paul Friche inside that tavern in observation—you told him what to do—"

"Well?"

"Paul Friche—the real Paul Friche—was taken to the infirmary some hours ago—with a cracked skull, dealt him by your Englishman, I've no doubt—"

"Impossible," reiterated Chauvelin with a curse.

"Impossible? why impossible?"

"The man I spoke to outside Le Bouffay—"

"Was not Paul Friche."

"He was on guard in the Place with two other Marats."

"He was not Paul Friche—the others were not Marats."

"Then the man who was inside the tavern?—"

"Was not Paul Friche."

"—who climbed the gutter pipe—?"

"Malediction!"

And the chase continued—waxing hotter every minute. The hare had gained slightly on the hounds—there were more than a hundred hot on the trail by now—having crossed the bridge he was on the Isle

Feydeau, and without hesitating a moment he plunged at once into the network of narrow streets which cover the island in the rear of La Petite Hollande and the Hôtel de le Villestreux, where lodged Carrier, the representative of the people. The hounds after him had lost some ground by halting—if only for a second or two—first at the head of the bridge, then at the corners of the various streets, while they peered into the darkness to see which way had gone that fleet-footed hare.

"Down this way!"

"No! That!"

"There he goes!"

It always took a few seconds to decide, during which the man on ahead with his burden on his shoulder had time mayhap to reach the end of a street and to turn a corner and once again to plunge into darkness and out of sight. The street lanthorns were few in this squalid corner of the city, and it was only when perforce the running hare had to cross a circle of light that the hounds were able to keep hot on the trail.

"To the bridges for your lives!" now shouted Fleury to the men nearest to him. "Leave him to wander on the island. He cannot come off it, unless he jumps into the Loire."

The Marats—intelligent and ferociously keen on the chase—had already grasped the importance of this order: with the bridges guarded that fleet-footed Englishman might run as much as he liked, he was bound to be run to earth like a fox in his burrow. In a moment they had dispersed along the quays, some to one bridge-head, some to another—the Englishman could not double back now, and if he had already crossed to the Isle Gloriette, which was not joined to the left bank of the river by any bridge, he would be equally caught like a rat in a trap.

"Unless he jumps into the Loire," reiterated Fleury triumphantly.

"The proconsul will have more excitement than he hoped for," he added with a laugh. "He was looking forward to the capture of the English spy, and in deadly terror lest he escaped. But now meseems that we shall run our fox down in sight of the very gates of la Ville-streux."

Martin-Roget's thoughts ran on Yvonne and the *duc*.

"You will remember, citizen *commandant*," he contrived to say to Fleury, "that the *ci-devant* Kernogans were found inside the Rat Mort."

Fleury uttered an exclamation of rough impatience. What did he, what did anyone care at this moment for a couple of *aristos* more or less when the noblest game that had ever fallen to the bag of any Terrorist was so near being run to earth? But Chauvelin said nothing. He walked on at a brisk pace, keeping close to Commandant Fleury's side, in the immediate wake of the pursuit. His lips were pressed tightly together and a hissing breath came through his wide-open nostrils. His pale eyes were fixed into the darkness and beyond it, where the most bitter enemy of the cause which he loved was fighting his last battle against Fate.

"He cannot get off the island!" Fleury had said a while ago. Well! there was of a truth little or nothing now between the hunted hare and capture. The bridges were well guarded: the island swarming with hounds, the Marats at their posts and the Loire an impassable barrier all round.

And Chauvelin, the most tenacious enemy man ever had, Fleury keen on a reward and Martin-Roget with a private grudge to pay off, all within two hundred yards behind him.

True for the moment the Englishman had disappeared. Burden and all, the gloom appeared to have swallowed him up. But there was nowhere he could go; mayhap he had taken refuge under a doorway in one of the narrow streets and hoped perhaps under cover of the darkness to allow his pursuers to slip past him and then to double back.

Fleury was laughing in the best of humours. He was gradually collecting all the Marats together and sending them to the bridge-heads under the command of their various sergeants. Let the Englishman spend the night on the islands if he had a mind. There was a full company of Marats here to account for him as soon as he attempted to come out in the open.

The idlers and night hawks as well as the municipal town guard continued to run excitedly up and down the streets—sometimes there would come a lusty cry from a knot of pursuers who thought they spied the Englishman through the darkness, at others there would be a call of halt, and feverish consultation held at a street corner as to the best policy to adopt.

The town guard, jealous of the Marats, were pining to lay hands on the English spy for the sake of the reward. Fleury, coming across their provost, called him a fool for his pains.

"My Marats will deal with the English spies, citizen," he said roughly, "he is no concern of yours."

The provost demurred: an altercation might have ensued when

Chauvelin's suave voice poured oil on the troubled waters.

"Why not," he said, "let the town guard continue their search on the island, citizen *commandant?* The men may succeed in digging our rat out of his hole and forcing him out into the open all the sooner. Your Marats will have him quickly enough after that."

To this suggestion the provost gave a grudging assent. The reward when the English spy was caught could be fought for later on. For the nonce he turned unceremoniously on his heel, and left Fleury cursing him for a meddlesome busybody.

"So long as he and his rabble does not interfere with my Marats," growled the *commandant.*

"Will you see your sergeants, citizen?" queried Chauvelin tentatively. "They will have to keep very much on the alert and will require constant prodding to their vigilance. If I can be of any service—"

"No," retorted Fleury curtly, "you and Citizen Martin-Roget had best try and see the proconsul and tell him what we have done."

"He'll be half wild with terror when he hears that the English spy is at large upon the island."

"You must pacify him as best you can. Tell him I have a score of Marats at every bridge head and that I am looking personally to every arrangement. There is no escape for the devil possible save by drowning himself and the wench in the Loire."

Chauvelin and Martin-Roget turned from the quay on to the Petite Hollande—the great open ground with its converging row of trees which ends at the very apex of the Isle of Feydeau. Opposite to them at the further corner of the Place was the Hôtel de la Villestreux. One or two of the windows in the hotel were lighted from within. No doubt the proconsul was awake, trembling in the remotest angle of his lair, with the spectre of assassination rampant before him—aroused by the continued disturbance of the night, by the feverishness of this man-hunt carried on almost at his gates.

Even through the darkness it was easy to perceive groups of people either rushing backwards and forwards on the Place or congregating in groups under the trees. Excitement was in the air. It could be felt and heard right through the soughing of the north-westerly wind which caused the bare branches of the trees to groan and to crackle, and the dead leaves, which still hung on the twigs, to fly wildly through the night.

In the centre of the Place, two small lights, gleaming like eyes in the midst of the gloom, betrayed the presence of the proconsul's coach, which stood there as always, ready to take him away to a place of safety—away from this city where he was mortally hated and dreaded—whenever the spectre of terror became more insistent than usual, and drove him hence out of his stronghold. The horses were pawing the frozen ground and champing their bits—the steam from their nostrils caught the rays of the carriage lamps, which also lit up with a feeble flicker the vague outline of the coachman on his box and of the postilion rigid in his saddle.

The citizens of Nantes were never tired of gaping at the carriage—a huge C-springed *barouche*—at the coachman's fine caped coat of bottle-green cloth and at the horses with their handsome harness set off with heavy brass bosses: they never tired of bandying words with the successive coachmen as they mounted their box and gathered up the reins, or with the postilions who loved to crack their whips and to appear smart and well-groomed, in the midst of the squalor which reigned in the terror-stricken city. They were the guardians of the mighty proconsul: on their skill, quickness and presence of mind might depend his precious life.

Even when the shadow of death hangs over an entire community, there will be some who will stand and gape and crack jokes at an uncommon sight.

And now when the pall of night hung over the abode of the man-tiger and his lair and wrapped in its embrace the hunted and the hunters, there still was a knot of people standing round the carriage—between it and the hotel—gazing with lack-lustre eyes on the costly appurtenances wherewith the representative of a wretched people loved to surround himself. They could only see the solid mass of the carriage and of the horses, but they could hear the coachman clicking with his tongue and the postilion cracking his whip, and these sights broke the absolute dreary monotony of their lives.

It was from behind this knot of gaffers that there rose gradually a tumult as of a man calling out in wrath and lashing himself into a fury. Chauvelin and Martin-Roget were just then crossing La Petite Hollande from one bank of the river to the other: they were walking rapidly towards the hotel, when they heard the tumult which presently culminated in a hoarse cry and a volley of oaths.

"My coach! my coach at once—Lalouët, don't leave me—Curse you all for a set of cowardly oafs—My coach I say—"

"The proconsul," murmured Chauvelin as he hastened forward, Martin-Roget following closely on his heels.

By the time that they had come near enough to the coach to distinguish vaguely in the gloom what was going on, people came rushing to the same spot from end to end of the Place. In a moment there was quite a crowd round the carriage, and the two men had much ado to push their way through by a vigorous play of their elbows.

"Citizen Carrier!" cried Chauvelin at the top of his voice, trying to dominate the hubbub, "one minute—I have excellent news for you—The English spy—"

"Curse you for a set of blundering fools," came with a husky cry from out the darkness, "you have let that English devil escape—I knew it—I knew it—the assassin is at large—the murderer—my coach at once—my coach—Lalouët—do not leave me."

Chauvelin had by this time succeeded in pushing his way to the forefront of the crowd: Martin-Roget, tall and powerful, had effectually made a way for him. Through the dense gloom he could see the misshapen form of the proconsul, wildly gesticulating with one arm and with the other clinging convulsively to young Lalouët who already had his hand on the handle of the carriage door.

With a quick, resolute gesture Chauvelin stepped between the door and the advancing proconsul.

"Citizen Carrier," he said with calm determination, "on my oath there is no cause for alarm. Your life is absolutely safe—I entreat you to return to your lodgings—"

To emphasise his words, he had stretched out a hand and firmly grasped the proconsul's coat sleeve. This gesture, however, instead of pacifying the apparently terror-stricken maniac, seemed to have the effect of further exasperating his insensate fear. With a loud oath he tore himself free from Chauvelin's grasp.

"Ten thousand devils," he cried hoarsely, "who is this fool who dares to interfere with me? Stand aside man—stand aside or—"

And before Chauvelin could utter another word or Martin-Roget come to his colleague's rescue, there came the sudden sharp report of a pistol; the horses reared, the crowd was scattered in every direction, Chauvelin was knocked over by a smart blow on the head whilst a vigorous drag on his shoulder alone saved him from falling under the wheels of the coach.

Whilst confusion was at its highest, the carriage door was closed to with a bang and there was a loud, commanding cry hurled through the window at the coachman on his box.

"*En avant*, citizen coachman! Drive for your life! through the Savenay gate. The English assassins are on our heels."

The postilion cracked his whip. The horses, maddened by the report, by the pushing, jostling crowd and the confused cries and screams around, plunged forward, wild with excitement. Their hoofs clattered on the hard road. Some of the crowd ran after the coach across the Place, shouting lustily: "The proconsul! the proconsul!"

Chauvelin—dazed and bruised—was picked up by Martin-Roget.

"The cowardly brute!" was all that he said between his teeth, "he shall rue this outrage as soon as I can give my mind to his affairs. In the meanwhile—"

The clatter of the horses' hoofs was already dying away in the distance. For a few seconds longer, the rattle of the coach was still accompanied by cries of "The proconsul! the proconsul!" Fleury at the bridge head, seeing and hearing its approach, had only just time to order his Marats to stand at attention. A salvo should have been fired when the representative of the people, the high and mighty proconsul, was abroad, but there was no time for that, and the coach clattered over the bridge at breakneck speed, whilst Carrier with his head out of the window was hurling anathemas and insults at Fleury for having allowed the paid spies of that cursed British Government to threaten the life of a representative of the people.

"I go to Savenay," he shouted just at the last, "until that assassin has been thrown in the Loire. But when I return—look to yourself Commandant Fleury."

Then the carriage turned down the Quai de la Fosse and a few minutes later was swallowed up by the gloom.

Chauvelin, supported by Martin-Roget, was hobbling back across the Place. The crowd was still standing about, vaguely wondering why it had got so excited over the departure of the proconsul and the rattle of a coach and pair across the bridge, when on the island there was still an assassin at large—an English spy, the capture of whom would be one of the great events in the chronicles of the city of Nantes.

"I think," said Martin-Roget, "that we may as well go to bed now and leave the rest to Commandant Fleury. The Englishman may not be captured for some hours, and I for one am over-fatigued."

"Then go to bed an you desire, Citizen Martin-Roget," retorted Chauvelin drily, "I for one will stay here until I see the Englishman in the hands of commandant Fleury."

"Hark," interposed Martin-Roget abruptly. "What was that?"

Chauvelin had paused even before Martin-Roget's restraining

hand had rested on his arm. He stood still in the middle of the Place and his knees shook under him so that he nearly fell prone to the ground.

"What is it?" reiterated Martin-Roget with vague puzzlement. "It sounds like young Lalouët's voice."

Chauvelin said nothing. He had forgotten his bruises: he no longer hobbled—he ran across the Place to the front of the hotel whence the voice had come which was so like that of young Lalouët.

The youngster—it was undoubtedly he—was standing at the angle of the hotel: above him a lanthorn threw a dim circle of light on his bare head with its mass of dark curls, and on a small knot of idlers with two or three of the town guard amongst them. The first words spoken by him which Chauvelin distinguished quite clearly were:

"You are all mad—or else drunk—The citizen proconsul is up-stairs in his room—He has just sent me down to hear what news there is of the English spies—"

No one made reply. It seemed as if some giant and spectral hand had passed over this mass of people and with its magic touch had stilled their turbulent passions, silenced their imprecations and cooled their ardour—and left naught but a vague fear, a subtle sense of awe as when something unexplainable and supernatural has manifested itself before the eyes of men.

From far away the roll of coach wheels rapidly disappearing in the distance alone broke the silence of the night.

"Is there no one here who will explain what all this means?" que-ried young Lalouët, who alone had remained self-assured and calm, for he alone knew nothing of what had happened. "Citizen Fleury, are you there?"

Then as once again he received no reply, he added peremptorily:

"Hey! someone there! Are you all louts and oafs that not one of you can speak?"

A timid voice from the rear ventured on explanation.

"The citizen proconsul was here a moment ago—We all saw him, and you citizen Lalouët were with him—"

An imprecation from young Lalouët silenced the timid voice for the nonce—and then another resumed the halting narrative.

"We all could have sworn that we saw you, citizen Lalouët, also the citizen proconsul—He got into his coach with you—you—that is—they have driven off—"

"This is some awful and treacherous hoax," cried the youngster now in a towering passion; "the citizen proconsul is upstairs in bed, I tell you—and I have only just come out of the hotel —! Name of a name of a dog! am I standing here or am I not?"

Then suddenly he bethought himself of the many events of the day which had culminated in this gigantic feat of *leger-de-main*.

"Chauvelin!" he exclaimed. "Where in the name of h—ll is Citizen Chauvelin?"

But Chauvelin for the moment could nowhere be found. Dazed, half-unconscious, wholly distraught, he had fled from the scene of his discomfiture as fast as his trembling knees would allow. Carrier searched the city for him high and low, and for days afterwards the soldiers of the Compagnie Marat gave *aristos* and rebels a rest: they were on the look-out for a small, wizened figure of a man—the man with the pale, keen eyes who had failed to recognise in the pseudo-Paul Friche, in the dirty, out-at-elbows *sans-culotte*—the most exquisite dandy that had ever graced the *salons* of Bath and of London: they were searching for the man with the acute and sensitive brain who had failed to scent in the pseudo-Carrier and the pseudo-Lalouët his old and arch enemy Sir Percy Blakeney and the charming wife of my Lord Anthony Dewhurst.

CHAPTER 10

Lord Tony

A quarter of an hour later Citizen-Commandant Fleury was at last ushered into the presence of the proconsul and received upon his truly innocent head the full torrent of the despot's wrath. But Martin-Roget had listened to the counsels of prudence: for obvious reasons he desired to avoid any personal contact for the moment with Carrier, whom fear of the English spies had made into a more abject and more craven tyrant than ever before. At the same time, he thought it wisest to try and pacify the brute by sending him the ten thousand *francs*—the bribe agreed upon for his help in the undertaking which had culminated in such a disastrous failure.

At the self-same hour whilst Carrier—fuming and swearing—was for the hundredth time uttering that furious "How?" which for the hundredth time had remained unanswered, two men were taking leave of one another at the small postern gate which gives on the cemetery of St. Anne. The taller and younger one of the two had just dropped a heavy purse into the hand of the other. The latter stooped and kissed the kindly hand.

"Milor," he said, "I swear to you most solemnly that M. le Duc de Kernogan will rest in peace in hallowed ground. M. le Curé de Vertou—ah! he is a saint and a brave man, milor—comes over whenever he can prudently do so and reads the offices for the dead—over those who have died as Christians, and there is a piece of consecrated ground out here in the open which those fiends of Terrorists have not discovered yet."

"And you will bury *M. le Duc* immediately," admonished the younger man, "and apprise *M. le Curé* of what has happened."

"Aye! aye! I'll do that, milor, within the hour. Though *M. le Duc* was never a very kind master to me in the past, I cannot forget that I served him and his family for over thirty years as coachman. I drove Mlle. Yvonne in the first pony-cart she ever possessed. I drove her— ah! that was a bitter day!—her and *M. le Duc* when they left Kernogan never to return. I drove Mlle. Yvonne on that memorable night when a crowd of miserable peasants attacked her coach, and that brute Pierre Adet started to lead a rabble against the *château*. That was the beginning of things, milor. God alone knows what has happened to Pierre Adet. His father Jean was hanged by order of *M. le Duc*. Now *M. le Duc* is destined to lie in a forgotten grave. I serve this abominable Republic by digging graves for her victims. I would be happier, I think, if I knew what had become of Mlle. Yvonne."

"Mlle. Yvonne is my wife, old friend," said the younger man softly. "Please God she has years of happiness before her, if I succeed in making her forget all that she has suffered."

"Amen to that, milor!" rejoined the man fervently. "Then I pray you tell the noble lady to rest assured. Jean-Marie—her old coachman whom she used to trust implicitly in the past—will see that M. le Duc de Kernogan is buried as a gentleman and a Christian should be."

"You are not running too great a risk by this, I hope, my good Jean-Marie," quoth Lord Tony gently.

"No greater risk, milor," replied Jean-Marie earnestly, "than the one which you ran by carrying my old master's dead body on your shoulders through the streets of Nantes."

"Bah! that was simple enough," said the younger man, "the hue and cry is after higher quarry tonight. Pray God the hounds have not run the noble game to earth."

Even as he spoke there came from far away through the darkness the sound of a fast trotting pair of horses and the rumble of coach-wheels on the unpaved road.

"There they are, thank God!" exclaimed Lord Tony, and the tremor in his voice alone betrayed the torturing anxiety which he had been enduring, ever since he had seen the last both of his adored young wife and of his gallant chief in the squalid tap-room of the Rat Mort.

With the dead body of Yvonne's father on his back he had quietly worked his way out of the tavern in the wake of his chief. He had his orders, and for the members of that gallant League of the Scarlet Pimpernel there was no such word as "disobedience" and no such word as "fail." Through the darkness and through the tortuous streets of Nantes Lord Anthony Dewhurst—the young and wealthy exquisite, the hero of an hundred *fêtes* and galas in Bath, in London—staggered under the weight of a burden imposed upon him only by his loyalty and a noble sense of self-prescribed discipline—and that burden the dead body of the man who had done him an unforgivable wrong. Without a thought of revolt he had obeyed—and risked his life and worse in the obedience.

The darkness of the night was his faithful handmaiden, and the excitement of the chase after the other quarry had fortunately drawn every possible enemy from his track. He had set his teeth and accomplished his task, and even the deathly anxiety for the wife whom he idolised had been crushed, under the iron heel of a grim resolve. Now his work was done, and from far away he heard the rattle of the coach wheels which were bringing his beloved nearer and nearer to him.

Five minutes longer and the coach came to a halt. A cheery voice called out gaily:

"Tony! are you there?"

"Percy!" exclaimed the young man.

Already he knew that all was well. The gallant leader, the loyal and loving friend, had taxed every resource of a boundlessly fertile brain in order to win yet another wreath of immortal laurels for the League which he commanded, and the very tone of his merry voice proclaimed the triumph which had crowned his daring scheme.

The next moment Yvonne lay in the arms of her dear milor. He had stepped into the carriage, even while Sir Percy climbed nimbly on the box and took the reins from the bewildered coachman's hands.

"Citizen proconsul—" murmured the latter, who of a truth thought that he was dreaming.

"Get off the box, you old noodle," quoth the pseudo-proconsul peremptorily. "Thou and thy friend the postilion will remain here in the road, and on the morrow you'll explain to whomsoever it may concern that the English spy made a murderous attack on you both and left you half dead outside the postern gate of the cemetery of Ste. Anne. Here," he added as he threw a purse down to the two men—who half-dazed and overcome by superstitious fear had indeed scrambled down, one from his box, the other from his horse—"there's a hundred *francs* for each of you in there, and mind you drink to the health of the English spy and the confusion of your brutish proconsul."

There was no time to lose: the horses—still very fresh—were fretting to start.

"Where do we pick up Hastings and Ffoulkes?" asked Sir Percy Blakeney finally as he turned toward the interior of the *barouche*, the hood of which hid its occupants from view.

"At the corner of the rue de Gigan," came the quick answer. "It is only two hundred metres from the city gate. They are on the lookout for you."

"Ffoulkes shall be postilion," rejoined Sir Percy with a laugh, "and Hastings sit beside me on the box. And you will see how at the city gate and all along the route soldiers of the guard will salute the equipage of the all-powerful proconsul of Nantes. By Gad!" he added under his breath, "I've never had a merrier time in all my life—not even when—"

He clicked his tongue and gave the horses their heads—and soon the coachman and the postilion and Jean-Marie the gravedigger of the cemetery of Ste. Anne were left gaping out into the night in the direction where the barouche had so quickly disappeared.

"Now for Le Croisic and the *Daydream*," sighed the daring adventurer contentedly, "—and for Marguerite!" he added wistfully.

Under the hood of the *barouche* Yvonne, wearied but immeasurably happy, was doing her best to answer all her dear milor's impassioned questions and to give him a fairly clear account of that terrible chase and flight through the streets of the Isle Feydeau.

"Ah, milor, how can I tell you what I felt when I realised that I was being carried along in the arms of the valiant Scarlet Pimpernel? A word from him and I understood. After that I tried to be both resourceful and brave. When the chase after us was at its hottest we slipped into a ruined and deserted house. In a room at the back there were several bundles of what looked like old clothes. 'This is my storehouse,' milor said to me; 'now that we have reached it we can just make long noses at the whole pack of bloodhounds.' He made me slip into some boy's clothes which he gave me, and whilst I donned these he disappeared. When he returned I truly did not recognise him. He looked horrible, and his voice—!

"After a moment or two he laughed, and then I knew him. He explained to me the *rôle* which I was to play, and I did my best to obey him in everything. But oh! I hardly lived while we once more emerged into the open street and then turned into the great Place which was full—oh full!—of people. I felt that at every moment we might be suspected. Figure to yourself, my dear milor—"

What Yvonne Dewhurst was about to say next will never be recorded. My Lord Tony had closed her lips with a kiss.

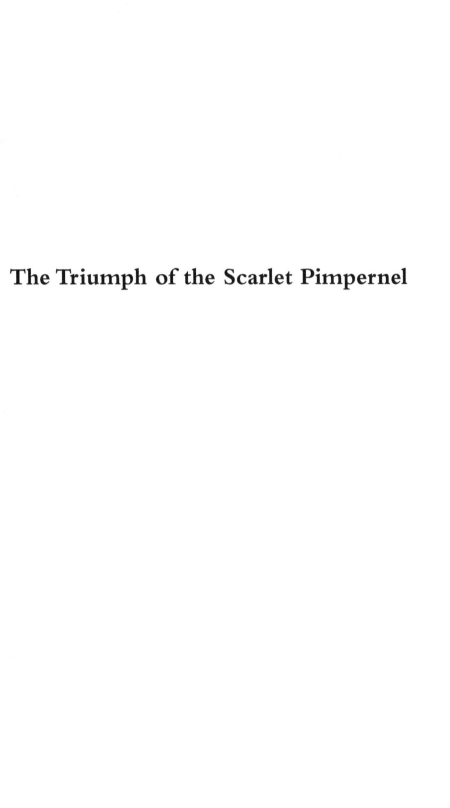

The Triumph of the Scarlet Pimpernel

Contents

Introduction   223

Feet of Clay   225

The Fellowship of Grief   237

One Dram of Joy must have a Pound of Care   243

Rascality Rejoices   251

One Crowded Hour of Glorious Life   260

Two Interludes   267

The Beautiful Spaniard   272

A Hideous, Fearful Hour   280

The Grim Idol that the World Adores   288

Strange Happenings   297

Chauvelin   302

The Fisherman's Rest   305

The Castaway   311

The Nest   313

A Lover of Sport   324

Reunion   332

Night and Morning   338

A Rencontre   342

Departure   347

Memories   353

Waiting   357

Mice and Men   361

By Order of the State   368

Four Days   376

A Dream   386

Terror or Ambition   392

In the Meanwhile   395

The Close of the Second Day   398

When the Storm Burst   404

Our Lady of Pity   409

Grey Dawn   416

The Cataclysm   421

The Whirlwind   425

CHAPTER 1

Introduction

"The everlasting stars look down, like glistening eyes bright with immortal pity, over the lot of man"

Nearly five years have gone by!

Five years, since the charred ruins of grim Bastille—stone image of Absolutism and of Autocracy—set the seal of victory upon the expression of a people's will and marked the beginning of that marvellous era of Liberty and of Fraternity which has led us step by step from the dethronement of a king, through the martryrdom of countless innocents, to the tyranny of an oligarchy more arbitrary, more relentless, above all more cruel, than any that the dictators of Rome or Stamboul ever dream of in their wildest thirst for power. An era that sees a populace always clamouring for the millennium, which ranting demagogues have never ceased to promise: a millennium to be achieved alternatively through the extermination of aristocracy, of titles, of riches, and the abrogation of priesthood: through dethroned royalty and desecrated altars, through an army without leadership, or an assembly without power.

They have never ceased to prate, these frothy rhetoricians! And the people went on, vaguely believing that one day, soon, that millennium would surely come, after seas of blood had purged the soil of France from the last vestige of bygone oppression, and after her sons and daughters had been massacred in their thousands and their tens of thousands, until their headless bodies had built up a veritable scaling ladder for the tottering feet of lustful climbers, and these in their turn had perished to make way for other ranters, other speech-makers, a new Demosthenes or long-tongued Cicero.

Inevitably these too perished, one by one, irrespective of their virtues or their vices, their errors or their ideals: Vergniaud, the enthusiast, and Desmoulins, the irresponsible; Barnave, the just, and Chaumette, the blasphemer; Hébert, the carrion, and Danton, the power. All, all have perished, one after the other: victims of their greed and of their

223

crimes—they and their adherents and their enemies. They slew and were slain in their turn. They struck blindly, like raging beasts, most of them for fear lest they too should be struck by beasts more furious than they. All have perished; but not before their iniquities have for ever sullied what might have been the most glorious page in the history of France—her fight for Liberty. Because of these monsters—and of a truth there were only a few—the fight, itself sublime in its ideals, noble in its conception, has become abhorrent to the rest of mankind.

But they, arraigned at the bar of history, what have they to say, what to show as evidence of their patriotism, of the purity of their intentions?

On this day of April, 1794, year II of the New Calendar, eight thousand men, women, and not a few children, are crowding the prisons of Paris to overflowing. Four thousand heads have fallen under the guillotine in the past three months. All the great names of France, her noblesse, her magistracy, her clergy, members of past Parliaments, shining lights in the sciences, the arts, the universities, men of substance, poets, brain-workers, have been torn from their homes, their churches or their places of refuge, dragged before a travesty of justice, judged, condemned and slaughtered; not singly, not individually, but in batches—whole families, complete hierarchies, entire households: one lot for the crime of being right, another for being nobly born; some because of their religion, others because of professed free-thought. One man for devotion to his friend, another for perfidy; one for having spoken, another for having held his tongue, and another for no crime at all—just because of his family connexions, his profession, or his ancestry.

For months it had been the innocents; but since then it has also been the assassins. And the populace, still awaiting the millennium, clamour for more victims and for more—for the aristocrat and for the *sans-culotte*, and howl with execration impartially at both.

But through this mad orgy of murder and of hatred, one man survives, stands apart indeed, wielding a power which the whole pack of infuriated wolves thirsting for his blood are too cowardly to challenge. The Girondists and the Extremists have fallen. Hébert, the idol of the mob, Danton its hero and its mouthpiece, have been hurled from their throne, sent to the scaffold along with *ci-devant* nobles, aristocrats, royalists and traitors. But this one man remains, calm in the midst of every storm, absolute in his will, indigent where others have grasped riches with both hands, adored, almost deified, by a few, dreaded by all, sphinx-like, invulnerable, sinister—Robespierre!

Robespierre at this time was at the height of his popularity and of his power. The two great Committees of Public Safety and of General Security were swayed by his desires, the Clubs worshipped him, the Convention was packed with obedient slaves to his every word. The Dantonists, cowed into submission by the bold *coup* which had sent their leader, their hero, their idol, to the guillotine, were like a tree that has been struck at the root. Without Danton, the giant of the Revolution, the colossus of crime, the maker of the Terror, the thunderbolt of the Convention, the part was atrophied, robbed of its strength and its vitality, its last few members hanging, servile and timorous, upon the great man's lips.

Robespierre was in truth absolute master of France. The man who had dared to drag his only rival down to the scaffold was beyond the reach of any attack. By this final act of unparalleled despotism, he had revealed the secrets of his soul, shown himself to be rapacious as well as self-seeking. Something of his aloofness, of his incorruptibility, had vanished, yielding to that ever-present and towering ambition which hitherto none had dared to suspect. But ambition is the one vice to which the generality of mankind will always accord homage, and Robespierre, by gaining the victory over his one in the convention, in the clubs and in the committees, had tacitly agreed to obey. The tyrant out of his vaulting ambition had brought forth the slaves.

Faint hearted and servile, they brooded over their wrongs, gazed with smouldering wrath on Danton's vacant seat in the convention, which no one cared to fill. But they did not murmur, hardly dared to plot, and gave assent to every decree, every measure, every suggestion promulgated by the dictator who held their lives in the hollow of his thin white hand; who with a word, a gesture, could send his enemy, his detractor, a mere critic of his actions, to the guillotine.

Chapter 2

Feet of Clay

On this 26th day of April, 1794, which in the newly constituted calendar is the 7th *Floreal*, year II of the Republic, three women and one man were assembled in a small, closely curtained room on the top floor of a house in the Rue de la Planchette, which is situated in a remote and dreary quarter of Paris. The man sat upon a chair which was raised on a dais. He was neatly, indeed immaculately, dressed, in dark cloth coat and tan breeches, with clean linen at throats and wrists, white stockings and buckled shoes. His own hair was concealed under a mouse-coloured wig. He sat quite still, with one leg crossed over the other, and his thin, bony hands were clasped in front of him.

Behind the dais there was a heavy curtain which stretched right across the room, and in front of it, at opposite corners, two young girls, clad in grey, clinging draperies, sat upon their heels, with the palms of their hands resting flat upon their thighs. Their hair hung loose down their backs, their chins were uplifted, their eyes fixed, their bodies rigid in an attitude of contemplation. In the centre of the room a woman stood, gazing upwards at the ceiling, her arms folded across her breast. Her grey hair, lank and unruly, was partially hidden by an ample floating veil of an indefinite shade of grey, and from her meagre shoulders and arms, her garment—it was hardly a gown—descended in straight, heavy, shapeless folds. In front of her was a small table, on it a large crystal globe, which rested on a stand of black wood, exquisitely carved and inlaid with mother-of-pearl, and beside it a small metal box.

Immediately above the old woman's head an oil lamp, the flame of which was screened by a piece of crimson silk, shed a feeble and lurid light upon the scene. Against the wall half a dozen chairs, on the floor a threadbare carpet, and in one corner a broken-down chiffonier represented the sum total of the furniture in the stuffy little room. The curtains in front of the window, as well as the *portières* which masked both the doors, were heavy and thick, excluding all light and most of the outside air.

The old woman, with eyes fixed upon the ceiling, spoke in a dull, even monotone.

"Citizen Robespierre, who is the Chosen of the Most High, hath deigned to enter the humble abode of his servant," she said. "What is his pleasure today?"

"The shade of Danton pursues me," Robespierre replied, and his voice too sounded toneless, as if muffled by the heavily weighted atmosphere. "Can you not lay him to rest?"

The woman stretched out her arms. The folds of her woollen draperies hung straight from shoulder to wrist down to the ground, so that she looked like a shapeless bodiless, grey ghost in the dim, red light.

"Blood!" she exclaimed in a weird, cadaverous wail. "Blood around thee and blood at thy feet! But not upon thy head, O Chosen of the

Almighty! Thy decrees are those of the Most High! Thy hand wields His Avenging Sword! I see thee walking upon a sea of blood, yet thy feet are as white as lilies and thy garments are spotless as the driven snow. *Avaunt!*" she cried in sepulchral tones, "ye spirits of evil! *Avaunt! ye vampires and ghouls! and venture not with your noxious breath to disturb the serenity of our Morning Star!"

The girls in front of the dais raised their arms above their heads and echoed the old soothsayer's wails.

"*Avaunt!*" they cried solemnly. "*Avaunt!*"

Now from a distant corner of the room, a small figure detached itself out of the murky shadows. It was the figure of a young negro, glad in white from head to foot. In the semi-darkness the draperies which he wore were alone visible, and the whites of his eyes. Thus, he seemed to be walking without any feet, to have eyes without any face, and to be carrying a heavy vessel without using any hands. His appearance indeed was so startling and so unearthly that the man upon the dais could not suppress and exclamation of terror. Whereupon a wide row of dazzlingly white teeth showed somewhere between the folds of the spectral draperies, and further enhanced the spook-like appearance of the blackamoor. He carried a deep bowl fashioned of chased copper, which he placed upon the table in front of the old woman, immediately behind the crystal globe and the small metal box. The seer then opened the box, took out a pinch of something brown and powdery, and holding it between finger and thumb, she said solemnly:

"From out the heart of France rises the incense of faith, of hope, and of love!" and she dropped the powder into the bowl. "May it prove acceptable to him who is her chosen Lord!"

A bluish flame shot up from out the depth of the vessel, shed for the space of a second or two its ghostly light upon the gaunt features of the old hag, the squat and grinning face of the negro, and toyed with the will-o'-the-wisp-like fitfulness of the surrounding gloom. A sweet-scented smoke rose upwards to the ceiling. Then the flame died down again, making the crimson darkness around appear by contrast more lurid and more mysterious than before.

Robespierre had not moved. His boundless vanity, his insatiable ambition, blinded him to the effrontery, the ridicule of this mysticism. He accepted the tangible incense, took a deep breath, as if to fill his entire being with its heady fumes, just as he was always ready to accept the fulsome adulation of his devotees and of his sycophants.

The old charlatan then repeated her incantations. Once more she

227

took powder from the box, threw some of it into the vessel, and spoke in a sepulchral voice:

"From out of the heart of those who worship thee rises the incense of their praise!"

A delicate white flame rose immediately out of the vessel. It shed a momentary, unearthly brightness around, then as speedily vanished again. And for the third time the witch spoke the mystic words:

"From out the heart of an entire nation rises the incense of perfect joy in thy triumph over thine enemies!"

This time, however, the magic powder did not act quite so rapidly as it had done on the two previous occasions. For a few seconds the vessel remained dark and unresponsive; nothing came to dispel the surrounding gloom. Even the light of the oil lamp overhead appeared suddenly to grow dim. At any rate, so it seemed to the autocrat who, with nerves on edge, sat upon his throne-like seat, his bony hands, so like the talons of a bird of prey, clutching the arms of his chair, his narrow eyes fixed upon the *sybil*, who in her turn was gazing on the metal vessel as if she would extort some cabalistic mystery from its depth.

All at once a bright red flame shot out of the bowl. Everything in the room became suffused with a crimson glow. The old witch bending over her cauldron looked as if she were smeared with blood, her eyes appeared bloodshot, her long hooked nose cast a huge black shadow over her mouth, distorting the face into a hideous, cadaverous grin. From her throat issued strange sounds like those of an animal in the throes of pain.

"Red! Red!" she lamented, and gradually as the flame subsided and finally flickered out altogether, her words became more distinct. She raised the crystal globe and gazed fixedly into it. "Always red," she went on slowly. "Thrice yesterday did I cast the spell in the name of Our Chosen—thrice did the spirits cloak their identity in a blood-red flame—red—always red—not only blood—but danger—danger of death through that which is red—"

Robespierre had risen from his seat his thin lips were murmuring hasty imprecations. The kneeling figurants looked scared, and strange wailing sounds came from their mouths. The young blackamoor alone looked self-possessed. He stood by, evidently enjoying the scene, his white teeth gleaming in a huge, board grin.

"A truce on riddles, Mother!" Robespierre exclaimed at last impatiently and descended hastily from the dais. He approached the old necromancer, seized her by the arm, thrust his head in front of hers in an endeavour to see something which apparently was revealed to her in the crystal globe. "What is it you see in there?" he queried harshly.

But she pushed him aside, gazed with rapt intentness into the globe.

"Red!" she murmured. "Scarlet—aye, scarlet! And now it takes shape—Scarlet—and it obscures the Chosen One—the shape becomes more clear—the Chosen One appears more dim—"

Then she gave a piercing shriek.

"Beware!—beware!—that which is Scarlet is shaped like a flower—five petals, I see them distinctly—and the Chosen One I see no more—"

"Malediction!" the man exclaimed. "What foolery is this?"

"No foolery," the old charlatan resumed in a dull monotone. "Thou didst consult the oracle, oh thou, who art the Chosen of the people of France! and the oracle has spoken. Beware of a scarlet flower! From that which is scarlet comes danger of death for thee!"

Wherat Robespierre tried to laugh.

"Someone has filled thy head, Mother," he said in a voice which he vainly tried to steady, "with tales of the mysterious Englishman who goes by the name of the Scarlet Pimpernel—"

"Thy mortal enemy, O Messenger of the Most High!" the old blasphemer broke in solemnly. "In far-off fog-bound England he hath sworn thy death. Beware—"

"If that is the only danger which threatens me—" the other began, striving to speak carelessly.

"The only one, and the greatest one," the hag went on insistently. "Despise it not because it seems small and remote."

"I do not despise it; neither do I magnify it. A gnat is a nuisance, but not a danger."

"A gnat may wield a poisoned dart. The spirits have spoken. Heed their warning, O Chosen of the People! Destroy the Englishman ere he destroy thee!"

"*Pardi!*" Robespierre retorted, and despite the stuffiness of the room he gave a shiver as if he felt cold. "Since thou dost commune with the spirits, find out from them how I can accomplish that."

The woman once more raised the crystal globe to the level of her breast. With her elbows stretched out and her draperies falling straight all around her, she gazed into it for a while in silence. Then she began to murmur.

"I see the Scarlet Flower quite plainly—a small Scarlet Flower.— And I see the great Light which is like an aureole, the Light of the

Chosen One. It is of dazzling brightness—but over the Scarlet Flower casts a Stygian shadow."

"Ask them," Robespierre broke in peremptorily, "ask thy spirits how best I can overcome mine enemy."

"I see something," the witch went on in an even monotone, still gazing into the crystal globe "white and rose and tender—is it a woman—"

"A woman?"

"She is tall, and she is beautiful—a stranger in the land—with eyes dark as the night and tresses black as the raven's wing.—Yes, it is a woman.—She stands between the Light and that blood-red flower. She takes the flower in her hand—she fondles it, raises it to her lips.—Ah!" and the old seer gave a loud cry of triumph. "She tosses it mangled and bleeding into the consuming Light.—And now it lies faded, torn, crushed, and the Light grows in radiance and in brilliancy, and there is none now to dim its pristine glory—"

"But the woman? Who is she?" the man broke in impatiently. "What is her name?"

"The spirits speak no names," the seer replied. "Any woman would gladly be thy handmaid, O Elect of France! The spirits have spoken," she concluded solemnly. "Salvation will come to thee by the hand of a woman."

"And mine enemy?" he insisted. "Which of us two is in danger of death now—now that I am warned—which of us two?—mine English enemy, or I?"

Nothing loth, the old hag was ready to continue her sortilege. Robespierre hung breathless upon her lips. His whole personality seemed transformed. He appeared eager, fearful, credulous—a different man to the cold, calculating despot who sent thousands to their death with his measured oratory, the mere power of his presence. Indeed, history has sought in vain for the probably motive which drove this cynical tyrant into consulting this pitiable charlatan. That Catherine Théot had certain psychic powers has never been gainsaid, and since the philosophers of the eighteenth century had undermined the religious superstitions of the Middle Ages, it was only to be expected that in the great upheaval of this awful Revolution, men and women should turn to the mystic and the supernatural as to a solace and respite from the fathomless misery of their daily lives.

In this world of ours, the more stupendous the events, the more abysmal the catastrophes, the more do men realise their own impotence and the more eagerly do they look for the Hidden Hand that is powerful enough to bring about such events and to hurl upon them such devastating cataclysms. Indeed, never since the dawn of history had so many theosophies, demonologies, occult arts, spiritualism, exorcism of all sorts, flourished as they did now: The Theists, the Rosicrucians, the Illuminat, Swedenborg, the Count of Saint Germain, Weishaupt, and scores of others, avowed charlatans or earnest believers, had their neophytes, their devotees, and their cults.

Catherine Théot was one of many: for the nonce, one of the most noteworthy in Paris. She believed herself to be endowed with the gift of prophecy, and her fetish was Robespierre. In this at least she was genuine. She believed him now to be a new Messiah, the Elect of God. Nay! she loudly proclaimed him as such, and one of her earliest neophytes, an ex-Carthusian monk named Gerle, who sat in the convention next to the great man, had whispered in the latter's ear the insidious flattery which had gradually led his footsteps to the witch's lair.

Whether his own vanity—which was without limit and probably without parallel—caused him to believe in his own heaven-sent mission, or whether he only desire to strengthen his own popularity by endowing it with supernatural prestige, is a matter of conjecture. Certain it is that he did lend himself to Catherine Thao's cabalistic practices and that he allowed himself to be flattered and worshipped by the numerous nepohytes who flocked to this new temple of magic, either from mystical fervour or merely to serve their own ends by fawning on the most dreaded man in France.

Catherine Théot had remained rigidly still, in rapt contemplation. It seemed as if she pondered over the Chosen One's last peremptory demand.

"Which of us two," he had queried, in a dry, hard voice, "is in danger of death now—now that I am warned—mine English enemy, or I?"

The next moment, as if moved by inspiration, she took another pinch of powder out of the metal box. The nigger's bright black eyes followed her every movement, as did the dictator's half-contemptuous gaze. The girls had begun to intone a monotonous chant. As the seer dropped the powder into the metal bowl, a highly scented smoke shot upwards and the interior of the vessel was suffused with a golden glow. The smoke rose in spirals. Its fumes spread through the airless room, rendering the atmosphere insufferably heavy.

The dictator of France felt a strange exultation running through him, as with deep breaths he inhaled the potent fumes. It seemed to him as if his body had suddenly become etherealised, as if he were in truth the Chosen of the Most High as well as the idol of France. Thus disembodied, he felt in himself boundless strength! the power to rise triumphant over all his enemies, whoever they may be. There was a mighty buzzing in his ears like the reverberation of thousands of trumpets and drums ringing and beating in unison to his exaltation and to his might. His eyes appeared to see the whole of the people of France, clad in white robes, with ropes round their necks, and bowing as slaves to the ground before him. He was riding on a cloud. His throne was of gold. In his hand he had a sceptre of flame, and beneath his feet lay, crushed and mangled, a huge scarlet flower. The *sybil's* voice reached his ears as if through a supernal trumpet:

"Thus, lie for ever crushed at the feet of the Chosen One, those who have dared to defy his power!"

Greater and greater became his exultation. He felt himself uplifted high, high above the clouds, until he could see the world as a mere crystal ball at his feet. His head had touched the portals of heaven; his eyes gazed upon his own majesty, which was second only to that of God. An eternity went by. He was immortal.

Then suddenly, through all the mystic music, the clarion sounds and songs of praise, there came a sound, so strange and yet so human, that the almighty dictator's wandering spirit was in an instant hurled back to earth, brought down with a mighty jerk which left him giddy, sick, with throat dry and burning eyes. He could not stand on his feet, indeed would have fallen but that the negro had hastily pulled a chair forward, into which he sank, swooning with unaccountable horror.

And yet that sound had been harmless enough: just a peal of laughter, merry and inane—nothing more. It came faintly echoing form beyond the heavy *portière*. Yet it had unnerved the most ruthless despot in France. He looked about him, scared and mystified. Nothing had been changed since he had gone wandering into Elysian fields. He was still in a stuffy, curtained room; there was the dais on which he had sat; the two women still chanted their weird lament; and there was the old necromancer in her shapeless, colourless robe, coolly setting down the crystal globe upon its carved stand. There was the blackamoor, grinning and mischievous, the metal vessel, the oil lamp, the threadbare carpet. What of all this had been a dream? The clouds and the trumpets, or that peal of human laughter with the quaint, inane catch in it? No one looked scared: the girls chanted, the old hag mumbled vague directions to her black attendant, who tried to look solemn, since he was paid to keep his impish mirth in check.

"What was that?" Robespierre murmured at last.

The old woman looked up.

"What was what, O Chosen One?" she asked.

"I heard a sound——" he mumbled. "A laugh—Is anyone else in the room?"

She shrugged her shoulders.

"People are waiting in the antechamber," she replied carelessly, "until it is the pleasure of the Chosen One to go. As a rule, they wait patiently, and in silence. But one of them may have laughed." Then, as he made no further comment but still stood there silent, as if irresolute, she queried with a great show of deference: "What is thy next pleasure, O thou who art beloved of the people of France?"

"Nothing—nothing!" he murmured. "I'll go now."

She turned straight to him and made him elaborate obeisance, waving her arms about her. The two girls struck the ground with their foreheads. The Chosen One, in his innermost heart vaguely conscious of ridicule, frowned impatiently.

"Do not," he said peremptorily, "let anyone know that I have been here."

"Only those who idolise thee——" she began.

"I know—I know," he broke in more gently, for the fulsome adulation soothed his exacerbated nerves. "But I have many enemies—and thou too art watched with malevolent eyes.—Let not our enemies make capital of our intercourse."

"I swear to thee, O Mighty Lord, that thy servant obeys thy behests in all things."

"That is well," he retorted drily. "But thy adepts are wont to talk too much. I'll not have my name bandied about for the glorification of thy necromancy."

"Thy name is sacred to thy servants," she insisted with ponderous solemnity. "As sacred as is thy person. Thou art the regenerator of the true faith, the Elect of the First Cause, the high priest of a new religion. We are but thy servants, thy handmaids, thy worshippers."

All this charlatanism was precious incense to the limitless vanity of the despot. His impatience vanished, as did his momentary terror. He became kind, urbane, condescending. At the last, the old hag almost prostrated herself before him, and clasping her wrinkled hands together, she said in tones of reverential entreaty:

"In the name of thyself, of France, of the entire world, I adjure thee to lend ear to what the spirits have revealed this day. Beware the danger that comes to thee from the scarlet flower. Set thy almighty mind to compass its destruction. Do not disdain a woman's help, since the spirits have proclaimed that through a woman thou shalt be saved. Remember! Remember!" she adjured him with ever-growing earnestness. "Once before, the world was saved through a woman. A woman crushed the serpent beneath her foot. Let a woman now crush that scarlet flower beneath hers. Remember!"

She actually kissed his feet; and he, blinded by self-conceit to the folly of this fetishism and the ridicule of his own acceptance of it, raised his hand above her head as if in the act of pronouncing a benediction.

Then without another word he turned to go. The young negro brought him his hat and cloak. The latter he wrapped closely round his shoulders, his hat he pulled down well over his eyes. Thus, muffled and, he hoped, unrecognisable, he passed with a firm tread out of the room.

For a while the old witch waited, strainer her ears to catch the last sound of those retreating footsteps; then, with a curt word and an impatient clapping of her hands, she dismissed her attendants, the negro as well as her neophytes. These young women at her word lost quickly enough their air of rapt mysticism, became very human indeed, stretched out their limbs, yawned lustily, and with none too graceful movements uncurled themselves and struggled to their feet. Chattering and laughing like so many magpies let out of a cage, they soon disappeared through the door in the rear.

Again, the old woman waited silent and motionless until that merry sound too gradually subsided. Then she went across the room to the dais and drew aside the curtain which hung behind it.

"Citizen Chauvelin!" she called peremptorily.

A small figure of a man stepped out from the gloom. He was dressed in black, his hair, of a nondescript blonde shade and his crumpled linen alone told light in the general sombreness of his appearance.

"Well?" he retorted drily.

"Are you satisfied?" the old woman went on with eager impatience. "You heard what I said?"

"Yes, I heard," he replied. "Think you he will act on it?"

"I am certain of it."

"But why not have named Theresia Cabarrus? Then, at least, I would have been sure—"

"He might have recoiled at an actual name," the woman replied, "suspected me of connivance. The Chosen of the people of France is shrewd as well as distrustful. And I have my reputation to consider. But, remember what I said: 'tall, dark, beautiful, a stranger in this land!' So, if indeed you require the help of the Spaniard—"

"Indeed, I do!" he rejoined earnestly. And, as if speaking to his own inward self, "Theresia Cabarrus is the only woman I know who can really help me."

"But you cannot force her consent, Citizen Chauvelin," the *sybil* insisted.

The eyes of Citizen Chauvelin lit up suddenly with a flash of that old fire of long ago, when he was powerful enough to compel the consent or the co-operation of any man, woman or child on whom he had deigned to cast an appraising glance. But the flash was only momentary. The next second, he had once more resumed his unobtrusive, even humbled, attitude.

"My friends, who are few," he said, with a quick sigh of impatience; "and mine enemies, who are without number, will readily share your conviction, Mother, that Citizen Chauvelin can compel no one to do his bidding these days. Least of all the affianced wife of powerful Tallien."

"Well, then," the *sybil* argued, "how think you that—"

"I only hope, Mother," Chauvelin broke in suavely, "that after your *séance* today, Citizen Robespierre himself will see to it that Theresia Cabarrus gives me the help I need."

Catherine Théot shrugged her shoulders.

"Oh!" she said drily, "the Cabarrus knows no law save that of her caprice. And as Tallien's *fiancée* she is almost immune."

"Almost, but not quite! Tallien is powerful, but so was Danton."

"But Tallien is prudent, which Danton was not."

"Tallien is also a coward; and easily led like a lamb, with a halter. He came back from Bordeaux tied to the apron-strings of the fair Spaniard. He should have spread fire and terror in the region; but at her bidding he dispensed justice and even mercy instead. A little more airing of his moderate views, a few more acts of unpatriotic clemency, and powerful Tallien himself may become 'suspect.'"

"And you think that, when he is," the old woman rejoined with grim sarcasm, "you will hold his fair betrothed in the hollow of your hand?"

"Certainly!" he assented, and with an acid smile fell to contemplating his thin, talon-like palms. "Since Robespierre, counselled by Mother Théot, will himself have placed her there."

Whereupon Catherine Théot ceased to argue, since the other appeared so sure of himself. Once more she shrugged her shoulders.

"Well, then, if you are satisfied—" she said.

"I am. Quite," he replied, and at once plunged his hand in the breast-pocket of his coat. He had caught the look of avarice and of greed which had glittered in the old hag's eyes. From his pocket he drew a bundle of notes, for which Catherine immediately stretched out a grasping hand. But before giving her the money, he added a stern warning.

"Silence, remember! And, above all, discretion!"

"You may rely on me, citizen," the *sybil* riposted quietly. "I am not likely to blab."

He did not place the notes in her hand but threw them down on the table with a gesture of contempt, without deigning to count. But Catherine Théot cared nothing for his contempt. She coolly picked up the notes and hid them in the folds of her voluminous draperies. Then as Chauvelin, without another word, had turned unceremoniously to go, she placed a bony hand upon his arm.

"And I can rely on you, citizen," she insisted firmly, "that when the Scarlet Pimpernel is duly captured—"

"There will be ten thousand *livres* for you," he broke in impatiently, "if my scheme with Theresia Cabarrus is successful. I never go back on my word."

"And I'll not go back on mine," she concluded drily. "We are dependent on one another, Citizen Chauvelin. You want to capture the English spy, and I want ten thousand *livres*, so that I may retire from active life and quietly cultivate a plot of cabbages somewhere in the sunshine. So, you may leave the matter to me, my friend. I'll not allow the great Robespierre to rest till he has compelled Theresia Cabarrus to do your bidding. Then you may use her as you think best. That gang of English spies must be found and crushed. We cannot have the Chosen of the Most High threatened by such vermin. Ten thousand *livres*, you say?" the *sybil* went on, and once again, as in the presence of the dictator, a mystic exultation appeared to possess her soul. Gone was the glitter of avarice from her eyes; her wizened face seemed transfigured, her shrunken form to gain in stature. "Nay! I would serve you on my knees and accord you worship, if you avert the scarlet danger that hovers over the head of the Beloved of France!"

But Chauvelin was obviously in no mood to listen to the old hag's jeremiads, and while with arms uplifted she once more worked herself up to a hysterical burst of enthusiasm for the bloodthirsty monster whom she worshipped, he shook himself free from her grasp and finally slipped out of the room, without further wasting his breath.

Chapter 3

The Fellowship of Grief

In the antechamber of Catherine Théot's abode of mysteries some two hours later, half a dozen persons were sitting. The room was long, narrow and bare, its walls dank and colourless, and save for the rough wooden benches on which these persons sat, was void of any furniture. The benches were ranged against the walls; the one window at the end was shuttered as to exclude all daylight, and from the ceiling there hung a broken-down wrought-iron chandelier, wherein a couple of lighted tallow candles were set, the smoke from which rose in irregular spirals upwards to the low and blackened ceiling.

These persons who sat or sprawled upon the benches did not speak to one another. They appeared to be waiting. One or two of them were seemingly asleep; others, from time to time, would rouse themselves from their apathy, look with dim, inquiring eyes in the direction of a heavy *portière*. When this subsided again all those in the bare waiting-room resumed their patient, lethargic attitude, and a silence—weird and absolute—reigned once more over them all. Now and then somebody would sigh, and at one time one of the sleepers snored.

Far away a church clock struck six.

A few minutes later, the *portière* was lifted, and a girl came into the room. She held a shawl, very much the worse for wear, tightly wrapped around her meagre shoulders, and from beneath her rough woollen skirt her small feet appeared clad in well-worn shoes and darned worsted stockings. Her hair, which was fair and soft, was partially hidden under a white muslin cap, and as she walked with a brisk step across the room, she looked neither to right nor left, appeared to move as in a dream. And her large grey eyes were brimming over with tears.

Neither her rapid passage across the room nor her exit through a door immediately opposite the window created the slightest stir amongst those who were waiting. Only one of the men, a huge ungainly giant, whose long limbs appeared to stretch half-across the bare wooden floor, looked up lazily as she passed.

After the girl had gone, silence once more fell on the small assembly. Not a sound came from behind the *portière*; but from beyond the other door the faint patter of the girl's feet could be heard gradually fading away as she went slowly down the stone stairs.

A few more minutes went by, then the door behind the *portière* was opened and a cadaverous voice spoke the word, "Enter!"

There was a faint stir among those who waited. A woman rose from her seat, said dully: "My turn, I think?" and, gliding across the room like some bodiless spectre, she presently vanished behind the *portière*.

"Are you going to the Fraternal Supper tonight, Citizen Langlois?" the giant said, after the woman had gone. His tone was rasping and harsh and his voice came with a wheeze and an obviously painful effort from his broad, doubled-up chest.

"Not I!" Langlois replied. "I must speak with Mother Théot. My wife made me promise. She is too ill to come herself, and the poor unfortunate believes in the Théot's incantations."

"Come out and get some fresh air, then," the other rejoined. "It is stifling in here!"

It was indeed stuffy in the dark, smoke-laden room. The man put his bony hand up to his chest, as if to quell a spasm of pain. A horrible, rasping cough shook his big body and brought a sweat to his brow. Langlois, a wizened little figure of a man, who looked himself as if he had one foot in the grave, waited patiently until the spasm was over, then, with the indifference peculiar to these turbulent times, he said lightly:

"I would just as soon sit here as wear out shoe-leather on the cobblestones of this God-forsaken hole. And I don't want to miss my turn with Mother Théot."

"You'll have another four hours mayhap to wait in this filthy atmosphere."

"What an *aristo* you are, Citizen Rateau!" the other retorted drily. "Always talking about the atmosphere!"

"So, would you, if you had only one lung wherewith to inhale this filth," growled the giant through a wheeze.

"Then don't wait for me, my friend," Langlois concluded with a careless shrug of his narrow shoulders. "And, if you don't mind missing your turn—"

"I do not," was Rateau's curt reply. "I would as soon be last as not. But I'll come back presently. I am the third from now. If I'm not back you can have my turn, and I'll follow you in. But I can't—"

His next words were smothered in a terrible fit of coughing, as he struggled to his feet. Langlois swore at him for making such a noise, and the women, roused from their somnolence, sigh with impatience or resignation. But all those who remained seated on the benches watched with a kind of dull curiosity the ungainly figure of the asthmatic giant as he made his way across the room and anon went out through the door.

His heavy footsteps were heard descending the stone stairs with a shuffling sound, and the clatter of his wooden shoes. The women once more settled themselves against the dank walls, with feet stretched out before them and arms folded over their breasts, and in that highly uncomfortable position prepared once more to go to sleep.

Langlois buried his hands in the pockets of his breeches, spat contentedly upon the floor, and continued to wait.

In the meanwhile, the girl who, with tear-filled eyes, had come out of the inner mysterious room in Mother Théot's apartments, had, after a slow descent down the interminable stone stairs, at last reached the open air.

The Rue de la Planchette is only a street in name, for the houses in it are few and far between. One side of it is taken up for the major portion of its length by the dry moat which at this point forms the boundary of the Arsenal and of the military ground around the Bastille. The house wherein lodged Mother Théot is one of a small group situated behind the Bastille, the grim ruins of which can be distinctly seen from the upper windows. Immediately facing those houses is the Porte St. Antoine, through which the wayfarer in this remote quarter of Paris has to pass in order to reach the more populous parts of the city. This is just a lonely and squalid backwater, broken up by undeveloped land and timber yards. One end of the street abuts on the river, the other becomes merged in the equally remote suburb of Popincourt.

But, for the girl who had just come out of the heavy, fetid atmosphere of Mother Théot's lodgings, the air which reached her nostrils as she came out of the wicket-gate, was positive manna to her lungs. She stood for a while quite still, drinking in the balmy spring air, almost dizzy with the sensation of purity and of freedom which came to her from over the vast stretch of open ground occupied by the

Arsenal. For a minute or two she stood there, then walked deliberately in the direction of the Porte St. Antoine.

She was very tired, for she had come to the Rue de la Planchette on foot all the way from the small apartment in the St. Germain quarter, where she lodged with her mother and sister and a young brother; she had become weary and jaded by sitting for hours on a hard wooden bench, waiting her turn to speak with Mother Théot, and then standing for what seemed an eternity of time in the presence of the soothsayer, who had further harassed her nerves by weird prophecies and mystic incantations.

But for the nonce weariness was forgotten. Régine de Serval was going to meet the man she loved, at a trysting-place which they had marked as their own: the porch of the church of Petit St. Antoine, a secluded spot where neither prying eyes could see them nor ears listen to what they had to say. A spot which to poor little Régine was the very threshold of Paradise, for here she had Bertrand all to herself, undisturbed by the prattle of Joséphine or Jacques or the querulous complaints of *maman*, cooped up in that miserable apartment in the old St. Germain quarter of the city.

So, she walked briskly and without hesitation. Bertrand had agreed to meet her at five o'clock. It was now close on half-past six. It was still daylight, and a brilliant April sunset tinged the cupola of Ste. Marie with gold and drew long fantastic shadows across the wide Rue St. Antoine.

Régine had crossed the Rue des Balais, and the church porch of Petit St. Antoine was bust a few paces farther on, when she became conscious of heavy, dragging footsteps some little way behind her. Immediately afterwards, the distressing sound of a racking cough reached her ears, followed by heartrending groans as of a human creature in grievous bodily pain. The girl, not in the least frightened, instinctively turned to look, and was moved to pity on seeing a man leaning against the wall of a house, in a state bordering on collapse, his hands convulsively grasping his chest, which appeared literally torn by a violent fit of coughing. Forgetting her own troubles, as well as the joy which awaited her so close at hand, Régine unhesitatingly recrossed the road, approached the sufferer, and in a gentle voice asked him if she could be of any assistance to him in his distress.

"A little water," he gasped, "for mercy's sake!"

Just for a second or two she looked about her, doubtful as to what to do, hoping perhaps to catch sight of Bertrand, if he had not given up all hope of meeting her. The next, she had stepped boldly through the wicket-gate of the nearest *porte-cochère* and finding her way to the lodge of the *concierge*, she asked for a drop of water for a passer-by who was in pain. A jug of water was at once handed to her by a sympathetic *concierge*, and with it she went back to complete her simple act of mercy.

For a moment she was puzzled, not seeing the poor vagabond there, where she had left him half-swooning against the wall. But soon she spied him, in the very act of turning under the little church porch of Petit St. Antoine, the hallowed spot of her frequent meetings with Bertrand.

He seemed to have crawled there for shelter, and there he collapsed upon the wooden bench, in the most remote angle of the porch. Of Bertrand there was not a sign.

Régine was soon by the side of the unfortunate. She held up the jug of water to his quaking lips, and he drank eagerly. After that he felt better, muttered vague words of thanks. But he seemed so weak, despite his stature, which appeared immense in this narrow enclosure, that she did not like to leave him. She sat down beside him, suddenly conscious of fatigue. He seemed harmless enough, and after a while began to tell her of his trouble. This awful asthma, which he had contracted in the campaign against the English in Holland, where he and his comrades had to march in snow and ice, often shoeless and with nothing but bass mats around their shoulders. He had but lately been discharged out of the army as totally unfit, and he had no money wherewith to pay a doctor, he would no doubt have been dead by now but that a comrade had spoken to him of Mother Théot, a marvellous sorceress, who knew the art of drugs and simples, and could cure all ailments of the body by the mere laying on of hands.

"Ah, yes," the girl sighed involuntarily, "of the body!"

Through the very act of sitting still, a deadly lassitude had crept into her limbs. She was thankful not to move, to say little, and to listen with half an ear to the vagabond's jeremiads. Anyhow, she was sure that Bertrand would no longer be waiting. He was ever impatient if he thought that she failed him in anything, and it was she who had appointed five o'clock for their meeting. Even now the church clock way above the porch was striking half-past six. And the asthmatic giant went glibly on. He had partially recovered his breath.

"Aye!" he was saying, in response to her lament, "and of the mind, too. I had a comrade whose sweetheart was false to him while he was fighting for his country. Mother Théot gave him a potion which he administered to the faithless one, and she returned to him as full of ardour as ever before."

"I have no faith in potions," the girl said, and shook her head sadly the while tears once more gathered in her eyes.

"No more have I," the giant assented carelessly. "But if my sweetheart was false to me I know what I would do."

This he said in so droll a fashion, and the whole idea of this ugly, ungainly creature having a sweetheart was so comical, that despite her will, the ghost of a smile crept round the young girl's sensitive mouth.

"What would you do, citizen?" she queried gently.

"Just take her away, out of the reach of temptation," he replied sententiously. "I should say, 'This must stop,' and 'You come away with me, *ma mie!*'"

"Ah!" she retorted impulsively, "it is easy to talk. A man can do so much. What can a woman do?"

She checked herself abruptly, ashamed of having said so much. What was this miserable caitiff to her that she should as much as hint her troubles in his hearing? In these days of countless spies, of innumerable confidence tricks set to catch the unwary, it was more than foolhardy to speak of one's private affairs to any stranger, let alone to an out-at-elbows vagabond who was just the sort of refuse of humanity who would earn a precarious livelihood by the sale of information, true or false, wormed out of some innocent fellow-creature. Hardly, then, were the words out of her mouth than the girl repented of her folly, turned quick, frightened eyes on the abject creature beside her.

But he appeared not to have heard. A wheezy cough came out of his bony chest. Nor did he meet her terrified gaze.

"What did you say, *citoyenne?*" he muttered fretfully. "Are you dreaming?—or what?—"

"Yes—yes!" she murmured vaguely, her heart still beating with that sudden fright. "I must have been dreaming.—But you—you are better—?"

"Better? Perhaps," he replied, with a hoarse laugh. "I might even be able to crawl home."

"Do you live very far?" she asked.

"No. Just by the Rue de l'Anier."

He made no attempt to thank her for her gentle ministration, and she thought of how ungainly he looked—almost repellent—sprawling right across the porch, with his long legs stretched out before him and his hands buried in the pockets of his breeches. Nevertheless, he looked so helpless and so pitiable that the girl's kind heart was again stirred with compassion, and when presently he struggled with difficulty to his feet, she said impulsively:

"The Rue de l'Anier is on my way. If you will wait, I'll return the jug to the kind *concierge* who let me have it and I'll walk with you. You really ought not to be about the street alone."

"Oh, I am better now," he muttered, in the same ungracious way. "You had best leave me alone. I am not a suitable gallant for a pretty wench like you."

But already the girl had tripped away with the jug and returned two minutes later to find that the curious creature had already started on his way and was fifty yards or more farther up the street by now. She shrugged her shoulders, feeling mortified at his ingratitude, and not a little ashamed that she had forced her compassion where it was so obviously unwelcome.

Chapter 4

One Dram of Joy must have a Pound of Care

She stood for a moment, gazing mechanically on the retreating figure of the asthmatic giant. The next moment she heard her name spoken and turned quickly with a little cry of joy.

"Régine!"

A young man was hurrying towards her, was soon by her side and took her hand.

"I have been waiting," he said reproachfully, "for more than an hour."

In the twilight his face appeared pinched and pale, with dark, deep-sunken eyes that told of a troubled soul and a consuming, inward fire. He wore cloth clothes that were very much the worse for wear, and boots that were down at hell. A battered tricorne hat was pushed back from his high forehead, exposing the veined temples with the line of brown hair, and the arched, intellectual brows that proclaimed the enthusiast rather than the man of action.

"I am sorry, Bertrand," the girl said simply. "But I had to wait such a long time at Mother Théot's, and—"

"But what were you doing now?" he queried with an impatient frown. "I saw you from a distance. You came out of yonder house, and then stood here like one bewildered. You did not hear when first I called."

"I have had quite a funny adventure," Régine explained; "and I am very tired. Sit down with me, Bertrand, for a moment. I'll tell you all about it."

A flat refusal hovered palpably on his lips.

"It is too late—" he began, and the frown of impatience deepened upon his brow. He tried to protest, but Régine did look very tired. Already, without waiting for his consent, she had turned into the little porch, and Bertrand perforce had to follow her.

The shades of evening now were fast gathering in, and the length-ened shadows stretched out away, right across the street. The last rays of the sinking sun still tinged the roofs and chimney pots opposite with a crimson hue. But here, in the hallowed little trysting-place, the kingdom of night had already established its sway. The darkness lent an air of solitude and of security to this tiny refuge, and Régine drew a happy little sigh as she walked deliberately to its farthermost recess and sat down on the wooden bench in it extreme and darkest angle.

Behind her, the heavy oaken door of the church was closed. The church itself, owning to the contumaciousness of its parish priest, had been desecrated by the ruthless hands of the Terrorists and left derelict, to fall into decay. The stone walls themselves appeared cut off from the world, as if ostracized. But between them Régine felt safe, and when Bertrand Moncrif somewhat reluctantly sat down beside her, she also felt almost happy.

"It is very late," he murmured once more, ungraciously.

She was leaning her head against the wall, looked so pale, with eyes closed and bloodless lips, that the young man's heart was suddenly filled with compunction.

"You are not ill, Régine?" he asked, more gently.

"No," she replied, and smiled bravely up at him. "Only very tired and a little dizzy. The atmosphere in Catherine Théot's rooms was stifling, and then when I came out—"

He took her hand, obviously making an effort to be patient and to be kind; and she, not noticing the effort or his absorption, began to tell him about her little adventure with the asthmatic giant.

"Such a droll creature," she explained. "He would have frightened me but for that awful, churchyard cough."

But the matter did not seem to interest Bertrand very much; and presently he took advantage of a pause in her narrative to ask abruptly:

"And Mother Théot, what had she to say?"

Régine gave a shudder.

"She foretells danger for us all," she said.

"The old charlatan!" he retorted with a shrug of the shoulders. "As if everyone was not in danger these days!"

"She gave me a powder," Régine went on simply, "which she thinks will calm Joséphine's nerves."

"And that is folly," he broke in harshly. "We do not want Joséphine's nerves to be calmed."

But at his words, which in truth sounded almost cruel, Régine roused herself with a sudden air of authority.

"Bertrand," she said firmly, "you are doing a great wrong by dragging the child into your schemes. Joséphine is too young to be used as a tool by a pack of thoughtless enthusiasts."

A bitter, scornful laugh from Bertrand broke in on her vehemence.

"Thoughtless enthusiasts!" he exclaimed roughly. "Is that how you call us, Régine? My God! where is your loyalty, your devotion? Have you no faith, no aspirations? Do you no longer worship God or reverence your king?"

"In heaven's name, Bertrand, take care!" she whispered hoarsely, looked about her as if the stone walls of the porch had ears and eyes fixed upon the man she loved.

"Take care!" he rejoined bitterly. "Yes! that is your creed now. Caution! Circumspection! You fear—"

"For you," she broke in reproachfully; "for Joséphine; for *maman*; for Jacques—not for myself, God knows!"

"We must all take risks, Régine," he retorted more composedly. "We must all risk our miserable lives in order to end this awful, revolting tyranny. We must have a wider outlook, think not only of ourselves, of those immediately round us, but of France, of humanity, of the entire world. The despotism of a bloodthirsty autocrat has made of the people of France a people of slaves, cringing, fearful, abject—swayed by his word, too cowardly now to rebel."

"And what are you? My God!" she cried passionately. "You and your friends, my poor young sister, my foolish little brother? What are you, that you think you can stem to torrent of this stupendous Revolution? How think you that your feeble voices will be heard above the roar of a whole nation in the throes of misery and of shame?"

"It is the still small voice," Bertrand replied, in the tone of a visionary, who sees mysteries and who dreams dreams, "that is heard by its persistence even above the fury of thousands in full cry. Do we not call our organisation 'the Fatalists'? Our aim is to take every opportunity by quick, short speeches, by mixing with the crowd and putting in a word here and there, to make propaganda against the fiend Robespierre. The populace are like sheep; they'll follow a lead. One day, one of us—it may be the humblest, the weakest, the youngest; it may be Joséphine or Jacques; I pray God it may be me—but one of us will find the word and speak it at the right time, and the people will follow us and turn against that execrable monster and hurl him from his throne, down into Gehenna."

He spoke below his breath, in a hoarse whisper which even she had to strain her ears to hear.

"I know, I know, Bertrand," she rejoined, and her tiny hand stole out in a pathetic endeavour to capture his. "Your aims are splendid. You are wonderful, all of you. Who am I, that I should even with a word or a prayer, try to dissuade you to do what you think is right? But Joséphine is so young, so hot-headed! What help can she give you? She is only seventeen. And Jacques! He is just an irresponsible boy! Think, Bertrand, think! If anything were to happen to these children, it would kill *maman!*"

He gave a shrug of the shoulders and smothered a weary sigh. She had succeeded in capturing his hand, clung to it with the strength of a passionate appeal.

"You and I will never understand one another, Régine," he began; then added quickly, "over these matters," because, following on his cruel words, he had heard the tiny cry of pain, so like that of a wounded bird, which much against her will had escaped her lips. "You do not understand," he went on, more quietly, "that in a great cause the sufferings of individuals are nought beside the glorious achievement that is in view."

"The sufferings of individuals," she murmured, with a pathetic little sigh. "In truth 'tis but little heed you pay, Bertrand, to my sufferings these days." She paused awhile, then added under her breath: "Since first you met Theresia Cabarrus, three months ago, you have eyes and ears only for her."

He smothered an angry exclamation.

"It is useless, Régine—" he began.

"I know," she broke in quietly. "Theresia Cabarrus is beautiful; she has charm, wit, power—all things which I do not possess."

"She has fearlessness and a heart of gold," Bertrand rejoined and, probably despite himself, a sudden warmth crept into his voice. "Do you not know of the marvellous influence which she exercised over that fiend Tallien, down in Bordeaux? He went there filled with a veritable tiger's fury, ready for a wholesale butchery of all the royalists, the aristocrats, the *bourgeois*, over there—all those, in fact, whom he chose to believe were conspiring against this hideous Revolution. Well! under Theresia's influence he actually modified his views and became so lenient that he was recalled. You know, or should know, Régine," the young man added in a tone of bitter reproach, "that Theresia is as good as she is beautiful."

"I do know that, Bertrand," the girl rejoined with an effort. "Only—"

"Only what?" he queried roughly.

"I do not trust her—that is all." Then, as he made no attempt at concealing his scorn and his impatience, she went on in a tone which was much harsher, more uncompromising than the one she had adopted hitherto: "your infatuation blinds you, Bertrand, or you—an enthusiastic royalist, an ardent loyalist—would not place your trust in an avowed Republican. Theresia Cabarrus may be kind-hearted—I don't deny it. She may have done and she may be all that you say; but she stands for the negation of every one of your ideals, for the destruction of what you exalt, the glorification of the principles of this execrable Revolution."

"Jealousy blinds you, Régine," he retorted moodily.

She shook her head.

"No, it is not jealousy, Bertrand—not common, vulgar jealousy— that prompts me to warn you, before it is too late. Remember," she added solemnly, "that you have not only yourself to think of, but that you are accountable to God and to me for the innocent lives of Joséphine and of Jacques. By confiding in that Spanish woman—"

"Now you are insulting her," he broke in mercilessly. "Making her out to be a spy."

"What else is she?" the girl riposted vehemently. "You know that she is affianced to Tallien, whose influence and whose cruelty are second only to those of Robespierre. You know it, Bertrand!" she insisted, seeing that at last she had silenced him and that he sat beside her, sullen and obstinate. "You know it, even though you choose to close your eyes and ears to what is common knowledge."

There was silence after that for a while in the narrow porch, where two hearts once united were filled now with bitterness, one against the other. Even out in the street it had become quite dark, the darkness of a spring night, full of mysterious lights and grey, indeterminate shadows. The girl shivered as with cold and drew her tattered shawl more closely round her shoulders. She was vainly trying to swallow her tears. Goaded into saying more than she had ever meant to, she felt the finality of what she had said. Something had finally snapped just now: something that could never in after years be put together again. The boy and girl love which had survived the past two years of trouble and of stress, lay wounded unto death, bleeding at the foot of the shrine of a man's infatuation and a woman's vanity. How impossible this would have seemed but a brief while ago!

Through the darkness, swift visions of past happy times came fleeting before the girl's tear-dimmed gaze: visions of walks in the woods round Auteuil, of drifting down-stream in a boat on the Seine on hot August days—aye! even of danger shared and perilous moments passed together, hand in hand, with bated breath, in darkened rooms, with curtains drawn and ears straining to hear the distant cannonade, the shouts of an infuriated populace or the rattle of death carts upon the cobblestones. Swift visions of past sorrows and past joys! An immense self-pity filled the girl's heart to bursting. An insistent sob that would not be suppressed rose to her throat.

"Oh, Mother of God, have mercy!" she murmured through her tears.

Bertrand, shamed and confused, his heart stirred by the misery of this girl whom he had so dearly loved, his nerves strained beyond endurance through the many mad schemes which his enthusiasm was for ever evolving, felt like a creature on the rack, torn between compunction and remorse on the one hand and irresistible passion on the other.

"Régine," he pleaded, "forgive me! I am a brute, I know—a brute to you, who have been the kindest little friend a man could possibly hope for. Oh, my dear," he added pitiably, "if you would only understand—"

At once her tender, womanly sentiment was to the fore, sweeping pride and just resentment out of the way. Hers was one of those motherly natures that are always more ready to comfort than to chide. Already she had swallowed her tears, and now that with a wearied gesture he had buried his face in his hands, she put her arm around his neck, pillowed his head against her breast.

"I do understand, Bertrand," she said gently. "And you must never ask my forgiveness, for you and I have loved one another too well to bear anger or grudge one toward the other. There!" she said, and rose to her feet, and seemed by that sudden act to gather up all the moral strength of which she stood in such sore need. "It is getting late, and *maman* will be anxious. Another time we must have a more quiet talk about our future. But," she added, with renewed seriousness, "if I concede you Theresia Cabarrus without another murmur, you must give me back Joséphine and Jacques, If—if I—am to lose you—I could not bear to lose them as well. They are so young—"

"Who talks of losing them?" he broke in, once more impatient, enthusiastic—his moodiness gone, his remorse smothered, his conscience dead to all save to his schemes. "And what have I to do with it all? Joséphine and Jacques are members of the Club. They may be young, but they are old enough to know the value of an oath. They are pledged just like I am, just like we all are. I could not, even if I would, make them false to their oath." Then, as she made no reply, he leaned over to her, took her hands in his, tried to read her inscrutable face through the shadows of night. He thought that he read obstinacy in her rigid attitude, the unresponsive placidity of her hands. "You would not have them false to their oath?" he insisted.

She made no reply to that, only queried dully:

"What are you going to do tonight?"

"Tonight," he said with passionate earnestness, his eyes glowing with the fervid ardour of self-immolation, "we are going to let hell loose around the name of Robespierre."

"Where?"

"At the open-air supper in the Rue St. Honoré. Joséphine and Jacques will be there."

She nodded mechanically, quietly disengaged her hands from his feverish grasp.

"I know," she said quietly. "They told me they were going. I have no influence to stop them."

"You will be there, too?" he asked.

"Of course. So, will poor *maman*," she replied simply.

"This may be the turning point, Régine," he said with passionate earnestness, "in the history of France!"

"Perhaps!"

"Think if it, Régine! Think of it! Your sister, your young brother! Their name may go down to posterity as the saviours of France!"

"The saviours of France!" she murmured vaguely.

"One word has swayed a multitude before now. It may do so again—tonight!"

"Yes," she said. "And those poor children believe in the power of their oratory."

"Do not you?"

"I only remember that you, Bertrand, have probably spoken of your plan to Theresia Cabarrus, that the place will be swarming with the spies of Robespierre, and that you and the children will be recognised, seized, dragged into prison, then to the guillotine! My God!" she added, in a pitiful murmur. "And I am powerless to do anything but look on like an insentient log, whilst you run your rash heads into a noose, and then follow you all to death, whilst *maman* is left alone to perish in misery and in want."

"A pessimist again, Régine!" he said with a forced laugh, and in his turn rose to his feet. "'Tis little we have accomplished this evening," he added bitterly, "by talking."

She said nothing more. An icy chill had hold of her heart. Not only of her heart, but of her brain and her whole being. Strive as she might, she could not enter into Bertrand's schemes, and as his whole entity was wrapped up in them she felt estranged from him, out of touch, shut out from his heart. Unspeakable bitterness filled her soul. She hated Theresia Cabarrus, who had enslaved Bertrand's fancy, and above all she mistrusted her. At this moment she would gladly have given her life to get Bertrand away from the influence of that woman and away from that madcap association which called itself "the Fatalists," and into which he had dragged both Joséphine and Jacques.

Silently she preceded him out of the little church porch, the habitual trysting-place, where at one time she had spent so many happy hours. Just before she turned off into the street, she looked back, as if through the impenetrable darkness which enveloped it now she would conjure up, just once more, those happy images of the past, but the darkness made no response to the mute cry of her fancy, and with a last sigh of intense bitterness, she followed Bertrand down the street.

Less than five minutes after Bertrand and Régine had left the porch of Petit St. Antoine, the heavy oak door of the church was cautiously opened. It moved noiselessly upon its hinges, and presently through the aperture the figure of a man emerged, hardly discernible in the gloom. He slipped through the door into the porch, then closed the former noiselessly behind him.

A moment or two later his huge, bulky figure was lumbering up the Rue St. Antoine, in the direction of the Arsenal, his down-at-heel shoes making a dull clip-clop on the cobblestones. There were but very few passers-by at this hour, and the man went along with his peculiar shuffling gait until he reached the Porte St. Antoine. The city gates were still open at this hour, for it was only a little while ago that the many church clocks of the quartier had struck eight, nor did the sergeant at the gate pay much heed to the beggarly caitiff who went by; only he and the half-dozen men of the National Guard who were in charge of the gate, did remark that the belated wayfarer appeared to be in distress with a terrible asthmatic cough which caused one of the men to say with grim facetiousness:

"*Pardi!* but here's a man who will not give *maman* guillotine any trouble!"

They all noticed, moreover, that after the asthmatic giant had passed through the city gate, he turned his shuffling footsteps in the direction of the Rue de la Planchette.

CHAPTER 5

Rascality Rejoices

The Fraternal Suppers were a great success. They were the invention of Robespierre, and the unusual warmth of these early spring evenings lent the support of their balmy atmosphere to the scheme.

Whole Paris is out in the streets on these mild April nights. Families out on a holiday, after the daily spectacle of the death-cart taking the enemies of the people, the conspirators against their liberty, to the guillotine.

And *maman* brings a basket filled with whatever scanty provisions she can save from the maximum per day allowed for the provisioning of her family. Beside her, papa comes along, dragging his youngest by the hand—the latter no longer chubby and rosy, as were his prototypes in the days gone by, because food is scarce and dear, and milk unobtainable; but looking a man for all that, though bare-footed and bare-kneed, with the red cap upon his lank, unwashed locks, and hugging against his meagre chest a tiny toy guillotine, the latest popular fancy, all complete with miniature knife and pulleys, and frame artistically painted a vivid crimson.

The Rue St. Honoré is a typical example of what goes on all over the city. Though it is very narrow and therefore peculiarly inconvenient for the holding of outdoor entertainments, the Fraternal Suppers there are extensively patronized, because the street itself is consecrated as holding the house wherein lives Robespierre.

Here, as elsewhere, huge braziers are lit at intervals, so that materfamilias may cook the few herrings she has brought with her if she be so minded, and all down the narrow street tables are set, innocent of cloths or even of that cleanliness which is next to the equally neglected virtue of godliness. But the tables have an air of cheeriness nevertheless, with resin torches, tallow candles, or old stable lanthorns set here and there, the flames flickering in the gentle breeze, adding picturesqueness to the scene which might otherwise have seemed sordid, with those pewter mugs and tin plates, the horn-handled knives and iron spoons.

The scanty light does little more than accentuate the darkness around, the deep shadows under projecting balconies or lintels of *portes-cochères* carefully closed and barred for the night; but it glints with weird will-o'-the-wisp-like fitfulness on crimson caps and tricolour cockades, on drawn and begrimed faces, bony arms, or lean, brown hands.

A motley throng, in truth! The workers of Paris, its proletariat, all conscripted servants of the State—slaves, we might call them, though they deem themselves free men—all driven into hard manual labour, partly by starvation and wholly by the decree of the committees, who decide how and when and in what form the nation requires the arms or hands—not the brains, mind you!—of its citizens. For brains the nation has no use, only in the heads of those who sit in convention or on committees. "The State hath no use for science," was grimly said to Lavoisier, the great chemist, when he begged for a few days' surcease from death in order to complete some important experiments.

But coal-heavers are useful citizens of the State; so are smiths and armourers and gunmakers, and those who can sew and knit stockings, do anything in fact to clothe and feed the national army, the defenders of the sacred soil of France. For them, for those workers—the honest, the industrious, the sober—are the Fraternal Suppers invented; but not for them only. There are the "*tricotteuses*," sexless hags, who, by order of the State, sit at the foot of the scaffold surrounded by their families and their children and knit, and knit, the while they jeer—still by order of the State—at the condemned—old men, young women, children even, as they walk up to the guillotine.

There are the "*insulteuses publiques*," public insulters, women mostly—save the mark!—paid to howl and blaspheme as the death-carts rattle by. There are the "*tappe-durs*," the hit-hards, who, armed with weighted sticks, form the body-guard around the sacred person of Robespierre. Then, the members of the *Société Révolutionnaire*, recruited from the refuse of misery and of degradation of this great city; and—oh, the horror of it all!—the "*Enfants Rouges*," the red children, who cry "Death" and "à la lanterne" with the best of them—precocious little offsprings of the new Republic. For them, too, are the Fraternal Suppers established: for all the riff-raff, all the sweepings of abject humanity. For they too must be amused and entertained, lest they sit in clusters and talk themselves into the belief that they are more wretched, more indigent, more abased, than they were in the days of monarchical oppression.

And so, on these balmy evenings of mid-April, family parties are gathered in the open air, around meagre suppers that are "fraternal" by order of the State. Family parties which make for camaraderie between the honest man and the thief, the sober citizen and the homeless vagabond, and help one to forget awhile the misery, the starvation, the slavery, the daily struggle for bare existence, in anticipation of the belated Millennium.

There is even laughter around the festive boards, fun and frolic. jokes are cracked, mostly of a grim order. There is intoxication in the air: spring has got into the heads of the young. And there is even kissing under the shadows, love-making, sentiment; and here and there perhaps a shred of real happiness.

The provisions are scanty. Every family brings its own. Two or three herrings, sprinkled with shredded onions and wetted with a little vinegar, or else a few boiled prunes or a pottage of lentils and beans.

"Can you spare some of that bread, citizen?"

"Aye! if I can have a bite of your cheese."

They are fraternal suppers! Do not, in the name of Liberty and Equality, let us forget that. And the whole of it was Robespierre's idea. He conceived and carried it through, commanded the voices in the Convention that voted the money required for the tables, the benches, the tallow candles. He lives close by, in this very street, humbly, quietly, like a true son of the people, sharing house and board with Citizen Duplay, the cabinet-maker, and with his family.

A great man, Robespierre! The only man! Men speak of him with bated breath, young girls with glowing eyes. He is the fetish, the idol, the demigod. No benefactor of mankind, no saint, no hero-martyr was ever worshipped more devotedly than this death-dealing monster by his votaries. Even the shade of Danton is reviled in order to exalt the virtues of his successful rival.

"Danton was gorged with riches: his pockets full, his stomach satisfied! But look at Robespierre!"

"Almost a wraith!—so thin, so white!"

"An ascetic!"

"Consumed by the fire of his own patriotism."

"His eloquence!"

"His selflessness!"

"You have heard him speak, citizen?"

A girl, still in her 'teens, her elbows resting on the table, her hands supporting her rounded chin, asks the question with bated breath. Her large grey eyes, hollow and glowing, are fixed upon her *vis-à-vis*, a tall, ungainly creature, who sprawls over the table, vainly trying to dispose of his long limbs in a manner comfortable to himself.

His hair is lank and matted with grease, his face covered in coal-dust; a sennight's growth of beard, stubbly and dusty, accentuates the squareness of his jaw even whilst it fails to conceal altogether the cruel, sarcastic curves of his mouth. But for the moment, in the rapt eyes of the young enthusiast, he is a prophet, a seer, a human marvel: he has heard Robespierre speak.

"Was it in the Club, Citizen Rateau?" another woman asks—a young matron with a poor little starveling at her breast.

The man gives a loud guffaw, displays in the feeble, flickering light of the nearest torch a row of hideous uneven teeth, scored with gaps and stained with tobacco juice.

"In the Club?" he says with a curse, and spits in a convenient direction to show his contempt for that or any other institution. "I don't belong to any Club. There's no money in my pocket. And the Jacobins and the Cordeliers like to see a man with a decent coat on his back."

His guffaw broke in a rasping cough which seemed to tear his broad chest to ribbons. For a moment speech was denied him; even oaths failed to reach his lips, trembling like an unset jelly in this distressing spasm. His neighbours alongside the table, the young enthusiast opposite, the comely matron, paid no heed to him—waited indifferently until the clumsy lout had regained his breath. This, mark you, was not an era of gentleness or womanly compassion, and an asthmatic mudlark was not like to excite pity. Only when he once more stretched out his long limbs, raised his head and looked about him, panting and blear-eyed, did the girl insist quietly:

"But you have heard *Him* speak!"

"Aye!" the ruffian replied drily. "I did."

"When?"

"Night before last. *Tenez!* He was stepping out of Citizen Duplay's house yonder. He saw me leaning against the wall close by. I was tired, half asleep, what? He spoke to me and asked me where I lived."

"Where you lived?' the girl echoed, disappointed.

"Was that all?" the matron added with a shrug of her shoulders.

The neighbours laughed. The men enjoyed the discomfiture of the women, who were all craning their necks to hear something great, something palpitating, about their idol.

The young enthusiast sighed, clasped her hands in favour.

"He saw that you were poor, Citizen Rateau," she said with conviction; "and that you were tired. He wished to help and comfort you."

"And where did you saw you lived, citizen?" the young matron went on, in her calm, matter-of-fact tone.

"I live far from here, the other side of the water, not in an aristocratic quarter like this one—what?"

"You told *Him* you lived there?" the girl still insisted. Any scrap or crumb of information even remotely connected with her idol was manna to her body and balm to her soul.

"Yes, I did," Citizen Rateau assented.

"Then," the girl resumed earnestly, "solace and comfort will come to you very soon, citizen. He never forgets. His eyes are upon you. He knows your distress and that you are poor and weary. Leave it to him, Citizen Rateau. He will know how and when to help."

"He will know, more like," here broke in a harsh voice, vibrating with excitement, "how and when to lay his talons on an obscure and helpless citizen whenever his Batches for the guillotine are insufficient to satisfy his lust!"

A dull murmur greeted this tirade. Only those who sat close by the speaker knew which he was, for the lights were scanty and burnt dim in the open air. The others only heard—received this arrow-shot aimed at their idol—with for the most part a kind of dull resentment. The women were more loudly indignant. One or two young devotees gave a shrill cry or so of passionate indignation.

"Shame! Treason!"

"Guillotine, forsooth! The enemies of the people all deserve the guillotine!"

And the enemies of the people were those who dared raise their voice against their Chosen, their Fetish, the great, incomprehensible Mystery.

Citizen Rateau was once more rendered helpless by a tearing fit of coughing.

But from afar, down the street, there came one or two assenting cries.

"Well spoken, young man! As for me, I never trusted that blood-hound!"

And a woman's voice added shrilly: "His hands reek of blood. A butcher, I call him!"

"And a tyrant!" assented the original spokesman. "His aim is a dictatorship, with his minions hanging around him like abject slaves. Why not Versailles, then? How are we better off now than in the days of kingship? Then, at least, the streets of Paris did not stink of blood. Then, at least—"

But the speaker got no father. A hard crust of very dry, black bread, aimed by a sure hand, caught him full in the face, whilst a hoarse voice shouted lustily:

"Hey there, citizen! If thou'lt not hold thy tongue 'tis thy neck that will be reeking with blood o'er soon, I'll warrant!"

"Well said, Citizen Rateau!" put in another, speaking with his mouth full, but with splendid conviction. "Every word uttered by that jackanapes yonder reeks of treason!"

"Shame!" came from every side.

"Where are the agents of the Committee of Public Safety? Men have been thrown into prison for less than this."

"Shame!"

"Denounce him!"

"Take him to the nearest Section!"

"Ere he wreaks mischief more lasting than words!" cried a woman, who tried as she spoke to give her utterance its full, sinister meaning.

"Shame! Treason!" came soon from every side. Voices were raised all down the length of the tables—shrill, full-throated, even dull and indifferent. Some really felt indignation—burning, ferocious indignation; others only made a noise for the sheer pleasure of it, and because the past five years had turned cries of "Treason!" and of "Shame!" into a habit. Not that they knew what the disturbance was about. The street was long and narrow, and the cries came some way from where they were sitting; but when cries of "Treason!" flew through the air these days, 'twas best to join in, lest those cries turned against one, and the next stage in the proceedings became the approach of an Agent of the Sûreté, the nearest prison, and the inevitable guillotine.

So, everyone cried "Shame!" and "Treason!" whilst those who had first dared to raise their voices against the popular demagogue drew together into a closer batch, trying no doubt to gather courage through one another's proximity. Eager, excited, a small compact group of two men—one a mere boy—and three women, it almost seemed as if they were suffering from some temporary hallucination. How else would five isolated persons—three of them in their first youth—have dared to brave a multitude?

In truth Bertrand Moncrif, face to face as he believed with martyrdom, was like one transfigured. Always endowed with good looks, he appeared like a veritable young prophet, haranguing the multitude and foretelling its doom. The gloom partly hid his figure, but his hand was outstretched, and the outline of an avenging finger pointing straight out before him, appeared in the weird light of the resin torch, as if carved in glowing lava. Now and then the fitful light caught the sharp outline of his face—the straight nose and pointed chin, and brown hair matted with the sweat of enthusiasm.

Beside him Régine, motionless and white as a wraith, appeared alive only by her eyes, which were fixed on her beloved. In the hulking giant with the asthmatic cough she had recognised the man to whom she had ministered earlier in the day. Somehow, his presence here and now seemed to her sinister and threatening. It seemed as if all day he had been dogging her footsteps: first at the soothsayer's then he surely must have followed her down the street. Then he had inspired her with pity; now his hideous face, his grimy hands, that croaking voice and churchyard cough, filled her with nameless terror.

He appeared to her excited fancy like a veritable spectre of death, hovering over Bertrand and over those she loved. With one arm she tried to press her brother Jacques closer to her breast, to quench his eagerness and silence his foolhardy tongue. But he, like a fierce, impatient young animal, fought to free himself from her loving embrace, shouted approval to Bertrand's oratory, played his part of the young propagandist, heedless of Régine's warnings and of his mother's tears. Next to Régine, her sister Joséphine—a girl not out of her 'teens, with all the eagerness and exaggeration of extreme youth, was shouting quite as loudly as her brother Jacques, clapping her small hands together, turning glowing, defying, arrogant eyes on the crowd of great unwashed whom she hoped to sway with her ardour and her eloquence.

"Shame on us all!" she cried with passionate vehemence. "Shame

257

on us French women and French men that we should be the abject slaves of such a bloodthirsty tyrant!"

Her mother, pale-faced, delicate, had obviously long since given up all hope of controlling this unruly little crowd. She was too listless, too anaemic, had no doubt suffered too much already, to be afraid for herself or for her children. She was past any thought or fear. Her wan face only expressed despair—despair that was absolutely final—and the resignation of silent self-immolation, content to suffer beside those she loved, only praying to be allowed to share their martyrdom, even though she had no part in their enthusiasm.

Bertrand, Joséphine and Jacques had all the ardour of martyrdom. Régine and her mother all its resignation.

The Fraternal Supper threatened to end in a free fight, wherein the only salvation for the young fire-eaters would lie in a swift taking to their heels. And even then, the chances would be hopelessly against them. Spies of the convention, spies of the committees, spies of Robespierre himself, swarmed all over the place. They were marked men and women, those five. It was useless to appear defiant and high-minded and patriotic. Even Danton had gone to the guillotine for less.

"Shame! Treason!"

The balmy air of mid-April seemed to echo the sinister words, but Bertrand appeared unconscious of all danger. Nay! it almost seemed as if he courted it.

"Shame on you all!" he called out loudly, and his fresh, sonorous voice rang out above the tumult and the hoarse murmurings. "Shame on the people of France for bowing their necks to such monstrous tyranny. Citizens of Paris, think on it! Is not Liberty a mockery now? Do you call your bodies your own? They are but food for cannon at the bidding of the Convention. Your families? You are parted from those you love. Your wife? You are torn from her embrace. Your children? They are taken from you for the service of the State. And by whose orders? Tell me that! By whose orders, I say?"

He was lashing himself into a veritable fury of self-sacrifice, stood up beside the table and with a gesture even bade Joséphine and Jacques be still. As for Régine, she hardly was conscious that she lived, so acute, so poignant was her emotion, so gaunt and real the approach of death which threatened her beloved.

This of course was the end—this folly, this mad, senseless, useless folly! Already through the gloom she could see as in a horrible vision all those she cared for dragged before a tribunal that knew of no mercy; she could hear the death-carts rattling along the cobblestones, she could see the hideous arms of the guillotine, ready to receive this unique, this believed, this precious prey. She could feel Joséphine's arms clinging pitiably to her for courage; she could see Jacques' defiant young face, glorying in martyrdom; she could see *maman*, drooping like a faded flower, bereft of what was life to her—the nearness of her children. She could see Bertrand, turning with a dying look of love, not to her but to the beautiful Spaniard who had captured his fancy and then sold him without compunction to the spies of Robespierre and of her own party.

But for the fact that this was a "Fraternal Supper," that people had come out here with their families, their young children, to eat and to make merry and to forget all their troubles as well as the pall of crime that hung over the entire city, I doubt not but what the young Hotspur and his crowd of rashlings would ere now have been torn from their eats, trampled underfoot, at best been dragged to the nearest Commissary, as the asthmatic Citizen Rateau had already threatened. Even as it was, the temper of many a paterfamilias was sorely tried by this insistence, with wilful twisting of the tigers' tails. And the women were on the verge of reprisals. As for Rateau, he just seemed to gather his huge limbs together, uttered an impatient oath and an angry: "By all the cats and dogs that render this world hideous with their howls, I have had about enough of this screeching oratory."

Then he threw one long leg over the bench on which he had been sitting, and in an instant was lost in the gloom, only to reappear in the dim light a few seconds later, this time on the farther side of the table, immediately behind the young rhetorician, his ugly, begrimed face with its grinning, toothless mouth and his broad, bent shoulders towering above the other's slender figure.

"Knock him down, citizen!" a young woman cried excitedly. "Hit him in the face! Silence his abominable tongue!"

But Bertrand was not to be silenced yet. No doubt the fever of notoriety, of martyrdom, had got into his blood. His youth, his good looks—obvious even in the fitful light and despite his tattered clothes—were an asset in his favour, no doubt; but a man-eating tiger is apt to be indiscriminate in his appetites and will devour a child with as much gusto as a gaffer; and this youthful firebrand was teasing the man-eating tiger with reckless insistence.

"By whose orders," he reiterated, with passionate vehemence, "by whose orders are we, free citizens of France, dragged into this abomi-

nable slavery? Is it by those of the representatives of the people? No!
Of the committees chosen by the people? No! Of your municipalities? your clubs? your sections? No! and again No! Your bodies, citizens, your freedom, your wives, your children, are all slaves, the property, the toys of one man—real tyrant and traitor, the oppressor of the weak, the enemy of the people; and that man is—"

Again, he was interrupted, this time more forcibly. A terrific blow on the head deprived him of speech and of sight. His senses reeled, there was a mighty buzzing in his ears, which effectually drowned the cries of execration or of approval that greeted his tirade, as well as a new and deafening tumult which filled the whole narrow street with its weird and hideous sounds.

Whence the blow had come, Bertrand had no notion. It had all been so swift. He had expected to be torn limb from limb, to be dragged to the nearest commissariat: he courted condemnation, envisaged the guillotine; 'stead of which, he was prosily knocked down by a bow which would have felled an ox.

Just for a second, his fast-fading perceptions struggled back into consciousness. He had a swift vision of a giant form towering over him, with grimy fist uplifted and toothless mouth grinning hideously, and of the crowd, rising from their seats, turning their backs upon him, waving their arms and caps frantically, and shouting, shouting, with vociferous lustiness. He also had an equally swift pang of remorse as the faces of his companions—of Régine and Mme de Serval, of Joséphine and Jacques—whom he dragged with him into this mad and purposeless outburst, rose prophetically before him from out the gloom, with wide-eyed, scared faces and arms uplifted to ward off vengeful blows.

But the next moment these lightning-like visions faded into complete oblivion. He felt something hard and heavy hitting him in the back. All the lights, the faces, the outstretched hands, danced wildly before his eyes, and he sank like a log on the greasy pavement, dragging pewter plates, mugs and bottles down with him in his fall.

CHAPTER 6

One Crowded Hour of Glorious Life

And all the while, the people were shouting:
"*Le violà!*"
"Robespierre!"
The Fraternal Supper was interrupted. Men and women pushed

and jostled and screamed, the while a small, spare figure in dark cloth coat and immaculate breeches, with smooth brown hair and pale-ascetic face, stood for a moment under the lintel of a gaping *porte-cochère*. He had two friends with him; handsome, enthusiastic St. Just, the right hand and the spur of the bloodthirsty monster, own kinsman to Armand St. Just the renegade, whose sister was married to a rich English millor; and Couthon, delicate, half-paralysed, wheeled about in a chair, with one foot in the grave, whose devotion to the tyrant was partly made up of ambition, and wholly of genuine admiration.

At the uproarious cheering which greeted his appearance, Robespierre advanced into the open, whilst a sudden swift light of triumph darted from his narrow, pale eyes.

"And you still hesitate!" St. Just whispered excitedly in his ear. "Why, you hold the people absolutely in the hollow of your hand!"

"Have patience, friend!" Couthon remonstrated quietly. "Robespierre's hour is about to strike. To hasten it now, might be courting disaster."

Robespierre himself would, in the meanwhile, have been in serious danger through the exuberant welcome of his admirers. Their thoughtless crowding around his person would easily have given some lurking enemy or hot-headed, would-be martyr the chance of wielding an assassin's knife with success, but for the presence amongst the crowd of his *"tappe-durs"*—hid-hards—a magnificent bodyguard composed of picked giants from the mining districts of Eastern France, who rallied around the great man, and with their weighted sticks kept the enthusiastic crowd at bay.

He walked a few steps down the street, keeping close to the houses on his left; his two friends, St. Just and Couthon in his carrying chair, were immediately behind him, and between these three and the mob, the *tappe-durs*, striding two abreast, formed a solid *phalanx*.

Then, all of a sudden, the great man came to a halt, faced the crowd, and with an impressive gesture, imposed silence and attention. His bodyguard cleared a space for him and he stood in the midst of them, with the light of a resin torch striking full upon his spare figure and bringing into bold relief that thin face so full of sinister expression, the cruel mouth and the coldly glittering eyes. He was looking straight across the table, on which the *débris* of Fraternal Suppers lay in unsavoury confusion.

On the other side of the table, Mme de Serval with her three children sat, or rather crouched, closely huddled against one another.

Joséphine was clinging to her mother, Jacques to Régine. Gone was the eagerness out of their attitude now, gone the enthusiasm that had reviled the bloodthirsty tyrant in the teeth of a threatening crowd. it seemed as if, with that terrific blow dealt by a giant hand to Bertrand who was their leader in this mad adventure, the awesome fear of death had descended upon their souls. The two young faces as well as that of Mme de Serval appeared distorted and haggard, whilst Régine's eyes, dilated with terror, strove to meet Robespierre's steady gaze, which was charged with sinister mockery.

And for one short interval of time the crowd was silent; and the everlasting stars looked down from above on the doings of men. To these trembling, terrified young creatures, suddenly possessed with youth's passionate desire to live, with a passionate horror of death, these few seconds of tense silence must have seemed like an eternity of suffering. Then Robespierre's thin face lighted up in a portentous smile—a smile that caused those pale cheeks yonder to take on a still more ashen hue.

"And where is our eloquent orator of a while ago?" the great man asked quietly. "I heard my name, for I sat at my window looking with joy on the fraternization of the people of France. I caught sight of the speaker and came down to hear more clearly what he had to say. But, where is he?"

His pale eyes wandered slowly along the crowd; and such was the power exercised by the extraordinary man, so great the terror that he inspired, that everyone there—men, women and children, workers and vagabonds—turned their eyes away, dared not meet his glance lest in it they read an accusation or a threat.

Indeed, no one dared to speak. The young rhetorician had disappeared, and every one trembled lest they should be implicated in his escape. He had evidently got away under cover of the confusion and the noise. But his companions were still there—four of them; the woman and the boy and the two girls, crouching like frightened beasts before the obvious fury, the certain vengeance of the people. The murmurs were ominous. "Death! Guillotine! Traitors!" were words easily distinguishable in the confused babbling of the sullen crowd.

Robespierre's cruel, appraising glance rested on those four pathetic forms, so helpless, so desperate, so terrified.

"Citizens," he said coldly, "did you not hear me ask where your eloquent companion is at this moment?"

Régine alone knew that he lay like a log under the table, close to her feet. She had seen him fall, struck by that awful blow from a brutal fist; but at the ominous query she instinctively pressed her trembling lips close together, whilst Joséphine and Jacques clung to her with the strength of despair.

"Do not parley with the rabble, citizen," St. Just whispered eagerly. "This is a grand moment for you. Let the people of their own accord condemn those who dared to defame you."

And even Couthon, the prudent, added sententiously:

"Such an opportunity may never occur again."

The people, in truth, were over-ready to take vengeance into their own hands.

"*À la lanterne, les aristos!*"

Gaunt, bedraggled forms leaned across the table, shook begrimed fists in the direction of the four crouching figures. With the blind instinct of trapped beasts, they retreated into the shadows step by step, as those threatening fists appeared to draw closer, clutching at the nearest table and dragging it with them, in an altogether futile attempt at a barricade.

"Holy Mother of God, protect us!" murmured Mme de Serval from time to time.

Behind them there was nothing but the rows of houses, no means of escape even if their trembling knees had not refused them service; whilst vaguely, through their terror, they were conscious of the proximity of that awful asthmatic creature with the wheezy cough and the hideous, toothless mouth. At times he seemed so close that they shut their eyes, almost feeling his grimy hands around their throat, his huge, hairy arms dragging them down to death.

It all happened in the space of a very few minutes, far fewer even than it would take completely to visualize the picture. Robespierre, like an avenging wraith, theatrical yet impassive, standing in the light of a huge resin torch, which threw alternate lights and shadows, grotesque and weird, upon his meagre figure, now elongating the thin, straight nose, now widening the narrow mouth, misshaping the figure till it appeared like some fantastic ghoul-form from the nether world. Behind him, his two friends were lost in the gloom, as were now Mme de Serval and her children. They were ensconced against a heavy *porte-cochère*, a rickety table alone standing between them and the mob, who were ready to drag them to the nearest lanthorn and immolate them before the eyes of their outraged idol.

"Leave the traitors alone!" Robespierre commanded. "Justice will deal with them as they deserve."

"*À la lanterne!*" the people—more especially the women—demanded insistently.

Robespierre turned to one of his "*tappe-durs.*"

"Take the *aristos* to the nearest commissariat," he said. "I'll have no bloodshed to mar our Fraternal Supper."

"The commissariat, forsooth!" a raucous voice positively bellowed. "Who is going to stand between us and our vengeance? Robespierre has been outraged by this rabble. Let them perish in sight of all!"

How it all happened after that, none who were there could in truth have told you. The darkness, the flickering lights, the glow of the braziers, which made the inky blackness around more pronounced, made everything indistinguishable to ordinary human sight. Certain it is that Citizen Rateau—who had constituted himself the spokesman of the mob—was at one time seen towering behind the four unfortunates, with his huge arms stretched out, his head thrown back, his mouth wide open, screaming abuse and vituperation, demanding the people's right to take the law into its own sovereign hands.

At that moment the light of the nearest resin torch threw his hulking person into bold relief against a heavy *porte-cochère* which was immediately behind him. The mob acclaimed him, cheered him to the echoes, agreed with him that summary justice in such a case was lone satisfying. The next instant a puff of wind blew the flame of the torch in a contrary direction, and darkness suddenly enveloped the ranting colossus and the cowering prey all ready to his hand.

"Rateau!" shouted someone.

"Hey, there! Citizen Rateau! Where art thou?" came soon from every side.

No answer came from the spot where Rateau had last been seen, and it seemed as if just then a strong current of air had slammed a heavy door to somewhere in the gloom. Citizen Rateau had disappeared, and the four traitors along with him.

It took a few seconds of valuable time ere the mob suspected that it was being robbed of its prey. Then a huge upheaval occurred, a motion of the human mass densely packed in the Rue St. Honoré, that was not unlike the rush of water through a narrow gorge.

"Rateau!" People were yelling the name from end to end of the street.

Superstition, which was rampant in these days of carnage and of crime, had possession of many a craven soul. Rateau had vanished. It seemed as if the Evil One, whose name had been so freely invoked during the course of the Fraternal Supper, had in very truth spirited Rateau away.

On the top of the tumult came a silence as complete as that of a graveyard at midnight. The "*tappe-durs*," who at their chief's command had been forging their way through the crowd, in order to reach the traitors, ceased their hoarse calls of "Make way there, in the name of the Convention!" whilst St. Just, who still stood close to his friend, literally saw the cry stifled on Robespierre's lips.

Robespierre himself had not altogether realised what had happened. In his innermost heart he had already yielded to his friends' suggestion and was willing to let mob-law run its course. As St. Just had said: what a triumph for himself if his detractors were lynched by the mob! When Rateau towered above the four unfortunates, hurling vituperation above their heads, the tyrant smiled, well satisfied; and when the giant thus incontinently vanished, Robespierre for a moment or two remained complacent and content.

Then the whole crowd oscillated in the direction of the mysterious *porte-cochère*. Those who were in the front ranks threw themselves against the heavy panels, whilst those in the rear pushed with all their might. But the *porte-cochères* of old Paris are heavily constructed. Woodwork that had resisted the passage of centuries withheld the onslaught of a pack of half-starved caitiffs. But only for a while.

The mob, fearing that it was getting foiled, broke into a howl of execration, and Robespierre, his face more drawn and grey than before, turned to his companions, trying to read their thoughts.

"If it should be—" St. Just murmured yet dared not put his surmise into words.

Nor had he time to do so, or Robespierre the leisure to visualise his own fears. Already the massive oak panels were yielding to persistent efforts. The mighty woodwork began to crack under the pressure of this living battering ram; when suddenly the howls of those who were in the rear turned to a wild cry of delight. Those who were pushing against the *porte-cochère* paused in their task. All necks were suddenly craned upwards. The weird lights of torches and the glow of braziers glinted on gaunt necks and upturned chins, turned heads and faces into phantasmagoric, unearthly shapes.

Robespierre and his two companions instinctively looked up too. There, some few metres lower down the street, on the third-floor balcony of a neighbouring house, the figure of Rateau had just appeared.

The window immediately behind him was wide open and the room beyond was flooded with light, so that his huge person appeared distinctly silhouetted—a black and gargantuan mass—against the vivid and glowing background. His head was bare, his lank hair fluttered in the breeze, his huge chest was bare and his ragged shirt hung in tatters from his brawny arms. Flung across his left shoulder, he held an inanimate female form, whilst with his right hand he dragged another through the open window in his wake. Just below him, a huge brazier was shedding its crimson glow.

The sight of him—gaunt, weird, a veritable tower of protean revenge—paralyzed the most ebullient, silenced every clamour. For the space of two seconds only did he stand there, in full view of the crowd, in full view of the almighty tyrant whose defamation he had sworn to avenge. Then he cried in stentorian tones:

"Thus, perish all conspirators against the liberty of the people, all traitors to its cause, by the hands of the people and for the glory of their chosen!"

And, with a mighty twist of his huge body, he picked up the inanimate form that lay lifeless at his feet. For a moment he held the two in his arms, high above the iron railing of the balcony; for a moment those two lifeless, shapeless forms hung in the darkness in mid-air, whilst an entire crowd of fanatics held their breath and waited, awed and palpitating, only to break out into frantic cheering as the giant hurled the two lifeless bodies down, straight into the glowing brazier.

"Two more to follow!" he shouted lustily.

There was pushing and jostling and cheering. Women screamed, men blasphemed and children cried. Shouts of "*Vive Rateau!*" mingled with those of "*Vive* Robespierre!" a circle was formed, hands holding hands, and a wild saraband danced around the glowing brazier. And this mad orgy of enthusiasm lasted for full three minutes, until the foremost among those who, awestruck and horrified, had approached the brazier in order to see the final agony of the abominable traitor, burst out with a prolonged "Malediction!"

Beyond that exclamation, they were speechless—pointed with trembling hands at the shapeless bundles on which the dull fire of the braziers had not yet obtained a purchase.

The bundles were shapeless indeed. Rags hastily tied together to represent human forms; but rags only! No female traitors, no *aristos* beneath! The people had been fooled, hideously fooled by a traitor all the more execrable, as he had seemed one of themselves.

"Malediction! Death to the traitor!"

Aye, death indeed! The giant, whoever he might be, would have to bear a charmed life if he were to escape the maddened fury of a foiled populace.

"Rateau!" they shouted hoarsely.

They looked up to that third-floor balcony which had so fascinated them a while ago. But now the window was shut and no light from within chased the gloom that hung over the houses around.

"Rateau!" the people shouted.

But Rateau had disappeared. It all seemed like a dream, a nightmare. Had Rateau really existed, or was he a wraith, sent to tease and to scare those honest patriots who were out for liberty and for fraternity? Many there were who would have liked to hold on to that theory—men and women whose souls, warped and starved by the excesses and the miseries of the past five years, clung to any superstition, any so-called supernatural revelations, that failed to replace the old religion that had been banished from their hearts.

But in this case not even superstition could be allowed free play. Rateau had vanished, it is true. The house from whence he had thus mocked and flouted the people was searched through and through by a mob who found nothing but bare boards and naked walls, empty rooms and disused cupboards on which to wreak its fury.

But down there, lying on the top of the brazier, were those two bundles of rags slowly being consumed by the smouldering embers, silent proofs of the existence of that hulking creature whose size and power had, with that swiftness peculiar to human conceptions, already become legendary.

And in a third-floor room, a lamp that had recently been extinguished, a coil of rope, more rages, male and female clothes, a pair of boots, a battered hat, were mute witnesses to the swift passage of the mysterious giant with the wheezy cough—the trickster who had fooled a crowd and thrown the great Robespierre himself into ridicule.

Chapter 7

Two Interludes

Two hours later the Rue St. Honoré had resumed its habitual graveyard-like stillness. The stillness had to come at last. Men in their wildest passions, in their most ebullient moods, must calm down sooner or later, if only temporarily. Blood aglow with enthusiasm, or rage, or idolatry, cannot retain its fever-pitch uninterruptedly for long. And so, silence and quietude descended once more upon the setting of that turbulent scene of a while ago.

Here, as in other quarters of Paris, the fraternal suppers had come to an end; and perspiring matrons, dragging weary children at their skirts, wended their way homewards, whilst their men went to consummate the evening's entertainment at one of the numerous clubs or cabarets where the marvellous doings in the Rue St. Honoré could be comfortably lived over again or retailed to those, less fortunate, who had not been there to see.

In the early morning the "*nettoyeurs publiques*" would be coming along, to clear away the *débris* of the festivities and to gather up the tables and benches which were the property of the several Municipal sections and put them away for the next occasion.

But these "*nettoyeurs*" were not here yet. They, too, were spending an hour or two in the nearest cabarets, discussing the startling events that had rendered notorious one corner of the Rue St. Honoré.

And so the streets were entirely deserted, save here and there for the swift passage of a furtive form, hugging the walls, with hands in pockets and a crimson cap pulled over the eyes, anxious only to escape the vigilance of the night-watchman, swift of foot and silent of tread; and anon, in the Rue St. Honoré itself, when even these nightbirds had ceased to flutter, the noiseless movement of a dark and mysterious form that stirred cautiously upon the greasy cobblestones. More silent, more furtive than any hunted beast creeping out of its lair, this mysterious form emerged from under one of the tables that was standing nearly opposite the house where Robespierre lived and close to the one where the superhuman colossus had wrought his magic trick.

It was Bertrand Moncrif. No longer a fiery Desmosthenes now, but a hunted, terror-filled human creature, whom a stunning blow from a giant fist had rendered senseless, even whilst it saved him from the consequences of his own folly. His senses still reeling, his limbs cramped and aching, he had lain stark and still under the table just where he had fallen, not sufficiently conscious to realise what was happening beyond his very limited range of vision or to marvel what was the ultimate fate of his companions.

His only instinct throughout this comatose condition was the blind one of self-preservation. Feeling rather than hearing the tumult around him, he had gathered his limbs close together, lain as still as a mouse, crouching within himself in the shelter of the table above. It was only when the silence around had lasted an eternity of time that he ventured out of his hiding-place. With utmost caution, hardly daring to breathe, he crept on hands and knees and looked about him, up and down the street. There was no one about. The night fortunately was moonless and dark; nature had put herself on the side of those who wished to pass unperceived.

Bertrand struggled to his feet, smothering a cry of pain. His head ached furiously, his knees shook under him; but he managed to crawl as far as the nearest house and rested for a while against its wall. The fresh air did him good. The April breeze blew across his burning forehead.

For a few minutes he remained thus, quite still, his eyes gradually regaining their power of vision. He recollected where he was and all that had happened. An icy shiver ran down his spine, for he also remembered Régine and Mme de Serval and the two children. But he was still too much dazed, really only half conscious, to do more than vaguely marvel what had become of them.

He ventured to look fearfully up and down the street. Tables scattered pell-mell, the unsavoury remnants of fraternal suppers, a couple of smouldering braziers, collectively met his gaze. And at one point, sprawling across a table, with head lost between outstretched arms, a figure, apparently asleep, perhaps dead.

Bertrand, now nothing but a bundle of nerves, could hardly suppress a cry of terror. It seemed to him as if his life depended on whether that sprawling figure was alive or dead. But he dared not approach in order to make sure. For a while he waited, sinking more and more deeply into the shadows, watching that motionless form on which his life depended.

The figure did not move, and gradually Bertrand nerved himself up to confidence and then to action. He buried his head in the folds of his coat-collar and his hands in the pockets of his breeches, and with silence, stealthy footsteps he started to make his way down the street. At first, he looked back once or twice at the immobile figure sprawling across the table. It had not moved, still appeared as if it might be dead. Then Bertrand took to his heels and, no longer looking either behind him or to the right or left, with elbows pressed close to his side, he started to run in the direction of the Tuileries.

A minute later, the motionless figure came back to life, rose quickly and with swift, noiseless tread, started to run in the same direction.

In the cabarets throughout the city, the chief topic of conversation was the mysterious events of the Rue St. Honoré. Those who had seen it all had marvellous tales to tell of the hero of the adventure.

"The man was eight or else nine feet high; his arms reached right across the street from house to house. Flames spurted out of his mouth when he coughed. He had horns on his head; cloven feet; a forked tail!"

These were but a few of the asseverations which rendered the person of the fictitious Citizen Rateau a legendary one in the eyes of those who had witnessed his amazing prowess. Those who had not been thus favoured listened wide-eyed and open-mouthed.

But all agreed that the mysterious giant was in truth none other than the far-fame Englishman—that spook, that abominable trickster, that devil incarnate, known to the Committees as the Scarlet Pimpernel.

"But how could it be the Englishman?" was suddenly put forward by Citizen Hottot, the picturesque landlord of the Cabaret de la Liberté, a well-known rendezvous close to the Carrousel. "How could it be the Englishman who played you that trick, seeing that you all say it was Citizen Rateau who—The devil take it all!" he added, and scratched his bald head with savage vigour, which he always did whene'er he felt sorely perplexed. "A man can't be two at one and the same time; nor two men become one. Nor—Name of a name of a dog!" concluded the worthy citizen, puffing and blowing in the maze of his own puzzlement like an old walrus that is floundering in the water.

"It was the Englishman, I tell thee!" one of his customers asserted indignantly. "Ask anyone who saw him! Ask the *tappe-durs*! Ask Robespierre himself! He saw him, and turned as grey as—as putty, I tell thee! he concluded, with more conviction than eloquence.

"And *I* tell thee," broke in Citizen Sical, the butcher—he with the bullet-head and bull-neck and a fist that could in truth have felled an ox; "I tell thee that it was Citizen Rateau. Don't I know Citizen Rateau?" he added and brought that heavy fist of his down upon the upturned cask on which stood pewter mugs and bottles of *eau de vie* and glared aggressively round upon the assembly. He had only one eye; the other presented a hideous appearance, scarred and blotched, the result of a terrible fatality in his early youth. The one eye leered with a glance of triumph as well as of a challenge, daring any less muscular person to impugn his veracity.

One man alone was bold enough to take up the challenge—a wizened little fellow, a printer by trade, with skin of the texture of grained oak and a few unruly curls that tumbled over one another above a highly polished forehead.

"And I tell thee, citizen Sical," he said with firm decision; "I tell thee and those who aver, as thou dost, that Citizen Rateau had anything to do with those monkey-tricks, that ye lie. Yes!" he reiterated emphatically and paying no heed to the glowering looks and blasphemies of Sical and his friends. "Yes, ye lie! Not consciously, I grant you; but you lie nevertheless. Because—" He paused and glanced around him, like a clever actor conscious of the effect which he produced. His tiny beady eyes blinked in the glare of the lamp before him.

"Because what?" came in an eager chorus from every side.

"Because," resumed the other sententiously, "all the while that ye were supping at the expense of the State in the open, and had your gizzards stirred by the juggling devices of some unknown mountebank, Citizen Rateau was lying comfortably drunk and snoring lustily in the antechamber of Mother Théot, the soothsayer, right at the other end of Paris!"

"How do you know that, Citizen Langlois?" queried the host with icy reproval, for butcher Sical was his best customer, and Sical did not like being contradicted. But little Langlois with the shiny forehead and tiny, beady, humorous eyes, continued unperturbed.

"*Pardi!*" he said gaily, "because I was at Mother Théot myself, and saw him there."

That certainly was a statement to stagger even the great Sical. It was received in complete silence. Every one promptly felt that the moment was propitious for another drink; nay! that the situation demanded it.

Sical, and those who had fought against the Scarlet Pimpernel theory, were too staggered to speak. They continued to imbibe Citizen Hottot's *eau de vie* in sullen brooding. The idea of the legendary Englishman, which has so unexpectedly been strengthened by citizen Langlois' statement concerning Rateau, was repugnant to their common sense. Superstition was all very well for women and weaklings like Langlois; but for men to be asked to accept the theory that a kind of devil in human shape had so thrown dust in the eyes of a number of perfectly sober patriots that they literally could not believe what they saw, was nothing short of an insult.

And they had *seen* Rateau at the fraternal supper, had talking with him, until the moment when—Then who in Satan's name had they been talking with?

"Here, Langlois! Tell us—"

And Langlois, who had become the hero of the hour, told all he knew, and told it, we are told, a dozen times and more. How he had gone to Mother Théot's at about four o'clock in the afternoon, and had sat patiently waiting beside his friend Rateau, who wheezed and snored alternately for a couple of hours. How, at six o'clock or a little after, Rateau went out because—the *aristo*, forsooth!—had found the atmosphere filthy in Mother Théot's antechamber—no doubt he went to get another drink.

"At about half-past seven," the little printer went on glibly, "my turn came to speak with the old witch. When I came out it was long past eight o'clock and quite dark. I saw Rateau sprawling upon a bench, half asleep. I tried to speak with him, but he only grunted. However, I went out then to get a bit of supper at one of the open-air places, and at ten o'clock I was once more past Mother Théot's place. One or two people were coming out of the house. They were all grumbling because they had been told to go. Rateau was one who was for making a disturbance, but I took him by the arm. We went down the street together, and parted company in the Rue de l'Anier, where he lodges. And here I am!" concluded Langlois and turned triumphantly to challenge the gaze of every one of the sceptics around him.

There was not a single doubtful point in his narrative, and though he was questioned—aye! and severely cross-questioned, too—he never once swerved from his narrative or in any manner did he contradict himself. Later on, it transpired that there were others who had been in Mother Théot's antechamber that day. They too subsequently corroborated all that the little printer had said. One of them was the wife of Sical's own brother; and there were others. So, what would you?

"Name of a name of a dog, then, who was it when spirited the *aristos* away?"

Chapter 8

The Beautiful Spaniard

In the Rue Villedot, which is in the Louvre quarter of Paris, there is a house, stone built and five-storeyed, with grey shutters to all the windows and balconies of wrought iron—a house exactly similar to hundreds and thousands of others in every quarter of Paris. During the day the small wicket in the huge *porte-cochère* is usually kept open; it allows a peep into a short dark passage, and beyond it to the lodge of the concierge. Beyond this again there is a courtyard, into which, from every one of its four sides, five rows of windows, all adorned with grey shutters, blink down like so many colourless eyes. The inevitable wrought-iron balconies extend along three sides of the quadrangle on every one of the five floors, and on the balustrade of these, pieces of carpet in various stages of decay are usually to be seen hanging out to air. From shutter to shutter clothes lines are stretched and support fantastic arrays of family linen that flap lazily in the sultry, vitiated air which alone finds its way down the shaft of the quadrangle.

On the left of the entrance passage and opposite the lodge of the concierge there is a tall glass door, and beyond it the vestibule and primary staircase, which gives access to the principal apartments—those that look out upon the street and are altogether more luxurious and more airy than those which give upon the courtyard. To the latter, two back stairways give access. They are at the far corners of the courtyard; both are pitch dark and reek of stuffiness and evil smells. The apartments which they serve, especially those on the lower floors, are dependent for light and air on what modicum of these gifts of heaven comes down the shaft into the quadrangle.

After dark, of course, *porte-cochère* and wicket are both closed, and if a belated lodger of visitor desires to enter the house, he must ring the bell and the concierge in his lodge will pull a communicating cord that will unlatch the wicket. It is up to the belated visitor or lodger to close the wicket after him, and he is bound by law to give his name, together with the number of the apartment to which he is going, in to the *concierge* as he goes past the lodge. The *concierge*, on the other hand, will take a look at him so that he may identify him should trouble or police inquiry arise.

On this night of April, somewhere near midnight, there was a ring at the outer door. Citizen Leblanc, the *concierge*, roused from his first sleep, pulled the communicating cord. A young man, hatless and in torn coat and muddy breeches, slipped in through the wicket and hurried past the lodge, giving only one name, but that in a clear voice, as he passed:

"Citoyenne Cabarrus."

The *concierge* turned over in his bed and grunted, half asleep. His duty clearly was to run after the visitor, who had failed to give his own name; but to begin with, the worthy *concierge* was very tired; and then the name which the belated caller had given was one requiring special consideration.

The Citoyenne Cabarrus was young and well favoured, and even in these troublous days, youth and beauty demanded certain privileges which no patriotic *concierge* could refuse to grant. Moreover, the aforesaid lady had visitors at all hours of the day and late into the night—visitors for the most part with whom it was not well to interfere. Citizen Tallien, the popular Representative in the Convention was, as everyone knew, her ardent adorer. 'Twas said by all and sundry that since the days when he met the fair Cabarrus in Bordeaux and she exercised such a mellowing influence upon his bloodthirsty patriotism, he had no thought save to win her regard.

But he was not the only one who came to the dreary old apartment in the Rue Villedot, with a view to worshipping at the Queen of Beauty's shrine. Citizen Leblanc had seen many a great Representative of the People pass by his lodge since the beautiful Theresia came to dwell here. And if he became very confidential and his interlocutor very insistent, he would throw out a hint that the greatest man in France today was not infrequent visitor in the house.

Obviously, therefore, it was best not to pry too closely into secrets, the keeping of which might prove uncomfortable for one's peace of mind. And Citizen Leblanc, tossing restlessly in his sleep, dreamed of the fair Cabarrus and wished himself in the place of those who were privileged and pay their court to her.

And so, the belated visitor was able to make his way across the courtyard and up the dark back stairs unmolested, but even this reassuring fact failed to give him confidence. He hurried on with the swift and stealthy footstep which had become habitual to him, glancing over his shoulder from time to time, wide-eyed and with ears alert, and heart quivering with apprehension.

Up the dark and narrow staircase, he hurried, dizzy and sick, his head reeling in the dank atmosphere, his shaking hands seeking the support of the walls as he climbed wearily up to the third floor. Here he almost measured his length upon the landing, tottered up again and came down sprawling on his knees against one of the doors—the one which had the number 22 painted upon it. For the moment it seemed as if he would once more fall into a swoon. Terror and relief were playing havoc with his whirling brain. He had not sufficient strength to stretch out an arm in order to ring the bell, but only beat feebly against the panel of the door with his moist palm.

A moment later the door was opened, and the unfortunate fell forward into the vestibule at the feet of a tall apparition clad in white and holding a small table lamp above her head. The apparition gave a little scream which was entirely human and wholly feminine, hastily put down the lamp on a small console close by, and by retreating forcefully farther into the vestibule, dragged the half-animate form of the young man along too; for he was now clinging to a handful of white skirt with the strength of despair.

"I am lost, Theresia!" he moaned pitiably. "Hide me, for God's sake!—only for tonight!"

Theresia Cabarrus was frowning now, looked more perplexed than kindly, and certainly made no attempt to raise the crouching figure from the ground. *Anon* she called loudly: "Pepita!" and whilst waiting for an answer to this call, she remained quite still, and the frown of puzzlement on her face yielded to one of fear. The young man, obviously only half conscious, continued to moan and to implore.

"Silence, you fool!" she said peremptorily. "The door is still open. Anyone on the stairs could hear you. Pepita!" she called again, more harshly this time.

The next moment an old woman came from somewhere out of the darkness, threw up her hands at sight of that grovelling figure on the floor, and would no doubt have broken out in loud lament but that her young mistress ordered her at once to close the door.

"Then help the Citoyen Moncrif to a sofa in my room," the beautiful Theresia went on peremptorily. "Give him a restorative and see above all to it that he hold his tongue!"

With a quick imperious jerk, she freed herself from the convulsive grasp of the young man, and walking quickly across the small vestibule, she went through a door at the end of it that had been left ajar, leaving the unfortunate Moncrif to the ministrations of Pepita.

Theresia Cabarrus, who had obtained a divorce from her husband, the Marquis de Fontenay (by virtue of a decree of the former Legislative Assembly, which allow—nay, encouraged—the dissolution of a marriage with an *émigré* who refused to return to France). Theresia Cabarrus was, in this year 1794, in her twenty-fourth year, and perhaps in the zenith of her beauty and in the plenitude of that power which had subjugated so many men. In what that power consisted the historian has vainly tried to guess; for it was not her beauty only that brought so many to her feet. In the small oval face, the pointed chin, the full, sensuous lips, so typically Spanish, we look in vain for traces of that beauty which we are told surpassed that of other women of her time; whilst in the dark, velvety eyes, more tender than spiritual, and in the narrow arched brows, we fail to find an expression of the *esprit* which had moulded Tallien to her will and even brought Robespierre out of the shell of his asceticism—a willing victim to her wiles.

But who would be bold enough to analyse that subtle quality, acknowledged by all, possessed by a very few, which is vaguely denoted by the word "charm"? Theresia Cabarrus must have possessed it to a marvellous degree—that, and an utter callousness for the feelings of her victims, which would leave her mind cool and keen to pursue her own ends, whilst theirs was thrown into that maze of jealousy and of passion wherein prudence flies to the winds and the fever of self-immolation gets into the blood.

At this moment, in the sparsely furnished room of her dingy apartment, she looked like an angry goddess. Her figure, which undeniably was superb, was drawn to its full height, its splendid proportions accentuated by the clinging folds of her modish gown—a marvel of artistic scantiness, which only have concealed the perfectly modelled bust, and left the rounded thigh, in its skin-tight, flesh-coloured undergarment, unblushingly exposed. Her blue-black hair was dressed in the new fashion, copied from ancient Greece and snooded by a glittering antique fillet; and her small bare feet were encased in satin sandals. Truly a lovely woman, but for that air of cold displeasure coupled with fear, which marred the harmony of the dainty, child-like features.

After a while Pepita came back.

"Well?" queried Theresia impatiently.

"Poor M. Bertrand is very ill," the old Spanish woman replied with unconcealed sympathy. "He has fever, the poor cabbage. Bed is the only place for him—"

"He cannot stay here, as thou well knowest, Pepita," the imperious beauty retorted drily. "Thy head and mine are in danger every moment that he spends under this roof."

"But thou couldst not turn a sick man out into the streets in the middle of the night."

"Why not?" Theresia riposted coldly. "It is a beautiful and balmy night. Why not?" she reiterated fretfully.

"Because he would die on thy doorstep," was old Pepita's muttered reply.

Theresia shrugged her shoulders.

"He dies if he goes," she said slowly, "and we die if he stays. Tell him to go, Pepita, ere Citizen Tallien comes."

A shudder went through the old woman's spare frame.

"It is late," she protested. "Citizen Tallien will not come tonight."

"Not only he," Theresia rejoined coldly, "but—but—the other—Thou knowest well, Pepita—those two arranged to meet here in my lodgings tonight."

"But not at this hour!"

"*After* the sitting of the Convention."

"It is nearly midnight. They'll not come," the old woman persisted obstinately.

"They arranged to meet here, to talk over certain matters which interest their party," Citoyenne Cabarrus went on, equally firmly. "They'll not fail. So, tell Citoyen Moncrif to go, Pepita. He endangers my life by staying here."

"Then do the dirty work thyself," the old woman muttered sullenly. "I'll not be a part to cold-blooded murder."

"Well, since Citoyen Moncrif's life is more valuable to thee than mine—"

Theresia began, but got no father. The words died on her lips.

Bertrand Moncrif, very pale, still looking scared and wild, had quietly entered the room.

"You wish me to go, Theresia," he said simply. "You did not think surely that I would do anything that might endanger your safety. My God!" he added with passionate vehemence, "Do you not know that I would at any time lay down my life for yours?"

Theresia shrugged her statuesque shoulders.

"Of course, of course, Bertrand," she said a little impatiently, though obviously trying to be kind. "But I do entreat you not to go into heroics at this hour, and not to put on tragic airs. You must see that for yourself as well as for me it would be fatal if you were found here, and—"

"And I am going, Theresia," he broke in seriously. "I ought never to have come. I was a fool, as usual!" he added with bitterness. "But after that awful fracas I was dazed and hardly knew what I was doing."

The frown of vexation reappeared upon the woman's fair, smooth brow.

"The fracas?" she asked quickly. "What fracas?"

"In the Rue St. Honoré. I thought you knew."

"No. I know nothing," she retorted, and her voice was now trenchant and hard. "What happened?"

"They were deifying that brute Robespierre—"

"Silence!" she broke in harshly. "Name no names."

277

"And they were deifying a bloodthirsty tyrant, and I—"

"And you rose from your seat," she broke in again, and this time with a laugh that was cruel in its biting irony; "and lashed yourself into a fury of eloquent vituperation. Oh, I know! I know!" she went on excitedly. "You and your Fatalists, or whatever you call yourselves! And that rage for martyrdom!—Senseless, stupid, and selfish! Oh, my God! how selfish! And then you came here to drag me down with you into an abyss of misery, along with you to the guillotine—to—"

It seemed as if she were choking, and her small white hands, with a gruesome and pathetic gesture, went up to her neck, smoothed it and fondled it, as if to shield it from that awful fate.

Bertrand tried to pacify her. It was he who was the more calm of the two now. It seemed as if her danger had brought him back to full consciousness. He forgot his own danger, the threat of death which lay in wait for him, probably on the very threshold of this house. He was a marked man now; martyrdom had ceased to be a dream: it had become a grim reality. But of this he did not think. Theresia was in danger, compromised by his own callous selfishness, his mind was full of her; and Régine, the true and loyal friend, the beloved of past happier years, had no place in his thoughts beside the exquisite enchantress, whose very nearness was paradise.

"I am going," he said earnestly. "Theresia, my beloved, try to forgive me. I was a fool—a criminal fool! But lately—since I thought that you—you did not really care; that all my hopes of future happiness were naught but senseless dreams; since then I seem to have lost my head—I don't know *what* I am doing!—And so—"

He got no farther. Ashamed of his own weakness, he was too proud to let her see that she made him suffer. For the moment, he only bent the knee and kissed the hem of her diaphanous gown. He looked so handsome then, despite his bedraggled, woebegone appearance—so young, so ardent, that Theresia's egotistical heart was touched, as it had always been when the incense of his perfect love rose to her sophisticated nostrils. She put out her hand and brushed with a gentle, almost maternal, gesture the matted brown hair from his brow.

"Dear Bertrand," she murmured vaguely. "What a foolish boy to think that I do not care!"

Already he had been brought back to his senses. The imminence of her danger lent him the courage which he had been lacking, and unhesitatingly now he jumped to his feet and turned to go. But she, quick in the transition of her moods, had already seized him by the arm.

"No, no!" she murmured in a hoarse whisper. "Don't go just yet—not before Pepita has seen if the stairs are clear."

Her small hand held him as in a vice, whilst Pepita, obedient and silent, was shuffling across the vestibule in order to execute her mistress's commands. But, even so, Bertrand struggled to get away. An epitome of their whole life, this struggle between them!—he trying to free himself from those insidious bonds that held him one moment and loosed him the next; that numbed him to all that he was wont to hold sacred and dear—his love for Régine, his loyalty, his honour. An epitome of her character and his: he, weak and yielding, ever a ready martyr thirsting for self-immolation; and she, just a bundle of feminine caprice, swayed by sentiment one moment and by considerations of ambition or of personal safety the next.

"You must wait, Bertrand," she urged insistently. "Citizen Tallien may be on the stairs—he or—or the other. If they saw you!—My God!"

"They would conclude that you had turned me out of doors," he riposted simply. "Which would, in effect, be the truth. I entreat you to let me go!" he added earnestly. "'Twere better they met me on the stairs than in here."

The old woman's footsteps were heard hurrying back. Bertrand struggled to free himself—did in truth succeed; and Theresia smothered a desperate cry of warning as he strode rapidly through the door and across the vestibule only to be met here by Pepita, who pushed him with all her might incontinently back.

Theresia held her tiny handkerchief to her mouth to deaden the scream that forced itself to her lips. She had followed Bertrand out of the salon, and now stood in the doorway, a living statue of fear.

"Citizen Tallien," Pepita had murmured hurriedly. "He is on the landing. Come this way."

She dragged Bertrand by the arm, not waiting for orders from her mistress this time, along a narrow dark passage, which at its extreme end gave access to a tiny kitchen. Into this she pushed him and locked the door upon him.

"Name of a name!" she muttered as she shuffled back to the vestibule. "If they should find him here!"

Citoyenne Cabarrus had not moved. Her eyes, dilated with terror, mutely questioned the old woman as the latter made ready to admit the visitor. Pepita gave reply as best she could, by silent gestures, in-

279

dicating the passage and the action of turning a key in the lock. Her wrinkled old lips hardly stirred, and then only in order to murmur quickly and with a sudden assumption of authority:

"Self-possession, my cabbage, or you'll endanger yourself and us all!"

Theresia pulled herself together. Obviously, the old woman's warning was not to be ignored, nor had it been given a moment too soon. Outside, the visitor had renewed his impatient rat-tat against the door. The eyes of mistress and maid met for one brief second. Theresia was rapidly regaining her presence of mind; whereupon Pepita smoothed out her apron, readjusted her cap, and went to open the door, even whilst Theresia said in a firm voice, loudly enough for the new visitor to hear:

"One of my guests, at last! Open quickly, Pepita!"

Chapter 9

A Hideous, Fearful Hour

A young man—tall, spare, with sallow skin and shifty, restless eyes—pushed unceremoniously past the old servant, threw his hat and cane down on the nearest chair, and hurrying across the vestibule, entered the *salon* where the beautiful Spaniard, a picture of serene indifference, sat ready to receive him.

She had chosen for the setting of this scene a small settee covered in old rose brocade. On this she half sat, half reclined, with an open book in her hand, her elbow resting on the frame of the settee, her cheek leaning against her hand. Immediately behind her, the light from an oil lamp tempered by a shade of rose-coloured silk, outlined with a brilliant, glowing pencil the contour of her small head, one exquisite shoulder, and the mass of her raven hair, whilst it accentuated the cool half-tones of her diaphanous gown, on the round bare arms and bust, the tiny sandalled feet and cross-gartered legs.

A picture in truth to dazzle the eyes of any man! Tallien should have been at her feet in an instant. The fact that he paused in the doorway bore witness to the unruly thoughts that ran riot in his brain.

"Ah, Citizen Tallien!" the fair Theresia exclaimed with a perfect assumption of *sang-froid*. "You are the first to arrive and are indeed welcome; for I was nearly swooning with *ennui*. Well!" she added, with a provocative smile, and extended a gracious arm in his direction. "Are you not going to kiss my hand?"

"I heard a voice," was all the response which he gave to this seductive invitation. "A man's voice. Who was it?"

She raised a pair of delicately pencilled eyebrows. Her eyes became as round and as innocent-looking as a child's.

"A man's voice?" she riposted with a perfect air of astonishment. "You are crazy, *mon ami;* or else are crediting my faithful Pepita with a virile bass, which in truth she doth not possess!"

"Whose voice was it?" Tallien reiterated, making an effort to speak calmly, even though he was manifestly shaking with choler.

Whereupon the fair Theresia, no longer gracious or arch, looked him up and down as if he were no better than a lacquey.

"*Ah, ça!*" she rejoined coldly. "Are you perchance trying to cross-question me? By what right, I pray you, Citizen Tallien, do you assume this hectoring tone in my presence? I am not yet your wife, remember; and 'tis not you, I image, who are the dictator of France."

"Do not tease me, Theresia!" the man interposed hoarsely. "Bertrand Moncrif is here."

For the space of a second, or perhaps less, Theresia gave no reply to the taunt. Her quick, alert brain had already faced possibilities, and she was far too clever a woman to take the risks which a complete evasion of the truth would have entailed at this moment. She did not, in effect, know whether Tallien was speaking from positive information given to him by spies, or merely from conjecture born of jealousy. Moreover, another would be here presently—another, whose spies were credited with omniscience, and whom she might not succeed in dominating with a smile or a frown, as she could the love-sick Tallien. Therefore, after that one brief instant's reflection she decided to temporize, to shelter behind a half-truth, and replied, with a quick glance from under her long lashes:

"I am not teasing you, Citizen Bertrand came here for shelter a while ago."

Tallien drew a quick sigh of satisfaction, and she went on carelessly:

"But, obviously, I could not keep him here. He seemed hurt and frightened.—He has been gone this past half-hour."

For a moment it seemed as if the man, in face of this obvious lie, would flare out into a hot retort; but Theresia's luminous eyes subdued him, and before the cool contempt expressed by those exquisite lips, he felt all his blustering courage oozing away.

"The man is an abominable and an avowed traitor," he said sullenly. "Only two hours ago—"

"I know," she broke in coldly. "He vilified Robespierre. A dangerous thing to do. Bertrand was ever a fool, and he lost his head."

"He will lose it more effectually tomorrow," Tallien retorted grimly.

"You mean that you would denounce him?"

"That I will denounce him. I would have done so tonight, before coming here, only—only—"

"Only what?"

"I was afraid he might be here."

Theresia broke into a ringing if somewhat artificial peal of laughter.

"I must thank you, citizen, for this consideration of my feelings. It was, in truth, thoughtful of you to think of sparing me a scandal. But, since Bertrand is *not* here—"

"I know where he lodges. He'll not escape, *citoyenne*. My word on it!"

Tallien spoke very quietly, but with that concentrated fury of which a fiercely jealous man is ever capable. He had remained standing in the doorway all this while, his eyes fixed on the beautiful woman before him, but his attention feverishly divided between her and what might be going on in the vestibule behind him.

In answer to his last threatening words, the lovely Theresia rejoined, more seriously:

"So as to make sure I do not escape either!" And a flash of withering anger shot from her dark eyes on the unromantic figure of her adorer. "Or you, *mon ami!* You are determined that Mme Roland's fate shall overtake me, eh? And no doubt you will be thrilled to the marrow when you see my head fall into your precious salad-bowl. Will yours follow mine, think you? Or will you prefer to emulate Citizen Roland's more romantic ending?"

Even while she spoke, Tallien had been unable to repress a shudder.

"Theresia, in heaven's name—!" he murmured.

"Bah, *mon ami!* There is no longer a heaven these days. You and your party have carefully abolished the Hereafter. So, after you and I have taken our walk up the steps of the scaffold—"

"Theresia!"

"Eh, what?" she went on coolly. "Is that not perchance what you have in contemplation? Moncrif, you say, is an avowed traitor. Has openly vilified and insulted your demi-god. He has been seen coming to my apartments. Good! I tell you that he is no longer here. But let that pass. He is denounced. Good! Sent to the guillotine. Good again!

And Theresia Cabarrus in whose house he tried to seek refuge, much against her will, goes to the guillotine in his company. The prospect may please you, *mon ami,* because for the moment you are suffering from a senseless attack of jealousy. But I confess that it does not appeal to me."

The man was silent now; awed against his will. His curiously restless eyes swept over the graceful apparition before him. Insane jealousy was fighting a grim fight in his heart with terror for his beloved. Her argument was a sound one. Even he was bound to admit that. Powerful though he was in the Convention, his influence was as nothing compared with that of Robespierre. And he knew his redoubtable colleague well enough that an insult such as Moncrif had put upon in the Rue St. Honoré this night would never be forgiven, neither in the young hot-head himself nor in any of his friends, adherents, or mere pitying sympathizers.

Theresia Cabarrus was clever enough and quick enough to see that she had gained one point.

"Come and kiss my hand," she said, with a little sight of satisfaction.

This time the man obeyed, without an instant's hesitation. Already he was down on his knees, repentant and humiliated. She gave him her small, sandalled foot to kiss. After that, Tallien became abject.

"You know that I would die for you, Theresia!" he murmured passionately.

This is the second time tonight that such an assertion had been made in this room. And both had been made in deadly earnest, whilst the fair listener had remained equally indifferent to both. And for the second time tonight, Theresia passed her cool white hand over the bent head of an ardent worshipper, whilst her lips murmured vaguely:

"Foolish! Oh, how foolish! Why do men torture themselves, I wonder, with senseless jealousy?"

Instinctively she turned her small head in the direction of the passage and the little kitchen, where Bertrand Moncrif had found temporary and precarious shelter. Self-pity and a kind of fierce helplessness not untinged with remorse made her eyes appear resentful and hard.

There, in the stuffy little kitchen at the end of the dark, dank passage, love in its pure sense, happiness, brief perhaps but unalloyed, and certainly obscure, lay in wait for her. Here, at her feet, was security in the present turmoil, power, and a fitting background for her beauty and her talents. She did not want to lose Bertrand; indeed, she did not intend to lose him. She sighed a little regretfully as she thought of his good looks, his enthusiasm, his selfless ardour. Then she looked down once more on the narrow shoulders, the lank, colourless hair, the bony hands of the erstwhile lawyer's clerk to whom she had already promised marriage, and she shuddered a little when she remembered that those same hands into which she had promised to place her own and which now grasped hers in passionate adoration had, of a certainty, signed the order for those execrable massacres which had for ever sullied the early days of the Revolution. For a moment—a brief one, in truth—she marvelled if union with such a man was not too heavy a price to pay for immunity and for power.

But the hesitancy only lasted a few seconds. The next, she had thrown back her head as if in defiance of the whisperings of conscience and of heart. She need not lose her youthful lover at all. He was satisfied with so little! A few kind words here, an occasional kiss, a promise or two, and he would always remain her willing slave.

It were foolish indeed, and far, far too late, to give way to sentiment at this hour, when Tallien's influence in the Convention was second only to that of Robespierre, whilst Bertrand Moncrif was a fugitive, a suspect, a poor miserable fanatic, whose hot-headedness was for ever landing him from one dangerous situation into another.

So, after indulging in the faintest little sigh of yearning for the might-have-been, she met her latest adorer's worshipping glance with coquettish air of womanly submission, which completed his subjugation, and said lightly:

"And now give me my orders for tonight, *mon ami*."

She settled herself down more comfortably upon the settee, and graciously allowed him to sit on a low chair beside her.

The turbulent little incident was closed. Theresia had *her* way, and poor, harassed Tallien succeeded in shutting away in the innermost recesses of his heart the pangs of jealousy which still tortured him. His goddess was now all smiles, and the subtle flattery implied by her preference for him above his many rivals warmed his atrophied heart and soothed his boundless vanity.

We must accept the verdict of history that Theresia Cabarrus never loved Tallien. In truth appears to be that what love she was capable of had undoubtedly been given to Bertrand Moncrif, whom she would not entirely dismiss from his allegiance, even though she had at last been driven into promising marriage to the powerful Terrorist.

It is doubtful if, despite that half-hearted and wholly selfish love for the young royalist, she had ever intended that he should be more to her than a slavish worshipper, a friend on whom she could count for perpetual adoration or mere sentimental dalliance; but a husband— never! Certain it is that even Tallien, influential as he was, was only a *pis-aller.* The lovely Spaniard, we make no doubt, would have preferred Robespierre as a future husband, or, failing him, Louise-Antoine St. Just, but the latter was deeply enamoured of another woman; and Robespierre was too cautious, too ambitious, to allow himself to be enmeshed.

So, she fell back on Tallien.

"Give me my orders for tonight," the lovely woman had said to her future lord. And he—a bundle of vanity and egoism—was flattered and soothed by this submission, though he knew in his heart of hearts that it was only pretence.

"You will help me, Theresia?" he pleaded.

She nodded, and asked coldly: "How?"

"You know that Robespierre suspects me," he went on, and in- stinctively, at the mere breathing of that awe-inspiring name his voice sank to a murmur. "Ever since I came back from Bordeaux."

"I know. Your leniency there is attributed to me."

"It was your influence, Theresia—" he began.

"That turned you," she broke in coldly, "from a bloodstained beast into a right-minded justiciary. Do you regret it?"

"No, no!" he protested; "since it gained me your love."

"Could I love a beast of prey?" she retorted. "But if you do not regret, you are certainly afraid."

"And he had sent me to Bordeaux to punish, not to pardon."

"Then you are afraid!" she insisted. "Has anything happened?"

"No; only his usual hints—his vague threats. You know them."

She nodded.

"The same," he went on sombrely, "that he used ere he struck Danton."

"Danton was hot-headed. He was too proud to appeal to the pop- ulace who idolised him."

"And I have no popularity to which I can appeal. If Robespierre strikes at me in the Convention, I am doomed—"

"Unless you strike first."

"I have no following. We none of us have. Robespierre sways the Convention with one word."

"You mean," she broke in more vehemently, "that you are all cringing cowards—the abject slaves of one man. Two hundred of you are longing for this era of bloodshed to cease; two hundred would stay the pitiless work of the guillotine—and not one is plucky enough to cry, 'Halt! It is enough!'"

"The first man who cries 'Halt!' is called a traitor," Tallien retorted gloomily. "And the guillotine will not rest until Robespierre himself had said, 'It is enough!'"

"He alone knows what he wants. He alone fears no one," she exclaimed, almost involuntarily giving grudging admiration where in truth she felt naught but loathing.

"I would not fear either, Theresia," he protested, and there was a note of tender reproach in his voice, "if it were not for you."

"I know that, *mon ami*," she rejoined with an impatient little sight. "Well, what do you want me to do?"

He leaned forward in his chair, closer to her, and did not mark— poor fool!—that, as he drew near, she recoiled ever so slightly from him.

"There are two things," he said insinuatingly, "which you could do, Theresia, either of which would place Robespierre under such lasting obligation to you that he would admit us into the inner circle of his friends, trust us and confide in us as he does in St. Just or Couthon."

"Trust you, you mean. He never would trust a woman."

"It means the same thing—security for us both."

"Well?" she rejoined. "What are these two things?"

He paused a moment, appeared to hesitate; then said resolutely:

"Firstly, there is Bertrand Moncrif—and his Fatalists—"

Her face hardened. She shook her head.

"I warned Robespierre about tonight," she said. "I knew that a lot of young fools meant to cause a fracas in the Rue St. Honoré. But the whole thing has been a failure, and Robespierre has no use for failures."

"It need not be a failure—even yet."

"What do you mean?"

"Robespierre will be here directly," he urged, in a whisper rendered hoarse with excitement. "Bertrand Moncrif is here—Why not deliver the young traitor, and earn Robespierre's gratitude?"

"Oh!" she broke in indignant protest. Then, as she caught the look of jealous anger which at her obvious agitation suddenly flared up in his narrow eyes again, she went on with a careless shrug of her statuesque shoulders: "Bertrand is not here, as I told you, my friend. So, these means of serving your cause are out of my reach."

"Theresia," he urged, "by deceiving me—"

"By tantalising me," she broke in harshly, "you do yourself no good. Let us understand one another, my friend," she went on more gently. "You wish me to serve you by serving the dictator of France. And I tell you you'll not gain your ends by taunting me."

"Theresia, we must make friends with Robespierre! He has the power; he rules over France. Whilst I—"

"Ah!" she retorted with vehemence. "That is where you and your weak-kneed friends are wrong! You say that Robespierre rules France. 'Tis not true. It is not Robespierre, the man, who rules; it is his name! The name of Robespierre has become a fetish, an idolatry. Before it every head is bent and every courage cowed. It rules by the fear which it evokes and by the slavery which it compels under the perpetual threat of death. Believe me," she insisted, "'tis not Robespierre who rules, but the guillotine which he wields! And we are all of us helpless—you and I and your friends. And all the others who long to see the end of this era of bloodshed and of revenge, we have got to do as he tells us—pile up crime upon crime, massacre upon massacre, and bear the odium of it all, while he stands aloof in darkness and in solitude, the brain that guides, whilst you and your party are only the hands that strike. Oh! the humiliation of it! And if you were but men, all of you, instead of puppets—"

"Hush, Theresia, in heaven's name!" Tallien broke in peremptorily at last. He had vainly tried to pacify her while she poured forth the vials of her resentment and her contempt. But now his ears, attuned to sensitiveness by an ever-present danger, had caught a sound which proceeded from the vestibule—a sound which made him shudder—a footstep—the opening of a door—a voice. "Hush!" he entreated. "Every dumb wall has ears, these days!"

She broke into a harsh, excited little laugh.

"You are right, my friend," she said under her breath. "What do I care, after all? What do any of us care now, so long as our necks are fairly safe upon our shoulders? But I'll not sell Bertrand," she added firmly. "If I did it I should despise myself too much and hate you worse. So, tell me quickly what else I can do to propitiate the ogre!"

"He'll tell you himself," Tallien murmured hurriedly, as the sounds in the vestibule became more loud and distinctive. "Here they are! And, in heaven's name, Theresia, remember that our lives are at that one man's mercy!"

CHAPTER 10

The Grim Idol that the World Adores

Theresia, being a woman, was necessarily the more accomplished actor. While Tallien retired into a gloomy corner of the room, vainly trying to conceal his agitation, she rose quite serene in order to greet her visitors.

Pepita had just admitted into her mistress's apartments a singular group, composed of two able-bodied men supporting a palsied one. One of the former was St. Just, one of the most romantic figures of the Revolutionary period, the confidant and intimate friend of Robespierre and own cousin to Armand St. Just and to the beautiful Marguerite, who had married the fastidious English milord, Sir Percy Blakeney. The other was Chauvelin, at one time one of the most influential members of the Committee of Public Safety, now little more than a hanger-on of Robespierre's party. A man of no account, to whom not even Tallien and his colleagues thought it worth while to pay their court. The palsied man was Couthon, despite his crimes an almost pathetic figure in his helplessness, after his friends had deposited him in an armchair and wrapped a rug around his knees. The carrying chair in which he spent the greater part of his life had been left down below in the concierge's lodge, and St. Just and Chauvelin had carried him up the three flights of stairs to Citoyenne Cabarrus's apartment.

Close behind these three men came Robespierre.

Heavens! if a thunderbolt had fallen from the skies on that night of the 26th of April, 1794, and destroyed house No. 22 in the Rue Villedot, with all those who were in it, what a torrent of blood would have been stemmed, what horrors averted, what misery forefended!

But nothing untoward happened. The four men who sat that night and well into the small hours of the morning in the dingy apartment, occupied for the present by the beautiful Cabarrus, were allowed by inscrutable Providence to discuss their nefarious designs unchecked.

In truth, there was no discussion. One man dominated the small assembly, even though he sat for the most part silent and apparently self-absorbed, wrapped in that taciturnity and even occasional somnolence which seemed to have become a pose with him of late. He sat on a high chair, prim and upright. Immaculately dressed in blue cloth coat and white breeches, with clean linen at throat and wrist, his hair neatly tied back with a black silk bow, his nails polished, his shoes free from mud, he presented a marked contrast to the ill-conditioned appearance of those other products of revolutionary ideals.

St. Just, on the other hand—young, handsome, a brilliant talker and convinced enthusiast—was only too willing to air his compelling eloquence, was in effect the mouthpiece of the great man as he was his confidant and his right hand. He had acquired in the camps which he so frequently visited a breezy, dictatorial manner that pleased his friends and irritated Tallien and his clique, more especially when sententious phrases fell from his lips which were obviously the echo of some of Robespierre's former speeches in the Convention.

Then there was Couthon, sarcastic and contemptuous, delighting to tease Tallien and to affect a truculent manner, which brought abject flattery from the other's lips.

St. just the fiery young demagogue, and Couthon the half-paralysed enthusiast, were known to be pushing their leader toward the proclamation of a triumvirate, with Robespierre as chief dictator and themselves as his two hands; and it amused the helpless cripple to see just how far the obsequiousness to Tallien and his colleagues would go in subscribing to so monstrous a project.

As for Chauvelin, he said very little, and the deference wherewith he listened to the others, the occasional unctuous words which he let fall, bore testimony to the humiliating subservience to which he had sunk.

And the beautiful Theresia, presiding over the small assembly like a goddess who listens to the prattle of men, sat for the most part quite still, on the one dainty piece of furniture of which her dingy apartment boasted. She was careful to sit so that the rosy glow of the lamp fell on her in the direction most becoming to her attitude. From time to time she threw in a word; but all the while her whole attention was concentrated on what was said. At her future husband's fulsome words of flattery, at his obvious cowardice before the popular idol and his cringing abjectness, a faint smile of contempt would now and then force itself up to her lips. But she neither reproved nor encouraged him. And when Robespierre appeared to be flattered by Tallien's obsequiousness she even gave a little sigh of satisfaction.

St. Just, now as always the mouthpiece of his friend, was the first to give a serious turn to the conversation. Compliments, flatteries, had gone their round; platitudes, grandiloquent phrases on the subject of country, intellectual revolution, liberty, purity, and so on, had been spouted with varying eloquence. The fraternal suppers had been alluded to with servile eulogy of the giant brain who had conceived the project.

Then it was that St. Just broke into a euphemistic account of the disorderly scene in the Rue St. Honoré.

Theresia Cabarrus, roused from her queen-like indifference, at once became interested.

"The young traitor!" she exclaimed, with a great show of indignation. "Who was he? What was he like?"

Couthon gave quite a minute description of Bertrand, and accurate one, too. He had faces the blasphemer—thus was he called by this compact group of devotees and sycophants—for fully five minutes, and despite the flickering and deceptive light, had studied his features, distorted by fury and hate, and was quite sure that he would know them again.

Theresia listened eagerly, caught every inflection of the voices as they discussed the strange events that followed. The keenest observer there could not have detected the slightest agitation in her large, velvety eyes—not even when they met Robespierre's coldly inquiring gaze. No one—not even Tallien—could have guessed what an effort it cost her to appear unconcerned, when all the while she was straining every sense in the direction of the small kitchen at the end of the passage, where the much-discussed Bertrand was still lying concealed.

However, the certainty that Robespierre's spies and those of the Committees had apparently lost complete track of Moncrif, did much to restore her assurance, and her gaiety became after a while somewhat more real.

At one time she turned boldly to Tallien.

"You were there, too, citizen," she said provokingly. "Did you not recognise any of the traitors?"

Tallien stammered out an evasive answer, implored her with a look not to taunt him and not to play like a thoughtless child within sight and hearing of a man-eating tiger. Thereisa's dalliance with the young and handsome Bertrand must in truth be known to Robespierre's army of spies, and he—Tallien—was not altogether convinced that the fair Spaniard, despite her assurances to the contrary, was not harbouring Moncrif in her apartment even now.

Therefore, he would not meet her tantalising glance; and she, delighted to tease, threw herself with greater zest than before into the discussion, amused to see sober Tallien, whom in her innermost heart she despised, enduring tortures of apprehension.

"Ah!" she exclaimed, apparently enraptured by St. Just's glowing account of the occurrence, "what would I not give to have seen it all! In truth, we do not often get such thrilling incidents every day in this dull and dreary Paris. The death-carts with their load of simpering *aristos* have ceased to entertain us. But the drama in the Rue St. Honoré! *à la bonne heure!* What a palpitating scene!"

"Especially," added Couthon, "the spiriting away of the company of traitors through the agency of that mysterious giant, who some aver was just a coal-heaver named Rateau, well known to half the night-birds of the city as an asthmatic reprobate; whilst others vow that he was—"

"Name him not, friend Couthon," St. Just broke in with a sarcastic chuckle. "I pray thee, spare the feelings of Citizen Chauvelin." And his bold, provoking eyes shot a glance of cool irony on the unfortunate victim of his taunt.

Chauvelin made no retort, pressed his thin lips more tightly together as if to smother any incipient expression of the resentment which he felt. Instinctively his glance sought those of Robespierre, who sat by, still apparently disinterested and impassive, with head bent and arms cross over his narrow chest.

"Ah, yes!" here interposed Tallien unctuously. "Citizen Chauvelin has had one or two opportunities of measuring his prowess against that of the mysterious Englishman; but we are told that, despite his talents, he has met with no success in that direction."

"Do not tease our modest friend Chauvelin, I pray you, citizen," Theresia broke in gaily. "The Scarlet Pimpernel—that is the name of the mysterious Englishman, is it not?—is far more elusive and a thousand times more resourceful and daring than any mere man can possibly conceive. 'Tis woman's wits that will bring him to his knees one day. You can take my word for that!"

"*Your* wits, *citoyenne?*"

Robespierre had spoken. It was the first time, since the discussion had turned on the present subject, that he had opened his lips. All eyes were at once reverentially turned to him. His own, cold and sarcastic, were fixed upon Theresia Cabarrus.

She returned his glance with provoking coolness, shrugged her splendid shoulders, and retorted airily:

"Oh, you want a woman with some talent as a sleuthhound—a female counterpart of Citizen Chauvelin. I have no genius in that direction."

"Why not?" Robespierre went on drily. "You, fair *citoyenne*, would be well qualified to deal with the Scarlet Pimpernel, seeing that your adorer, Bertrand Moncrif, appears to be a *protégé* of the mysterious League."

At this taunt, uttered by the dictator with deliberate emphasis, like one who knows what he is talking about, Tallien gave a gasp and his sallow cheeks became the colour of lead. But Theresia placed her cool, reassuring hand upon his.

"Bertrand Moncrif," she said serenely, "is no adorer of mine. He foreswore his allegiance to me on the day that I plighted my troth to Citizen Tallien."

"That is as may be," Robespierre retorted coldly. "But he certainly was the leader of the gang of traitors whom that meddlesome English rabble chose to snatch away tonight from the vengeance of a justly incensed populace."

"How do you know that, Citizen Robespierre?" Theresia asked. She was still maintaining an outwardly calm attitude; her voice was apparently quite steady, her glance absolutely serene. Only Tallien's keen perceptions were able to note the almost wax-like pallor which had spread over her cheeks and the strained, high-pitched tone of her usually mellow voice. "Why do you suppose, citizen," she insisted, "that Bertrand Moncrif had anything to do with the fracas tonight? Methought he had emigrated to England—or somewhere," she added airily, "after—after I gave him his definite *congé*."

"Did you think that, *citoyenne?*" Robespierre rejoined with a wry smile. "Then let me tell you that you are under a misapprehension. Moncrif, the traitor, was the leader of the gang that tried to rouse the people against me tonight. You ask me how I know it?" he added icily. "Well, I saw him—that is all!"

"Ah!" exclaimed Theresia, in well-played mild astonishment. "You say Bertrand Moncrif, citizen? He is in Paris, then?"

"Seemingly."

"Strange, he never came to see me!"

"Strange, indeed!"

"What does he look like? Some people have told me that he is getting fat."

The discussion had now resolved itself into a duel between these two: the ruthless dictator, sure of his power, and the beautiful woman, conscious of hers. The atmosphere of the drably furnished room had become electrical. Everyone felt it. Every man instinctively held his breath, conscious of the quickening of his pulses, of the accelerated beating of his heart.

Both the duellists appeared perfectly calm. Of the two, in truth, Robespierre appeared the most moved. His *staccato* voice, the drumming of his pointed fingers upon the arms of his chair, suggested that the banter of the beautiful Theresia was getting on his nerves. It was like the lashing of a puma's tail, the irritation of a tempter unaccustomed to being provoked, and Theresia was clever enough—above all, woman enough—to note that, since the dictator was moved, he could not be perfectly sure of his ground. He would not display this secret irritation if by a word he could confound his beautiful adversary, and openly threaten where now he only insinuated.

"He saw Bertrand in the Rue St. Honoré," was the sum total of her quick reasoning; "but does not know that he is here. I wonder what it is he does want!" came as an afterthought.

The one that really suffered throughout, and suffered acutely, was Tallien. He would have given all that he possessed to know for a certainty that Bertrand Moncrif was no longer in the house. Surely Theresia would not be foolhardy enough to provoke the powerful dictator into one of those paroxysms of spiteful fury for which he was notorious—fury wherein he might be capable of anything—insulting his hostess, setting his spies to search her apartments for a traitor if he suspected one of lying hidden away somewhere. In truth, Tallien, trembling for his beloved, was ready to swoon. How marvellous she was! how serene! While men held their breath before the inexorable despot, she went on teasing the tiger, even though he had already begun to snarl.

"I entreat you, Citizen Robespierre," she said, with a pout, "to tell me if Bertrand Moncrif has grown fat."

"That I cannot tell you, *citoyenne*," Robespierre replied curtly. "Having recognised my enemy, I no longer paid heed to him. My attention was arrested by his rescuer—"

"That elusive Scarlet Pimpernel," she broke in gaily. "Unrecognisable to all save to Citizen Robespierre, under the disguise of an asthmatic gossoon. Ah, would I had been there!"

"I would you had, *citoyenne*," he retorted. "You would have realised that to refuse your help to unmask an abominable spy after such an episode is tantamount to treason."

Her gaiety dropped from her like a mantle. In a moment she was serious, puzzled. A frown appeared between her brows. Her dark eyes flashed, rapidly inquiring, suspicious, fearful, upon Robespierre.

"To refuse my help?" she asked slowly. "My help in unmasking a spy? I do not understand."

She looked from one man to the other. Chauvelin was the only one who would not meet her gaze. No, not the only one. Tallien, too, appeared absorbed in contemplating his finger nails.

"Citizen Tallien," she queried harshly. "What does this mean?"

"It means just what I said," Robespierre intervene coldly. "That abominable English spy has fooled us all. You said yourself that 'tis a woman's wit that will bring that elusive adventurer to his knees one day. Why not yours?"

Theresia gave no immediate reply. She was meditating. Here, then, was this other means to her hand, whereby she was to propitiate the man-eating tiger, turn his snarl into a purr, obtain immunity for herself and her future lord, but what a prospect!

"I fear me, Citizen Robespierre," she said after a while, "that you overestimate the keenness of my wits."

"Impossible!" he retorted drily.

And St. Just, ever the echo of his friend's unspoken words, added with a great show of gallantry:

"The Citoyenne Cabarrus, even from her prison in Bordeaux, succeeded in snaring our friend Tallien, and making him the slave of her beauty."

"Then why not the Scarlet Pimpernel?" was Couthon's simple conclusion.

"The Scarlet Pimpernel!" Theresia exclaimed with a shrug of her handsome shoulders. "The Scarlet Pimpernel, forsooth! Why, meseems that no one knows who he is! Just now you all affirmed that he was a coal-heaver named Rateau. I cannot make love to a coal-heaver, can I?"

"Citizen Chauvelin knows who the Scarlet Pimpernel is," Couthon went on deliberately. "He will put you on the right track. All that we want is that he should be at your feet. It is so easy for the Citoyenne Cabarrus to accomplish that."

"But if you know who he is," she urged, "why do you need my help?"

"Because," St. Just replied, "the moment that he lands in France he sheds his identity, as a man would a coat. Here, there, everywhere—he is more elusive than a ghost, for a ghost is always the same, whilst the Scarlet Pimpernel is never twice alike. A coal-heaver one day; a prince of dandies the next. He has lodgings in every quarter of Paris and quits them at a moment's notice. He has confederates everywhere: *concierges*, cabaret-keepers, soldiers, vagabonds. He has been a public letter-writer, a sergeant of the National Guard, a rogue, a thief! 'Tis only in England that he is always the same, and Citizen Chauvelin can identify him there. 'Tis there that you can see him, *citoyenne*, there that you can spread your nets for him; from thence that you can lure him to France in your train, like you lured Citizen Tallien to obey your every whim in Bordeaux. Once a man hath fallen a victim to the charms of beautiful Theresia Cabarrus," added the young demagogue gallantly, "she need only to beckon and he will follow, as does Citizen Tallien, as did Bertrand Moncrif, as do so many others. Bring the Scarlet Pimpernel to your feet, here in Paris, *citoyenne*, and we will do the rest."

While his young devotee spoke thus vehemently, Robespierre had relapsed into his usual pose of affected detachment. His head was bent, his arms were folded across his chest. He appeared to be asleep. When St. Just paused, Theresia waiting awhile, her dark eyes fixed on the great man who had conceived this monstrous project. Monstrous, because of the treachery that it demanded.

Theresia Cabarrus had in truth identified herself with the Revolutionary government. She had promised to marry Tallien, who outwardly at least was as bloodthirsty and ruthless as was Robespierre himself; but she was a woman and not a demon. She had refused to sell Bertrand Moncrif in order to pander to Tallien's fear of Robespierre. To entice a man—whoever he was—into making love to her, and then to betray him to his death, was in itself an abhorrent idea. What she might do if actual danger of death threatened her, she did not know. No human soul can with certainty say, "I would not do this or that, under any circumstances whatever!" Circumstance and impulse are the only two forces that create cowards or heroes. Principles, will-power, virtue, are really subservient to those two. If they prove the stronger, everything in man must yield to them.

And Theresia Cabarrus had not yet been tried by force of circumstance or driven by force of impulse. Self-preservation was her dominant law, and she had not yet been in actual fear of death.

This is not a justification on the part of this veracious chronicle of Theresia's subsequent actions; it is an explanation. Faced with this demand upon her on the part of the most powerful despot in France, she hesitated, even though she did not altogether dare to refuse. Womanlike, she tried to temporize.

She appeared puzzled; frowned. Then asked vaguely:

"Is it then that you wish me to go to England?"

St. Just nodded.

"But," she continued, in the same indeterminate manner, "me-seems that you talk very glibly of my—what shall I say?—my pro-posed dalliance with the mysterious Englishman. Suppose he—he does not respond?"

"Impossible!" Couthon broke in quickly.

"Oh!" she protested. "Impossible? Englishmen are known to be prudish—moral—what? And if the man is married—what then?"

"The Citoyenne Cabarrus underrates her powers," St. Just riposted glibly.

"Theresia, I entreat!" Tallien put in dolefully.

He felt that the interview, from which he had hoped so much, was proving a failure—nay, worse! For he realised that Robespierre, thwarted in this desire, would bitterly resent Theresia's positive refusal to help him.

"Eh, what?" she riposted lightly. "And it is you, Citizen Tallien, who would push me into this erotic adventure? I' faith, your trust in me is highly flattering! Have you not thought that in the process I might fall in love with the Scarlet Pimpernel myself? He is young, they say, handsome, adventurous; and I am to try and capture his fan-cy—the butterfly is to dance around the flame.—No, no! I am too much afraid that I may singe my wings!"

"Does that mean," Robespierre put in coldly, "that you refuse us your help, Citoyenne Cabarrus?"

"Yes—I refuse," she replied calmly. "The project does not please me, I confess—"

"Not even if we guaranteed immunity to your lover, Bertrand Moncrif?"

She gave a slight shudder. Her lips felt dry, and she passed her tongue rapidly over them.

"I have no lover, except Citizen Tallien," she said steadily, and placed her fingers, which had suddenly become ice-cold, upon the clasped hands of her future lord. Then she rose, thereby giving the signal for the breaking-up of the little party.

In truth, she knew as well as Tallien that the meeting had been a failure. Tallien was looking sallow and terribly worried. Robespierre, taciturn and sullen, gave her one threatening glance before he took his leave.

"You know, *citoyenne*," he said coldly, "that the nation has means at its disposal for compelling its citizens to do their duty."

"Ah, bah!" retorted the fair Spaniard, shrugging her shoulders. "I am not a citizen of France. And even your unerring Public Prosecutor would find it difficult to frame an accusation against me."

Again, she laughed, determined to appear gay and inconsequent through it all.

"Think how the accusation would sound, Citizen Robespierre!" she went on mockingly. "'The Citoyenne Cabarrus, for refusing to make amorous overtures to the mysterious Englishman known as the Scarlet Pimpernel, and for refusing to administer a love-philtre to him as prepared by Mother Théot at the bidding of Citizen Robespierre!' Confess! Confess!" she added, and her rippling laugh had a genuine note of merriment in it at last, "that we none of us would survive such ridicule!"

Theresia Cabarrus was a clever woman, and by speaking the word "ridicule," she had touched the one weak chink in the tyrant's armour. But it is not always safe to prod a tiger, even with a child's cane, or even from behind protecting bars. Tallien knew this well enough. He was on tenterhooks, longing to see the others depart so that he might throw himself once again at Theresia's feet and implore her to obey the despot's commands.

But Theresia appeared unwilling to give him such another chance. She professed intense fatigue, bade him "goodnight" with such obvious finality, that he dared not outstay his welcome. A few moments later they had all gone. Their gracious hostess accompanied them to the door, since Pepita had by this time certainly gone to bed. The little procession was formed, with St. Just and Chauvelin supporting their palsied comrade, Robespierre detached and silent, and finally Tallien, whose last appealing look to his beloved would have melted a heart of stone.

Chapter 11

Strange Happenings

Now the dingy little apartment in the Rue Villedot was silent and dark. The elegant little lamp with its rose-coloured shade was turned down in the withdrawing-room, leaving only a tiny glimmer of light, which failed to dispel the gloom around. The nocturnal visitors had departed more than a quarter of an hour ago; nevertheless, the beautiful hostess had not yet gone to bed. In fact, she had hardly moved since she bade the final *adieu* to her timorous lover. The enforced gaiety of the last few moments still sat like a mask upon her face. All that she had done was to sink with a sigh of weariness upon the settee.

And there she remained, with neck craned forward, listening, straining every nerve to listen, even though the heavy, measured footsteps of the five men had long since ceased to echo up and down the stone passages and stairs. Her foot, in its quaint small sandal, beat now and then an impatient tattoo upon the threadbare carpet. Her eyes at intervals cast anxious looks upon the old-fashioned clock above the mantelpiece.

It struck half-past two. Whereupon Theresia rose and went out into the vestibule. Here a tallow candle flickered faintly in its pewter sconce and emitted an evil-smelling smoke, which rose in spirals to the blackened ceiling.

Theresia paused, glanced inquiringly down the narrow passage which gave access to the little kitchen beyond. Between the kitchen and the corner of the vestibule where she was standing, two doors gave on the passage: her bedroom, and that of her maid Pepita. Theresia was vividly conscious of the strange silence which reigned in the whole apartment. The passage was pitch dark save at its farthest end, where a tiny ray of light found its way underneath the kitchen door.

The silence was oppressive, almost terrifying. In a hoarse, anxious voice, Theresia called:

"Pepita!"

But there came no answer. Pepita apparently had gone to bed, was fast asleep by now. But what had become of Bertrand?

Full of vague misgivings, her nerves tingling with a nameless fear, Theresia picked up the candle and tiptoed down the passage. Outside Pepita's door she paused and listened. Her large dark eyes looked weird in their expression of puzzlement and of awe, the flickering light of the candle throwing gleams of orange-coloured lights into the depths of the widely dilated pupils.

"Pepita!" she called; and somehow the sound of her own voice added to her terror. Strange that she should be frightened like this in her own familiar apartment, and with a faithful, sturdy maid sleeping the other side of this thin partition wall!

"Pepita!" Theresia's voice was shaking. She tried to open the door, but it was locked. Why had Pepita, contrary to her habit, locked herself in? Had she, too, been a prey to some unexplainable panic? Theresia knocked against the door, rattled the handle in its socket, called more loudly and more insistently, "Pepita!" and, receiving no reply, fell, half-swooning with fear, against the partition wall, whilst the candle slipped out of her trembling grasp and fell with a clatter to the ground.

She was now in complete darkness, with senses reeling and brain paralysed. How long she remained thus, in a state bordering on collapse, she did not know; probably not more than a minute or so. Consciousness returned quickly, and with it the cold sweat of an abject fear; for through this returning consciousness she had perceived a groan issuing from behind the locked door. But her knees were still shaking; she felt unable to move.

"Pepita!" she called again; and to her own ears her voice sounded hoarse and muffled. Straining her ears and holding her breath, she once more caught the sound of a smothered grown.

Whereupon, driven into action by the obvious distress of her maid, Theresia recovered a certain measure of self-control. Pulling herself vigorously together, she began by groping for the candle which had dropped out of her hand a while ago. Even as she stooped down for this she contrived to say in a moderately clear and firm voice:

"Courage, Pepita! I'll find the light and come back." Then she added: "Are you unable to unlock the door?"

To this, however, she received no reply save another muffled groan.

Theresia now was on her hands and knees, groping for the candlestick. Then a strange thing happened. Her hands, as they wandered vaguely along the flagged floor, encountered a small object, which proved to be a key. In an instant she was on her feet again, her fingers running over the door until they encountered the keyhole. Into this she succeeded, after further groping, in inserting the key; it fitted and turned the lock. She pushed open the door and remained paralysed with surprise upon the threshold.

Pepita was reclining in an armchair, her hands tied behind her, a woollen shawl wound loosely around her mouth. In a distant corner of the room, a small oil-lamp, turned very low, cast a glimmer of light upon the scene. For Theresia to run to the pinioned woman and undo the bonds that held her was but the work of a few seconds.

"Pepita!" she cried. "What in heaven's name has happened?"

The woman seemed not much the worse for her enforced duress. She groaned, and even swore under her breath, and indeed appeared more dazed than hurt. Theresia, impatient and excited, had to shake her more than once vigorously by the shoulder before she was able to gather her scattered wits together.

"Where is M. Bertrand?" Theresia asked repeatedly, ere she got a reply from her bewildered maid.

At last Pepita was able to speak.

"In very truth, *Madame*," she said slowly, "I do not know."

"How do you mean, you do not know?" Theresia queried, with a deepened frown.

"Just what I saw, my pigeon," Pepita retorted with marked acerbity. "You ask me what has happened, and I say I do not know. You want to know what has become of M. Bertrand. Then go and look for yourself. When I last saw him, he was in the kitchen, unfit to move, the poor cabbage!"

"But, Pepita," Theresia insisted, and stamped her foot with impatience, "you must know how you came to be sitting here, pinioned and muffled. Who did it? Who has been here? God preserve the woman; will she never speak!"

Pepita by now had fully recovered her senses. She had struggled to her feet, and went to take up the lamp, then led the way toward the door, apparently intent on finding out for herself what had become of M. Bertrand and in no way sharing her mistress's unreasoning terror. She halted on the threshold and turned to Theresia, who quite mechanically started to follow her.

"M. Bertrand was sitting in the armchair in the kitchen," she said simply. "I was arranging a cushion for his head, to make him more comfortable, when suddenly a shawl was flung over my head without the slightest warning. I had seen nothing; I had not heard the merest sound. And I had not the time to utter a scream before I was muffled up in the shawl. Then I was lifted off the ground as if I were a sack of feathers, and I just remember smelling something acrid which made my head spin round and round. But I remember nothing more after until I heard voices in the vestibule when thy guests were going away. Then I heard thy voice and tried to make thee hear mine. And that is all!"

"When did that happen, Pepita?"

"Soon after the last of thy guests had arrived. I remember I looked at the clock. It must have been half an hour after midnight."

While the woman spoke, Theresia had remained standing in the middle of the room, looking in the gloom like an elfin apparition, with her clinging, diaphanous draperies. A frown of deep puzzlement lay between her brows and her lips were tightly pressed together as if in wrath; but she said nothing more, and when Pepita, lamp in hand, went out of the room, she followed.

When, the kitchen door being opened, that room was found to be empty, Theresia was no longer surprised. Somehow, she had expected this. She knew that Bertrand would be gone. The windows of the kitchen gave on the ubiquitous wrought-iron balcony, as did all the other windows of the apartment. That those windows were unfastened, had only been pushed to from the outside, appeared to her as a matter of course. It was not Bertrand who had thrown the shawl over Pepita's head; therefore, someone had come in from the outside and had kidnapped Bertrand—someone who was peculiarly bold and daring. He had not come in from the balcony and through the window, because the latter had been fastened as usual by Pepita much earlier in the evening. No! He had gone that way, taking Bertrand with him; but he must have entered the place in some other mysterious manner, like a disembodied sprite bent on mischief or mystery.

Whilst Pepita fumbled and grumbled, Theresia started on a tour of inspection. Still deeply puzzled, she was no longer afraid. With Pepita to speak and the lamps all turned on, her habitual courage and self-possession had quickly returned to her. She had no belief in the supernatural. Her materialistic, entirely rational mind at once rejected the supposition, hinted at by Pepita, that magical powers had been at work to take Bertrand Moncrif to a place of safety.

Something was going on in her brain, certain theories, guesses, conjectures, which she was passionately eager to set at rest. Nor did it take her long. Candle in hand, she had gone round to explore. No sooner had she entered her own bedroom than the solution of the mystery lay revealed before her, in a shutter, forced open from the outside, a broken pane of glass which had allowed a hand to creep in and surreptitiously turn the handle of the tall French window to allow of easy ingress. It had been quickly and cleverly done; the splinters of glass had made no noise as they fell upon the carpet. But for the disappearance of Bertrand, the circumstances suggested a nimble housebreaker rather than a benevolent agency for the rescue of young rashlings in distress.

The frown of puzzlement deepened on Theresia Cabarrus's brow, and her mobile mouth with the perfectly arched if somewhat thin lips expressed a kind of feline anger, whilst the hand that held the pewter candlestick trembled perceptibly.

Pepita's astonishment expressed itself by sundry exclamations: "Name of a name!" and "Is it possible?" The explanation of the mystery had loosened her tongue, and while she set stolidly to work to clear up the debris of glass in her mistress's bedroom, she allowed free rein to her indignation against the impudent marauder, who in doubt had only been foiled in his attempt at wholesale robbery by some lucky circumstance which would presently come to light.

The worthy old peasant absolutely refused to connect the departure of M. Bertrand with so obvious an attempt at housebreaking.

"M. Bertrand was determined to go, the poor cabbage!" she said decisively; "since thou didst make him understand that his staying here was a danger to the front door whilst thou wast engaged in conversation with that pack of murderers, whom may the good God punish one of these days!"

From which remark we may gather that Pepita had not imbibed revolutionary ideals with the air of her native Andalusia.

Theresia Cabarrus, wearied beyond endurance by all the events of this night, as well as by her old servant's incessant gabble, finally sent her, still muttering and grumbling, to bed.

CHAPTER 12

Chauvelin

Theresia had opposed a stern refusal to Pepita's request that she might put her mistress to bed before she herself went to rest. She did not want to go to bed: she wanted to think, and now that that peculiar air of mystery, that silence and semi-darkness no longer held their gruesome sway in her apartment, she did not feel afraid.

Pepita went to bed. For a while, Theresia could hear her moving about, with ponderous, shuffling footsteps; then, presently everything was still. The clock of old St. Roch struck three. Not much more than half an hour had gone by since her guests had been departed. To Theresia it seemed like an infinity of time. The sense of a baffling mystery being at work around her had roused her ire and killed all latent fear.

But what was the mystery?

And was there a mystery at all? Or was Pepita's rational explanation of the occurrence of this night the right one after all?

Citoyenne Cabarrus, unable to sit still, wandered up and down the passage, in and out of the kitchen; in and out of her bedroom, and thence into the vestibule. Then back again. At one moment, when standing in the vestibule, she thought she heard someone moving on the landing outside the front door. Her heart beat a little more rapidly, but she was not afraid. She did not believe in housebreakers and she felt that Pepita, who was a very light sleeper, was well within call.

So, she went to the front door and opened it. The quick cry which she gave was one of surprise rather than of fear. In her belated visitor she had recognised Citizen Chauvelin; and somehow, by a vague process of reasoning, his presence just at this moment seemed quite rational—in keeping with the unsolved mystery that was so baffling to the fair Theresia.

"May I come in, *citoyenne?*" Chauvelin said in a whisper. "It is late, I know; but there is urgency."

He was standing on the threshold, and she, a few paces away from him in the vestibule. The candle, which now burned low in its socket, was behind her. Its light touched with a weird, flickering glow on the pale face of the once noted Terrorist, with its pale eyes and sharply hooked nose, which gave him the air of a gaunt bird of prey.

"It is late," she murmured vaguely. "What do you want?"

"Something has happened," he replied, still speaking below his breath. "Something which concerns you. And, before speaking of it to Citizen Robespierre—"

At the dread name Theresia stepped farther back into the vestibule.

"Enter!" she said curtly.

He came in, and she closed the door carefully behind him. Then she led the way into the withdrawing room and turned up the wick of the lamp under its rosy shade. She sat down and motioned to him to do the same.

"What is it?" she asked.

Before replying, Chauvelin's finger and thumb—thin and pointed like the talons of a vulture—went fumbling in the pocket of his waistcoat. From it he extracted a small piece of neatly folded paper.

"When we left your apartment, *citoyenne*—my friend St. Just and I supporting poor palsied Couthon, and Robespierre following close behind us—I spied this scrap of paper, which St. Just's careless foot had just kicked to one side when he was stepping across the threshold. Some unknown hand must have insinuated it underneath the door. Now, I never despise stray bits of paper. I have had so many through my hands that proved after examination to be of paramount importance. So, whilst the others were busy with their own affairs I, unseen by them, had already stooped and picked the paper up."

He paused for a moment or two, then, satisfied that he held the beautiful woman's undivided attention, he went on in his habitual dry, urbane monotone:

"Now, though I was quite sure in my own mind, *citoyenne*, that this *billet-doux* was intended for your fair hands, I felt that, as its finder, I had some sort of lien upon it—"

"To the point, citizen, I pray you!" Theresia broke in harshly, tried by a show of impatience and of fatigue to hide the anxiety which had once more taken possession of her heart. "You found a letter addressed to me; you read it. As you have brought it here, I presume that you wish me to know its contents. So, get on, man, get on!" she added more vehemently. "It is not at three in the morning that one cares for dalliance."

By way of reply, Chauvelin slowly unfolded the note and began to read:

"'Bertrand Moncrif is a young fool, but he is too good to be the plaything of a sleek black pantheress, however beautiful she might be. So, I am taking him away to England where, in the arms of his long-suffering and loyal sweetheart, he will soon forget the brief madness which so nearly landed him on the guillotine and made of him a tool to serve the selfish whims of Theresia Cabarrus.'"

Theresia had listened to the brief, enigmatic epistle without displaying the slightest sign of emotion or surprise. Now, when Chauvelin had finished reading, and with his strange, dry smile had handed her the tiny note, she took it and for a while contemplated it in silence, her face perfectly placid save for a curious and ominous contraction of the brows and a screwing-up of the fine eyes, which gave her a curious, snake-like expression.

"You know, of course, *citoyenne*," Chauvelin said after a while, "who the writer of this—shall we say?—impudent epistle happens to be?"

She nodded.

"The man," he went on placidly, "who goes by the name of the Scarlet Pimpernel. The impudent English adventurer whom Citizen Robespierre has asked you, *citoyenne*, to lure into the net which we may spread for him."

Still Theresia was silent. She did not look at Chauvelin, but kept her eyes fixed upon the scrap of paper, which she had folded into a long, narrow ribbon and was twining in and out between her fingers.

"A while ago, *citoyenne*," Chauvelin continued, "in this very room, you refused to lend us a helping hand."

Still no reply from Theresia. She had just smoothed out the mysterious epistle, carefully folded it into four, and was in the act of slipping it into the bosom of her gown. Chauvelin waited quite patiently. He was accustomed to waiting, and patience was an integral part of his stock in trade. Opportunism was another.

Theresia was sitting on her favourite settee, leaning forward with her hands clasped between her knees, her head was bent, and the tiny rose-shaded lamp failed to throw its glimmer of light upon her face. The clock on the mantelshelf behind her was ticking with insentient monotony. *Anon*, a distant chime struck the quarter after three. Whereupon Chauvelin rose.

"I think we understand one another, *citoyenne*," he said quietly, and with a sigh of complete satisfaction. "It is late now. At what hour may I have the privilege of seeing you alone?"

"At three in the afternoon?" she replied tonelessly, like one speaking in a dream. "Citizen Tallien is always at the Convention then, and my door will be denied to everybody else."

"I'll be here at three o'clock," was Chauvelin's final word.

Theresia had not moved. He made her a deep bow and went out of the room. The next moment, the opening and shutting of the outer door proclaimed that he had gone.

After that, Theresia Cabarrus went to bed.

CHAPTER 13

The Fisherman's Rest

And whilst the whole of Europe was in travail with the repercussion of the gigantic upheaval that was shaking France to its historic foundations, the last few years had seen by very little change in this little corner of England.

The Fisherman's Rest stood where it had done for two centuries and long before thrones had tottered and anointed heads fallen on the scaffold. The oak rafters, black with age, the monumental hearth, the tables and high-backed benches, seemed like mute testimonies to good order and to tradition, just as the shiny pewter mugs, the foaming ale, the brass that glittered like gold, bore witness to unimpaired prosperity and an even, well-regulated life.

Over in the kitchen yonder, Mistress Sally Waite, as she now was, still ruled with a firm if somewhat hasty hand, the weight of which, so the naughty gossips averred, even her husband, Master Harry Waite, had experienced more than once. She still queened it over her father's household, presided over his kitchen, and drove the young scullery wenches to their task with her sharp tongue and an occasional slap. But The Fisherman's Rest could not have gone on without her. The copper saucepans would in truth not have glittered so, nor would the home-brewed ale have tasted half so luscious to Master Jellyband's faithful customers, had not Mistress Sally's strong brown hands drawn it for them, with just the right amount of creamy foam on the top and not a bit too much.

And so, it was still many a "Ho, Sally! 'Ere Sally! 'Ow long'll you be with that there beer!" or "Say, Sally! A cut of your cheese and home-baked bread; and look sharp about it!" that resounded from end to end of the long, low-raftered coffee-room of "The Fisherman's Rest," on this fine May day of the year of grace 1794.

Sally Waite, her muslin cap set at a becoming angle, her kerchief primly folded over her well-developed bosom, and her kirtle neatly raised above a pair of exceedingly shapely ankles, was in and out of the room, in and out of the kitchen, tripping it like a benevolent if somewhat substantial fairy, bandying chaff here, administering rebuke there, hot, panting and excited.

The while mine host, Master Jellyband—perhaps a shade more portly of figure, a thought more bald of pate, these last two years—stood with stubby legs firmly planted upon his own hearth, wherein, despite the warmth of a glorious afternoon, a log fire blazed away merrily. He was giving forth his views upon the political situation of Europe generally with the self-satisfied assurance born of complete ignorance and true British insular prejudice.

Believe me, Mr. Jellyband was in no two minds about "them murderin' furriners over yonder" who had done away with their king and queen and all their nobility and quality, and whom England had at last decided to lick into shape.

"And not a moment too soon, hark'ee, Mr. 'Empseed," he went on sententiously. "And if I 'ad my way, we should 'ave punished 'em proper long before this—blown their bloomin' Paris into smithereens and carried off the pore queen afore those murderous villains 'ad 'er pretty 'ead off 'er shoulders!"

Mr. Hempseed, from his own privileged corner in the inglenook, was not altogether prepared to admit that.

"I am not for interfering with other folks' ways," he said, raising his quaking treble so as to stem effectually the torrent of Master Jellyband's eloquence. "As the Scriptures say—"

"Keep your dirty fingers from off my waist!" came in decisive tones from Mistress Sally Waite, whilst the shrill sound made by the violent contact of a feminine hand against a manly cheek froze the Scriptural quotation on Mr. Hempseed's lips.

"Now then, now then, Sally!" Mr. Jellyband thought fit to say in stern tones, not liking his customers to be thus summarily dealt with.

"Now then, father," Sally retorted, with a toss of her brown curls, "you just attend to your politics, and Mr. 'Empseed to ''is Scriptures and leave me to deal with them impudent jackanapes. You wait!" she added, turning once more with a parting shot directed against the discomfited offender. "If my 'Arry catches you at them tricks, you'll see what you get—that's all!"

"Sally!" Mr. Jellyband admonished, more sternly this time. "You'll 'ave my Lord Hastings 'ere before 'is dinner is ready."

Which suggestion so overawed Mistress Sally that she promptly forgot the misdoings of the forward swain and failed to hear the sarcastic chuckle which greeted the mention of her husband's name. With an excited little cry, she ran quickly out of the room.

Mr. Hempseed, loftily unaware of interruption, concluded his sententious remark:

"As the Scriptures say, Mr. Jellyband: ''Ave no fellowship with the unfruitful work of darkness.' I don't 'old not with interfering. Remember what the Scriptures say: ''E that committeth sin is of the devil, and the devil sinneth from the beginning,'" he concluded with sublime irrelevance, sagely nodding his head.

But Mr. Jellyband was not thus lightly to be confounded in his argument—no, not by any quotation, relevant or otherwise!

"All very fine, Mr. 'Empseed," he said, "and good enough for them 'oo, like yourself, are willin' to side with them murderin' reprobates—"

"Like myself, Mr. Jellyband?" protested Mr. Hempseed, with as much vigour as his shrill treble would allow. "Nay, but I'm not for them children of darkness—"

"You may be or you may not," Mr. Jellyband went on, nothing daunted. "There be many as are, and 'oo'd say 'Let 'em murder,' even now, but I say that them as 'oo talk that way are not true Englishmen; for 'tis we Englishmen 'oo can teach the furriner just what 'e may do and what 'e may not. And as we've got the ships and the men and the money, we can just fight 'em as are not of our way o' thinkin'. And let me tell you, Mr. 'Empseed, that I'm prepared to back my opinions 'gainst any man as don't agree with me!"

For the nonce Mr. Hempseed was silent. True, a Scriptural text did hover on his thin, quivering lips; but as no one paid any heed to him for the moment its appositeness will for ever remain doubtful. The honours of victory rested with Mr. Jellyband. Such lofty patriotism, coupled with so much sound knowledge of political affairs, could not fail to leave its impress upon the more ignorant and the less fervent amongst the frequenters of The Fisherman's Rest.

Indeed, who was more qualified to pass an opinion on current events than the host of that much-frequented resort, seeing that the ladies and gentlemen of quality who came to England from over the water, so as to escape all them murtherin' reprobates in their own country, did most times halt at The Fisherman's Rest on their way to London or to Bath? And though Mr. Jellyband did not know a word of French—no furrin lingo for him, thank 'ee!—he nevertheless had mixed with all that nobility and gentry for over two years now, and had learned all that there was to know about the life over there, and about Mr. Pitt's intentions to put a stop to all those abominations.

Even now, hardly had mine hosts conversation with his favoured customers assumed a more domestic turn, than a loud clatter on the cobblestones outside, a jingle and a rattle, shouts, laughter and bustle, announced the arrival of guests who were privileged to make as much noise as they pleased.

Mr. Jellyband ran to the door, shouted for Sally at the top of his voice with a "Here's my lord Hastings!" to add spur to Sally's hustle. Politics were forgotten for the nonce, arguments set aside, in the excitement of welcoming the quality.

Three young gallants in travelling clothes, smart of appearance and debonair of mien, were ushering a party of strangers—three ladies and two men—into the hospitable porch of The Fisherman's Rest. The little party had walked across from the inner harbour, where the graceful masts of an elegant schooner lately arrived in port were seen gently swaying against the delicately coloured afternoon sky. Three or four sailors from the schooner were carrying luggage, which they deposited in the hall of the inn, then touched their forelocks in response to a pleasant smile and nod from the young lords.

"This way, my lord," Master Jellyband reiterated with jovial obsequiousness. "Everything is ready. This way! Hey, Sallee!" he called again; and Sally, hot, excited, blushing, came tripping over from the kitchen, wiping her hot plump palms against her apron in anticipation of shaking hands with their lordships.

"Since Mr. Waite isn't anywhere about," my Lord Hastings said gaily, as he put a bold arm round Mistress Sally's dainty waist, "I'll e'en have a kiss, my pretty one."

"And I, too, by gad, for old sake's sake!" Lord Tony asserted, and planked a hearty kiss on mistress Sally's dimpled cheek.

"At your service, my lords, at your service!" Master Jellyband rejoined, laughing. Then added more soberly: "Now then, Sally, show the ladies up into the blue room, the while their lordships 'ave a first shake down in the coffee-room. This way, gentlemen—your lordships—this way!"

The strangers in the meanwhile had stood by, wide-eyed and somewhat bewildered in face of this exuberant hilarity which was so unlike what they had pictured to themselves of dull, fog-ridden England—so unlike, too, the dreary moroseness which of late had replaced the erstwhile light-hearted gaiety of their own countrymen. The porch and the narrow hall of The Fisherman's Rest appeared to them seething and vitality. Everyone was talking, nobody seemed to listen; everyone was merry, and everyone knew everybody else and was pleased to meet them. Sonorous laughter echoed from end to end along the solid beams, black and shiny with age. it all seemed so homely, so happy. The deference paid to the young gallants and to them as strangers by the sailors and the innkeeper was so genuine and hearty without the slightest sign of servility, that those five people who had left behind them so much class-hatred, enmity and cruelty in their own country, felt an unaccountable tightening of the heart, a few hot tears rise to their eyes, partly of joy, but partly too of regret.

Lord Hastings, the youngest and merriest of the English party, guided the two Frenchmen toward the coffee-room, with many a jest in atrocious French and kindly words of encouragement, all intended to put the strangers at their ease.

Lord Anthony Dewhurst and Sir Andrew Ffoulkes—a trifle more serious and earnest, yet equally happy and excited at the success of their perilous adventure and at the prospect of reunion with their wives—lingered a moment longer in the hall, in order to speak with the sailors who had brought the luggage along.

"Do you know aught of Sir Percy?" Lord Tony asked.

"No, my lord," the sailor gave answer; "not since he went ashore early this morning. 'Er Ladyship was waitin' for 'im on the pier. Sir Percy just ran up the steps and then 'e shouted to us to get back quickly. 'Tell their lordships,' 'e says, 'I'll meet them at "The Rest".' And then Sir Percy and 'er ladyship just walked off and we saw naun more of them."

"That was many hours ago," Sir Andrew Ffoulkes mused, with an inward smile. He too saw visions of meeting his pretty Suzanne very soon and walking away with her into the land of dreams.

"'Twas just six o'clock when Sir Percy 'ad the boat lowered," the sailor rejoined. "And we rowed quick back after we landed 'im, but the *Daydream*, she 'ad to wait for the tide. We wurr a long while gettin' into port."

Sir Andrew nodded.

"You don't know," he said, "if the skipper had any further orders?"

"I don't know, sir," the man replied. "But we mun be in readiness always. No one knows when Sir Percy may wish to set sail again."

The two young men said nothing more, and presently the sailors touched their forelocks and went away. Lord Tony and Sir Andrew exchanged knowing smiles. They could easily picture to themselves their beloved chief, indefatigable, like a boy let out from school, exhilarated by the deadly danger through which he had once more passed unscathed, clasping his adored wife in his arms and wandering off with her, heaven knew whither, living his life of joy and love and happiness during the brief hours which his own indomitable energy, his reckless courage, accorded to the sentimental side of his complex nature.

Far too impatient to wait until the tide allowed the *Daydream* to get into port, he had been rowed ashore in the early dawn, and his beautiful Marguerite—punctual to the assignation conveyed to her by one of those mysterious means of which Percy alone knew the secret—was ready there to receive him, to forget in the shelter of his arms the days of racking anxiety and of cruel terror for her beloved through which she had again and again been forced to pass.

Neither Lord Tony nor Sir Andrew Ffoulkes, the Scarlet Pimpernel's most faithful and devoted lieutenants, begrudged their chief these extra hours of bliss, the while they were left in charge of the party so lately rescued from horrible death. They knew that within a day or two—within a few hours, perhaps—Blakeney would tear himself away once more from the clinging embrace of his exquisite wife, from the comfort of luxury of an ideal home, from the adulation of friends, the pleasures of wealth and of fashion, in order mayhap to grovel in the squalor and filth of some outlandish corner of Pairs, where he could be in touch with the innocents who suffered—the poor, the terror-stricken victims of the merciless revolution. Within a few hours, mayhap, he would be risking his life again every moment of the day, in order to save some poor hunted fellow-creature—man, woman or child—from death that threatened them at the hands of inhuman monsters who knew neither mercy nor compunction.

And for the nineteen members of the League, they took it in turns to follow their leader where danger was thickest. It was a privilege eagerly sought, deserved by all, and accorded to those who were most highly trusted. It was invariably followed by a period of rest in happy England, with wife, friends, joy and luxury. Sir Andrew Ffoulkes, Lord Anthony Dewhurst and my lord Hastings had been of the expedition which brought Mme de Serval with her three children and Bertrand Moncrif safely to England, after adventures more perilous, more reckless of danger, than most. Within a few hours they would be free to forget in the embrace of clinging arms every peril and every adventure save the eternal one of love, free to forswear everything outside that, save their veneration for their chief and their loyalty to his cause.

CHAPTER 14

The Castaway

An excellent dinner served by Mistress Sally and her attendant little wenches put everybody into rare good-humour. Madame de Serval—pale, delicate, with gentle, plaintive voice and eyes that had acquired a pathetically furtive look—even contrived to smile, her heart warmed by the genuine welcome, the rare gaiety that irradiated this fortunate corner of God's earth. Wars and rumours of war reached it only as an echo of great things that went on in the vast outside world; and though more than one of Dover's gallant sons had perished in one or the other of the Duke of York's unfortunate incursions into Holland, or in one of the numerous naval engagements off the Western shores of France, on the whole, the war, intermittent and desultory, had not yet cast its heavy gloom over the entire country.

Joséphine and Jacques de Serval, whose enthusiasm for martyrdom had received so severe a check in the course of the Fraternal Supper in the Rue. St. Honoré, had at first with the self-consciousness of youth adopted an attitude of obstinate and irreclaimable sorrow, until the antics of Master Harry Waite, pretty Sally's husband—jealous as a young turkey-cock of every gallant who dared to ogle his buxom wife—brought laughter to their lips. My Lord Hastings' comical attempts at speaking French, the droll mistakes he made, easily did the rest; and soon their lively, high-pitched Latin voices mingled with unimpaired gaiety with the more mellow sound of Anglo-Saxon tongues.

Even Régine de Serval had smiled when my lord Hastings had asked her with grave solemnity whether Mme de Serval would wish

311

"*le fou de descendre*"—the lunatic to the come downstairs—meaning all the while whether she wanted the fire in the big hearth to be let down, seeing that the atmosphere in the coffee-room was growing terribly hot.

The only one who seemed quite unable to shake off his moroseness was Bertrand Moncrif. He sat next to Régine, silent, somewhat sullen, a look that seemed almost one of dull resentment lingering in his eyes. From time to time, when he appeared peculiarly moody or when he refused to eat, her little hand would steal out under the table and press his with a gentle, motherly gesture.

It was when the merry meal was over and while Master Jellyband was going the round with a fine bottle of smuggled brandy, which the young gentlemen sipped with unmistakable relish, that a commotion arose outside the inn; whereupon Master Harry Waite ran out of the coffee-room in order to see what was amiss.

Nothing very much apparently. Waite came back after a moment or two and said that two sailors from the barque *Angela* were outside with a young French lad, who seemed more dead than alive, and whom it appears the barque had picked up just outside French waters, in an open boat, half perished with terror and inanition. As the lad spoke nothing but French, the sailors had brought him along to The Fisherman's Rest, thinking that maybe some of the quality would care to interrogate him.

At once Sir Andrew Ffoulkes, my Lord Tony and Lord Hastings were on the *qui vive*. A lad in distress, coming from France, found alone in an open boat, suggested one of those tragedies in which the League of the Scarlet Pimpernel was wont to play a *rôle*.

"Let the lad be taken into the parlour, Jellyband," Sir Andrew commanded. "You've got a fire in there, haven't you?"

"Yes, yes, Sir Andrew! We always keep fires going here until past the 15th of May."

"Well then, get him in there. Then give him some of your smuggled brandy first, you old dog! then some wine and food. After that we'll find out something more about him."

He himself went along in order to see that his orders were carried out. Jellyband, as usual, had already deputed his daughter to do the necessary, and in the hall, there was Mistress Sally, capable and compassionate, supporting, almost carrying, a youth who in truth appeared scarce able to stand.

She led him gently into the small private parlour, where a cheerful log-fire was blazing, sat him down in an armchair beside the hearth, after which Master Jellyband himself poured half a glass of brandy down the poor lad's throat. This revived him a little, and he looked about him with huge, scared eyes.

"*Sainte Mére de Dieu!*" he murmured feebly. "Where am I?"

"Never mind about that now, my lad," replied Sir Andrew, whose knowledge of French was of a distinctly higher order than that of his comrades. "You are among friends. That is enough. Have something to eat and drink now. Later we'll talk."

He was eyeing the boy keenly. Contact with suffering and misery over there in France, under the leadership of the most selfless, most understanding man of this or any time, had intensified his powers of perception. Even the first glance had revealed to him the fact that here was no ordinary waif. The lad spoke with a gentle, highly refined voice; his skin was delicate, and his face exquisitely beautiful; his hands, though covered with grime, and his feet, encased in huge, coarse boots, were small and daintily shaped, like those of a woman. Already Sir Andrew had made up his mind that if the oilskin cap which sat so extraordinarily tightly on the boy's head were to be removed, a wealth of long hair would certainly be revealed.

However, all these facts, which threw over the young stranger a further veil of mystery, could not in all humanity be investigated now. Sir Andrew Ffoulkes, with the consummate tact born of kindliness, left the lad alone as soon as he appeared able to sit up and eat, and himself rejoined his friends in the coffee-room.

CHAPTER 15

The Nest

No one, save a very few intimates, knew of the little nest wherein Sir Percy Blakeney and his lady hid their happiness on those occasions when the indefatigable Scarlet Pimpernel was only able to spend a few hours in England, and when a journey to their beautiful home in Richmond could not be thought of. The house—it was only a cottage, timbered and creeper-clad—lay about a mile and a half outside Dover, off the main road, perched up high on rising ground over a narrow lane. It had a small garden round it, which in May was ablaze with daffodils and bluebells, and in June with roses. Two faithful servants, a man and his wife, looked after the place, kept the nest cosy and warm whenever her ladyship weared of fashion, or else, actually expecting Sir Percy, would come down from London for a day or two in order to dream of that elusive and transient happiness for which her soul hungered, even while her indomitable spirit accepted the inevitable.

A few days ago, the weekly courier from France had brought her a line from Sir Percy, together with the promise that she should rest in his arms on the 1st of May. And Marguerite had come down to the creeper-covered cottage knowing that, despite obstacles which might prove insuperable to others, Percy would keep his world.

She had stolen out at dawn to wait for him on the pier; and sure enough, as soon as the May-day sun, which had risen today in his glory as if to crown her brief happiness with warmth and radiance, had dissipated the morning mist, her yearning eyes had spied the smart white gig which had put off from the *Daydream* leaving the graceful ship to await the turn of the tide before putting into port.

Since then, every moment of the day had been one of rapture. The first sight of her husband in his huge caped coat, which seemed to add further inches to his great height, his call of triumph when he saw her, his arms outstretched, there, far away in the small boat, with a gesture of such infinite longing that for a second or two tears obscured Marguerite's vision. Then the drawing up of the boat against the landing-stage; Percy's spring ashore; his voice, his look; the strength of his arms; the ardour of his embrace. Rapture, in truth, to which the thought of its brief duration alone lent a touch of bitterness.

But of parting again Marguerite would not think—not today, while the birds were singing a deafening paean of joy; not while the scent of growing grass, of moist, travailing earth, was in her nostrils; not while the sap was in the trees, and the gummy crimson buds of the chestnuts were bursting into leaf. Not while she wandered up the narrow lane between hedges of black-thorn in bloom, with Percy's arm around her, his loved voice in her ear, his merry laughter echoing through the sweet morning air.

After that, breakfast in the low, raftered room—the hot, savoury milk, the home-baked bread, the home-churned butter. Then the long, delicious, intimate talk of love, and of yearnings, of duty and of gallant deeds. Blakeney kept nothing secret from his wife; and what he did not tell her, that she easily guessed. But it was from the members of the League that she learned all there was to know of heroism and selflessness in the perilous adventures through which her husband passed with so light-hearted a gaiety.

"You should see me as an asthmatic reprobate, m'dear," he would say, with his infectious laugh. "And hear that cough! Lud love you, but I am mightily proud of that cough! Poor old Rateau does not do it better himself; and he is genuinely asthmatic."

He gave her an example of his prowess; but she would not allow him to go on. The sound was too weird and conjured up visions which today she would fain forget.

"Rateau was a real find," he went on more seriously; "because he is three parts an imbecile and as obedient as a dog. When some of those devils are on my track, lo! the real Rateau appears and yours truly vanishes where no one can find him!"

"Pray God," she murmured involuntarily, "they never may!"

"They won't, m'dear, they won't!" he asserted with light-hearted conviction. "They have become so confused now between Rateau the coalheaver, the mysterious Scarlet Pimpernel, and the problematic English milor, that all three of these personalities can appear before their eyes and they will let 'em all escape! I assure you that the confusion between the Scarlet Pimpernel who was in the ante-chamber of Mother Théot on that fateful afternoon, and again at the Fraternal Supper in the Rue St. Honoré, and the real Rateau who was at Mother Théot's while that same exciting supper party was going on, was so great that not one of those murdering reprobates could trust his own eyes and ears, and that we got away as easily as rabbits out of a torn net."

Thus, did he explain and laugh over the perilous adventure where he had faced a howling mob disguised as Rateau the coalheaver, and with almost superhuman pluck and boldness had dragged Mme de Serval and her children into the derelict house which was one of the League's headquarters. That is how he characterized the extraordinary feat of audacity when, in order to give his gallant lieutenants time to smuggle the unfortunates out of the house through a back and secret way, he showed himself on the balcony above the multitude, and hurled dummy figures into the brazier below.

Then came the story of Bertrand Moncrif, snatched half-unconscious out of the apartment of the fair Theresia Cabarrus, whilst Robespierre himself sat not half a dozen yards away, with only the thickness of a wall between him and his arch enemy.

"How the woman must hate you!" Marguerite murmured, with a slight shudder of acute anxiety which she did her best to conceal. "There are things that a woman like the Cabarrus will never forgive. Whether she cares for Bertrand Moncrif or no, her vanity will suffer intensely, and she will never forgive you for taking him out of her clutches."

He laughed.

"Lud, m'dear!" he said lightly. "If we were to take heed of all the people who hate us we should spend our lives pondering rather than doing. And all I want to ponder over," he added, whilst his glance of passionate earnestness seemed to envelop her like an exquisite warm mantle, "is your beauty, your eyes, the scent of your hair, the delicious flavour of your kiss!"

It was some hours later on that same glorious day, when the shadows of ash and chestnut lay right across the lane and the arms of evening folded the cosy nest in their mysterious embrace, that Sir Percy and Marguerite sat in the deep window-embrasure of the tiny living-room. He had thrown open wide the casements, and hand resting in hand, they watched the last ray of golden light lingering in the west and listened to the twitterings which came like tender "good nights" from the newly-built nests among the trees.

It was one of those perfect spring evenings, rare enough in northern climes, without a breath of wind, when every sound carries clear and sharp through the stillness around. The air was soft and slightly moist, with a tang in it of wakening life and of rising sap, and with the scent of wild narcissus and of wood violets rising like intoxicating incense to the nostrils. It was in truth one of those evening when happiness itself seems rudely out of place, and nature—exquisite, but so cruelly, transient in her loveliness—demands the tribute of gentle melancholy.

A thrust said something to its mate—something insistent and tender that lulled them both to rest. After that, Nature became quite still, and Marguerite, with a catch in her throat which she would have given much to suppress, laid her head upon her husband's breast.

Then it was that suddenly a man's voice, hoarse but distant, broke in upon the perfect peace around. What it said could not at first be gathered. It took some time ere Marguerite became sufficiently conscious of the disturbing noise to raise her head and listen. As for Sir Percy, he was wrapped in the contemplating of the woman he worshipped, and nothing short of an earthquake would have dragged him back to reality, had not Marguerite raised herself on her knees and quickly whispered:

"Listen!"

The man's voice had been answered by a woman's, raised as if in defiance that seemed both pitiful and futile.

"You cannot harm me now. I am in England!"

Marguerite leaned out of the window, tried to peer into the darkness which was fast gathering over the lane. The voices had come from there: first the man's, then the woman's, and now the man's again; both speaking in French, the woman obviously terrified and pleading, the man harsh and commanding. Now it was raised again, more incisive and distinct than before, and Marguerite had in truth some difficulty in repressing the cry that rose to her lips. She had recognised the man's voice.

"Chauvelin!" she murmured.

"Aye, in England, *citoyenne!*" that ominous voice went on drily. "But the arm of justice is long. And remember that you are not the first who has tried—unsuccessfully, let me tell you!—to evade punishment by flying to the enemies of France. Wherever you may hide, I will know how to find you. Have I not found you here, now?—and you but a few hours in Dover!"

"But you cannot touch me!" the woman protested with the courage of one in despair.

The man laughed.

"Are you really simple enough, *citoyenne,*" he said, "to be convinced of that?"

This sarcastic retort was followed by a moment or two of silence, then by a woman's cry; and in an instant Sir Percy was on his feet and out of the house. Marguerite followed him as far as the porch, whence the sloping ground, aided by flagged steps here and there, led down to the gate and thence on to the lane.

It was close beside the gate that a human-looking bundle lay huddled, when Sir Percy came upon the scene, even whilst, some fifty yards away at the sharp bend of the lane, a man could be seen walking rapidly away, his pace well-nigh at a run. Sir Percy's instinct was for giving chase, but the huddle-up figure put out a pair of arms and clung to him so desperately, with smothered cries of: "For pity's sake, don't leave me!" that it would have been inhuman to go. And so, he bent down, raised the human bundle from the ground, and carried it bodily up into the house.

Here he deposited his burden upon the window seat, where but a few moments ago he had been wrapped in the contemplation of Marguerite's eyelashes, and with his habitual quaint good-humour, said:

"I leave the rest to you, m'dear. My French is too atrocious for

317

dealing with the case."

Marguerite understood the hint. Sir Percy, whose command of French was nothing short of phenomenal, never used the language save when engaged in his perilous undertakings. His perfect knowledge of every idiom would have set any ill-intentioned eavesdropper thinking.

The human bundle looked very pathetic lying there upon the window seat, propped up with cushions. It appeared to be a youth, dressed in rough fisherman's clothes and with a cap that fitted tightly round the head; but with hands delicate as a woman's and a face of exquisite beauty.

Without another word, Marguerite quietly took hold of the cap and gently removed it. A wealth of blue-black hair fell like a cascade over the recumbent shoulders. "I thought as much!" Sir Percy remarked quietly, even whilst the stranger, apparently terrified, jumped up and burst into tears, moaning piteously:

"*Oh, mon Dieu! mon Dieu! Sainte Vierge, protégez-moi!*"

There was nothing to do but to wait; and *anon* the first paroxysm of grief and terror passed. The stranger, with a wry little smile, took the handkerchief which Lady Blakeney was holding out to her and proceeded to dry her tears. Then she looked up at the kind Samaritans who had befriended her.

"I am an impostor, I know," she said, with lips that quivered like those of a child in grief. "But if you only knew—!"

She sat bolt upright now, squeezing and twirling the wet handkerchief between her fingers.

"Some kind English gentlemen were good to me, down in the town," she went on more glibly. "They gave me food and shelter, and I was left alone to rest. But I felt stifled in the narrow room. I could hear every one talking and laughing, and the evening air was so beautiful. So, I ventured out. I only meant to breathe a little fresh air; but it was all so lovely, so peaceful—here in England—so different to—"

She shuddered a little and looked as if she was going to cry again. But Marguerite interposed gently:

"So, you prolonged your walk, and found this lane?"

"Yes. I prolonged my walk," the woman replied. "I did not notice that the road had become lonely. Then suddenly I realised that I was being followed, and I ran. *Mon Dieu*, how I ran! Whither, I knew not! I just felt that something horrible was at my heels!"

Her eyes, dilated with terror, looked as black as sloes. They were fixed upon Marguerite, never once raised on Sir Percy, who, standing some way apart from the two women, was looking down on them, silent and apparently unmoved.

The stranger shuddered again; her face was almost grey in its expression of fear, and her lips seemed quite bloodless. Marguerite gave her trembling hands an encouraging pat.

"It was lucky," she said gently, "that you found your way here."

"I had seen the light," the woman continued more calmly. "And I believe that at the back of my mind there was the instinct to run for shelter. Then suddenly my foot knocked against a stone, and I fell. I tried to raise myself quickly, but I had not the time, for the next moment I felt a hand on my shoulder, and a voice—oh, a voice I dread, *citoyenne!*—called to me by name."

"The voice of Citizen Chauvelin?" Marguerite asked simply.

The woman looked up quickly.

"You knew-?" she murmured.

"I knew his voice."

"But you know him?" the other insisted.

"I know him—yes," Marguerite replied. "I am a compatriot of yours. Before I married, I was Marguerite St. Just."

"St. Just?"

"We are cousins, my brother and I, of the young deputy, the friend of Robespierre."

"God help you!" the woman murmured.

"He has done so already, by bringing us both to England. My brother is married, and I am Lady Blakeney now. You too will feel happy and safe now that you are here."

"Happy?" the woman ejaculated, with a piteous sob. "And safe? *Mon Dieu*, if only I could think it!"

"But what have you to fear? Chauvelin may have retained some semblance of power over in France. He has none over here."

"He hates me!" the other murmured. "Oh, how he hates me!"

"Why?"

The stranger made no immediate reply. Her eyes, dark as the night, glowing and searching, seemed to read the very soul behind Marguerite's serene brow. Then after a while she went on, with seeming irrelevance:

"It all began so foolishly!—*mon Dieu*, how foolishly! And I really meant nothing treacherous to my own country—nothing unpatriotic, quoi?" she suddenly seized Marguerite's two hands and exclaimed

319

with childlike enthusiasm: "You have heard of the Scarlet Pimpernel, have you not?"

"Yes," Marguerite replied. "I have heard of him."

"You know then that he is the finest, bravest, most wonderful man in all the world?"

"Yes, I know that," Marguerite assented with a smile.

"Of course, in France they hate him. Naturally! He is the enemy of the republic, *quoi?* He is against all those massacres, the persecution of the innocent. He saves them and helps them when he can. So, they hate him. Naturally."

"Naturally!"

"But I have always admired him," the woman continued, enthusiasm glowing in her dark eyes. "Always; always! Ever since I heard what he had done, and how he saved the Comte de Tournay, and Juliette Marny, and Esther Vincent, and—and countless others. Oh, I knew about them all! For I knew Chauvelin well, and one or two of the men on the Committee of Public Safety quite intimately, and I used to worm out of them all the true facts about the Scarlet Pimpernel. Can you wonder that with my whole soul I admired him? I worshipped him! I could have laid down my life to help him! He has been the guiding star of my dreary life—my hero and my king!"

She paused, and those deep, dark eyes of her were fixed straight out before her, as if in truth she beheld the hero of her dreams. There was a glow now in her cheeks, and her marvellous hair fell like a sable mantle around her, framing the perfect oval of the face and enhancing by vivid contrast the creamy whiteness of chin and throat and the rose-like bloom that had spread over her face. Indeed, this was an exquisitely beautiful creature, and Marguerite, herself one of the loveliest women of her time, was carried away by genuine, wholehearted admiration for the stranger, as well as by her enthusiasm, which, in very truth, seeing its object, was a perfectly natural feeling.

"So now," the woman concluded, coming back to the painful realities of life with a shudder, which extinguished the light in her eyes and took all the glow out of her cheeks, "so now you understand perhaps why Chauvelin hates me!"

"You must have been rather indiscreet," Marguerite remarked with a smile.

"I was, I suppose. And Chauvelin is so vindictive. He hates the Scarlet Pimpernel. Out of a few words, foolishly spoken perhaps, he has made out a case against me. A friend gave me warning. My name was already in the hands of Foucquier-Tinville. You know what that means! Perquisition! Arrest! Judgment! Then the guillotine! Oh, *mon Dieu!* And I had done nothing!—nothing! I fled out of Paris. An influential friend just contrived to arrange this for me. A faithful servant accompanied me. We reached Boulogne. How, I know not! I was so weak, so ill, so wretched, I hardly lived. I just allowed François—that was my servant—to take me whithersoever he wished. But we had no passports, no papers—nothing! And Chauvelin was on our track. We had to hide—in barns—in pigsties—anywhere! But we reached Boulogne at last—I had some money, fortunately. We bribed a fisherman to let us have his boat. Only a small boat—imagine! A rowing boat! And François and I alone in it! But it meant our lives if we didn't go; and perhaps it meant our lives if we went! A rowing boat on the great, big sea!—Fortunately the weather was fine, and François lifted me into the boat. And I just remember seeing the coast of France receding, receding, receding—farther and farther from me. I was so tired. It is possible that I slept. Then suddenly something woke me. I was wide awake. I had heard a cry. I knew I had heard a cry, and then a splash—an awful splash! I was wet through. One oar hung in the rowlock; the other had gone. And François was not there. I was all alone."

She spoke in hard, jerky sentences, as if every word hurt her physically as she uttered it. For the most part she was looking down on her hands, that twitched convulsively and twisted the tiny wet handkerchief into a ball. But now and again she looked up, not at Marguerite always, rather at Sir Percy. Her glowing, tear-wet eyes fastened themselves on him from time to time with an appealing or a defiant gaze. He appeared silent and sympathetic, and his glance rested on her the whole while that she spoke, with an expression of detached if kindly interest, as if he did not quite understand everything that she said. Marguerite as usual was full of tenderness and compassion.

"How terribly you must have suffered!" she said gently. "But what happened after that?"

"Oh, I don't know! I don't know!" the poor woman resumed. "I was too numbed, too dazed with horror and fear, to suffer very much. The boat drifted on, I suppose. It was a beautiful, calm night. And the moon was lovely. You remember the moon last night?"

Marguerite nodded.

"But I remember nothing after—after that awful cry—and the splash! I suppose my poor François fainted or fell asleep—and that he fell into the water. I never saw him again.—And I remember nothing until—until I found myself on board a ship with a lot of rough sailors around me, who seemed very kind.—They brought me ashore and took me to a nice warm place, where some English gentlemen took compassion on me. And—and—I have already told you the rest."

She leaned back against the cushions of the seat as if exhausted with the prolonged effort. Her hands seemed quite cold now, almost blue, and Marguerite rose and closed the window behind her.

"How kind and thoughtful you are!" the stranger exclaimed, and after a moment added with a weary sigh, "I must not trespass any longer on your kindness. It is late now, and—I must go."

She struggled to her feet, rose with obvious reluctance.

"The inn where I was," she said, "it is not far?"

"But you cannot go out alone," Marguerite reckoned. "You do not even know the way!"

"Ah, no! But perhaps your servant could accompany me—only as far as the town.—After that I can ask the way—I should no longer be frightened."

"You speak English then, *Madame?*"

"Oh, yes! My father was a diplomat. He was in England once for four years. I learned a little English. I have not forgotten it."

"One of the servants shall certainly go with you. The inn you speak of must be "The Fisherman's Rest," since you found English gentlemen there."

"If *Madame* will allow me?" Sir Percy broke in, for the first time since the stranger had embarked upon her narrative.

The stranger looked up at him with a half-shy, half-eager smile.

"You, milor!" she exclaimed. "Oh no! I would be ashamed——"

She paused, and her cheeks became crimson whilst she looked down in utter confusion on her extraordinary attire.

"I had forgotten," she murmured tearfully. "François made me put on these awful clothes when we left Paris."

"Then I must lend you a cloak for tonight," Marguerite interposed with a smile. "But you need not mind your clothes, *Madame*. On this coast our people are used to seeing unfortunate fugitives landing in every sort of guise. Tomorrow we must find you something wherein to travel to London."

"To London?" the stranger said with some eagerness. "Yes! I would wish to go to London."

"It will be quite easy. Mme de Serval, with her son and two daughters and another friend, is travelling by the coach tomorrow. You could join them, I am sure. Then you would not be alone. You have money, *Madame?*" Marguerite concluded, with practical solicitude.

"Oh, yes!" the other replied. "I have plenty for present needs—in a wallet—under my clothes. I was able to collect a little—and I have not lost it. I am not dependent," she added, with a smile of gratitude. "And as soon as I have found my husband—"

"Your husband?" Marguerite exclaimed.

"M. le Marquis de Fontenay," the other answered simply. "Perhaps you know him. You have seen him—in London?—Not?"

Marguerite shook her head.

"Not to my knowledge."

"He left me—two years ago—cruelly—emigrated to England—and I was left alone in the world.—He saved his own life by running away from France; but I—I could not go just then—and so—"

She seemed on the verge of breaking down again, then recovered herself and continued more quietly:

"That was my idea, you see; to find my husband one day. Now a cruel Fate has forced me to fly from France; so, I thought I would go to London and perhaps some kind friends will help me to find M. de Fontenay. I have never ceased to love him, though he was so cruel. And I think that—perhaps—he also has not quite forgotten me."

"That were impossible," Marguerite rejoined gently. "But I have friends in London who are in touch with most of the *emigrés* here. We will see what can be done. It will not be difficult, methinks, to find M. de Fontenay."

"You are an angel, milady!" the stranger exclaimed; and with a gesture that was perfect in its suggestion of gracious humility, she took Marguerite's hand and raised it to her lips. Then she once more mopped her eyes, picked up her cap and hastily hid the wealth of her hair beneath it. After which, she turned to Sir Percy.

"I am ready, milor," she said. "I have intruded far too long as it is upon your privacy.—But I am not brave enough to refuse your escort. Milady, forgive me! I will walk fast, very fast, so that milor will return to you very soon!"

She wrapped herself up in a cloak which, at Lady Blakeney's bidding, one of the servants had brought her, and a moment or two later the stranger and Sir Percy were out of the house, whilst Marguerite remained for a while on the porch, listening to their retreating footsteps.

There was a frown of puzzlement between her brows, a look

of troubled anxiety in her eyes. Somehow, the brief sojourn of that strange and beautiful woman in her house had filled her soul with a vague feeling of dread, which she tried vainly to combat. There was no real suspicion against the woman in her heart—how could there be?—but she—Marguerite—who as a rule was so compassionate, so understanding of those misfortunes, to alleviate which Sir Percy was devoting his entire life, felt cold and unresponsive in this case—most unaccountably so. Mme de Fontenay's story differed but little in all its grim detail of misery and humiliation from the thousand and one other similar tales which had been poured for the past three years into her sympathetic ear. She had always understood, had always been ready to comfort and to help. But this time she felt very much as if she had come across a sick or wounded reptile, something weak and dumb and helpless, and yet withal unworthy of compassion.

However, Marguerite Blakeney was surely not the woman to allow such fancies to dry the well of her pity. The gallant Scarlet Pimpernel was not wont to pause in his errands of mercy in order to reflect whether the objects of his selfless immolation were worthy of it or no. So, Marguerite, with a determined little sigh, chided herself for her disloyalty and cowardice, and having dried her tears she went within.

Chapter 16

A Lover of Sport

For the first five minutes, Sir Percy Blakeney and Madame de Fontenay walked side by side in silence. Then she spoke.

"You are silent, milor?" she queried, speaking in perfect English.

"I was thinking," he replied curtly.

"What?"

"What a remarkably fine actress is lost in the fashionable Theresia Cabarrus."

"Madame de Fontenay, I pray you, milor," she retorted drily.

"Theresia Cabarrus nevertheless. Madame Tallien probably tomorrow: for Madame divorced that weak-kneed marquis as soon as the lay 'contre les emigrés' allowed her to regain her freedom."

"You seem very well informed, milor."

"Almost as well as *Madame* herself," he riposted with a pleasant laugh.

"Then you do not believe my story?"

"Not one word of it!" he replied.

"Strange!" she mused. "For every word of it is true."

"Demmed strange!" he assented.

"Of course, I did not tell all," she went on, with sudden vehemence. "I could not. My lady would not understand. She has become—what shall I say?—very English. Marguerite St. Just would understand—Lady Blakeney—no?"

"What would Lady Blakeney not understand?"

"*Eh bien!* About Bertrand Moncrif."

"Ah?"

"You think I did harm to the boy—I know—you took him away from me—You! The Scarlet Pimpernel!—You see, I know! I know everything! Chauvelin told me—"

"And guided you most dexterously to my door," he concluded with a pleasant laugh. "There to enact a delicious comedy of gruff-voiced bully and pathetic victim of merciless persecution. It was all excellently done! Allow me to offer you my sincere congratulations!"

She said nothing for a moment or two, then queried abruptly:

"You think that I am here in order to spy upon you?"

"Oh!" he riposted lightly, "how could I be so presumptuous as to suppose that the beautiful Cabarrus would bestow attention on so unworthy an object as I?"

"'Tis you now, milor," she rejoined drily, "who choose to play a *rôle*. A truce on it, I pray you; and rather tell me what you mean to do."

To this query he gave no reply, and his silence appeared to grate on Theresia's nerves, for she went on harshly:

"You will betray me to the police, of course. And as I am here without papers—"

He put up his hand with that gently deprecating gesture which was habitual to him.

"Oh!" he said, with his quiet little laugh, "why should you think I would do anything so unchivalrous?"

"Unchivalrous?" she retorted with a pathetic sigh of weariness. "I suppose, here in England, it would be called an act of patriotism or self-preservation—like fighting an enemy—or denouncing a spy—"

She paused a moment or two, and as he once more took refuge in silence, she resumed with sudden, moving passion:

"So, it is to be a betrayal after all! The selling of an unfortunate woman to her bitterest enemy! Oh, what wrong have I ever done you, that you should persecute me thus?"

"Persecute you?" he exclaimed. "*Pardi, Madame;* but this is a subtle joke which by your leave my dull wits are unable to fathom."

"It is no joke, milor," she rejoined earnestly. "Will you let me explain? For indeed it seems to me that we are at cross purposes, you and I."

She came to a halt, and he perforce had to do likewise. They had come almost to the end of the little lane; a few yards farther on it debouched on the main road. Beyond that, the lights of Dover Town and the Harbour lights glinted in the still, starry night. Behind them the lane, sunk between grassy slopes and overhung by old elms of fantastic shapes, appeared dark and mysterious. But here, where they stood, the moon shed its full radiance on the broad highway, the clump of copper beeches over on the left, that tiny cottage with its thatched roof nestling at the foot of the cliff; and far away, on the picturesque mass of Dover Castle, the church and towers. Every bit of fencing, every tiny twig in the hawthorn hedges, stood out clear cut, sharp like metal in the cold, searching light. Theresia—divinely slender and divinely tall, graceful despite the rough masculine clothes which she wore—stood boldly in the full light; the tendrils of her jet black hair were gently stirred by an imperceptible breeze, her eyes, dark and luminous, were fixed upwards at the man whom she had set out to subjugate.

"That boy," she went on quite gently, "Bertrand Moncrif, was just a young fool. But I liked him, and I could see the abyss to which his folly was tending. There was never anything but friendship between us; but I knew that sooner or later he would run his head into a noose, and then what good would his pasty-faced sweetheart have been to him? Whilst I—I had friends, influence—*quoi?* And I liked the boy; I was sorry for him. Then the catastrophe came—the other night. There was what those ferocious beasts over in Paris were pleased to call a Fraternal Supper. Bertrand Moncrif was there. Like a young food, he started to vilify Robespierre—Robespierre, who is the idol of France! There!—in the very midst of the crowd! They would have torn him limb from limb, it seems.

"I don't know just what happened, for I wasn't there; but he came to my apartment—at midnight—dishevelled—his clothes torn— more dead than alive. I gave him shelter; I tended him. Yes, I!—even whilst Robespierre and his friends were in my house, and I risked my life every moment that Bertrand was under my roof! Chauvelin suspected something then. Oh, I knew it! Those awful pale, deep-set eyes of his seemed to be searching my soul all the time! At which precise moment you came and took Bertrand away, I know not. But Chauvelin knew. He saw—he saw, I tell you! He had not been with us the whole time, but in and out of the apartment on some pretext or other.

"Then, after the others had left, he came back, accused me of having harboured not only Bertrand, but the Scarlet Pimpernel himself!—swore that I was in league with the English spies and had arranged with them to smuggle my lover out of the house. Then he went away. He did not threaten. You know him as well as I do. Threatening is not his way. But from his look I knew that I was doomed. Luckily, I had François. We packed up my few belongings then and there. I left my woman Pepita in charge, and I fled. As for the rest, I swear to you that it all happened just as I told it to milady.

"You say you do not believe me. Very well! Will you then take me away from this sheltered land, which I have reached after terrible sufferings? Will you send me back to France, and drive me to the arms of a man who but waits to throw me into the tumbril with the next batch of victims for the guillotine? You have the power to do it, of course. You are in England; you are rich, influential, a power in your own country; whilst I am an alien, a political enemy, a refugee, penniless and friendless. You can do with me what you will, of course. But if you do that, milor, my blood will stain your hands for ever; and all the good you and your League have ever done in the cause of humanity will be wiped out by this execrable crime."

She spoke very quietly and with soul-moving earnestness. So was also exquisitely beautiful. Sir Percy Blakeney had been more than human if he had been proof against such an appeal, made by such perfect lips. Nature itself spoke up for Theresia: the softness and stillness of the night; the starlit sky and the light of the moon; the scent of wood violets and of wet earth, and the patter of tiny, mysterious feet in the hedgerows. And the man whose whole life was consecrated to the relief of suffering humanity and whose ears were for ever strained to hear the call of the weak and of the innocent—he could far, far sooner have believed that this beautiful woman was speaking the truth, rather than allow his instinct of suspicion, his keen sense of what was untrustworthy and dangerous, to steel his heart against her appeal.

But whatever his thoughts might be, when she paused, wearied and shaken with sobs which she vainly tried to suppress, he spoke to her quite gently.

"Believe me, dear lady," he said, "that I had no thought of wronging you when I owned to disbelieving your story. I have seen so many strange things in the course of my checkered career that, in verity, I ought to know by now how unbelievable truth often appears."

"Had you known me better, milor—" she began.

"Ah, that is just it!" he rejoined quaintly. "I did not know you, *Madame*. And now, meseems, that Fate has intervened, and that I shall never have the chance of knowing you."

"How is that?" she asked.

But to this he gave to immediate answer, suggested irrelevantly:

"Shall we walk on? It is getting late."

She gave a little cry, as if startled out of a dream, then started to walk by his side with her long, easy stride, so full of sinuous grave. They went on in silence for a while, down the main road now. Already they had passed the first group of town houses, and The Running Footman, which is the last inn outside the town. There was only the High Street now to follow and the Old Place to cross, and The Fisherman's Rest would be in sight.

"You have not answered my question, milor," Theresia said presently.

"What question, *Madame?*" he asked.

"I asked you how Fate could intervene in the matter of our meeting again."

"Oh!" he retorted simply. "You are staying in England, you tell me."

"If you will deign to grant me leave," she said, with gentle submission.

"It is not in my power to grant or to refuse."

"You will not betray me—to the police?"

"I have never betrayed a woman in my life."

"Or to Lady Blakeney?"

He made no answer.

"Or to Lady Blakeney?" she insisted.

Then, as he still gave no answer, she began to plead with passionate earnestness.

"What could she gain—or you—by her knowing that I am that unfortunate, homeless waif, without kindred and without friends, Theresia Cabarrus—the beautiful Cabarrus!—once the *fiancée* of the great Tallien, now suspect of trafficking with her country's enemies in France—and suspect of being a suborned spy in England!—My God, where am I to go? What am I to do? Do not tell Lady Blakeney, milor! On my knees I entreat you, do not tell her! She will hate me—fear me—despise me! Oh, give me a chance to be happy! Give me—a chance—to be happy!"

Again, she had paused and placed her hand on his arm. Once more she was looking up at him, her eyes glistening with tears, her full red lips quivering with emotion. And he returned her appealing, pathetic glance for a moment or two in silence; then suddenly, without any warning, he threw back his head and laughed.

"By Gad!" he exclaimed. "But you are a clever woman!"

"Milor!" she protested, indignant.

"Nay: you need have no fear, fair one! I am a lover of sport. I'll not betray you."

She frowned, really puzzled this time.

"I do not understand," she murmured.

"Let us get back to The Fisherman's Rest," he retorted with characteristic irrelevance. "Shall we?"

"Milor," she insisted, "will you explain?"

"There is nothing to explain, dear lady. You have asked me—nay! challenged me—not to betray you to anyone, not even to Lady Blakeney. Very well! I accept your challenge. That is all."

"You will not tell anyone—anyone, mind you!—that Mme de Fontenay and Theresia Cabarrus are one and the same?"

"You have my word for that."

She drew a scarce perceptible sigh of relief.

"Very well then, milor," she rejoined. "Since I am allowed to go to London, we shall meet there, I hope."

"Scarcely, dear lady," he replied, "since I go to France tomorrow."

This time she gave a little gasp, quickly suppressed—for she hoped milor had not noticed.

"You go to France tomorrow, milor?" she asked.

"As I had the honour to tell you, I go to France tomorrow, and I leave you a free hand to come and go as you please."

She chose not to notice the taunt; but suddenly, as if moved by an uncontrollable impulse, she said resolutely:

"If you go, I shall go too."

"I am sure you will, dear lady," he retorted with a smile. "So there really is no reason why we should linger here. Our mutual friend M. Chauvelin must be impatient to hear the result of this interview."

She gave a cry of horror and indignation.

"Oh! You—you still think *that of me?*"

He stood there, smiling, looking down on her with that half-amused, lazy glance of his. He did not actually say anything, but she felt that she had her answer. With a moan of pain, like a child who has been badly hurt, she turned abruptly, and burying her face in her hands she sobbed as if her heart would break. Sir Percy waited quietly for a moment or two, until the first paroxysm of grief had quieted down, and he said gently:

"*Madame*, I entreat you to compose yourself and to dry your tears. If I have wronged you in my thoughts, I humbly crave your pardon. I pray you to understand that when a man holds human lives in his hands, when he is responsible for the life and safety of those who trust in him, he must be doubly cautious and in his turn trust no one. You have said yourself that now at last in this game of life and death, which I and my friends have played so successfully these last three years, I hold the losing cards. Then must I watch every trick all the more closely, for a sound player can win through the mistakes of his opponent, even if he hold a losing hand."

But she refused to be comforted.

"You will never know, milor—never—how deeply you have wounded me," she said through her tears. "And I, who for months past—ever since I knew!—have dreamed of seeing the Scarlet Pimpernel one day! He was the hero of my dreams, the man who stood alone in the mass of self-seeking, vengeful, cowardly humanity as the personification of all that was fine and chivalrous. I longed to see him—just once—to hold his hand—to look into his eyes—and feel a better woman for the experience. Love? It was not love I felt, but hero-worship, pure as one's love for a starlit night or a spring morning, or a sunset over the hills. I dreamed of the Scarlet Pimpernel, milor; and because of my dreams, which were too vital for perfect discretion, I had to flee from home, suspected, vilified, already condemned. Chance brings me face to face with the hero of my dreams, and he looks on me as that vilest thing on earth: a spy!—a woman who could lie to a man first and send him afterwards to his death!"

Her voice, though more passionate and intense, had nevertheless become more steady. She had at last succeeded in controlling her tears. Sir Percy had listened—quite quietly, as was his wont—to her strange words. There was nothing that he could say to this beautiful woman who was so ingenuously avowing her love for him. It was a curious situation, and in truth he did not relish it—would have given quite a great deal to see it end as speedily as possible. Theresia, fortunately, was gradually gaining the mastery over her own feelings. She dried her eyes, and after a moment or two, of her own accord, she started once more on her way.

Nor did they speak again with one another until they were under the porch of The Fisherman's Rest. Then Theresia stopped, and with a perfectly simple gesture she held out her hand to Sir Percy.

"We may never meet again on this earth, milor," she said quietly. "Indeed, I shall pray to *le bon Dieu* to keep me clear of your path."

He laughed good-humouredly.

"I very much doubt, dear lady," he said, "that you will be in earnest when you utter that prayer!"

"You choose to suspect me, milor; and I'll no longer try to combat your mistrust. But to one more word you must listen: Remember the fable of the lion and the mouse. The invincible Scarlet Pimpernel might one day need the help of Theresia Cabarrus. I would wish you to believe that you can always count on it."

She extended her hand to him, and he took it, the while his inveterately mocking glance challenged her earnest one. After a moment or two he stooped and kissed her finger-tips.

"Let me rather put it differently, dear lady," he said. "One day the exquisite Theresia Cabarrus—the Egeria of the Terrorists, the *fiancée* of the Great Tallien—might need the help of the League of the Scarlet Pimpernel."

"I would sooner die than seek your help, milor," she protested earnestly.

"Here in Dover, perhaps—but in France?—And you said you were going back to France, in spite of Chauvelin and his pale eyes, and his suspicions of you."

"Since you think so ill of me," she retorted, "why should you offer me your help?"

"Because," he replied lightly, "with the exception of my friend Chauvelin, I have never had so amusing an enemy; and if would afford me intense satisfaction to render you a signal service."

"You mean, that you would risk your life to save mine?"

"No. I should not risk my life, dear lady," he said with his puzzling smile. "But I should—God help me!—do my best, if the need arose, to save yours."

After which, with another ceremonious bow, he took final leave of her, and she was left standing there, looking after his tall, retreating figure until the turn of the street hid him from view.

Who could have fathomed her thoughts and feelings at that moment? No one, in truth; not even herself. Theresia Cabarrus had met many men in her day, subjugated and fooled not a few. But she had never met anyone like this before. At one moment she had thought she had him: he appeared moved, serious, compassionate, gave her his word that he would not betray her; and in that word, her unerring instinct—the instinct of the adventuress, the woman who succeeds by her wits as well by her charm—told her that she could trust. Did he fear her, or did he not? Did he suspect her? Theresia could not say. She had no experience of such men. As for the word "sport," she hardly knew its meaning; and yet he had talked of not betraying her because he was "a lover of sport"! It was all very puzzling; very mysterious.

For a long while she remained standing in the porch. From the square bay window on her right came the sound of laughter and chatter, issuing from the coffee-room, whilst one or two noisy groups of sailors and their girls passed her by, singing and laughing, down the street. But in the porch, where she stood, the noisy world appeared distant, as if she were alone in one of her own creation. She could, just by closing her eyes and ears to the life around her, imagine she could still hear the merry, lazy, drawling voice of the man she had set out to punish. She could still see his tall figure and humorous face, with those heavy eyes that lit up now and again with a strange, mysterious light, and the firm lips every ready to break into a smile. She could still see the man who so loved sport that he swore not to betray her, and risked the chance, in his turn, of falling into a trap.

Well! he had defied and insulted her. The letter which he left for her after he had smuggled Bertrand Moncrif out of her apartment, rankled and stung her pride as nothing had ever done before. Therefore, the man must be punished, and in a manner that would leave no doubt in his mind as to whence came the blow that struck him. But it was all going to be very much more difficult than the beautiful Theresia Cabarrus had allowed herself to believe.

CHAPTER 17

Reunion

It was a thoughtful Theresia who turned into the narrow hall of The Fisherman's Rest a few moments later. The inn, when she left it earlier in the evening, had still been all animation and bustle consequent on the arrival of their lordships with the party of ladies and gentlemen over from France, and the excitement of making all these grand folk comfortable for the night. Theresia Cabarrus, in her disguise as a young stowaway, had only aroused passing interest—refugees of every condition and degree were frequent enough in these

332

parts—and when a while ago she had slipped out in order to enact the elaborate *rôle* devised by her and Chauvelin, she had done so unperceived. Since then, no doubt there had been one or two cursory questions about the mysterious stowaway, who had been left to feed and rest in the tiny living-room; but equally no doubt, interest in him waned quickly when it was discovered that he had gone, without as much as thanking those who had befriended him.

The travellers from France had long since retired to their rooms, broken with fatigue after the many terrible experiences they had gone through. The young English gallants had gone, either to friends in the neighbourhood or—in the case of Sir Andrew Ffoulkes and Lord Anthony Dewhurst—ridden away in the early part of the evening, so as to reach Ashford mayhap or Maidstone before nightfall, and thus lessen the distance which still separated them from the loved ones at home.

A good deal of noise and laughter was still issuing from the coffee-room. Through the glass door Theresia could see the *habitués* of The Fisherman's Rest—yokels and fisherfolk—sitting over their ale, some of them playing cards or throwing dice. Mine host was there too, engaged as usual in animated discussion with some privileged guests who sat in the ingle-nook.

Theresia slipped noiselessly past the glass door. Straight in front of her a second passage ran at right angles; two or three steps led up to it. She tip-toed up these, and then looked about her, trying to reconstruct in her mind the disposition of the various rooms. On her left a glass partition divided the passage from the small parlour wherein she had found shelter on her arrival. On her right the passage obviously led to the kitchen, for much noise of crockery and shrill feminine voices and laughter came from there.

For a moment Theresia hesitated. Her original intention had been to find Mistress Waite and see if a bed for the night were still available; but a slight noise or movement issuing from the parlour caused her to turn. She peeped through the glass partition. The room was dimly lighted by a small oil-lamp which hung from the ceiling. A fire still smouldered in the hearth, and beside it, sitting on a low stool staring into the embers, his hands held between his knees, was Bertrand Moncrif.

Theresia Cabarrus had some difficulty in smothering the cry of surprise which had risen to her throat. Indeed, for the moment she thought that the dim light and her own imaginative fancy was playing

333

her a fantastic trick. The next, she had opened the door quite noise-lessly and slipped into the room. Bertrand had not moved. Apparently, he had not heart; or if he had cursorily glanced up, he had disdained to notice the roughly clad fellow who was disturbing his solitude. Certain it is that he appeared absorbed in gloomy meditations; whilst Theresia, practical and deliberate, drew the curtains together that hung in front of the glass partition, and thus made sure that intruding eyes could not catch her unawares. Then she murmured softly:

"Bertrand!"

He woke as from a dream, looked up and saw her. He passed a shaking hand once or twice across his forehead, then suddenly realised that she was actually there, near him, in the flesh. A hoarse cry escaped him, and the next moment he was down on his knees at her feet, his arms around her, his face buried in the folds of her mantle.

Everything—anxiety, sorrow, even surprise—was forgotten in the joy of seeing her. He was crying like a child and murmuring her name in the intervals of covering her knees, her hands, her feet in their rough boots with kisses. She stood there, quite still, looking down on him, yielding her hands to his caresses. Around her full red lips there was an undefinable smile; but the light in her eyes was certainly one of triumph.

After a while he rose, and she allowed him to lead her to an arm-chair by the hearth. She sat down, and he knelt at her feet with one arm around her waist, and his head against her breast. He had never in his life been quite so exquisitely happy. This was not the imperious Theresia, impatient and disdainful, as she had been of late—cruel even sometimes, as on that last evening when he thought he would never see her again. It was the Theresia in the early days in Paris, when first she came back from Bordeaux, with a reputation for idealism as well as for beauty and wit, and with a gracious acceptance of his homage which had completely subjugated him.

She insisted on hearing every detail of his escape out of Paris and out of France, under the protection of the League of the Scarlet Pimpernel. In truth, he did not know who his rescuer was. He remembered by little of that awful night when, after the terrible doings at the Fraternal Supper, he had sought refuge in her apartment and then realised that, like a criminal and selfish fool, he was compromising her precious life by remaining under her roof.

He had resolved to go as soon as he was able to stand—resolved if need be to give himself up at the nearest Poste de Section, when in a semi-conscious state, he became aware that someone was in the room with him. He had not the time or the power to rouse himself and to look about, when a cloth was thrown over his face and he felt himself lifted off the chair bodily and carried away by powerful arms, whither he knew not.

After that, a great deal had happened—it all seemed indeed like a dream. At one time he was with Régine de Serval in a coach, at others with her brother Jacques, in a hut at night, lying on straw, trying to get some sleep, and tortured with thoughts of Theresia and fear for her safety. There were halts and delays, and rushes through the night. He himself was quite dazed, felt like a puppet that was dragged hither and thither in complete unconsciousness. Régine was constantly with him. She did her best to comfort him, would try to wile away the weary hours in the coach or in various hiding-places by holding his hand and talking of the future—the happy future in England, when they would have a home of their own, secure from the terrors of the past two years, peaceful in complete oblivion of the cruel past. Happy and peaceful! My God! As if there could be any happiness or peace for him, away from the woman he worshipped!

Theresia listened to the tale, for the most part in silence. From time to time she would stroke his hair and forehead with her cool, gentle hand. She did ask one or two questions, but these chiefly on the subject of his rescuer: Had he seen him? Had he seen any of the English gentlemen who effected his escape?

Oh, yes! Bertrand saw a good deal of the three or four young gallants who accompanied him and the party all the way from Paris. He only saw the last of them here, in this inn, a few hours ago. One of them gave him some money to enable him to reach London in comfort. They were very kind, entirely unselfish. Mme de Serval, Régine, and the others were overwhelmed with gratitude, and oh, so happy! Joséphine and Jacques had forgotten all about their duty to their country in their joy at finding themselves united and safe in this new land.

But the Scarlet Pimpernel himself, Theresia insisted, trying to conceal her impatience under a veneer of tender solicitude—had Bertrand seen him?

"No!" Bertrand replied. "I never once set eyes on him, though it was he undoubtedly who dragged me helpless out of your apartment. The others spoke of him—always as 'the chief.' They seemed to reverence him. He must be fine and brave. Régine and her mother and the two young ones have learned to worship him. Small wonder! seeing what he did for them at that awful Fraternal Supper."

"What did he do?" Theresia queried.

And the story had to be told by Bertrand, just as he had had it straight from Régine. The asthmatic coal-heaver—the quarrel—Robespierre's arrival on the scene—the shouts—the mob. The terror of that awful giant who had dragged them into the empty house, and there left them in the care of others scarce less brave than himself. Then the disguises—the wanderings through the streets—the deathly anxiety at the gates of the city—the final escape in a laundry cart. Miracles of self-abnegation! Wonders of ingenuity and of daring! What wonder that the name of the Scarlet Pimpernel was one to be revered!

"On my knees will I pay homage to him," Bertrand concluded fervently; "since he brought you to my arms!"

She had him by the shoulders, held him from her at arm's length, whilst she looked—inquiring, slightly mocking—into his eyes.

"Brought me to your arms, Bertrand?" she said slowly. "What do you mean?"

"You are here, Theresia," he riposted. "Safe in England—through the agency of the Scarlet Pimpernel."

She gave a hard, mirthless laugh.

"Aye!" she said drily; "through his agency. But not as you imagine, Bertrand."

"What do you mean?"

"The Scarlet Pimpernel, my friend, after he had dragged you away from the shelter which you had found under my roof, sent an anonymous denunciation of me to the nearest Poste de Section, as having harboured the traitor Moncrif and conspiring with him to assassinate Robespierre whilst the latter was in my apartment."

Bertrand uttered a cry of horror.

"Impossible!" he exclaimed.

"The chief Commissary of the Section," she went on glibly, earnestly—never taking her eyes off his, "at risk of his life, gave me warning. Aided by him and a faithful servant, I contrived to escape—out of Paris first, then across country in the amidst of unspeakable misery, and finally out of the country into an open boat, until I was picked up by a chance vessel and brought to this inn more dead than alive."

She fell back against the cushion of the chair, her sinuous body shaken with sobs. Bertrand, speechless with horror, could but try and soothe his beloved as she had soothed him a while ago, when past terrors and past bitter experiences had unmanned him. After a while she became more calm, contrived to smile through her tears.

"You see, Bertrand, that your gallant Scarlet Pimpernel is as merciless in hate as he is selfless in love."

"But why?" the young man ejaculated vehemently. "Why?"

"Why he should hate me?" she rejoined with a pathetic little sigh and a shrug of the shoulders. "*Chien sabe*, my friend! Of course, he does not know that of late—ever since I have gained the regard of Citizen Tallien—my life has been devoted to intervening on behalf of the innocent victims of our revolution. I suppose he takes me for the friend and companion of all those ruthless Terrorists whom he abhors. He has forgotten what I did in Bordeaux, and how I risked my life there, and did so daily in Paris for the sake of those whom he himself befriends. It may all be a question of misunderstanding," she added, with gentle resignation, "but 'tis one that well-nigh did cost me my life."

Bertrand folded her in his arms, held her against him, as if to shield her with his body against every danger. It was his turn now to comfort and to console, and she rested her head against his shoulder—a perfect woman rather than an unapproachable divinity, giving him through her weakness more exquisite bliss than he had ever dreamed of before. The minutes sped on, winged with happiness, and time was forgotten in the infinity of joy.

Theresia was the first to rouse herself from this dream of happiness and oblivion. She glanced up at the clock. It was close upon ten. Confused, adorable, she jumped to her feet.

"You will ruin my reputation, Bertrand," she said with a smile, "thus early in a strange land!"

She would arrange with the landlord's daughter, she said, about a bed for herself, as she was very tired. What did he mean to do?

"Spend the night in this room," he replied, "if mine host will let me. I could have such happy dreams here! These four walls will reflect your exquisite image, and 'tis your dear face will smile down on me ere I close mine eyes in sleep."

She had some difficulty in escaping fro his clinging arms, and 'twas only the definite promise that she gave him to come back in a few minutes and let him know what she had arranged, that ultimately enabled him to let her go. Even so, he felt inexpressibly sad when she went, watched her retreating figure, so supple and so quaint in the rough, masculine clothes and the heavy mantle, as she walked resolutely down the passage in the direction of the kitchen. From the coffee-room there still came the sound of bustle and of merriment; but this little room seemed so peaceful, so remote—a shrine, now that his goddess had hallowed it by her presence.

Bertrand drew a deep sigh, partly of happiness, partly of utter weariness. He was more tired than he knew. She had promised to come back and say goodnight—in a few minutes.—But the minutes seemed leaden-footed now—and he was half-dead with fatigue. He threw himself down on the hard, uncomfortable horsehair sofa, whereon he hoped to pass the night if the landlord would let him and glanced up at the clock. Only three minutes since she had gone—of course she would not be long—only a few more minutes—a very few.—He closed his eyes, for the lids felt heavy—of a surety he would hear her come—

CHAPTER 18

Night and Morning

Theresia waited for a moment or two at the turn of the passage, until her keen ear had told her that Bertrand was no longer on the watch and had closed the door behind him. Then she retraced her steps—on tiptoe, lest he should hear.

She found her way to the front door; it was still on the latch. She opened it and peered out into the night. The little porch was deserted, but out there on the quay a few passers-by still livened the evening with chatter or song. Theresia was on the point of steeping out of the porch, when a familiar voice hailed her softly by name:

"Citoyenne Cabarrus!"

A man, dressed in dark clothes, with high boots and sugar-loaf hat, came out from the dark angle behind the porch.

"Not here!" Theresia whispered eagerly. "Out on the quay. Wait for me there, my little Chauvelin. I'll be with you *anon*. I have so much to tell you!"

Silently, he did as she desired. She waited for a moment in the porch, watching the meagre figure in the dark cloak making its way across to the quay, then walking rapidly in the direction of the Pent. The moon was dazzlingly brilliant. The harbour and the distant sea glistened like diamond-studded sheets of silver. From afar there came the sound of the castle clock striking ten. The groups of passers-by had dwindled down to an occasional amorous couple strolling homewards, whispering soft nothings and gazing enraptured at the moon;

or half-a-dozen sailors lolling down the quays arm in arm, on their way back to their ship, obstructing the road, yelling and singing the refrain of the newest ribald song; or perhaps a belated pedlar, weary of an unprofitable beat, wending his way dejectedly home.

One of these poor wretches—a cripple with a wooden leg and bent nearly doubt with the heavy load on his pack—paused for a moment beside the porch, held out a grimy hand to Theresia, with a pitiable cry.

"Of your charity, kind sir! Buy a little something from the pore ole man, to buy a bit of bread!"

He looked utterly woebegone, with lank grey hair blown about by the breeze and a colourless face covered with sweat, that shone like painted metal in the moon-light.

"Buy a little something, kind sir!" he went on, in a shrill, throaty voice. "I've a sick wife at 'ome, and pore little gran'childen!"

Theresia—a little frightened, and not at all charitably inclined at this hour—turned hastily away and went back into to house, whither the cripple's vigorous curses followed her.

"May Satan and all his armies—"

She shut the door on him and hastened up the passage. That cadaverous old reprobate had caused her to shudder as with the presentiment of coming evil.

With infinite precaution, Theresia peeped into the room where she had left Bertrand. She saw him lying on the sofa, fast asleep.

On the table in the middle of the room there was an old ink-horn, a pen, and few loose sheets of paper. Noiseless as a mouse, Theresia slipped into the room, sat at the table, and hurriedly wrote a few lines. Bertrand had not moved. Having written her missive, Theresia folded it carefully, and still on tiptoe, more stealthily even than before, she slipped the paper between the young man's loosely clasped fingers. Then, as soundlessly as she had come, she glided out of the room, ran down the passage, and was out in the porch once more, breathless but relieved.

Bertrand had not moved; and no one had seen her. Theresia only paused in the porch long enough to recover her breath, then, without hesitation and with rapid strides, she crossed over to the water's edge and walked along in the direction of the Pent.

Whereupon, the figure of the old cripple emerged from out the shadows. He gazed after the fast retreating figure of Theresia for a moment or two, then threw down his load, straightened out his back, and stretched out his arms from the shoulders with a sigh of content. After which amazing proceedings he gave a soft, inward chuckle, unstrapped his wooden leg, slung it with his discarded load across his broad shoulders, and turning his back upon harbour and sea, turned up the High Street and strode rapidly away.

When Bertrand Moncrif woke, the dawn was peeping in through the uncurtained window. He felt cold and stiff. It took him some time to realise where he was, to collect his scattered senses. He had been dreaming—here in this room—Theresia had been here—and she had laid her head against his breast and allowed him to soothe and comfort her. Then she said that she would come back—and he—like a fool— had fallen asleep.

He jumped up, fully awake now; and as he did so a folded scrap of paper fell out of his hand. He had not known that it was there when first he woke, and somehow it appeared to be a part of his dream. As it lay there on the sanded floor at his feet, it looked strangely ghostlike, ominous; and it was with a trembling hand that, presently, he picked it up.

Every minute now brought fuller daylight into the room; a grey, cold light, for the window faced the south-west, showing a wide stretch of the tidal harbour and the open sea beyond. The sun, not fully risen, had not yet shed warmth over the landscape, and to Bertrand this colourless dawn, the mysterious stillness which earth assumes just before it wakens to the sun's kiss, seemed inexpressibly dreary and desolate.

He went to the window and threw open the casement. Down below, a kitchen wench was busy scrubbing the flagged steps of the porch; over in the inner harbour, one or two fishing vessels were preparing to put out to sea; and from the tidal harbour, the graceful yacht which yesterday had brought him—Bertrand—and his friends safely to this land of refuge, was majestically gliding out, like a beautiful swan with gleaming wings outspread.

Controlling his apprehension, his nervousness, Bertrand at last contrived to unfold the mysterious epistle. He read the few lines that were traced with a delicate, feminine hand, and with a sigh of infinite longing and of ardent passion, he pressed the paper to his lips. Theresia had sent him a message. Finding him asleep, she had slipped it into his hand. The marvel was that he did not wake when she stooped over him, and perhaps even touched his forehead with her lips.

"A kind soul," so the message ran, "hath taken compassion on me.

There was no room for me at the inn, and she has offered me a bed in her cottage, somewhere close by. I do not know where it is. I have arranged with the landlord that you shall be left undisturbed in the small room where he found one another, and where the four walls will whisper to you of me. Good night, my beloved! Tomorrow you will go to London with the de Servals. I will follow later. It is better so. In London you will find me at the house of Mme de Neafchateau, a friend of my father's who lives at No. 54 in the Soho Square, and who offered me hospitality in the days when I thought I might visit London for pleasure. She will receive me now that I am poor and an exile. Come to me there. Until then my heart will feed on the memory of your kiss."

The letter was signed "Theresia."

Bertrand pressed it time and again to his lips. Never in his wildest dreams had he hoped for this; never even in those early days of rapture had he tasted such perfect bliss. The letter he hid against his breast. He was immeasurably happy, felt as if he were treading on air. The sea, the landscape, no longer looked grey and dreary. This was England, the land of the free, the land wherein he had regained his beloved. Ah, the mysterious Scarlet Pimpernel, while seeking ignoble vengeance against her, for sins which she never had committed, did in truth render him and her a priceless service. Theresia, courted, adulated, over in Paris, had been as far removed from Bertrand Moncrif as the stars; but here, where she was poor and lonely, a homeless refugee like himself, she turned instinctively to the faithful lover, who would gladly die to ensure her happiness.

With that letter in his possession, Bertrand felt that he could not remain indoors. He was pining for open spaces, the sea, the mountains, God's pure air—the air which she too was breathing even now. He snatched up his hat and made his way out of the little building. The kitchen wench paused in her scrubbing and looked up smiling as he ran past her, singing and shouting for joy. For Régine—the tender, loving heart that pined for him and for his love—he had not a thought. She was the past, the dull, drabby past wherein he had dwelt before he knew how glorious a thing life could be, how golden the future, how rosy that horizon far away.

By the time he reached the harbour, the sun had risen in all its glory. Way out against the translucent sky, the graceful silhouette of the schooner swayed gently in the morning breeze, her outspread sails gleaming like wings that are tinged with gold. Bertrand watched her for a while. He thought of the mysterious Scarlet Pimpernel and the hideous vengeance which he had wrought against his beloved. And the rage which possessed his soul at the thought obscured for a moment the beauty of the morning and the glory of the sky. With a gesture characteristic of his blood and of his race, he raised his fist and shook it in the direction of the distant ship.

CHAPTER 19

A Rencontre

For Marguerite, that wonderful May-day, like so many others equally happy and equally wonderful, came to an end all too soon. To dwell on those winged hours were but to record sorrow, anxiety, a passionately resentment coupled with an equally passionate acceptance of the inevitable. Her intimate friends often marvelled how Marguerite Blakeney bore the strain of these constantly recurring farewells. Every time that in the early dawn she twined her loving arms round the neck of the man she worshipped, feeling that mayhap she was looking into those dear, lazy, laughing eyes for the last time on earth—every time, it seemed to her as if earth could not hold greater misery.

Then after that came that terrible half-hour, whilst she stood on the landing-stage—his kisses still hot upon her lips, her eyes, her throat—and watched and watched that tiny speck, that fast-sailing ship that bore him away on his errand of mercy and self-sacrifice, leaving her lonely and infinitely desolate. And then the days and hours, when he was away and it was her task t smile and laugh, to appear to know nothing of her husband save that he was a society butterfly, the pet of the salons, an exquisite, something of a fool, whose frequent absences were accounted for by deer-stalking in Scotland or fishing in the Tweed, or hunting in the shires—anything and everything that would throw dust in the eyes of the fashionable crowd of whom she and he formed an integral part.

"Sir Percy not with you tonight, dear Lady Blakeney?"

"With me? Lud love you, no! I have not seen him these three weeks past."

"The dog!"

People would talk and ask questions, throw out suggestions and innuendoes. Society a few months ago had been greatly agitated because the beautiful Lady Blakeney, the most fashionable woman about town, had taken a mad fancy for—you'll never believe it, my dear!—for her own husband. She had him by her side at routs and river-parties, in her opera-box and on the Mall. It was positively indecent! Sir Percy was the pet of Society, his sallies, his inane laugh, his lazy, delicious, impertinent ways and his exquisite clothes, made the success of every salon in which he chose to appear. His Royal Highness was never so good-tempered as when Sir Percy was by his side. Then, for his own wife to monopolize him was preposterous, abnormal, extravagant! Some people put it down to foreign eccentricity; others to Lady Blakeney's shrewdness in thus throwing dust in the eyes of her none-too-clever lord, in order to mask some intrigue or secret amour, of which Society had not as yet the key.

Fortunately for the feelings of the fashionable world, this phase of conjugal affection did not last long. It had been at its height last year and had waned perceptibly since. Of late, so it was averred, Sir Percy was hardly ever at home, and his appearances at Blakeney Manor—his beautiful house at Richmond—were both infrequent and brief. He had evidently tired of playing second fiddle to his exquisite wife, or been irritated by her caustic wit, which she was wont to sharpen at his expense; and the *ménage* of these two leaders of fashion had, in the opinion of those in the know, once more resumed a more normal aspect.

When Lady Blakeney was in Richmond, London or Bath, Sir Percy was shooting or fishing or yachting—which was just as it should be. And when he appeared in society, smiling, elegant, always an exquisite, Lady Blakeney would scarce notice him, save for making him a butt for her lively tongue.

What it cost Marguerite to keep up this *rôle* none but a very few ever knew. The identity of one of the greatest heroes of this or any time was known to his most bitter enemy—not to his friends. So, Marguerite went on smiling, joking, flirting, while her heart ached and her brain was at times well-nigh numb with anxiety. His intimates rallied round her, of course: the splendid little band of heroes who formed the League of the Scarlet Pimpernel—Sir Andrew Ffoulkes and his pretty wife; Lord Anthony Dewhurst and his lady, whose great dark eyes still wore the impress of the tragedy which had darkened the first month of her happy wedded life. Then there was my lord Hastings; and Sir Evan Cruche, the young Squire of Holt, and all the others.

And for the Prince of Wales, it is more than surmised by those competent to judge that His Royal Highness did indeed guess at the identity of the Scarlet Pimpernel, even if he had no actually been apprised of it. Certain it is that his tact and discretion did on more than one occasion save a situation which might have proved embarrassing for Marguerite.

In all these friends then—in their conversation, their happy laughter, their splendid pluck and equally splendid gaiety, the echo of the chief whom they adored—Marguerite found just the solace that she needed. With Lady Ffoulkes and Lady Anthony Dewhurst she had everything in common. With those members of the League who happened to be in England, she could talk over and in her mind trace the various stages of the perilous adventure on which her beloved and the others were even then engaged.

And there were always the memories of those all too brief days at Dover or in Richmond, when her loving heart tasted such perfect happiness as is granted only to the elect: the happiness that comes from perfect love, perfect altruism, a complete understanding and measureless sympathy. On those memories her hungering soul could subsist in the intervals, and with them as her unalienable property, she could even bid the grim spectre of unhappiness begone.

Of Madame de Fontenay—for as such Marguerite still knew her— she saw but little. Whether the beautiful Theresia had gone to London or no, whether she had succeeded in finding her truant husband, Marguerite did not know and cared less. The unaccountable antipathy which she had felt on that first night of her acquaintance with the lovely Spaniard still caused her to hold herself aloof. Sir Percy, true to his word, had not betrayed the actual identity of Theresia Cabarrus to his wife; but in his light, insouciant manner had dropped a word or two of warning, which had sharpened Marguerite's suspicions and strengthened her determination to avoid Mme de Fontenay as far as possible. And since monetary or other material help was apparently not required, she had no reason to resume an intercourse which, in point of fact, was not courted by Theresia either.

But one day, walking alone in Richmond Park, she came face to face with Theresia. It was a beautiful late afternoon in July, the end of a day which had been a comparatively happy one for Marguerite—the day when a courier had come from France with news of Sir Percy; a letter from him, telling her that he was well and hinting at the possibility of another of those glorious days together at Dover.

With that message from her beloved just to hand, Marguerite had felt utterly unable to fulfil her social engagements in London. There was nothing of any importance that claimed her presence. His Royal

Highness was at Brighton; the opera and the rout at Lady Portarles' could well get on without her. The evening promised to be more than ordinarily beautiful, with a radiant sunset and the soft, sweet-scented air of a midsummer's evening.

After dinner, Marguerite had felt tempted to stroll out alone. She threw a shawl over her head and stepped out on to the terrace. The vista of velvet lawns, of shady paths and rose borders in full bloom, stretched out into the dim distance before her; and beyond these, the boundary wall, ivy-clad, overhung with stately limes, and broken into by the finely wrought iron gates that gave straight into the Park.

The shades of evening were beginning to draw in, and the garden was assuming that subtle veil of mysterious melancholy which perfect beauty always lends. In the stately elms far away, a blackbird was whistling his evensong. The night was full of sweet odours—roses and heliotrope, lime and mignonette—whilst just below the terrace a bed of white tobacco swung ghost-like its perfumed censer into the air. Just an evening to lure a lonely soul into the open, away from the indifferent, the casual, into the heart of nature, always potent enough to soothe and to console.

Marguerite strolled through the grounds with a light foot, and *anon* reached the monumental gates, through which the exquisite peace and leafy solitude of the Park seemed to beckon insistently to her. The gate was on the latch; she slipped through and struck down a woodland path bordered by tangled undergrowth and tall bracken, and thus reached the pond, when suddenly she perceived Mme de Fontenay.

Theresia was dressed in a clinging gown of diaphanous black silk, which gave value to the exquisite creamy whiteness of her skin and to the vivid crimson of her lips. She wore a transparent shawl round her shoulders, which with the new-modish, high-waisted effect of her gown, suited her sinuous grace to perfection. But she wore no jewellery, no ornaments of any kind: only a magnificent red rose at her breast.

The sight of her at this place and at this hour was so unexpected that, to Marguerite's super-sensitive intuition, the appearance of this beautiful woman, strolling listless and alone beside the water's edge, seemed like a presage of evil. Her first instinct had been to run away before Mme de Fontenay was aware of her presence; but the next moment she chided herself for this childish cowardice, and stood her ground, waiting for the other woman to draw near.

A minute or two later, Theresia had looked up and, in her turn had perceived Marguerite. She did not seem surprised, rather came forward with a glad little cry, and her two hands outstretched.

"Milady!" she exclaimed. "Ah, I see you at last! I have oft wondered why we never met."

Marguerite took her hands, greeted her as warmly as she could. Indeed, she did her best to appear interested and sympathetic.

Mme de Fontenay had not much to relate. She had found refuge in the French convent of the Assumption at Twickenham, where the Mother Superior had been an intimate friend of her mother's in the happy olden days. She went out very little, and never in society. But she was fond of strolling in this beautiful Park. The sisters had told her that Lady Blakeney's beautiful house was quite near. She would have liked to call—but never dared—hoping for a chance *recontre* which hitherto had never come.

She asked kindly after milor and seemed to have heard a rumour that he was at Brighton, in attendance on his royal friend. Of her husband, Mme de Fontenay had as yet found no trace. He must be living under an assumed name, she thought—no doubt in dire poverty— Theresia feared it but did not know—would give worlds to find out.

Then she asked Lady Blakeney whether she knew aught of the de Servals.

"I was so interested in them," she said, "because I had heard something of them while I was in Paris and seeing that we arrived in England the same day, though under such different circumstances. But we could not journey to London together, as you, milady, so kindly suggested, because I was very ill the next day.—Ah, can you wonder?—A kind friend in Dover took care of me. But I remember their name and have oft marvelled if we should ever meet."

Yes; Marguerite did see the de Servals from time to time. They rented a small cottage not very far from here—just outside of town. One of the daughters, Régine, was employed all day at the fashionable dress-maker's in Richmond. The younger girl, Joséphine, and the boy, Jacques, was doing work in a notary's office. It was all very dreary for them, but their courage was marvellous; and though the children did not earn much, it was sufficient for their wants.

Madame de Fontenay was vastly interested. She hoped that Régine's marriage with the man of her choice would bring a ray of real happiness into the household.

"I hope so too," Lady Blakeney assented.

"Milady has seen the young man—Régine's *fiancé?*"

"Oh, yes! once or twice. But he is engaged in business all day, it seems. He is inclined to be morbid and none too full of ardour. It is a pity; for Régine is a sweet girl and deserves happiness."

"We have so much sorrow in common," she said with a pathetic smile. "So many misfortunes. We ought to be friends."

Then she gave a slight little shiver.

"The weather is extraordinarily cold for July," she said. "Ah, how one misses the glorious sunshine of France!"

She wrapped her thin, transparent shawl closer round her shoulders. She was delicate, she explained. Always had been. She was a child of the South, and fully expected the English climate would kill her. In any case, it was foolish of her to stand thus talking, when it was so cold.

After which she took her leave, with a gracious inclination of the head and a cordial *au revoir*. Then she turned off into a small path under the trees, cut through the growing bracken; and Marguerite watched the graceful figure thoughtfully, until the leafy undergrowth hid her from view.

CHAPTER 20

Departure

The next morning's sun rose more radiant than before. Marguerite greeted it with a sigh that was entirely a happy one. Another round of the clock had brought her a little nearer to the time when she would see her beloved. The next courier might indeed bring a message naming the very day when she could rest once more in his arms for a few brief hours, which were so like the foretaste of heaven.

Soon after breakfast she ordered her coach, intending to go to London in order to visit Lady Ffoulkes and give Sir Andrew the message which was contained for him in Percy's last letter. Whilst waiting for the coach, she strolled out into the garden, which was gay with roses and blue larkspur, sweet william and heliotrope, alive with a deafening chorus of blackbirds and thrushes, the twittering of sparrows and the last call of the cuckoo. It was a garden, brim-full of memories, filled in rich abundance with the image of the man she worship. Every bird-song seemed to speak his name, the soughing of the breeze amidst the trees seemed to hold the echo of his voice; the perfume of thyme and mignonette to bring back the savour of his kiss.

Then suddenly she became aware of hurrying footsteps on the gravelled path close by. She turned, and saw a young man whom at first, she did not recognise, running with breathless haste towards her. He was hatless, his linen crumpled, his coat-collar awry. At sight of her he gave a queer cry of excitement and relief.

"Lady Blakeney! Thank God! Thank God!"

Then she recognised him. It was Bertrand Moncrif.

He fell on his knees and seized her gown. He appeared entirely overwrought, unbalanced, and Marguerite tried in vain at first to get a coherent word out of him. All that he kept on repeating was:

"Will you help me? Will you help us all?"

"Indeed, I will, if I can, M. Moncrif," Marguerite said gently. "Do try and compose yourself and tell me what is amiss."

She persuaded him to rise, and presently to follow her to a garden seat, where she sat down. He remained standing in front of her. His eyes still looked wild and scared, and he passed a shaking hand once or twice through his unruly hair. But he was obviously making an effort to compose himself, and after a little while, during which Marguerite waited with utmost patience, he began more coherently:

"Your servants said, milady," he began more quietly, "that you were in the garden. I could not wait until they called you, so I ran to find you. Will you try and forgive me? I ought not to have intruded."

"Of course, I will forgive you," Marguerite rejoined with a smile, "if you will only tell me what is amiss."

He paused a moment, then cried abruptly:

"Régine has gone!"

Marguerite frowned, puzzled, and murmured slowly, not understanding:

"Gone? Whither?"

"To Dover," he replied, "with Jacques."

"Jacques?" she reiterated, still uncomprehending.

"Her brother," he rejoined. "You know the boy?"

Marguerite nodded.

"Hot-headed, impulsive," Moncrif went on, trying to speak calmly. "He and the girl Joséphine always had it in their minds that they were destined to liberate France from her present state of anarchy and bloodshed."

"Like you yourself, M. Moncrif!" Marguerite put in with a smile.

"Oh, I became sobered, reasonable, when I realised how futile it all was. We all owe our lives to that noble Scarlet Pimpernel. They were no longer ours to throw away. At least, that was my theory, and Régine's. I have been engaged in business; and she works hard.—Oh, but you know!" he exclaimed impulsively.

"Yes, I know all your circumstances. But to the point, I pray you!"

"Jacques of late has been very excited, feverish. We did not know what was amiss. Régine and I oft spoke of him. And Mme de Serval has been distraught with anxiety. She worships the boy. He is her only son. But Jacques would not say what was amiss. He spoke to no one. Went to his work every day as usual. Last night he did not come home. A message came for Mme de Serval to say that a friend in London had persuaded him to go to the play and spend the night with him. Mme de Serval thought nothing of that. She was pleased to think that Jacques had some amusement to distract him from his brooding thoughts. But Régine, it seems, was not satisfied. After her mother had gone to bed, she went into Jacque's room; found some papers, it seems—letters—I know not—proof in fact that the boy was even then on his way to Dover, having made arrangements to take ship for France."

"*Mon Dieu!*" Marguerite exclaimed involuntarily. "What senseless folly!"

"Ah! but that is not the worst. Folly, you say! But there is worse folly still!"

With the same febrile movements that characterized his whole attitude, he drew a stained and crumpled letter from his pocket.

"She sent me this, this morning," he said. "That is why I came to you."

"You mean Régine?" Marguerite asked and took the letter which he was handing to her.

"Yes! She must have brought it round herself—to my lodgings—in the early dawn. I did not know what to do—whom to consult.—A blind instinct brought me here—I have no other friend—"

In the meanwhile, Marguerite was deciphering the letter, turning a deaf ear to his ramblings.

"My Bertrand," so the letter ran, "Jacques is going to France. Nothing will keep him back. He says it is his duty. I think that he is mad, and I know that it will kill *maman*. So, I go with him. Perhaps at the last—at Dover—my tears and entreaties might yet prevail. If not, and he puts this senseless project in execution, I can watch over him there, and perhaps save him from too glaring a folly. We go by coach to Dover, which starts in an hour's time. Farewell, my beloved, and forgive me for causing you the anxiety; but I feel that Jacques has more need of me than you."

Below the signature "Régine de Serval" there were a few more lines, written as if with an afterthought:

"I have told *maman* that my employer is sending me down into the country about some dresses for an important customer, and that as Jacques can get a few days' leave from his work, I am taking him with me, for I feel the country air would do him good.

"*Maman* will be astonished and no doubt hurt that Jacques did not send her word of farewell, but it is best that she should not learn the truth too suddenly. If we do not return to Dover within the week, you will have to break the news as gently as you can."

Whilst Marguerite read the letter, Bertrand had sunk upon the seat and buried his head in his hands. He looked utterly dejected and forlorn, and she felt a twinge of remorse at thought how she had been wronging him all this while by doubting his love for Régine. She placed a kindly hand on the young man's shoulder.

"What was your idea," she asked, "in coming to me? What can I do?"

"Give me advice, milady!" he implored. "I am so helpless, so friendless. When I had the letter, I could think of nothing at first. You see, Régine and Jacques started early this morning, by the coach from London, long before I had it. I thought you could tell me what to do, how to overtake them. Régine loves me—oh, she loves me! If I knelt at her feet I could bring her back. But they are marked people, those two. The moment they attempt to enter Paris, they will be recognised, arrest. Oh, my God! have mercy on us all!"

"You think you can persuade Régine, M. Moncrif?"

"I am sure," he asserted firmly. "And you, milady! Régine thinks the whole world of you!"

"But there is the boy—Jacques!"

"He is just a child—he acted on impulse—and I always had great authority over him. And you, milady! The whole family worship you!—they know what they owe you. Jacques has not thought of his mother; but if he did—"

Marguerite rose without another word.

"Very well," she said simply. "We go together and see what we can do with those two obstinate, young folk."

Bertrand gave a gasp of surprise and of hope. His whole face lighted up and he gazed upon the beautiful woman before him as a worshipper would on his divinity.

"You, milady?" he murmured. "You would—really—help me—

like that?"

Marguerite smiled.

"I really would help you like that," she said. "My coach is ordered; we can start at once. We'll get relays at Maidstone and at Ashford, and easily reach Dover tonight, before the arrival of the public coach. In any case, I know every one of any importance in Dover. We could not fail to find the runaways."

"But you are an angel, milady!" Bertrand contrived to stammer, although obviously he was over-whelemed with gratitude.

"You are ready to start?" Marguerite retorted, gently checking any further display of emotion.

He certainly was hatless, and his clothes were in an untidy condition; but such trifles mattered nothing at a moment like this. Marguerite's household, on the other hand, were accustomed to these sudden vagaries and departures of their mistress, either for Dover, Bath, or any known and unknown destination, often at a few minutes' notice.

In this case the coach was actually at the gates. The maids packed the necessary valise; her ladyship changed her smart gown for a dark travelling one, and less than half an hour after Bertrand Moncrif's first arrival at the Manor, he was seated beside Lady Blakeney in her coach. The coachman cracked his whip, the postilion swung himself into the saddle, and the servants stood at attention as the vehicle slowly swung out of the gates; and presently, the horses putting on the pace, disappeared along the road, followed by a cloud of dust.

Bertrand Moncrif, brooding, absorbed in thoughts, said little or nothing while the coach swung along at a very brisk pace. Marguerite, who always had plenty to think about, did not feel in the mood to try and make conversation. She was very sorry for the young man, who in very truth must have suffered also from remorse. His lack of ardour—obviously only an outward lack—toward his *fiancée* and the members of her family, must to a certain extent have helped to precipitate the present catastrophe. Coolness and moroseness on his part gave rise to want of confidence on the other. Régine, heart-sick at her lover's seeming indifference, was no doubt all the more ready to lavish love and self-sacrifice upon the young brother.

Marguerite was sorry enough for the latter—a young fool, with the *exalté* Latin temperament, brimming over with desires for self-immolation as futile as they were senseless—but her generous heart went out to Régine de Serval, a girl who appeared predestined to sorrow and disappointments, endowed with an exceptionally warm nature and cursed with the inability to draw whole-hearted affection to herself. She worshipped Bertrand Moncrif; she idolized her mother, her brother, her sister. But though they, one and all, relied on her, brought her the confidences of their troubles and their difficulties, it never occurred to any one of them to give up something—a distraction, a fancy, an ideal—for the sake of silent, thoughtful Régine.

Marguerite allowed her thoughts thus to dwell on these people, whom her husband's splendid sacrifice on their behalf had rendered dear. Indeed, she loved them like she loved so many others, because of the dangers which he had braved for their sakes. Their lives had become valuable because of his precious one, daily risked because of them. And at the back of her mind there was also the certainty that if these two young fools did put their mad project in execution and endeavoured to return to Paris, it would again be the gallant Scarlet Pimpernel who would jeopardize his life to save them from the consequences of their own folly.

Luncheon and a brief halt was taken at Farningham and Maidstone reached by three o'clock in the afternoon. Here Lady Blakeney's own servants took leave of her, and post-horses were engaged to take her ladyship on to Ashford. Two hours later, at Ashford, fresh relays were obtained. The public coach at this hour was only some nine or ten miles ahead, it seems, and there was now every chance that Dover would be reached by nightfall and the young runaways met by their pursuers on arrival.

All was then for the best. Bertrand, after the coach had rattled out of Ashford, appeared to find comfort and courage. He began to talk, long and earnestly—of himself, his plans and projects, his love for Régine, to which he always found it so difficult to give expression; of Régine herself and the de Servals, mother, son and daughters. His voice was toneless and very even. The monotony of his diction acted after a while as a soporific on Marguerite's nerves.

The rumble of the coach, the closeness of this long afternoon in July, the rocking of the springs, made her feel drowsy. After a while took, a curious scent pervaded the interior of the coach—a sweet, heady scent that appeared to weigh her eyelids down and gave her a feeling of delicious and lazy beatitude. Bertrand Moncrif droned on, and his voice came to her fast-fading senses as through a thick pulpy veil. She closed her eyes. That sweet, intoxicating scent came, more marked, more insistent, to her nostrils. She laid her head against the cushions, and still she heard the dreary monotone of Bertrand's voice, quite inarticulate now, like the hum of a swarm of bees—

Then, all of a sudden, she was fully conscious; only just in time to feel the weight of an iron hand against her mouth and to see Bertrand's face, ghastly of hue, eyes distorted more with fear than rage, quite close to her own. She had not the time to scream, and her limbs felt as heavy as lead, so that she could not struggle. The next moment a thick woollen scarf was wound quickly and tightly round her head, covering her mouth and eyes, only barely giving her room to breathe, and her hands and arms were tied together with cords.

This brutal assault had been so quick and so sudden that at first it seemed to Marguerite like part of a hideous dream. She was not fully conscious and was half suffocated by the thick folds of the scarf and that persistent odour, which by its sickened sweetness caused her wellnigh to swoon.

Through this semi-consciousness, however, she was constantly aware of her enemy, Bertrand Moncrif—the black-hearted traitor who had carried out this execrable outrage: why and for what purpose, Marguerite was too dazed to attempt to guess. He was there, that she knew. She was conscious of his hands making sure of the cords round her wrists, tightening the scarf around her mouth; then presently she felt him leaning across her body and throwing down the window, and she heard him shouting to the driver:

"Her ladyship as fainted. Drive as fast as ever you can till you come to that white house yonder on the right, the one with the green shutters and the tall yew at the gate!"

The driver's reply she could not hear, nor the crack of his whip. Certain it is that, though the coach had rattled on at a great pace before, the horses, as if in response to Bertrand's commands, now burned the ground under their hoofs. A few minutes went by—an eternity. Then that terrible cloying perfume was again held close to her nostrils; an awful dizziness and nausea seized her; after which she remembered nothing more.

CHAPTER 21

Memories

When Marguerite Blakeney finally recovered consciousness, the sun was low down in the west. She was in a coach—not her own—which was being whisked along the road at terrific speed. She was alone, her mouth gagged, her wrists and her ankles tied with cords, so that she could neither speak nor move—a helpless log, being taken—

whither?—and by whom?

Bertrand was not here. Through the front window of the coach she could perceive the vague outline of two men sitting on the driver's seat, whilst another was riding the off-leader. Four horses were harnessed to the light coach. It flew along in a south-easterly direction, the while the shades of evening were fast drawing in.

Marguerite had seen too much of the cruelties and barbarities of this world, too much of the hatred that existed between enemy countries, and too much of the bitter rancour felt by certain men against her husband and indirectly against herself, not to realise at once whence the blow had come that had struck her. Something too in the shape of that back which she perceived through the window in front of her, something in the cut of the threadbare coat, the set of the black bow at the nape of the neck, was too familiar to leave her even for a moment in doubt. Here was no ordinary foot-pad, no daring abduction with a view to reward or ransom. This was the work of her husband's enemies, who, through her, were once more striving to get at him.

Bertrand Moncrif had been the decoy. Whence had come the hatred which prompted him to raise his hand against the very man to whom he owed his life, Marguerite was still too dazed to conjecture. He had gone, and taken his secret of rancour with him, mayhap for ever. Lying pinioned and helpless as she was, Marguerite had but the one thought: in what way would those fiends who had her a prisoner use her as a leverage against the life and honour of the Scarlet Pimpernel? They had held her once before—not so very long ago—in Boulogne, and he had emerged unscathed, victorious over them all.

Marguerite, helpless and pinioned, forced her thoughts to dwell on that time, when his enemies had filled to the brim the cup of humiliation and of dread which was destined for each him through her hands, and his ingenuity and his daring dashed the cup to the ground ere it reached her lips. In truth, her plight then, at Boulogne, was in no way less terrible, less seemingly hopeless than now. She was a prisoner then, just as she was now; in the power of men whose whole life and entire range of thought had for the past two years been devoted to the undoing and annihilation of the Scarlet Pimpernel. And there was a certain grim satisfaction for the pinioned, helpless woman in recalling the many instances where the daring adventurer had so completely outwitted his enemies, as well as in the memory of those days at Boulogne when the life of countless innocents was to be the price of her own.

The embarkation took place somewhere on the coast around Birchington. When, at dead of night, the coach came to a halt, and the tang of sea air and salt spray reached Marguerite's burning cheeks and parched lips, she tried with all her might to guess at her exact position. But that was impossible.

She was lifted out of the coach, and at once a shawl was thrown over her face, so that she could not see. It was more instinct than anything else that guided her perceptions. Even in the coach she had been vaguely conscious of the direction in which she had been travelling. All that part of the country was entirely familiar to her. So often she had driven down with Sir Percy, either to Dover or more often to some lonely part of the coast, where he took ship for unknown destinations, that in her mind she could, even blinded with tears and half-conscious as she was, trace in her mind the various turnings and side-roads along which she was being borne at unabating speed.

Birchington—one of the favourite haunts of the smuggling fraternity, with its numberless caves and retreats dug by the sea in the chalk cliffs, as if for the express benefit of ne'er-do-wells—seemed the natural objective of the miscreants who had her in their power. In fact, at one moment she was quite sure that the square tower of old Minister church flitted past her vision through the window of the coach, and that the horses immediately after that sprinted the hill between Minster and Acoll.

Be that as it may, there was no doubt that the coach came to a halt at a desolate spot. The day which had begun in radiance and sunshine, had turned to an evening of squall and drizzle. A thin rain soon wetted Marguerite's clothes and the shawl on her head through and through, greatly adding to her misery and discomfort. Though she saw nothing, she could trace every landmark of the calvary to the summit of which she was being borne like an insentient log.

For a while she lay at the bottom of a small boat, aching in body as well as in mind, her eyes closed, her limbs cramped by the cords which owing to the damp were cutting into her flesh, faint with cold and want of food, wet to the skin yet with eyes and head and hands burning hot, and her ears filled with the dreary, monotonous sound of the oars creaking in the rowlocks and the boom of the water against the sides of the boat.

She was lifted out of the boat and carried, as she judged, by two men up a companion ladder, then down some steps and finally deposited on some hard boards; after which the wet shawl was removed from her face. She was in the dark. Only a tiny streak of light found its way through a chink somewhere close to the floor. A smell of tar and of stale food gave her a wretched sense of nausea. But she had by now reached a stage of physical and mental prostration wherein even acute bodily suffering counts as nothing and is endurable because it is no longer felt.

After a while the familiar motion, the well-known sound of a ship weighing anchor, gave another blow to her few lingering hopes. Every movement of the ship now bore her farther and farther from England and home and rendered her position more utterly miserable and hopeless.

Far be it from me to suggest even for a moment that Marguerite Blakeney lost either spirit or courage during this terrible ordeal. But she was so completely helpless that instinct forced her to remain motionless and quiescent, and not to engage in a fight against overwhelming odds. In mid-Channel, surrounded by miscreants who had her in their power, she could obviously do nothing except safeguard what dignity she could by silence and seeming acquiescence.

She was taken ashore in the early dawn, at a spot not very far from Boulogne. Precautions were no longer taken against her possible calls for help; even the cords had been removed from her wrists and ankles as soon as she was lowered into the boat that brought her to shore. Cramped and stiff though she was, she disdained the help of an arm which was held out to her to enable her to step out of the boat.

All the faces around her were unfamiliar. There were four or five men, surly and silent, who piloted her over the rocks and cliffs and then along the sands, to the little hamlet of Wimereux, which she knew well. The coast at this hour was still deserted; only at one time did the little party meet with a group of buxom young women, trudging along barefooted with their shrimping nets over their shoulders. They stared wide-eyed but otherwise indifferent, at the unfortunate woman in torn, damp clothes, and with golden hair all dishevelled, who was bravely striving not to fall whilst urged on by five rough fellows in ragged jerseys, tattered breeches, and bare-kneed.

Just for one moment—a mere flash—Marguerite at sight of these girls had the wild notion to run to them, implore their assistance in the name of their sweethearts, their husbands, their songs; to throw herself at their feet and beg them to help her, seeing that they were women and could not be without heart or pity. But it was a mere flash, the wild vagary of an over-excited brain, the drifting straw that mocks the drowning man. The next moment the girls had gone by, laughing and chattering. One of them intoned the "*Ca ira!*" and Marguerite, fortunately for her own dignity, was not seriously tempted to essay so futile, so senseless an appeal.

Later on, in a squalid little hovel on the outskirts of Wimereux, she was at last given some food which, though of the poorest and roughest description, was nevertheless welcome, for it revived her spirit and strengthened her courage, of which she had sore need.

The rest of the journey was uneventful. Within the first hour of making a fresh start, she had realised that she was being taken to Paris. A few words dropped casually by the men who had charge of her apprised her of the fact. Otherwise they were very reticent—not altogether rough or unkind.

The coach in which she travelled during this stage of the journey was roomy and not uncomfortable, although the cushions were ragged and the leatherwork mildewed. Above all, she had the supreme comfort of privacy. She was alone in the coach, alone during the halts at way-side hostelries when she was allowed food and rest, alone throughout those two interminable nights when, with brief intervals whilst relays of horses were put into the shafts or the men took it in turns to get food or drunk in some house unseen in the darkness, she vainly tried to get a snatch or two of sleep and a few moments of forgetfulness; alone throughout that next long day, whilst frequent summer showers sent heavy raindrops beating against the window-panes of the coach, and familiar landmarks on the way to Paris flitted like threatening ghouls past her aching eyes.

Paris was reached at dawn of the third day. Seventy-two hours had crept along leaden-footed, since the moment when she hat stepped into her own coach outside her beautiful home in Richmond, surrounded by her own servants, and with that traitor Moncrif by her side. Since then, what a load of sorrow, of anxiety, seemed as nothing beside the heartrending thoughts of her beloved, as yet ignorant of her terrible fate and of the schemes which those fiends who had so shamefully trapped her were even now concocting for the realisation of their vengeance against him.

CHAPTER 22

Waiting

The house to which Marguerite was ultimately driven, and where she presently found herself ushered up the stairs into a small, well-

furnished apartment, appeared to be situated somewhere in an outly-
ing quarter of Pairs.

The apartment consisted of three rooms—a bedroom, a sitting-
room, and small *cabinet de toilette*—all plainly but nicely furnished. The
bed looked clean and comfortable, there was a carpet on the floor, one
or two pictures on the wall, an arm-chair or two, even a few books in
an armoire. An old woman, dour of mien but otherwise willing and
attentive, did all she could to minister to the poor wearied woman's
wants. She brought up some warm milk and home-baked bread. Butter, she explained, was not obtainable these day, and the household had
not seen sugar for weeks.

Marguerite, tired out and hungry, readily ate some breakfast; but
what she longed for most and needed most was rest. So presently, at
the gruff invitation of the old woman, she undressed and stretched
her weary limbs between the sheets, with a sigh of content. Anxiety,
for the moment, had to yield to the sense of well-being, and with the
name of her beloved on her lips Marguerite went to sleep like a child.

When she woke, it was late afternoon. On a chair close by her
bedside was some clean linen laid out, a change of stockings, clean
shoes, and a gown—a perfect luxury, which made this silent and lonely house appear more like the enchanted abode of ogres or fairies than
before. Marguerite rose and dressed. The linen was fine, obviously the
property of a woman of refinement, whilst everything in the tiny
dressing-room—a comb, hand-mirror, soap, and scented water—suggested that the delicate hand of a cultured woman had seen to their
disposal. A while later, the dour attendant brought her some soup and
a dish of cooked vegetables.

Every phase of the situation became more and more puzzling as
time went one. Marguerite, with the sense of well-being further accentuated by the feel of warm, dry clothes and of wholesome food,
had her mind free enough to think and to ponder. She had thrown
open the window, and peeping out, noted that it obviously gave on
the back of the house and that the view consisted of rough, unculti-
vated land, broken up here and there by workshops, warehouses, and
timber-yards. Marguerite also noted that she was gazing out in the
direction of the north-west, that the apartment wherein she found
herself was on the top floor of a detached house which, judging by
certain landmarks vaguely familiar, was situated somewhere outside
the barrier of St. Antoine, and not very far from the Bastille and from
the Arsenal.

Again, she pondered. Where was she? Why was she being treated with a kindness and consideration altogether at variance with the tactics usually adopted by the enemies of the Scarlet Pimpernel? She was not in prison. She was not being starved, or threatened, or humiliated. The day wore on, and she was not confronted with one or other of those fiends who were so obviously using her as a decoy for her husband.

But though Marguerite Blakeney was not in prison, she was a prisoner. This she had ascertained five minutes after she was alone in the apartment. She could wander at will from room to room; but only in them, not out of them. The door of communication between the rooms was wide open; those that obviously gave on a landing outside were securely locked; and when a while ago the old woman had entered with the tray of food, Marguerite had caught sight of a group of men in the well-known tattered uniform of the National Guard, standing at attention in a wide, long antechamber.

Yes; she was a prisoner! She could open the windows of her apartment and inhale the soft moist air which came across the wide tract of a barren land; but these windows were thirty feet above the ground, and there was no projection in the outside wall of the house anywhere near that would afford a foothold to anything human.

Thus, for twenty-four hours she was left to meditate, thrown upon her own resources, with no other company save that of her own thoughts, and they were anything but cheerful. The uncertainty of the situation soon began to prey upon her nerves. She had been calm in the morning; but as the day wore on the loneliness, the mystery, the silence, began to tell upon her courage. Soon she got to look upon the woman who waited on her as upon her jailer, and when she was alone she was for ever straining her ears to hear what the men who were guarding her door might be saying among themselves.

The next night she hardly slept.

Twenty-four hours later she had a visiting from Citizen Chauvelin.

She had been expecting that visit all along, or else a message from him. When he came she had need of all her pluck and all her determination, not to let him see the emotion which his presence caused her. Dread! Loathing! These were her predominant sensations. But dread above all; because he was dressed with scrupulous care and affected the manners and graces of a society which had long since cast him out. It was not the rough, out-at-elbows Terrorist who stood before her, the revolutionary demagogue who hits out right and left against a caste that has always spurned him and held itself aloof; it was the broken-down gentleman at war with fortune, who strives by his wits to be revenged against the buffetings of Fate and the arrogance which ostracized him as soon as he was down.

He began by asking solicitously after her well-being; hoped the journey had not over-fatigued her; humbly begged her pardon for the discomfort which a higher power compelled him to put upon her. He talked platitudes in an even, unctuous voice until Marguerite, exasperated, and her nerves on edge, curtly bade him to come to the point.

"I have come to the point, dear lady," he retorted suavely. "The point is that you should be comfortable and have no cause to complain whilst you are under this roof."

"And how long am I to remain a prisoner under it?" she asked.

"Until Sir Percy has in his turn honoured this house with his presence," he replied.

To this she made no answer for a time, but sat quite still looking at him, as if detached and indifferent. He waited for her to speak, his pale eyes, slightly mocking, fixed upon her. Then she said simply:

"I understand."

"I was quite sure you would, dear lady," he rejoined blandly. "You see, the phase of heroics is past. I will confess to you that it proved of no avail when measured against the lofty coolness of that peerless exquisite. So, we over here have shed our ardour like a mantle. We, too, now are quite calm, quite unperturbed, quite content to wait. The beautiful Lady Blakeney is a guest under this roof. Well, sooner or later that most gallant of husbands will desire to approach his lady. Sooner or later he will learn that she is no longer in England. Then he will set his incomparable wits to work to find out where she is. Again, I may say that sooner or later, perhaps, even aided by us, he will know that she is here. Then he will come. Am I not right?"

Of course, he was right. Sooner or later Percy would learn where she was; and then he would come. He would come to her, despite every trap set for his undoing, despite every net laid to catch him, despite danger of death that waited for him if he came.

Chauvelin said little more. In truth, the era of heroics was at an end. At an end those ominous "either—ors" that he was wont to mete out with a voice quavering with rage and lust of revenge. Now there was no alternative, no deep-laid plot save one: to wait for the Scarlet Pimpernel until he came.

In the meanwhile, she, Marguerite, must remain helpless and a prisoner; she must eat and drink and sleep. She, the decoy!—who would never know when the crushing blow would fall that would mean a hundred deaths to her if it involved that of the husband whom she worshipped.

After a while, Chauvelin went away. In fact, she never knew actually when he did go. A while ago he had sat there on that upright chair, quiet, well groomed, suave of speech and bland of manner.

"Then he will come," he had said quite urbanely. "Am I not right?"

When Marguerite closed her eyes, she could still see him, his mocking gaze fixed upon her, his thin, white hands folded complacently before him. And presently, as the day wore on and the shades of evening blurred one object in the room after another, the straight-backed chair, still left in its place, assumed a fantastic human shape—the shape of a meagre figure with narrow shoulders and thin, carefully be-stockinged legs. And all the faint noises around her—the occasional creaking of the furniture, the movements of the men outside her door, the soughing of the evening breeze in the foliage of the elm trees—all were merged into a thin, bland human voice, that went on repeating in a kind of thin, dreary monotone:

"Then he will come. Am I not right?"

CHAPTER 23

Mice and Men

It was on her return from England that Theresia Cabarrus took to consulting the old witch in the Rue de la Planchette, driven thereto by ambition, and also no doubt by remorse. There was nothing of the hardened criminal about the fair Spaniard; she was just a spoilt woman who had been mocked and thwarted, and desired to be revenged. The Scarlet Pimpernel had appeared before her as one utterly impervious to her charms, and, egged on by Chauvelin, who used her for his own ends, she entered into a callous conspiracy, the aim of which was the destruction of that gang of English spies who were the enemies of France, and the first stage of which was the heartless abduction of Lady Blakeney and her incarceration as a decoy for the ultimate capture of her own husband.

A cruel, abominable act! Theresia, who had plunged headlong into this shameful crime, would a few days later have given much to undo the harm she had wrought. But she had yet to learn that, once used as a tool by the Committee of Public Safety and by Chauvelin, its most unscrupulous agent, no man or woman could hope to become free again until the work demanded had been accomplished to the end. There was no freedom from that taskmaster save in death; and Theresia's fit of compunction did not carry her to the lengths of self-sacrifice. Marguerite Blakeney was her prisoner, the decoy which would bring the English milor inevitably to the spot where his wife was incarcerated; and Theresia, who had helped to bring this state of things about, did her best to smother remorse, and having done Chauvelin's dirty work for him she set to see what personal advantage she could derive from it.

Firstly, the satisfaction of her petty revenge: The Scarlet Pimpernel caught in a trap, would surely regret his interference in Theresia's love affairs. Theresia cared less than nothing about Bertrand Moncrif and would have been quite grateful to the English milor for having spirited that embarrassing lover of hers away but for that letter which had wounded the beautiful Spaniard's vanity to the quick, and still rankled sufficiently to ease her conscience on the score of her subsequent actions. That the letter was a bogus one, concocted and written by Chauvelin himself in order to spur her on to a mean revenge, Theresia did not know.

But far stronger than thoughts of revenge where Theresia's schemes for her own future. She had begun to dream of Robespierre's gratitude, of her triumph over all those who had striven for over two years to bring that gang of English spies to book. She saw her name writ largely on the roll of fame; she even saw in her mind, the tyrant himself as her willing slave—and something more than that.

For her tool Bertrand she had no further use. By way of a reward for the abominable abduction of Lady Blakeney, he had been allowed to follow the woman he worshipped like a lackey attached to her train. Dejected, already spurned, he returned to Paris with her, here to resume the life of humiliation and of despised ardour which had broken his spirit and warped his nature, before his gallant rescuer had snatched him out of the toils of the beautiful Spaniard.

Within an hour of setting his foot on French soil, Bertrand had realised that he had been nothing in Theresia's sight but a lump of malleable wax, which she had moulded to her own design and now threw aside as cumbersome and useless. He had realised that her ambition soared far above linking her fate to an obscure and penniless lover, when the coming man of the hour—Citizen Tallien—was already at her feet.

Thus, Theresia had attained one of her great desires: the Scarlet

Pimpernel was as good as captured, and when he finally succumbed he could not fail to know whence came the blow that struck him.

With regard to her future, matters were more doubtful. She had not yet subjugated Robespierre sufficiently to cause him to give up his more humble love and to lay down his power and popularity at her feet; whilst the man who had offered her his hand and name—Citizen Tallien—was for ever putting a check upon her ambition and his own advancement by his pusillanimity and lack of enterprise.

Whilst she was aching to push him into decisive action, into seizing the supreme power before Robespierre and his friends had irrevocably established theirs, Tallien was for temporizing, fear that in trying to snatch a dictatorship he and his beloved with him would lose their heads.

"While Robespierre lives," Theresia would argue passionately, "no man's head is safe. Every rival, sooner or later, becomes a victim. St. Just and Couthon aim at a dictatorship for him. Sooner or later they will succeed; then death to every man who has ever dared oppose them."

"Therefore 'tis wiser not to oppose," the prudent Tallien would retort. "The time will come—"

"Never!" she riposted hotly. "While you plot, and argue and ponder, Robespierre acts or signs your death-warrant."

"Robespierre is the idol of the people; he sways the Convention with a word. His eloquence would drag an army of enemies to the guillotine!"

"Robespierre!" Theresia retorted with sublime contempt. "Ah, when you have said that, you think you have said everything! France, humanity, the people, sovereign power!—all that, you assert, is embodied in that one man. But, my friend, listen to me!" she went on earnestly. "Listen, when I assert that Robespierre is only a name, a fetish, a manikin set up on a pedestal! By whom? By you, and the Convention; by the Clubs and the Committees. And the pedestal is composed of that elusive entity which you call the people and which will disintegrate from beneath his feet as soon as the people have realised that those feet are less than clay. One touch of a firm finger against that manikin, I tell you, and he will fall as dust before you; and you can rise upon that same elusive pedestal—popularity, to the heights which he hath so easily attained."

But, though Tallien was at times carried away by her vehemence, he would always shake his head and counsel prudence, and assure her that the time was not yet. Theresia, impatient and dictatorial, had more than once hinted at rupture.

"I could not love a weakling," she would aver; and at the back of her mind there would rise schemes, which aimed at transferring her favours to the other man, who she felt would be more worthy of her.

"Robespierre would not fail me, as this coward does!" she mused, even while Tallien, blind and obedient, was bidding her farewell at the very door of the charlatan to whom Theresia had turned in her ambition and her difficulties.

Something of the glamour which had originally surrounded Mother Théot's incantations had vanished since sixty-two of her devotees had been sent to the guillotine on charge of conspiring for the overthrow of the Republic. Robespierre's enemies, too cowardly to attack him in the Convention or in the Clubs, had seized upon the mystery which hung over the *séances* in the Rue de la Planchette in order to undermine his popularity in the one and his power in the other.

Spies were introduced into the witch's lair. The names of its chief frequenters became known, and soon wholesale arrests were made, which were followed by the inevitable condemnations. Robespierre had not actually been named; but the identity of the sycophants who had proclaimed him the Messenger of the Most High, the Morning Star, or the Regenerator of Mankind, were hurled across from the tribune of the Convention, like poisoned arrows aimed at the tyrant himself.

But Robespierre had been too wary to allow himself to be dragged into the affair. His enemies tried to goad him into defending his worshippers, thus admitting his association with the gang; but he remained prudently silent, and with callous ruthlessness he sacrificed them to his own safety. He never raised his voice nor yet one finger to save them from death, and whilst he—bloodthirsty autocrat—remain firmly installed upon his self-constituted throne, those who had acclaimed him as second only to God, perished upon the scaffold.

Mother Théot, for some inexplicable reason, escaped this wholesale slaughter; but her *séances* were henceforth shorn of their splendour. Robespierre no longer dared frequent them even in disguise. The house in the Rue de la Planchette became a marked one to the agents of the Committee of Public Safety, and the witch herself was reduced to innumerable shifts to eke out a precarious livelihood and to keep herself in the good graces of those agents, by rendering them various unavowable services.

To those, however, who chose to defy public opinion and to disregard the dangers which attended the frequentation of Mother Théot's sorceries, these latter had lost little or nothing of their pristine solemnity. There was the closely curtained room; the scented, heavy atmosphere; the chants, the coloured flames, the ghost-like neophytes. Draped in her grey veils, the old witch still wove her spells and called on the powers of light and of darkness to aid her in foretelling the future. The neophytes chanted and twisted their bodies in quaint contortions; alone, the small blackamoor grinned at what experience had taught him was nothing by quackery and charlatanism.

Theresia, sitting on the dias, with the heady fumes of Oriental scents blurring her sight and the clearness of her intellect, was drinking in the honeyed words and flattering prophecies of the old witch.

"Thy name will be the greatest in the land! Before thee will bow the mightiest thrones! At thy word heads will fall and diadems will totter!" Mother Théot announced in sepulchral tones, whilst gazing into the crystal before her.

"As the wife of Citizen Tallien?" Theresia queried in an awed whisper.

"That the spirits do not say," the old witch replied. "What is a name to them? I see a crown of glory, and thy head surrounded by a golden light; and at thy feet lies something which once was scarlet, and now is crimson and crushed."

"What does it mean?" Theresia murmured.

"That is for thee to know," the *sybil* replied sternly. "Commune with the spirits; lose thyself in their embrace; learn from them the great truths, and the future will be made clear to thee."

With which cryptic utterance she gathered her veils around her, and with weird murmurs of, "*Evohe! Evohe! Sammael! Zamiel! Evohe!*" glided out of the room, mysterious and inscrutable, presumably in order to allow her bewildered client to meditate on the enigmatical prophecy in solitude.

But directly she had closed the door behind her, Mother Théot's manner underwent a chance. Here the broad light of day appeared to divest her of all her *sybilline* attributes. She became just an ugly old woman, wrinkled and hook-nosed, dressed in shabby draperies that were grey with age and dirt, and with claw-like hands that looked like the talons of a bird of prey.

As she entered the room, a man who had been standing at the window opposite, staring out into the dismal street below, turned quickly to her.

"Art satisfied?" she asked at once.

"From what I could hear, yes!" he replied, "though I could have wished thy pronouncements had been more clear."

The hag shrugged her lean shoulders and nodded in the direction of her lair.

"Oh!" she said. "The Spaniard understands well enough. She never consults me or invokes the spirits but they speak to her of that which is scarlet. She knows what it means. You need not fear, Citizen Chauvelin, that in the pursuit of her vaulting ambition, she will forget that her primary duty is to you!"

"No," Chauvelin asserted calmly, "she'll not forget that. The Cabarrus is no fool. She knows well enough that when citizens of the State have been employed to work on its behalf, they are no longer free agents afterwards. The work must be carried through to the end."

"You need not fear the Cabarrus, citizen," the *sybil* rejoined dryly. "She'll not fail you. Her vanity is immense. She believes that the Englishman insulted her by writing that flippant letter, and she'll not leave him alone till she has had her revenge."

"No!" Chauvelin assented. "She'll not fail me. Nor thou either, *citoyenne.*"

The old hag shrugged her shoulders.

"I?" she exclaimed, with a quiet laugh. "Is that likely? You promised me ten thousand *livres* the day the Scarlet Pimpernel is captured!"

"And the guillotine," Chauvelin broke in grimly, "if thou shouldst allow the woman upstairs to escape."

"I know that," the old woman rejoined dryly. "If she escapes 'twill not be through my connivance."

"In the service of the State," Chauvelin riposted, "even carelessness becomes a crime."

Catherine Théot was silent for a moment or two, pressed her thin lips together; then rejoined quite quietly:

"She'll not escape. Have no fear, Citizen Chauvelin."

"That's brave! And now, tell me what has become of the coalheaver Rateau?"

"Oh, he comes and goes. You told me to encourage him."

"Yes."

"So, I give him potions for his cough. He has one foot in the grave."

"Would he had both!" Chauvelin broke in savagely. "That man is a perpetual menace to my plans. It would have been so much better if we could have sent him last April to the guillotine."

"It was in your hands," Mother Théot retorted. "The Committee reported against him. His measure was full enough. Aiding that execrable Scarlet Pimpernel to escape—! Name of a name! it should have been enough!"

"It was not proved that he did aid the English spies," Chauvelin retorted moodily. "And Foucquier-Tinville would not arraign him. He vowed it would anger the people—the rabble—of which Rateau himself forms an integral part. We cannot afford to anger the rabble these days, it seems."

"And so Rateau, the asthmatic coalheaver, walked out of prison a free man, whilst my *neophytes* were dragged up to the guillotine, and I was left without means of earning an honest livelihood!" Mother Théot concluded with a doleful sigh.

"Honest?" Chauvelin exclaimed, with a sarcastic chuckle. Then, seeing that the old witch was ready to lose her temper, he quickly added: "Tell me more about Rateau. Does he often come here?"

"Yes; very often. He must be in my anteroom now. He came directly he was let out of prison and has haunted this place ever since. He thinks I can cure him of his asthma, and as he pays me well—"

"Pays you well?" Chauvelin broke in quickly. "That starveling?"

"Rateau is no starveling," the old woman asserted. "Many an English gold piece hath he given me."

"But not of late?"

"No later than yesterday."

Chauvelin swore viciously.

"Then he is still in touch with that cursed Englishman!"

Mother Théot shrugged her shoulders.

"Does one ever know which is the Englishman, and which is the asthmatic Rateau?" she queried, with a dry laugh.

Whereupon a strange thing happened—so strange indeed that Chauvelin's next words turned to savage curses, and that Mother Théot, white to the lips, her knees shaking under her, tiny beads of perspiration rising beneath her scanty locks, had to hold on to the table to save herself from falling.

"Name of a name of a dog!" Chauvelin muttered hoarsely, whilst the old woman, shaken but that superstitious dread which she liked to arouse in her clients, could only stare at him and mutely shake her head.

And yet nothing very alarming had occurred. Only a man had

laughed, light-heartedly and long; and the sound of that laughter had come from somewhere near—the next room probably, or the landing beyond Mother Théot's anteroom. It had come low and distinct, slightly muffled by the intervening wall. Nothing in truth to frighten the most nervous child!

A man had laughed. One of Mother Théot's clients probably, who in the company of a friend chose to wile away the weary hour of waiting on the *sybil* by hilarious conversation. Of course, that was it! Chauvelin, cursing himself now for his cowardice, passed a still shaking hand across his brow, and a wry smile distorted momentarily his thin, set lips.

"One of your clients is of good cheer," he said with well-assumed indifference.

"There is no one in the anteroom at this hour," the old hag murmured under her breath. "Only Rateau—and he is too scant of breath to laugh—he—"

But Chauvelin no longer heard what she had to say. With an exclamation which no one who heard it could have defined, he turned on his heel and almost ran out of the room.

CHAPTER 24

By Order of the State

The antechamber, wide and long, ran the whole length of Mother Théot's apartment. Her witch's lair and the room where she had just had her interview with Chauvelin gave directly on it on the one side, and two other living rooms on the other. At one end of the antechamber there were two windows, usually kept closely shuttered; and at the other was the main entrance door, which led to landing and staircase.

The antechamber was empty. It appeared to mock Chauvelin's excitement, with its grey-washed walls streaked with grime, its worm-eaten benches and tarnished chandelier. Mother Théot, voluble and quaking with fear, was close at his heels. Curtly he ordered her to be gone; her mutterings irritated him, her obvious fear of something unknown grated unpleasantly on his nerves. He cursed himself for his cowardice and cursed the one man who alone in this world had the power to unnerve him.

"I was dreaming, of course," he muttered aloud to himself between his teeth. "I have that arch-devil, his laugh, his voice, his affectations, on the brain!"

He was on the point of going to the main door, in order to peer

368

out on the landing or down the stairs, when he heard his name called immediately behind him. Theresia Cabarrus was standing under the lintel of the door which gave on the *sybil's* sanctum, her delicate hand holding back the *portière*.

"Citizen Chauvelin," she said, "I was waiting for you."

"And I, *citoyenne*," he retorted gruffly, "had in truth forgotten you."

"Mother Théot left me alone for a while, to commune with the spirits," she explained.

"Ah!" he riposted, slightly sarcastic. "With what result?"

"To help you further, Citizen Chauvelin," she replied; "if you have need of me."

"Ah!" he exclaimed with a savage curse. "In truth, I have need of every willing hand that will raise itself against mine enemy. I have need of you, citizeness; of that old witch; of Rateau, the coalheaver; of every patriot who will sit and watch this house, to which we have brought the one bait that will lure the goldfish to our net."

"Have I not proved my willingness, citizen?" she retorted, with a smile. "Think you 'tis pleasant to give up my life, my salon, my easy, contented existence, and become a mere drudge in your service?"

"A drudge," he broke in with a chuckle, "who will soon be greater than a queen."

"Ah, if I thought that!—" she exclaimed.

"I am as sure of it as that I am alive," he replied firmly. "You will never do anything with Citizen Tallien, *citoyenne*. He is too mean, too cowardly. But bring the Scarlet Pimpernel to his knees at the chariot wheel of Robespierre, and even the crown of the Bourbons would be yours for the asking."

"I know that, citizen," she rejoined dryly; "else I were not here."

"We hold all the winning cards," he went on eagerly. "Lady Blakeney is in our hands. So long as we hold her, we have the certainty that sooner or later the English spy will establish communication with her. Catherine Théot is a good jailer, and Captain Boyer upstairs has a number of men under his command—veritable sleuthhounds, whose efficiency I can guarantee and whose eagerness is stimulated by the promise of a magnificent reward. But experience has taught me that that accursed Scarlet Pimpernel is never so dangerous as when we think we hold him. His extraordinary histrionic powers have been our undoing hitherto. No man's eyes are keen enough to pierce his disguises.

"That is why, *citoyenne*, I dragged you to England; that is why I placed you face to face with him, and said to you, 'That is the man.' Since then, with your help, we hold the decoy. Now you are my co-adjutor and my help. In your eyes I place my trust; in your wits, your instinct. In whatever guise the Scarlet Pimpernel presents himself before you—and he will present himself before you, or he is no longer the impudent and reckless adventurer I know him to be!—I feel that you at least will recognise him."

"Yes; I think I should recognise him," she mused.

"Think you that I do not appreciate the sacrifice you make—the anxiety, the watchfulness to which you so nobly subject yourself? But 'tis you above all who are the lure which must inevitably attract the Scarlet Pimpernel into my hands."

"Soon, I hope," she sighed wearily.

"Soon," he asserted firmly. "I dare swear it! Until then, citizeness, in the name of your own future, and in the name of France, I adjure you to watch. Watch and listen! Oh, think of the stakes for which we are playing, you and I! Bring the Scarlet Pimpernel to his knees, *citoyenne*, and Robespierre will be as much your slave as he is now the prey to a strange dread of that one man. Robespierre fears the Scarlet Pimpernel. A superstitious conviction had seized hold of him that the English spy will bring about his downfall. We have all seen of late how aloof he holds himself. He no longer attends the Committees.

"He no longer goes to the Clubs; he shuns his friends; and his furtive glance is for ever trying to pierce some imaginary disguise, under which he alternately fears and hopes to discover his arch-enemy. He dreads assassination, anonymous attacks. In every obscure member of the Convention who walks up the steps of the tribune, he fears to find the Scarlet Pimpernel under a new, impenetrable mask. Ah, *citoyenne!* what influence you would have over him if through your agency all those fears could be drowned in the blood of that abominable Englishman!"

"Now, who would have thought that?" a mocking voice broke in suddenly, with a quiet chuckle. "I vow, my dear M. Chambertin, you are waxing more eloquent than ever before!"

Like the laughter of a while ago, the voice seemed to come from nowhere. It was in the air, muffled by the clouds of Mother Théot's perfumes, or by the thickness of doors and tapestries. Weird, yet human.

"By Satan, this is intolerable!" Chauvelin exclaimed; and paying no heed to Theresia's faint cry of terror, he ran to the main door. It was on the latch. He tore it open and dashed out upon the landing.

From here a narrow stone staircase, dank and sombre, led downwards as well as upwards, in a spiral. The house had only the two storeys, perched above some disused and dilapidated storage-rooms, to which a double outside door and wicket gave access from the street.

The staircase received its only light from a small window high up in the roof, the panes of which were coated with grime, so that the well of the stairs, especially past the first-floor landing, was almost in complete gloom. For an instant Chauvelin hesitated. Never a coward physically, he yet had no mind to precipitate himself down a dark staircase when mayhap his enemy was lying in wait for him down below.

Only for an instant however. The very next second had brought forth the positive reflection: "bah! Assassination, and in the dark, are not the Englishman's ways."

Scarce a few yards from where he stood, the other side of the door, was the dry moat which ran round the Arsenal. From there, at a call from him, a dozen men and more would surge from the ground—sleuthhounds, as he had told Theresia a moment ago, who were there on the watch and whom he could trust to do his work swiftly and securely—if only he could reach the door and call for help. Elusive as that accursed Pimpernel was, successful chase might even now be given to him.

Chauvelin ran down half a dozen steps, peered down the shaft of the staircase, and spied a tiny light, which moved swiftly to and fro. Then presently, below the light a bit of tallow candle, then a grimy hand holding the candle, an arm, the top of a shaggy head crowned by a greasy red cap, a broad back under a tattered blue jersey. He heard the thump of heavy soles upon the stone flooring below, and a moment or two later the weird, sepulchral sound of a churchyard cough. Then the light disappeared. For a second or two the darkness appeared more impenetrably dense; then one or two narrow streaks of daylight showed the position of the outside door. Something prompted him to call:

"Is that you, Citizen Rateau?"

It was foolish, of course. And the very next moment he had his answer. A voice—the mocking voice he knew so well—called up to him in reply:

"At your service, dear M. Chambertin! Can I do anything for you?"

Chauvelin swore, threw all prudence to the winds, and ran down the stairs as fast as his shaking knees would allow him. Some three steps from the bottom he paused for the space of a second, like one turned to stone by what he saw. Yet it was simple enough: just the same tiny light, the grimy hand holding the tallow candle, the shaggy head with the greasy red cap.—The figure in the gloom looked preternaturally large, and the flickering light threw fantastic shadows on the face and neck of the colossus, distorting the nose to a grotesque length and the chin to weird proportions.

The next instant Chauvelin gave a cry like an enraged bull and hurled his meagre person upon the giant, who, shaken at the moment by a tearing fit of coughing, was taken unawares and fell backwards, overborne by the impact, dropping the light as he fell and still wheezing pitiably whilst trying to give vent to his feelings by vigorous curses.

Chauvelin, vaguely surprised at his own strength or the weakness of his opponent, pressed his knee against the latter's chest, gripped him by the throat, smothering his curses and wheezes, turning the funeral cough into agonized gasps.

"At my service, in truth, my gallant Pimpernel!" he murmured hoarsely, feeling his small reserve of strength oozing away by the strenuous effort. "What you can do for me? Wait here, until I have you bound and gagged, safe against further mischief!"

His victim had in fact given a last convulsive gasp, lay now at full length upon the stone floor, with arms outstretched, motionless. Chauvelin relaxed his grip. His strength was spent, he was bathed in sweat, his body shook from head to foot. But he was triumphant! His mocking enemy, carried away by his own histrionics, had overtaxed his colossal strength. The carefully simulated fit of coughing had taken away his breath at the critical moment; the surprise attack had done the rest; and Chauvelin—meagre, feeble, usually the merest human insect beside the powerful Englishman—had conquered by sheer pluck and resource.

There lay the Scarlet Pimpernel, who had assumed the guise of asthmatic Rateau once too often, helpless and broken beneath the weight of the man whom he had hoodwinked and derided. And now at last all the intrigues, the humiliations, the schemes and the disappointments, were at an end. He—Chauvelin—free and honoured: Robespierre his grateful servant.

A wave of dizziness passed over his brain—the dizziness of coming glory. His senses reeled. When he staggered to his feet he could scarcely stand. The darkness was thick around him; only two streaks of daylight at right angles to one another came through the chinks of the outside door and vaguely illumined the interior of the dilapidated store-room, the last step or two of the winding stairway, the row of empty barrels on one side, the pile of rubbish on the other, and on the stone floor the huge figure in grimy and tattered rags, lying prone and motionless. Guided by those streaks of light, Chauvelin lurched up to the door, fumbled for the latch of the wicket-gate, and finding it pulled the gate open and almost fell out into the open.

The Rue de la Planchette was as usual lonely and deserted. It was a second or two before Chauvelin spied a passer-by. That minute he spent in calling for help with all his might. The passer-by he quickly dispatched across to the Arsenal for assistance.

"In the name of the Republic!" he said solemnly.

But already his cries had attracted the attention of the sentries. Within two or three minutes, half a dozen men of the National Guard were speeding down the street. Soon they had reached the house, the door where Chauvelin, still breathless but with his habitual official manner that brooked of no argument, gave them hasty instructions.

"The man lying on the ground in there," he commanded. "Seize him and raise him. Then one of you find some cord and bind him securely."

The men flung the double doors wide open. A flood of light illumined the store-room. There lay the huge figure on the floor, no longer motionless, but trying to scramble to his feet, once more torn by a fit of coughing. The man ran up to him; one of them laughed.

"Why, if it isn't old Rateau!"

They lifted him up by his arms. He was helpless as a child, and his face was of a dull purple colour.

"He will die!" another man said, with an indifferent shrug of the shoulders.

But, in a way, they were sorry for him. He was one of themselves. Nothing of the *aristo* about asthmatic old Rateau!

They had succeeded in propping him up and sitting him down upon a barrel. His fit of coughing was subsiding. He had breath enough now to swear. He raised his head and encountered the pale eyes of Citizen Chauvelin fixed as if sightlessly upon him.

"Name of a dog!" he began; but got no farther. Giddiness seized him, for he was weak from coughing and from that strangling grip round his throat, after he had been attacked in the darkness and thrown violently to the ground.

The men around him recoiled at sight of Citizen Chauvelin. His appearance was almost death-like. His cheeks and lips were livid; his hair dishevelled; his eyes of an unearthly paleness. One hand, clawlike and shaking, he held out before him, as if to ward off some horrible apparition.

This trance-like state made up of a ghastly fear and a sense of the most hideous, most unearthly impotence, lasted for several seconds. The men themselves were frightened. Unable to understand what had happened, they thought that Citizen Chauvelin, whom they all knew by sight, had suddenly lost his reason or was possessed of a devil. For in truth there was nothing about poor old Rateau to frighten a child!

Fortunately, the tension was over before real panic had seized on any of them. The next moment Chauvelin had pulled himself together with one of those mighty efforts of will of which strong natures are always capable. With an impatient gesture he passed his hand across his brow, then backwards and forwards in front of his face, as if to chase away the demon of terror that obsessed him. He gazed on Rateau for a moment or two, his eyes travelling over the uncouth, semi-conscious figure of the coalheaver with a searching, undefinable glance. Then, as if suddenly struck with an idea, he spoke to the man nearest him:

"Sergeant Chazot? Is he at the Arsenal?"

"Yes, citizen," the man replied.

"Run across quickly then," Chauvelin continued; "and bring him hither at once."

The soldier obeyed, and a few more minutes—ten, perhaps—went by in silence. Rateau, weary, cursing, not altogether in full possession of his faculties, sat huddled up on the barrel, his bleary eyes following every movement of Citizen Chauvelin with an anxious, furtive gaze. The latter was pacing up and down the stone floor, like a caged, impatient animal. From time to time he paused, either to peer out into the open in the direction of the Arsenal, or to search the dark angles of the store-room, kicking the piles of rubbish about with his foot.

Anon he uttered a sigh of satisfaction. The soldier had returned, was even now in the doorway with a comrade—a short, thick-set, powerful-looking fellow—beside him.

"Sergeant Chazot!" Chauvelin said abruptly.

"At your commands, citizen!" the sergeant replied, and at a sign from the other followed him to the most distant corner of the room.

"Bend your ear and listen," Chauvelin murmured peremptorily. "I don't want those fools to hear." And, having assured himself that he and Chazot could speak without being overheard, he pointed to Rateau, then went on rapidly: "You will take this lout over to the cavalry barracks. See the veterinary. Tell him—"

He paused, as if unable to proceed. His lips were trembling, his face, ashen-white, looked spectral in the gloom. Chazot, not understand, waited patiently.

"That lout," Chauvelin resumed more steadily after a while, "is in collusion with a gang of dangerous English spies. One Englishman especially—tall, and a master of histrionics—uses this man as a kind of double. Perhaps you heard—"

Chazot nodded.

"I know, citizen," he said sagely. "The Fraternal Supper in the Rue St. Honoré. Comrades have told me that no one could tell who was Rateau the coalheaver and who the English milor."

"Exactly!" Chauvelin rejoined dryly, quite firmly now. "Therefore, I want to make sure. The veterinary, you understand? He brands the horses for the cavalry. I want a brand on this lout's arm. Just a letter—a distinguishing mark—"

Chazot gave an involuntary gasp.

"But, citizen—!" he exclaimed.

"Eh? What?" the other retorted sharply. "In the service of the Republic there is no 'but,' Sergeant Chazot."

"I know that, citizen," Chazot, abashed, murmured humbly. "I only meant—it seems so strange—."

"Stranger things than that occur every day in Paris, my friend," Chauvelin said dryly. "We brand horses that are the property of the State; why not a man? Time may come," he added with a vicious snarl, "when the Republic may demand that every local citizen carry—indelibly branded in his flesh and by order of the State—the sign of his own allegiance."

"'Tis not for me to argue, citizen," Chazot rejoined, with a careless shrug of the shoulders. "If you tell me to take Citizen Rateau over to the veterinary at the cavalry barracks and have him branded like cattle, why. . ."

"Not like cattle, citizen," Chauvelin broke in blandly. "You shall commence proceedings by administering to Citizen Rateau a whole bottle of excellent *eau de vie*, at the government's expense. Then, when he is thoroughly and irretrievably drunk, the veterinary will put the brand upon his left forearm—just one letter.—Why, the drunken reprobate will never feel it!"

"As you command, citizen," Chazot assented with perfect indifference. "I am not responsible. I do as I'm told."

"Like the fine soldier that you are, citizen Chazot!" Chauvelin concluded. "And I know that I can trust to your discretion."

"Oh, as to that—!"

"It would not serve you to be otherwise; that's understood. So now, my friend, get you gone with the lout; and take these few words of instructions with you, for the citizen veterinary."

He took tablet and point from his pocket and scribbled a few words; signed it "Chauvelin" with that elegant flourish which can be traced to this day on so many secret orders that emanated from the Committee of Public Safety during the two years of its existence.

Chazot took the written order and slipped it into his pocket. Then he turned on his heel and briefly gave the necessary orders to the men. Once more they hoisted the helpless giant up on his feet. Rateau was willing enough to go. He was willing to do anything so long as they took him away from here, away from the presence of that small devil with the haggard face and the pale, piercing eyes. He allowed himself to be conducted out of the building without a murmur.

Chauvelin watched the little party—the six men, the asthmatic coalheaver and lastly the sergeant—file out of the place, then cross the Rue de la Planchette and take the turning opposite, the one that led through the Porte and the Rue St. Antoine to the cavalry barracks in the Quartier Bastille. After which, he carefully closed the double outside doors and, guided by instinct since the place down here was in darkness once more, he groped his way to the foot of the stairs and slowly mounted to the floor above.

He reached the first-floor landing. The door which led into Mother Théot's apartments was on the latch, and Chauvelin had just stretched out his hand with a view to pushing it open, when the door swung out on its hinges, as if moved by an invisible hand, and a pleasant, mocking voice immediately behind him said, with grave politeness:

"Allow me, my dear M. Chambertin!"

Chapter 25

Four Days

What occurred during the next few seconds Chauvelin himself would have been least able to say. Whether he stepped of his own accord into the antechamber of Catherine Théot's apartment, or whether an unseen hand pushed him in, he could not have told you. Certain it is that, when he returned to the full realisation of things, he was

376

sitting on one of the benches, his back against the wall, whilst immediately in front of him, looking down on him through half-closed, lazy eyes, *débonnair*, well groomed, unperturbed, stood his arch-enemy, Sir Percy Blakeney.

The antechamber was gloomy in the extreme. Someone in the interval had lighted the tallow candles in the centre chandelier, and these shed a feeble, flickering light on the dank, bare walls, the carpetless floor, the shuttered windows; whilst a thin spiral of evil-smelling smoke wound its way to the blackened ceiling above.

Of Theresia Cabarrus there was not a sign. Chauvelin looked about him, feeling like a goaded animal shut up in a narrow space with its tormentor. He was making desperate efforts to regain his composure, above all he made appeal to that courage which was wont never to desert him. In truth, Chauvelin had never been a physical coward, nor was he afraid of death or outrage at the hands of the man whom he had so deeply wronged, and whom he had pursued with a veritable lust of hate. No! he did not fear death at the hands of the Scarlet Pimpernel. What he feared was ridicule, humiliation, those schemes—bold, adventurous, seemingly impossible—which he knew were already seething behind the smooth, unruffled brow of his arch-enemy, behind those lazy, supercilious eyes, which had the power to irritate his nerves to the verge of dementia.

This impudent adventurer—no better than a spy, despite his aristocratic mien and air of lofty scorn—this meddlesome English brigand, was the one man in the world who had, when he measured his prowess against him, invariably brought him to ignominy and derision, made him a laughing-stock before those whom he had been wont to dominate; and at this moment, when once again he was being forced to look into those strangely provoking eyes, he appraised their glance as he would to sword of a proved adversary, and felt as he did so just that same unaccountable dread of them which had so often paralysed his limbs and atrophied his brain whenever mischance flung him into the presence of his enemy.

He could not understand why Theresia Cabarrus had deserted him. Even a woman, if she happened to be a friend, would by her presence have afforded him moral support.

"You are looking for Mme de Fontenay, I believe, dear M. Chambertin," Sir Percy said lightly, as if divining his thoughts. "The ladies—ah, the ladies! They add charm, piquancy, eh? to the driest conversations. Alas!" he went on with mock affectation, "that Mme de

377

Fontenay should have fled at first sound of my voice! Now she hath sought refuge in the old witch's lair, there to consult the spirits as to how best she can get out again, seeing that the door is now locked.—Deemed awkward, a locked door, when a pretty woman wants to be on the other side. What think you, M. Chambertin?"

"I only think, Sir Percy," Chauvelin contrived to retort, calling all his wits and all his courage to aid him in his humiliating position, "I only think of another pretty woman, who is in the room just above our heads and who would also be mightily glad to find herself the other side of a locked door."

"Your thoughts," Sir Percy retorted with a light laugh, "are always so ingenuous, my dear M. Chambertin. Strangely enough, mine just at this moment run on the possibility—not a very unlikely one, you will admit—of shaking the breath out of your ugly little body, as I would that of a rat."

"Shake, my dear Sir Percy, shake!" Chauvelin riposted with well-simulated calm. "I grant you that I am a puny rat and you are the most magnificent of lions; but even if I lie mangled and breathless on this stone floor at your feet, Lady Blakeney will still be a prisoner in our hands."

"And you will still be wearing the worst-cut pair of breeches it has ever been my bad fortune to behold," Sir Percy retorted, quite unruffled. "Lud love you, man! Have you guillotined all the good tailors in Paris?"

"You choose to be flippant, Sir Percy," Chauvelin rejoined dryly. "But, though you have chosen for the past few years to play the *rôle* of a brainless nincompoop, I have cause to know that behind your affectations there lurks an amount of sound common sense."

"Lud, how you flatter me, my dear sir!" quoth Sir Percy airily. "I vow you had not so high an opinion of me last time I had the honour of conversing with you. It was at Nantes; do you remember?"

"There, as elsewhere, you succeeded in circumventing me, Sir Percy."

"No, no!" he protested. "Not in circumventing you. Only in making you look a demmed fool!"

"Call it that, if you like, sir," Chauvelin admitted, with an indifferent shrug of the shoulders. "Luck has favoured you many a time. As I had the honour to tell you, you have had the laugh of us in the past, and no doubt you are under the impression that you will have it again this time."

"I am such a believer in impressions, my dear sir. The impression now that I have your charming personality is indelibly graven upon my memory."

"Sir Percy Blakeney counts a good memory as one of his many accomplishments. Another is his adventurous spirit, and the gallantry which must inevitably bring him into the net which we have been at pains to spread for him. Lady Blakeney—"

"Name her not, man!" Sir Percy broke in with affect deliberation; "or I verily believe that within sixty seconds you would be a dead man!"

"I am not worthy to speak her name, *c'est entendu*," Chauvelin retorted with mock humility. "Nevertheless, Sir Percy, it is around the person of that gracious lady that the Fates will spin their web during the next few days. You may kill me. Of course, I am at this moment entirely at your mercy. But before you embark on such a perilous undertaking, will you allow me to place the position a little more clearly before you?"

"Lud, man!" quoth Sir Percy with a quaint laugh. "That's what I'm here for! Think you that I have sought your agreeable company for the mere pleasure of gazing at your amiable countenance?"

"I only desired to explain to you, Sir Percy, the dangers to which you expose Lady Blakeney, if you laid violent hands upon me. 'Tis you, remember, who sought this interview—not I."

"You are right, my dear sir, always right; and I'll not interrupt again. I pray you to proceed."

"Allow me then to make my point clear. There are at this moment a score of men of the National Guard in the room above your head. Every one of them goes to the guillotine if they allow their prisoner to escape; every one of them receives a reward of ten thousand *livres* the day they capture the Scarlet Pimpernel. A good spur for vigilance, what? But that is not all," Chauvelin went on quite steadily, seeing that Sir Percy had apparently become thoughtful and absorbed. "The men are under the command of Captain Boyer, and he understands that ever day at a certain hour—seven in the evening, to be precise—I will be with him and interrogate him as to the welfare of the prisoner. If—mark me, Sir Percy!—if on any one day I do not appear before him at that hour, his orders are to shoot the prisoner on sight—"

The word was scarce out of his mouth; it broke in a hoarse spasm. Sir Percy had him by the throat, shook him indeed as he would a rat.

"You cur!" he said in an ominous whisper, his face quite close now to that of his enemy, his jaw set, his eyes no longer good-humoured and mildly scornful, but burning with the fire of a mighty, unbridled wrath. "You damned—insolent—miserable cur! As there is a Heaven above us—"

Then suddenly his grip relaxed, the whole face changed as if an unseen hand has swept away the fierce lines of anger and hate. The eyes softened beneath their heavy lids, the set lips broke into a mocking smile. He let go his hold of the Terrorist's throat; and the unfortunate man, panting and breathless, fell heavily against the wall. He tried to steady himself as best he could, but his knees were shaking, and faint and helpless, he finally collapses upon the nearest bench, the while Sir Percy straightened out his tall figure, with unruffled composure rubbed his slender hands one against the other, as if to free them from dust, and said, with gentle, good-humoured sarcasm:

"Do put your cravat straight, man! You look a disgusting object!"

He dragged the corner of a bench forward, sat astride upon it, and waited with perfect sang-froid, spy-glass in hand, while Chauvelin mechanically readjusted the set of his clothes.

"That's better?" he said approvingly. "Just the bow at the back of your neck—a little more to the right—now your cuffs.—Ah, you look quite tidy again!—a perfect picture, I vow, my dear M. Chambertin, of elegance and of a well-regulated mind!"

"Sir Percy—!" Chauvelin broke in with a vicious snarl.

"I entreat you to accept my apologies," the other rejoined with utmost courtesy. "I was on the verge of losing my temper, which we in England would call demmed bad form. I'll not transgress again. I pray you, proceed with what you were saying. So interesting—demmed interesting! You were talking about murdering a woman in cold blood, I think—"

"In hot blood, Sir Percy," Chauvelin rejoined more firmly. "Blood fired by thoughts of just revenge."

"Pardon! My mistake! As you were saying—"

"'Tis you who attack us. You—the meddlesome Scarlet Pimpernel, with your accursed gang!—We defend ourselves as best we can, using what weapons lie closest to our hand—"

"Such as murder, outrage, abduction—and wearing breeches the cut of which would provoke a saint to indignation."

"Murder, abduction, outrage, as you will, Sir Percy," Chauvelin retorted, as cool now as his opponent. "Had you ceased to interfere in the affairs of France when first you escaped punishment for your machinations, you would not now be in the sorry plight in which your own intrigues have at last landed you. Had you left us alone, we should by now have forgotten you."

"Which would have been such a pity, my dear M. Chambertin," Blakeney rejoined gravely. "I should not like you to forget me. Believe me, I have enjoyed life so much these past two years, I would not give up those pleasures even for that of seeing you and your friends have a bath or wear tidy buckles on your shoes."

"You will have cause to indulge in those pleasures within the next few days, Sir Percy," Chauvelin rejoined dryly.

"What?" Sir Percy exclaimed. "The Committee of Public Safety going to have a bath? Or the Revolutionary Tribunal? Which?"

But Chauvelin was determined not to lose his temper again. Indeed, he abhorred this man so deeply that he felt no anger against him, no resentment; only a cold, calculating hate.

"The pleasure of pitting your wits against the inevitable," he riposted dryly.

"Ah?" quoth Sir Percy airily. "The inevitable has always been such a good friend to me."

"Not this time, I fear, Sir Percy."

"Ah? You really mean this time to—?" and he made a significant gesture across his own neck.

"In as few days as possible."

Whereupon Sir Percy rose, and said solemnly:

"You are right there, my friend, quite right. Delays are always dangerous. If you mean to have my head, why—have if quickly. As for me, delays always bore me to tears."

He yawned and stretched his long limbs.

"I am getting so deemed fatigued," he said. "Do you not think this conversation has lasted quite long enough?"

"It was none of my seeking, Sir Percy."

"Mine, I grant you; mine, absolutely! But, hang it, man! I had to tell you that your breeches were badly cut."

"And I, that we are at your service, to end the business as soon as may be."

"To—?" And once more Sir Percy passed his firm hand across his throat. Then he gave a shudder.

"B-r-r-r!" he exclaimed. "I had no idea you were in such a demmed hurry."

"We await your pleasure, Sir Percy. Lady Blakeney must not be kept in suspense too long. Shall we say that, in three days—"

"Make if four, my dear M. Chambertin, and I am eternally your debtor."

"In four days then, Sir Percy," Chauvelin rejoined with pronounced sarcasm. "You see how ready I am to meet you in a spirit of conciliation! Four days, you say? Very well then; for four days more we keep our prisoner in those rooms upstairs.—After that—"

He paused, awed mayhap, in spite of himself, but the diabolical thought which had suddenly come into his mind—a sudden inspiration which in truth must have emanated from some unclean spirit with which he held converse. He looked the Scarlet Pimpernel—his enemy—squarely in the face. Conscious of his power, he was no longer afraid. What he longed for most at this moment was to see the least suspicion of a shadow dim the mocking light that danced in those lazy, supercilious eyes, or the merest tremor pass over the slender hand framed in priceless Mechlin lace.

For a while complete silence reigned in the bare, dank room—a silence broken only by the stertorous, rapid breathing of the one man who appeared moved. That man was not Sir Percy Blakeney. He indeed had remained quite still, spy-glass in hand, the good-humoured smile still dancing round his lips. Somewhere in the far distance a church clock struck the hour. Then only did Chauvelin put his full fiendish project into words.

"For four days," he reiterated with slow deliberation, "we keep our prisoner in the room upstairs.—After that, Captain Boyer has orders to shoot her."

Again there was silence—only for a second perhaps; whilst down by the Stygian creek, where Time never was, the elfish ghouls and impish demons set up a howl of delight at the hellish knavery of man.

Just one second, whilst Chauvelin waited for his enemy's answer to this monstrous pronouncement, and the very walls of the drabby apartment appeared to listen, expectant. Overhead, could be dimly heard the measured tramp of heavy feet upon the uncarpeted floor. And suddenly through the bare apartment there rang the sound of a quaint, light-hearted laugh.

"You really are the worst-dressed man I have ever come across, my good M. Chambertin," Sir Percy said with rare good-humour. "You must allow me to give you the address of a good little tailor I came across in the Latin Quarter the other day. No decent man would be seen walking up the guillotine in such a waistcoat as you are wearing.

382

Ad for your boots—" He yawned again. "You really must excuse me! I came home late from the theatre last night and have not had my usual hours of sleep. So, by your leave—"

"By all means, Sir Percy!" Chauvelin replied complacently. "At this moment you are a free man, because I happen to be alone and unarmed, and because this house is solidly built and my voice would not carry to the floor above. Also, because you are so nimble that no doubt you could give me the slip long before Captain Boyer and his men came to my rescue. Yes, Sir Percy; for the moment you are a free man! Free to walk out of this house unharmed. But even now, you are not as free as you would wish to be, eh? You are free to despise me, to overwhelm me with lofty scorn, to sharpen your wits at my expense; but you are not free to indulge your desire to squeeze the life out of me, to shake me as you would a rat. And shall I tell you why? Because you know now that if at a certain hour of the day I do not pay my daily visit to Captain Boyer upstairs, he will shoot his prisoner without the least compunction."

Whereupon Blakeney threw up his head and laughed heartily.

"You are absolutely priceless, my dear M. Chambertin!" he said gaily. "But you really must put your cravat straight. It has once again become disarranged—in the heat of your oratory, no doubt.—Allow me to offer you a pin."

And with inimitable affectation, he took a pin out of his own cravat and presented it to Chauvelin, who, unable to control his wrath, jumped to his feet.

"Sir Percy—!" he snarled.

But Blakeney placed a gentle, firm hand upon his shoulder, forcing him to sit down again.

"Easy, easy, my friend," he said. "Do not, I pray you, lose that composure for which you are so justly famous. There! Allow me to arrange your cravat for you. A gentle tug here," he added, suiting the action to the word, "a delicate flick there, and you are the most perfectly cravatted man in France!"

"Your insults leave me unmoved, Sir Percy," Chauvelin broke in savagely, and tried to free himself from the touch of those slender, strong hands that wandered so uncomfortably in the vicinity of his throat.

"No doubt," Blakeney riposted lightly, "that they are as futile as your threats. One does not insult a cur, any more than one threatens Sir Percy Blakeney—what?"

"You are right there, Sir Percy. The time for threats has gone by. And since you appear so vastly entertained—"

"I *am* vastly entertained, my dear M. Chambertin! How can I help it, when I see before me a miserable shred of humanity who does not even know how to keep his tie straight or his hair smooth, calmly—or almost calmly—talking of—Let me see, what were you talking of, my amiable friend?"

"Of the hostage, Sir Percy, which we hold until the happy day when the gallant Scarlet Pimpernel is a prisoner in our hands."

"'M, yes! He was that once before, was he not, my good sir? Then, too, you laid down mighty schemes for his capture."

"And we succeeded."

"By your usual amiable methods—lies, deceit, forgery. The latter has been useful to you this time too, eh?"

"What do you mean, Sir Percy?"

"You had need of the assistance of a fair lady for your schemes. She appeared disinclined to help you. So, when her inconvenient lover, Bertrand Moncrif, was happily dragged away from her path, you forged a letter, which the lady rightly looked upon as an insult. Because of that letter, she nourished a comfortable amount of spite against me, and lent you her aid in the fiendish outrage for which you are about to receive punishment."

He had raised his voice slightly while he spoke, and Chauvelin cast an apprehensive glance in the direction of the door behind which he guessed that Theresia Cabarrus must be straining her ears to listen.

"A pretty story, Sir Percy," he said with affected coolness. "And one that does infinite credit to your imagination. It is mere surmise on your part."

"What, my friend? What is surmise? That you gave a letter to Madame de Fontenay which you had concocted, and which I had never written? Why, man," he added with a laugh, "I saw you do it!"

"You? Impossible!"

"More impossible things than that will happen within the next few days, my good sir. I was outside the window of Madame de Fontenay's apartment during the whole of your interview with her. And the shutters were not as closely fastened as you would have wished. But why argue about it, my dear M. Chambertin, when you know quite well that I have given you a perfectly accurate *exposé* of the means which you employed to make a pretty and spoilt woman help you in your nefarious work?"

"Why argue, indeed?" Chauvelin retorted dryly. "The past is past. I'll answer to my country, which you outrage by your machinations, for the methods which I employ to circumvent them. Your concern and mine, my gallant friend, is solely with the future—with the next four days, in fact—After which, either the Scarlet Pimpernel is in our hands, or Lady Blakeney will be put against the wall upstairs and summarily shot."

Then only did something of his habitual lazy nonchalance go out of Blakeney's attitude. Just for the space of a few seconds he drew himself up to his full magnificent height, and from the summit of his splendid audacity and the consciousness of his own power, he looked down at the mean, cringing figure of the enemy who had hurled this threat of death against the woman he worshipped. Chauvelin vainly tried to keep up some semblance of dignity; he tried to meet the glance which no longer mocked, and to close his ears to the voice which, sonorous and commanding, now threatened in its turn.

"And you really believe," Sir Percy Blakeney said slowly and deliberately, "that you have the power to carry through your infamous schemes? That I—yes, I!—would allow you to come within measurable distance of their execution? Bah! my dear friend. You have learned nothing by past experience—not even this: that when you dared to lay your filthy hands upon Lady Blakeney, you and the whole pack of assassins who have terrorised this beautiful country far too long, struck the knell of your ultimate doom. You have dared to measure your strength against mine by perpetrating an outrage so monstrous in my sight that, to punish you, I—even I!—will sweep you off the face of the earth and send you to join the pack of unclean ghouls who have aided you in your crimes. After which—thank the Lord!—the earth, being purged of your presence, will begin to smell sweetly again."

Chauvelin made a vain effort to laugh, to shrug his shoulders, to put on those airs of insolence which came so naturally to his opponent. No doubt the strain of this long interview with his enemy had told upon his nerves. Certain it is that at this moment, though he was conscious enough to rail inwardly at his own cowardice, he was utterly unable to move or to retort. His limbs felt heavy as lead, an icy shudder was coursing down his spine. It seemed in truth as if some uncanny ghoul had entered the dreary, dank apartment and with gaunt, invisible hand was tolling a silent passing bell—the death-knell of all his ambitions and all his hopes. He closed his eyes, for he felt giddy and sick. When he opened his eyes again he was alone.

CHAPTER 26

A Dream

Chauvelin had not yet regained full possession of his faculties, when a few seconds later he saw Theresia Cabarrus glide swiftly across the antechamber. She appeared to him like a ghost—a pixie who had found her way through a keyhole. But she threw him a glance of contempt that was very human, very feminine indeed, and the next moment she was gone.

Outside on the landing she paused. Straining her ears, she caught the sound of a firm footfall slowly descending the stairs. She ran down a few steps, then called softly:

"Milor!"

The footsteps paused, and a pleasant voice gave quiet reply:

"At your service, fair lady!"

Theresia, shrewd as well as brave, continued to descend. She was not in the least afraid. Instinct had told her before now that no woman need ever have the slightest fear of that elegant milor with the quaint laugh and gently mocking mien, whom she had learned to know over in England.

Midway down the stairs she came face to face with him, and when she paused, panting, a little breathless with excitement, he said with perfect courtesy:

"You did me the honour to call me, *Madame?*"

"Yes, milor," she replied, in a quick, eager whisper. "I heard every word that passed between you and Citizen Chauvelin."

"Of course, you did, dear lady," he rejoined with a smile. "If a woman once resisted the temptation of putting a shell-like ear to a keyhole, the world would lose many a cause for entertainment."

"That letter, milor—" she broke in impatiently.

"Which letter, *Madame?*"

"That insulting letter to me—when you took Moncrif away.—You never wrote it?"

"Did you really think that I did?" he retorted.

"No. I ought to have guessed—the moment that I saw you in England—"

"And realised that I was not a cad—what?"

"Oh, milor!" she protested. "But why—why did you not tell me before?"

"It had escaped my memory. And if I remember rightly, you spent

386

most of the time when I had the honour of walking with you, in giving me elaborate and interesting accounts of your difficulties, and I, in listening to them."

"Oh!" she exclaimed vehemently. "I hate that man! I hate him!"

"In truth, he is not a lovable personality. But, by your leave, I presume that you did not desire to speak with me so that we might discuss our friend Chauvelin's amiable qualities."

"No, no, milor!" she rejoined quickly. "I called to you because—"

Then she paused for a moment or two, as if to collect her thoughts. Her eager eyes strove to pierce the gloom that enveloped the figure of the bold adventurer. She could only see the dim outline of his powerful figure, the light from above striking on his smooth hair, the elegantly tied bow at the nape of his neck, the exquisite filmy lace at his throat and wrists. His head was slightly bent, one arm in a curve supported his *chapeau-bras*, his whole attitude was one befitting a salon rather than this dank hovel, where death was even now at his elbow; it was as cool and unperturbed as it had been on that May-day evening, in the hawthorn scented lanes of Kent.

"Milor," she said abruptly, "you told me one—you remember?— that you were what you English call a sportsman. Is that so?"

"I hope always to remain that, dead lady," he replied with a smile.

"Does that mean," she queried, with a pretty air of deference and hesitation, "does that mean a man who would under no circumstances harm a woman?"

"I think so."

"Now even if she—if she has sinned—transgressed against him?"

"I don't quite understand, *Madame*," he rejoined simply. "And, time being short—Are you perchance speaking of yourself?"

"Yes. I have done you an injury, milor."

"A very great one indeed," he assented gravely.

"Could you," she pleaded, raising earnest, tear-filled eyes to his, "could you bring yourself to believe that I have been nothing but a miserable, innocent tool?"

"So was the lady upstairs innocent, *Madame*," he broke in quietly.

"I know," she retorted with a sigh. "I know. I would never dare to plead, as you must hate me so."

He shrugged his shoulders with an air of carelessness.

"Oh!" he said. "Does a man every hate a pretty woman?"

"He forgives her, milor," she entreated, "if he is a true sportsman."

"Indeed? You astonish me, dear lady. But in verity you all in this unhappy country are full of surprises for a plain, blunt-headed Britisher. Now what, I wonder," he added, with a light, good-humoured laugh, "would my forgiveness be worth to you?"

"Everything!" she replied earnestly. "I was deceived by that abominable liar, who knew how to play upon a woman's pique. I am ashamed, wretched.—Oh, cannot you believe me? And I would give worlds to atone!"

He laughed in his quiet, gently ironical way.

"You do not happen to possess worlds, dear lady. All that you have is youth and beauty and ambition, and life. You would forfeit all those treasures if you really tried to atone."

"But—"

"Lady Blakeney is a prisoner.—You are her jailer.—Her precious life is the hostage for yours."

"Milor—" she murmured.

"From my heart, I wish you well, fair one," he broke in lightly. "Believe me, the pagan gods that fashioned you did not design you for tragedy—And if you ran counter to your friend Chauvelin's desires, I fear me that that pretty neck of yours would suffer. A thing to be avoided at all costs! And now," he added, "have I your permission to go? My position here is somewhat precarious, and for the next four days I cannot afford the luxury of entertaining so fine a lady, by running my head into a noose."

He was on the point of going when she placed a restraining hand upon his arm.

"Milor!" she pleaded.

"At your service, dear lady!"

"Is there naught I can do for you?"

He looked at her for a moment or two, and even through the gloom she caught his quizzical look and the mocking lines around his firm lips.

"You can ask Lady Blakeney to forgive you," he said, with a thought more seriousness than was habitual to him. "She is an angel; she might do it."

"And if she does?"

"She will know what to do, to convey her thoughts to me."

"Nay! but I'll do more than that, milor," Theresia continued excitedly. "I will tell her that I shall pray night and day for your deliverance and hers. I will tell her that I have seen you, and that you are well."

"Ah, if you did that—" he exclaimed, almost involuntarily.

"You would forgive me, too?" she pleaded.

"I would do more than that, fair one. I would make you Queen of France, in all but name."

"What do you mean?" she murmured.

"That I would then redeem the promise which I made to you that evening, in the lane—outside Dover. Do you remember?"

She made no reply, closed her eyes; and her vivid fancy, rendered doubly keen by the mystery which seemed to encompass him as with a supernal mantle, conjured up the vision of that unforgettable evening: the moonlight, the scent of the hawthorn, the call of the thrush. She saw him stooping before her, and kissing her finger-tips, even whilst her ears recalled every word he had spoken and every inflexion of his mocking voice:

"Let me rather put it differently, dear lady," he had said then. "One day the exquisite Theresia Cabarrus, the Egeria of the Terrorists, the *fiancée* of the great Tallien, might need the help of the Scarlet Pimpernel."

And she, angered, piqued by his coolness, thirsting for revenge for the insult which she believed he had put upon her, had then protested earnestly:

"I would sooner die," she had boldly asserted, "than seek your help, milor!"

And now, at this hour, here in this house where Death lurked in every corner, she could still hear his retort:

"Here in Dover, perhaps.—But in France?"

How right he had been!—How right! She—who had thought herself so strong, so powerful—what was she indeed but a miserable tool in the hands of men who would break her without scruple if she ran counter to their will? Remorse was not for her—atonement too great a luxury for a tool of Chauvelin to indulge in. The black, hideous taint, the sin of having dragged this splendid man and that innocent woman to their death, must rest upon her soul for ever. Even now she was jeopardizing his life, every moment that she kept him talking in this house. And yet the impulse to speak with him, to hear him say a word of forgiveness, had been unconquerable. One moment she longed for him to go; the next she would have sacrificed much to keep him by her side. When he wished to go, she held him back. Now that, with his wonted careless disregard of danger, he appeared willing to linger, she sought for the right words wherewith to bid him go.

He seemed to divine her thoughts, remained quite still while she stood there with eyes closed, in one brief second reviewing the past. All! All! It all came back to her: her challenge to him, his laughing retort.

"You mean," she said at parting, "that you would risk your life to save mine?"

"I should not risk my life, dear lady," he had said, with his puzzling smile; "But I should—God help me!—do my best, if the need arose, to save yours."

Then he had gone, and she had stood under the porch of the quaint old English inn and watched his splendid figure as it disappeared down the street. She had watched, puzzled, uncomprehending, her heart already stirred by that sweet, sad ache which at this hour brought tears to her eyes—the aching sorrow of that which could never, never be. Ah! if it had been her good fortune to have come across such a man, to have aroused in him that admiration for herself which she so scorned in others, how different, how very different would life have been! And she fell to envying the poor prisoner upstairs, who owned the most precious treasure life can offer to any woman: the love of a fine man. Two hot tears came slowly through her closed eyes, coursing down her cheeks.

"Why so sad, dear lady?" he asked gently.

She could not speak for the moment, only murmured vaguely:

"Four days—"

"Four days," he retorted gaily, "as you say! In four days, either I or a pack of assassins will be dead."

"Oh, what will become of me?" she sighed.

"Whatever you choose."

"You are bold, milor," she rejoined more calmly. "And you are brave. Alas! what can you do, when the most powerful hands in France are against you?"

"Smite them, dear lady," he replied airily. "Smite them! Then turn my back upon this fair land. It will no longer have need of me." Then he made her a courteous bow. "May I have the honour of escorting you upstairs? Your friend M. Chauvelin will be awaiting you."

The name of her taskmaster brought Theresia back to the realities of life. Gone was the dream of a while ago, when subconsciously her mind had dwelt upon a sweet might-have-been. The man was nothing to her—less than nothing; a common spy, so her friends averred. Even if he had not presumed to write her an insulting letter, he was still the enemy—the foe whose hand was raised against her own country and against those with whose fortunes she had thrown in her lot. Even now, she ought to be calling loudly for help, rouse the house with her cries, so that this spy, this enemy, might be brought down before her eyes. Instead of which, she felt her heart beating with apprehension lest his quiet even voice be heard on the floor above, and he be caught in the snare which those who feared and hated him had laid for him.

Indeed, she appeared far more conscious of danger than he was; and while she chided herself for her folly in having called to him, he was standing before her as if he were in a drawing-room, holding out his arm to escort her in to dinner. His foot was on the step, ready to ascend, even whilst Theresia's straining ears caught the sound of other footsteps up above: footsteps of men—real men, those!—who were set up there to watch for the coming of the Scarlet Pimpernel, and whose vigilance had been spurred by promise of reward and by threat of death. She pushed his arm aside almost roughly.

"You are mad, milor!" she said, in a choked murmur. "Such fool-hardiness, when your life is in deadly jeopardy, becomes criminal folly—"

"The best of life," he said airily, "is folly. I would not miss this moment for a kingdom!"

She felt like a creature under a spell. He took her hand and drew it through his arm. She went up the steps beside him.

Every moment she thought that one or more of the soldiers would be coming down, or that Chauvelin, impatient at her absence, might step out upon the landing. The dank, murky air seemed alive with ominous whisperings, of stealthy treads upon the stone. Theresia dared not look behind her, fearful lest the grim presence of Death itself be suddenly made manifest before her.

On the landing he took leave of her, stooped and kissed her hand.

"Why, how cold it is!" he remarked with a smile.

His was perfectly steady and warm. The very feel of it seemed to give her strength. She raised her eyes to his.

"Milor," she entreated, "on my knees I beg of you not to toy with your life any longer."

"Toy with my life?" he retorted gaily. "Nothing is further from my thoughts."

"You must know that every second which you spend in this house if fraught with the greatest possible danger."

"Danger? Ne'er a bit, dear lady! I am no longer in danger, now that you are my friend."

The next moment he was gone. For a while, Theresia's straining ears still caught the sound of his form footfall upon the stone steps. Then all was still; and she was left wondering if, in very truth, the last few minutes on the dark stairs had not all been part of a dream.

CHAPTER 27

Terror or Ambition

Chauvelin had sufficiently recovered from the emotions of the past half-hour to speak coolly and naturally to Theresia. Whether he knew that she had waylaid Sir Percy Blakeney on the stairs or no, she could not conjecture. He made no reference to his interview with the Scarlet Pimpernel, nor did he question her directly as to whether she had overheard what passed between them.

Certainly, his attitude was a more dictatorial one than it had been before. Some of his first words to her contained a veiled menace. Whether the sense of coming triumph gave him a fresh measure of that arrogance which past failures had never wholly subdued, or whether terror for the future caused him to bluster and to threaten, it were impossible to say.

"Vigilance!" he said to Theresia, after a curt greeting. "Incessant vigilance, night and day, is what your country demands of you now, citizeness! All our lives now depend upon our vigilance."

"Yours perhaps, citizen," she rejoined coolly. "You seem to forget that I am not bound—"

"You? Not bound?" he broke in roughly, and with a strident laugh. "Not bound to aid in bringing the most bitter enemy of your country to his knees? Not bound, now that success is in sight?"

"You only obtained my help by a subterfuge," she retorted; "by a forged letter and a villainous lie—"

"Bah! Are you going to tell me, citizeness, that all means are not justifiable when dealing with those whose hands are raised against France? Forgery?" he went on, with passionate earnestness. "Why not? Outrage? Murder? I would commit every crime in order to serve the country which I love and hound her enemies to death. The only crime that is unjustifiable, *citoyenne*, is indifference. You? Not bound? Wait! Wait, I say! And if by your indifference or your apathy we fail once more to bring that elusive enemy to book, wait then until you stand at the bar of the people's tribunal, and in the face of France, who called to you for help, of France, who beset by a hundred foes, stretch appealing arms to you, her daughter, you turned a deaf ear to her entreaties, and, shrugging your fair shoulders, calmly pleaded, 'Bah! I was not bound!'"

He paused, carried away by his own enthusiasm, feeling perhaps that he had gone too far, or else had said enough to enforce the obedience which he exacted. After a while, since Theresia remained silent too, he added more quietly:

"If we capture the Scarlet Pimpernel this time, citizeness, Robespierre shall know from my lips that it is to you and to you alone that he owes this triumph over the enemy whom he fears above all. Without you, I could not have set the trap out of which he cannot now escape."

"He can escape! He can!" she retorted defiantly. "The Scarlet Pimpernel is too clever, too astute, too audacious, to fall into your trap."

"Take care, *citoyenne*, take care! Your admiration for that elusive hero carries you beyond the bounds of prudence."

"Bah! If he escapes, 'tis you who will be blamed—"

"And 'tis you who will suffer, *citoyenne*," he riposted blandly. With which parting shaft he left her certain that she would ponder over his threats as well as over his bold promise of a rich reward.

Terror and ambition! Death, or the gratitude of Robespierre! How well did Chauvelin gauge the indecision, the shallowness of a fickle woman's heart! Theresia, left to herself, had only those two alternatives over which to ponder. Robespierre's gratitude, which meant that the admiration which already he felt for her would turn to stronger passion. He was still heart-whole, that she knew. The regard which he was supposed to feel for the humble cabinet-maker's daughter could only be a passing fancy. The dictator of France must choose a mate worthy of his power and of his ambition; his friends would see to that. Robespierre's gratitude! What a vista of triumphs and of glory did that eventuality open up before her, what dizzy heights of satisfied ambition! And what a contrast if Chauvelin's scheme failed in the end!

"Wait," he had cried, "until you stand at the bar of the people's tribunal and plead indifference!"

Theresia shuddered. Despite the close atmosphere of the apartment, she was shivering with cold. Her loneliness, her isolation, here in this house, where an appalling and grim tragedy was even now in preparation, filled her with sickening dread. Overhead she could hear the soldiers moving about, and in one of the rooms close by her sensitive ear caught the sound of Mother Théot's shuffling tread.

But the sound that was most insistent, that hammered away at her heart until she could have screamed with the pain, was the echo of a lazy, somewhat inane laugh and of a gently mocking voice that said lightly:

"The best of life is folly, dear lady. I would not miss this moment for a kingdom."

Her hand went up to her throat to smother the sobs that would rise up against her will. Then she called all her self-control, all her ambition, to her aid. This present mood was sentimental nonsense, an abyss created by an over-sensitive heart, into which she might be falling headlong. What was this Englishman to her that thought of his death should prove such mental agony? As for him, he only laughed at her; despised her still, probably; hated her for the injury she had done to that woman upstairs whom he loved.

Impatient to get away from this atmosphere of tragedy and of mysticism which was preying on her nerves, Theresia called peremptorily to Mother Théot, and when the old woman came shuffling out of her room, demanded her cloak and hood.

"Have you seen aught of Citizen Moncrif?" she asked, just before going away.

"I caught sight of him over the way," Catherine Théot replied, "watching this house, as he always does when you, *citoyenne*, are in it."

"Ah!" the imperious beauty retorted, with a thought of spite in her mellow voice. "Would you could give him a potion, Mother, to cure him of his infatuation for me!"

"Despise no man's love, *citoyenne*," the witch retorted sententiously. "Even that poor vagabond's blind passion may yet prove thy salvation."

A moment or two later Theresia was once more on the dark stairs where she had dreamed of the handsome milor. She sighed as she ran swiftly down—sighed and looked half-fearfully about her. She still felt his presence through the gloom; and in the ghostly light that feebly illumined the corner whereon he had stood, she still vaguely saw in spirit his tall straight figure, stooping whilst he kissed her hand. At one moment she was quite sure that she heard his voice and the echo of his pleasant laugh.

Down below, Bertrand Moncrif was waiting for her, silent, humble, with the look of a faithful watch-dog upon his pale, wan face.

"You make yourself ill, my poor Bertrand," Theresia said, not unkindly, seeing that he stood aside to let her pass, fearful of a rebuff if he dared speak to her. "I am in no danger, I assure you; and this constant dogging of my footsteps can do no good to you or to me."

"But it can do no harm," he pleaded earnestly. "Something tells me, Theresia, that danger does threaten you, unbeknown to you, from a quarter least expected."

"Bah!" she retorted lightly. "And if it did, you could not avert it."

He made a desperate effort to check the words of passionate protestations which rose to his lips. He longed to protect her from harm, how happy he would be if he might die for her. But obviously he dared not say what lay nearest to his heart. All he could do now was to talk silently by her side as far as her lodgings in the Rue Villedot, grateful for this small privilege, uncomplaining and almost happy because she tolerated his presence, and because while she walked the ends of her long scarf stirred by the breeze would now and again flutter against his cheek.

Miserable Bertrand! He had laden his soul with an abominable crime for this woman's sake; and he had not even the satisfaction of feeling that she gave him an infinitesimal measure of gratitude.

CHAPTER 28

In the Meanwhile

Chauvelin, who, despite his many failures, was still one of the most conspicuous—since he was one of the most unscrupulous—members of the Committee of Public Safety, had not attended its sittings for some days. He had been too deeply absorbed in his own schemes to trouble about those of his colleagues. In truth, the coup which he was preparing was so stupendous, and if it succeeded his triumph would be so magnificent, that he could well afford to hold himself aloof. Those who were still inclined to scorn and to scoff at him today would be his most cringing sycophants on the morrow.

He knew well enough—none better—that during this time the political atmosphere in the Committees and the Clubs was nothing short of electrical. He felt, as everyone did, that something catastrophic was in the air, that death, more self-evident than ever before, lurked at every man's elbow, and stalked round the corner of every street.

Robespierre, the tyrant, the autocrat whose mere word swayed the multitude, remained silent and impenetrable, absent from every gathering. He only made brief appearances at the Convention, and there sat moody and self-absorbed. Everyone knew that this man, dictator in all but name, was meditating a Titanic attack upon his enemies. His veiled threats, uttered during his rare appearances at the speaker's tribune, embraced even the most popular, the most prominent, amongst the representatives of the people. Everyone, in fact, who was likely to stand in his way when he was ready to snatch the supreme power. His intimates—Couthon, St. Just, and the others—openly accused of planning a dictatorship for their chief, hardly took the trouble to deny the impeachment, even whilst Tallien and his friends, feeling that the tyrant had already decreed their doom, went about like ghostly shadows, not daring to raise their voice in the Convention lest the first word they uttered brought down the sword of his lustful wrath upon their heads.

The Committee of Public Safety—now re-named the Revolutionary Committee—strove on the other hand by a recrudescence of cruelty to ingratiate itself with the potential dictator and to pose before the people as alone pure and incorruptible, blind in justice, inexorable where the safety of the Republic was concerned. Thus, an abominable emulation of vengeance and of persecution went on between the Committee and Robespierre's party, wherein neither side could afford to give in, for fear of being accused of apathy and of moderation.

Chauvelin, for the most part, had kept out of the turmoil. He felt that in his hands lay the destiny of either party. His one thought was of the Scarlet Pimpernel and of his imminent capture, knowing that, with the most inveterate opponent of revolutionary excesses in his hands, he would within an hour be in a position to link his triumph with one or the other of the parties—either with Robespierre and his herd of butchers, or with Tallien and the Moderates.

He was the mysterious and invisible *deus ex machina,* who *anon,* when it suited his purpose, would reveal himself in his full glory as the man who had tracked down and brought to the guillotine the most dangerous enemy of the revolutionary government. And, so easily is a multitude swayed, that that one fact would bring him popularity transcending that of every other man in France. He, Chauvelin, the despised, the derided, whose name had become synonymous with Failure, would then with a word sweep those aside who had mocked him, hurl his enemies from their pedestals, and name at will the rulers of France All within four days!

And of these, two had gone by.

These days in mid-July had been more than usually sultry. It seemed almost as if Nature had linked herself with the passions of men, and hand in hand with Vengeance, Lust and Cruelty, had rendered the air hot and heavy with the presage of oncoming storm.

For Marguerite Blakeney these days had gone by like a nightmare. Cut off from all knowledge of the outside world, without news from her husband for the past forty-eight hours, she was enduring mental agony such as would have broken a weaker or less trusting spirit.

Two days ago, she had received a message, a few lines hastily scribbled by an unknown hand, and brought to her by the old woman who waited upon her.

"I have seen him," the message said. "He is well and full of hope. I pray God for your deliverance and his, but help can only come by a miracle."

The message was written in a feminine hand, with no clue as to the writer.

Since then, nothing.

Marguerite had not seen Chauvelin again, for which indeed she thanked Heaven on her knees. But every day at a given hour she was conscious of his presence outside her door. She heard his voice in the vestibule: there would be a word or two of command, the grounding of arms, then some whispered talking; and presently Chauvelin's stealthy footstep would slink up to her door. And Marguerite would remain still as a mouse that scents the presence of a cat, holding her breath, life almost at a standstill in this agony of expectation.

The remainder of the day time hung with a leaden weight on her hands. She was given no books to read, not a needle wherewith to busy herself. She had no one to speak to save old Mother Théot, who waited on her and brought her her meals, nearly always in silence, and with a dour mien which checked any attempt at conversation.

For company, the unfortunate woman had nothing but her own thoughts, her fears which grew in intensity, and her hopes which were rapidly dwindling, as hour followed hour and day succeeded day in dreary monotony. No sound around her save the incessant tramp, tramp of sentries at her door, and every two hours the changing of the guard in the vestibule outside; then the whispered colloquies, the soldiers playing at cards or throwing dice, the bibulous songs, the ribald laughter, the obscene words flung aloud like bits of filthy rag; the life, in fact, that revolved around her jailers and seemed at a standstill within her prison walls.

In the late afternoons the air would become insufferably hot, and Marguerite would throw open the window and sit beside it, her gaze fixed upon the horizon far away, her hands lying limp and moist upon her lap.

Then she would fall to dreaming. Her thoughts, swifter than flight of swallows, would cross the sea and go roaming across country to her stately home in Richmond, where at this house the moist, cool air was fragrant with the scent of late roses and of lime blossom, and the murmur of the river lapping the mossy bank whispered of love and of peace. In her dream she would see the tall figure of her beloved coming toward her. The sunset was playing upon his smooth hair and upon his strong, slender hands, always outstretched toward the innocent and the weak. She would hear his dear voice calling her name, feel his arms around her, and her senses swooning in the ecstasy of that perfect moment which comes just before a kiss.

She would dream—only to wake up the next moment to hear the church clock of St. Antoine striking seven, and a minute or two later that ominous shuffling footstep outside her door, those whisperings, the grounding of arms, a burst of cruel laughter, which brought her from the dizzy heights of illusive happiness back to the hideous reality of her own horrible position, and of the deadly danger which lay in wait for her beloved.

Chapter 29

The Close of the Second Day

Soon after seven o'clock that evening the storm which had threatened all day burst in its full fury. A raging gale tore at the dilapidated roofs of this squalid corner of the great city and lashed the mud of the streets into miniature cascades. Soon the rain fell in torrents; one clap of thunder followed on another with appalling rapidity, and the dull, leaden sky was rent with vivid flashes of lightning.

Chauvelin, who had paid his daily visit to the captain in charge of the prisoner in the Rue de la Planchette, was unable to proceed homewards. Wrapped in his cloak, he decided to wait in the disused storage-room below until it became possible for an unfortunate pedestrian to sally forth into the open.

There seems no doubt that at this time the man's very soul was on the rack. His nerves were stretched to breaking point, not only by incessant vigilance, by obsession of the one idea, the one aim, but also by multifarious incidents which his overwrought imagination magnified into attempts to rob him of his prey.

He trusted no one—not Mother Théot, not the men upstairs, not Theresia: least of all Theresia. And his tortured brain invented and elaborated schemes whereby he set one set of spies to watch another, one set of sleuthhounds to run after another, in a kind of vicious and demoniac circle of mistrust and denunciation. Nor did he trust himself any longer: neither his instinct nor his eyes, nor his ears. His intimates—and he had very few of these—said of him at that time that, if he had his way, he would have had every tatterdemalion in the city branded, like Rateau, lest they were bribed or tempted into changing identities with the Scarlet Pimpernel.

Whilst waiting for a lull in the storm, he was pacing up and down the dank and murky storage house, striving by febrile movements to calm his nerves. Shivering, despite the closeness of the atmosphere, he kept the folds of his mantle closely wrapped around his shoulders.

It was impossible to keep the outer doors open, because the rain beat in wildly on that side, and the place would have been in utter darkness but for an old grimy lanthorn which some prudent hand had set up on a barrel in the centre of the vast space, and which shed a feeble circle of light around. The latch of the wicket appeared to be broken, for the small door, driven by the wind, flapped backwards and forwards with irritating ceaselessness. At one time, Chauvelin tried to improvise some means of fastening it, for the noise helped to exacerbate his nerves and, leaning out into the street in order to seize hold of the door, he saw the figure of a man, bent nearly double in the teeth of the gale, shuffling across the street from the direction of the Porte St. Antoine.

It was then nearly eight o'clock, and the light treacherous, but despite the veil of torrential rain which intervene between him and that shuffling figure, something in the gait, the stature, the stoop of the wide, bony shoulders, appeared unpleasantly familiar. The man's head and shoulders were wrapped in a tattered piece of sacking, which he held close to his chest. His arms were bare, as were his shins, and on his feet, he had a pair of *sabots* stuffed with straw.

Midway across the street he paused, and a tearing fit of coughing seemed to render him momentarily helpless. Chauvelin's first instinct prompted him to run to the stairs and to call for assistance from the Captain Boyer. Indeed, he was halfway up to the first floor when, looking down, he saw that the man had entered the place through the wicket-door. Still coughing and spluttering, he had divested himself of his piece of sacking and was crouching down against the barrel in the centre of the room and trying to warm his hands by holding them against the glass sides of the old lanthorn.

From where he stood, Chauvelin could see the dim outline of the man's profile, the chin ornamented with a three-days' growth of beard, the lank hair plastered above the pallid forehead, the huge bones, coated with grime, that protruded through the rags that did duty for a shirt. The sleeves of this tattered garment hung away from the arm, displaying a fiery, inflamed weal, shaped like the letter "M," that had recently been burned into the flesh with a branding iron.

The sight of that mark upon the vagabond's arm caused Chauvelin to pause a moment, then to come down the stairs again.

"Citizen Rateau!" he called.

The man jumped as if he had been struck with a whip, tried to struggle to his feet, but collapsed on the floor, while a terrible fit of coughing took his breath away. Chauvelin, standing beside the barrel, looked down with a grim smile on this miserable wreckage of humanity whom he had so judiciously put out of the way of further mischief. The dim flicker of the lanthorn illumine the gaunt, bony arm, so that the charred flesh stood out like a crimson, fiery string against a coating of grime.

Rateau appeared terrified, scared by the sudden apparition of the man who had inflicted the shameful punishment upon him. Chauvelin's face, lighted from below by the lanthorn, did indeed appear grim and forbidding. Some few seconds elapsed before the coalheaver had recovered sufficiently to stand on his feet.

"I seem to have scared you, my friend," Chauvelin remarked dryly.

"I—I did not know," Rateau stammered with a painful wheeze, "that anyone was here—I came for shelter—"

"I am here for shelter, too," Chauvelin rejoined, "and did not see you enter."

"Mother Théot allows me to sleep here," Rateau went on mildly. "I have had no work for two days—not since..." And he looked down ruefully upon his arm. "People think I am an escaped felon," he explained with snivelling timidity. "And as I have always lived just from hand to mouth—"

He paused, and cast an obsequious glance on the Terrorist, who retorted dryly:

"Better men than you, my friend, live from hand to mouth these days. Poverty," he continued with grim sarcasm, "exalts a man in this glorious revolution of ours. 'Tis riches that shame him."

Rateau's branded arm went up to his lanky hair, and he scratched his head dubiously.

"Aye," he nodded, obviously uncomprehending; "perhaps! But I'd like to taste some of that shame!"

Chauvelin shrugged his shoulders and turned on his heel. The thunder sounded a little more distant and the rain less violent for the moment, and he strode toward the door.

"The children run after me now," Rateau continued dolefully. "In my quartier, the *concierge* turned me out of my lodging. They keep asking me what I have done to be branded like a convict."

Chauvelin laughed.

"Tell them you've been punished for serving the English spy," he said.

"The Englishman paid me well, and I am very poor," Rateau retorted meekly. "I could serve the State now—if it would pay me well."

"Indeed? How?"

"By telling you something, citizen, which you would like to know."

"What is it?"

At once the instinct of the informer, of the sleuthhound, was on the *qui vive*. The coalheaver's words, the expression of cunning on his ugly face, the cringing obsequiousness of his attitude, all suggested the spirit of intrigue, of underhand dealing, of lies and denunciations, which were as the breath of life to this master-spy. He retraced his steps, came and sat upon a pile of rubbish beside the barrel, and when Rateau, terrified apparently at what he had said, made a motion as if to slink away, Chauvelin called him back peremptorily.

"What is it, Citizen Rateau," he said curtly, "that you could tell me, and that I would like to know?"

Rateau was cowering in the darkness, trying to efface his huge bulk and to smother his rasping cough.

"You have said too much already," Chauvelin went on harshly, "to hold your tongue. And you have nothing to fear—everything to gain. What is it?"

For a moment Rateau leaned forward, struck the ground with his fist.

"Am I to be paid this time?" he asked.

"If you speak the truth—yes."

"How much?"

"That depends on what you tell me. And now, if you hold your tongue, I shall call to the citizen captain upstairs and send you to jail."

The coalheaver appeared to crouch yet further into himself. He looked like a huge, shapeless mass in the gloom. His huge yellow teeth could be heard chattering.

"Citizen Tallien will send me to the guillotine," he murmured.

"What has Citizen Tallien to do with it?"

"He pays great attention to the Citoyenne Cabarrus."

"And it is about her?"

Rateau nodded.

"What is it?" Chauvelin reiterated harshly.

"She is playing you false, citizen," Rateau murmured in a hoarse breath, and crawled like a long, bulky worm a little closer to the Terrorist.

"How?"

"She is in league with the Englishman."

"How do you know?"

"I saw her here—two days ago.—You remember, citizen—after you—"

"Yes, yes!" Chauvelin cried impatiently.

"Sergeant Chazot took me to the cavalry barracks.—They gave me to drink—and I don't remember much what happened. But when I was myself again, I know that my arm was very sore, and when I looked down I saw this awful mark on it.—I was just outside the Arsenal then.—How I got there I don't know.—I suppose Sergeant Chazot brought me back.—He says I was howling for Mother Théot.—She has marvellous salves, you know, citizen."

"Yes, yes!"

"I came in here.—My head still felt very strange—and my arm felt like living fire. Then I heard voices—they came from the stairs.—I looked about me, and saw them standing there—"

Rateau, leaning upon one arm, stretched out the other and pointed to the stairs, Chauvelin, with a violent gesture, seized him by the wrist.

"Who?" he queried harshly. "Who was standing there?"

His glance followed the direction in which the coalheaver was pointing, then instinctively wandered back and fastened on that fiery letter "M" which had been seared into the vagabond's flesh.

"The Englishman and Citoyenne Cabarrus," Rateau replied feebly, for he had winced with pain under the excited grip of the Terrorist.

"You are certain?"

"I heard them talking—"

"What did they say?"

"I do not know.—But I saw the Englishman kiss the *citoyenne's* hand before they parted."

"And what happened after that?"

"The *citoyenne* went to Mother Théot's apartment and the Englishman came down the stairs. I had just time to hide behind that pile of rubbish. He did not see me."

Chauvelin uttered a savage curse of disappointment.

"Is that all?" he exclaimed.

"The State will pay me?" Rateau murmured vaguely.

"Not a *sou!*" Chauvelin retorted roughly. "And if Citizen Tallien hears this pretty tale—"

"I can swear to it?"

"Bah! Citoyenne Cabarrus will swear that you lied. 'Twill be her word against that of a mudlark!"

"Nay!" Rateau retorted. "'Twill be more than that."

"What then?"

"Will you swear to protect me, citizen, if Citizen Tallien—"

"Yes, yes! I'll protect you.—And the guillotine has no time to trouble about suck muck-worms as you!"

"Well, then, citizen," Rateau went on in a hoarse murmur, "if you will go to the *citoyenne's* lodgings in the Rue Villedot, I can show you where the Englishman hides the clothes wherewith he disguises himself—and the letters which he writes to the *citoyenne* when—"

He paused, obviously terrified at the awesome expression of the other man's face. Chauvelin had allowed the coalheaver's wrist to drop out of his grasp. He was sitting quite still, silent and grim, his thin, claw-like hands closely clasped together and held between his knees. The flickering light of the lanthorn distorted his narrow face, lengthened the shadows beneath the nose and chin, threw a high light just below the brows, so that the pale eyes appeared to gleam with an unnatural flame. Rateau hardly dared to move. He lay like a huge bundle of rags in the inky blackness beyond the circle of light projected by the lanthorn; his breath came and went with a dragging, hissing sound, now and then broken by a painful cough.

For a moment or two there was silence in the great disused storeroom—a silence broken only by the thunder, dull and distant now, and the ceaseless, monotonous patter of the rain. Then Chauvelin murmured between his teeth:

"If I thought that she—" But he did not complete the sentence, jumped to his feet and approached the big mass of rags and humanity that coward in the gloom. "Get up, Citizen Rateau!" he commanded.

The asthmatic giant struggled to his knees. His wooden shoes had slipped off his feet. He groped for them, and with trembling hands contrived to put them on again.

"Get up!" Chauvelin reiterated, with a snarl like an angry tiger.

He took a small tablet and a leaden point from his pocket, and stooping toward the light he scribbled a few words, and then handed the tablet to Rateau.

"Take this over to the commissary of the Section in the Place du Carrousel. Half a dozen men and a captain will be detailed to go with you to the lodgings of the Citoyenne Cabarrus in the Rue Villedot. You will find me there. Go!"

Rateau's hand trembled visibly as he took the tablets. He was obviously terrified at what he had done. But Chauvelin paid no further heed to him. He had given him his orders, knowing well that they would be obeyed. The man had gone too far to draw back. It never entered Chauvelin's head that the coalheaver might have lied. He had no cause for spite against the Citoyenne Cabarrus, and the fair Spaniard stood on too high a pinnacle of influence for false denunciations to touch her. The Terrorist waited until Rateau had quietly slunk out by the wicket door; then he turned on his heel and quickly went up the stairs.

In the vestibule on the top floor he called to Capitaine Boyer.

"Citizen Captain," he said at the top of his voice, "You remember that tomorrow eve is the end of the third day?"

"*Pardi!*" the captain retorted gruffly. "Is anything changed?"

"No."

"Then, unless by the eve of the fourth day that cursed Englishman is not in our hands, my orders are the same."

"Your orders are," Chauvelin rejoined loudly, and pointed with grim intention at the door behind which he felt Marguerite Blakeney to be listening for every sound, "unless the English spy is in our hands on the evening of the fourth day, to shoot your prisoner."

"It shall be done, citizen!" Captain Boyer gave reply.

Then he grinned maliciously, because from behind the closed door there had come a sound like a quickly smothered cry.

After which, Chauvelin nodded to the captain and once more descended the stairs. A few seconds later he went out of the house into the stormy night.

CHAPTER 30

When the Storm Burst

Fortunately, the storm only broke after the bulk of the audience was inside the theatre. The performance was timed to commence at seven, and a quarter of an hour before that time the citizens of Paris who had come to applaud Citoyenne Vestris, Citoyen Talma, and their colleagues, in Chénier's tragedy, *Henri VIII,* were in their seats.

The theatre in the Rue de Richelieu was crowded. Talma and Vestris had always been great favourites with the public, and more so perhaps since their secession from the old and reactionary *Comédie Française.* Citizen Chénier's tragedy was in truth of a very poor order; but the audience was not disposed to be critical, and there was quite an excited hush in the house when Citoyenne Vestris, in the part of "Anne de Boulen," rolled off the meretricious verses:

"*Trop longtemps j'ai gardé le silence;*
Le poids qui m'accablait tombe avec violence."

But little was heard of the storm which raged outside; only at times the patter of the rain on the domed roof became unpleasantly apparent as an inharmonious accompaniment to the declamation of the actors.

It was a brilliant evening, not only because Citoyenne Vestris was in magnificent form, but also because of the number of well-known people who sat in the various boxed and in the parterre and who thronged the foyer during the *entr'actes.*

It seemed as if the members of the Convention and those who sat upon the Revolutionary Committees, as well as the more prominent speakers in the various Clubs, had made a point of showing themselves to the public, gay, unconcerned, interested in the stage and in the audience, at this moment when every man's head was insecure upon his shoulders and no man knew whether on reaching home he would not find a posse of the National Guard waiting to convey him to the nearest prison.

Death indeed lurked everywhere.

The evening before, at a supper party given in the house of Deputy Barrère, a paper was said to have dropped out of Robespierre's coat pocket and been found by one of the guests. The paper contained nothing but just forty names. What those names were the general public did not know, nor for what purpose the dictator carried the list about in his pocket; but during the representation of *Henri VIII,* the more obscure citizens of Pairs—happy in their own insignificance—noted that in the foyer during the *entr'actes*, Citizen Tallien and his friends appeared obsequious, whilst those who fawned upon Robespierre were more than usually arrogant.

In one of the proscenium boxes, Citizeness Cabarrus attracted a great deal of attention. Indeed, her beauty tonight was in the opinion of most men positively dazzling. Dressed with almost ostentatious simplicity, she drew all eyes upon her by her merry, ringing laughter, the ripple of conversation which flowed almost incessantly from her lips, and the graceful, provocative gestures of her bare hands and arms as she toyed with a miniature fan.

Indeed, Theresia Cabarrus was unusually light-hearted tonight. Sitting during the first two acts of the tragedy in her box, in the company of Citizen Tallien, she became the cynosure of all eyes, proud and happy when, during the third interval, she received the visit of Robespierre.

He only stayed with her a few moments and kept himself concealed for the most part at the back of the box; but he had been seen to enter, and Theresia's exclamation, "Ah, Citizen Robespierre! What a pleasant surprise! 'Tis not often you grace the theatre with your presence!" had been heard all over the house.

Indeed, with the exception of Eleonore Duplay, whose passionate admiration he rather accepted than reciprocated, the incorruptible and feline tyrant had never been known to pay attention to any woman. Great therefore was Theresia's triumph. Visions of that grandeur which she had always coveted and to which she had always felt herself predestined, danced before her eyes; and remembering Chauvelin's prophecies and Mother Théot's incantations, she allowed the dream-picture of the magnificent English milor to fade slowly from her ken, bidding it a reluctant adieu.

Though in her heart she still prayed for his deliverance—and did it with a passionate earnestness—some impish demon would hover at her elbow and repeat in her unwilling ear Chauvelin's inspired words: "Bring the Scarlet Pimpernel to his knees at the chariot-wheel of Robespierre, and the crown of the Bourbons will be yours for the asking."

And if, when she thought of that splendid head falling under the guillotine, a pang of remorse and regret shot through her heart, she turned with a seductive smile to the only man who could place that crown at her feet. His popularity was still at its zenith. Tonight, whenever the audience caught sight of him in the Cabarrus' box, a wild cheer rang out from gallery to pit of the house. Then Theresia would lean over to him and whisper insinuatingly:

"You can do anything with that crowd, citizen! You hold the people by the magnetism of your presence and of your voice. There is no height to which you cannot aspire."

"The greater the height," he murmured moodily, "the dizzier the fall—"

"'Tis on the summit you should gaze," she retorted; "not on the abyss below."

"I prefer to gaze into the loveliest eyes in Paris," he replied with a clumsy attempt at gallantry; "and remain blind to the summits as well as to the depths."

She tapped her daintily shod foot against the ground and gave an impatient little sigh. It seemed as if at every turn of fortune, she was confronted with pusillanimity and indecision. Tallien fawning on Robespierre; Robespierre afraid of Tallien; Chauvelin a prey to nerves. How different to them all was that cool, self-possessed Englishman with the easy good-humour and splendid self-assurance!

"I would make you Queen of France in all but name!" He said this as easily, as unconcernedly as if he were promising an invitation to a rout.

When, a moment or two later, Robespierre took leave of her and she was left for a while alone with her thoughts, Theresia no longer tried to brush away from her mental vision the picture on which her mind loved to dwell. The tall, magnificent figure; the lazy, laughing eyes; the slender hand that looked so firm and strong amidst the billows of exquisite lace.

Ah, well! The dream was over! It would never come again. He himself had wakened her; he himself had cast the die which must end his splendid life, even at the hour when love and fortune smiled at him through the lips and eyes of beautiful Cabarrus.

Fate, in the guise of the one man she could have loved, was throwing Theresia into the arms of Robespierre.

The next moment she was rudely awakened from her dreams. The door of her box was torn open by a violent hand, and turning, she saw Bertrand Moncrif, hatless, with hair dishevelled, clothes dripping and mud-stained, and linen soaked through. She was only just in time to arrest with a peremptory gesture the cry which was obviously hovering on his lips.

"Hush—sh—sh!" came at once from every portion of the audience, angered by this disturbing noise.

Tallien jumped to his feet.

"What is it?" he demanded in a quick whisper.

"A perquisition," Moncrif replied hurriedly, "in the house of the *citoyenne!*"

"Impossible!" she broke in harshly.

"Hush!—Silence!" the audience muttered audibly.

"I come from there," Moncrif murmured. "I have seen—heard—"

"Come outside," Theresia interjected. "We cannot talk here."

She led the way out, and Tallien and Moncrif followed.

The corridor fortunately was deserted. Only a couple of *ouvreuses* stood gossiping in a corner. Theresia, white to the lips—but more from anger than fear—dragged Moncrif with her to the foyer. Here there was no one.

"Now, tell me!" she commanded.

Bertrand passed his trembling hand through his soaking hair. His clothes were wet through. He was shaking from head to foot and appeared to have run till now he could scarcely stand.

"Tell me!" Theresia reiterated impatiently.

Tallien stood by, half paralysed with terror. He did not question the younger man, but gazed on him with compelling, horror-filled eyes, as if he would wrench the words out of him before they reached his throat.

"I was in the Rue Villedot," Moncrif stammered breathlessly at last, "when the storm broke. I sought shelter under the portico of a house opposite the *citoyenne's* lodgings.—I was there a long time. Then the storm subsided.—Men in uniform came along.—They were soldiers of the National Guard—I could see that, though the street was pitch-dark.—They passed quite close to me.—They were talking of the *citoyenne.*—Then they crossed over to her lodgings.—I saw them enter the house.—I saw Citizen Chauvelin in the doorway.—He chided them for being late.—There was a captain, and there were six soldiers, and that asthmatic coalheaver was with them."

"What!" Theresia exclaimed. "Rateau?"

"What in Satan's name does it all mean?" Tallien exclaimed with a savage curse.

"They went into the house," Moncrif went on, his voice rasping through his parched throat. "I followed at a little distance, to make quite sure before I came to warn you. Fortunately, I knew where you were—fortunately I always know—"

"You are sure they went up to my rooms?" Theresia broke in quickly.

"Yes. Two minutes later I saw a light in your apartment."

She turned abruptly to Tallien.

"My cloak!" she commanded. "I left it in the box."

He tried to protest.

"I am going," she rejoined firmly. "This is some ghastly mistake, for which that fiend Chauvelin shall answer with his life. My cloak!"

It was Bertrand who went back for the cloak and wrapped her in it. He knew—none better—that if his divinity desire to go, no power on earth would keep her back. She did not appear in the least afraid, but her wrath was terrible to see, and boded ill to those who had dared provoke it. Indeed, Theresia, flushed with her recent triumph and with Robespierre's rare if clumsy gallantries still ringing in her ear, felt ready to dare anything, to brave anyone—even Chauvelin and his threats. She even succeeded in reassuring Tallien, ordered him to remain in the theatre, and to show himself to the public as utterly unconcerned.

"In case a rumour of this outrage penetrates to the audience," she said, "you must appear to make light of it.—Nay! you must at once threaten reprisals against its perpetrators."

Then she wrapped her cloak about her and, taking Bertrand's arm, she hurried out of the theatre.

CHAPTER 31

Our Lady of Pity

It was like an outraged divinity in the face of sacrilege that Theresia Cabarrus appeared in the antechamber of her apartment, ten minutes later.

Her rooms were full of men; sentries were at the door; the furniture was overturned, the upholstery ripped up, cupboard doors swung open; even her bed and bedding lay in a tangled heap upon the floor. The lights in the rooms were dim, one single lamp shedding its feeble rays from the antechamber into the living-room, whilst another flickered on a wall-bracket in the passage. In the bedroom the maid Pepita, guarded by a soldier, was loudly lamenting and cursing in voluble Spanish.

Citizen Chauvelin was standing in the centre of the living-room, intent on examining some papers. In a corner of the antechamber cowered the ungainly figure of Rateau the coalheaver.

Theresia took in the whole tragic picture at a glance; then with a proud, defiant toss of the head she swept past the soldiers in the antechamber and confronted Chauvelin, before he had time to notice her approach.

"Something has turned your brain, Citizen Chauvelin," she said coolly. "What is it?"

He looked up, encountered her furious glance, and at once made her a profound, ironical bow.

"How wise was our young friend there to tell you of our visit, *citoyenne*," he said suavely.

And he looked with mild approval in the direction where Bertrand Moncrif stood between two soldiers, who had quickly barred his progress and were holding him tightly by the wrists.

"I came," Theresia retorted harshly, "as the forerunner of those who will know how to punish this outrage, Citizen Chauvelin."

Once more he bowed, smiling blandly.

"I shall be as ready to receive them," he said quietly, "as I am gratified to see the Citoyenne Cabarrus. When they come, shall I direct them to call and see their beautiful Egeria at the *Conciergerie*, whither we shall have the honour to convey her immediately?"

Theresia threw back her head and laughed; but her voice sounded hard and forced.

"At the *Conciergerie?*" she exclaimed. "I?"

"Even you, *citoyenne*," Chauvelin replied.

"On what charge, I pray you?" she demanded, with biting sarcasm.

"Of trafficking with the enemies of the Republic."

She shrugged her shoulders.

"You are mad, Citizen Chauvelin!" she riposted with perfect *sang-froid*. "I pray you, order your men to re-establish order to my apartment; and remember that I will hold you responsible for any damage that has been done."

"Shall I also," Chauvelin rejoined with equally perfect equanimity, "replace these letters and other interesting objects, there where we found them?"

"Letters?" she retorted, frowning. "What letters?"

"These, *citoyenne*," he replied, and held up to her gaze the papers which he had in his hand.

"What are they? I have never seen them before."

"Nevertheless, we found them in that bureau." And Chauvelin pointed to a small piece of furniture which stood against the wall, and the drawers of which had obviously been forcibly torn open. Then as Theresia remained silent, apparently un-understanding, he went on suavely: "They are letters written at different times to Mme de Fontenay, née Cabarrus—*Our Lady of Pity*, as she was called by grateful Bordeaux."

"By whom?" she asked.

"By the interesting hero of romance who is known to the world as the Scarlet Pimpernel."

"It is false!" she retorted firmly. "I have never received a letter from him in my life!"

"His handwriting is all too familiar to me, *citoyenne*; and the letters are addressed to you."

"It is false!" she reiterated with unabated firmness. "This is some devilish trick you have devised in order to ruin me. But take care, Citizen Chauvelin, take care! If this is a trial of strength 'twixt you and me, the next few hours will show who will gain the day."

"If it were a trail of strength 'twixt you and me, *citoyenne*," he rejoined blandly, "I would already be a vanquished man. But it is France this time who has challenged a traitor. That traitor is Theresia Fontenay, née Cabarrus. The trial of strength is between her and France."

"You are mad, Citizen Chauvelin! If there were letters writ by the Scarlet Pimpernel found in my rooms, 'tis you who put them there!"

"That statement you will be at liberty to substantiate tomorrow, *citoyenne*," he retorted coldly, "at the bar of the revolutionary tribunal. There, no doubt, you can explain away how Citizen Rateau knew of the existence of those letters and led me straight to their discovery. I have an officer of the National Guard, the commissary of the section, and half a dozen men, to prove the truth of what I say, and to add that in a wall-cupboard in your antechamber we also found this interesting collection, the use of which you, *citoyenne*, will no doubt be able to explain."

He stepped aside and pointed to a curious heap which littered the floor—rags for the most part: a tattered shirt, frayed breeches, a grimy cap, a wig made up of lank, colourless hair, the counterpart of that which adorned the head of the coalheaver Rateau.

Theresia looked on those rags for a moment in a kind of horrified puzzlement. Her cheeks and lips became the colour of ashes. She put her hand up to her forehead, as if to chase a hideous, ghoulish vision away, and smothered a cry of horror. Puzzlement had given place to a kind of superstitious dread. The room, the rags, the faces of the soldiers began to whirl around her—impish shapes to dance a wild saraband before her eyes. And in the midst of this witch's cauldron the figure of Chauvelin, like a weird hobgoblin, was executing elf-like contortions and brandishing a packet of letters writ upon scarlet paper.

She tried to laugh, to speak defiant words; but her throat felt as if it were held in a vice, and losing momentary consciousness she tottered, and only saved herself from measuring her length upon the floor by clinging with both hands to a a table immediately behind her.

As to what happened after that, she only had a blurred impression. Chauvelin gave a curt word of command, and a couple of soldiers came and stood to right and left of her. Then a piercing cry rang through the narrow rooms, and she saw Bertrand Moncrif for one moment between herself and the soldiers, fighting desperately, shielding her with his body, tearing and raging like a wild animal defending its young. The whole room appeared full of deafening noise: cries and more cries—words of command—calls of rage and of entreaty. Then suddenly the word "Fire!" and the detonation of a pistol at close range, and the body of Bertrand Moncrif sliding down limp and impotent to the floor.

After that, everything became dark around her. Theresia felt as if she were looking down an immeasurable abyss of inky blackness, and that she was falling, falling—

A thin, dry laugh brought her back to her senses, her pride to the fore, her vanity up in arms. She drew her statuesque figure up to its full height and once more confronted Chauvelin like an august and outraged divinity.

"And at whose word," she demanded, "is this monstrous charge to be brought against me?"

"At the word of a free citizen of the State," Chauvelin replied coldly.

"Bring him before me."

Chauvelin shrugged his shoulders and smiled indulgently, like one who is ready to humour a wayward child.

"Citizen Rateau!" he called.

From the anteroom there came the sound of much shuffling, spluttering, and wheezing; then the dull clatter of wooden shoes upon the carpeted floor; and presently the ungainly, grime-covered figure of the coalheaver appeared in the doorway.

Theresia looked on him for a few seconds in silence, then she gave a ringing laugh, and with exquisite bare arm outstretched she pointed to the scrubby apparition.

"That man's word against mine!" she called, with well-assumed mockery. "Rateau, the caitiff against Theresia Cabarrus, the intimate friend of Citizen Robespierre! What a subject for a lampoon!"

Then her laughter broke. She turned once more on Chauvelin like an angry goddess.

"That vermin!" she exclaimed, her voice hoarse with indignation. "That sorry knave with a felon's brand! In truth, Citizen Chauvelin, your spite must be hard put to it to bring up such a witness against me!"

Then suddenly her glance fell upon the lifeless body of Bertrand Moncrif, and on the horrible crimson stain which discoloured his coat. She gave a shudder of horror, and for a moment her eyes closed and her head fell back, as if she were about to swoon. But she quickly recovered herself. Her will-power at this moment was unconquerable. She looked with unutterable contempt on Chauvelin; then she raised her cloak, which had slipped down from her shoulders, and wrapped it with a queen-like gesture around her, and without another word led the way out of the apartment.

Chauvelin remained standing in the middle of the room, his face quite expressionless, his clawlike hands still fingering the fateful letters. Two soldiers remained with him beside the body of Bertrand Moncrif. The maid Pepita, still shrieking and gesticulating violently, had to be dragged away in the wake of her mistress.

In the doorway between the living-room and the antechamber, Rateau, humble, snivelling, more than a little frightened, stood aside in order to allow the guard and their imperious prisoner to pass. Theresia did not condescend to look at him again; and he, shuffling and stumbling in his clumsy wooden shoes, followed the soldiers down the stairs.

It was still raining hard. The captain who was in charge of Theresia told her that he had a chaise ready for her. It was waiting out in the street. Theresia ordered him to send for it; she would not, she said, offer herself as a spectacle to the riff-raff who happened to be passing by. The captain had probably received orders to humour the prisoner as far as was compatible with safety. Certain it is that he sent one of his men to fetch the coach and to order the *concierge* to throw open the *porte-cochère*.

Theresia remained standing in the narrow vestibule at the foot of the stairs. Two soldiers stood on guard over the maid, whilst another stood beside Theresia. The captain, muttering with impatience, paced up and down the stone-paved floor. Rateau had paused on the stairs, a step or two just above where Theresia was standing. On the wall opposite, supported by an iron bracket, a smoky oil-lamp shed a feeble, yellowish flicker around.

A few minutes went by; then a loud clatter woke the echoes of the dreary old house, and a coach drawn by two ancient, half-starved nags, lumbered into the courtyard and came to a halt in front of the open doorway. The captain gave a sigh of relief, and called out: "Now then, *citoyenne!*" whilst the soldier who had gone to fetch the coach jumped down from the box-seat and, with his comrades, stood at attention. The maid was summarily bundled into the coach, and Theresia was ready to follow.

Just then the draught through the open door blew her velvet cloak against the filthy rags of the miserable ruffian behind her. An unexplainable impulse caused her to look up, and she encountered his eyes fixed upon her. A dull cry rose to her throat, and instinctively she put up her hand to her mouth, striving to smother the sound. Horror dilated her eyes, and through her lips one word escaped like a hoarse murmur:

"You!"

He put a grimy finger to his lips. But already she had recovered herself. Here then was the explanation of the mystery which surrounded this monstrous denunciation. The English milor had planned it as revenge for the injury done to his wife.

"Captain!" she cried out shrilly. "Beware! The English spy is at your heels!"

But apparently the captain's complaisance did not go to the length of listening to the ravings of his fair prisoner. He was impatient to get this unpleasant business over.

"Now then, *citoyenne!*" was his gruff retort. "*En voiture!*"

"You fool!" she cried, bracing herself against the grip of the soldiers who were on the point of seizing her. "'Tis the Scarlet Pimpernel! If you let him escape——"

"The Scarlet Pimpernel?" the captain retorted with a laugh. "Where?"

"The coalheaver! Rateau! 'Tis he, I tell you!" And Theresia's cries became more frantic as she felt herself unceremoniously lifted off the ground. "You fool! You fool! You are letting him escape!"

"Rateau, the coalheaver?" the captain exclaimed. "We have heard that pretty story before. Here, Citizen Rateau!" he went on, and shouted at the top of his voice. "Go and report yourself to Citizen Chauvelin. Tell him you are the Scarlet Pimpernel! As for you, *citoy-*

enne, enough of this shouting—what? My orders are to take you to the *Conciergerie*, and not to run after spies—English, German, or Dutch. Now then, citizen soldiers!—"

Theresia, throwing her dignity to the winds, did indeed raise a shout that brought the other lodgers of the house to their door. But her screams had become inarticulate, as the soldiers, in obedience to the captain's impatient orders, had wrapped her cloak about her head. Thus, the inhabitants of the dreary old house in the Rue Villedot could only ascertain that the Citoyenne Cabarrus who lodged on the third floor had been taken to prison, screaming and fighting, in a manner that no self-respecting aristo had ever done.

Theresia Cabarrus was ignominiously lifted into the coach and deposited by the side of equally noisy Pepita. Through the folds of the cloak her reiterated cry could still faintly be heard:

"You fool! You traitor! You cursed, miserable fool!"

One of the lodgers on the second floor—a young woman who was on good terms with every male creature that wore uniform—leaned over the balustrade of the balcony and shouted gaily down:

"Hey, citizen captain! Why is the *aristo* screaming so?"

One of the soldiers looked up, and shouted back:

"She has hold of the story that Citizen Rateau is an English milor in disguise, and she wants to run after him!"

Loud laughter greeted this tale, and a lusty cheer was set up as the coach swung clumsily out of the courtyard.

A moment or two later, Chauvelin, followed by the two soldiers, came quickly down the stairs. The noise from below had at last reached his ears. At first, he too through that it was only the proud Spaniard who was throwing her dignity to the winds. Then a word or two sounded clearly above the din:

"The Scarlet Pimpernel! The English spy!"

The words acted like a sorcerer's charm—a call from the vast deep. In an instant the rest of the world ceased to have any importance in his sight. One thing and one alone mattered; his enemy.

Calling to the soldiers to follow him, he was out of the apartment and down in the vestibule below in a trice. The coach at that moment was turning out of the *porte-cochère*. The courtyard, wrapped in gloom, was alive with chattering and laughter which proceeded from the windows and balconies around. It was raining fast, and from the balconies the water was pouring down in torrents.

Chauvelin stood in the doorway and sent one of the soldiers to ascertain what the disturbance had all been about. The man returned with an account of how the *aristo* had screamed and raved like a mad-woman and tried to escape by sending the citizen captain on a fool's errand, vowing that poor old Rateau was an English spy in disguise.

Chauvelin gave a sigh of relief. He certainly need not rack his nerves or break his head over that! He had good cause to know that Rateau, with the branded arm, could not possibly be the Scarlet Pimpernel!

CHAPTER 32

Grey Dawn

Ten minutes later the courtyard and approach of the old house in the Rue Villedot were once more wrapped in silence and in darkness. Chauvelin had with his own hands affixed the official seals on the doors which led to the apartments of Citoyenne Cabarrus. In the living room, the body of the unfortunate Moncrif still lay uncovered and unwatched, awaiting what hasty burial the commissary of the section would be pleased to order for it. Chauvelin dismissed the soldiers at the door, and himself went his way.

The storm was gradually dying away. By the time that the audience filed out of the theatre, it was scarcely raining. Only from afar, dull rumblings of thunder could still faintly be heard. Citizen Tallien hurried along on foot to the Rue Villedot. The last hour had been positive torture for him. Although his reason told him that no man would be fool enough to trump up an accusation against Theresia Cabarrus, who was the friend, the Egeria of every influential man in the Convention or the Clubs, and that she herself had always been far too prudent to allow herself to be compromised in any way—although he knew all that, his overwrought fancy conjured up vision which made him sick with dread. His Theresia in the hands of rough soldiery—dragged to prison—he himself unable to ascertain what had become of her—until he saw her at the bar of that awful tribunal, from which there was no issue save the guillotine!

And with this dread came unendurable, gnawing remorse. He himself was one of the men who had helped to set up the machinery of wild accusations, monstrous tribunals and wholesale condemnations which had been set in motion now by an unknown hand against the woman he loved. He—Tallien—the ardent lover, the future husband of Theresia, had aided in the constitution of that abominable Revolutionary Committee, which could strike at the innocent as readily and as ruthlessly as at the guilty.

Indeed, at this hour, this man, who long since had forgotten how to pray, when he heard the tower-clock of a neighbouring church striking the hour, turned his eyes that were blurred with tears towards the sacred edifice which he had helped to desecrate, and found in his heart a half-remembered prayer which he murmured to the Fount of all Mercy and of Pardon.

Citizen Tallien turned into the Rue Villedot, the street where lodged his beloved. A minute or so later, he was making his way up the back staircase of the dingy house where his divinity had dwelt until now. On the second-floor landing two women stood gossiping. One of them recognised the influential Representative.

"It is Citizen Tallien," she said.

And the other woman at once volunteered the information:

"They have arrested the Citoyenne Cabarrus," she said; "and the soldiers did not know whither they were taking her."

Tallien did not wait to listen further. He stumbled up the stairs to the third floor, to the door which he knew so well. His trembling fingers wandered over the painted panels. They encountered the official seals, which told their own mute tale.

The whole thing, then, was not a dream. Those assassins had taken his Theresia and dragged her to prison, would drag her on the morrow to an outrageous mockery of a tribunal first, and then to death! Who shall say what wild thoughts of retrospection and of remorse coursed through the brain of this man—himself one of the makers of a bloody revolution? What visions of past ideals, good intentions, of honest purpose and incessant labour, passed before his mind? That glorious revolution, which was to mark the regeneration of mankind, which was to have given liberty to the oppressed, equality to the meek, fraternity in one vast human family! And what did it lead to but to oppression far more cruel than all that had gone before, to fratricide and to arrogance on the one side, servility on the other, to constant terror of death, to discouragement and sloth?

For hours Citizen Tallien sat in the dark, on the staircase outside Theresia's door, his head buried in his hands. The grey dawn, living and chill, which came peeping in through the skylight overhead, found him still sitting there, stiff and numb with cold.

Whether what happened after that was part of a dream, he never knew. Certain it is that presently something extraneous appeared to rouse him. He sat up and listened, leaned his back against the wall, for he was very tired. Then he heard—or thought he heard—firm, swift steps on the stairs, and soon after saw the figure of two men coming up the stairs. Both the men were very tall, one of them unusually so, and the ghostly light of dawn made him appear unreal and mysterious. He was dressed with marvellous elegance; his smooth, fair hair was tied at the nape of the neck with a satin bow; soft, billowy lace gleamed at his wrists and throat, and his hands were exquisitely white and slender. Both the men wore huge coats of fine cloth, adorned with many capes, and boots of fine leather, perfectly cut.

They paused on the vestibule outside the door of Theresia's apartment, and appeared to be studying the official seals affixed upon the door. Then one of them—the taller of the two—took a knife out of his pocket and cut through the tapes which held the seals together. Then together they stepped coolly into the apartment.

Tallien had watched them, dazed and fascinated. He was so numb and weary that his tongue—just like it does in dreams—refused him service when he tried to call. But now he struggled to his feet and followed in the wake of the two mysterious strangers. With him, the instinct of the official, the respect due to regulations and laws framed by his colleagues and himself, had been too strong to allow him to tamper with the seals, and there was something mysterious and awesome about that tall figure of a man, dressed with supreme elegance, whose slender, firm hands had so unconcernedly committed this flagrant breach of the law. It did not occur to Tallien to call for help. Somehow, the whole incident—the two men—were so ghostlike, that he felt that at a word they would vanish into thin air.

He stepped cautiously into the familiar little antechamber. The strangers had gone through to the living-room. One of them was kneeling on the floor. Tallien, who knew nothing of the tragedy which had been enacted inside the apartment of his beloved, marvelled what the men were doing. He crept stealthily forward and craned his neck to see. The window at the end of the room had been left unfastened. A weird grey streak of light came peeping in and illumined the awesome scene: the overturned furniture, the torn hangings; and on the ground, the body of a man, with the stranger kneeling beside it.

Tallien, weary and dazed, always of a delicate constitution, felt nigh to swooning. His knees were shaking, a cold dread of the supernatural held his heart with an icy grip and caused his hair to tingle at the roots. His tongue felt huge and as if paralysed, his teeth were chattering together. It was as much as he could do not to measure his length on the ground; and the vague desire to remain unobserved kept him crouching in the gloom.

He just could see the tall stranger pass his hands over the body on the floor and could hear the other ask him a question in English.

A few moments went by. The strangers conversed in a low tone of voice. From one or two words which came clearly to his ear, Tallien gathered that they spoke in English—a language with which he himself was familiar. The taller man of the two appeared to be giving his friend some orders, which the latter promised to obey. Then, with utmost precaution, he took the body in his arms and lifted it from the floor.

"Let me help you, Blakeney," the other said in a whisper.

"No, no!" the mysterious stranger replied quickly. "The poor worm is as light as a feather! "'Tis better he died as he did. His unfortunate infatuation was killing him."

"Poor little Régine!" the younger man sighed.

"It is better so," his friend rejoined. "We'll be able to tell her that he died nobly, and that we've given him Christian burial."

No wonder that Tallien thought that he was dreaming! These English were strange folk indeed! Heaven alone knew what they risked by coming here, at this hour, and into this house, in order to fetch away the body of their friend. They certainly were wholly unconscious of danger.

Tallien held his breath. He saw the splendid figure of the mysterious adventurer step across the threshold, bearing the lifeless body in his arms with as much ease as if he were carrying a child. The pale grey light of morning was behind him, and his fine head with its smooth fair hair was silhouetted against the neutral-tinted background. His friend came immediately behind him.

In the dark antechamber he paused, and called abruptly:

"Citizen Tallien!"

A cry rose to Tallien's throat. He had thought himself entirely unobserved, and the stranger a mere vision which he was watching in a dream. Now he felt that compelling eyes were gazing straight at him, piercing the darkness for a clearer sight of his face.

But the spell was still on him, and he only moved in order to straighten himself out and to force his trembling knees to be still.

"They have taken the Citoyenne Cabarrus to the *Conciergerie*," the stranger went on simply. "Tomorrow she will be charged before the Revolutionary Tribunal..—You know what is the inevitable end—"

It seemed as if some subtle magic was in the man's voice, in his very presence, in the glance wherewith he challenged that of the unfortunate Tallien. The latter felt a wave of shame sweep over him. There was something so splendid in these two men—exquisitely dressed, and perfectly deliberate and cool in all their movements—who were braving and daring death in order to give Christian burial to their friend; whilst he, in face of the outrage put upon his beloved, had only sat on her desecrated doorstep like a dumb animal pining for its master. He felt a hot flush rush to his cheeks. With quick, nervy movements he readjusted the set of his coat, passed his thin hands over his rumpled hair; whilst the stranger reiterated with solemn significance:

"You know what is the inevitable end.—The Citoyenne Cabarrus will be condemned—"

Tallien this time met the stranger's eyes fearlessly. It was the magic of strength and of courage that flowed into him from them. He drew up his meagre stature to its full height and threw up his head with an air of defiance and of conscious power.

"Not while I live!" he said firmly.

"Theresia Cabarrus will be condemned tomorrow," the stranger went on calmly. "Then the next day, the guillotine—"

"Never!"

"Inevitably!—Unless—"

"Unless what?" Tallien queried and hung breathless on the man's lips as he would on those of an oracle.

"Theresia Cabarrus, or Robespierre and his herd of assassins. Which shall it be, Citizen Tallien?"

"By Heaven!—" Tallien exclaimed forcefully.

But he got no further. The stranger, bearing his burden, had already gone out of the room, closely followed by his friend.

Tallien was alone in the deserted apartment, where every broken piece of furniture, every torn curtain, cried out for vengeance in the name of his beloved. He said nothing. He neither protested nor swore. But he tip-toed into the apartment and knelt down upon the floor close beside the small sofa on which she was wont to sit. Here he remained quite still for a minute or two, his eyes closed, his hands tightly clasped together. Then he stooped very low and pressed his lips against the spot where her pretty, sandalled foot was wont to rest.

After that he rose, strode with a firm step out of the apartment, carefully closing the doors behind him.

The strangers had vanished into the night; and Citizen Tallien went quietly back to his own lodgings.

CHAPTER 33

The Cataclysm

Forty names! Found on a list in the pocket of Robespierre's coat!

Forty names! And every one of these that of a known opponent of Robespierre's schemes of dictatorship: Tallien, Barrère, Vadier, Cambon, and the rest. Men powerful today, prominent Members of the Convention, leaders of the people, too—but opponents!

The inference was obvious, the panic general. That night—it was the 8th *Thermidor*, July the 26th of the old calendar—men talked of flight, of abject surrender, of appeal—save the mark!—to friendship, camaraderie, humanity! Friendship, camaraderie, humanity? An appeal to a heart of stone! They talked of everything, in face, save of defying the tyrant; for such talk would have been folly.

Defying the tyrant? Ye gods! When with a word he could sway the Convention, the Committees, the multitude, bend them to his will, bring them to heel like any tamer of beasts when he cracks his whip?

So, men talked and trembled. All night they talked and trembled; for they did not sleep, those forty whose names were on Robespierre's list. But Tallien, their chief, was nowhere to be found. 'Twas known that his *fiancée*, the beautiful Theresia Cabarrus, had been summarily arrested. Since then he had disappeared; and they—the others—were leaderless. But, even so, he was no loss. Tallien was ever pusillanimous, a temporiser—what?

And now the hour for temporizing is past. Robespierre then is to be dictator of France. He will be dictator of France, in spite of any opposition led by those forty whose names are on his list! He will be dictator of France! He has not said it; but his friends have shouted it form the housetops and have murmured under their breath that those who oppose Robespierre's dictatorship are traitors to the land. Death then must be their fate.

When then, ye gods? What then?

And so, the day broke—smiling, mark you! It was a beautiful warm July morning. It broke on what is perhaps the most stupendous cataclysm—save one—the world has ever known.

Behold the picture! A medley. A confusion. A whirl of everything that is passionate and cruel, defiant and desperate. Heavens, how desperate! Men who have thrown lives away as if lives were in truth grains of sand; men who have juggled with death dealt it and tossed it about like cards upon a gaming table. They are desperate now, because their own lives are at stake; and they find now that life can be very dear.

So, having greeted their leader, the forty draw together, watching the moment when humility will be most opportune.

Robespierre mounts the tribune. The hour has struck. His speech is one long, impassioned, involved tirade, full at first on vague accusations against the enemies of the Republic and the people, and is full of protestations of his own patriotism and selflessness. Then he warms to his own oratory; his words are prophetic of death, his voice becomes harsh—like a screech owl's, so we're told. His accusations are no longer vague. He begins to strike.

Corruption! Backsliding! Treachery! Moderatism!—oh, moderatism above all! Moderatism is treachery to the glorious revolution. Every victim spared form the guillotine is a traitor let loose against the people! A traitor, he who robs the guillotine of her prey! Robespierre stands alone incorruptible, true, faithful unto death!

And for all that treachery, what remedy is there? Why, death of course! Death! The guillotine! New power to the sovereign guillotine! Death to all the traitors!

And seven hundred faces became paler still with dread, and the sweat of terror rises on seven hundred brows. There were only forty names on that list—but there might be others somewhere else!

And still the voice of Robespierre thunders on. His words fall of seven hundred pairs of ears like on a sounding-board; his friends, his sycophants, echo them; they applaud, rise in wild enthusiasm. 'Tis the applause that is thundering now!

One of the tyrant's most abject slaves has put forward the motion that the great speech just delivered shall forthwith be printed, and distributed to every township, every village, throughout France, as a monument to the lofty patriotism of her greatest citizen.

The motion at one moment looks as if it would be carried with acclamations; after which, Robespierre's triumph would have risen to the height of deification. Then suddenly the note of dissension; the hush; the silence. The great Assembly is like a sounding-board that has ceased to respond. Something had turned the acclamations to mutterings, and then to silence. The sounding-board has given forth a dissonance. Citizen Tallien has demanded "delay in printing that speech," and asked pertinently:

"What has become of the Liberty of Opinion in this Convention?"

His face is the colour of ashes, and his eyes, ringed with purple, gleam with an unnatural fire. The coward has become bold; the sheep has donned the lion's skin.

There is a flutter in the Convention, a moment's hesitation. But the question is put to the vote, and the speech is not to be printed. A small matter, in truth—printing or not printing.—Does the Destiny of France hang on so small a peg?

It is a small matter; and yet how full of portent! Like the breath of mutiny blowing across a ship. But nothing more occurs just then. Robespierre, lofty in his scorn, puts the notes of his speech into his pocket. He does not condescend to argue. He, the master of France, will not deign to bandy words with his slaves. And he stalks out of the Hall surrounded by his friends.

There has been a breath of mutiny; but his is still the iron heel, powerful enough to crush a raging revolt. His withdrawal—proud, silent, menacing—is in keeping with his character and with the pose which he has assumed of late. But he is still the Chosen of the People; and the multitude is there, thronging the streets of Paris—there, to avenge the insult put upon their idol by a pack of slinking wolves.

And now the picture becomes still more poignant. It is painted in colours more vivid, more glowing than and again the Hall of the Convention is crowded to the roof, with Tallien and his friends, in a close *phalanx*, early at their post!

Tallien is there, pale, resolute, the fire of his hatred kept up by anxiety for his beloved. The night before, at the corner of a dark street, a surreptitious hand slipped a scrap of paper into the pocket of his coat. It was a message written by Theresia in prison and written with her own blood. How it ever came into his pocket Tallien never know; but the few impassioned, agonized words, seared his very soul and whipped up his courage:

"The Commissary of Police has just left me," Theresia wrote. "He came to tell me that tomorrow I must appear before the tribunal. This means the guillotine. And I, who thought that you were a *man*—!"

Not only is his own head in peril, not only that of his friends; but the life of the woman whom he worships hangs now upon the thread of his own audacity and of his courage.

St. Just on this occasion is the first to mount the tribune; and Robespierre, the very incarnation of lustful and deadly Vengeance, stands silently by. He has spent the afternoon and evening with his friends at the Jacobins' Club, where deafening applause greeted his every word, and wild fury raged against his enemies.

It is then to be a fight to the finish! To your tents, O Israel!

To the guillotine all those who have dared to say one word against the Chosen of the People! St. Just shall thunder Vengeance from the tribune at the Convention, whilst Henriot, the drunken and dissolute Commandant of the Municipal Guard, shall, but the might of the sword and fire, proclaim the sovereignty of Robespierre through the streets of Paris. That is the picture as it has been painted in the minds of the tyrant and of his sycophants: a picture of death paramount, and of Robespierre rising like a new Phoenix from out the fire of calumny and revolt, greater, more unassailable than before.

And lo! One sweep of the brush, and the picture is changed.

Ten minutes—less—and the whole course of the world's history is altered. No sooner had St. Just mounted the tribune than Tallien jumped to his feet. His voice, usually meek and cultured, rises in a harsh crescendo, until it drowns that of the younger orator.

"Citizens," he exclaims, "I ask for truth! Let us tear aside the curtain behind which lurk concealed the real conspirators and the traitors!"

"Yes, yes! Truth! Let us have the truth!" One hundred voices—not forty—have raised the echo.

The mutiny is on the verge of becoming open revolt, is that already, perhaps. It is like a spark fallen—who knows where?—into a powder magazine. Robespierre feels it, sees the spark. He knows that one movement, one word, one plunge into that magazine, foredoomed though it be to destruction, one stamp with a sure foot, may yet quench the spark, may yet smother the mutiny. He rushes to the tribune, tries to mount. But Tallien has forestalled him, elbows him out of the way, and turns to the seven hundred with a cry that rings far beyond the Hall, out into the streets.

"Citizens!" he thunders in his turn. "I begged of you just now to tear aside the curtains behind which lurk the traitors. Well, the curtain is already rent. And if you dare not strike at the tyrant now, then 'tis I who will dare!" And from beneath his coat he draws a dagger and raises it above his head. "And I will plunge this into his heart," he cries, "if you have not the courage to smite!"

His words, that gleaming bit of steal, fan the spark into a flame. Within a few seconds, seven hundred voices are shouting, "Down with the tyrant!" Arms are waving, hands gesticulate wildly, excitedly. Only a very few shout: "Behold the dagger of Brutus!" All the others retort with "Tyranny!" and "Conspiracy!" and with cries of "*Vive la*

Liberté!"

At this hour all is confusion and deafening uproar. In vain Robespierre tries to speak. He demands to speak. He hurls insults, anathema, upon the President, who relentless refuses him speech and jingles his bell against him.

"President of Assassins," the falling tyrant cries, "I demand speech of thee!"

But the bell goes jingling on, and Robespierre, choked with rage and terror, "turns blue" we are told, and his hand goes up to his throat.

"The blood of Danton chokes thee!" cries one man. And these words seem like the last blow dealt to the fallen foe. The next moment the voice of an obscure Deputy is raised, in order to speak the words that have been hovering on every lip:

"I demand a decree of accusation against Robespierre!"

"Accusation!" comes from seven hundred throats. "The decree of accusation!"

The President jingles his bell, puts the question, and the motion is passed unanimously.

Maximilien Robespierre—erstwhile master of France—is decreed *accused*.

Chapter 34

The Whirlwind

It was then noon. Five minutes later, the Chosen of the People, the fallen idol, is hustled out of the Hall into one of the Committee rooms close by, and with his friends—St. Just, Couthon, Lebas, his brother Augustin, and the others—all decreed accused and the order of arrest launched against them. As for the rest, 'tis the work of the Public Prosecutor—and of the guillotine.

At five o'clock the Convention adjourns. The deputies have earned food and rest. They rush to their homes, there to relate what has happened; Tallien to the *Conciergerie*, to get a sight of Theresia. This is denied him. He is not dictator yet; and Robespierre, though apparently vanquished, still dominates—and lives.

But from every church steeple the tocsin bursts; and a prolonged roll of drums ushers in the momentous evening.

In the city all is hopeless confusion. Men are running in every direction, shouting, brandishing pistols and swords. Henriot, *Commandant* of the Municipal Guard, rides through the streets at the head of his *gendarmes* like one possessed, bent on delivering Robespierre.

Women and children fly screaming in every direction; the churches, so long deserted, are packed with people who, terror-stricken, are trying to remember long-forgotten prayers.

Proclamations are read at street corners; there are rumours of a general massacre of all the prisoners. At one moment—the usual hour—the familiar tumbril with its load of victims for the guillotine rattles along the cobblestones of the Rue St. Antoine. The populace, vaguely conscious of something stupendous in the air—even though the decree of accusation against Robespierre has not yet transpired—loudly demand the release of the victims. They surround the tumbrils, crying, "Let them be free!"

But Henriot at the head of his *gendarmes* comes riding down the street, and while the populace shouts, "It shall not be! Let them be free!" he threatens with pistols and sabre, and retorts, bellowing: "It shall be! To the guillotine!" And the tumbrils, which for a moment had halted, lumber on, on their way.

Up in the attic of the lonely house in the Rue de la Planchette, Marguerite Blakeney heard but a mere faint echo of the confusion and of the uproar.

During the previous long, sultry afternoon, it had seemed to her as if her jailers had been unwontedly agitated. There was much more moving to and fro on the landing outside her door than there had been in the last three days. Men talked, mostly in whispers; but at times a word, a phrase here and there, a voice raised above the others, reached her straining ears. She glued her ear to the keyhole and listened; but what she heard was all confusion, sentences that conveyed but little meaning to her. She distinguished the voice of the Captain of the Guard. He appeared impatient about something and talked about "missing all the fun." The other soldiers seemed to agree with him. Obviously, they were all drinking heavily, for their voices sounded hoarse and thick, and often would break into bibulous song. From time to time, too, she would hear the patter of wooden shoes, together with a wheezy cough, as from a man troubled with asthma.

But it was all very vague, for her nerves by this time were on the rack. She had lost count of time, of place; she knew nothing. She was unable even to think. All her instincts were merged in the dead of that silent evening hour, when Chauvelin's furtive footsteps would once more resound upon the stone floor outside her door, when she would hear the quick word of command that heralded his approach, the grounding of arms, the sharp query and quick answer, and when he would feel again the presence of the relentless enemy who lay in wait to trap her beloved.

At one moment that evening he had raised his voice, obviously so that she might hear.

"Tomorrow is the fourth day, citizen captain," she had heard him say. "I may not be able to come."

"Then," the voice of the captain had said in reply, "if the Englishman is not here by seven o'clock—"

Chauvelin had given a harsh, dry laugh, and retorted:

"Your orders are as they were, citizen. But I think that the Englishman will come."

What it all meant Marguerite could not fail to conjecture. It meant death to her or to her husband—to both, in fact. And all today she had sat by the open window, her hands clasped in silent, constant prayer, her eyes fixed upon the horizon far away, longing with all her might for one last sight of her beloved, fighting against despair, striving for trust in him and for hope.

At this hour, the centre of interest is the Place de l'Hôtel de Ville, where Robespierre and his friends sit entrenched and—for the moment—safe. The prisons have refused one by one to close their gates upon the Chosen of the People; governors and jailers alike have quaked in the face of so monstrous a sacrilege. And the same *gendarmes* who have been told off to escort the fallen tyrant to his penultimate resting-place, have had a touch of the same kind of scruple—or dread—and at his command have conveyed him to the Hôtel de Ville.

In vain does the Convention hastily reassemble. In vain—apparently—does Tallien demand that the traitor Robespierre and his friends be put outside the pale of the law. They are for the moment safe, redacting proclamations, sending out messengers in every direction; whilst Henriot and his *gendarmes*, having struck terror in the hearts of all peaceable citizens, hold the place outside the Town Hall and proclaim Robespierre dictator of France.

The sun sinks towards the west behind a veil of mist. Ferment and confusion are at their height. All around the city there is an invisible barrier that seems to confine agitation within its walls. Outside this barrier, no one knows what is happening. Only a vague dread has filtrated through and gripped every heart. The guard at the several gates appear slack and undisciplined. Sentries are accosted by passers-by, eager for news. And, from time to time, from every direction, troops of the Municipal *gendarmes* ride furiously by, with shouts of "Robespierre!

Robespierre! Death to the traitors! Long live Robespierre!"

They raise a cloud of dust around them, trample unheedingly over every obstacle, human or otherwise, that happens to be in their way They threaten peaceable citizens with their pistols and strike and women and children with the flat of their sabres.

As soon as they have gone by, excited groups close up in their wake.

"Name of a name, what is happening?" everyone queries in affright.

And gossip, conjectures, rumours, hold undisputed sway.

"Robespierre is dictator of France!"

"He has ordered the arrest of all the Members of the Convention."

"And the massacre of all the prisoners."

"*Pardi*, a wise decree! As for me, I am sick of the eternal tumbrils and the guillotine!"

"Better finish with the lot, say I!"

"Robespierre! Robespierre!" comes as a far-off echo, to the accompaniment of thundering hoofs upon the cobble-stones.

And so, from mouth to mouth! The meek and the peace-loving magnify these rumours into approaching cataclysm; the opportunists hold their tongue, ready to fall in with this party or that; the cowards lie in hiding and shout "Robespierre!" with Henriot's horde or "Tallien!" in the neighbourhood of the Tuileries.

Here the Convention has reassembled, and here they are threatened presently by Henriot and his artillery. The members of the great Assembly remain at their post. The President has harangued them.

"Citizen deputies!" he calls aloud. "The moment has come to die at our posts!"

As they sit waiting for Henriot's cannonade, and calmly decree all the rebels "outside the pale of the law."

Tallien, moved by a spirit of lofty courage, goes, followed by a few intimates, to meet Henriot's gunners boldly face to face.

"Citizen soldiers!" he calls aloud, and his voice has the resonance of undaunted courage. "After covering yourselves with glory on the fields of honour, are you going to disgrace your country?" He points a scornful finger at Henriot who, bloated, purple in the face, grunting and spluttering like an old seal, is reeling in his saddle. "Look at him, citizen soldiers!" Tallien commands. "He is drunk and besotted! What man is there who, being sober, would dare to order fire against the representatives of the people?"

The gunners are moved, frightened too by the decree which has placed them "outside the pale of the law." Henriot, fearing mutiny if he persisted in the monstrous order to fire, withdraws his troops back to the Hôtel de Ville.

Some follow him; some do not. And Tallien goes back to the Hall of the Convention covered with glory.

Citizen Barras is promoted Commandant of the National Guard and of all forces at the disposal of the Convention and ordered to recruit loyal troops that will stand up to the traitor Henriot and his ruffianly *gendarmes*. The latter are in open revolt against the government; but, name of a name! Citizen Barras, with a few hundred patriots, will soon put reason—and a few charges of gun-powder—into them!

So, at five o'clock in the afternoon, whilst Henriot has once more collected his *gendarmes* and the remnants of his artillery outside the Hôtel de Ville, Citizen Barras, accompanied by two *aides-de-camp*, goes forth on his recruiting mission. He makes the round of the city gates, wishing to find out what loyal soldiers amongst the National Guard the Convention can rely upon.

Chauvelin, on his way to the Rue de la Planchette, meets Barras at the Porte St. Antoine; and Barras is full of the news.

"Why were you not at your place at the Assembly, Citizen Chauvelin?" he asks of his colleague. "It was the grandest moment I have ever witnessed! Tallien was superb, and Robespierre ignoble! And if we succeed in crushing that bloodthirsty monster once and for all, it will be a new era of civilization and liberty!"

He halts, and continues with a fretful sigh:

"But we want soldiers—loyal soldiers! All the troops that we can get! Henriot has the whole of the Municipal Gendarmerie at his command, with muskets and guns; and Robespierre can always sway that rabble with a word. We want men!—Men!—"

But Chauvelin is in no mood to listen. Robespierre's fall or his triumph, what are they to him at this hour, when the curtain is about to fall on the final act of his own stupendous drama of revenge? Whatever happens, whoever remains in power, vengeance is his! The English spy in any event is sure of the guillotine. He is not the enemy of a party, but of the people of France. And the sovereignty of the people is not in question yet. Then, what matters if the wild beasts in the Convention are at one another's throat?

So Chauvelin listens unmoved to Barras' passionate tirades, and when the latter, puzzle at his colleague's indifference, reiterates frowning:

"I must have all the troops I can get. You have some capable soldiers at your command always, Citizen Chauvelin. Where are they now?"

Chauvelin retorts drily:

"At work. On business at least as important as taking side in a quarrel between Robespierre and Tallien."

"*Pardi!*—" Barras protests hotly.

But Chauvelin pays no further attention to him. A neighbouring church clock has just struck six. Within the hour and his arch enemy will be in his hands! Never for a moment does he doubt that the bold adventurer will come to the lonely house in the Rue de la Planchette. Even hating the Englishman as he does, he knows that the latter would not endanger his wife's safety by securing his own.

So Chauvelin turns on his heel, leaving Barras to fume and to threaten. At the angle of the Porte St. Antoine, he stumbles against and nearly knocks over a man who sits on the ground, with his back to the wall, munching a straw, his knees drawn up to his nose, a crimson cap pulled over his eyes, and his two long arms encircling his shins.

Chauvelin swore impatiently. His nerves were on the rack, and he was in no pleasant mood. The man, taken unawares, had uttered an oath, which died away in a racking fit of coughing. Chauvelin looked town and saw the one long arm branded with the letter "M," the flesh still swollen and purple with the fire of the searing iron.

"Rateau!" he ejaculated roughly. "What are you doing here?"

Meek and servile, Rateau struggled with some difficulty to his feet.

"I have finished my work at Mother Théot's, citizen," he said humbly. "I was resting."

Chauvelin kicked at him with the toe of his boot.

"Then go and rest elsewhere," he muttered. "The gates of the city are not refuges for vagabonds."

After which act of unnecessary brutality, his temper momentarily soothed, he turned on his heel and walked rapidly through the gate.

Barras had stood by during this brief interlude, vaguely interested in the little scene. But now, when the coalheaver lurched past him, one of his *aides-de-camp* remarked audibly:

"An unpleasant customer, Citizen Chauvelin! Eh, friend?"

"I believe you!" Rateau replied readily enough. Then, with the mulish persistence of a gabby who is smarting under a wrong, he thrust out his branded arm right under citizen Barras' nose. "See what he has done to me!"

Barras frowned.

"A convict, what? Then, how is it you are at large?"

"I am not a convict," Rateau protested with sullen emphasis. "I am an innocent man, and a free citizen of the Republic. But I got in Citizen Chauvelin's way, what? He is always full of schemes—"

"You are right there!" Barras retorted grimly. But the subject was not sufficiently interesting to engross his attention further. He had so many and such momentous things to do. Already he had nodded to his men and turned his back on the grimy coalheaver, who, shaken by a fit of coughing, unable to speak for the moment, had put out his grimy hand and gripped the deputy firmly by the sleeve.

"What is it now?" Barras ejaculated roughly.

"If you will but listen, citizen," Rateau wheezed painfully, "I can tell you—"

"What?"

"You were asking Citizen Chauvelin where you could find some soldiers of the Republic to do you service."

"Yes; I did."

"Well," Rateau rejoined, and an expression of malicious cunning distorted his ugly face. "I can tell you."

"What do you mean?"

"I lodge in an empty warehouse over yonder," Rateau went on eagerly, and pointed in the direction where Chauvelin's spare figure had disappeared a while ago. "The floor above is inhabited by Mother Théot, the witch. You know her, citizen?"

"Yes, yes! I thought she had been sent to the guillotine along with—"

"She was let out of prison and has been doing some of Citizen Chauvelin's spying for him."

Barras frowned. This was none of his business, and the dirty coalheaver inspired him with an unpleasant sense of loathing.

"To the point, citizen!" he said curtly.

"Citizen Chauvelin has a dozen or more soldiers under his command, in that house," Rateau went on with a leer. "They are trained troops of the National Guard—"

"How do you know?" Barras broke in harshly.

"*Pardi!*" was the coalheaver's dry reply. "I clean their boots for them."

"Where is the house?"

"In the Rue de la Planchette. But there is an entrance into the warehouse at the back of it."

"*Allons!*" was Barras' curt word of command, to the two men who accompanied him.

He strode up the street toward the gate, not caring whether Rateau came along or no. But the coalheaver followed in the wake of the three men. He had buried his grimy fists once more in the pocket of his tattered breeches; but not before he had shaken them, each in turn, in the direction of the Rue de la Planchette.

Chauvelin in the meanwhile had turned into Mother Théot's house, and without speaking to the old charlatan, who was watching for him in the vestibule, he mounted to the top floor. Here he called peremptorily to Captain Boyer.

"There is half an hour yet," the latter murmured gruffly; "and I am sick of all this waiting! Let me finish with that cursed *aristo* in there. My comrades and I want to see what is going on in the city, and join in the fun, if there is any."

"Half an hour, citizen," Chauvelin rejoined drily. "You'll lose little of the fun, and you'll certainly lose your share of the ten thousand *livres* if you shoot the woman and fail to capture the Scarlet Pimpernel."

"Bah! He'll not come now," Boyer riposted. "It is too late. He is looking after his own skin, *pardi!*"

"He will come, I swear!" Chauvelin said firmly, as if in answer to his own thoughts.

Inside the room, Marguerite has heard every word of this colloquy. Its meaning is clear enough. Clear and horrible! Death awaits her at the hands of those abominable ruffians—here—within half an hour—unless—Her thoughts are becoming confused; she cannot concentrate. Frightened? No, she is not frightened. She has looked death in the face before now. That time in Boulogne. And there are worse things than death.—There is, for instance, the fear that she might never see her husband again—in this life.—There is only half an hour or less than that—and—and he might not come.—She prays that he might not come. But, if he does, then what chance has he? My God, what chance?

And her tortured mind conjures up visions of his courage, his coolness, his amazing audacity and luck.—She thinks and thinks—if he does not come—and if he does—

A distant church clock strikes the half-hour—a short half-hour now—

The evening is sultry. Another storm is threatening, and the sun has tinged the heat-mist with red. The air smells foul, as in the midst of a huge, perspiring crowd. And through the heat, the lull, above the hideous sounds of those ruffians outside her door, there is a rumbling noise as of distant, unceasing thunder. The city is in travail.

Then suddenly Boyer, the captain of the ruffians, exclaims loudly:

"Let me finish with the *aristo*, Citizen Chauvelin! I want to join in the fun."

And the door of her room is torn open by a savage, violent hand.

The window behind Marguerite is open, and she, facing the door, clings with both hands to the sill. Her cheeks bloodless, her eyes glowing, her head erect, she waits, praying with all her might for courage—only courage.

The ruffianly captain, in his tattered, mud-stained uniform, stands in the doorway—for one moment only. The next, Chauvelin has elbowed him out of the way, and in his turn faces the prisoner—the innocent woman whom he has pursued with such relentless hatred. Marguerite prays with all her might and does not flinch. Not for one second. Death stands there before her in the guise of this man's vengeful lust, which gleams in his pale eyes. Death is there waiting for her, under the guise of the ignoble soldiers in the scrubby rags, with their muskets held in stained, filthy hands.

Courage—only courage! The power to die as he would wish her to—could he but know!

Chauvelin speaks to her; she does not hear. There is a mighty buzzing in her ears as of men shouting—shouting what, she does not know, for she is still praying for courage. Chauvelin has ceased talking. Then it must be the end. Thank God! she has had the courage not to speak and not to flinch. Now she closes her eyes, for there is a red mist before her and she feels that she might fall into it—straight into that mist.

With closed eyes, Marguerite suddenly seems able to hear. She hears shouts which come from below—quite close and coming nearer every moment. Shouts, and the tramp, the scurry of many feet; and now and then that wheezing, asthmatic cough, that strange, strange cough, and the click of wooden shoes. Then a voice, harsh and peremptory:

"Citizen soldiers, your country needs you! Rebels have defied her laws. To arms! Every man who hangs back is a deserter and a traitor!"

After this, Chauvelin's sharp, dictatorial voice raised in protest:

"In the name of the Republic, Citizen Barras!—"

But the other breaks in more peremptorily still:

"*Ah, ça,* Citizen Chauvelin Do you presume to stand between me and my duty? By order of the Convention now assembled, every soldier must report at once at his section. Are you perchance on the side of the rebels?"

At this point, Marguerite opens her eyes. Through the widely open door she sees the small, sable-clad figure of Chauvelin, his pale face distorted with rage to which he obviously dare not give rein; and beside him a short, stoutish man in cloth coat and cord breeches, and with the tricolour scarf around his waist. His round face appears crimson with choler and in his right hand he grasps a heavy Malacca stick with a grip that proclaims the desire to strike. The two men appear to be defying one another; and all around them are the vague forms of the soldiers silhouetted against a distant window, through which the crimson afternoon glow comes peeping in on a cloud of flickering dust.

"Now then, citizen soldiers!" Barras resumes, and incontinently turns his back on Chauvelin, who, white to the lips, raises a final and menacing word of warning.

"I warn you, citizen Barras," he says firmly, "that by taking these men away from their post, you place yourself in league with the enemy of your country and will have to answer to her for this crime."

His accent is so convinced, so firm, and fraught with such dire menace, that for one instant Barras hesitates.

"*Eh bien!*" he exclaims. "I will humour you thus far, Citizen Chauvelin. I will leave you a couple of men to wait on your pleasure until sundown. But, after that—"

For a second or two there was silence. Chauvelin stands there, with his thin lips pressed tightly together. Then Barras adds, with a shrug of his wide shoulders:

"I am contravening my duty in doing even so much; and the responsibility must rest with you, Citizen Chauvelin. *Allons*, my men!" he says once more; and without another glance on his discomfited colleague, he strides down the stairs, followed by Captain Boyer and the soldiers.

For a while the house is still filled with confusion and sounds: men tramping down the stone stairs, words of command, click of sabres and muskets, opening and slamming of doors. Then the sounds slowly die away, out in the street in the direction of the Porte St. Antoine. After which, there is silence.

Chauvelin stands in the doorway with his back to the room and to Marguerite, his claw-like hands intertwined convulsively behind him. The silhouette of the two remaining soldiers are still visible; they stand silently and at attention with their muskets in their hands. Between them and Chauvelin hovers the tall, ungainly figure of a man, clothed in rags and covered in soot and coal-dust. His feet are thrust into wooden shoes, his grimy hands are stretched out each side of him; and on his left arm, just above the wrist, there is an ugly mark like the brand seared into the flesh of a convict.

Just now he looks terribly distressed with a tearing fit of coughing. Chauvelin curtly bids him stand aside; and at the same moment the church clock of St. Louis, close by, strikes seven.

"Now then, citizen soldiers!" Chauvelin commands.

The soldiers grasp their muskets more firmly, and Chauvelin raises his hand. The next instant he is thrust violently back into the room, loses his balance, and falls backward against a table, whilst the door is slammed to between him and the soldiers. From the other side of the door there comes the sound of a short, sharp scuffle. Then silence.

Marguerite, holding her breath, hardly realised that she lived. A second ago she was facing death; and now—

Chauvelin struggled painfully to his feet. With a mighty effort and a hoarse cry of rage, he threw himself against the door. The impetus carried him further than he intended, no doubt; for at that same moment the door was opened, and he fell up against the massive form of the grimy coalheaver, whose long arms closed round him, lifted him off the floor, and carried him like a bundle of straw to the nearest chair.

"There, my dear Mr. Chambertin!" the coalheaver said, in exceedingly light and pleasant tones. "Let me make you quite comfortable!"

Marguerite watched—dumb and fascinated—the dexterous hands that twined the length of rope round the arms and legs of her helpless enemy and wound his own tricolour scarf around that snarling mouth.

She scarcely dared trust her eyes and ears.

There was the hideous, dust-covered mudlark with bare feet thrust into *sabots*, with ragged breeches and tattered shirt; there was the cruel, mud-stained face, the purple lips, the toothless mouth; and those huge, muscular arms, one of them branded like the arm of a convict, the flesh still swollen with the searing of the iron.

"I must indeed crave your ladyship's forgiveness. In very truth, I

435

am a disgusting object!"

Ah, there was the voice!—the dear, dear, merry voice! A little weary perhaps, but oh! so full of laughter and of boyish shamefacedness! To Marguerite it seemed as if God's own angels had opened to her the gates of Paradise. She did not speak; she scarce could move. All that she could do was to put out her arms.

He did not approach her, for in truth he looked a dusty object; but he dragged his ugly cap off his head, then slowly, and keeping his eyes fixed upon her, he put one knee to the ground.

"You did not doubt, m'dear, that I would come?" he asked quaintly.

She shook her head. The last days were like a nightmare now; and in truth she ought never to have been afraid.

"Will you ever forgive me?" he continued.

"Forgive? What?" she murmured.

"These last few days. I could not come before. You were safe for the time being.—That fiend was waiting for me—"

She gave a shudder and closed her eyes.

"Where is he?"

He laughed his gay, irresponsible laugh, and with a slender hand, still covered with coal-dust, he pointed to the helpless figure of Chauvelin.

"Look at him!" he said. "Doth he not look a picture?"

Marguerite ventured to look. Even at sight of her enemy bound tightly with ropes to a chair, his own tricolour scarf wound loosely round his mouth, she could not altogether suppress a cry of horror.

"What is to become of him?"

He shrugged his broad shoulders.

"I wonder!" he said lightly.

Then he rose to his feet, and went on with quaint bashfulness:

"I wonder," he said, "how I dare stand thus before your ladyship!"

And in a moment, she was in his arms, laughing, crying, covered herself now with coal-dust and with grime.

"My beloved!" she exclaimed with a shudder of horror. "What you must have gone through!"

He only laughed like a schoolboy who had come through some impish adventure without much harm.

"Very little, I swear!" he asserted gaily. "But for thoughts of you, I have never enjoyed anything so much as this last phase of a glorious adventure. After our clever friend here ordered the real Rateau to be branded, so that he might know him again wherever he say him, I had to bribe the veterinary who had done the deed, to do the same thing for me. It was not difficult. For a thousand *livres* the man would have branded his own mother on the nose; and I appeared before him as a man of science, eager for an experiment. He asked no questions. And, since then, whenever Chauvelin gazed contentedly on my arm, I could have screamed for joy!"

"For the love of Heaven, my lady!" he added quickly, for he felt her soft, warm lips against his branded flesh; "don't shame me over such a trifle! I shall always love that scar, for the exciting time it recalls and because it happens to be the initial of your dear name."

He stooped down to the ground and kissed the hem of her gown.

After which he had to tell her as quickly and as briefly as he could, all that had happened in the past few days.

"It was only by risking the fair Theresia's life," he said, "that I could save your own. No other spur would have goaded Tallien into open revolt."

He turned and looked down for a moment on his enemy, who lay pinioned and helpless, with hatred and baffled revenge writ plainly on the contorted face and pale, rolling eyes.

And Sir Percy Blakeney sighed, a quaint sigh of regret.

"I only regret one thing, my dear M. Chambertin," he said after a while. "And that is, that you and I will never measure wits again after this. Your damnable revolution is dead—I am glad I was never tempted to kill you. I might have succumbed, and in very truth robbed the guillotine of an interesting prey. Without any doubt, they will guillotine the lot of you, my good M. Chambertin. Robespierre tomorrow; then his friends, his sycophants, his imitators—you amongst the rest.—'Tis a pity! You have so often amused me. Especially after you had put a brand on Rateau's arm and thought you would always know him after that. Think it all out, my dear sir!

"Remember our happy conversation in the warehouse down below, and my denunciation of Citoyenne Cabarrus—You gazed upon my branded arm then and were quite satisfied. My denunciation was a false one, of course! 'Tis I who put the letters and the rags in the beautiful Theresia's apartments. But she will bear me no malice, I dare swear; for I shall have redeemed my promise. Tomorrow, after Robespierre's head has fallen, Tallien will be the greatest man in France and his Theresia a virtual queen. Think it all out, my dear Monsieur Chambertin! You have plenty of time. Someone is sure to drift up here presently, and will free you and the two soldiers, whom

I left out on the landing. But no one will free you from the guillotine when the time comes, unless I myself—"

He did not finish; the rest of the sentence was merged in a merry laugh.

"A pleasant conceit—what?" he said lightly. "I'll think on it, I promise you!"

And the next day Paris went crazy with joy. Never had the streets looked more gay, more crowded. The windows were filled with spectators; the very roofs were crowded with an eager, shouting throng.

The seventeen hours of agony were ended. The tyrant was a fallen, broken man, maimed, dumb, bullied and insulted. Aye! He, how yesterday was the Chosen of the People, the Messenger of the Most High, now sat, or rather lay, in the tumbril, with broken jaw, eyes closed, spirit already wandering on the shores of the Styx; insulted, railed at, cursed—aye, cursed!—by every woman, reviled by every child.

The end came at four in the afternoon, in the midst of acclamations from a populace drunk with gladness—acclamations which found their echo in the whole of France and have never ceased to re-echo to this day.

But of all that tumult, Marguerite and her husband heard but little. They lay snugly concealed the whole of that day in the quiet lodgings in the Rue de l'Anier, which Sir Percy had occupied during these terribly anxious times. Here they were waited on by that asthmatic reprobate Rateau and his mother, both of whom were now rich for the rest of their days.

When the shades of evening gathered in over the jubilant city, whilst the church bells were ringing and the cannons booming, a market gardener's cart, driven by a worthy farmer and his wife, rattled out of the Porte St. Antoine. It created no excitement, and suspicion was far from everybody's mind. The passports appeared in order; but even if they were not, who cared, on this day of all days, when tyranny was crushed and men dared to be men again?

e obtained

9 781782 827341